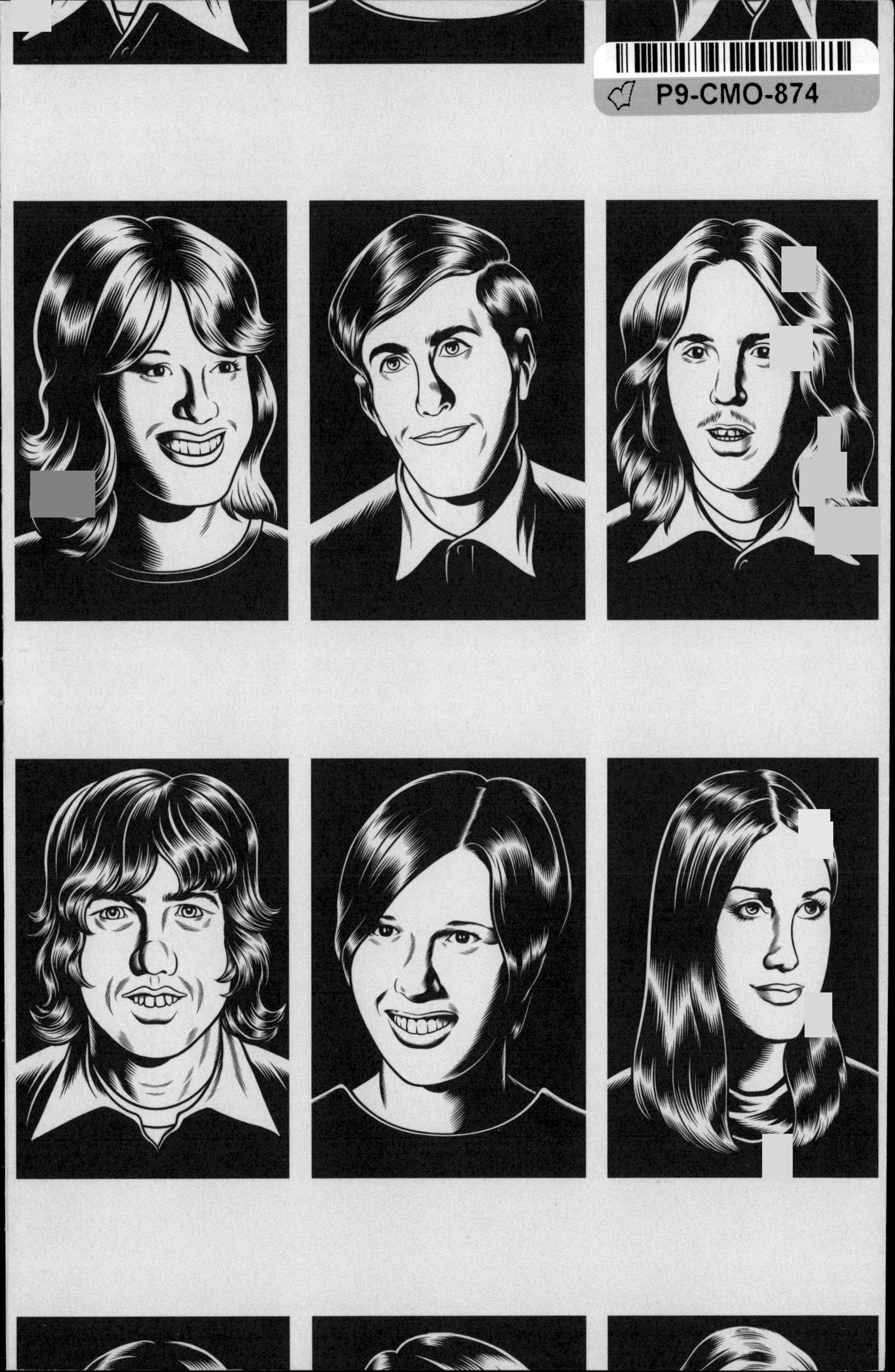

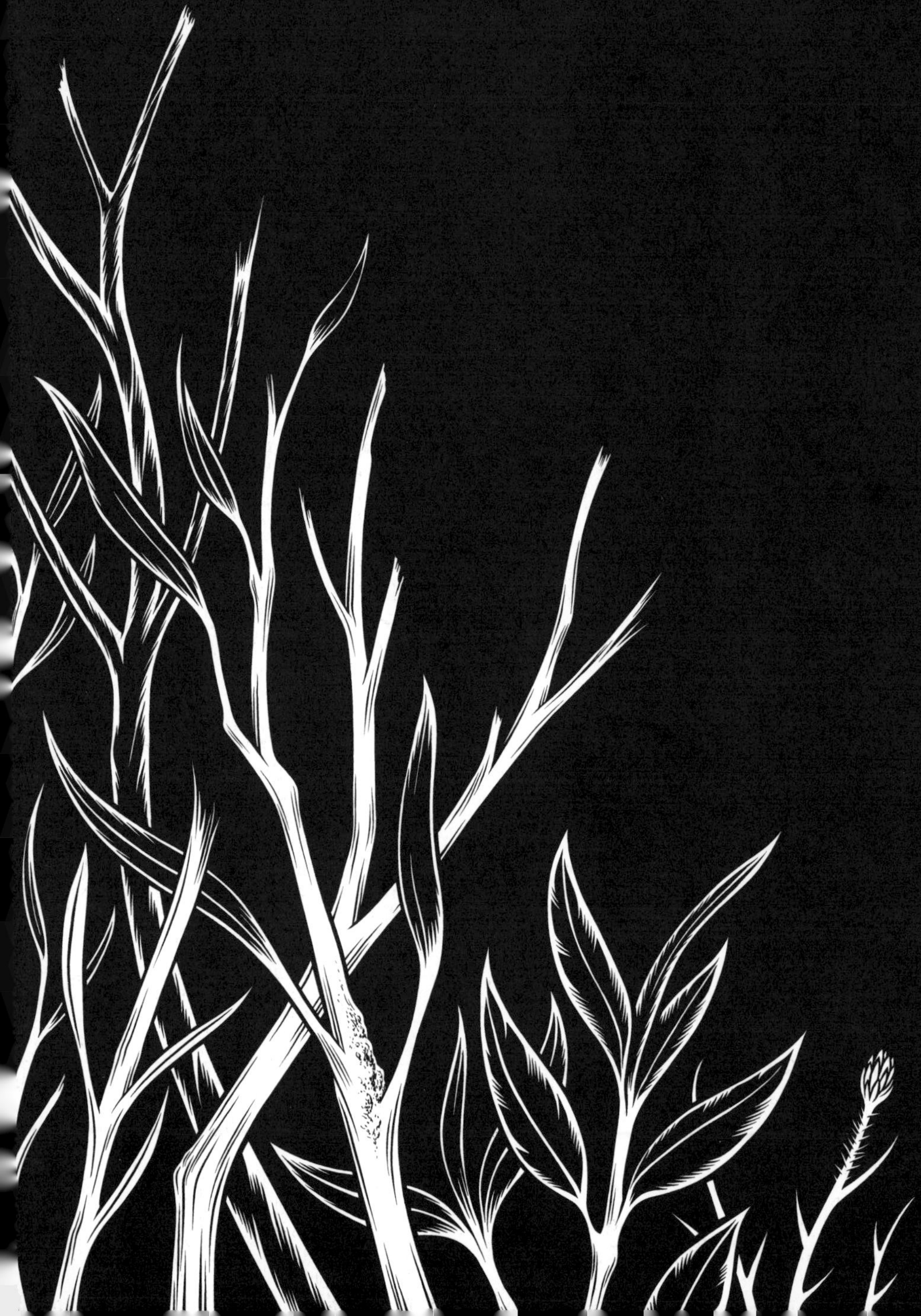

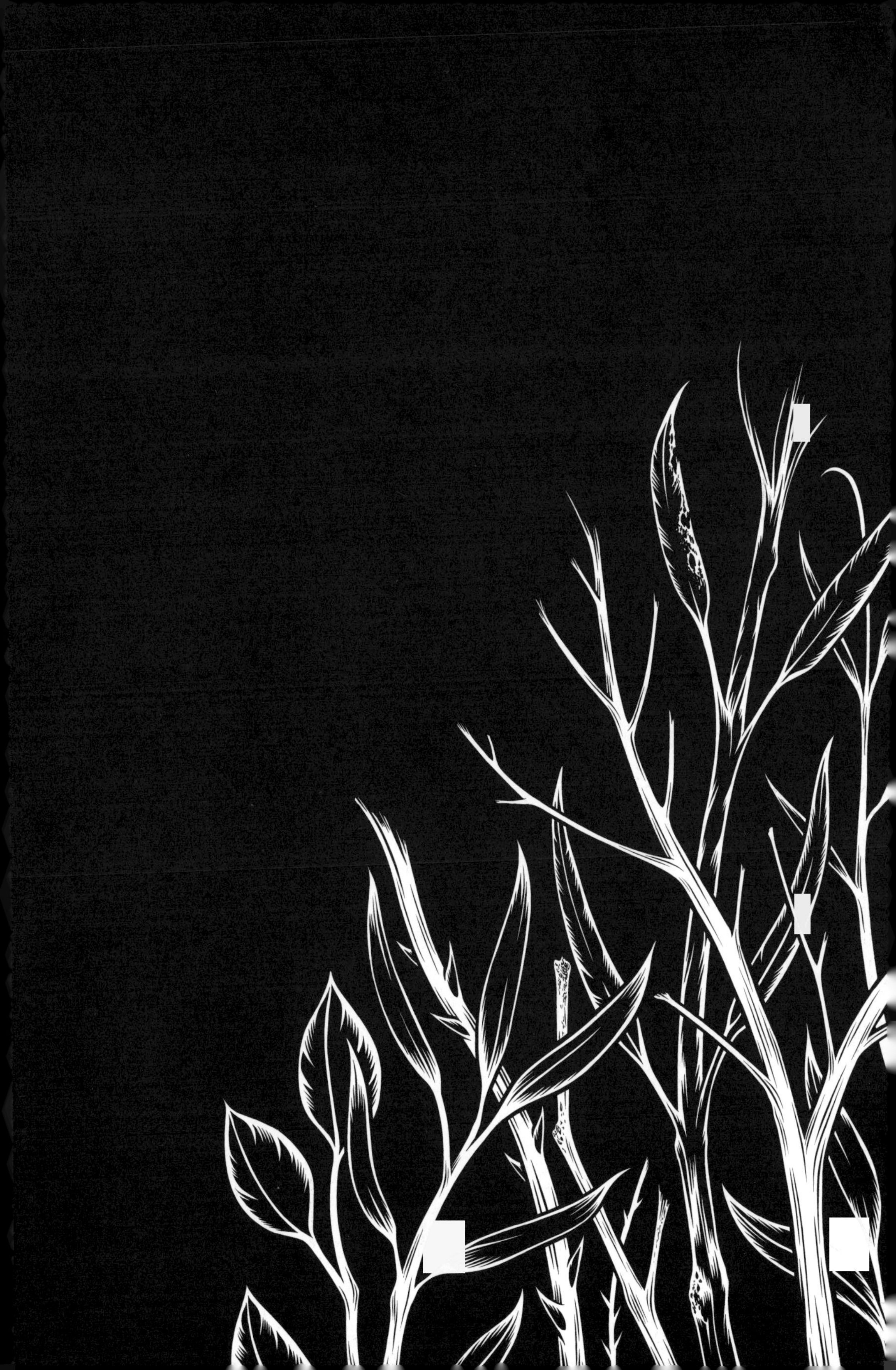

BLACK HOLE

CHARLES BURNS

THIS BOOK IS DEDICATED TO DEAN, MARK, J., PHIL, CASEY, COLLEEN, VICKIE, MIKE, PATTY, JANET, PENNY, LISA, JERI, JOHN, KAREN, KATHY, RETA, CLAUDIA, TED, TERRI, DOUG, PAUL, JAN, TOM, SCOTT, KURT, ANN, KIM, DIANE, SALLY, KATHLEEN, MARI, LIBBY, JON, JIM, PAT AND PETE. I NEVER FORGOT YOU.

THANKS TO JOHN KURAMOTO FOR HIS TECHNICAL ASSISTANCE AND TO SUSAN MOORE WHO LETTERED THIS ENTIRE BOOK.

 PUBLISHED IN THE UNITED STATES BY PANTHEON BOOKS, A DIVISION OF RANDOM HOUSE, INC., NEW YORK, AND IN CANADA BY RANDOM HOUSE OF CANADA LIMITED, TORONTO. SUBSEQUENTLY COMPILED IN HARDCOVER BY PANTHEON BOOKS, A DIVISION OF RANDOM HOUSE, INC., NEW YORK, IN 2005.

THIS WORK WAS ORIGINALLY PUBLISHED AS 12 SEPARATE COMIC BOOKS BY FANTAGRAPHICS BOOKS, SEATTLE, FROM 1995–2004.

LIBRARY OF CONGRESS CATALOGING-IN-PUBLICATION DATA
BURNS, CHARLES
BLACK HOLE / CHARLES BURNS.
P. CM.
ISBN 978-0-375-71472-6
1. GRAPHIC NOVEL. I. TITLE.
PN6727.887853 2005 641.5'973--DC22
2005046431

WWW.PANTHEONBOOKS.COM
PRINTED IN MALAYSIA
FIRST PAPERBACK EDITION
15 14 13 12 11

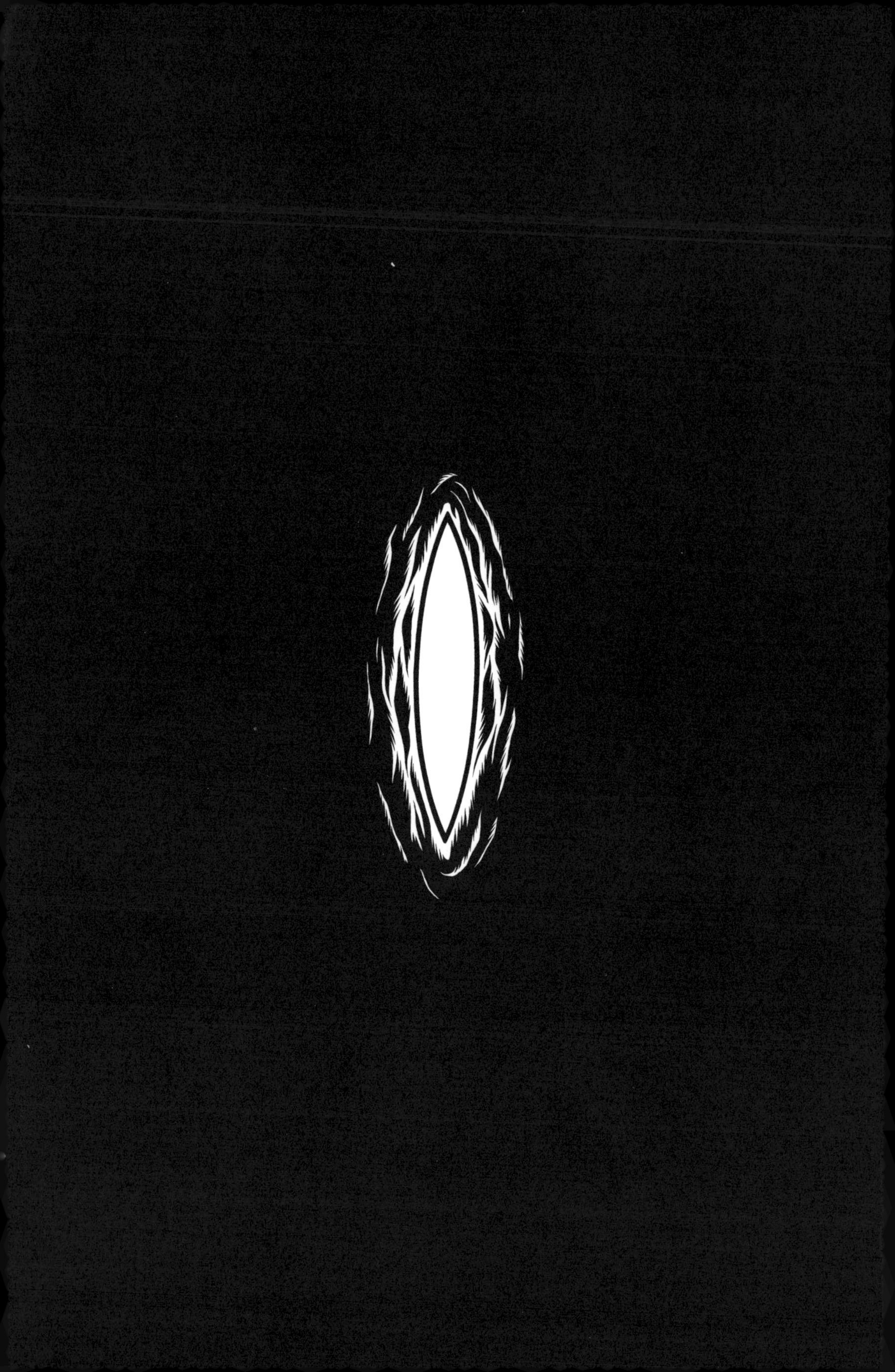

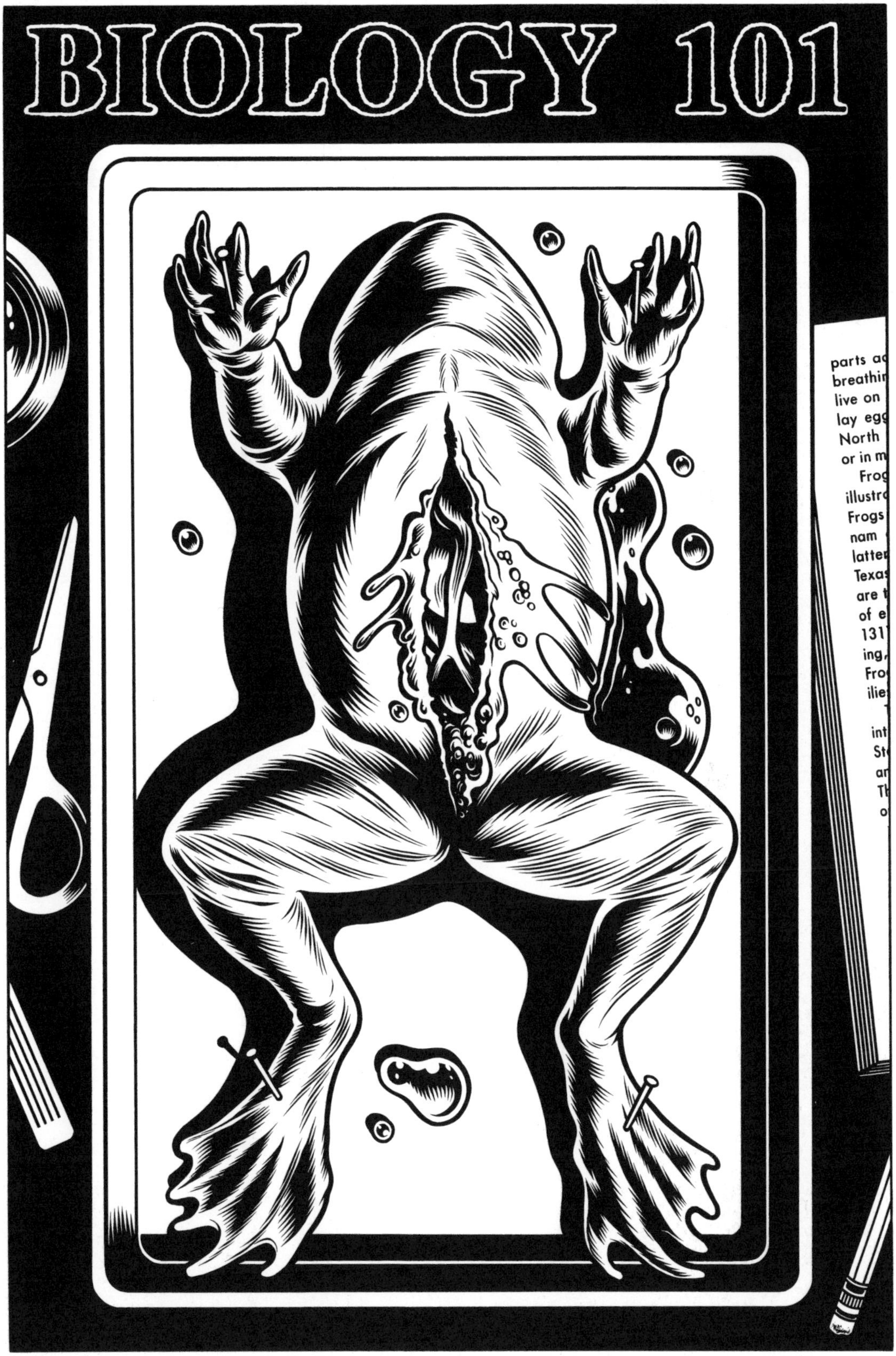
BIOLOGY 101

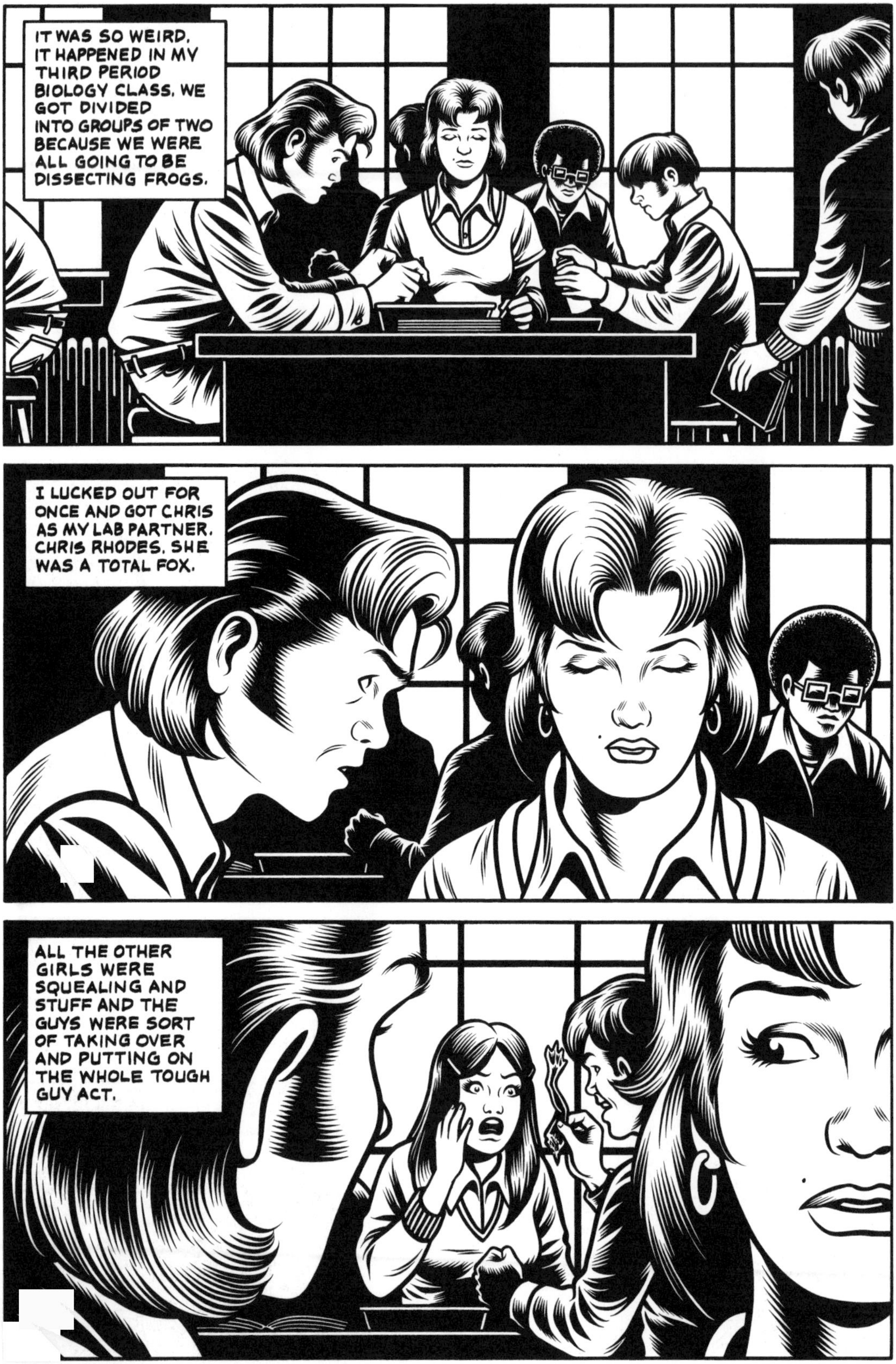
IT WAS SO WEIRD. IT HAPPENED IN MY THIRD PERIOD BIOLOGY CLASS. WE GOT DIVIDED INTO GROUPS OF TWO BECAUSE WE WERE ALL GOING TO BE DISSECTING FROGS.
I LUCKED OUT FOR ONCE AND GOT CHRIS AS MY LAB PARTNER. CHRIS RHODES. SHE WAS A TOTAL FOX.
ALL THE OTHER GIRLS WERE SQUEALING AND STUFF AND THE GUYS WERE SORT OF TAKING OVER AND PUTTING ON THE WHOLE TOUGH GUY ACT.

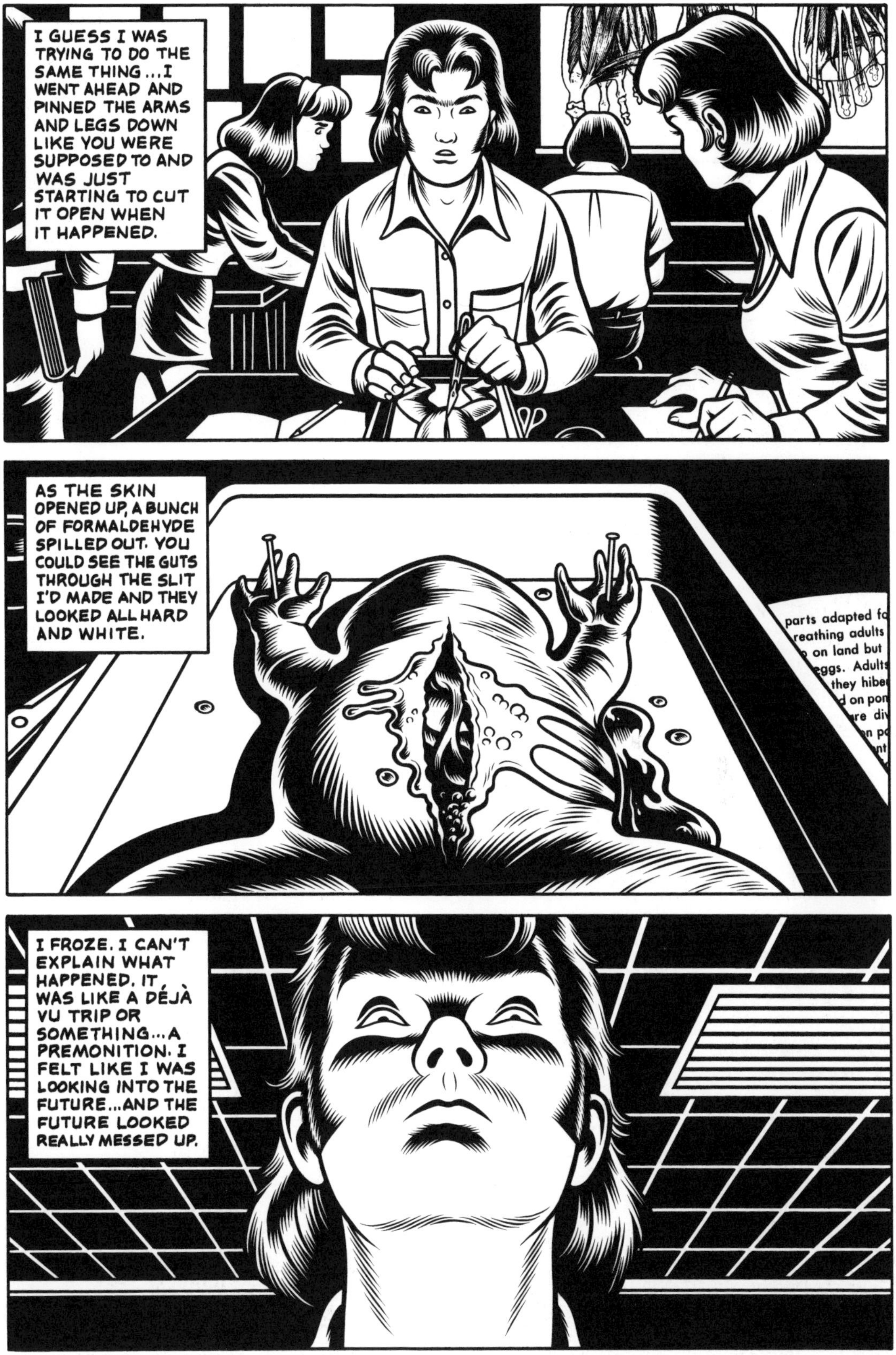
I GUESS I WAS TRYING TO DO THE SAME THING... I WENT AHEAD AND PINNED THE ARMS AND LEGS DOWN LIKE YOU WERE SUPPOSED TO AND WAS JUST STARTING TO CUT IT OPEN WHEN IT HAPPENED.
AS THE SKIN OPENED UP, A BUNCH OF FORMALDEHYDE SPILLED OUT. YOU COULD SEE THE GUTS THROUGH THE SLIT I'D MADE AND THEY LOOKED ALL HARD AND WHITE.
parts adapted fo
reathing adults
o on land but
eggs. Adults
they hibe
I FROZE. I CAN'T EXPLAIN WHAT HAPPENED. IT WAS LIKE A DÉJÀ VU TRIP OR SOMETHING... A PREMONITION. I FELT LIKE I WAS LOOKING INTO THE FUTURE... AND THE FUTURE LOOKED REALLY MESSED UP.

I WAS LOOKING AT A HOLE...A *BLACK* HOLE AND AS I LOOKED, THE HOLE OPENED UP...

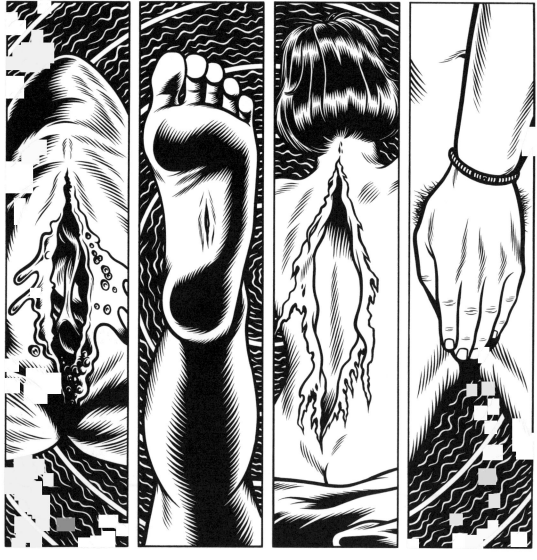

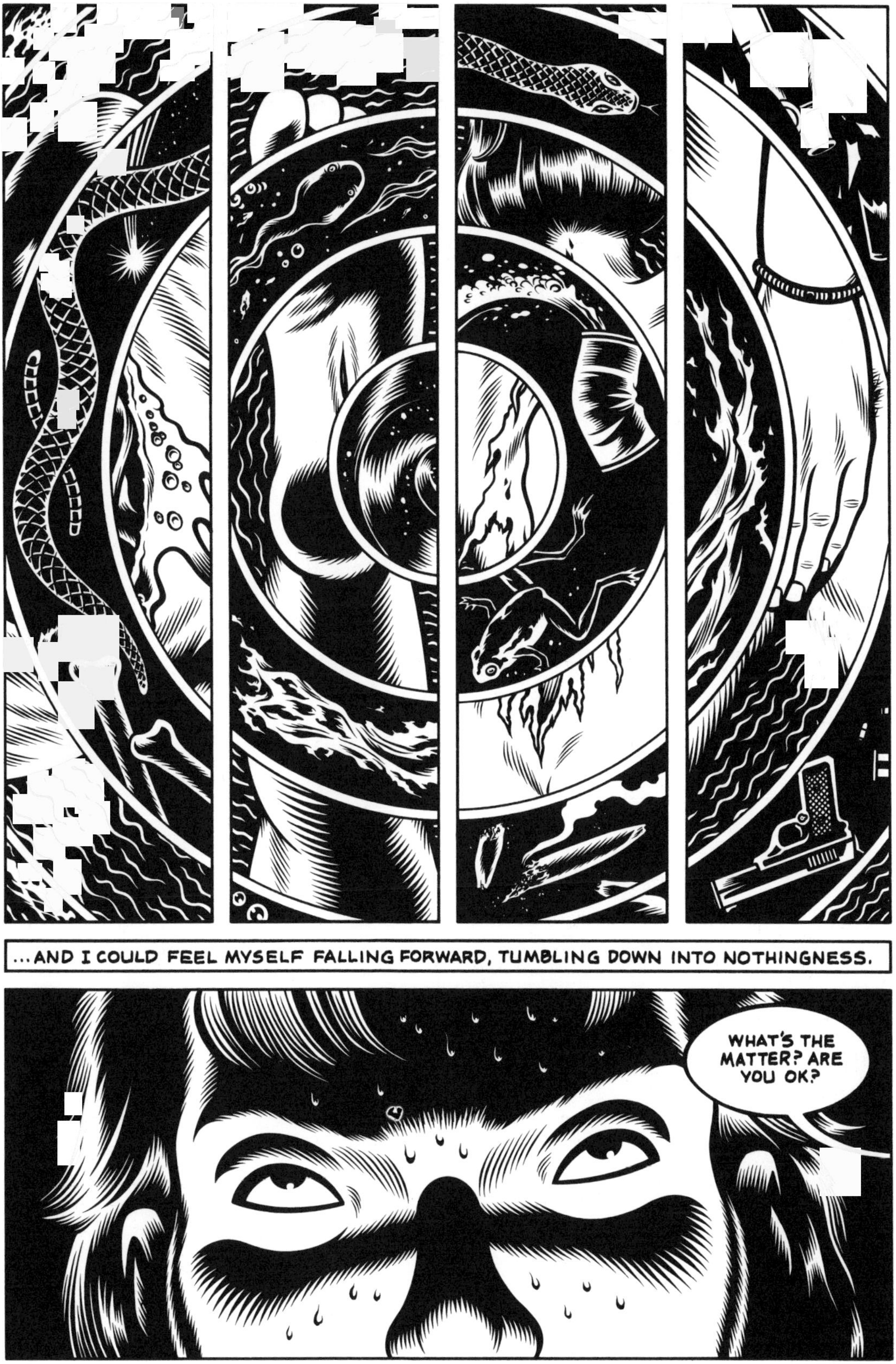
...AND I COULD FEEL MYSELF FALLING FORWARD, TUMBLING DOWN INTO NOTHINGNESS.
WHAT'S THE MATTER? ARE YOU OK?

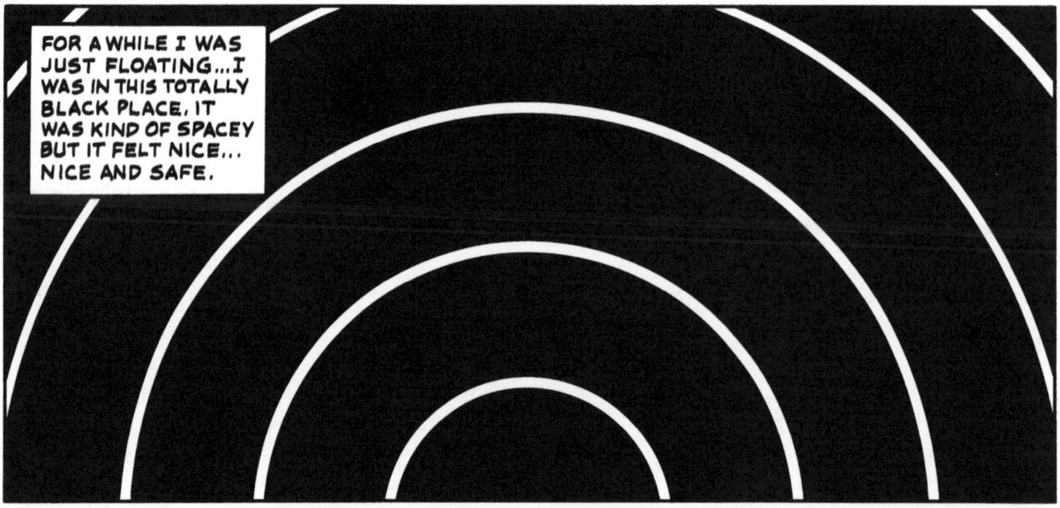
FOR A WHILE I WAS JUST FLOATING...I WAS IN THIS TOTALLY BLACK PLACE. IT WAS KIND OF SPACEY BUT IT FELT NICE... NICE AND SAFE.

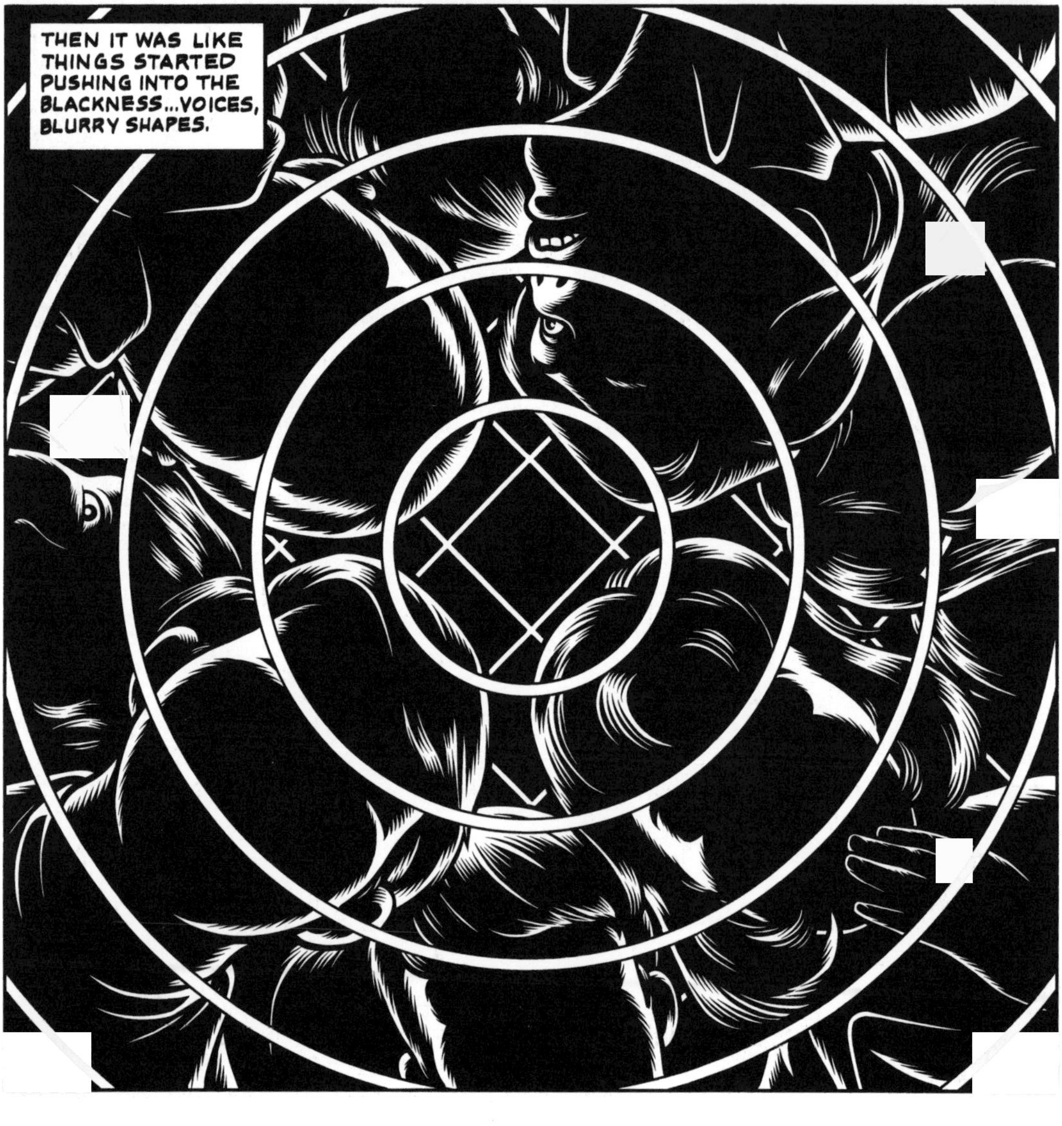
THEN IT WAS LIKE THINGS STARTED PUSHING INTO THE BLACKNESS...VOICES, BLURRY SHAPES.

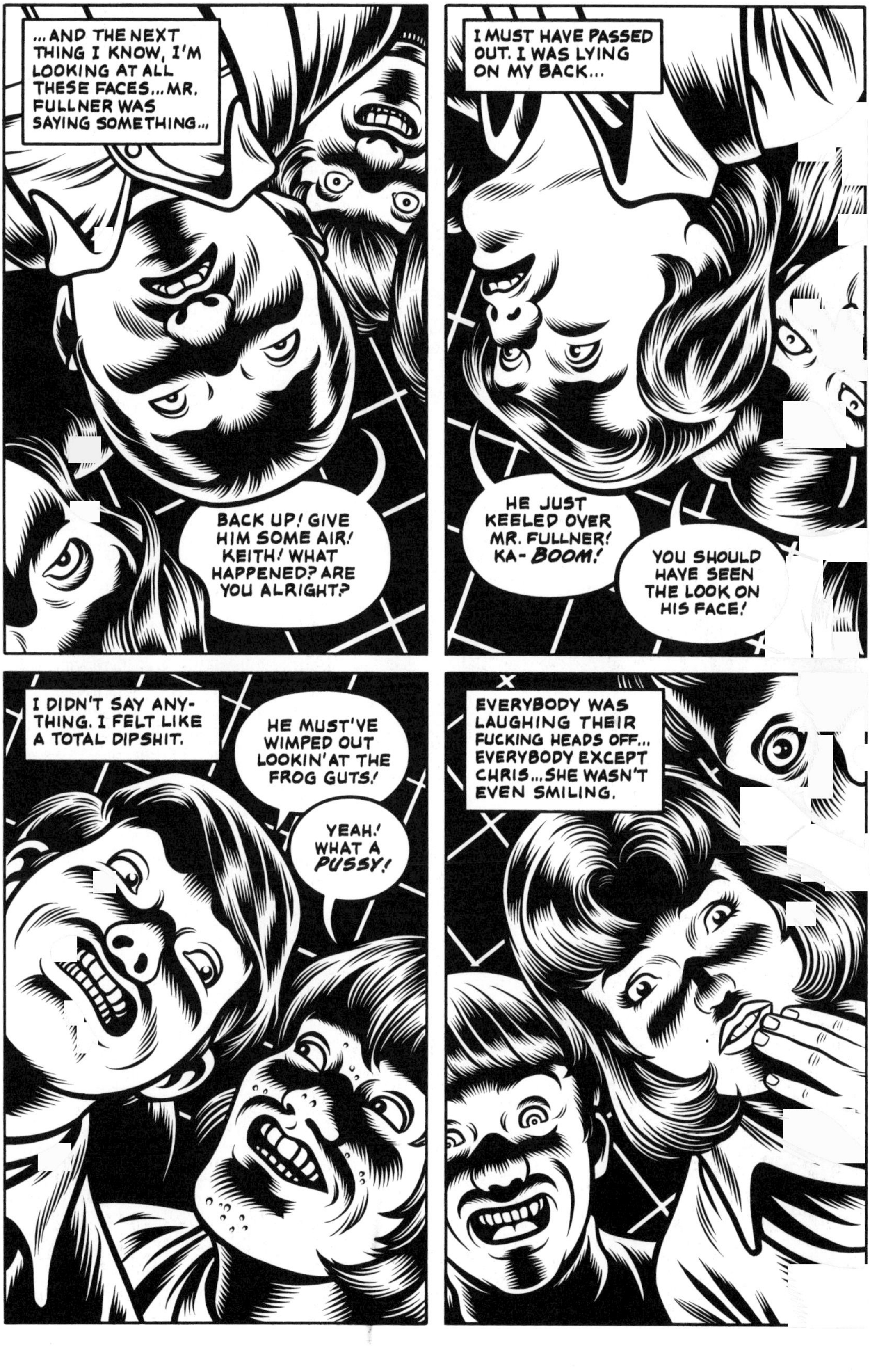
...AND THE NEXT THING I KNOW, I'M LOOKING AT ALL THESE FACES... MR. FULLNER WAS SAYING SOMETHING...
BACK UP! GIVE HIM SOME AIR! KEITH! WHAT HAPPENED? ARE YOU ALRIGHT?
I MUST HAVE PASSED OUT. I WAS LYING ON MY BACK...
HE JUST KEELED OVER MR. FULLNER! KA-BOOM!
YOU SHOULD HAVE SEEN THE LOOK ON HIS FACE!
I DIDN'T SAY ANYTHING. I FELT LIKE A TOTAL DIPSHIT.
HE MUST'VE WIMPED OUT LOOKIN' AT THE FROG GUTS!
YEAH! WHAT A PUSSY!
EVERYBODY WAS LAUGHING THEIR FUCKING HEADS OFF... EVERYBODY EXCEPT CHRIS... SHE WASN'T EVEN SMILING.

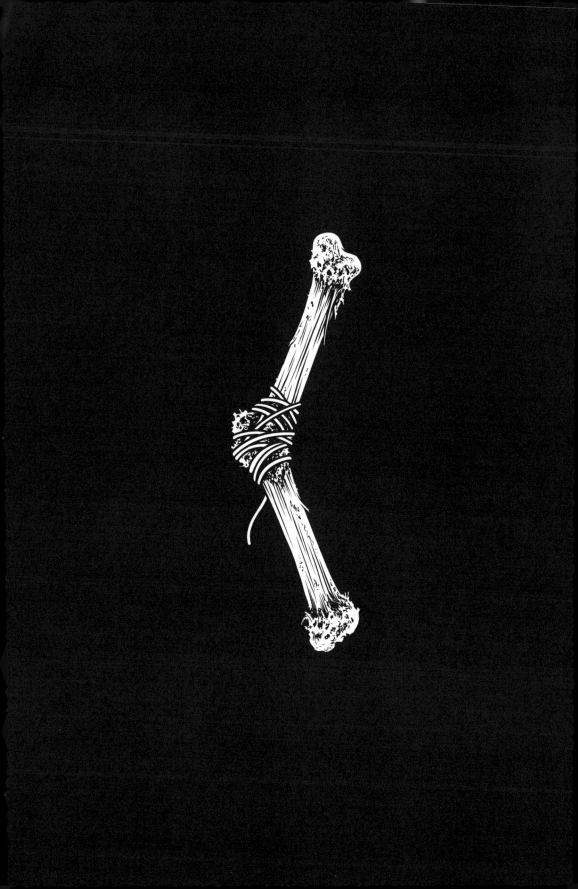

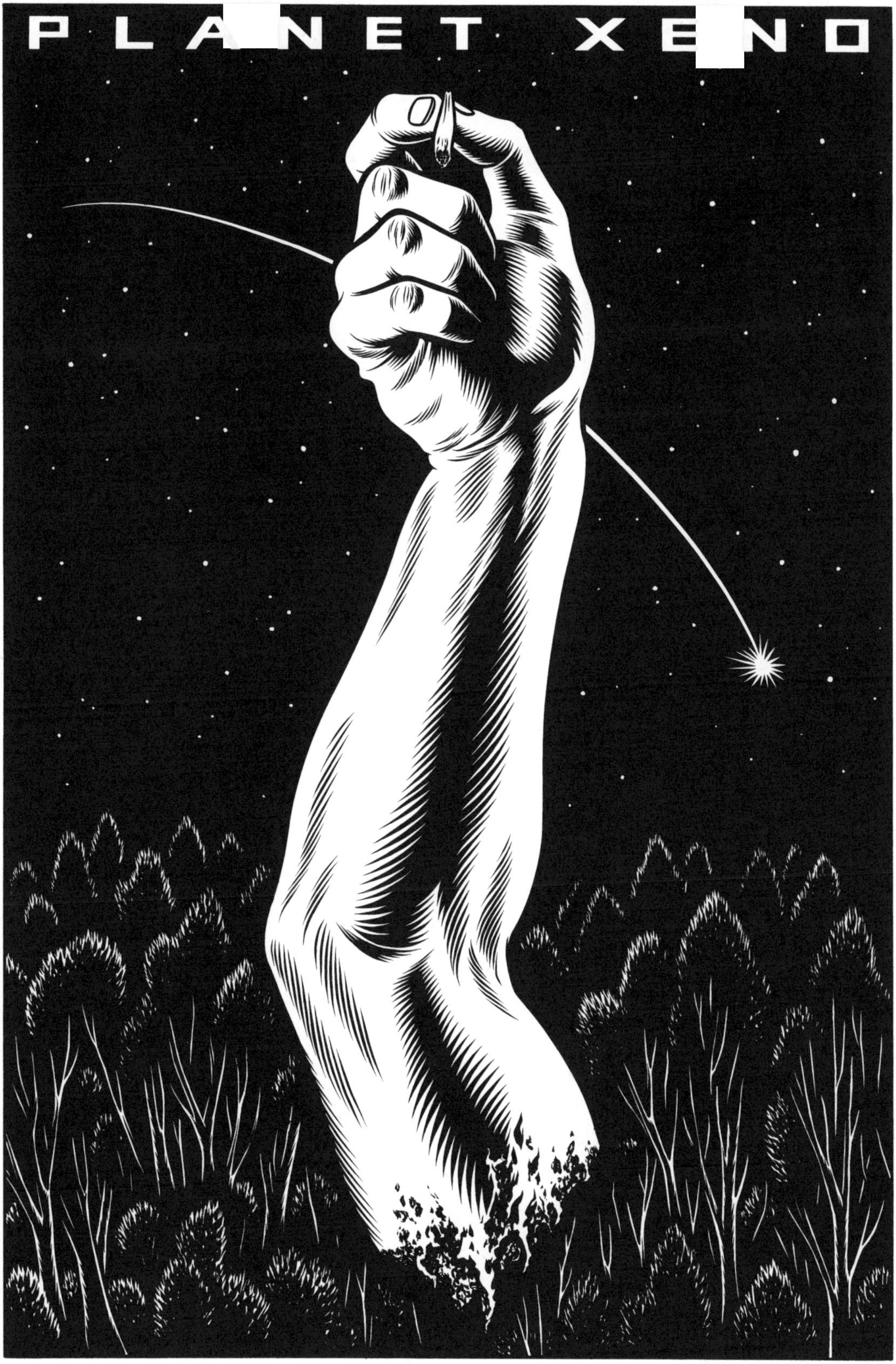
PLANET XENO

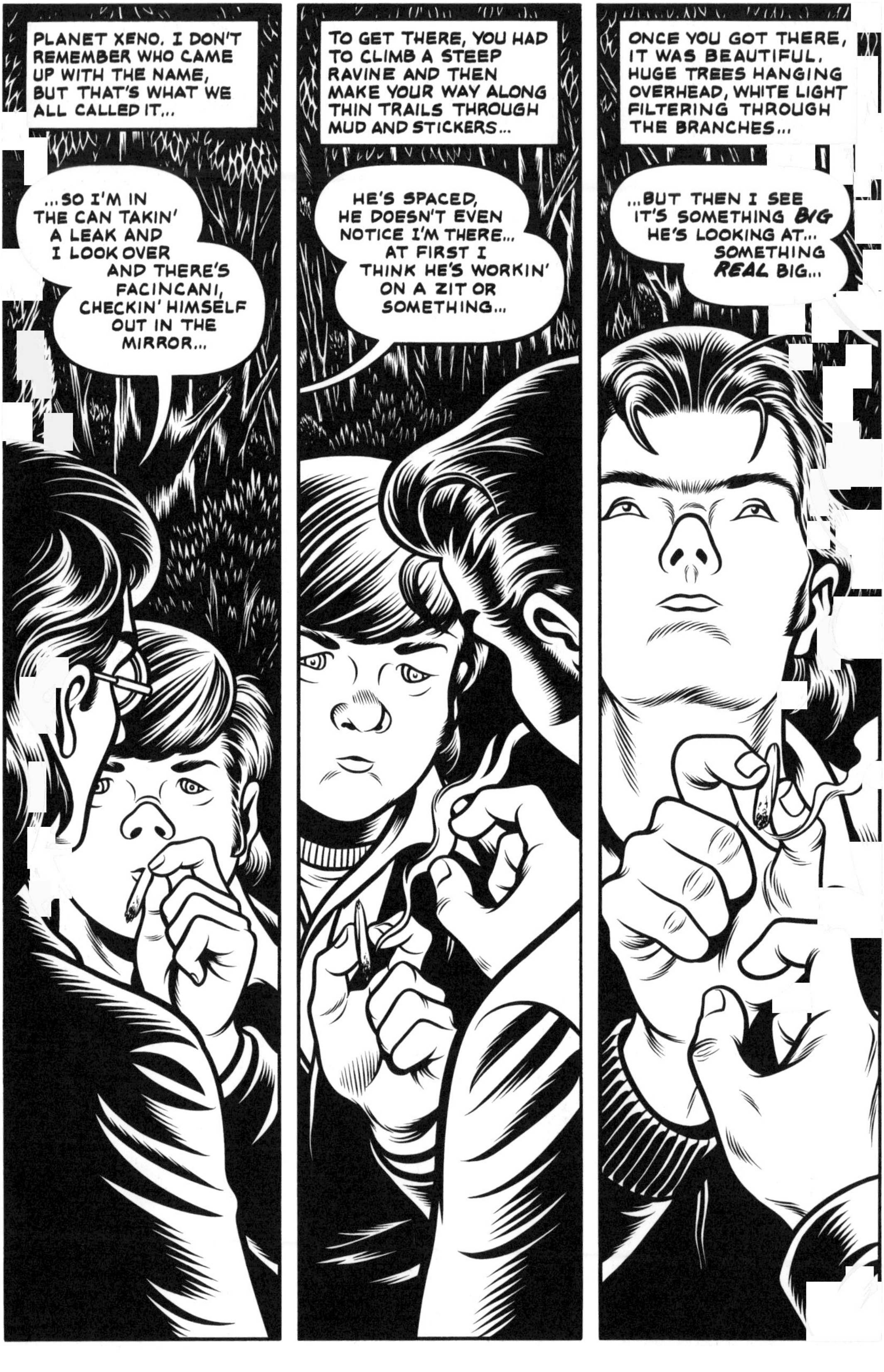
PLANET XENO. I DON'T REMEMBER WHO CAME UP WITH THE NAME, BUT THAT'S WHAT WE ALL CALLED IT...
...SO I'M IN THE CAN TAKIN' A LEAK AND I LOOK OVER AND THERE'S FACINCANI, CHECKIN' HIMSELF OUT IN THE MIRROR...
TO GET THERE, YOU HAD TO CLIMB A STEEP RAVINE AND THEN MAKE YOUR WAY ALONG THIN TRAILS THROUGH MUD AND STICKERS...
HE'S SPACED, HE DOESN'T EVEN NOTICE I'M THERE... AT FIRST I THINK HE'S WORKIN' ON A ZIT OR SOMETHING...
ONCE YOU GOT THERE, IT WAS BEAUTIFUL. HUGE TREES HANGING OVERHEAD, WHITE LIGHT FILTERING THROUGH THE BRANCHES...
...BUT THEN I SEE IT'S SOMETHING BIG HE'S LOOKING AT... SOMETHING REAL BIG...

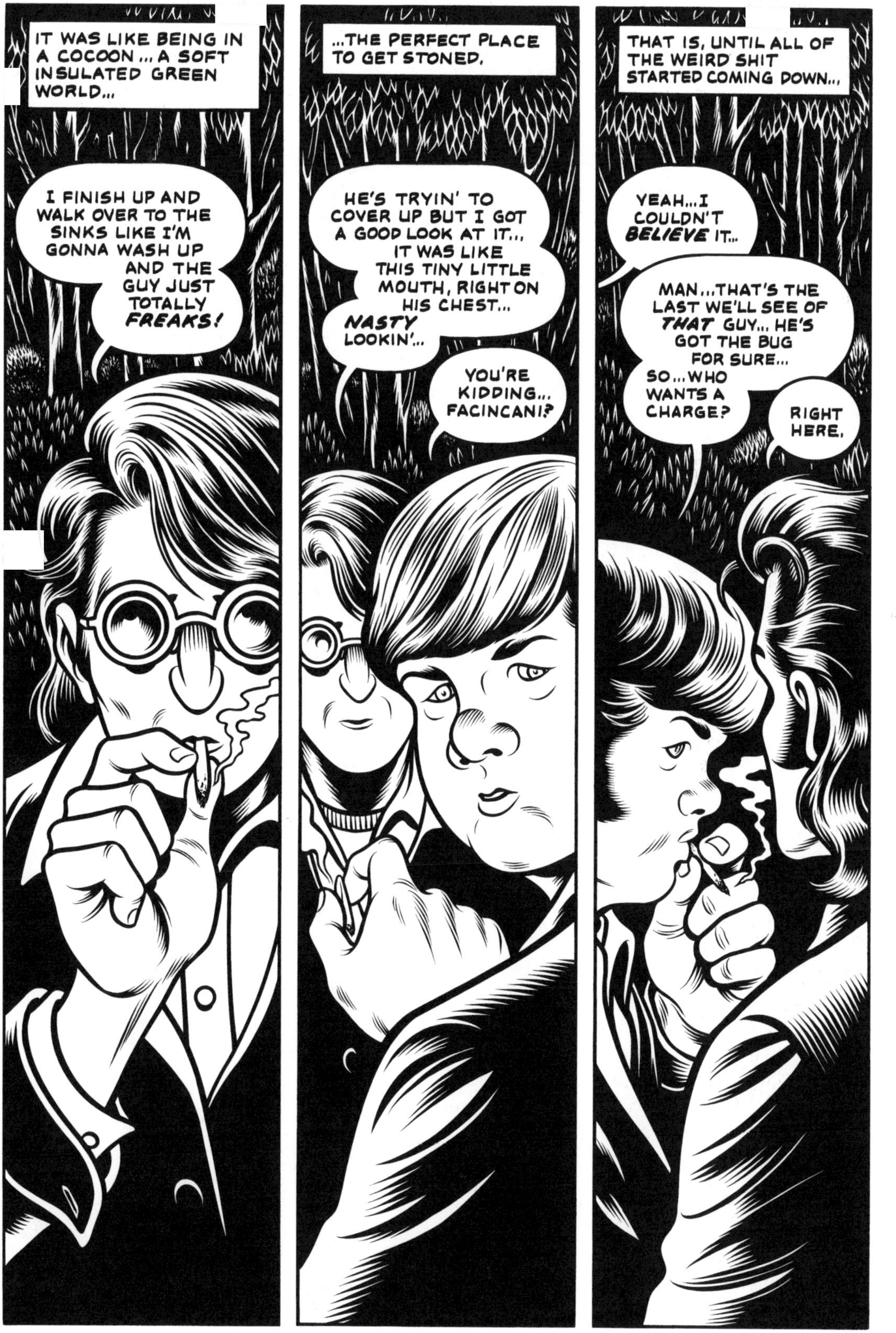
IT WAS LIKE BEING IN A COCOON... A SOFT INSULATED GREEN WORLD...
I FINISH UP AND WALK OVER TO THE SINKS LIKE I'M GONNA WASH UP AND THE GUY JUST TOTALLY FREAKS!
...THE PERFECT PLACE TO GET STONED.
HE'S TRYIN' TO COVER UP BUT I GOT A GOOD LOOK AT IT... IT WAS LIKE THIS TINY LITTLE MOUTH, RIGHT ON HIS CHEST... NASTY LOOKIN'...
YOU'RE KIDDING... FACINCANI?
THAT IS, UNTIL ALL OF THE WEIRD SHIT STARTED COMING DOWN...
YEAH...I COULDN'T BELIEVE IT...
MAN...THAT'S THE LAST WE'LL SEE OF THAT GUY... HE'S GOT THE BUG FOR SURE... SO...WHO WANTS A CHARGE?
RIGHT HERE.

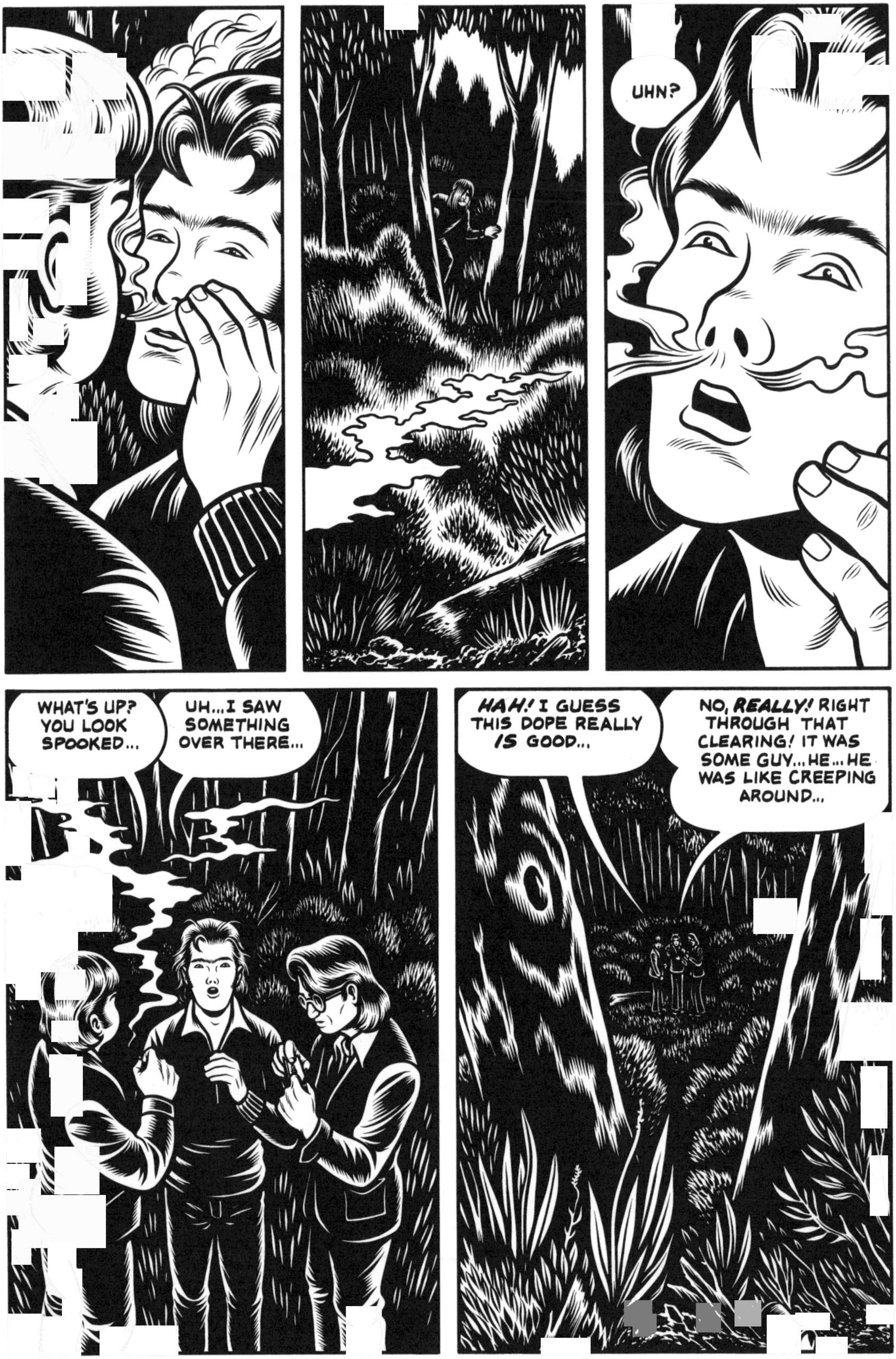
UHN?
WHAT'S UP? YOU LOOK SPOOKED...
UH...I SAW SOMETHING OVER THERE...
HAH! I GUESS THIS DOPE REALLY IS GOOD...
NO, REALLY! RIGHT THROUGH THAT CLEARING! IT WAS SOME GUY...HE...HE WAS LIKE CREEPING AROUND...

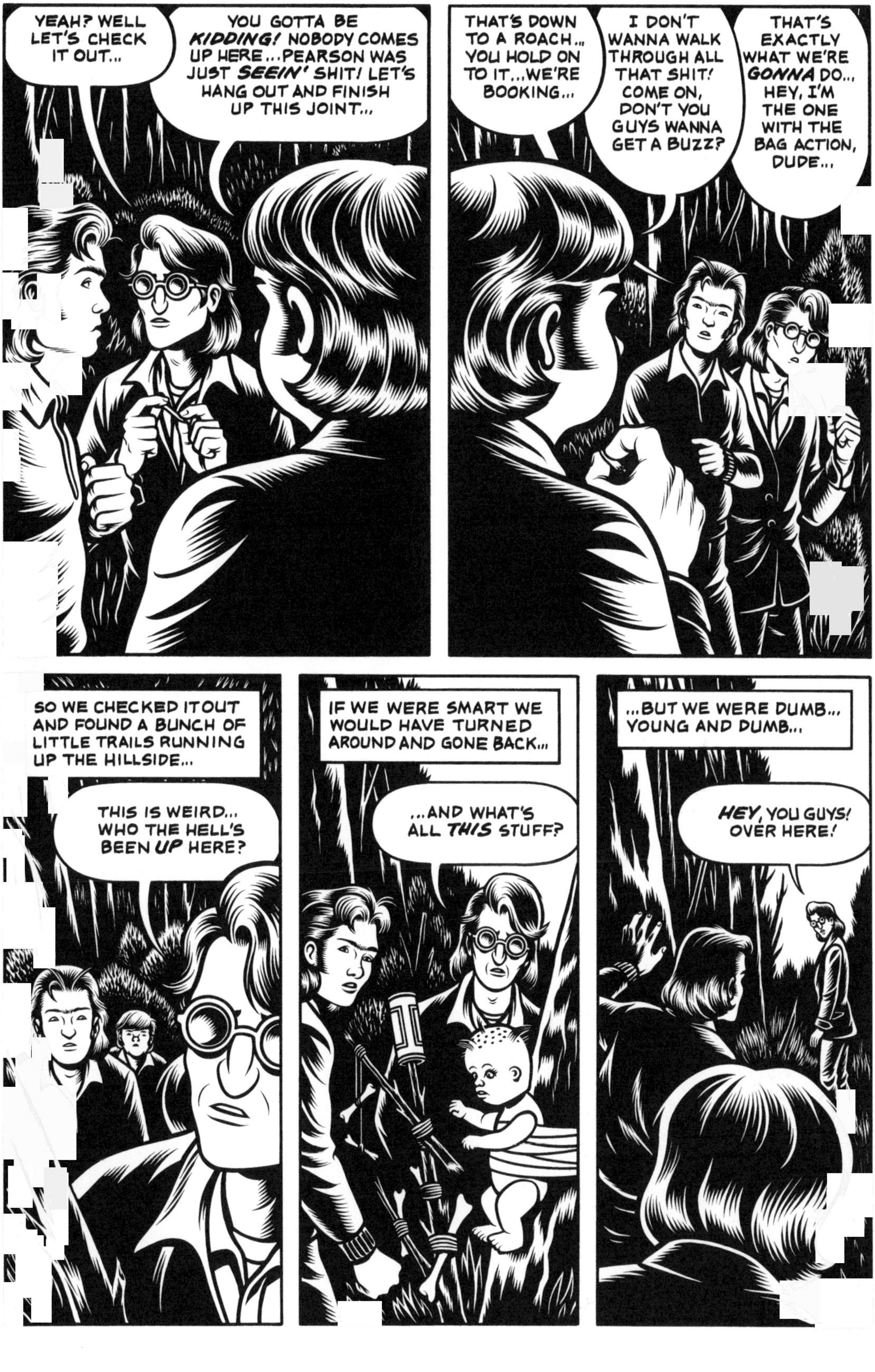
YEAH? WELL LET'S CHECK IT OUT...
YOU GOTTA BE KIDDING! NOBODY COMES UP HERE...PEARSON WAS JUST SEEIN' SHIT! LET'S HANG OUT AND FINISH UP THIS JOINT...
THAT'S DOWN TO A ROACH... YOU HOLD ON TO IT...WE'RE BOOKING...
I DON'T WANNA WALK THROUGH ALL THAT SHIT! COME ON, DON'T YOU GUYS WANNA GET A BUZZ?
THAT'S EXACTLY WHAT WE'RE GONNA DO... HEY, I'M THE ONE WITH THE BAG ACTION, DUDE...
SO WE CHECKED IT OUT AND FOUND A BUNCH OF LITTLE TRAILS RUNNING UP THE HILLSIDE...
THIS IS WEIRD... WHO THE HELL'S BEEN UP HERE?
IF WE WERE SMART WE WOULD HAVE TURNED AROUND AND GONE BACK...
...AND WHAT'S ALL THIS STUFF?
...BUT WE WERE DUMB... YOUNG AND DUMB...
HEY, YOU GUYS! OVER HERE!

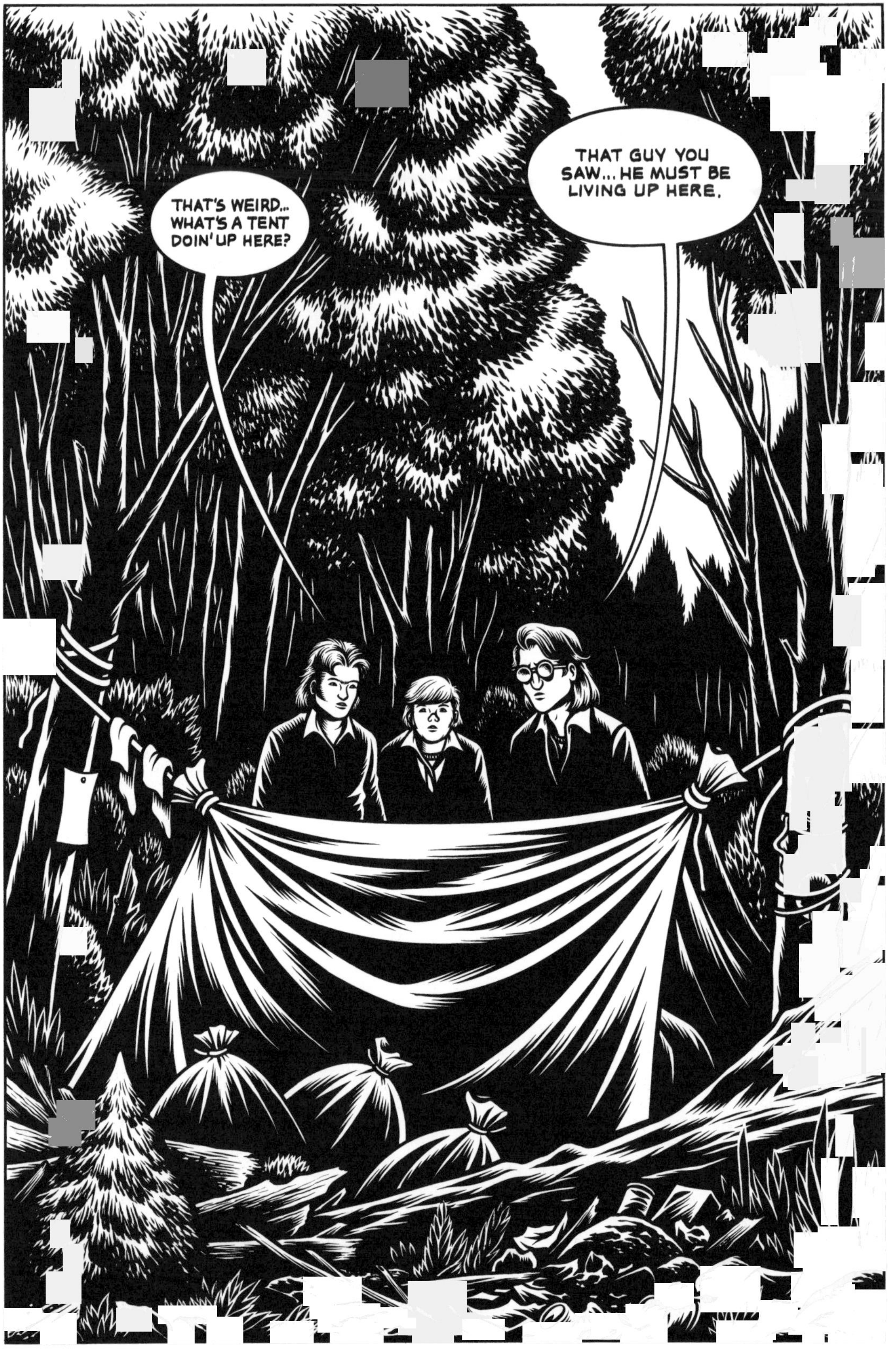
THAT'S WEIRD...
WHAT'S A TENT
DOIN' UP HERE?
THAT GUY YOU
SAW... HE MUST BE
LIVING UP HERE.

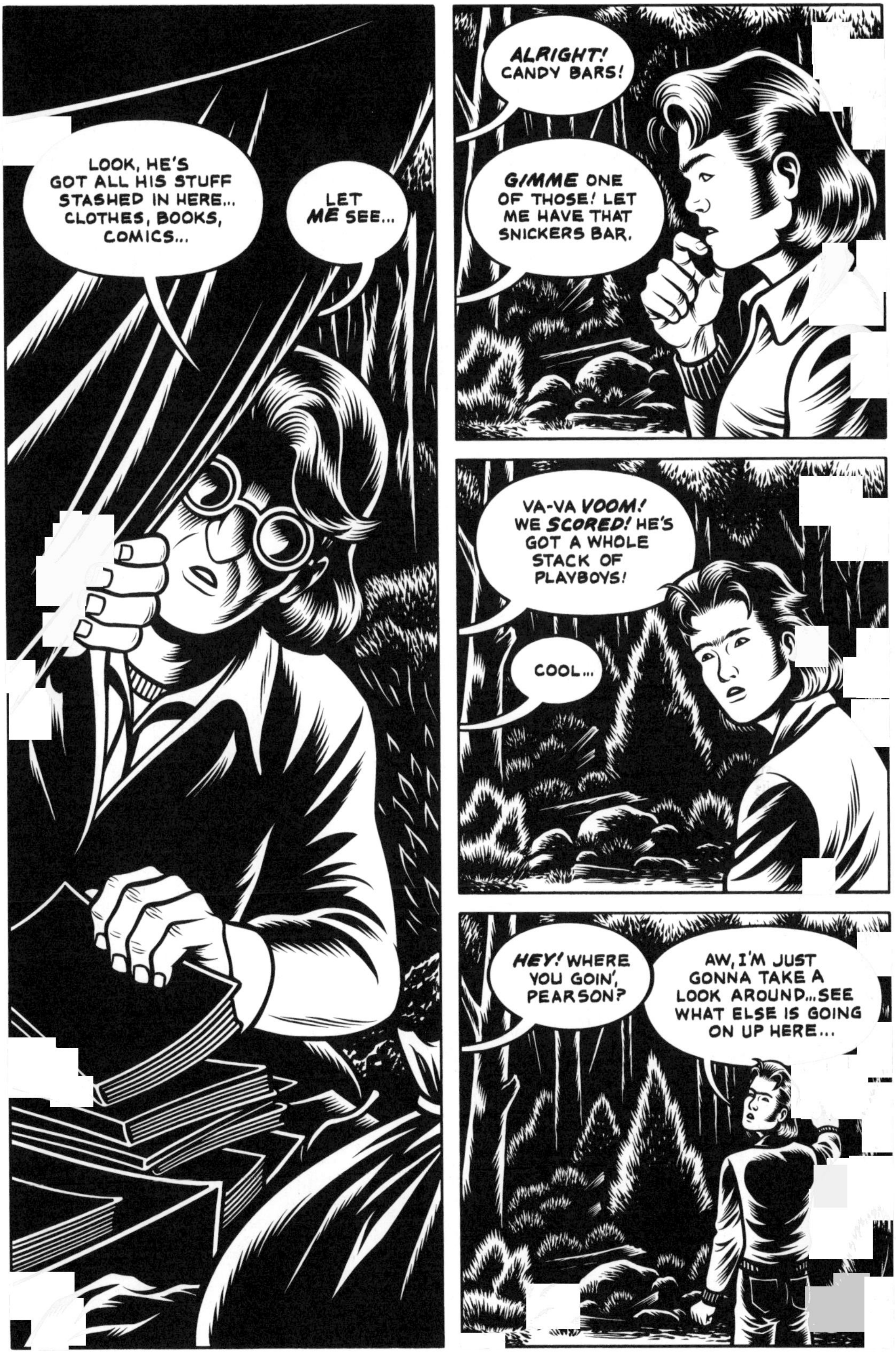
LOOK, HE'S GOT ALL HIS STUFF STASHED IN HERE... CLOTHES, BOOKS, COMICS...
LET ME SEE...
ALRIGHT! CANDY BARS!
GIMME ONE OF THOSE! LET ME HAVE THAT SNICKERS BAR.
VA-VA VOOM! WE SCORED! HE'S GOT A WHOLE STACK OF PLAYBOYS!
COOL...
HEY! WHERE YOU GOIN', PEARSON?
AW, I'M JUST GONNA TAKE A LOOK AROUND...SEE WHAT ELSE IS GOING ON UP HERE...

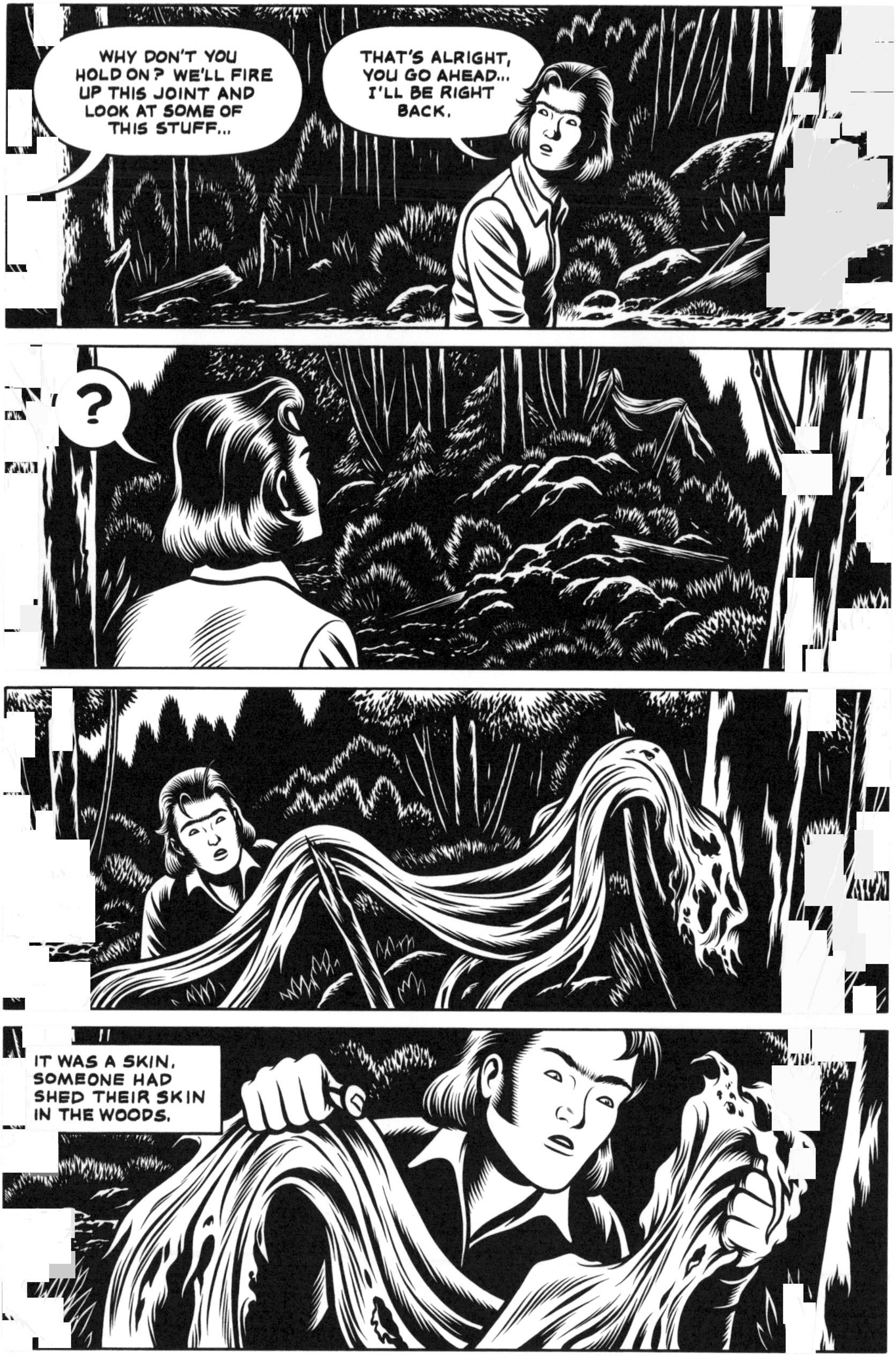
WHY DON'T YOU HOLD ON? WE'LL FIRE UP THIS JOINT AND LOOK AT SOME OF THIS STUFF...
THAT'S ALRIGHT, YOU GO AHEAD... I'LL BE RIGHT BACK.
?
IT WAS A SKIN. SOMEONE HAD SHED THEIR SKIN IN THE WOODS.

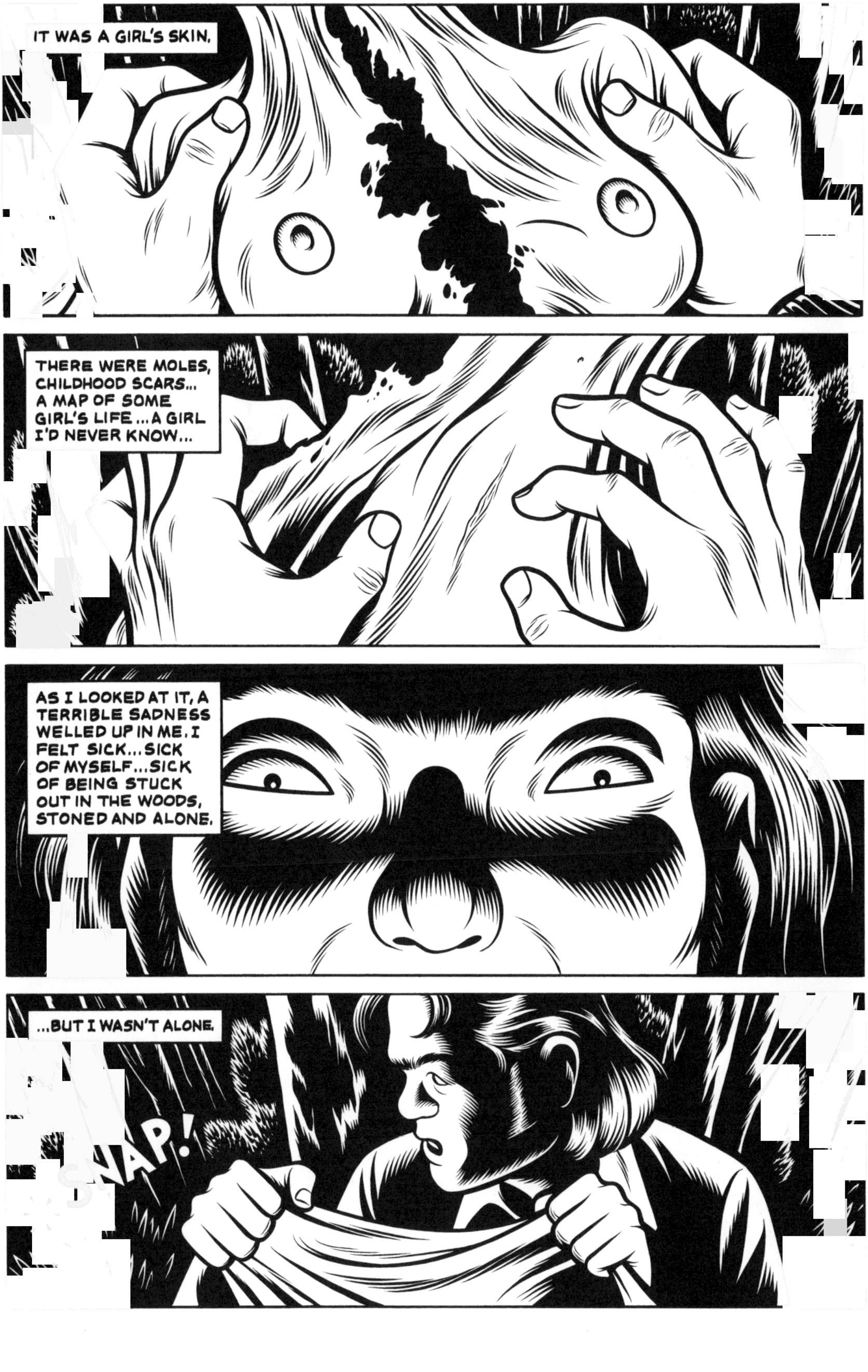

IT WAS A GIRL'S SKIN.
THERE WERE MOLES, CHILDHOOD SCARS... A MAP OF SOME GIRL'S LIFE... A GIRL I'D NEVER KNOW...
AS I LOOKED AT IT, A TERRIBLE SADNESS WELLED UP IN ME. I FELT SICK... SICK OF MYSELF... SICK OF BEING STUCK OUT IN THE WOODS, STONED AND ALONE.
...BUT I WASN'T ALONE.
SNAP!

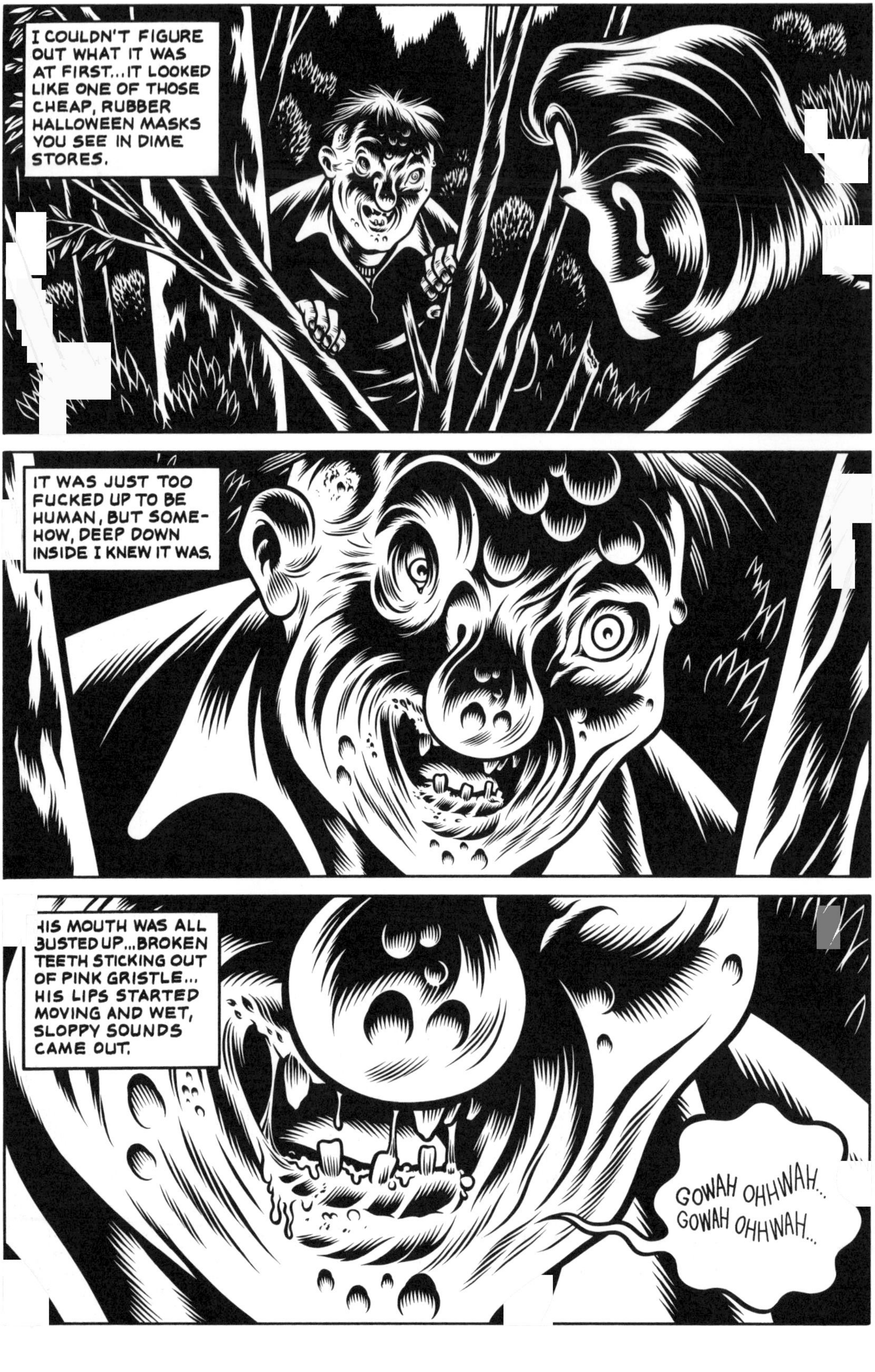
I COULDN'T FIGURE OUT WHAT IT WAS AT FIRST...IT LOOKED LIKE ONE OF THOSE CHEAP, RUBBER HALLOWEEN MASKS YOU SEE IN DIME STORES.
IT WAS JUST TOO FUCKED UP TO BE HUMAN, BUT SOMEHOW, DEEP DOWN INSIDE I KNEW IT WAS.
HIS MOUTH WAS ALL BUSTED UP...BROKEN TEETH STICKING OUT OF PINK GRISTLE... HIS LIPS STARTED MOVING AND WET, SLOPPY SOUNDS CAME OUT.
GOWAH OHHWAH... GOWAH OHHWAH...

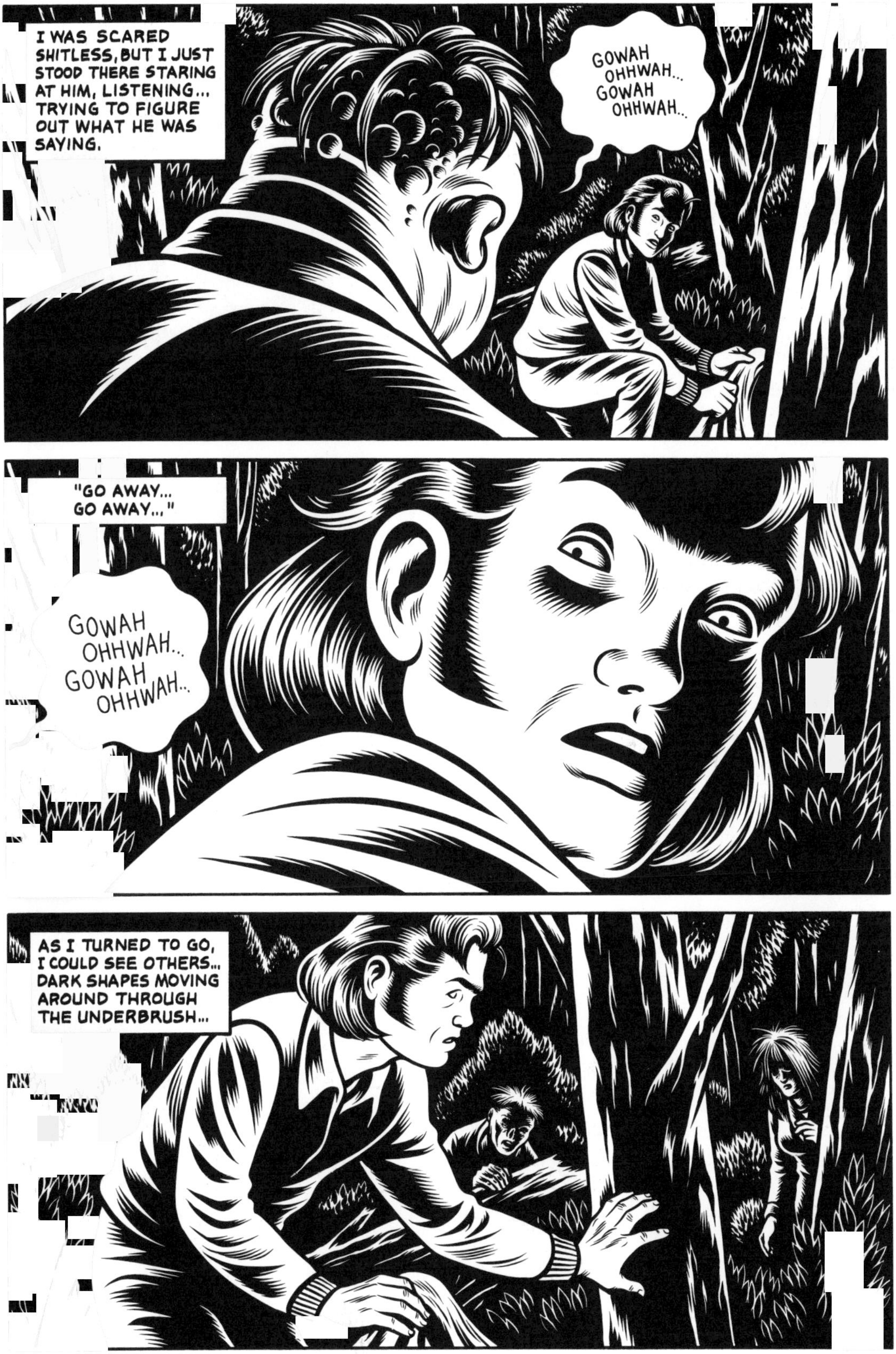
I WAS SCARED SHITLESS, BUT I JUST STOOD THERE STARING AT HIM, LISTENING... TRYING TO FIGURE OUT WHAT HE WAS SAYING.
GOWAH OHHWAH... GOWAH OHHWAH...
"GO AWAY... GO AWAY..."
GOWAH OHHWAH... GOWAH OHHWAH...
AS I TURNED TO GO, I COULD SEE OTHERS... DARK SHAPES MOVING AROUND THROUGH THE UNDERBRUSH...

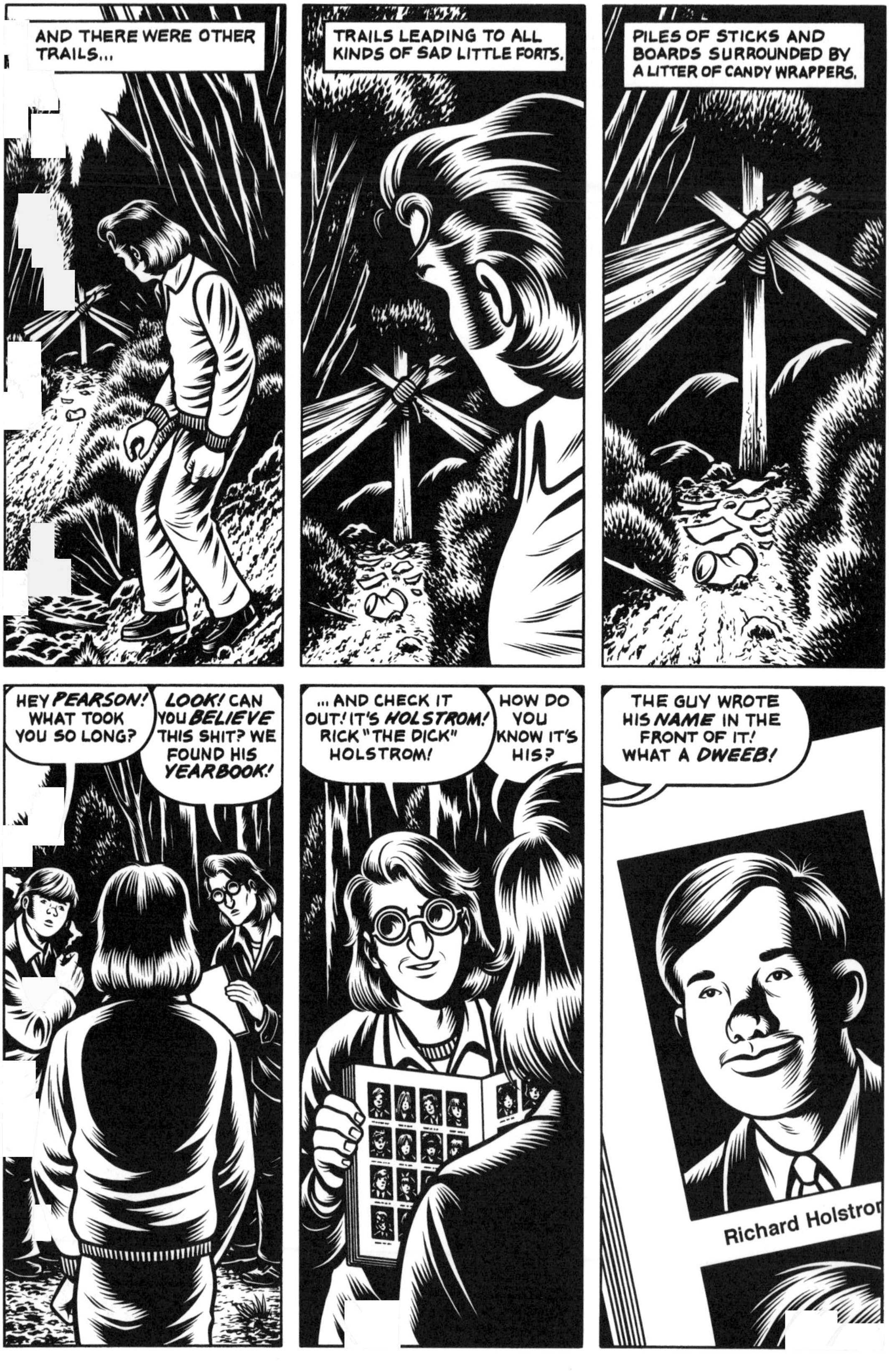
AND THERE WERE OTHER TRAILS...
TRAILS LEADING TO ALL KINDS OF SAD LITTLE FORTS.
PILES OF STICKS AND BOARDS SURROUNDED BY A LITTER OF CANDY WRAPPERS.
HEY PEARSON! WHAT TOOK YOU SO LONG?
LOOK! CAN YOU BELIEVE THIS SHIT? WE FOUND HIS YEARBOOK!
...AND CHECK IT OUT! IT'S HOLSTROM! RICK "THE DICK" HOLSTROM!
HOW DO YOU KNOW IT'S HIS?
THE GUY WROTE HIS NAME IN THE FRONT OF IT! WHAT A DWEEB!
Richard Holstrom

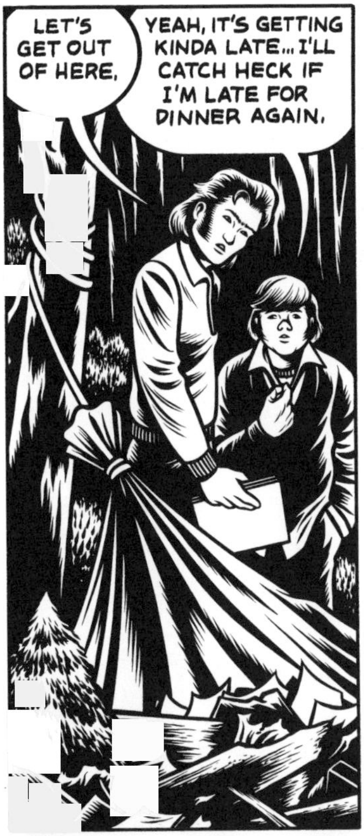
LET'S GET OUT OF HERE.
YEAH, IT'S GETTING KINDA LATE... I'LL CATCH HECK IF I'M LATE FOR DINNER AGAIN.

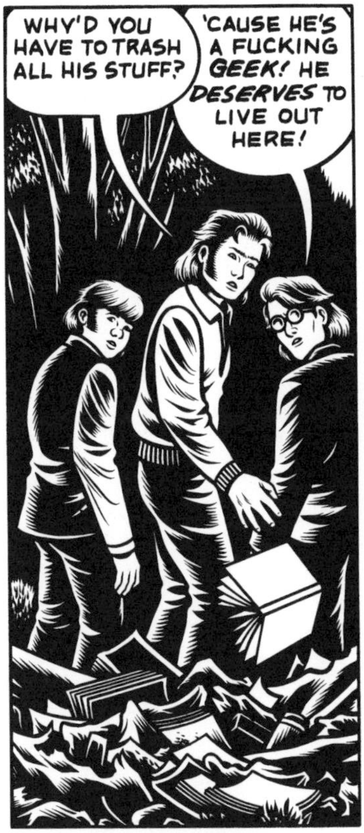
WHY'D YOU HAVE TO TRASH ALL HIS STUFF?
'CAUSE HE'S A FUCKING GEEK! HE DESERVES TO LIVE OUT HERE!

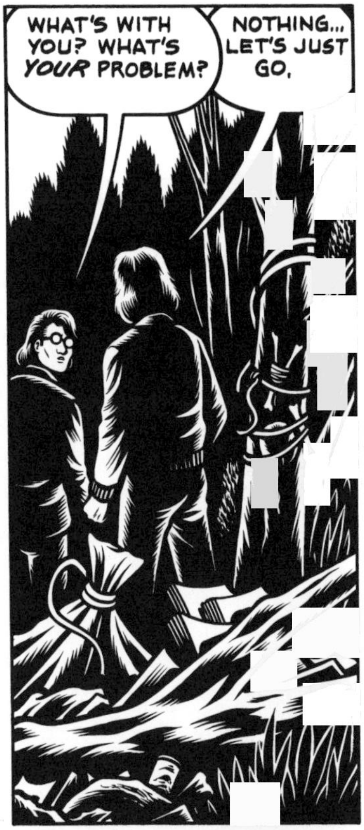
WHAT'S WITH YOU? WHAT'S YOUR PROBLEM?
NOTHING... LET'S JUST GO.

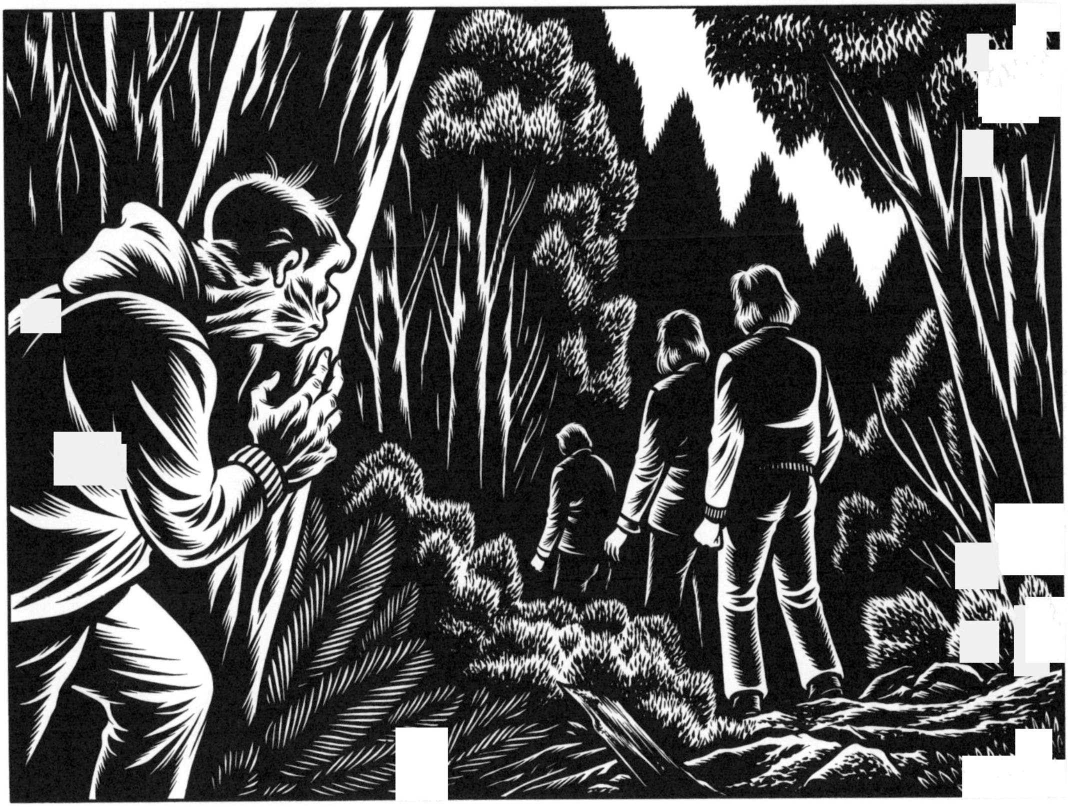

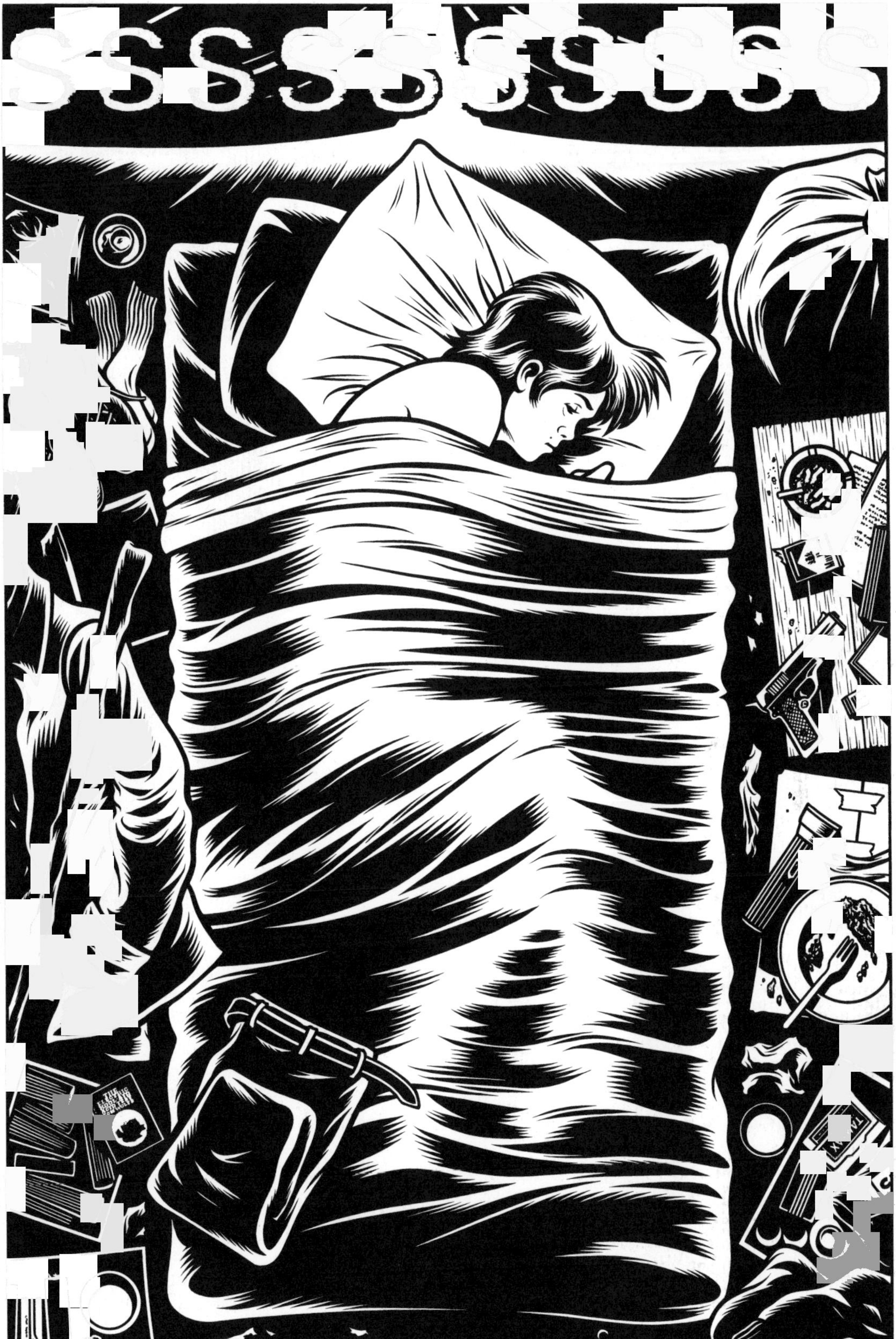
SSSSSSSSSS

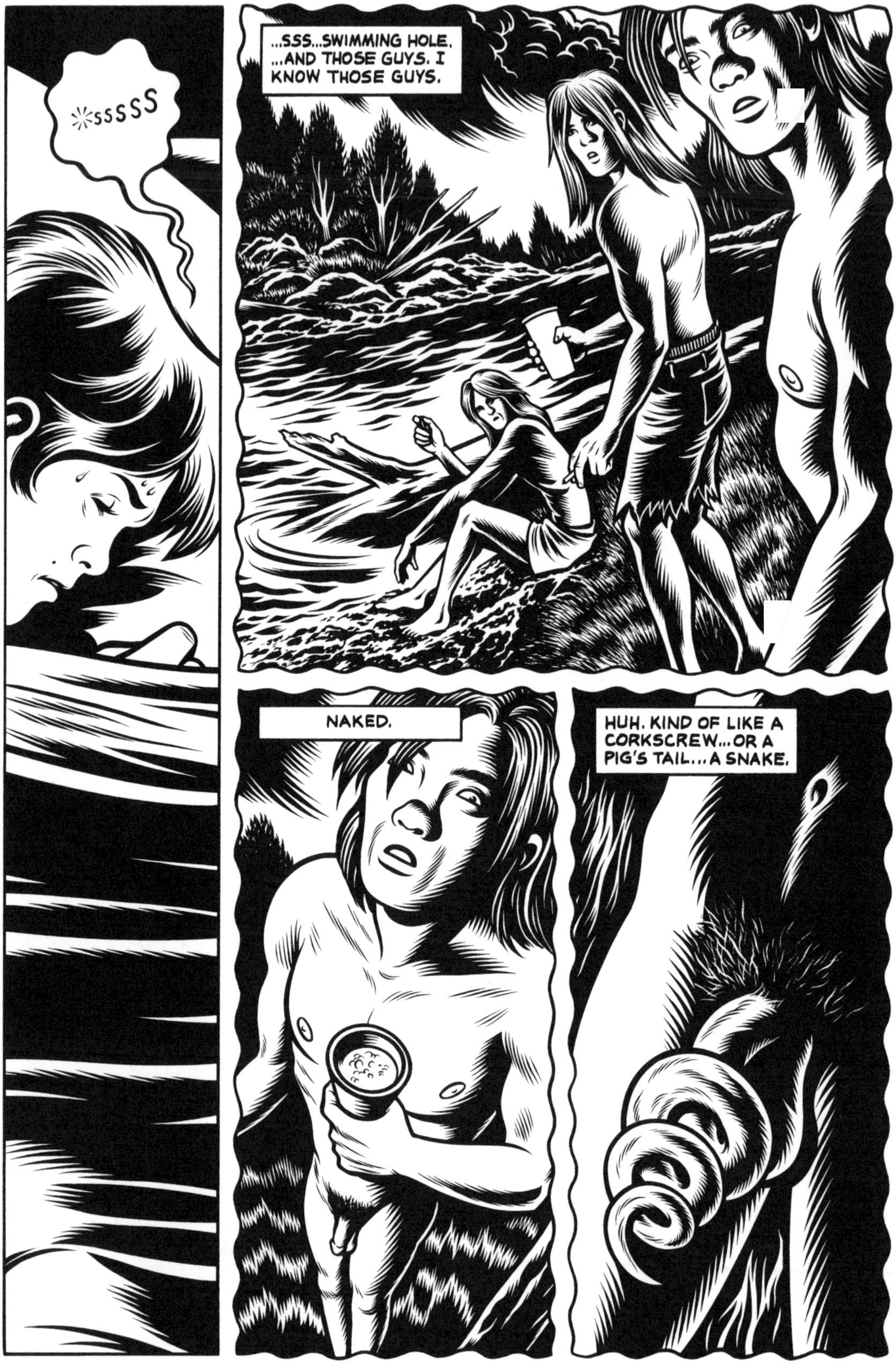
sssss
...SSS...SWIMMING HOLE.
...AND THOSE GUYS. I KNOW THOSE GUYS.
NAKED.
HUH. KIND OF LIKE A CORKSCREW...OR A PIG'S TAIL...A SNAKE.

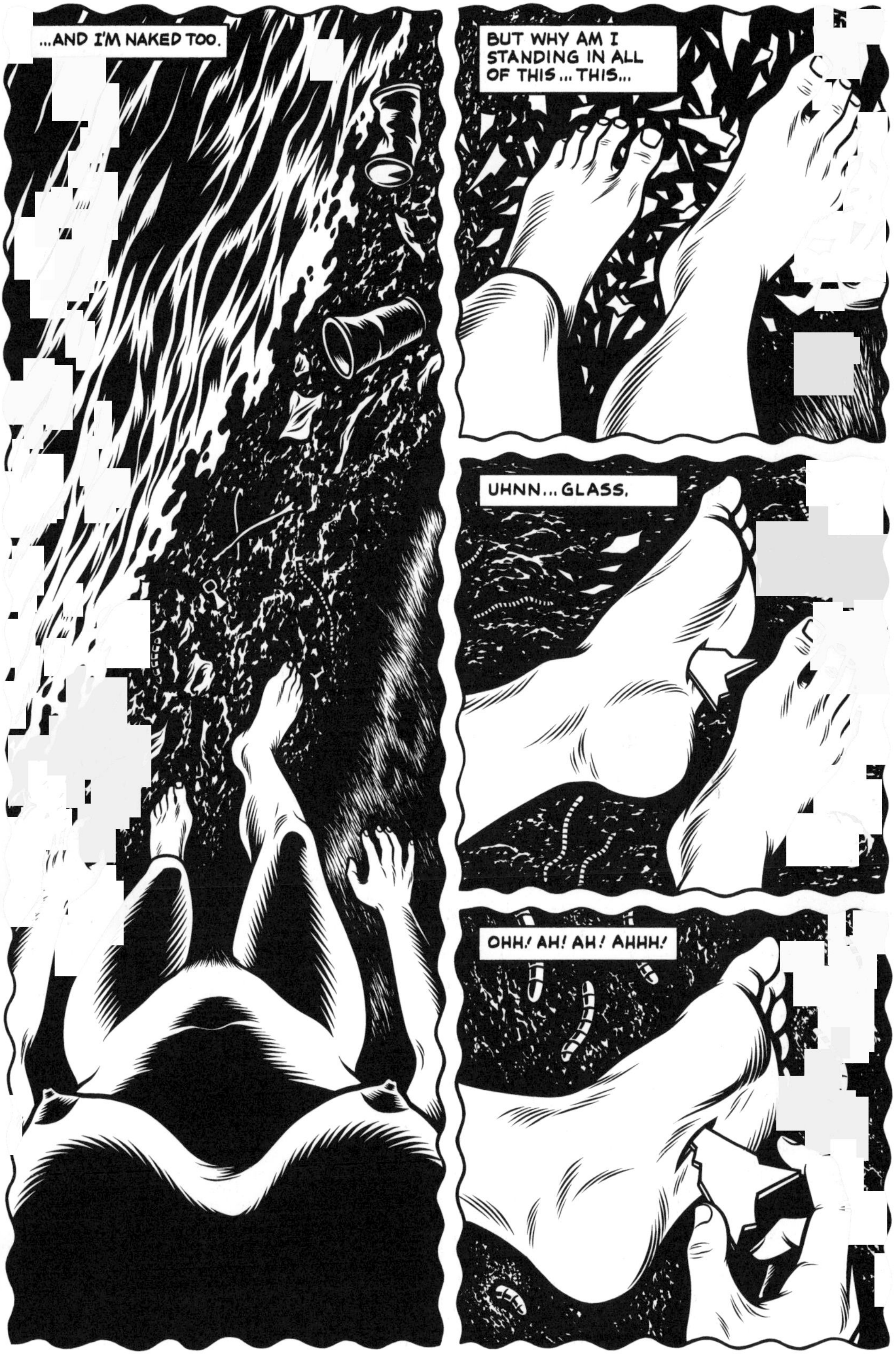
...AND I'M NAKED TOO.
BUT WHY AM I STANDING IN ALL OF THIS... THIS...
UHNN... GLASS.
OHH! AH! AH! AHHH!

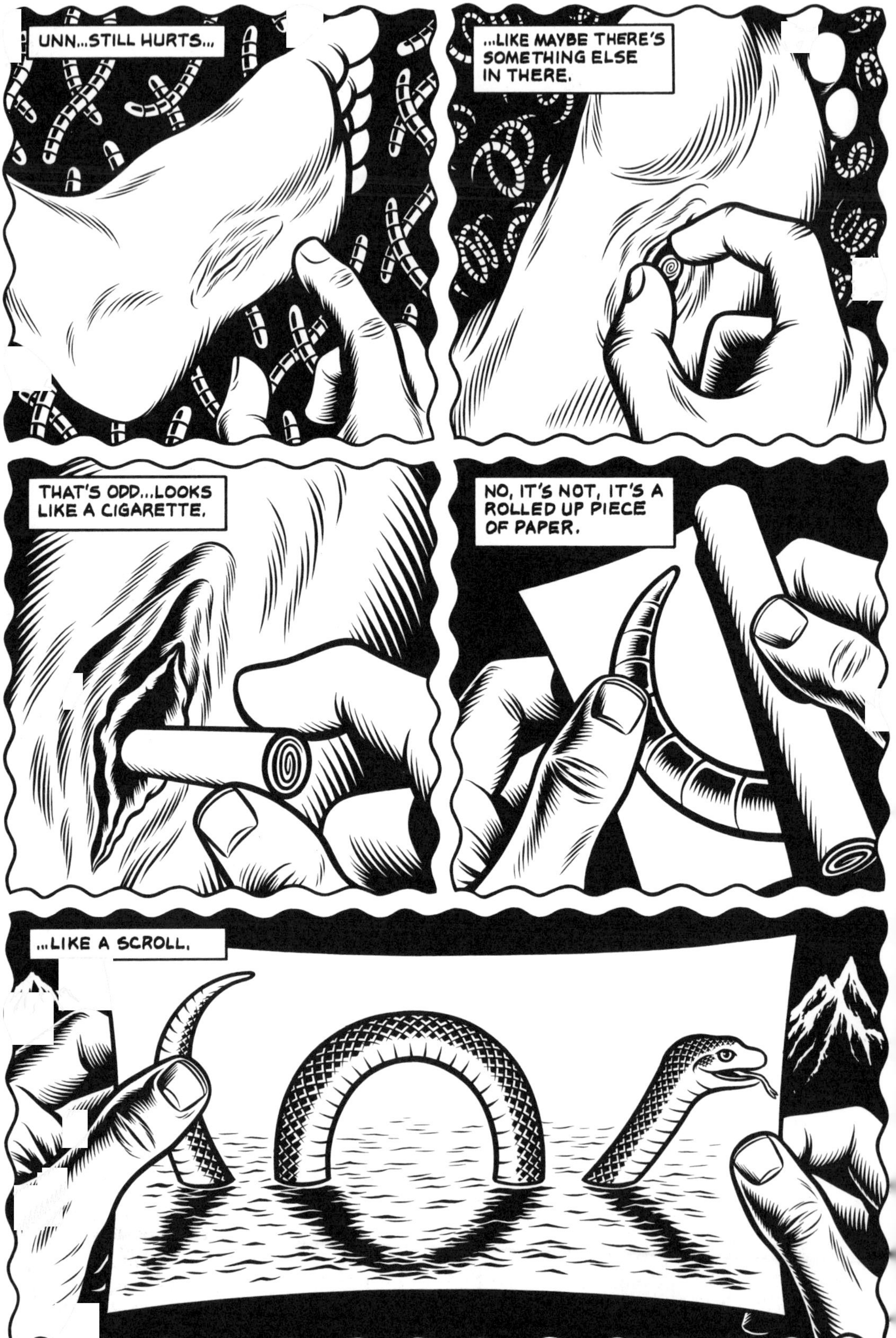
UNN...STILL HURTS...
...LIKE MAYBE THERE'S SOMETHING ELSE IN THERE.
THAT'S ODD...LOOKS LIKE A CIGARETTE.
NO, IT'S NOT, IT'S A ROLLED UP PIECE OF PAPER.
...LIKE A SCROLL.

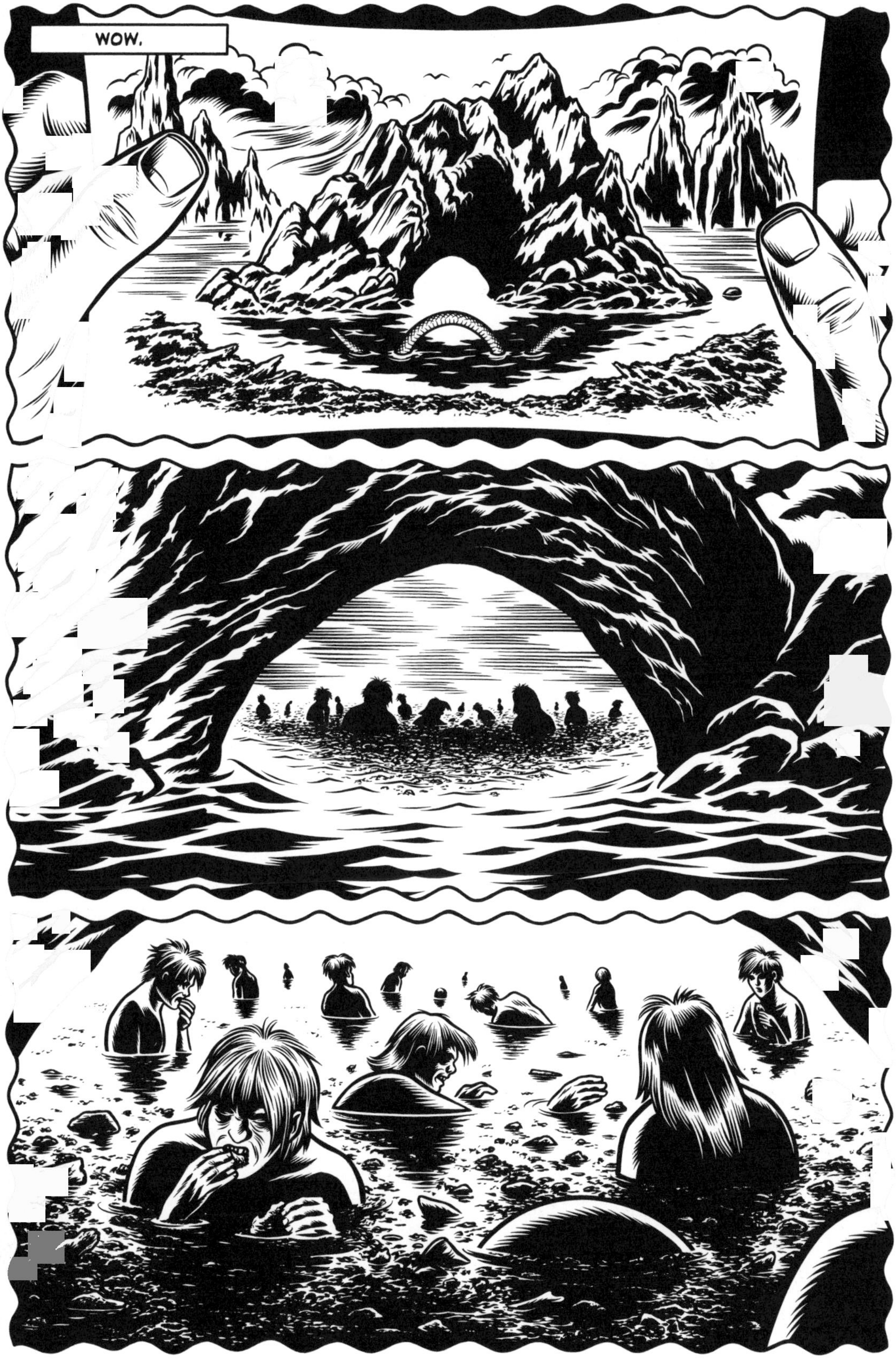
WOW.

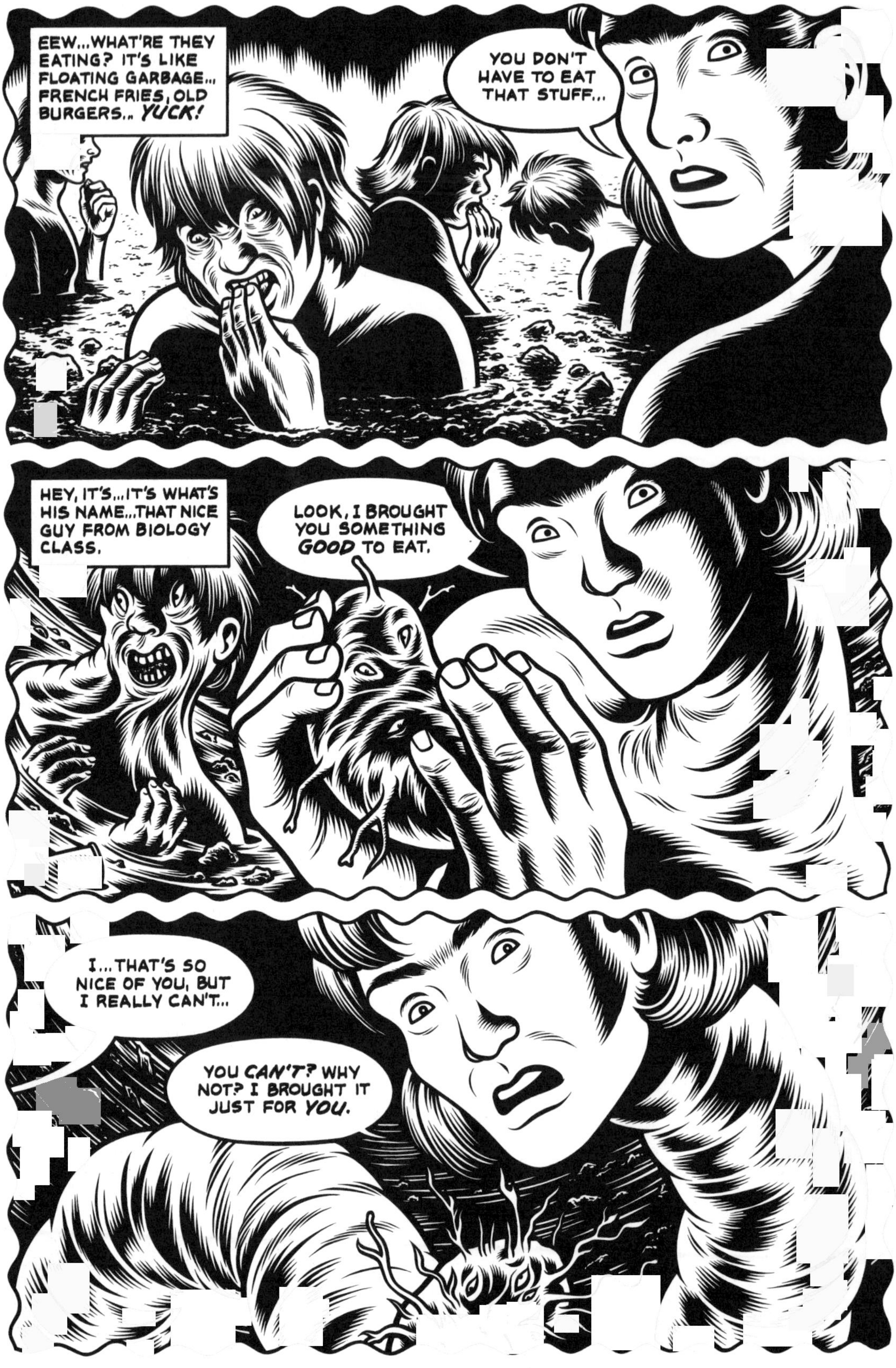
EEW...WHAT'RE THEY EATING? IT'S LIKE FLOATING GARBAGE... FRENCH FRIES, OLD BURGERS... YUCK!
YOU DON'T HAVE TO EAT THAT STUFF...
HEY, IT'S...IT'S WHAT'S HIS NAME...THAT NICE GUY FROM BIOLOGY CLASS.
LOOK, I BROUGHT YOU SOMETHING GOOD TO EAT.
I...THAT'S SO NICE OF YOU, BUT I REALLY CAN'T...
YOU CAN'T? WHY NOT? I BROUGHT IT JUST FOR YOU.

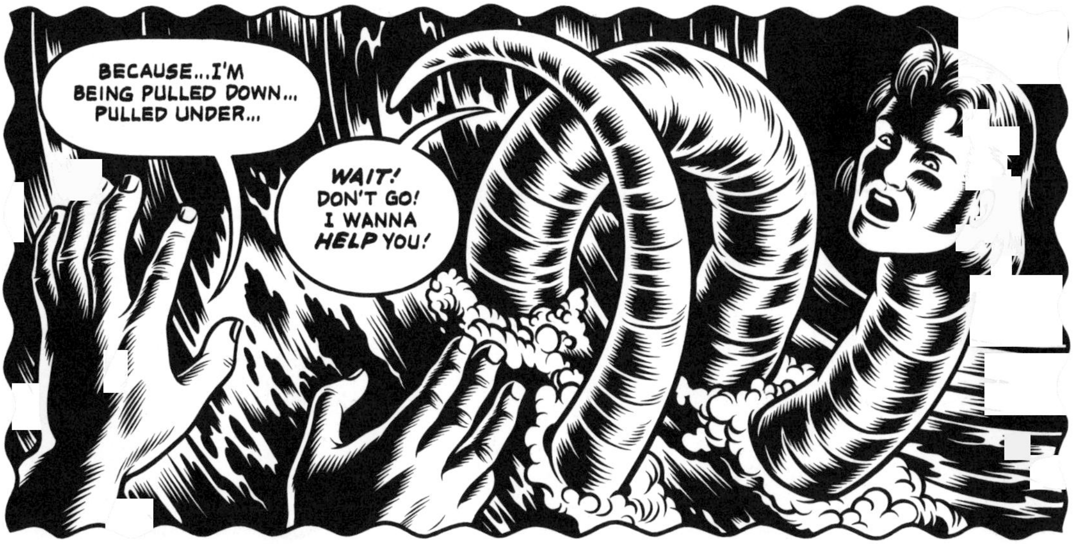
BECAUSE...I'M BEING PULLED DOWN... PULLED UNDER...
WAIT! DON'T GO! I WANNA HELP YOU!

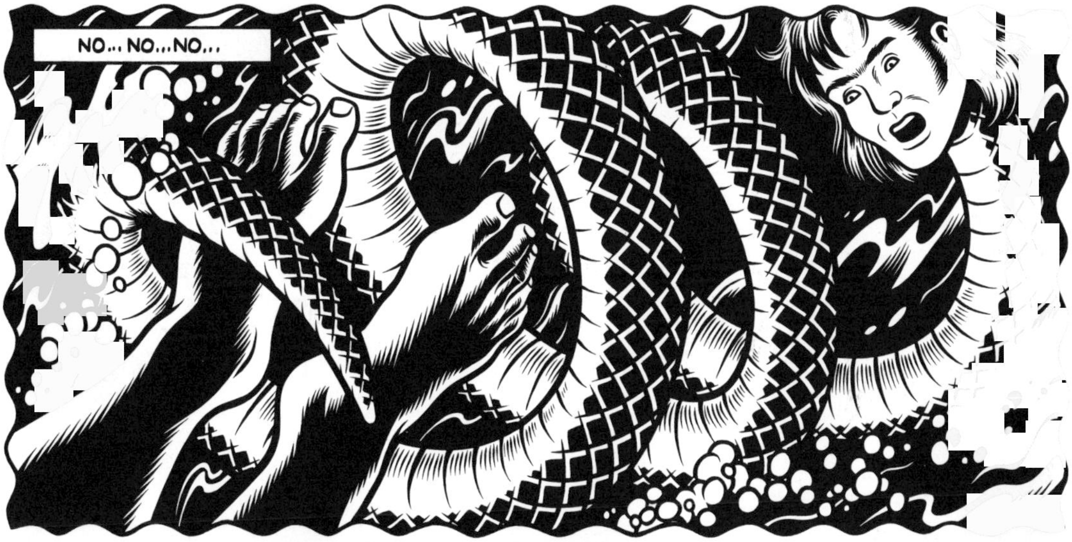
NO... NO...NO...

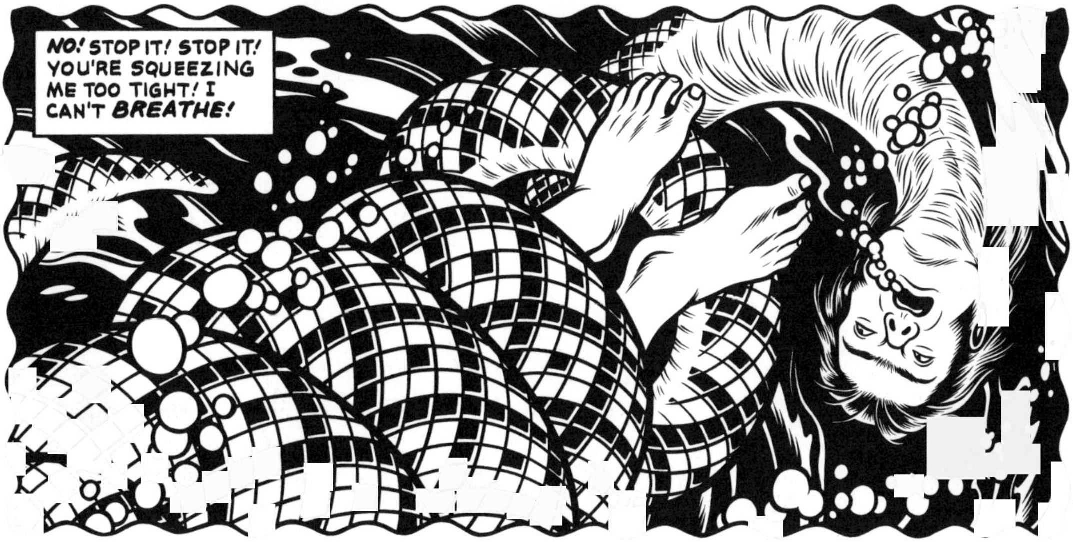
NO! STOP IT! STOP IT! YOU'RE SQUEEZING ME TOO TIGHT! I CAN'T BREATHE!

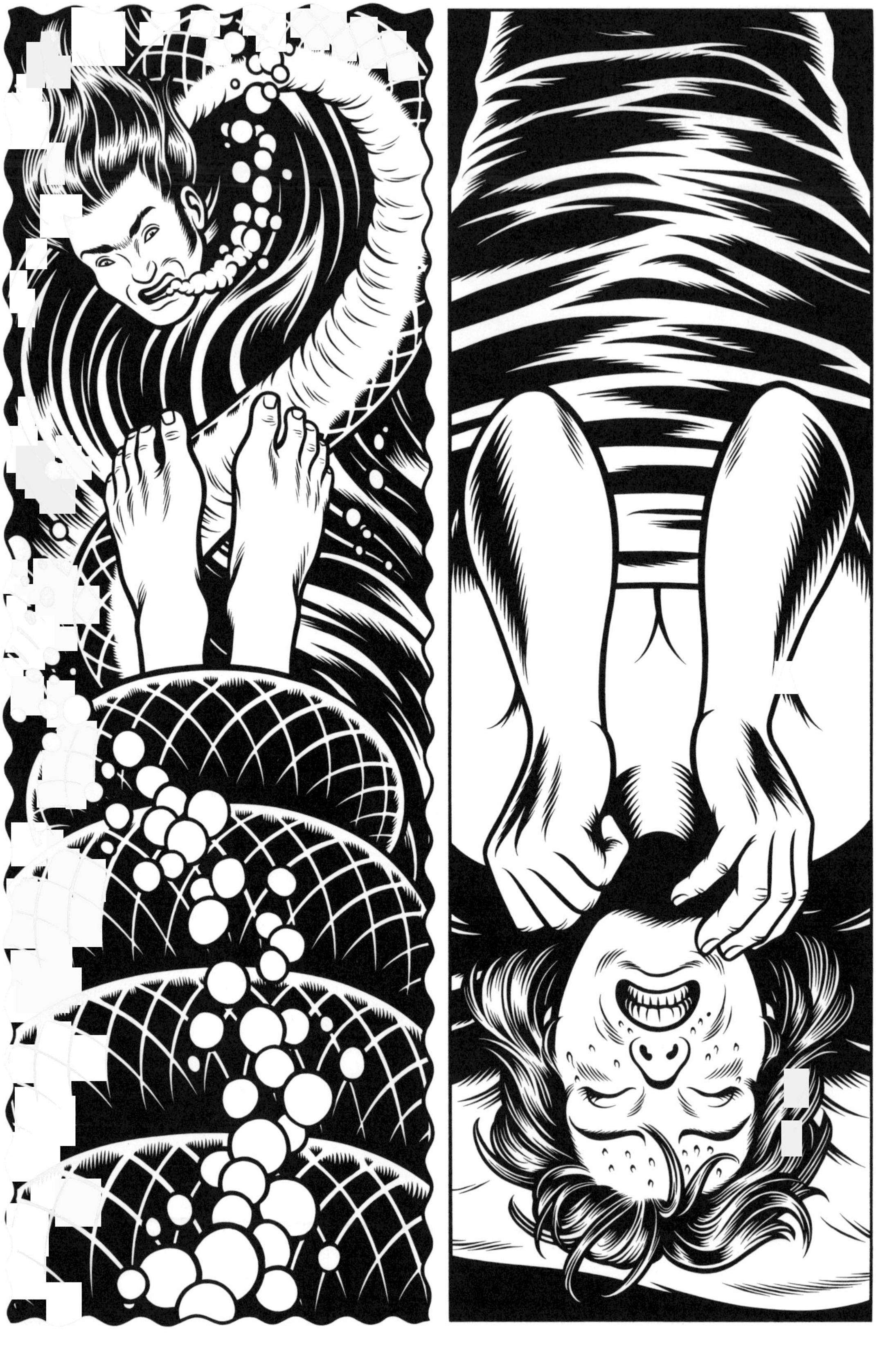

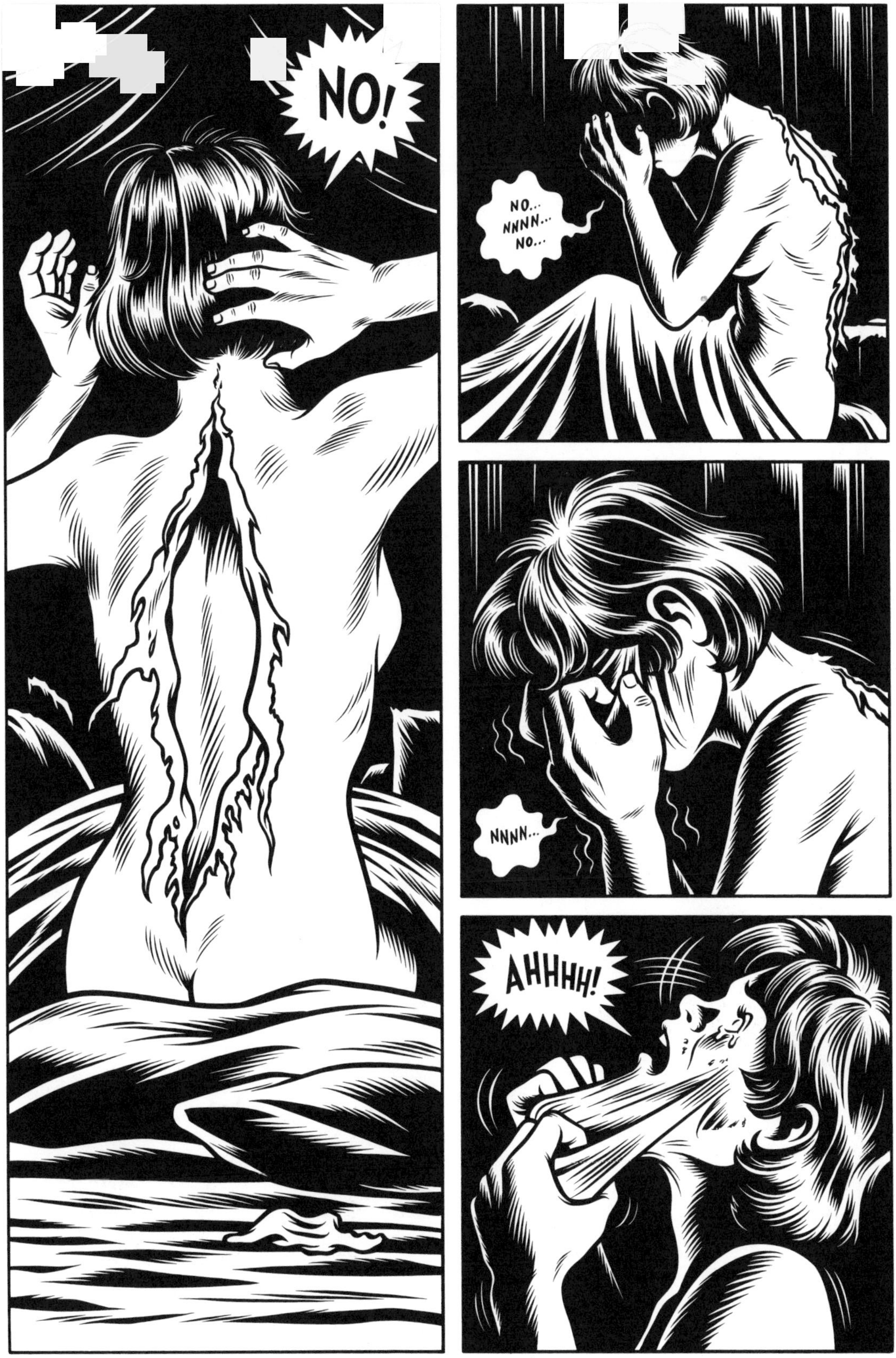
NO!
NO... NNNN... NO...
NNNN...
AHHHH!

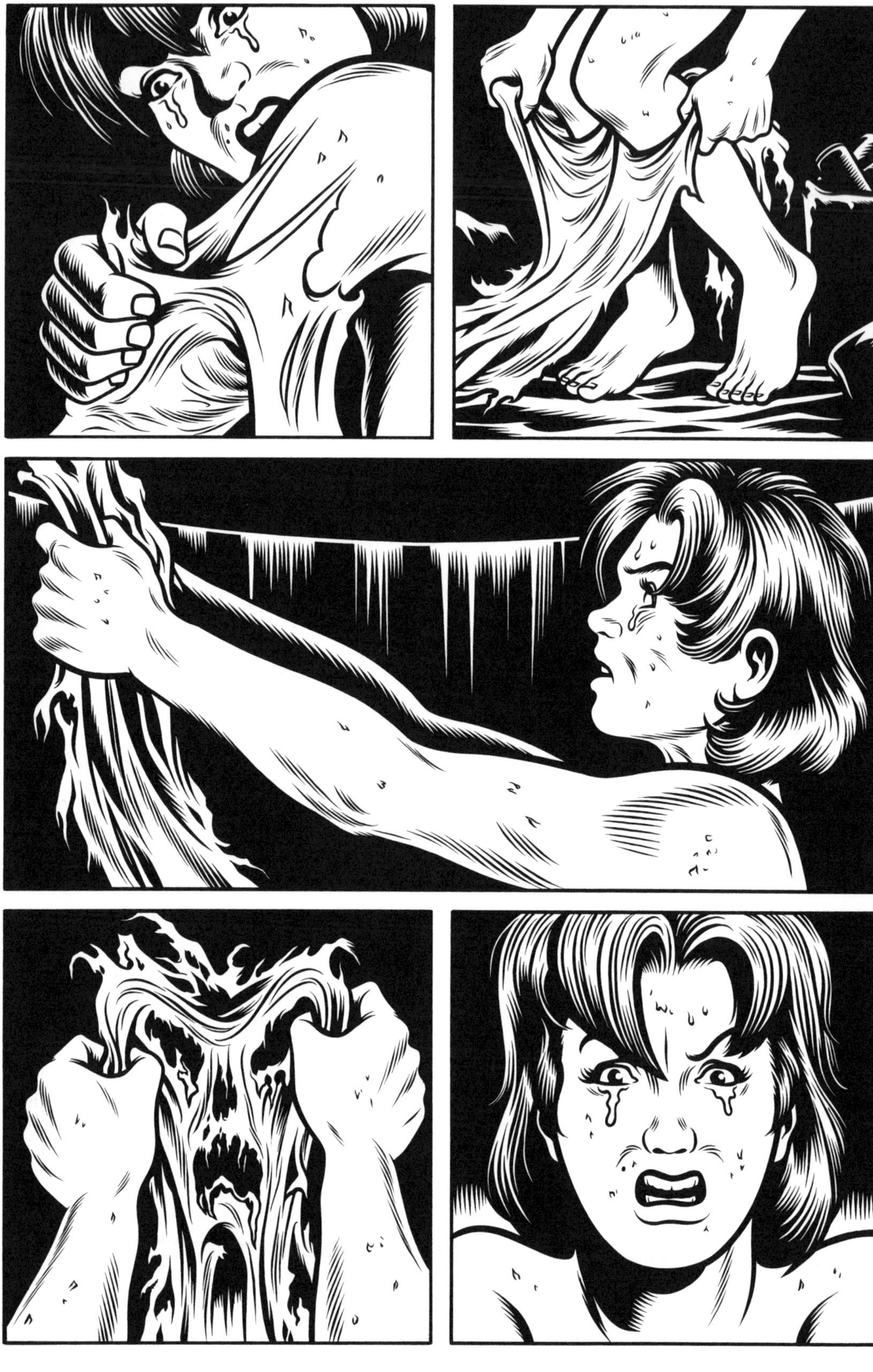

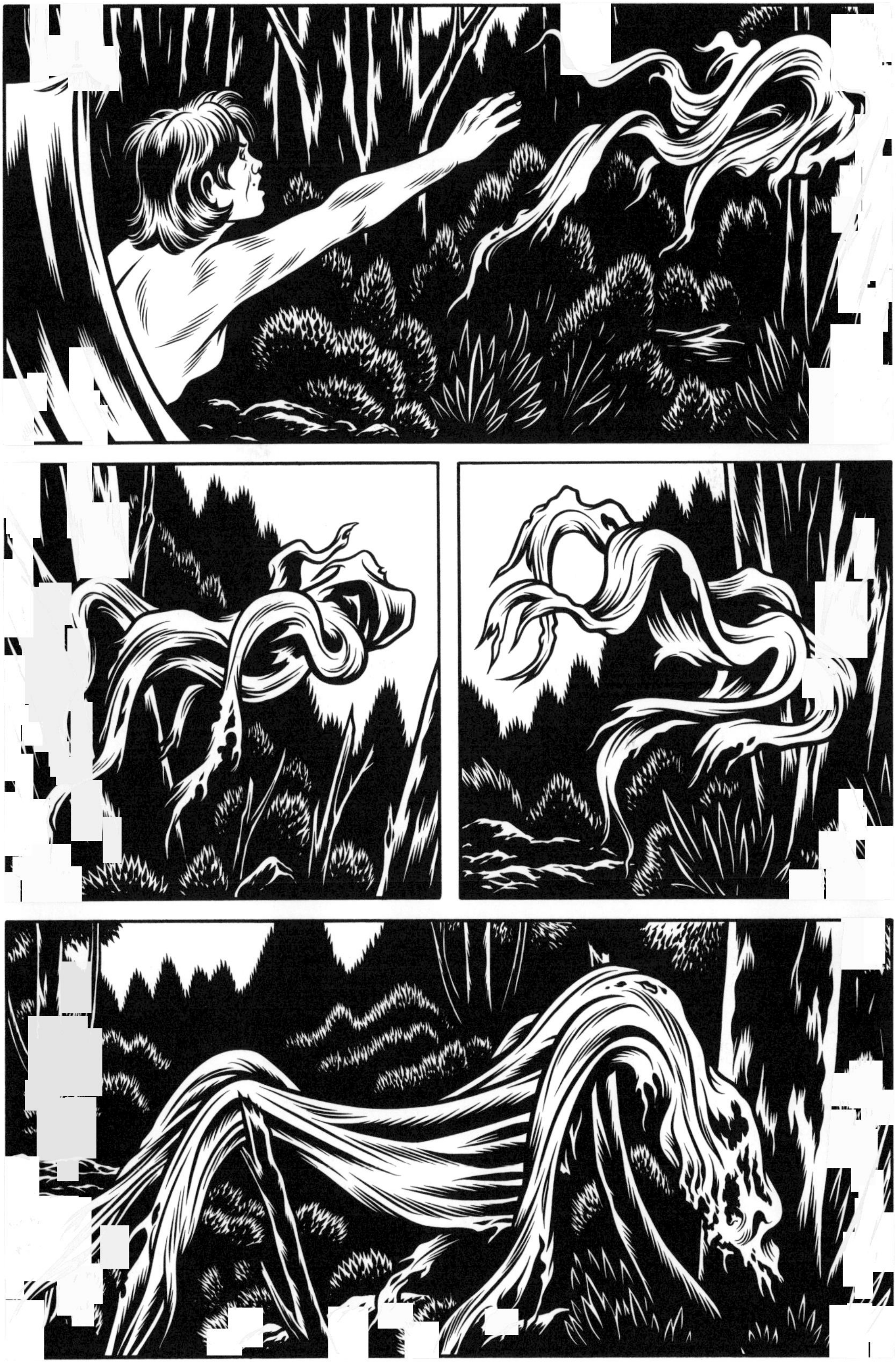

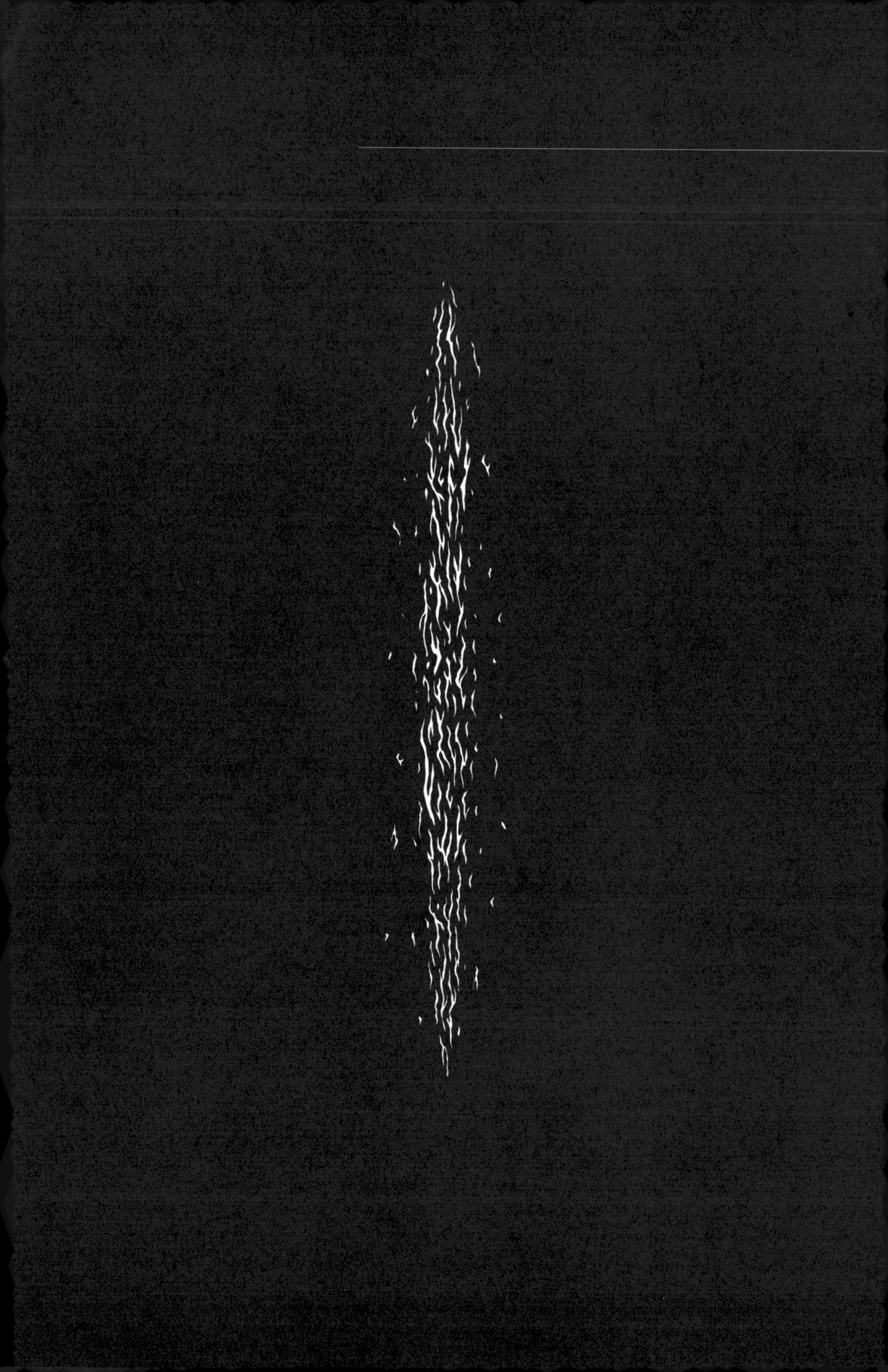

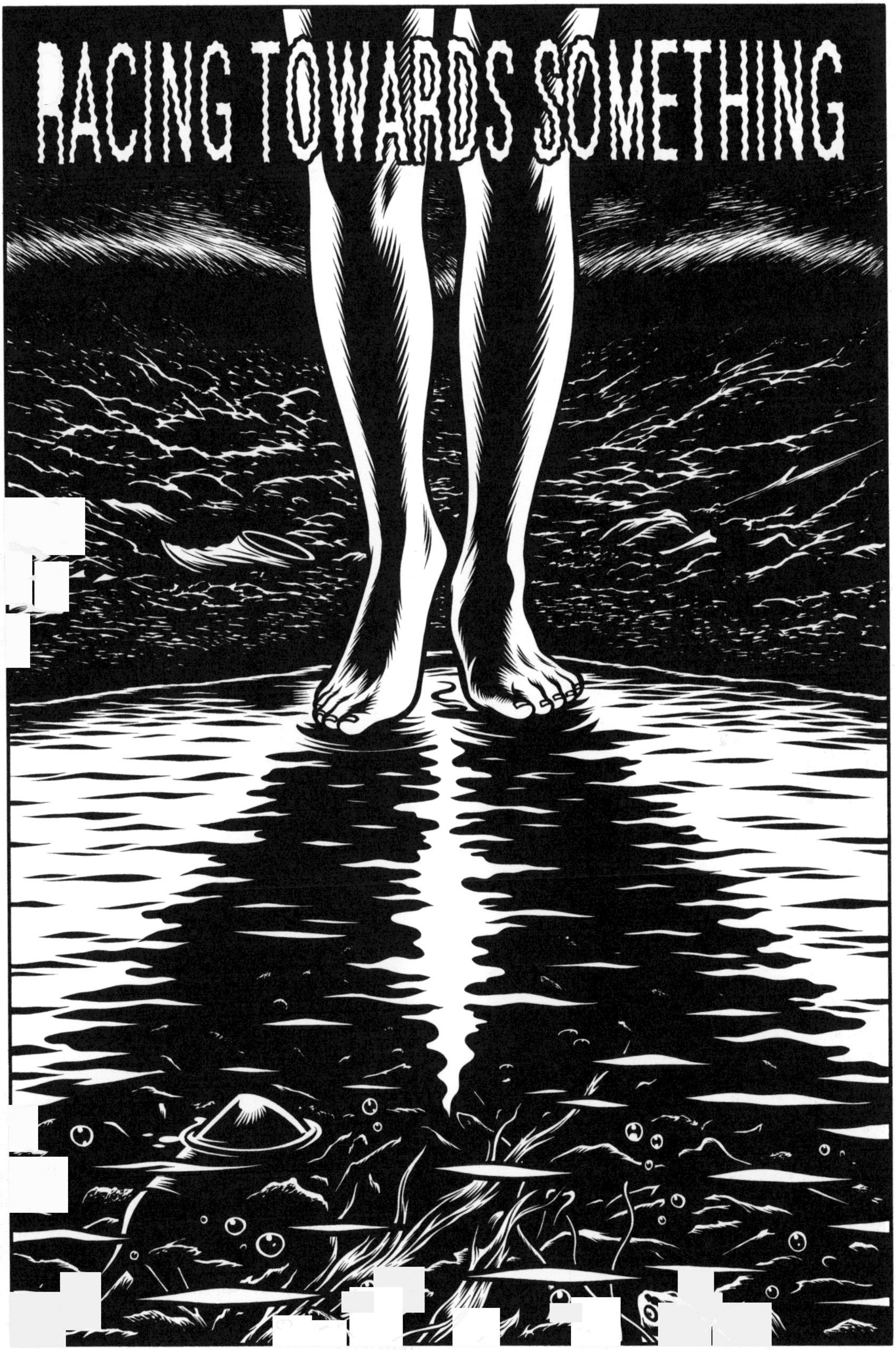
RACING TOWARDS SOMETHING

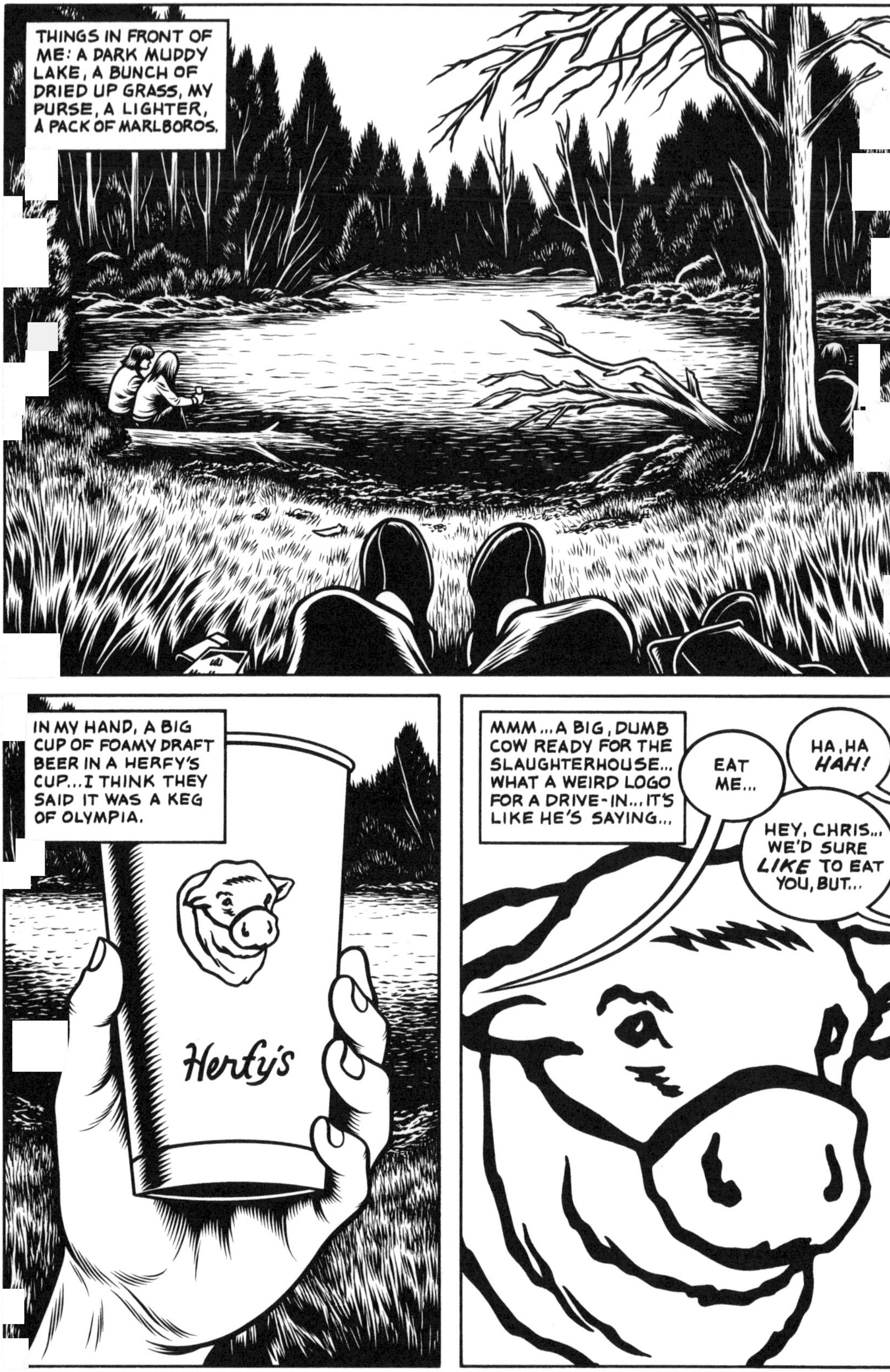
THINGS IN FRONT OF ME: A DARK MUDDY LAKE, A BUNCH OF DRIED UP GRASS, MY PURSE, A LIGHTER, A PACK OF MARLBOROS.
IN MY HAND, A BIG CUP OF FOAMY DRAFT BEER IN A HERFY'S CUP... I THINK THEY SAID IT WAS A KEG OF OLYMPIA.
Herfy's
MMM... A BIG, DUMB COW READY FOR THE SLAUGHTERHOUSE... WHAT A WEIRD LOGO FOR A DRIVE-IN... IT'S LIKE HE'S SAYING...
EAT ME...
HA, HA *HAH!*
HEY, CHRIS... WE'D SURE *LIKE* TO EAT YOU, BUT...

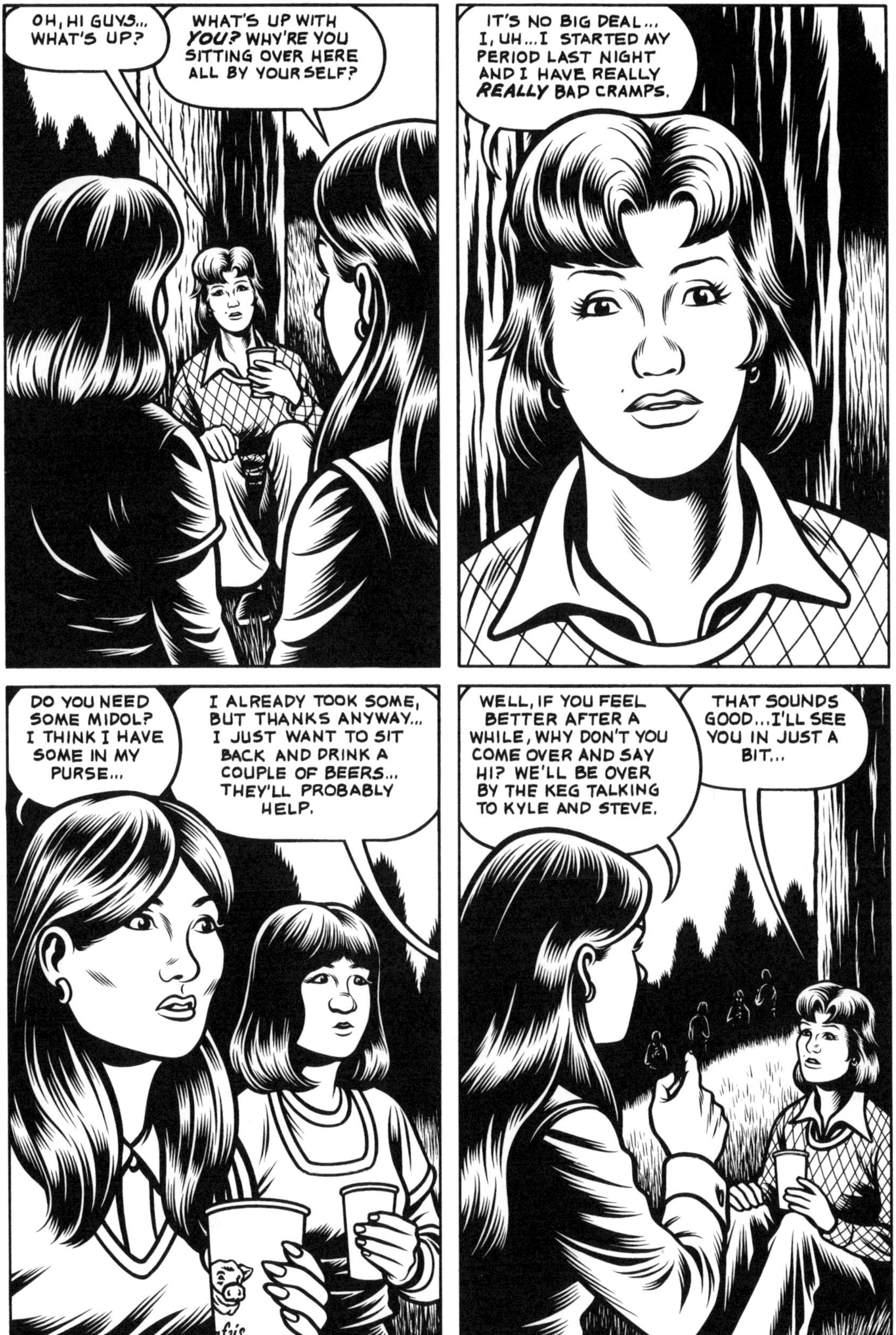
OH, HI GUYS... WHAT'S UP?
WHAT'S UP WITH YOU? WHY'RE YOU SITTING OVER HERE ALL BY YOURSELF?
IT'S NO BIG DEAL... I, UH... I STARTED MY PERIOD LAST NIGHT AND I HAVE REALLY REALLY BAD CRAMPS.
DO YOU NEED SOME MIDOL? I THINK I HAVE SOME IN MY PURSE...
I ALREADY TOOK SOME, BUT THANKS ANYWAY... I JUST WANT TO SIT BACK AND DRINK A COUPLE OF BEERS... THEY'LL PROBABLY HELP.
WELL, IF YOU FEEL BETTER AFTER A WHILE, WHY DON'T YOU COME OVER AND SAY HI? WE'LL BE OVER BY THE KEG TALKING TO KYLE AND STEVE.
THAT SOUNDS GOOD... I'LL SEE YOU IN JUST A BIT...

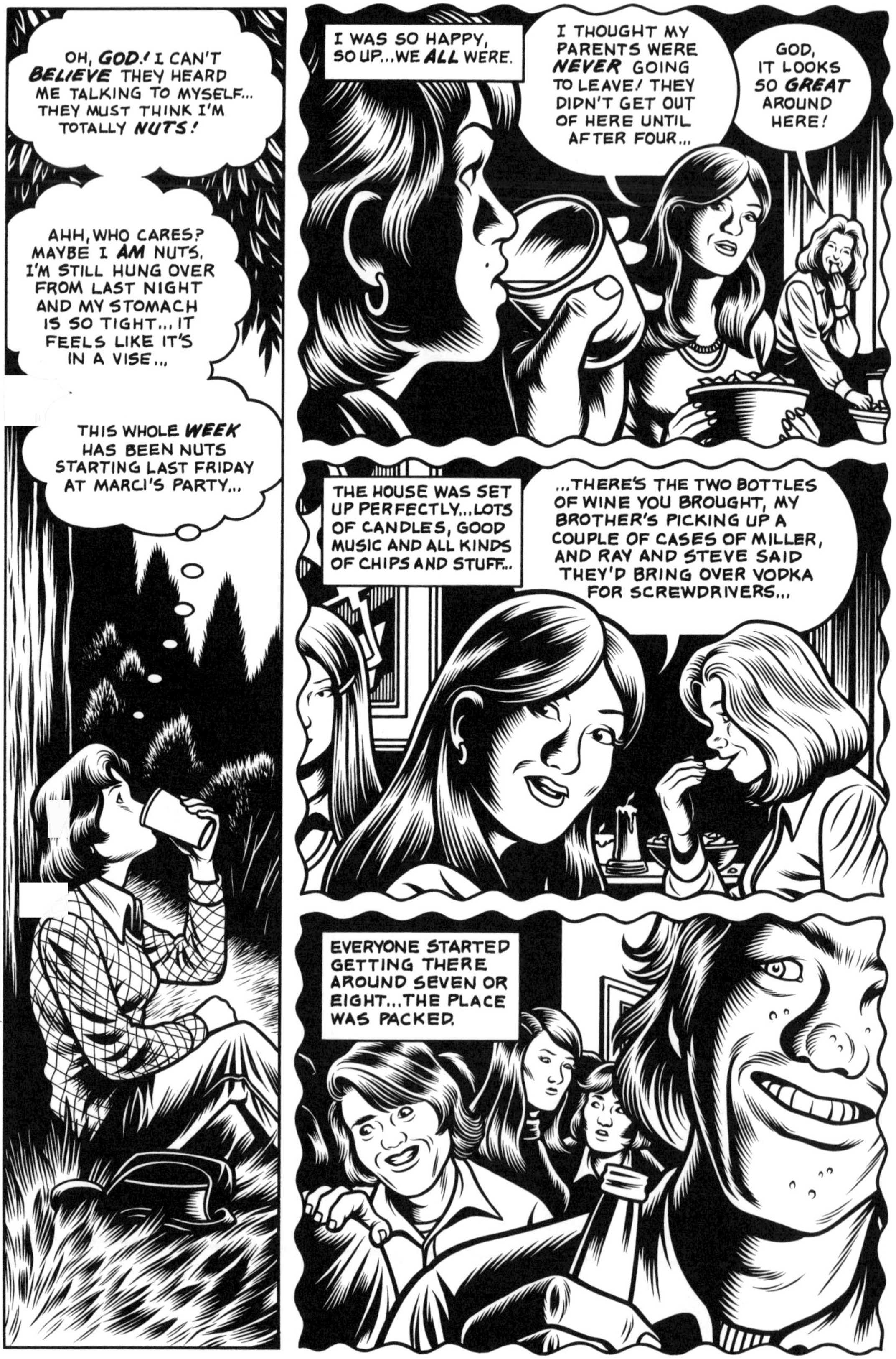
OH, GOD! I CAN'T BELIEVE THEY HEARD ME TALKING TO MYSELF... THEY MUST THINK I'M TOTALLY NUTS!
AHH, WHO CARES? MAYBE I AM NUTS. I'M STILL HUNG OVER FROM LAST NIGHT AND MY STOMACH IS SO TIGHT... IT FEELS LIKE IT'S IN A VISE...
THIS WHOLE WEEK HAS BEEN NUTS STARTING LAST FRIDAY AT MARCI'S PARTY...
I WAS SO HAPPY, SO UP... WE ALL WERE.
I THOUGHT MY PARENTS WERE NEVER GOING TO LEAVE! THEY DIDN'T GET OUT OF HERE UNTIL AFTER FOUR...
GOD, IT LOOKS SO GREAT AROUND HERE!
THE HOUSE WAS SET UP PERFECTLY... LOTS OF CANDLES, GOOD MUSIC AND ALL KINDS OF CHIPS AND STUFF...
...THERE'S THE TWO BOTTLES OF WINE YOU BROUGHT, MY BROTHER'S PICKING UP A COUPLE OF CASES OF MILLER, AND RAY AND STEVE SAID THEY'D BRING OVER VODKA FOR SCREWDRIVERS...
EVERYONE STARTED GETTING THERE AROUND SEVEN OR EIGHT... THE PLACE WAS PACKED.

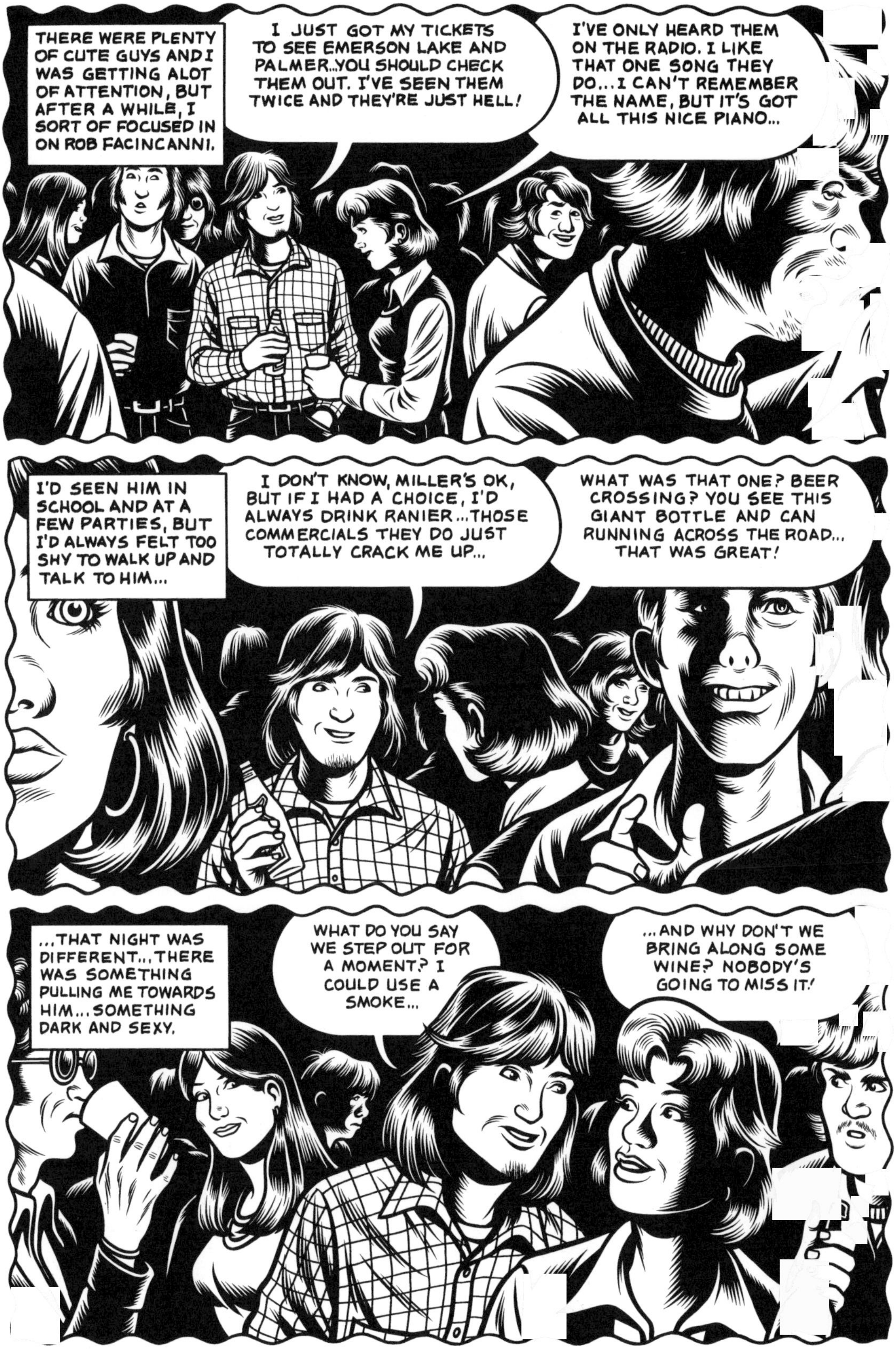
THERE WERE PLENTY OF CUTE GUYS AND I WAS GETTING ALOT OF ATTENTION, BUT AFTER A WHILE, I SORT OF FOCUSED IN ON ROB FACINCANNI.
I JUST GOT MY TICKETS TO SEE EMERSON LAKE AND PALMER...YOU SHOULD CHECK THEM OUT. I'VE SEEN THEM TWICE AND THEY'RE JUST HELL!
I'VE ONLY HEARD THEM ON THE RADIO. I LIKE THAT ONE SONG THEY DO... I CAN'T REMEMBER THE NAME, BUT IT'S GOT ALL THIS NICE PIANO...
I'D SEEN HIM IN SCHOOL AND AT A FEW PARTIES, BUT I'D ALWAYS FELT TOO SHY TO WALK UP AND TALK TO HIM...
I DON'T KNOW, MILLER'S OK, BUT IF I HAD A CHOICE, I'D ALWAYS DRINK RANIER... THOSE COMMERCIALS THEY DO JUST TOTALLY CRACK ME UP...
WHAT WAS THAT ONE? BEER CROSSING? YOU SEE THIS GIANT BOTTLE AND CAN RUNNING ACROSS THE ROAD... THAT WAS GREAT!
...THAT NIGHT WAS DIFFERENT... THERE WAS SOMETHING PULLING ME TOWARDS HIM... SOMETHING DARK AND SEXY.
WHAT DO YOU SAY WE STEP OUT FOR A MOMENT? I COULD USE A SMOKE...
...AND WHY DON'T WE BRING ALONG SOME WINE? NOBODY'S GOING TO MISS IT!

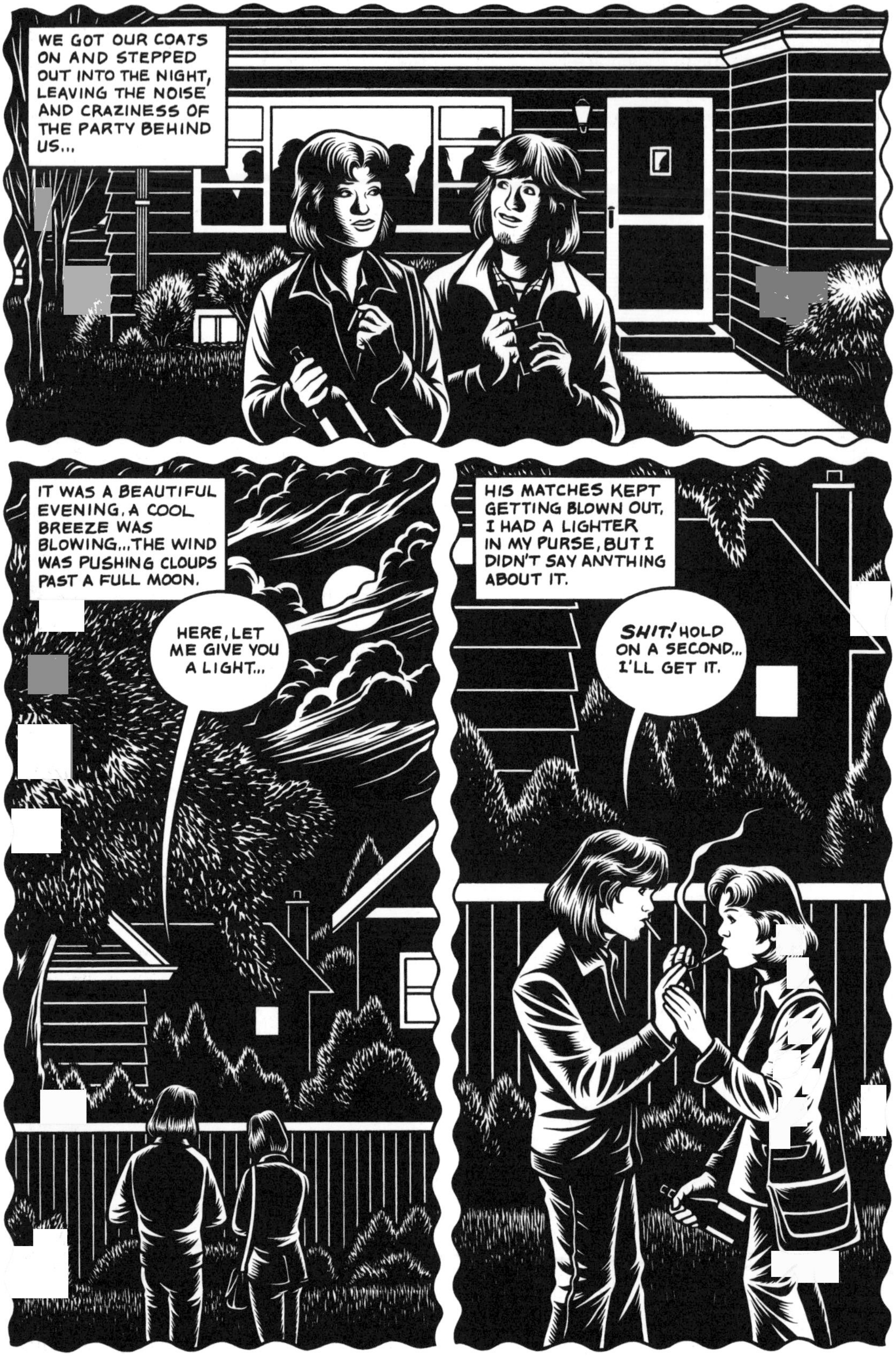
WE GOT OUR COATS ON AND STEPPED OUT INTO THE NIGHT, LEAVING THE NOISE AND CRAZINESS OF THE PARTY BEHIND US...
IT WAS A BEAUTIFUL EVENING. A COOL BREEZE WAS BLOWING... THE WIND WAS PUSHING CLOUDS PAST A FULL MOON.
HERE, LET ME GIVE YOU A LIGHT...
HIS MATCHES KEPT GETTING BLOWN OUT. I HAD A LIGHTER IN MY PURSE, BUT I DIDN'T SAY ANYTHING ABOUT IT.
SHIT! HOLD ON A SECOND... I'LL GET IT.

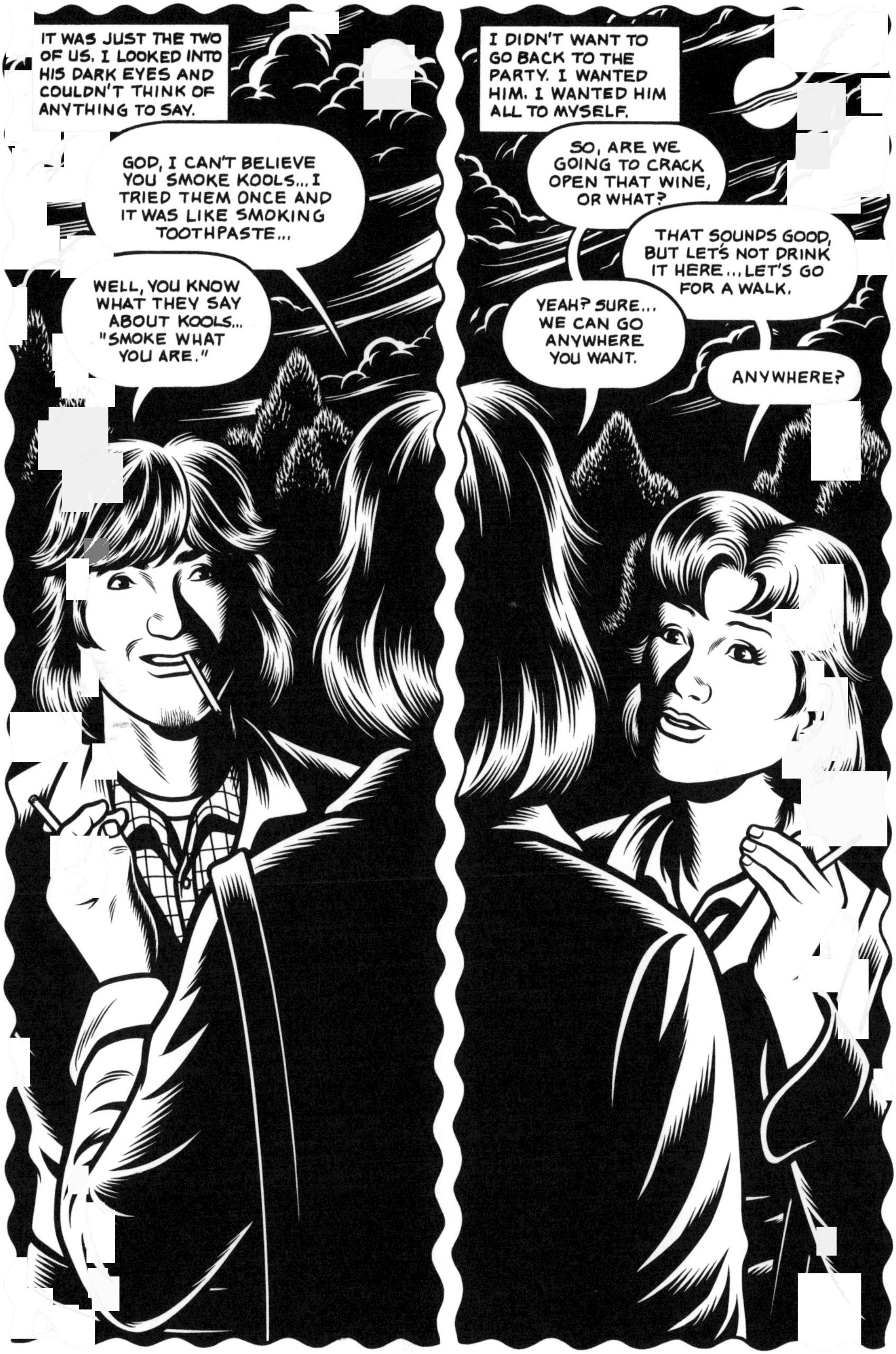
IT WAS JUST THE TWO OF US. I LOOKED INTO HIS DARK EYES AND COULDN'T THINK OF ANYTHING TO SAY.
GOD, I CAN'T BELIEVE YOU SMOKE KOOLS... I TRIED THEM ONCE AND IT WAS LIKE SMOKING TOOTHPASTE...
WELL, YOU KNOW WHAT THEY SAY ABOUT KOOLS... "SMOKE WHAT YOU ARE."
I DIDN'T WANT TO GO BACK TO THE PARTY. I WANTED HIM. I WANTED HIM ALL TO MYSELF.
SO, ARE WE GOING TO CRACK OPEN THAT WINE, OR WHAT?
THAT SOUNDS GOOD, BUT LET'S NOT DRINK IT HERE... LET'S GO FOR A WALK.
YEAH? SURE... WE CAN GO ANYWHERE YOU WANT.
ANYWHERE?

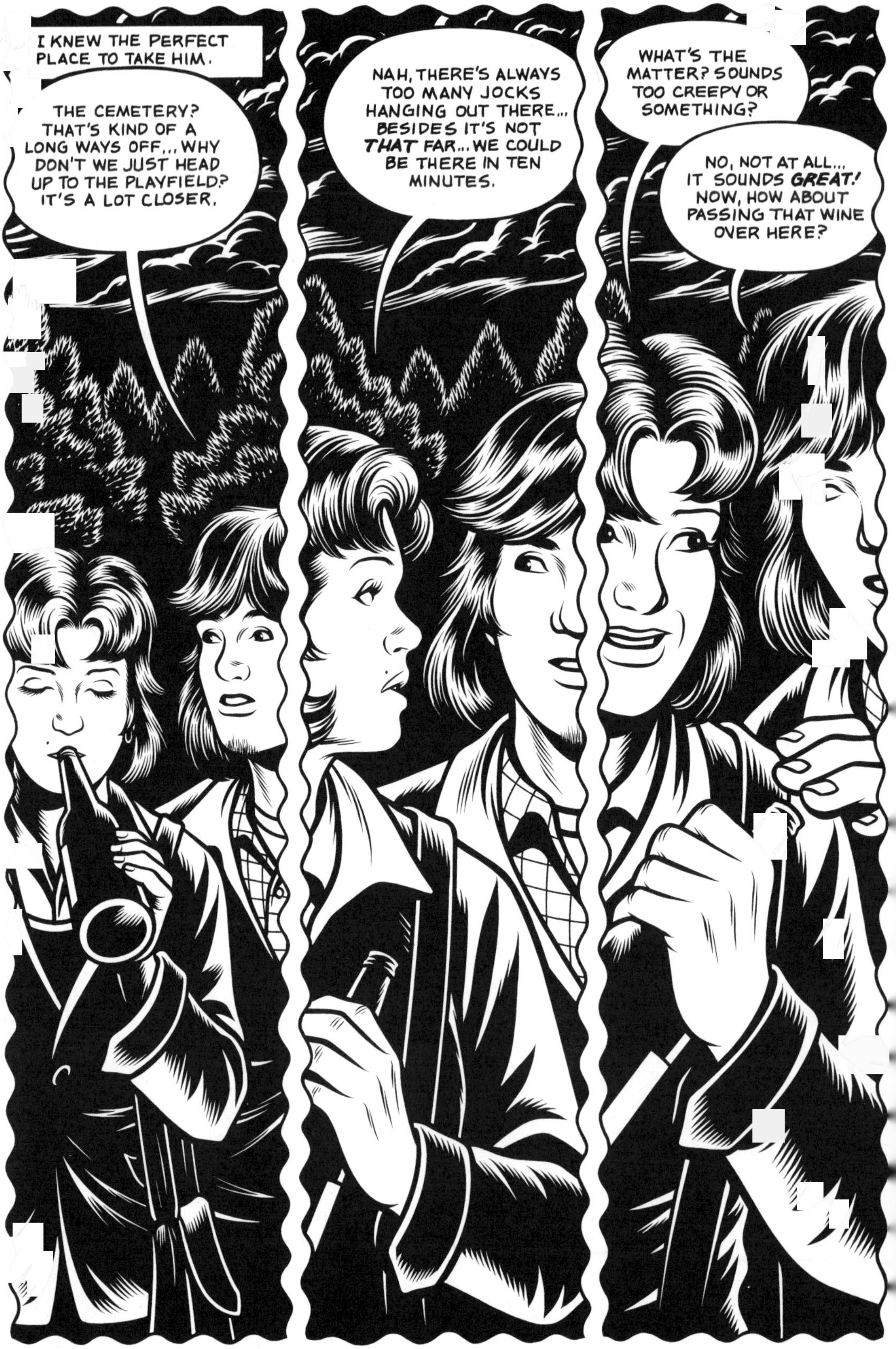
I KNEW THE PERFECT PLACE TO TAKE HIM.
THE CEMETERY? THAT'S KIND OF A LONG WAYS OFF... WHY DON'T WE JUST HEAD UP TO THE PLAYFIELD? IT'S A LOT CLOSER.
NAH, THERE'S ALWAYS TOO MANY JOCKS HANGING OUT THERE... BESIDES IT'S NOT THAT FAR... WE COULD BE THERE IN TEN MINUTES.
WHAT'S THE MATTER? SOUNDS TOO CREEPY OR SOMETHING?
NO, NOT AT ALL... IT SOUNDS GREAT! NOW, HOW ABOUT PASSING THAT WINE OVER HERE?

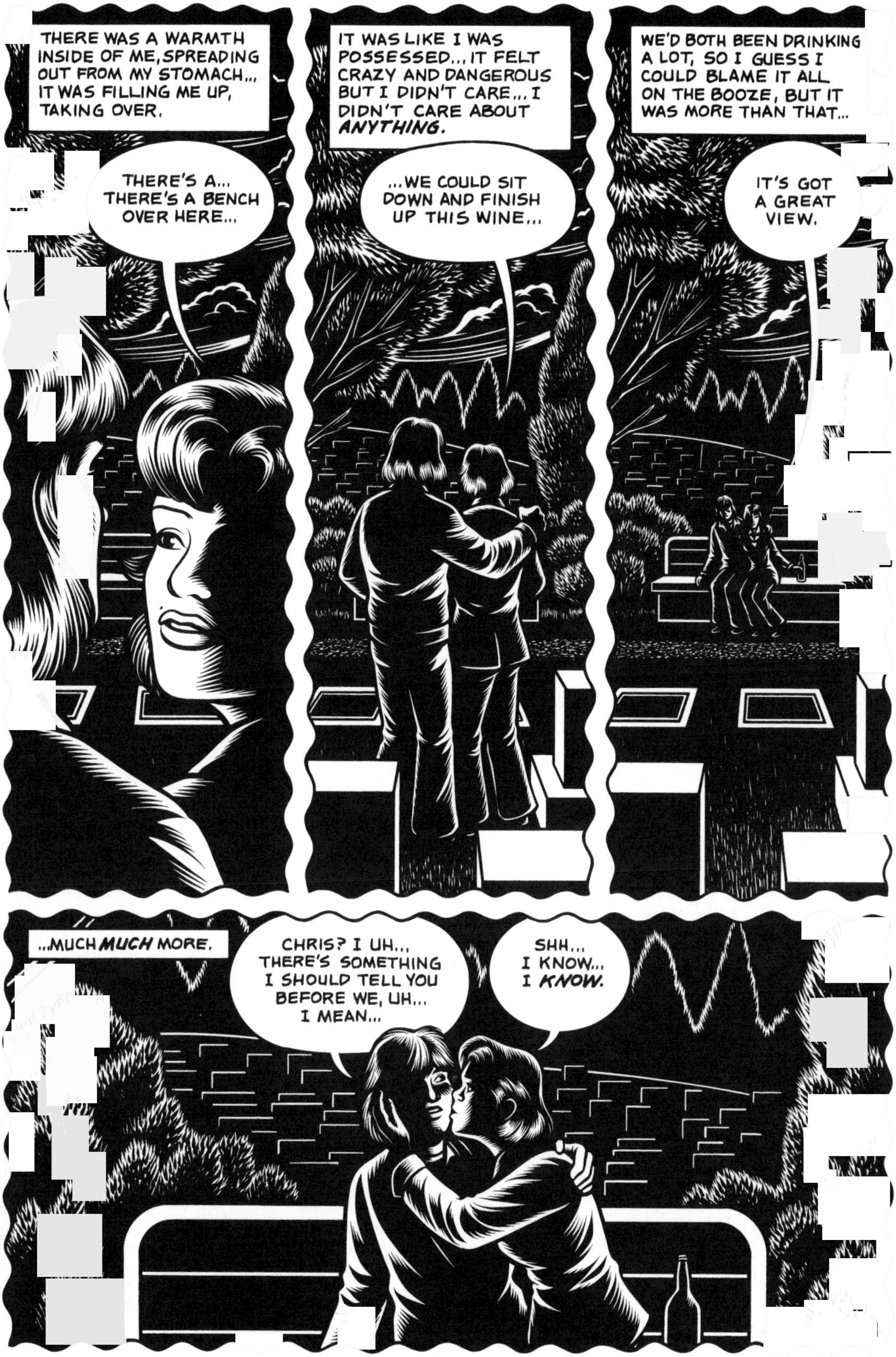
THERE WAS A WARMTH INSIDE OF ME, SPREADING OUT FROM MY STOMACH... IT WAS FILLING ME UP, TAKING OVER.
THERE'S A... THERE'S A BENCH OVER HERE...
IT WAS LIKE I WAS POSSESSED... IT FELT CRAZY AND DANGEROUS BUT I DIDN'T CARE... I DIDN'T CARE ABOUT *ANYTHING*.
...WE COULD SIT DOWN AND FINISH UP THIS WINE...
WE'D BOTH BEEN DRINKING A LOT, SO I GUESS I COULD BLAME IT ALL ON THE BOOZE, BUT IT WAS MORE THAN THAT...
IT'S GOT A GREAT VIEW.
...MUCH *MUCH* MORE.
CHRIS? I UH... THERE'S SOMETHING I SHOULD TELL YOU BEFORE WE, UH... I MEAN...
SHH... I KNOW... I *KNOW*.

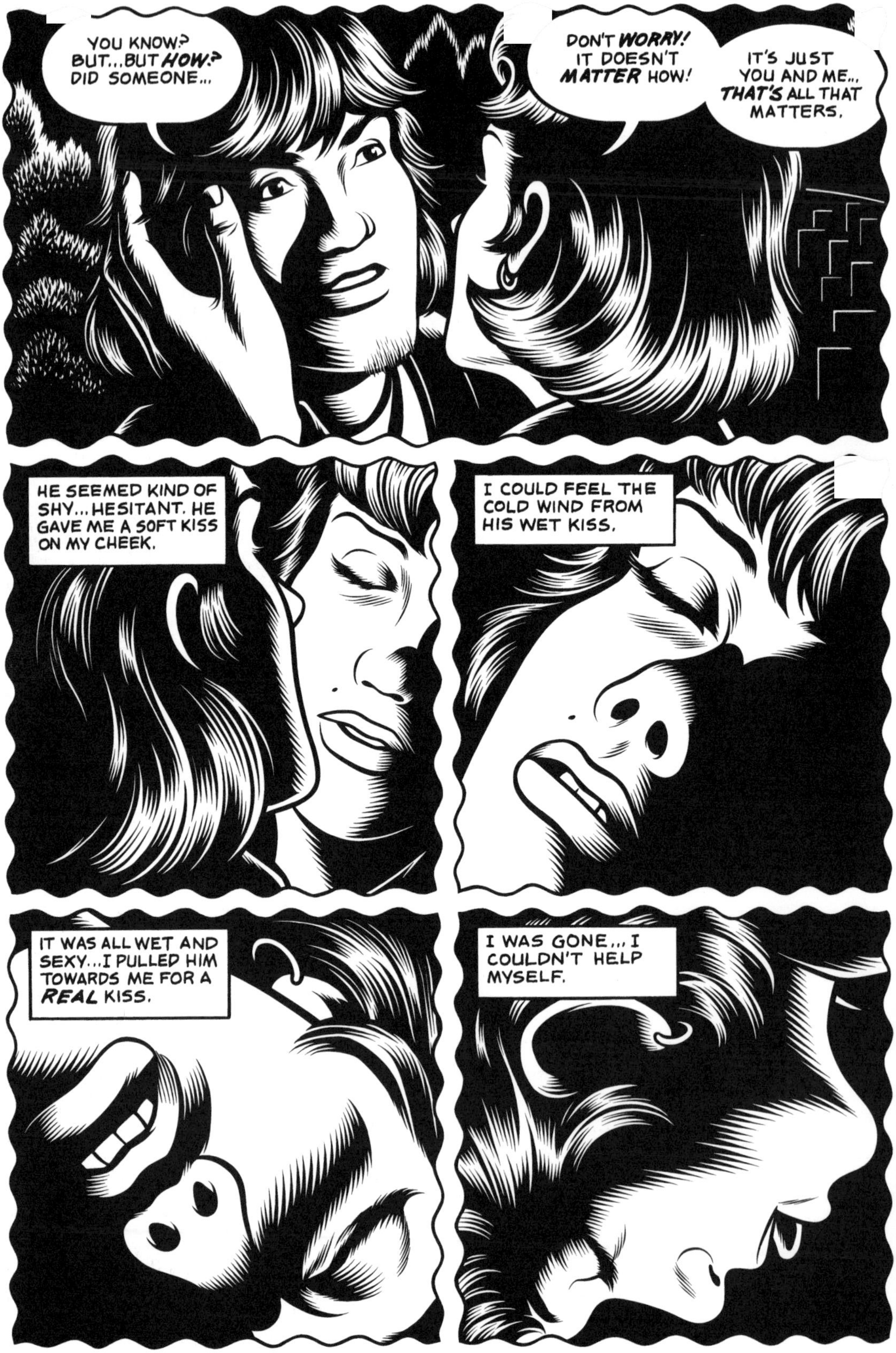
YOU KNOW? BUT...BUT HOW? DID SOMEONE...
DON'T WORRY! IT DOESN'T MATTER HOW!
IT'S JUST YOU AND ME... THAT'S ALL THAT MATTERS.
HE SEEMED KIND OF SHY... HESITANT. HE GAVE ME A SOFT KISS ON MY CHEEK.
I COULD FEEL THE COLD WIND FROM HIS WET KISS.
IT WAS ALL WET AND SEXY...I PULLED HIM TOWARDS ME FOR A REAL KISS.
I WAS GONE... I COULDN'T HELP MYSELF.

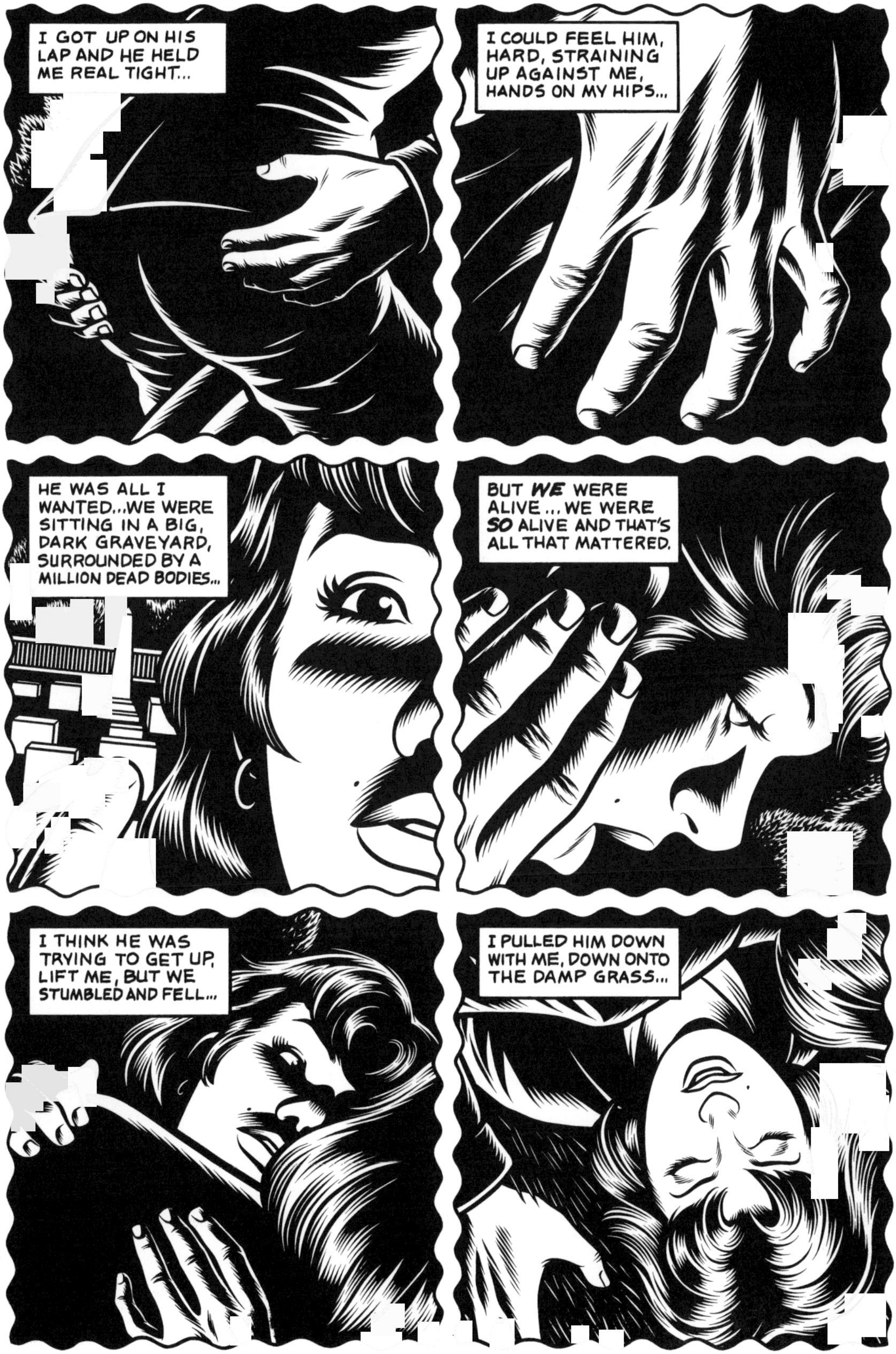
I GOT UP ON HIS LAP AND HE HELD ME REAL TIGHT...
I COULD FEEL HIM, HARD, STRAINING UP AGAINST ME, HANDS ON MY HIPS...
HE WAS ALL I WANTED...WE WERE SITTING IN A BIG, DARK GRAVEYARD, SURROUNDED BY A MILLION DEAD BODIES...
BUT *WE* WERE ALIVE... WE WERE *SO* ALIVE AND THAT'S ALL THAT MATTERED.
I THINK HE WAS TRYING TO GET UP, LIFT ME, BUT WE STUMBLED AND FELL...
I PULLED HIM DOWN WITH ME, DOWN ONTO THE DAMP GRASS...

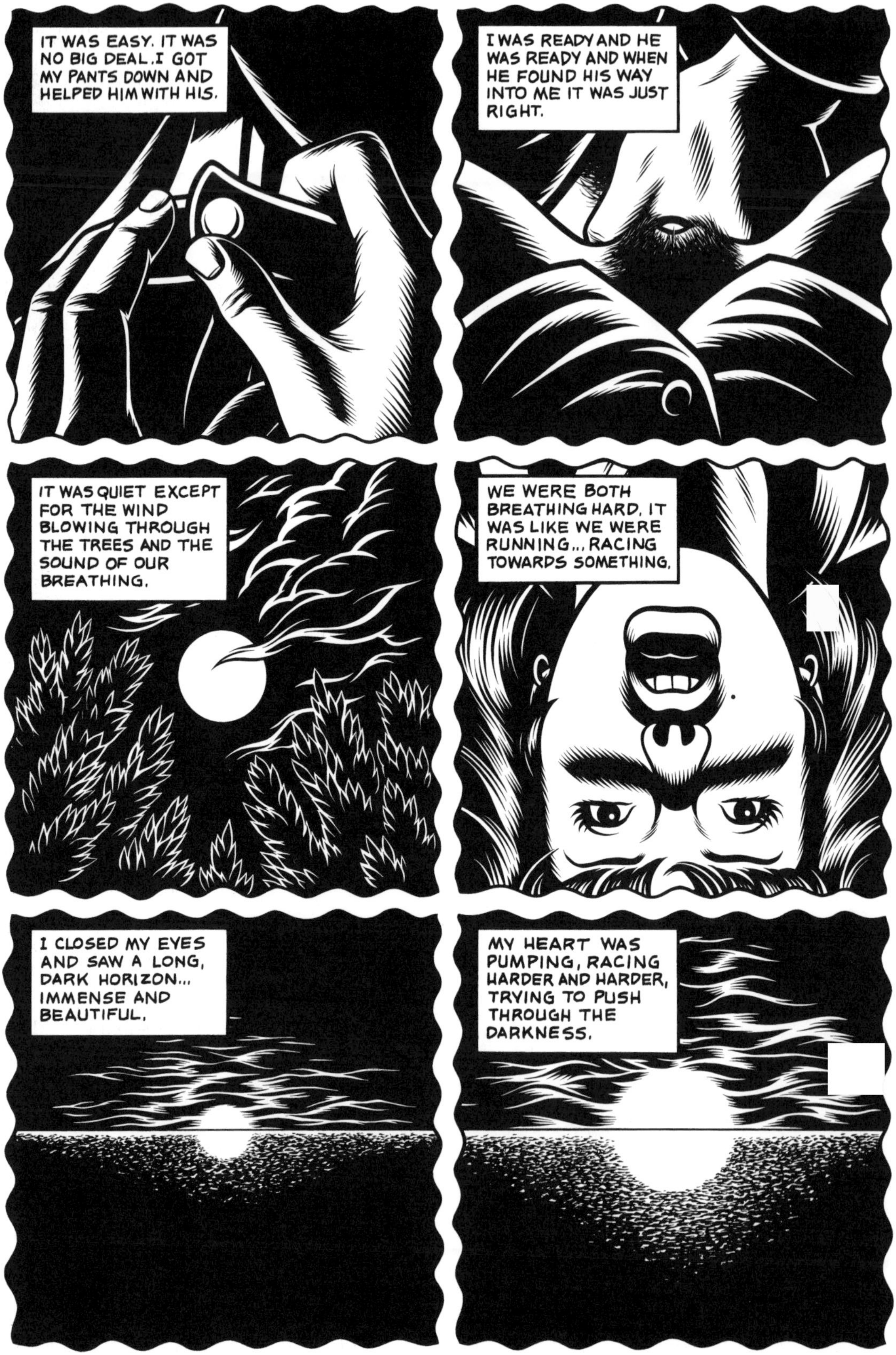
IT WAS EASY. IT WAS NO BIG DEAL. I GOT MY PANTS DOWN AND HELPED HIM WITH HIS.
I WAS READY AND HE WAS READY AND WHEN HE FOUND HIS WAY INTO ME IT WAS JUST RIGHT.
IT WAS QUIET EXCEPT FOR THE WIND BLOWING THROUGH THE TREES AND THE SOUND OF OUR BREATHING.
WE WERE BOTH BREATHING HARD, IT WAS LIKE WE WERE RUNNING... RACING TOWARDS SOMETHING.
I CLOSED MY EYES AND SAW A LONG, DARK HORIZON... IMMENSE AND BEAUTIFUL.
MY HEART WAS PUMPING, RACING HARDER AND HARDER, TRYING TO PUSH THROUGH THE DARKNESS.

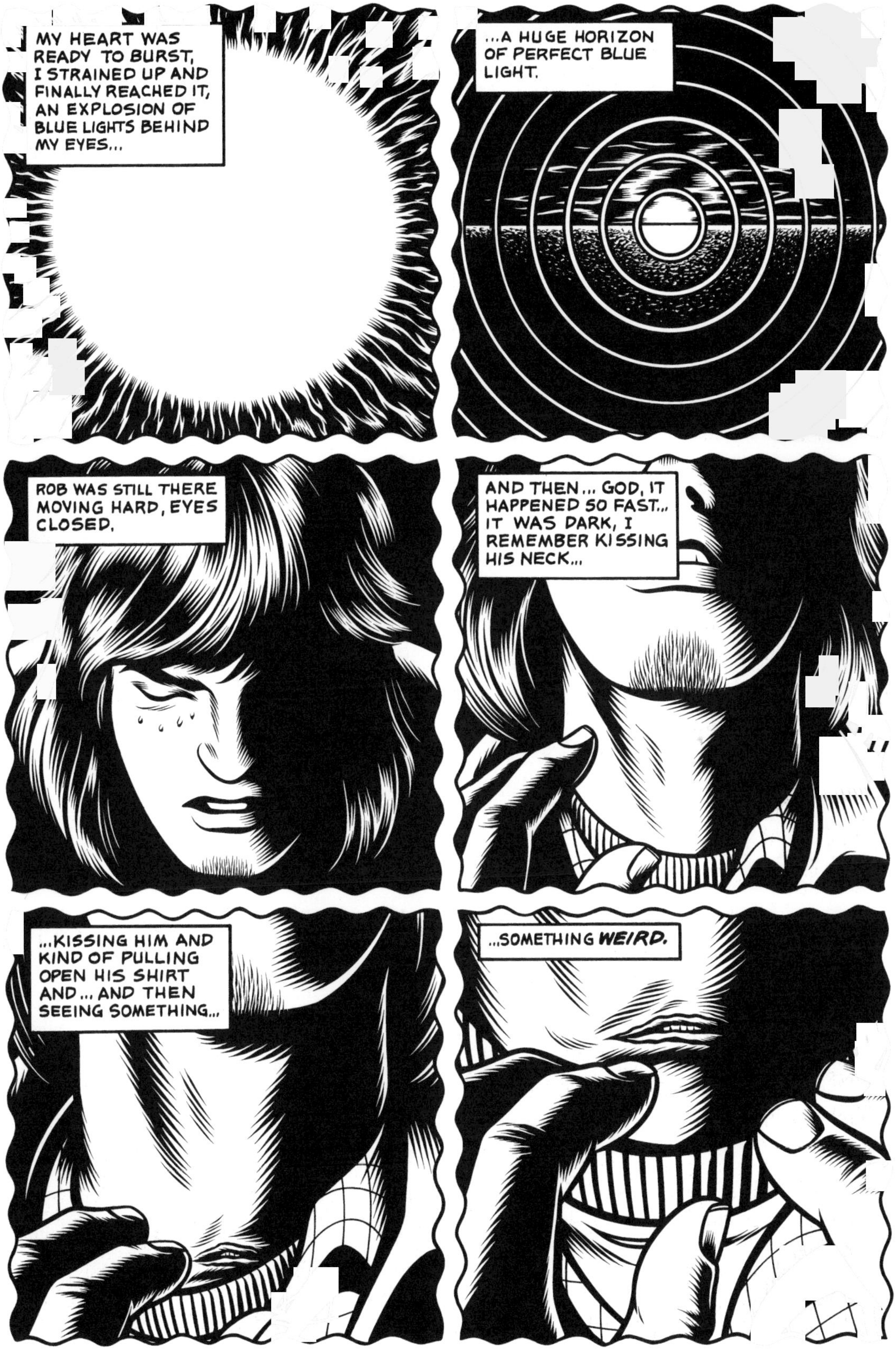
MY HEART WAS READY TO BURST, I STRAINED UP AND FINALLY REACHED IT, AN EXPLOSION OF BLUE LIGHTS BEHIND MY EYES...
...A HUGE HORIZON OF PERFECT BLUE LIGHT.
ROB WAS STILL THERE MOVING HARD, EYES CLOSED.
AND THEN... GOD, IT HAPPENED SO FAST... IT WAS DARK, I REMEMBER KISSING HIS NECK...
...KISSING HIM AND KIND OF PULLING OPEN HIS SHIRT AND... AND THEN SEEING SOMETHING...
...SOMETHING WEIRD.

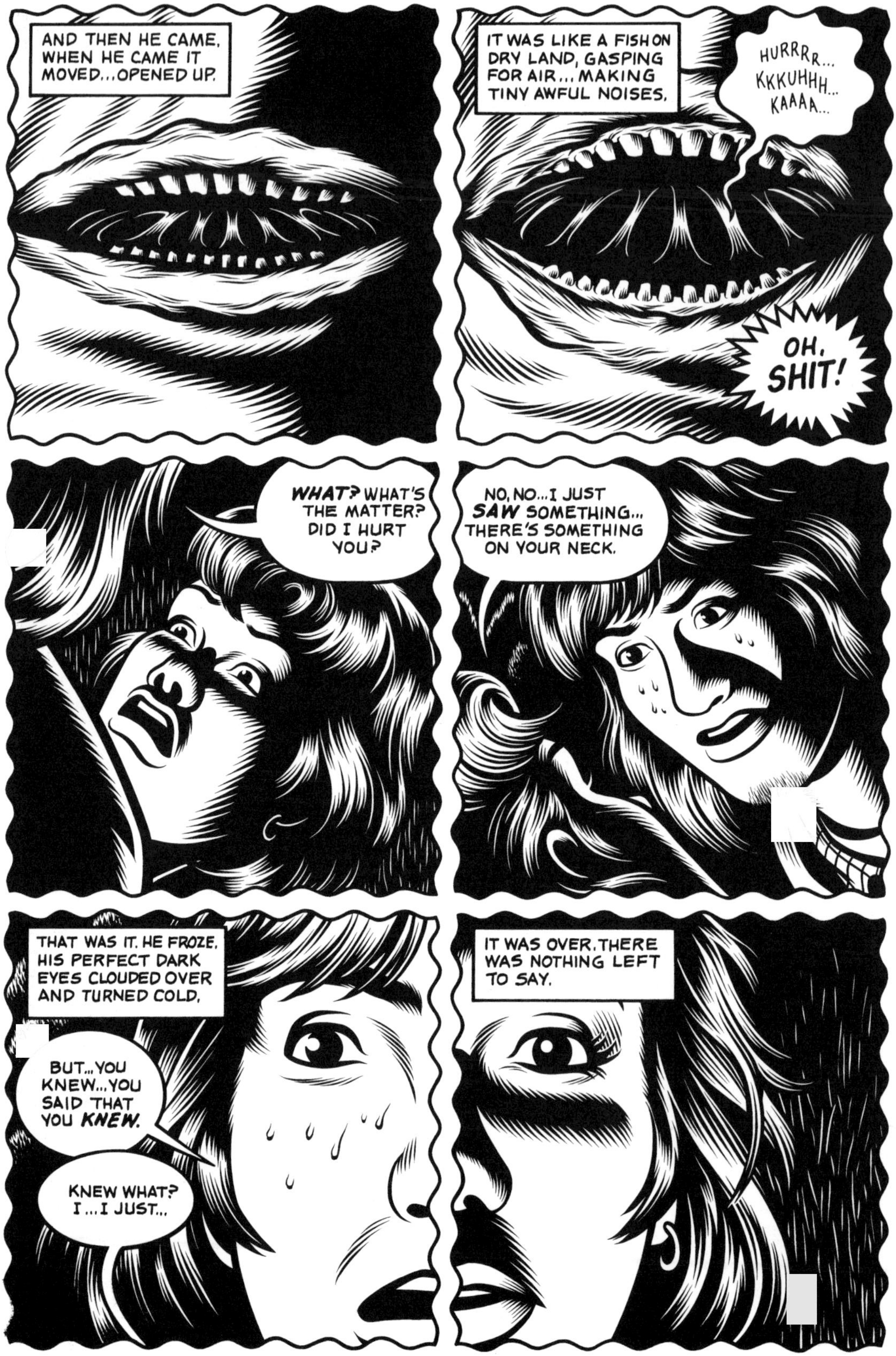
AND THEN HE CAME. WHEN HE CAME IT MOVED...OPENED UP.
IT WAS LIKE A FISH ON DRY LAND, GASPING FOR AIR... MAKING TINY AWFUL NOISES.
HURRRR... KKKUHHH... KAAAA...
OH, SHIT!
WHAT? WHAT'S THE MATTER? DID I HURT YOU?
NO, NO...I JUST SAW SOMETHING... THERE'S SOMETHING ON YOUR NECK.
THAT WAS IT. HE FROZE. HIS PERFECT DARK EYES CLOUDED OVER AND TURNED COLD.
BUT... YOU KNEW... YOU SAID THAT YOU KNEW.
KNEW WHAT? I... I JUST...
IT WAS OVER. THERE WAS NOTHING LEFT TO SAY.

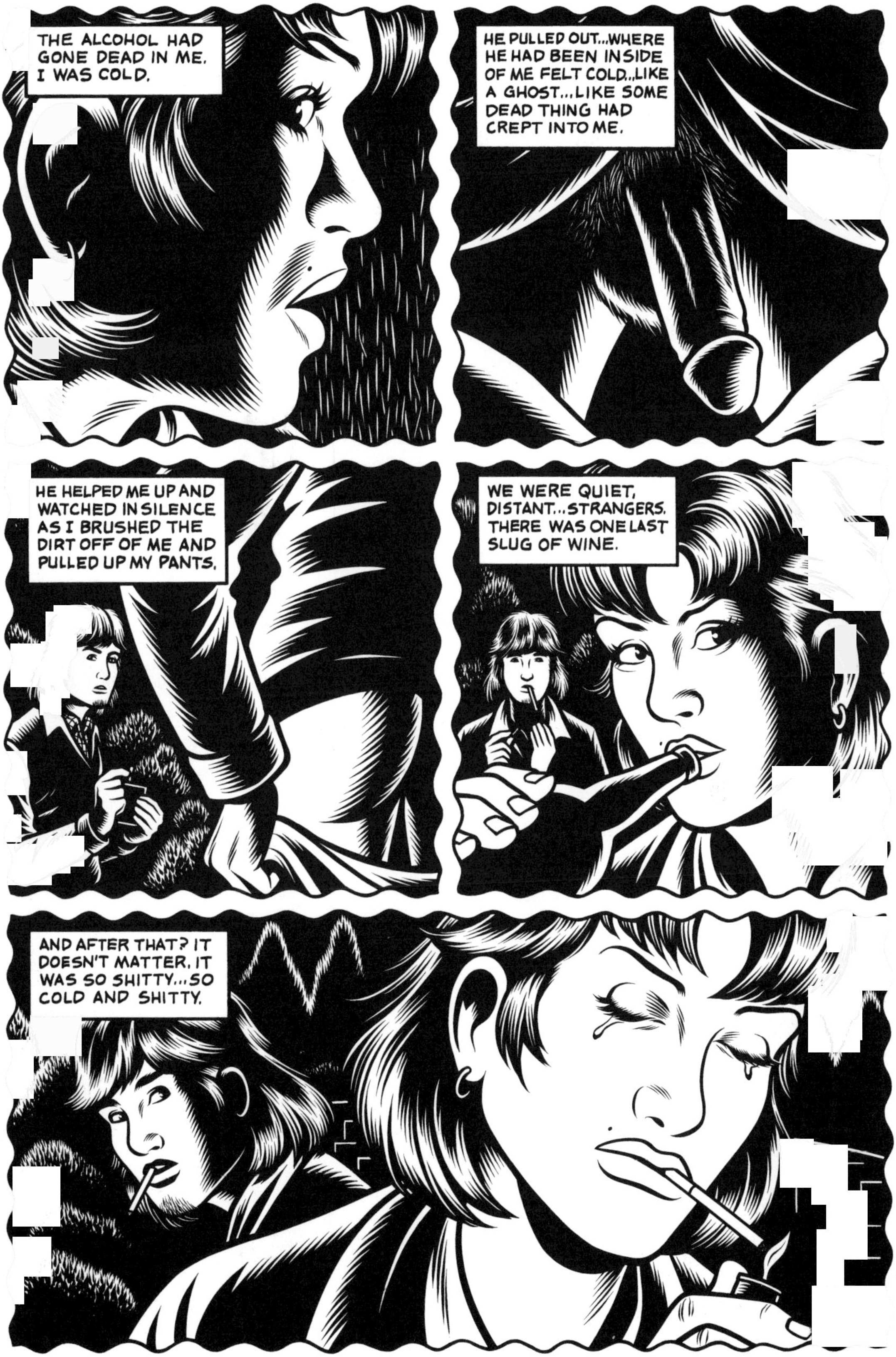
THE ALCOHOL HAD GONE DEAD IN ME. I WAS COLD.
HE PULLED OUT...WHERE HE HAD BEEN INSIDE OF ME FELT COLD...LIKE A GHOST...LIKE SOME DEAD THING HAD CREPT INTO ME.
HE HELPED ME UP AND WATCHED IN SILENCE AS I BRUSHED THE DIRT OFF OF ME AND PULLED UP MY PANTS.
WE WERE QUIET, DISTANT...STRANGERS. THERE WAS ONE LAST SLUG OF WINE.
AND AFTER THAT? IT DOESN'T MATTER. IT WAS SO SHITTY...SO COLD AND SHITTY.

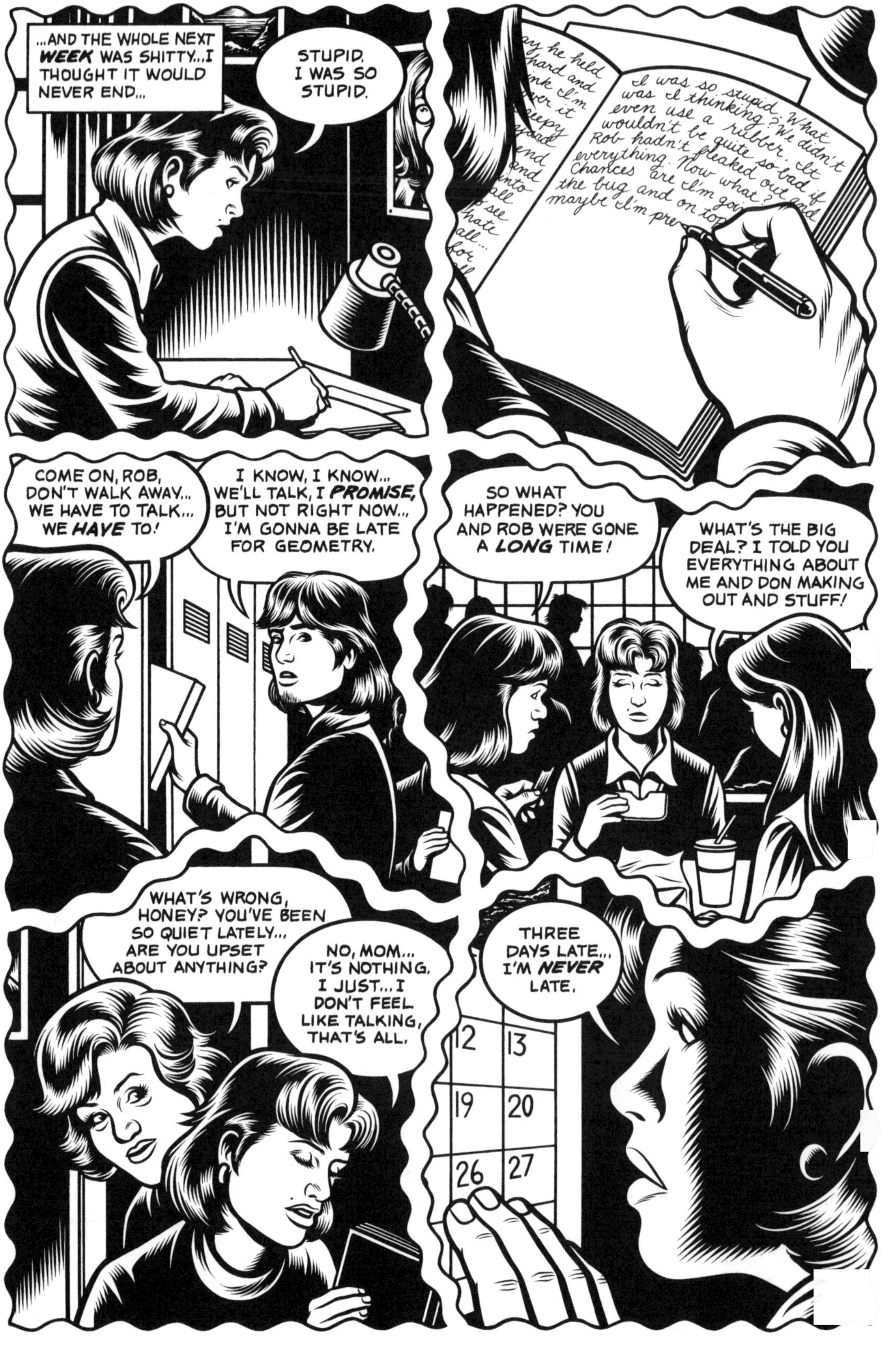
...AND THE WHOLE NEXT WEEK WAS SHITTY...I THOUGHT IT WOULD NEVER END...
STUPID. I WAS SO STUPID.
I was so stupid. What was I thinking? We didn't even use a rubber. It wouldn't be quite so bad if Rob hadn't freaked out and everything. Now what? Chances are I'm
the bug and on
maybe I'm
COME ON, ROB, DON'T WALK AWAY... WE HAVE TO TALK... WE HAVE TO!
I KNOW, I KNOW... WE'LL TALK, I PROMISE, BUT NOT RIGHT NOW... I'M GONNA BE LATE FOR GEOMETRY.
SO WHAT HAPPENED? YOU AND ROB WERE GONE A LONG TIME!
WHAT'S THE BIG DEAL? I TOLD YOU EVERYTHING ABOUT ME AND DON MAKING OUT AND STUFF!
WHAT'S WRONG, HONEY? YOU'VE BEEN SO QUIET LATELY... ARE YOU UPSET ABOUT ANYTHING?
NO, MOM... IT'S NOTHING. I JUST...I DON'T FEEL LIKE TALKING, THAT'S ALL.
THREE DAYS LATE... I'M NEVER LATE.
12 13
19 20
26 27

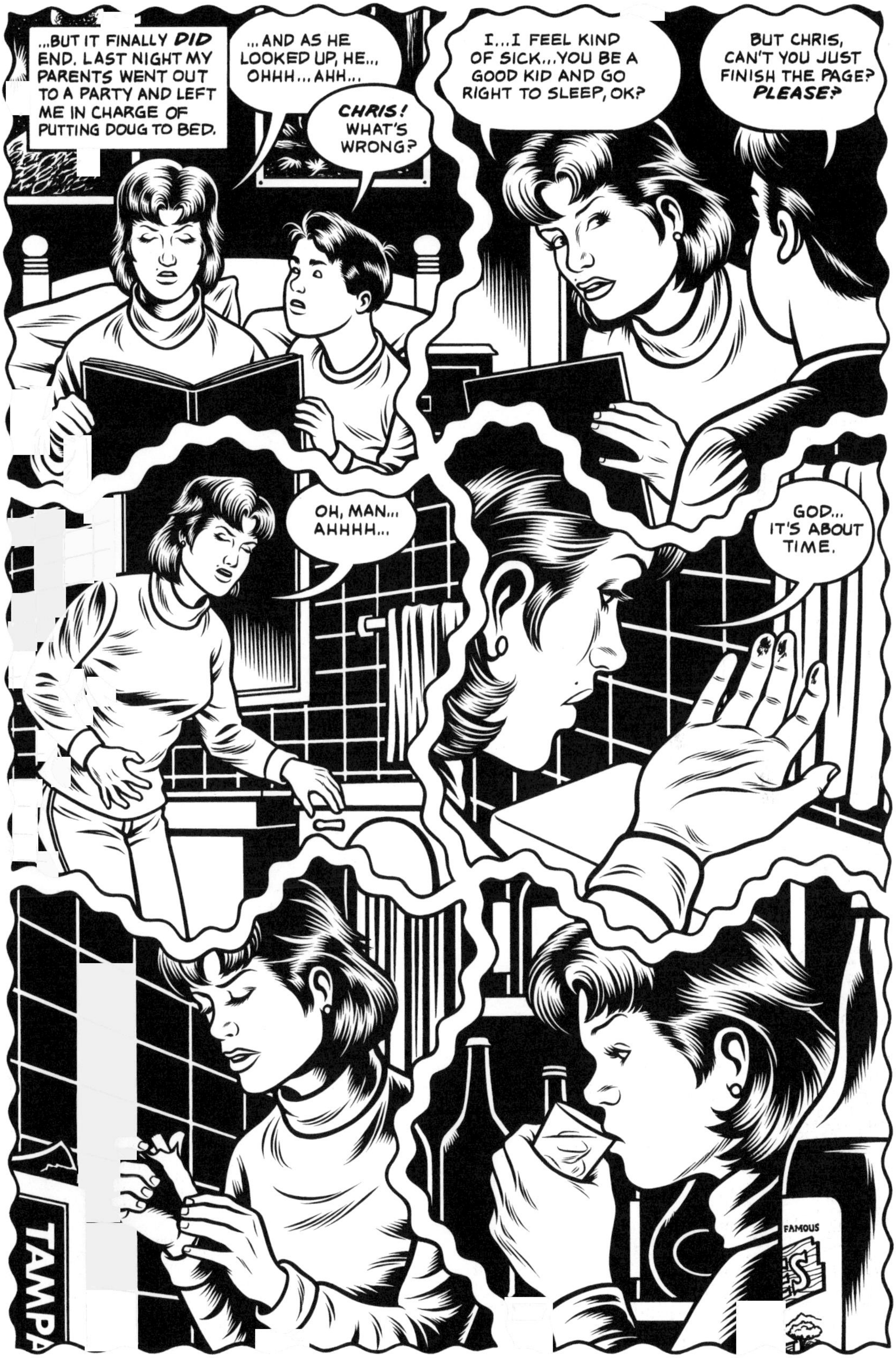
...BUT IT FINALLY DID END. LAST NIGHT MY PARENTS WENT OUT TO A PARTY AND LEFT ME IN CHARGE OF PUTTING DOUG TO BED.
...AND AS HE LOOKED UP, HE... OHHH...AHH...
CHRIS! WHAT'S WRONG?
I...I FEEL KIND OF SICK...YOU BE A GOOD KID AND GO RIGHT TO SLEEP, OK?
BUT CHRIS, CAN'T YOU JUST FINISH THE PAGE? PLEASE?
OH, MAN... AHHHH...
GOD... IT'S ABOUT TIME.
TAMPA
FAMOUS

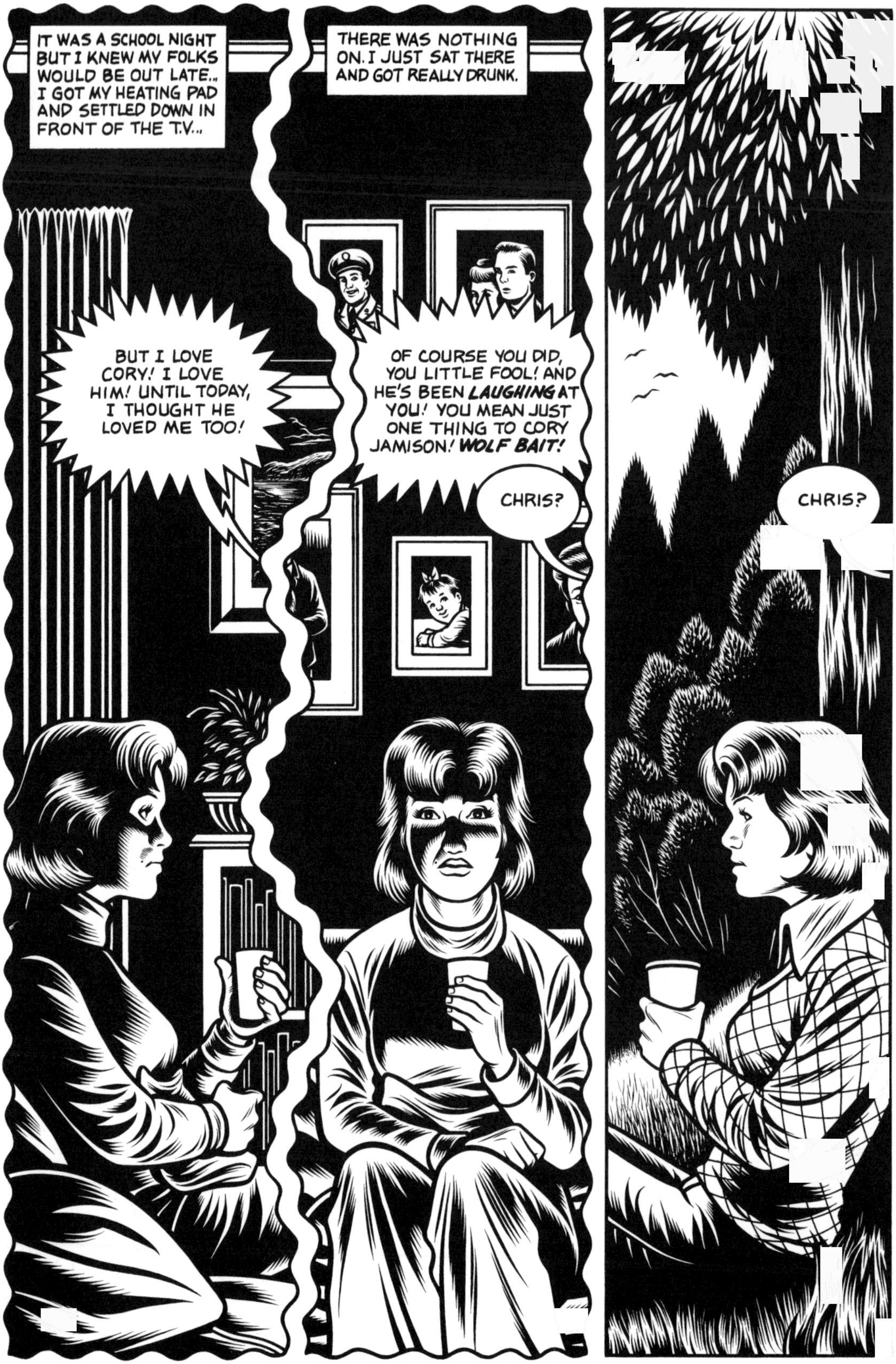
IT WAS A SCHOOL NIGHT BUT I KNEW MY FOLKS WOULD BE OUT LATE.. I GOT MY HEATING PAD AND SETTLED DOWN IN FRONT OF THE T.V...
BUT I LOVE CORY! I LOVE HIM! UNTIL TODAY, I THOUGHT HE LOVED ME TOO!
THERE WAS NOTHING ON. I JUST SAT THERE AND GOT REALLY DRUNK.
OF COURSE YOU DID, YOU LITTLE FOOL! AND HE'S BEEN LAUGHING AT YOU! YOU MEAN JUST ONE THING TO CORY JAMISON! WOLF BAIT!
CHRIS?
CHRIS?

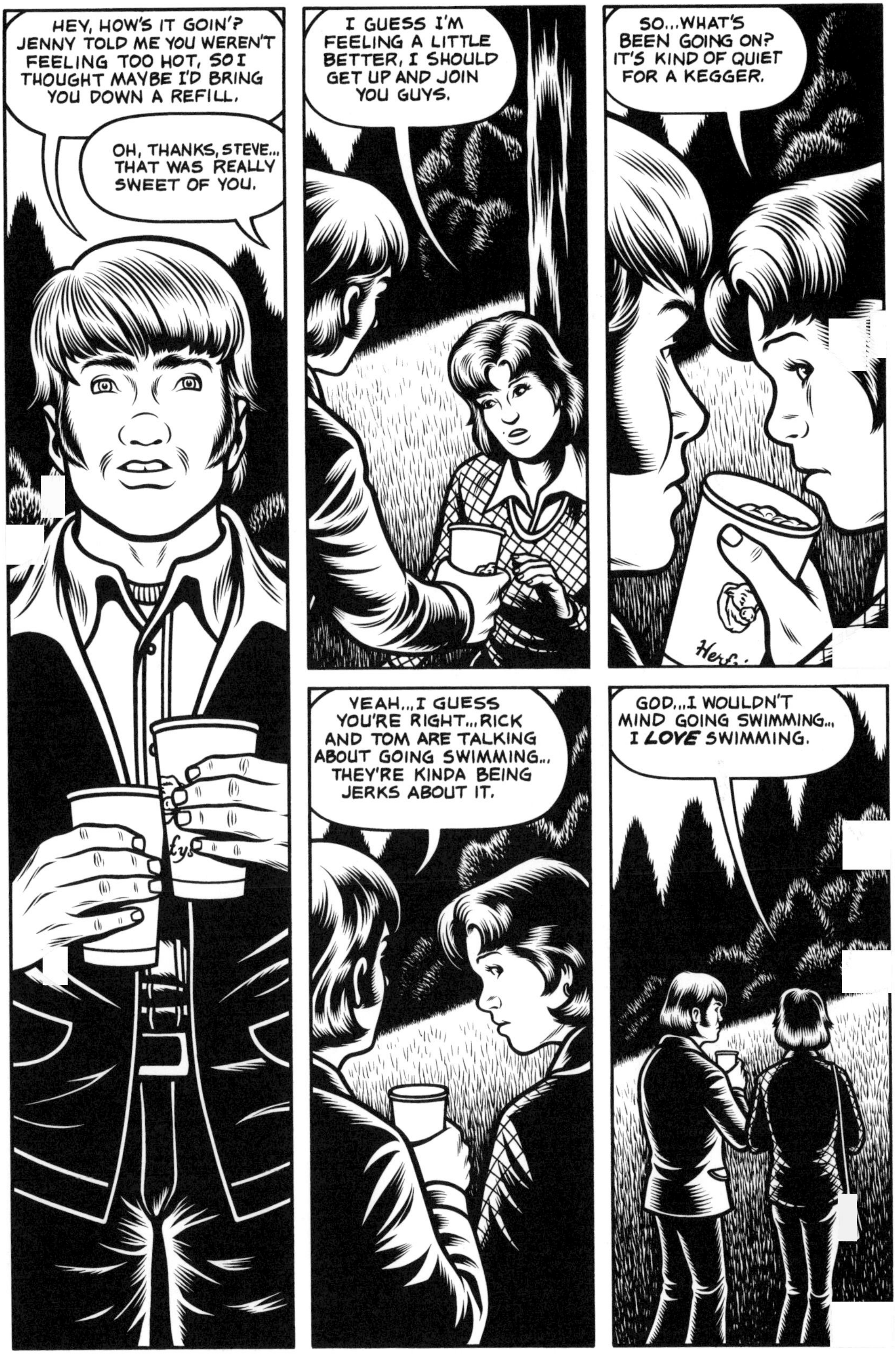
HEY, HOW'S IT GOIN'? JENNY TOLD ME YOU WEREN'T FEELING TOO HOT, SO I THOUGHT MAYBE I'D BRING YOU DOWN A REFILL.
OH, THANKS, STEVE... THAT WAS REALLY SWEET OF YOU.
I GUESS I'M FEELING A LITTLE BETTER, I SHOULD GET UP AND JOIN YOU GUYS.
SO... WHAT'S BEEN GOING ON? IT'S KIND OF QUIET FOR A KEGGER.
YEAH... I GUESS YOU'RE RIGHT... RICK AND TOM ARE TALKING ABOUT GOING SWIMMING... THEY'RE KINDA BEING JERKS ABOUT IT.
GOD... I WOULDN'T MIND GOING SWIMMING... I *LOVE* SWIMMING.

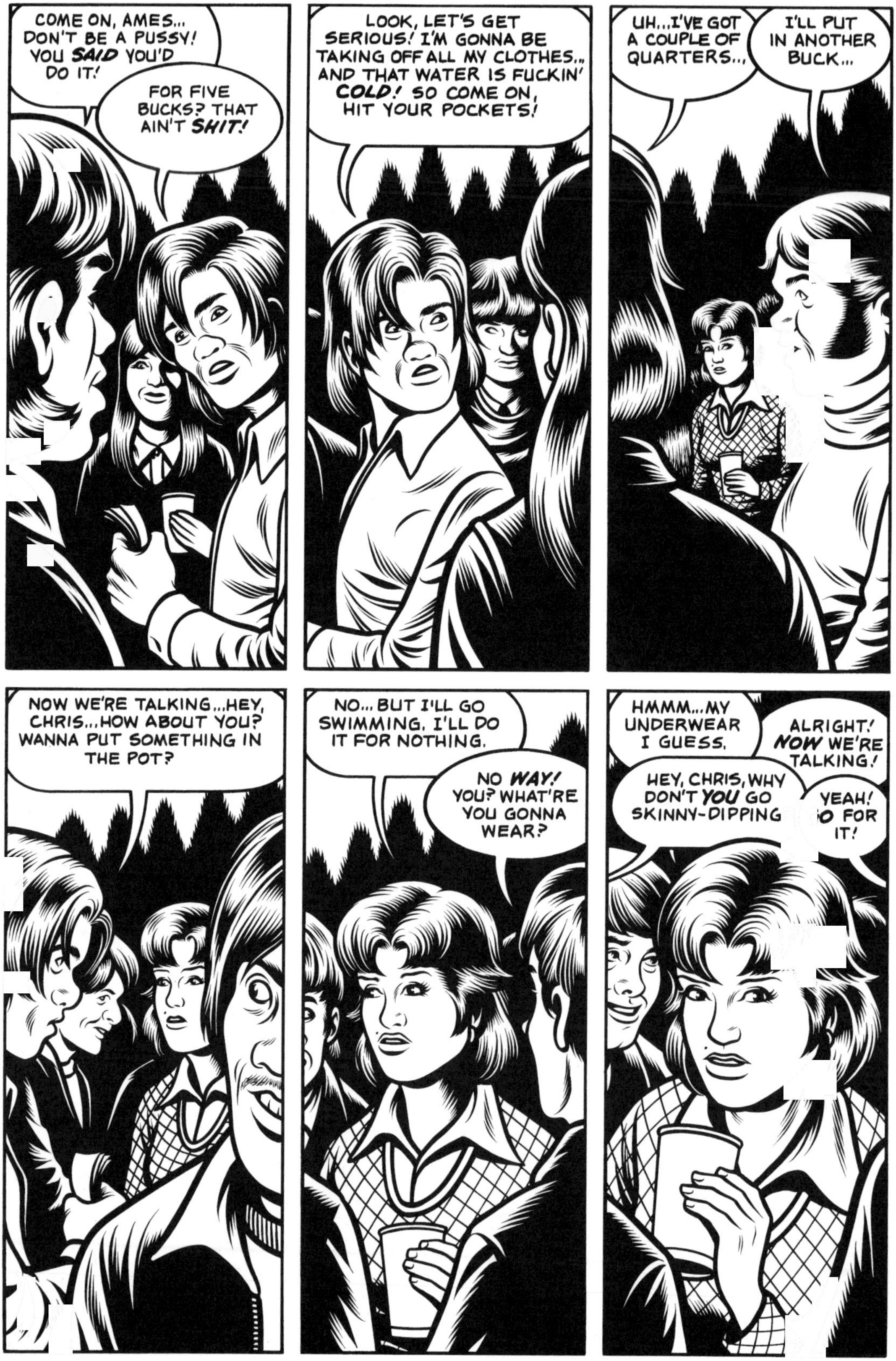
COME ON, AMES... DON'T BE A PUSSY! YOU SAID YOU'D DO IT!
FOR FIVE BUCKS? THAT AIN'T SHIT!
LOOK, LET'S GET SERIOUS! I'M GONNA BE TAKING OFF ALL MY CLOTHES... AND THAT WATER IS FUCKIN' COLD! SO COME ON, HIT YOUR POCKETS!
UH...I'VE GOT A COUPLE OF QUARTERS...,
I'LL PUT IN ANOTHER BUCK...
NOW WE'RE TALKING...HEY, CHRIS...HOW ABOUT YOU? WANNA PUT SOMETHING IN THE POT?
NO... BUT I'LL GO SWIMMING. I'LL DO IT FOR NOTHING.
NO WAY! YOU? WHAT'RE YOU GONNA WEAR?
HMMM...MY UNDERWEAR I GUESS.
ALRIGHT! NOW WE'RE TALKING!
HEY, CHRIS, WHY DON'T YOU GO SKINNY-DIPPING
YEAH! O FOR IT!

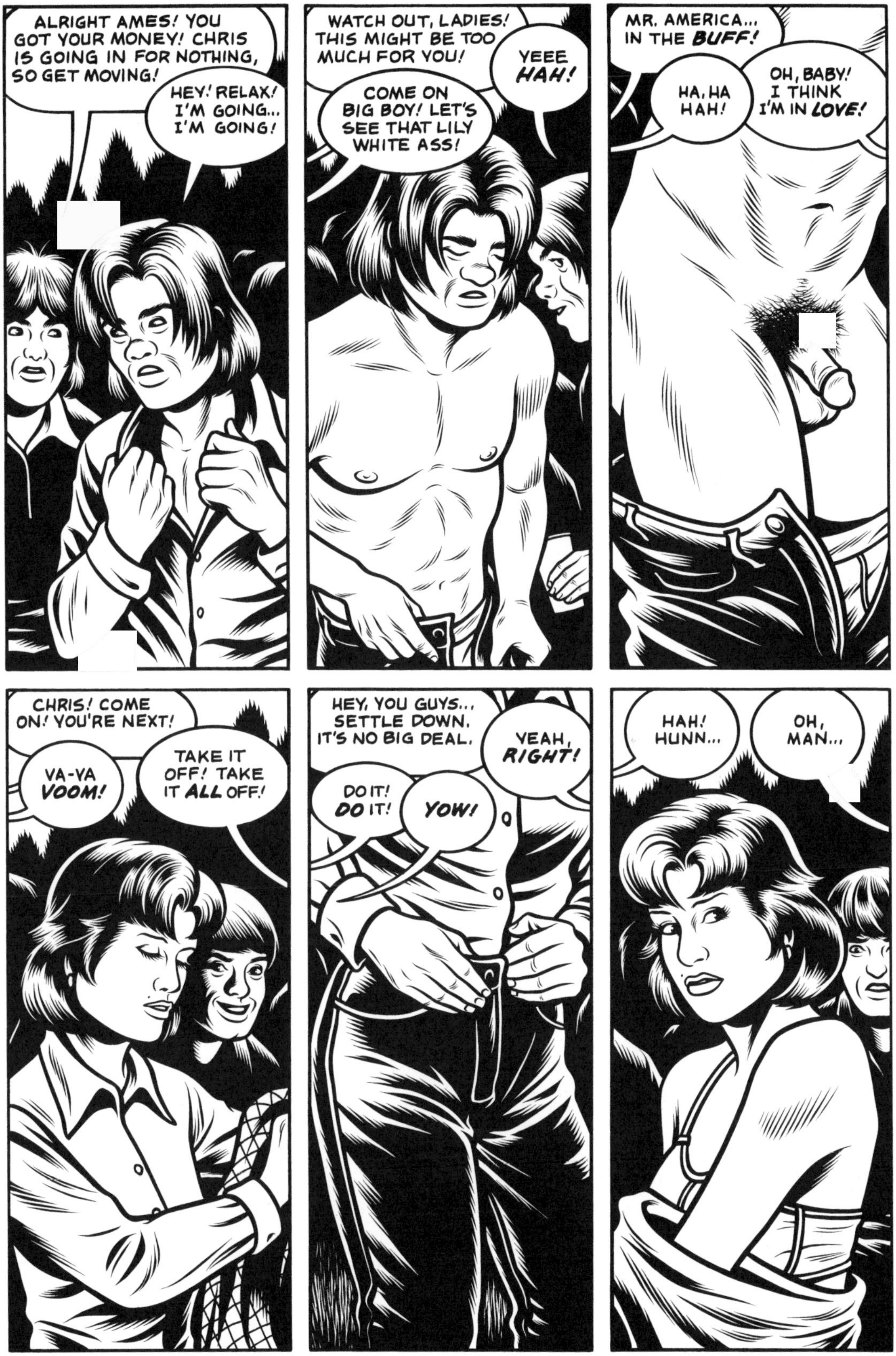
ALRIGHT AMES! YOU GOT YOUR MONEY! CHRIS IS GOING IN FOR NOTHING, SO GET MOVING!
HEY! RELAX! I'M GOING... I'M GOING!
WATCH OUT, LADIES! THIS MIGHT BE TOO MUCH FOR YOU!
YEEE HAH!
COME ON BIG BOY! LET'S SEE THAT LILY WHITE ASS!
MR. AMERICA... IN THE BUFF!
HA, HA HAH!
OH, BABY! I THINK I'M IN LOVE!
CHRIS! COME ON! YOU'RE NEXT!
VA-VA VOOM!
TAKE IT OFF! TAKE IT ALL OFF!
HEY, YOU GUYS... SETTLE DOWN. IT'S NO BIG DEAL.
YEAH, RIGHT!
DO IT! DO IT!
YOW!
HAH! HUNN...
OH, MAN...

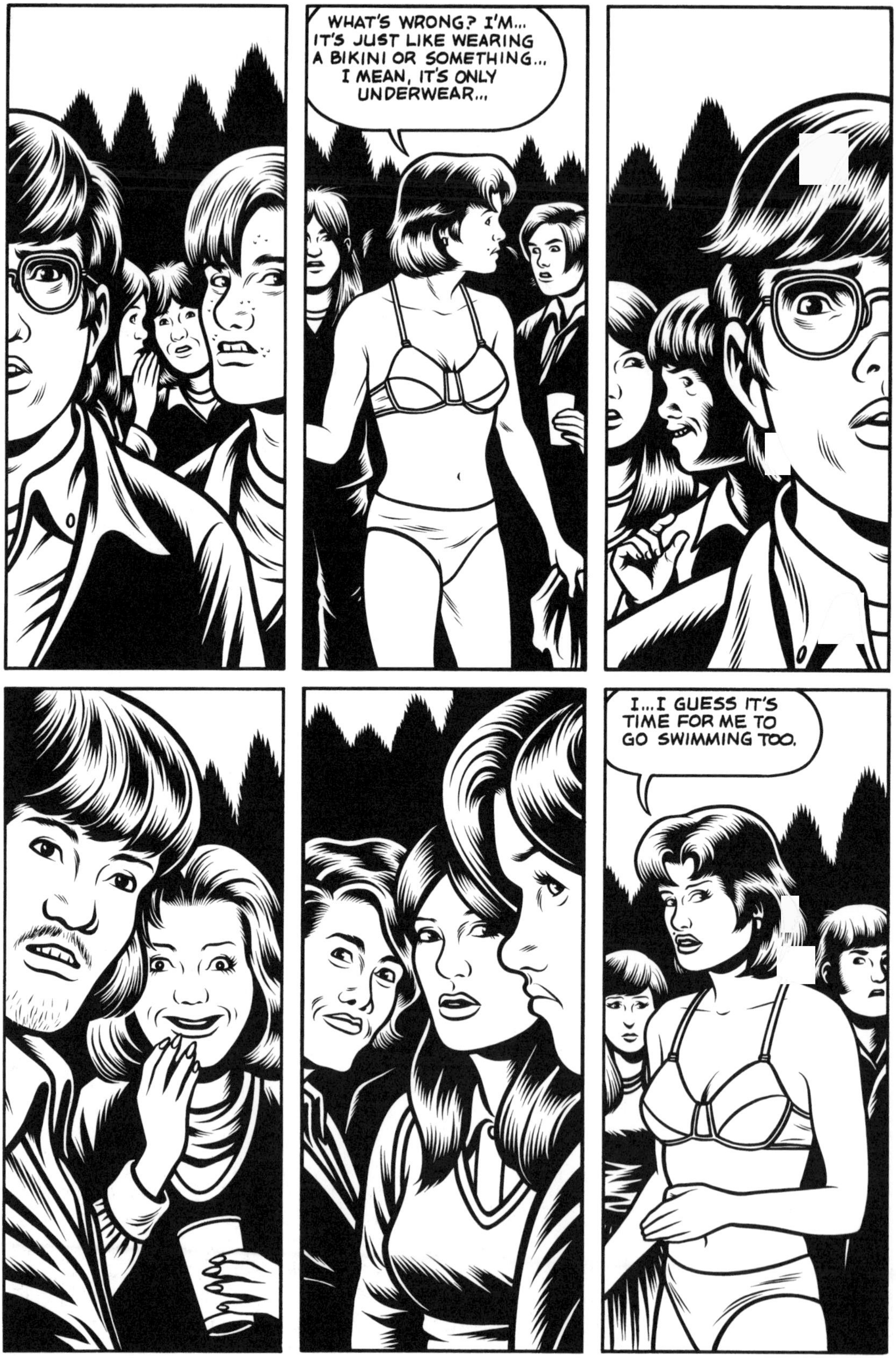
WHAT'S WRONG? I'M... IT'S JUST LIKE WEARING A BIKINI OR SOMETHING... I MEAN, IT'S ONLY UNDERWEAR...
I...I GUESS IT'S TIME FOR ME TO GO SWIMMING TOO.

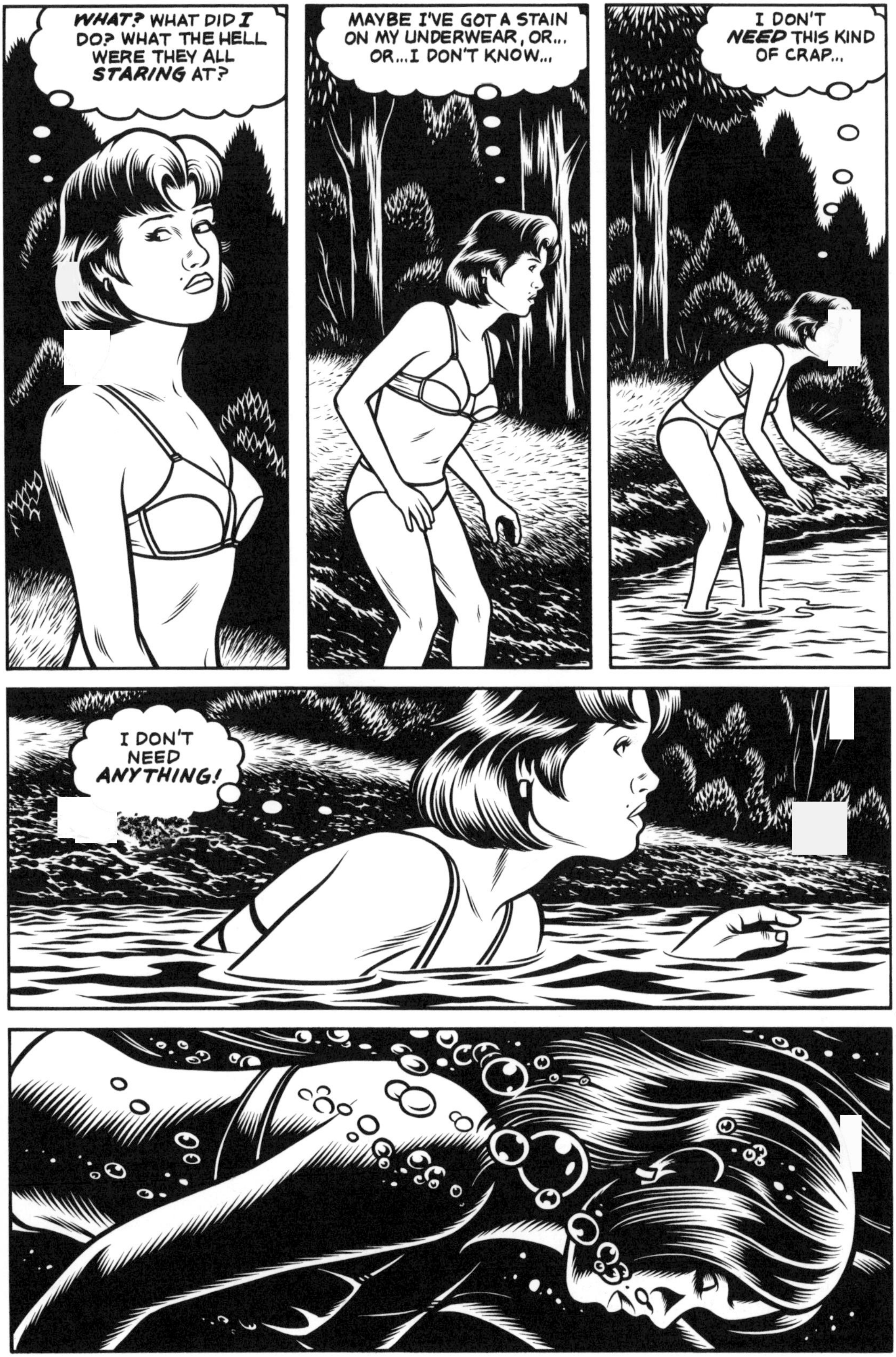

WHAT? WHAT DID I DO? WHAT THE HELL WERE THEY ALL STARING AT?
MAYBE I'VE GOT A STAIN ON MY UNDERWEAR, OR... OR...I DON'T KNOW...
I DON'T NEED THIS KIND OF CRAP...
I DON'T NEED ANYTHING!

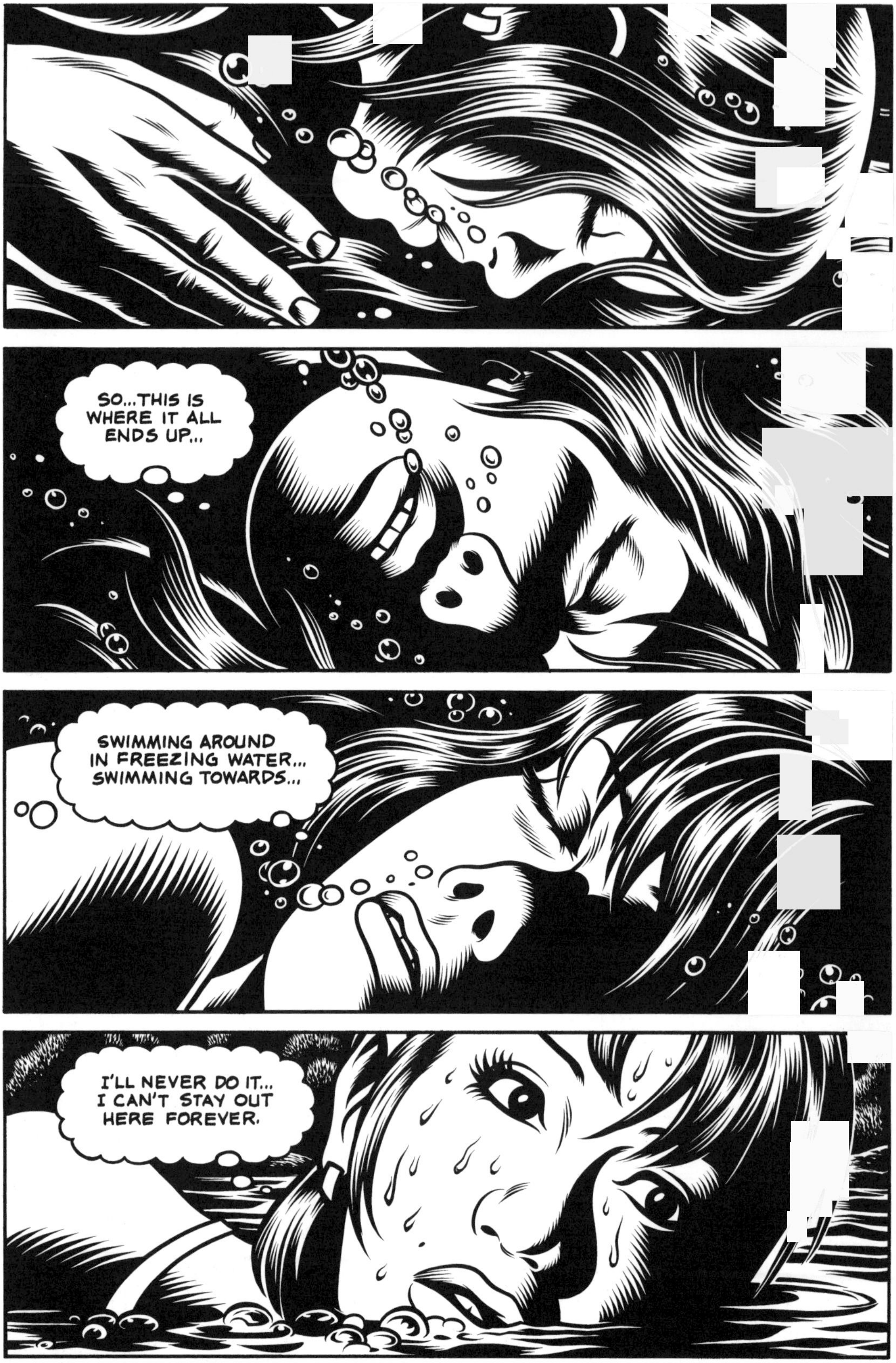
SO...THIS IS WHERE IT ALL ENDS UP...
SWIMMING AROUND IN FREEZING WATER... SWIMMING TOWARDS...
I'LL NEVER DO IT... I CAN'T STAY OUT HERE FOREVER.

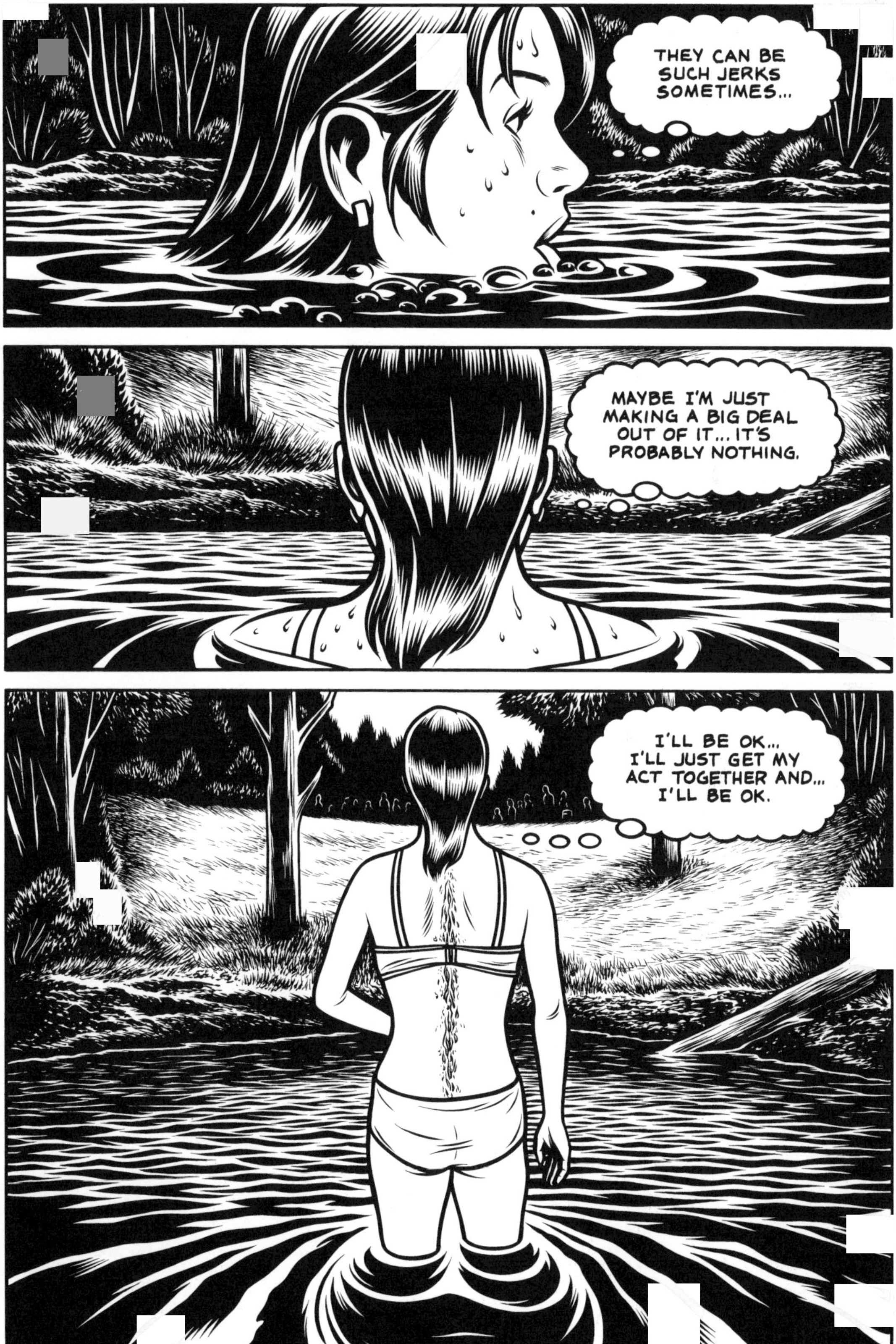
THEY CAN BE SUCH JERKS SOMETIMES...
MAYBE I'M JUST MAKING A BIG DEAL OUT OF IT... IT'S PROBABLY NOTHING.
I'LL BE OK... I'LL JUST GET MY ACT TOGETHER AND... I'LL BE OK.

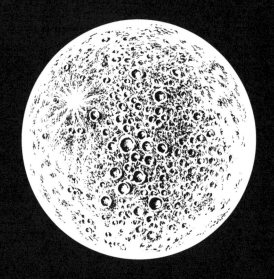

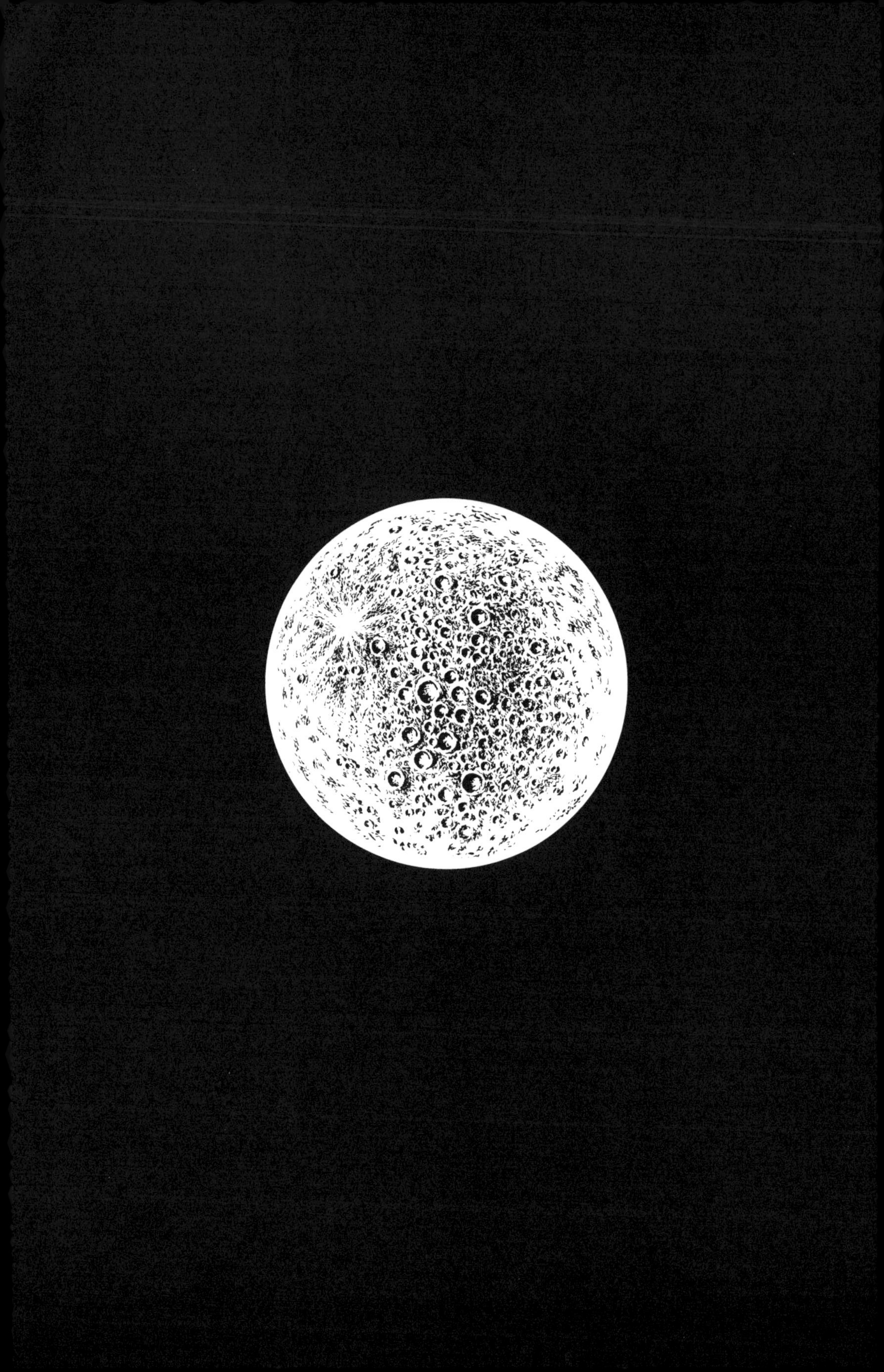

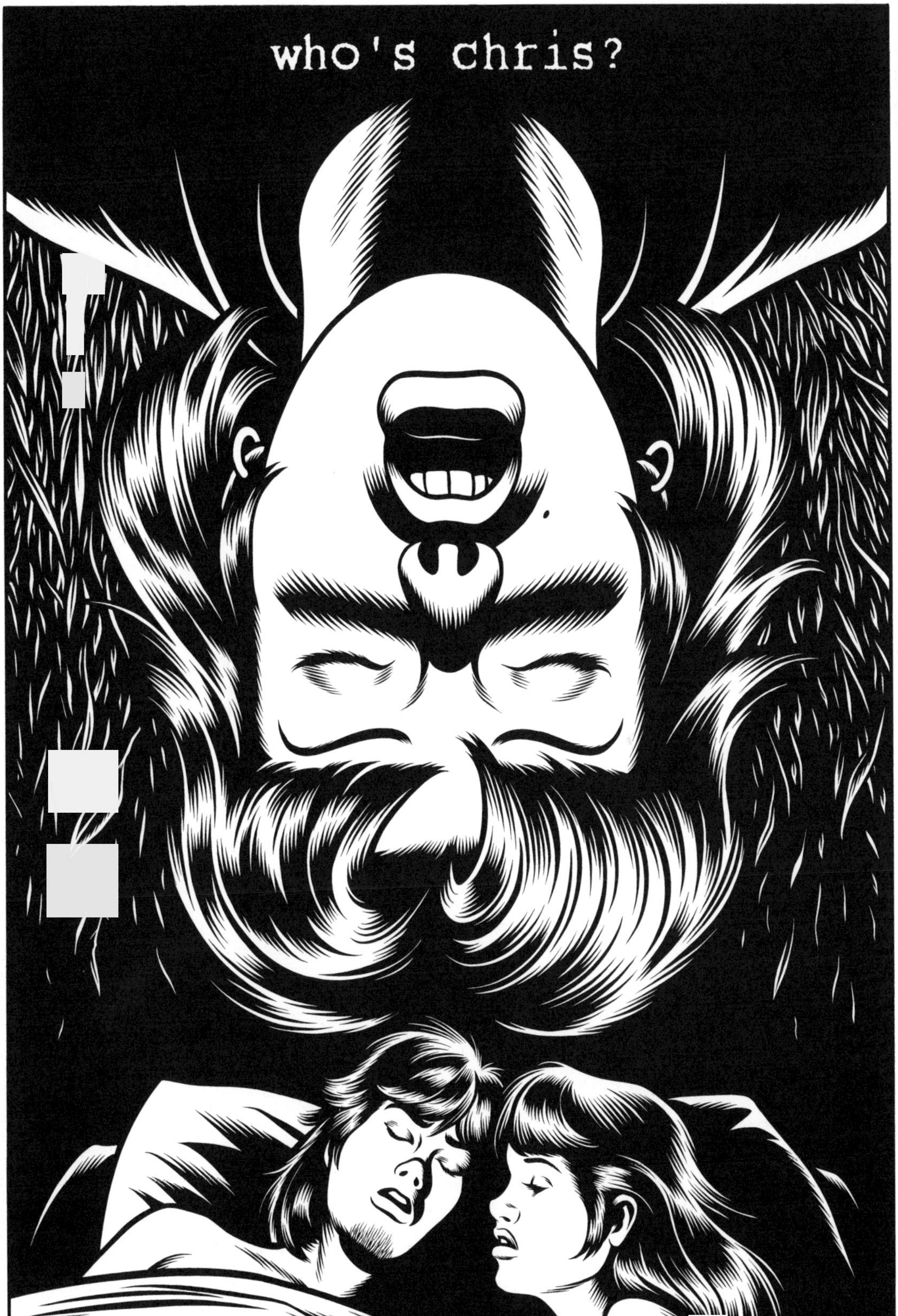
who's chris?

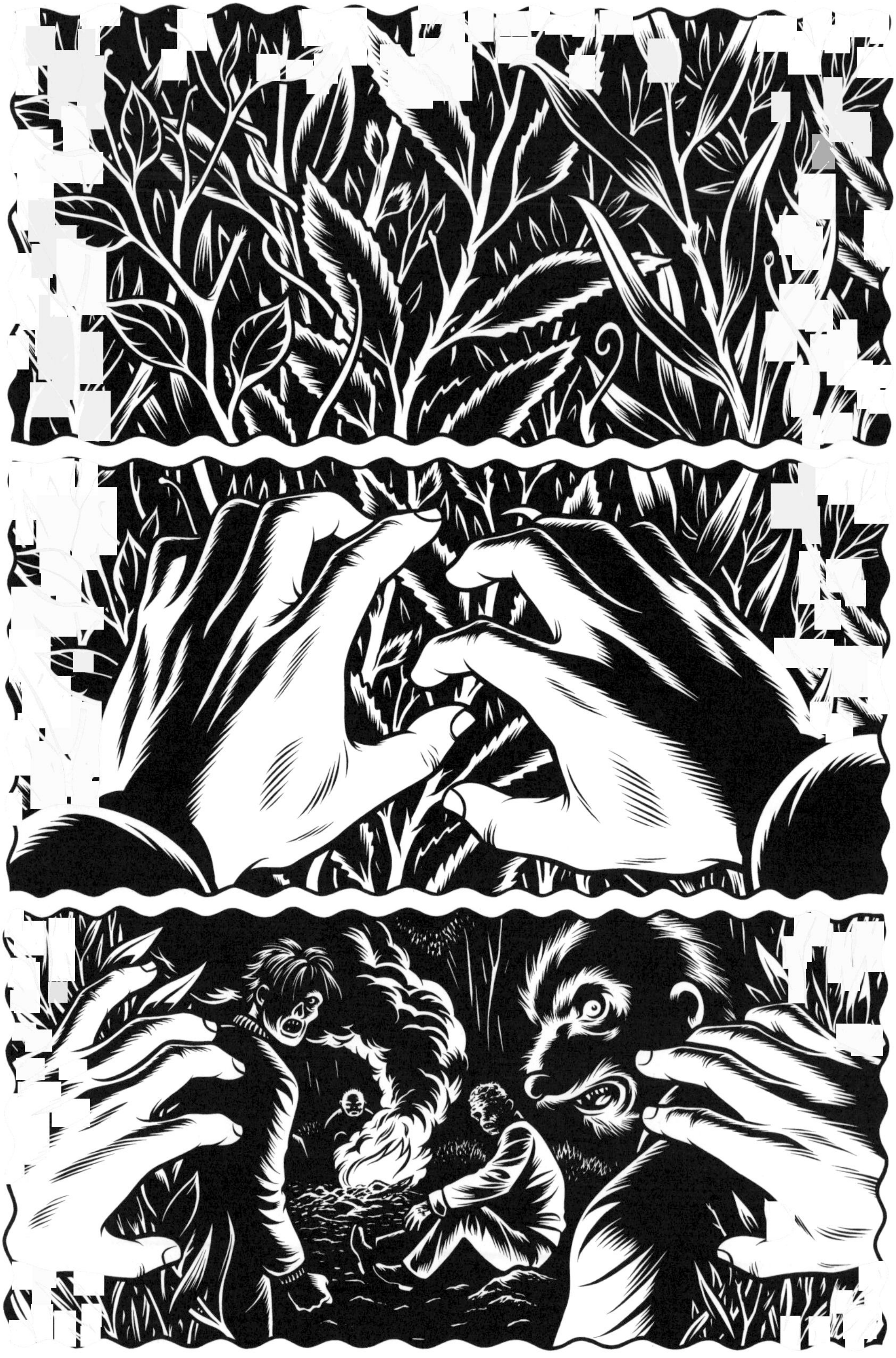

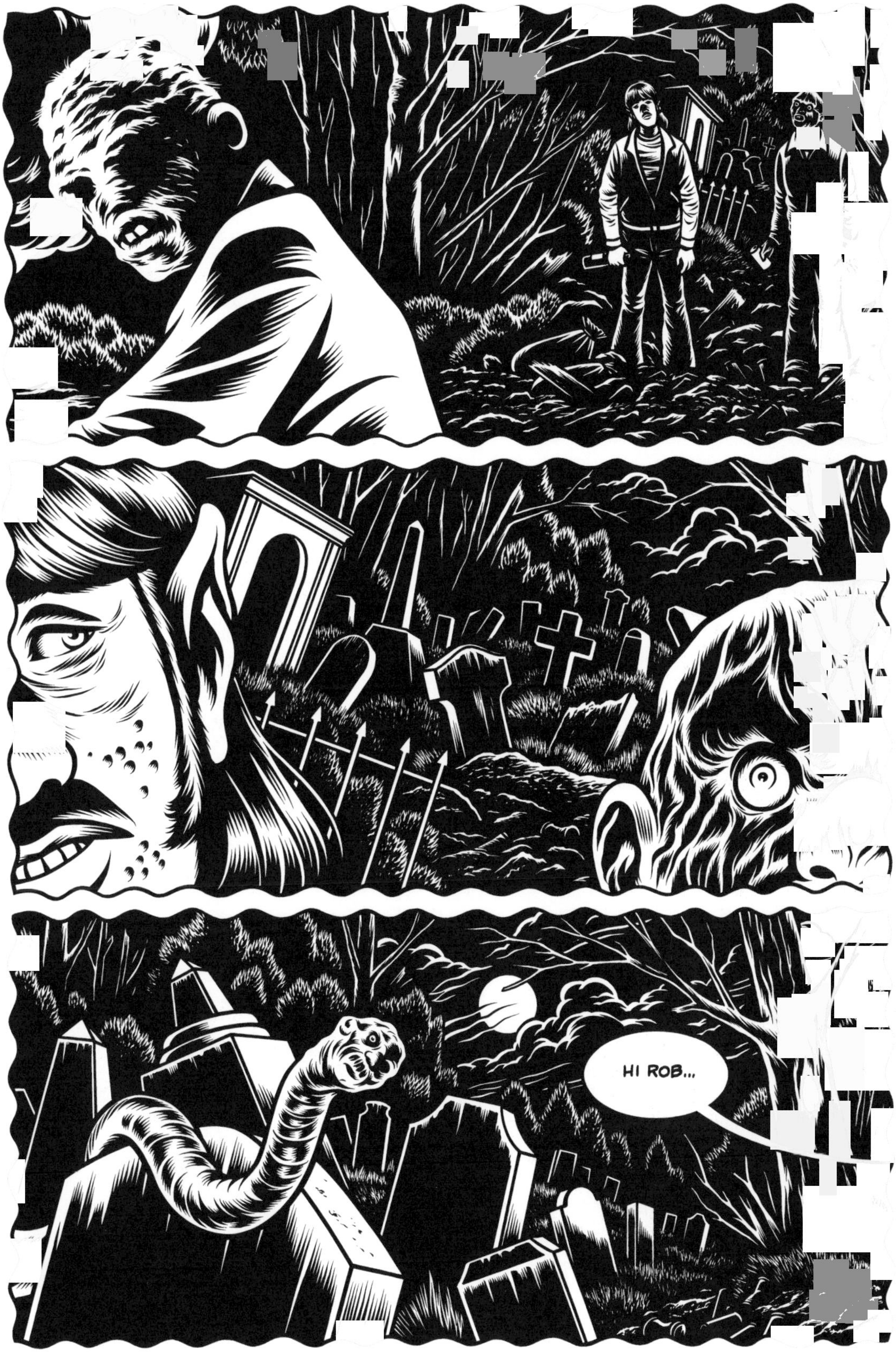
HI ROB...

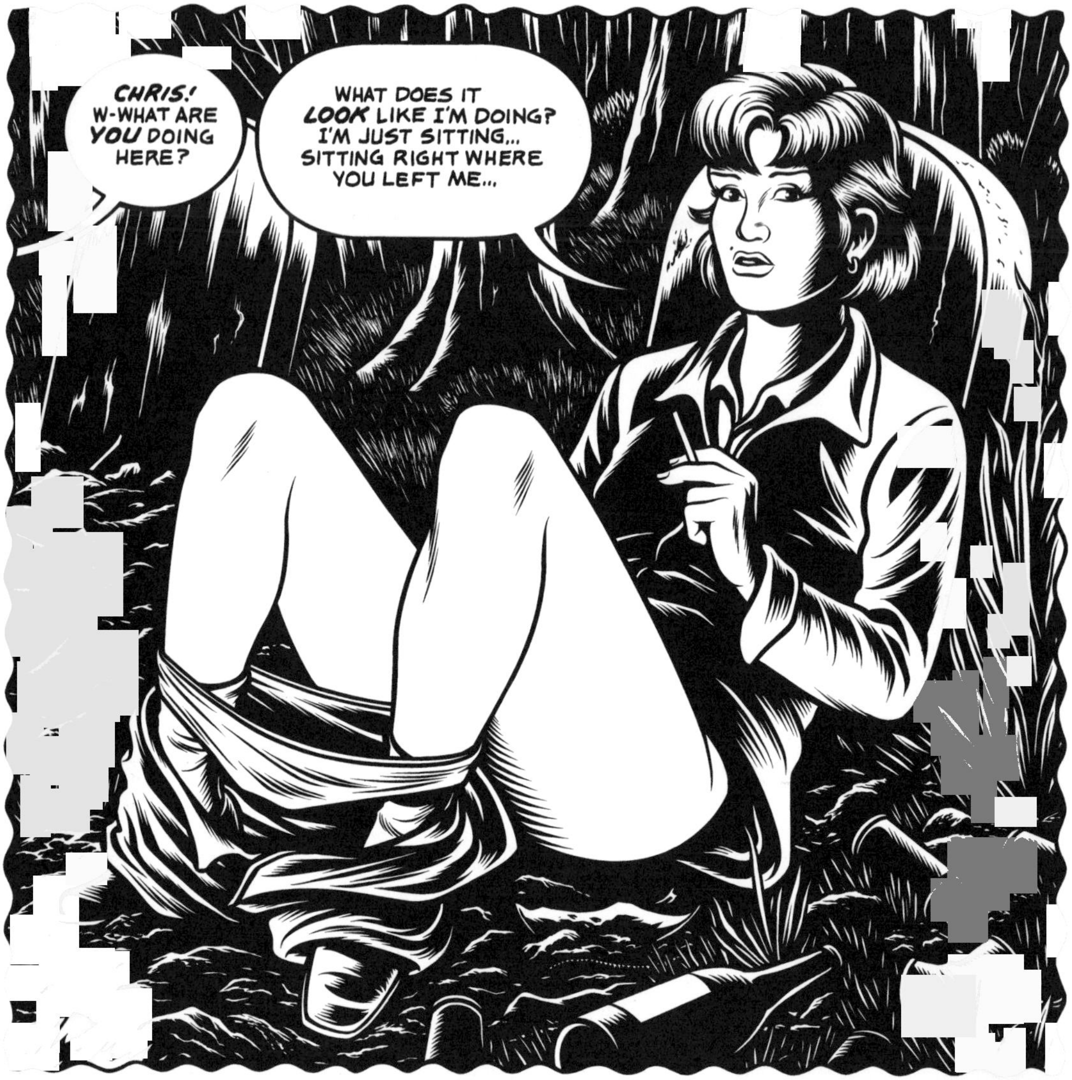
CHRIS! W-WHAT ARE YOU DOING HERE?
WHAT DOES IT LOOK LIKE I'M DOING? I'M JUST SITTING... SITTING RIGHT WHERE YOU LEFT ME...

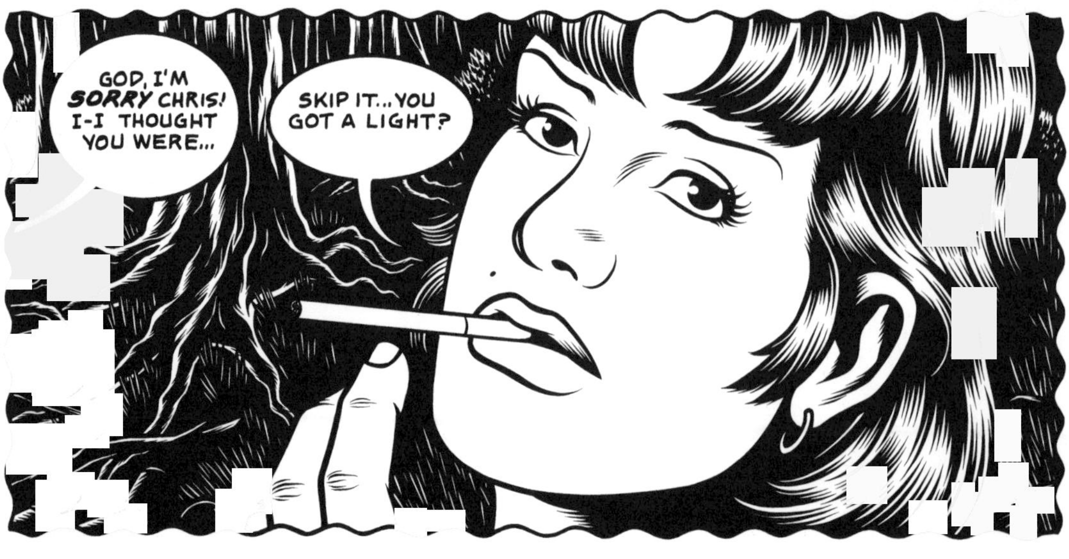
GOD, I'M SORRY CHRIS! I-I THOUGHT YOU WERE...
SKIP IT... YOU GOT A LIGHT?

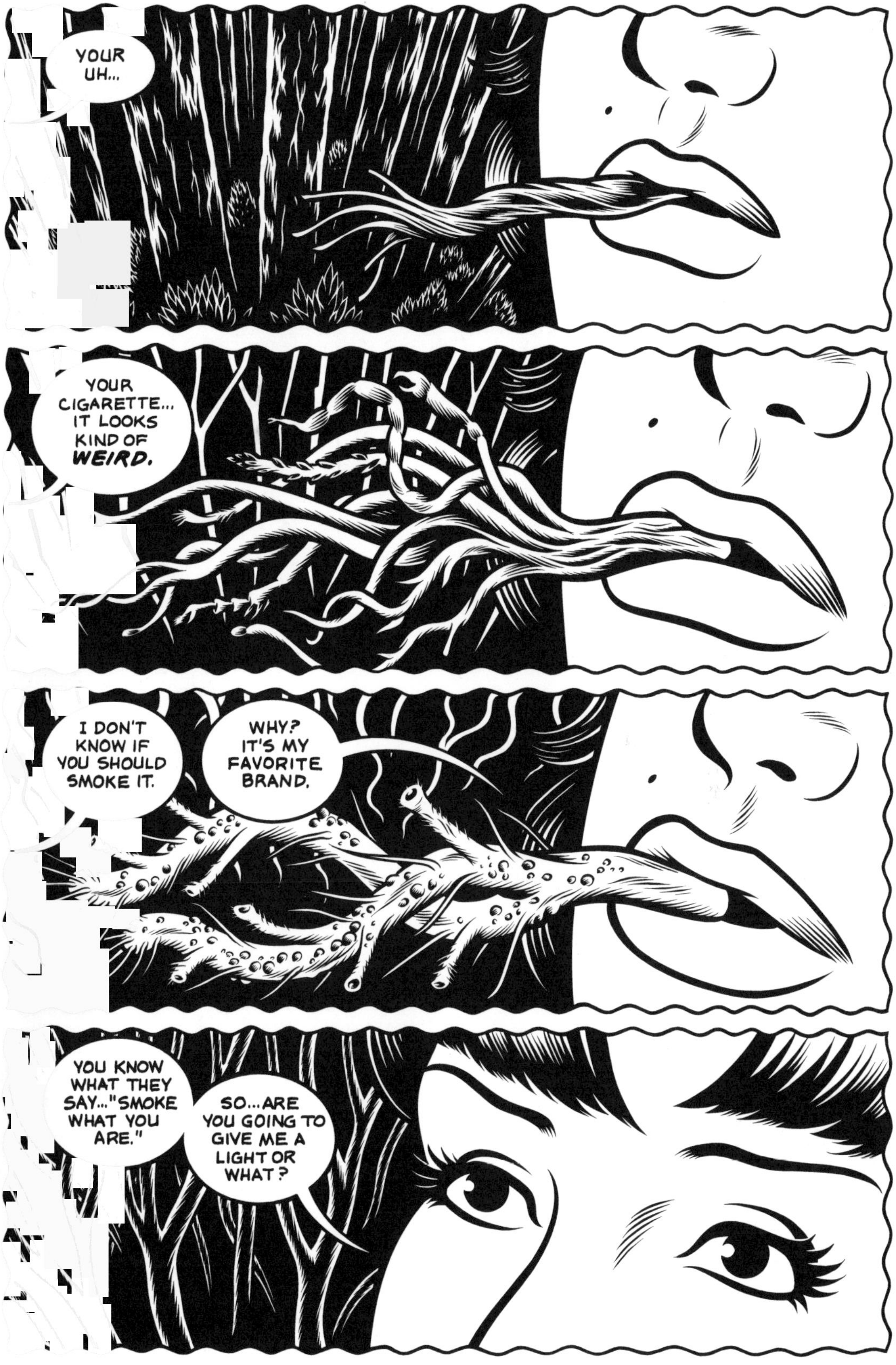
YOUR UH...
YOUR CIGARETTE... IT LOOKS KIND OF WEIRD.
I DON'T KNOW IF YOU SHOULD SMOKE IT.
WHY? IT'S MY FAVORITE BRAND.
YOU KNOW WHAT THEY SAY..."SMOKE WHAT YOU ARE."
SO...ARE YOU GOING TO GIVE ME A LIGHT OR WHAT?

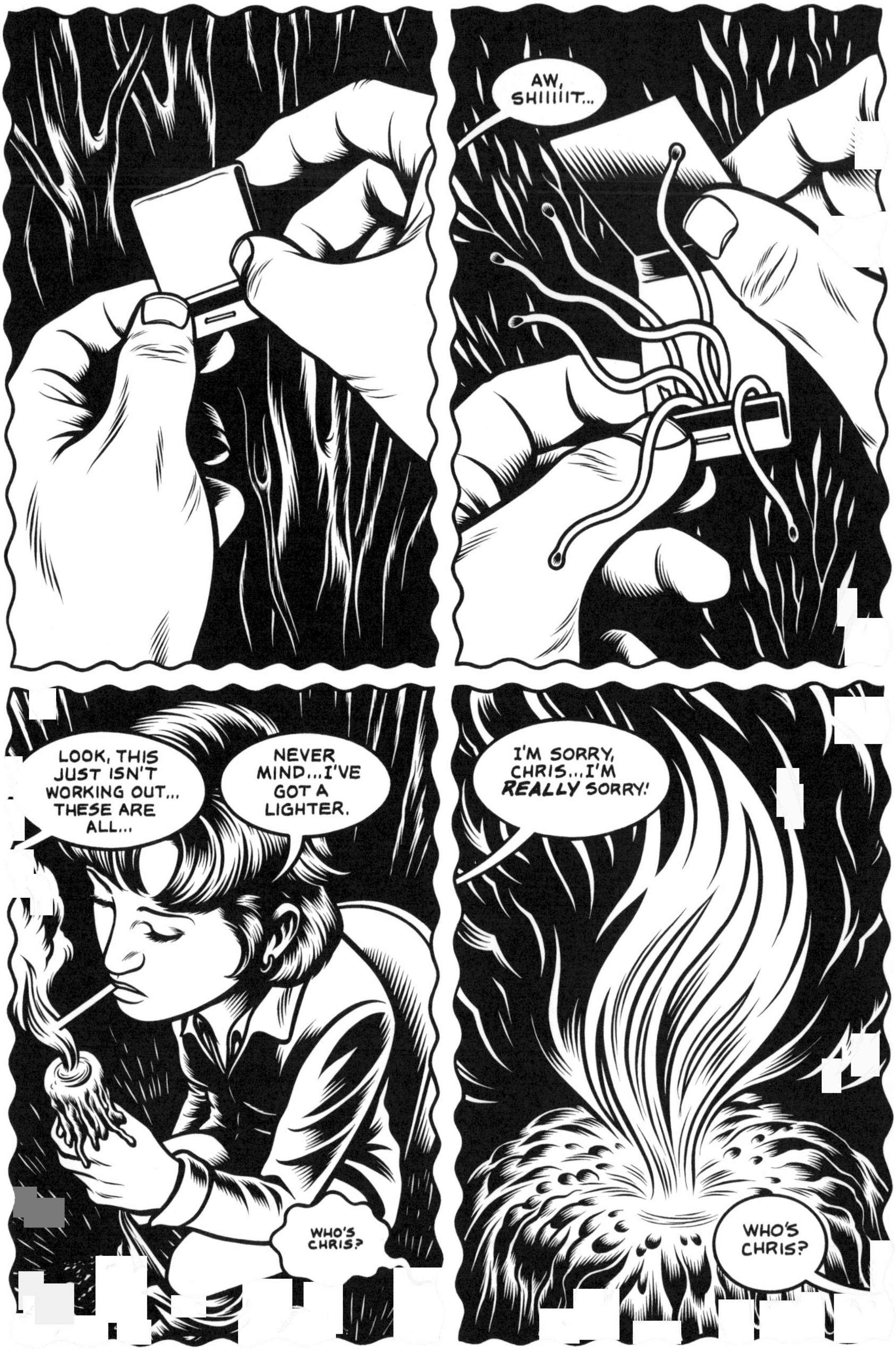
AW, SHIIIIIT...
LOOK, THIS JUST ISN'T WORKING OUT... THESE ARE ALL...
NEVER MIND...I'VE GOT A LIGHTER.
WHO'S CHRIS?
I'M SORRY, CHRIS...I'M REALLY SORRY!
WHO'S CHRIS?

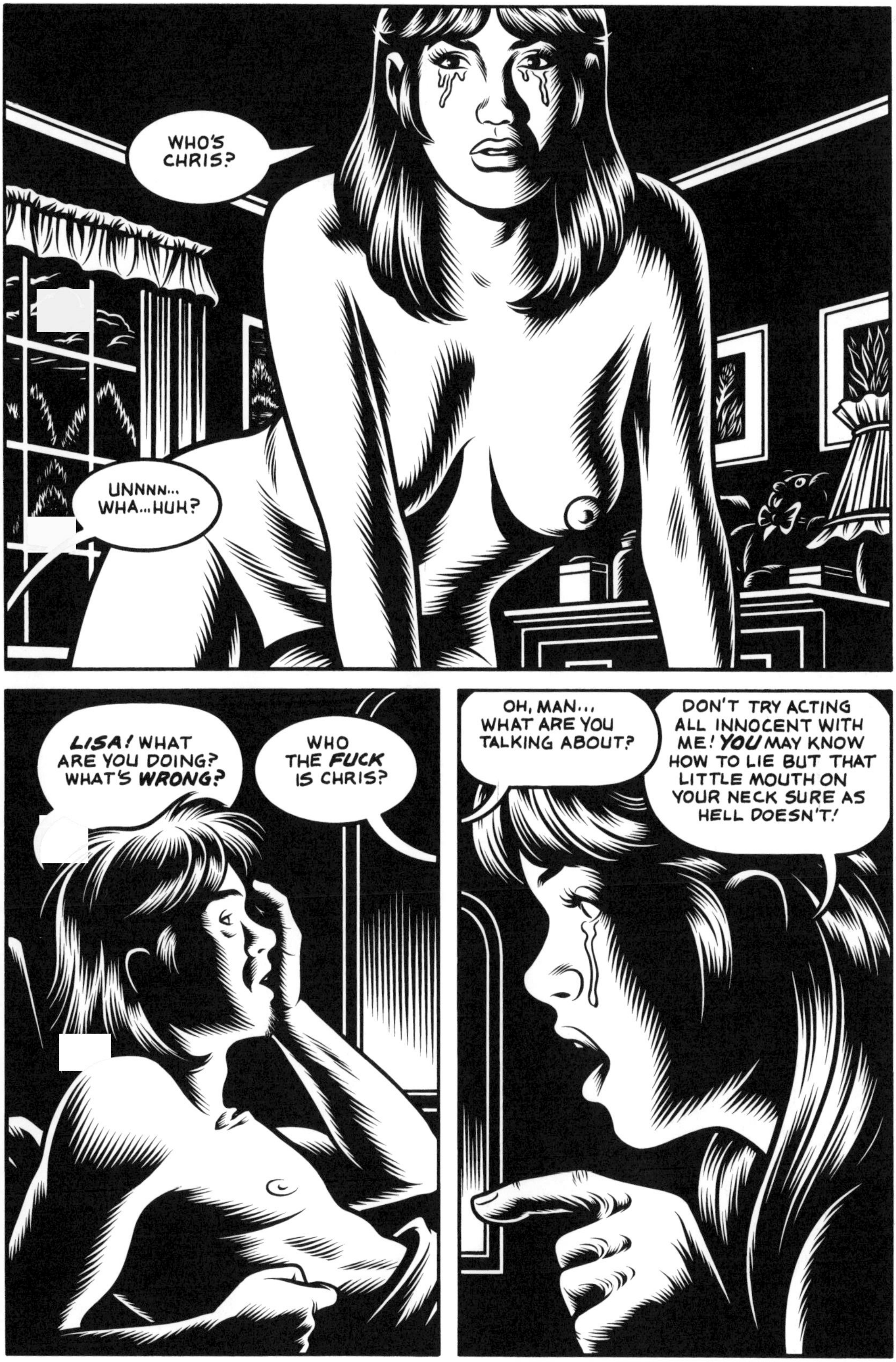
WHO'S CHRIS?
UNNNN... WHA...HUH?
LISA! WHAT ARE YOU DOING? WHAT'S WRONG?
WHO THE FUCK IS CHRIS?
OH, MAN... WHAT ARE YOU TALKING ABOUT?
DON'T TRY ACTING ALL INNOCENT WITH ME! YOU MAY KNOW HOW TO LIE BUT THAT LITTLE MOUTH ON YOUR NECK SURE AS HELL DOESN'T!

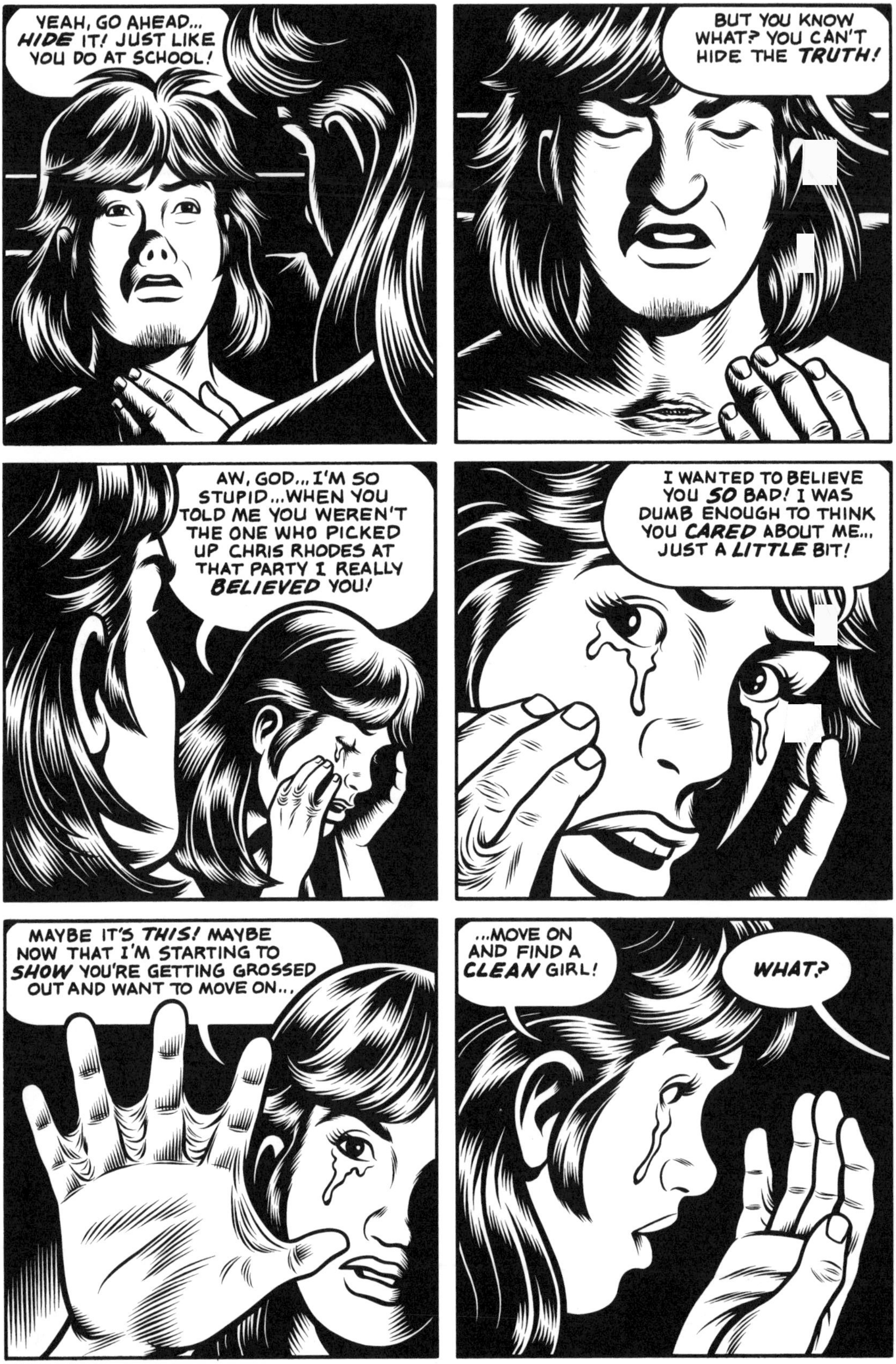
YEAH, GO AHEAD... HIDE IT! JUST LIKE YOU DO AT SCHOOL!
BUT YOU KNOW WHAT? YOU CAN'T HIDE THE TRUTH!
AW, GOD... I'M SO STUPID... WHEN YOU TOLD ME YOU WEREN'T THE ONE WHO PICKED UP CHRIS RHODES AT THAT PARTY I REALLY BELIEVED YOU!
I WANTED TO BELIEVE YOU SO BAD! I WAS DUMB ENOUGH TO THINK YOU CARED ABOUT ME... JUST A LITTLE BIT!
MAYBE IT'S THIS! MAYBE NOW THAT I'M STARTING TO SHOW YOU'RE GETTING GROSSED OUT AND WANT TO MOVE ON...
...MOVE ON AND FIND A CLEAN GIRL!
WHAT?

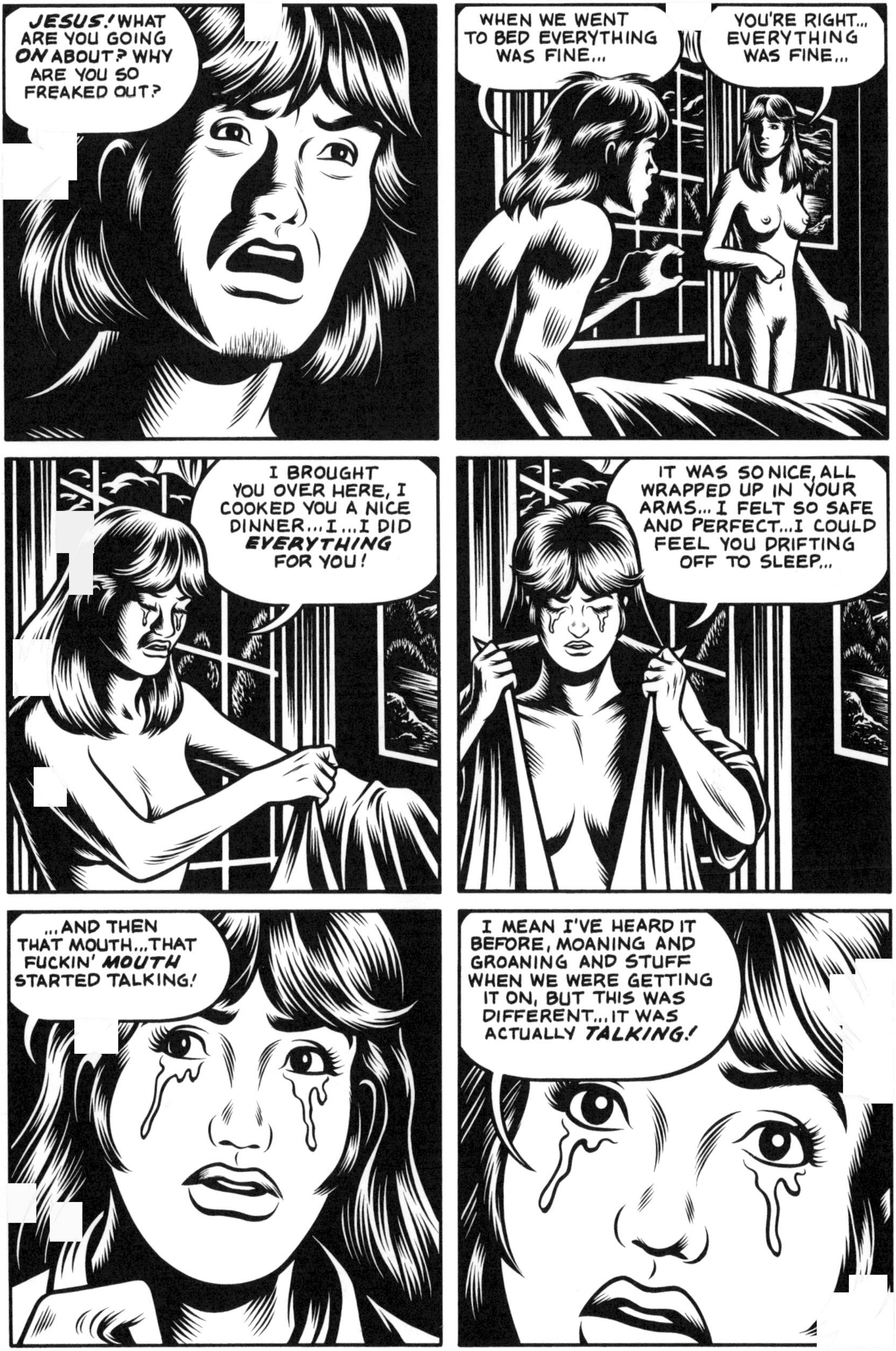

JESUS! WHAT ARE YOU GOING ON ABOUT? WHY ARE YOU SO FREAKED OUT?
WHEN WE WENT TO BED EVERYTHING WAS FINE...
YOU'RE RIGHT... EVERYTHING WAS FINE...
I BROUGHT YOU OVER HERE, I COOKED YOU A NICE DINNER... I... I DID EVERYTHING FOR YOU!
IT WAS SO NICE, ALL WRAPPED UP IN YOUR ARMS... I FELT SO SAFE AND PERFECT... I COULD FEEL YOU DRIFTING OFF TO SLEEP...
...AND THEN THAT MOUTH... THAT FUCKIN' MOUTH STARTED TALKING!
I MEAN I'VE HEARD IT BEFORE, MOANING AND GROANING AND STUFF WHEN WE WERE GETTING IT ON, BUT THIS WAS DIFFERENT... IT WAS ACTUALLY TALKING!

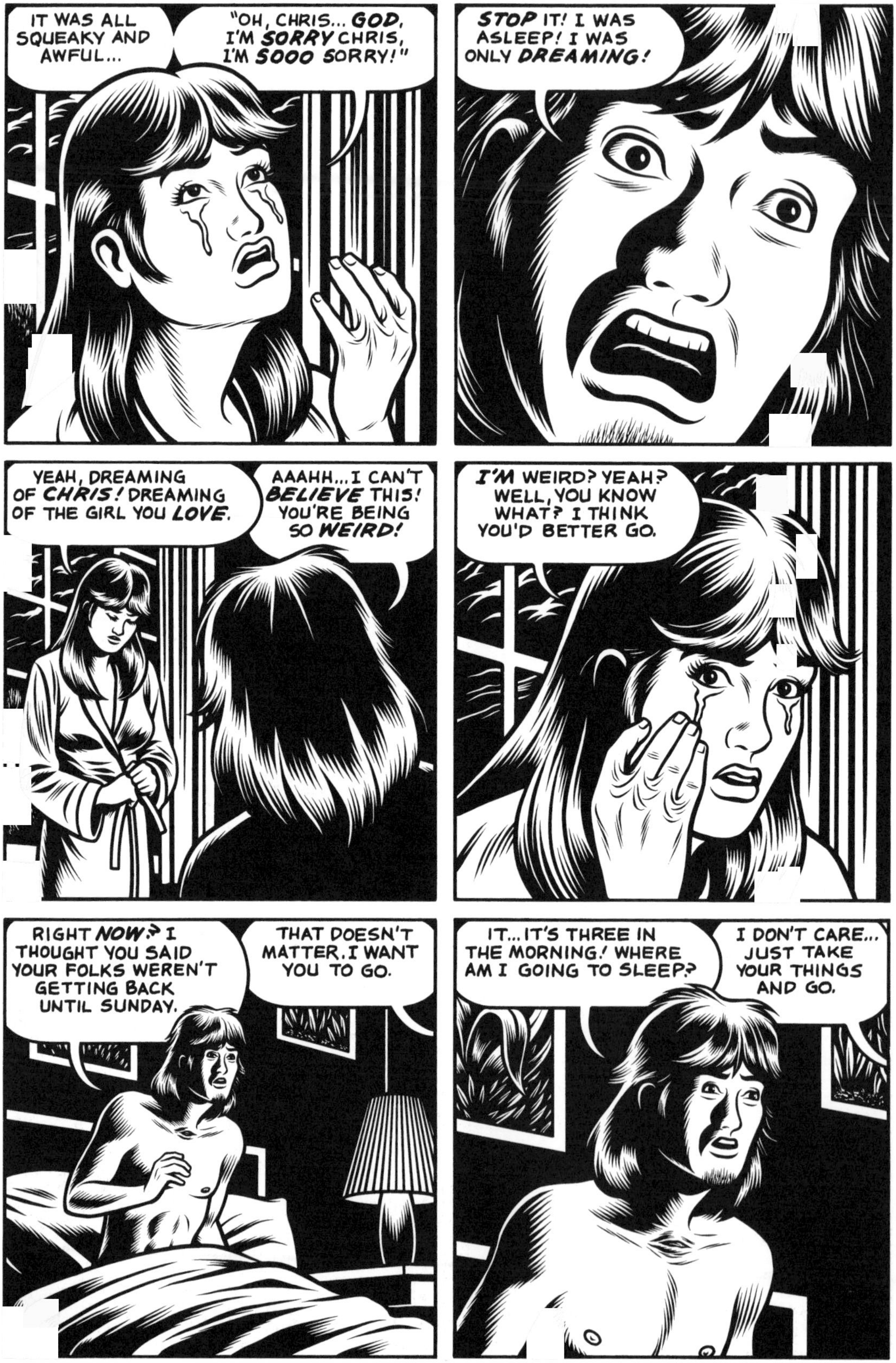
IT WAS ALL SQUEAKY AND AWFUL...
"OH, CHRIS... GOD, I'M SORRY CHRIS, I'M SOOO SORRY!"
STOP IT! I WAS ASLEEP! I WAS ONLY DREAMING!
YEAH, DREAMING OF CHRIS! DREAMING OF THE GIRL YOU LOVE.
AAAHH... I CAN'T BELIEVE THIS! YOU'RE BEING SO WEIRD!
I'M WEIRD? YEAH? WELL, YOU KNOW WHAT? I THINK YOU'D BETTER GO.
RIGHT NOW? I THOUGHT YOU SAID YOUR FOLKS WEREN'T GETTING BACK UNTIL SUNDAY.
THAT DOESN'T MATTER. I WANT YOU TO GO.
IT... IT'S THREE IN THE MORNING! WHERE AM I GOING TO SLEEP?
I DON'T CARE... JUST TAKE YOUR THINGS AND GO.

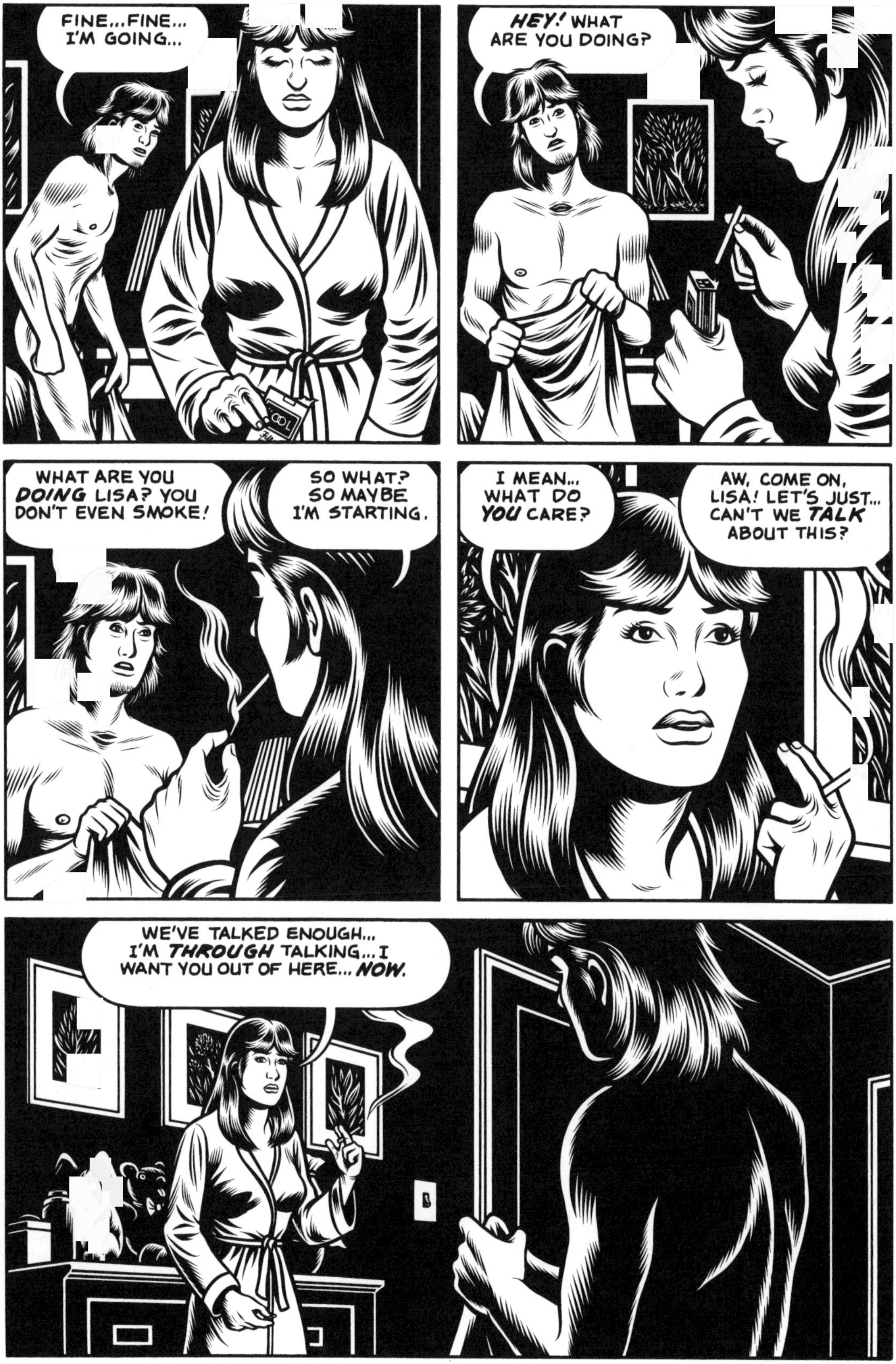
FINE...FINE... I'M GOING...
HEY! WHAT ARE YOU DOING?
WHAT ARE YOU DOING LISA? YOU DON'T EVEN SMOKE!
SO WHAT? SO MAYBE I'M STARTING.
I MEAN... WHAT DO YOU CARE?
AW, COME ON, LISA! LET'S JUST... CAN'T WE TALK ABOUT THIS?
WE'VE TALKED ENOUGH... I'M THROUGH TALKING... I WANT YOU OUT OF HERE... NOW.

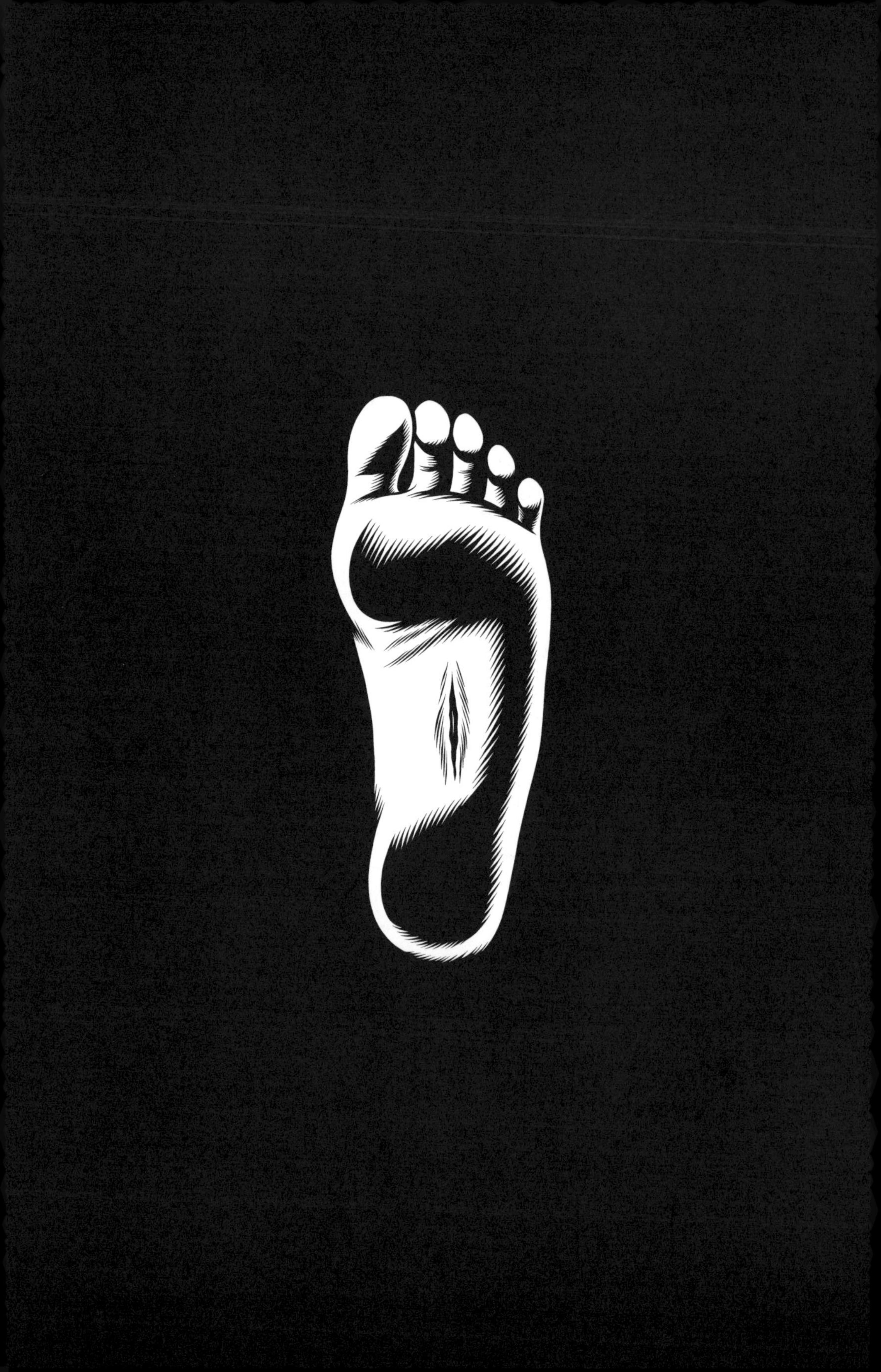

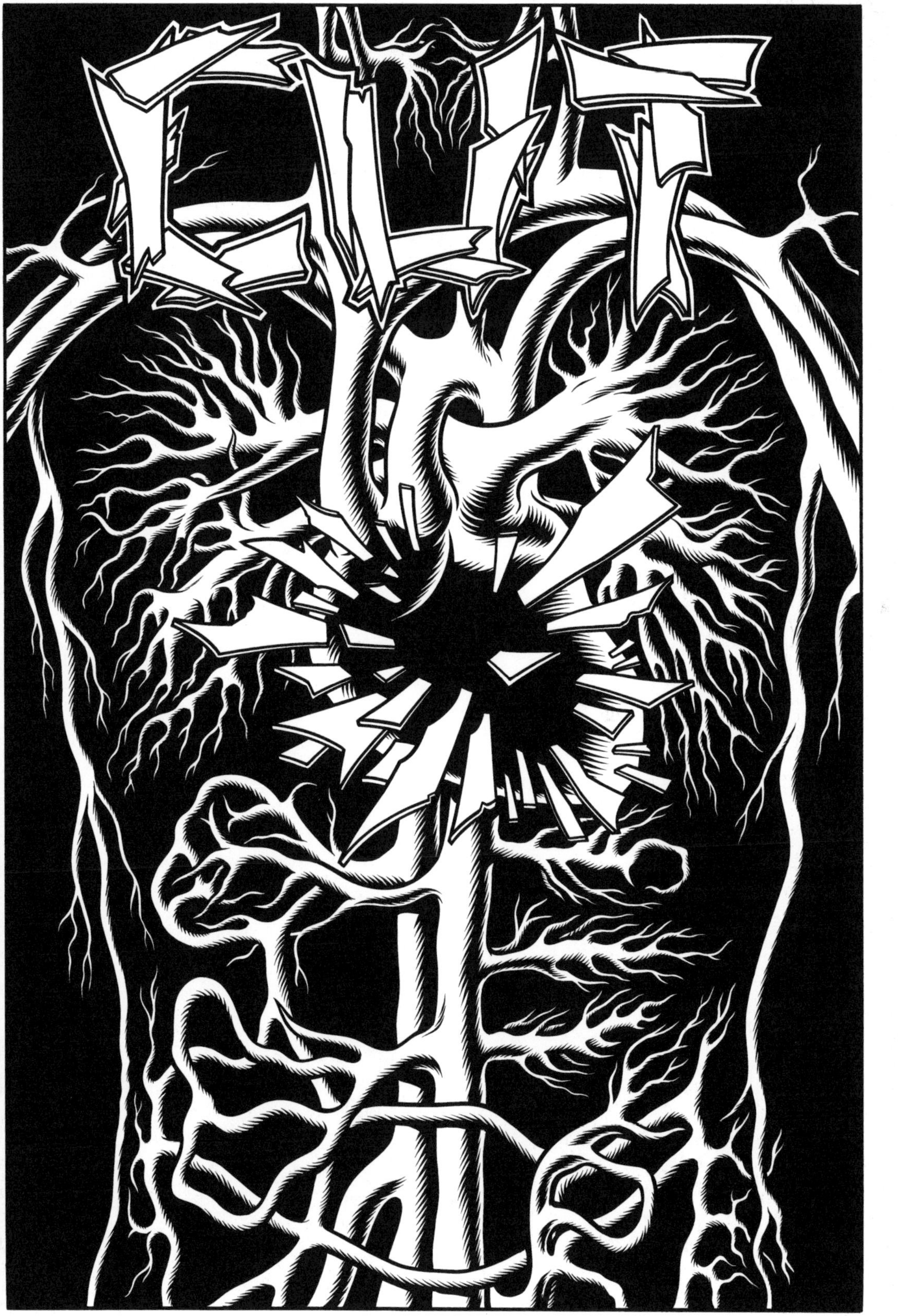
CUT

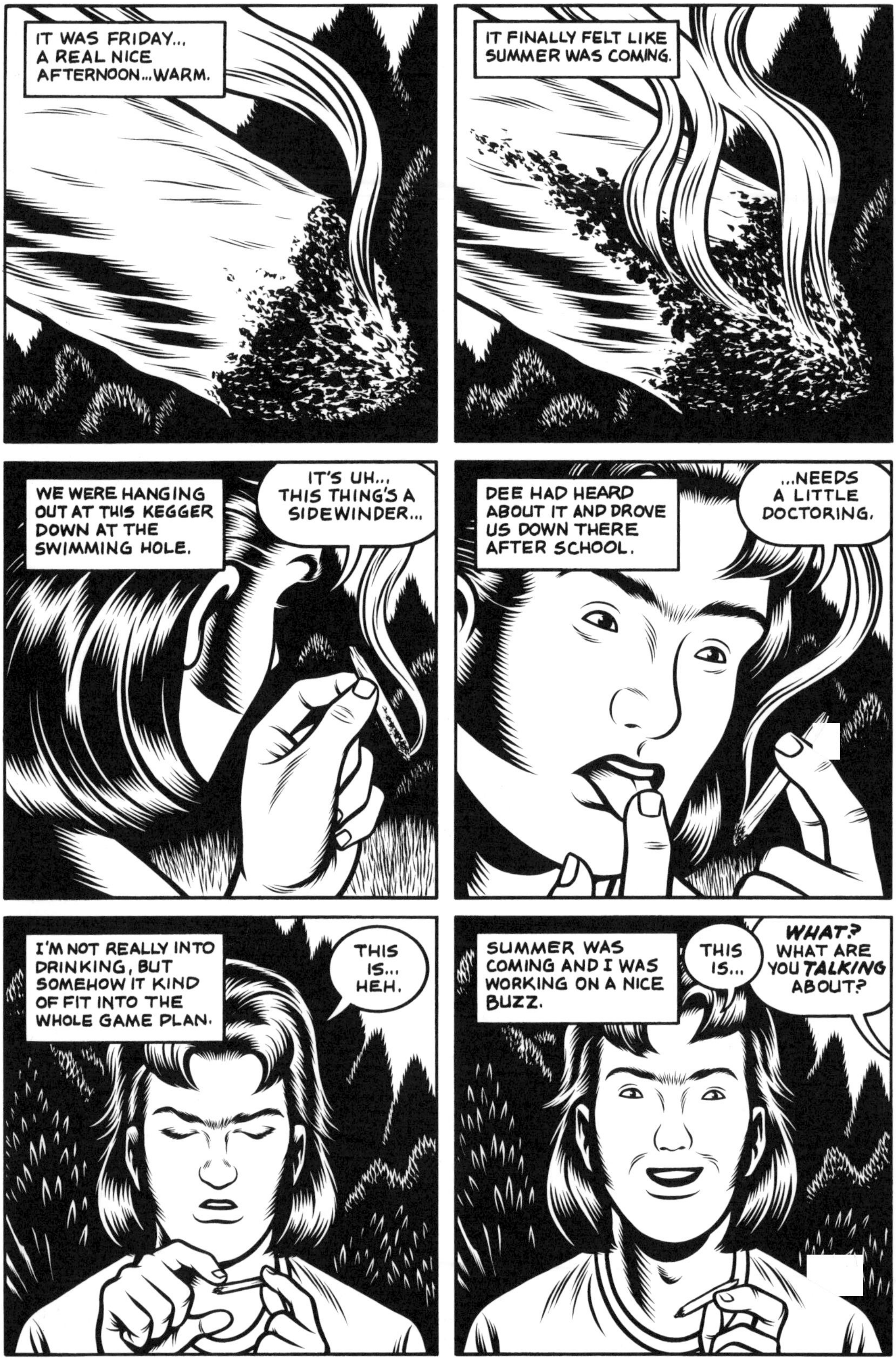
IT WAS FRIDAY... A REAL NICE AFTERNOON...WARM.
IT FINALLY FELT LIKE SUMMER WAS COMING.
WE WERE HANGING OUT AT THIS KEGGER DOWN AT THE SWIMMING HOLE.
IT'S UH... THIS THING'S A SIDEWINDER...
DEE HAD HEARD ABOUT IT AND DROVE US DOWN THERE AFTER SCHOOL.
...NEEDS A LITTLE DOCTORING.
I'M NOT REALLY INTO DRINKING, BUT SOMEHOW IT KIND OF FIT INTO THE WHOLE GAME PLAN.
THIS IS... HEH.
SUMMER WAS COMING AND I WAS WORKING ON A NICE BUZZ.
THIS IS...
WHAT? WHAT ARE YOU ***TALKING*** ABOUT?

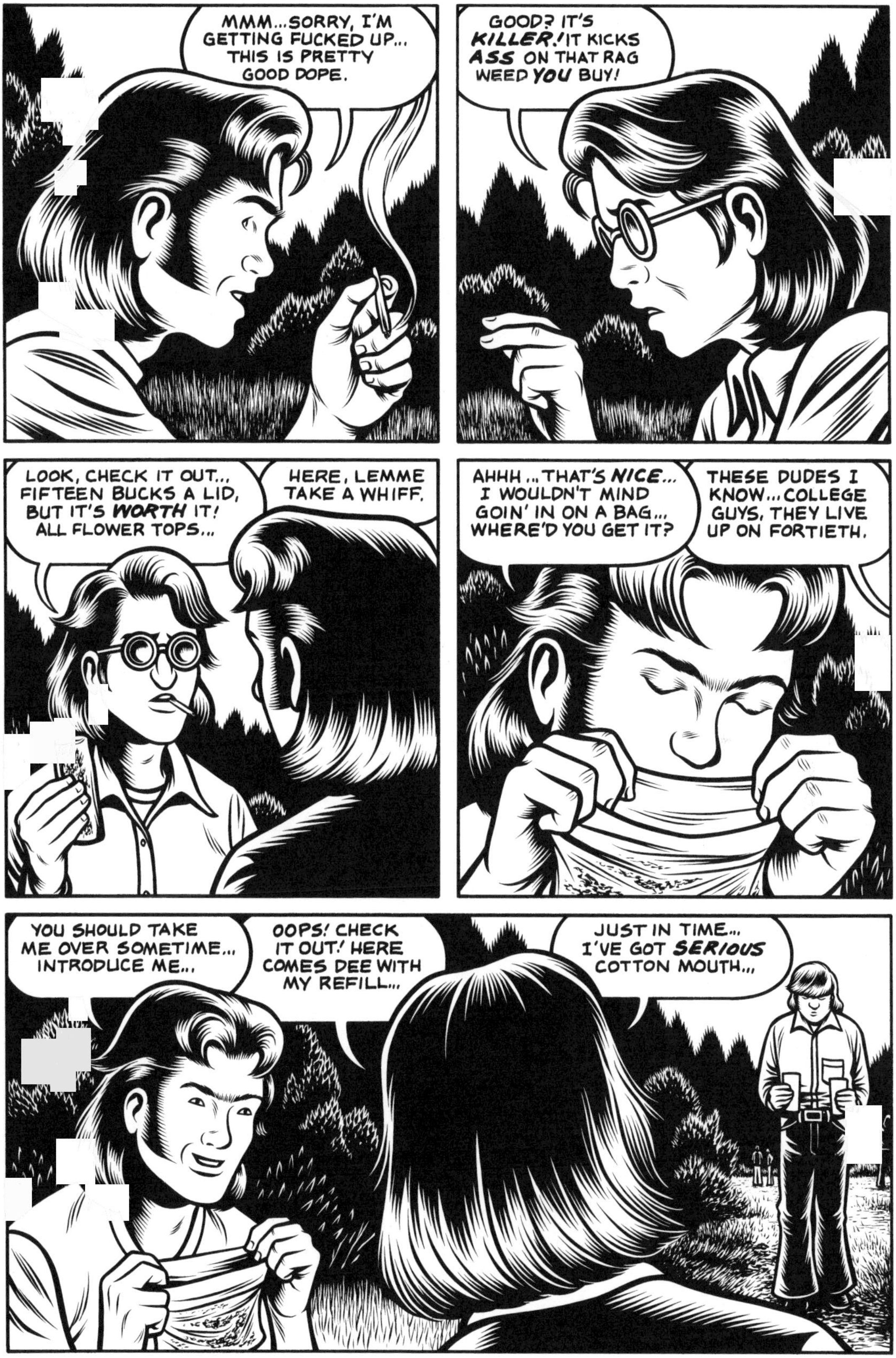
MMM... SORRY, I'M GETTING FUCKED UP... THIS IS PRETTY GOOD DOPE.
GOOD? IT'S KILLER! IT KICKS ASS ON THAT RAG WEED YOU BUY!
LOOK, CHECK IT OUT... FIFTEEN BUCKS A LID, BUT IT'S WORTH IT! ALL FLOWER TOPS...
HERE, LEMME TAKE A WHIFF.
AHHH... THAT'S NICE... I WOULDN'T MIND GOIN' IN ON A BAG... WHERE'D YOU GET IT?
THESE DUDES I KNOW... COLLEGE GUYS, THEY LIVE UP ON FORTIETH.
YOU SHOULD TAKE ME OVER SOMETIME... INTRODUCE ME...
OOPS! CHECK IT OUT! HERE COMES DEE WITH MY REFILL...
JUST IN TIME... I'VE GOT SERIOUS COTTON MOUTH...

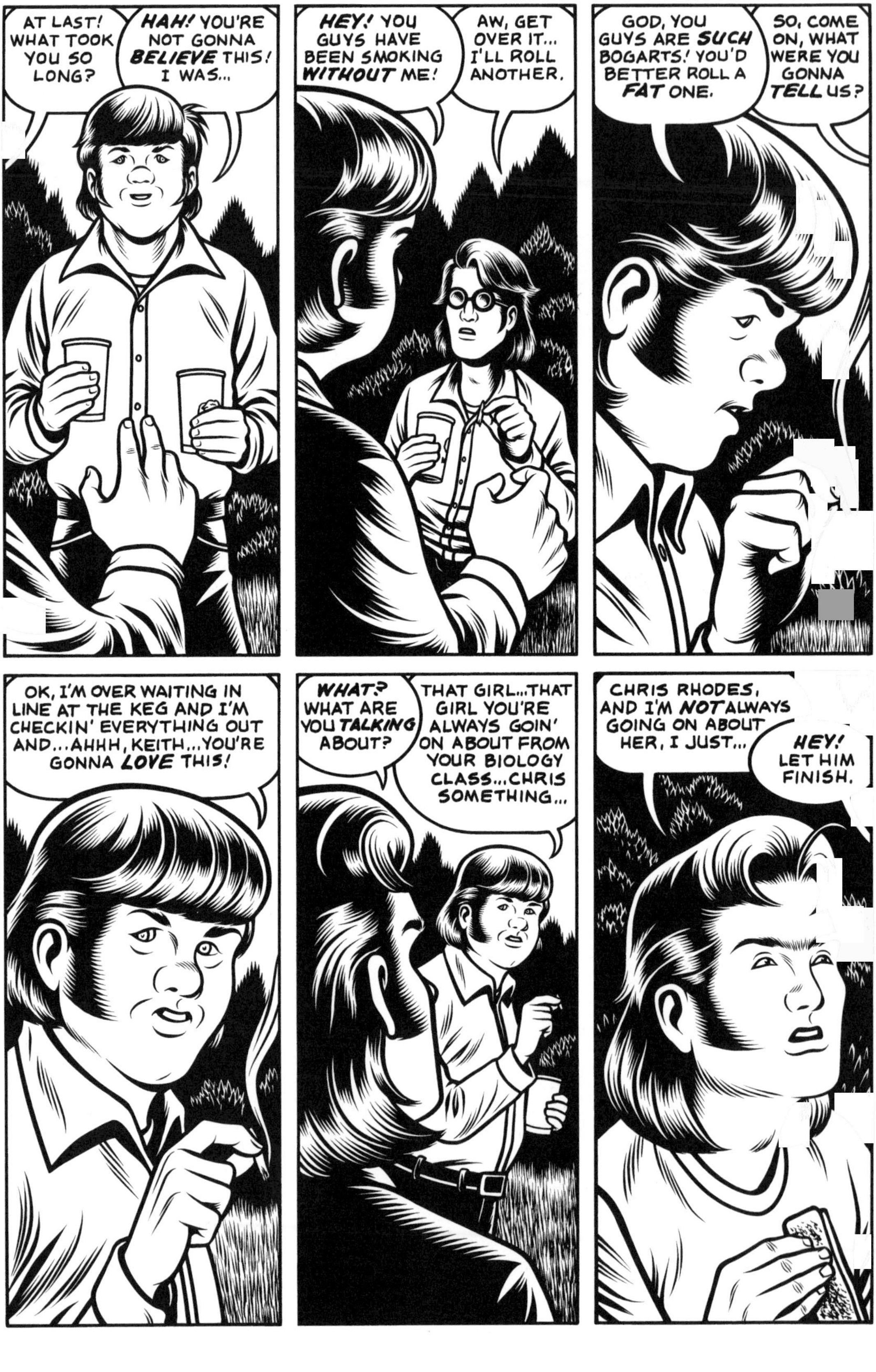
AT LAST! WHAT TOOK YOU SO LONG?
HAH! YOU'RE NOT GONNA BELIEVE THIS! I WAS...
HEY! YOU GUYS HAVE BEEN SMOKING WITHOUT ME!
AW, GET OVER IT... I'LL ROLL ANOTHER.
GOD, YOU GUYS ARE SUCH BOGARTS! YOU'D BETTER ROLL A FAT ONE.
SO, COME ON, WHAT WERE YOU GONNA TELL US?
OK, I'M OVER WAITING IN LINE AT THE KEG AND I'M CHECKIN' EVERYTHING OUT AND... AHHH, KEITH... YOU'RE GONNA LOVE THIS!
WHAT? WHAT ARE YOU TALKING ABOUT?
THAT GIRL... THAT GIRL YOU'RE ALWAYS GOIN' ON ABOUT FROM YOUR BIOLOGY CLASS... CHRIS SOMETHING...
CHRIS RHODES, AND I'M NOT ALWAYS GOING ON ABOUT HER, I JUST...
HEY! LET HIM FINISH.

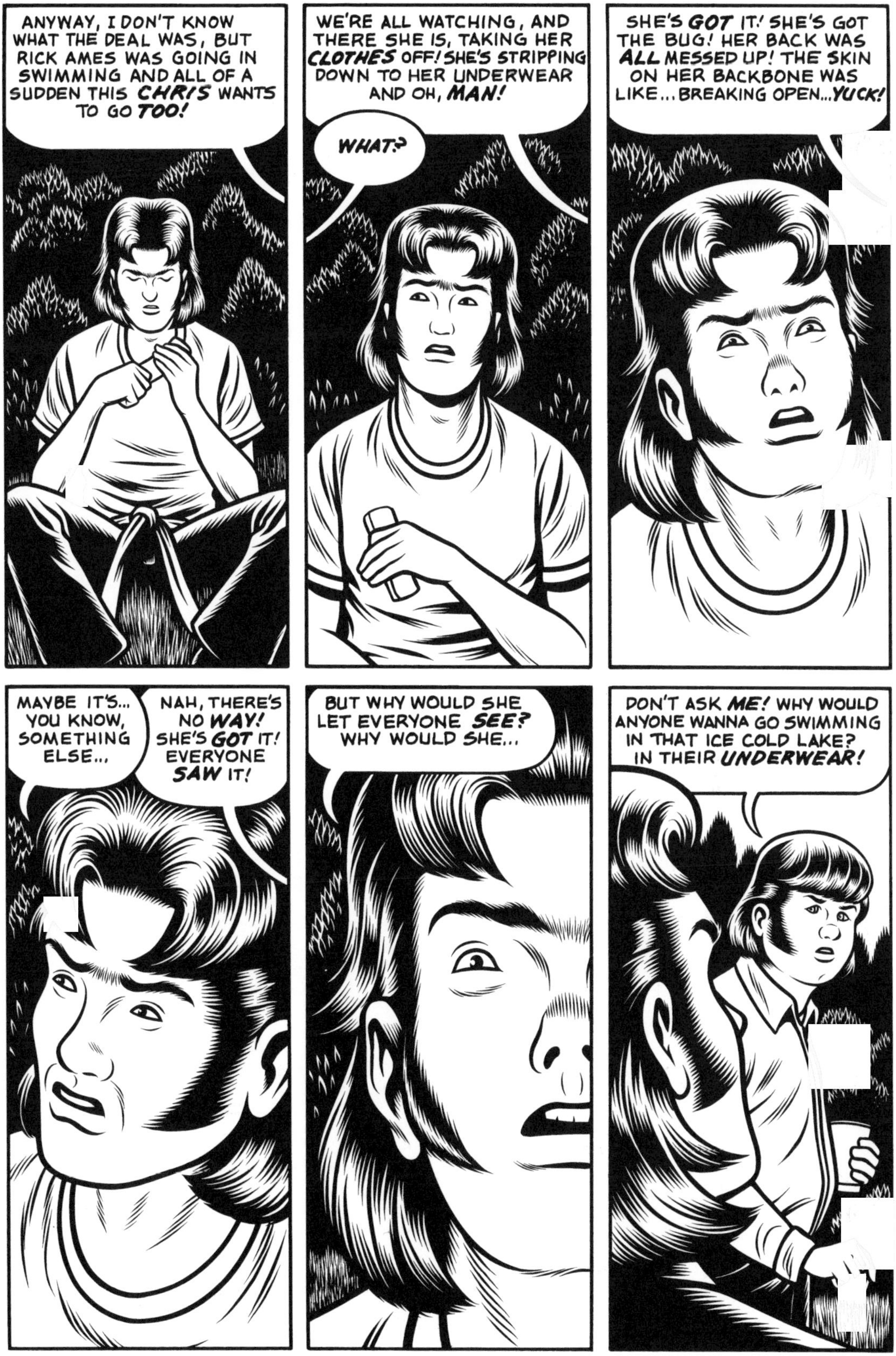
ANYWAY, I DON'T KNOW WHAT THE DEAL WAS, BUT RICK AMES WAS GOING IN SWIMMING AND ALL OF A SUDDEN THIS CHRIS WANTS TO GO TOO!
WE'RE ALL WATCHING, AND THERE SHE IS, TAKING HER CLOTHES OFF! SHE'S STRIPPING DOWN TO HER UNDERWEAR AND OH, MAN!
WHAT?
SHE'S GOT IT! SHE'S GOT THE BUG! HER BACK WAS ALL MESSED UP! THE SKIN ON HER BACKBONE WAS LIKE... BREAKING OPEN... YUCK!
MAYBE IT'S... YOU KNOW, SOMETHING ELSE...
NAH, THERE'S NO WAY! SHE'S GOT IT! EVERYONE SAW IT!
BUT WHY WOULD SHE LET EVERYONE SEE? WHY WOULD SHE...
DON'T ASK ME! WHY WOULD ANYONE WANNA GO SWIMMING IN THAT ICE COLD LAKE? IN THEIR UNDERWEAR!

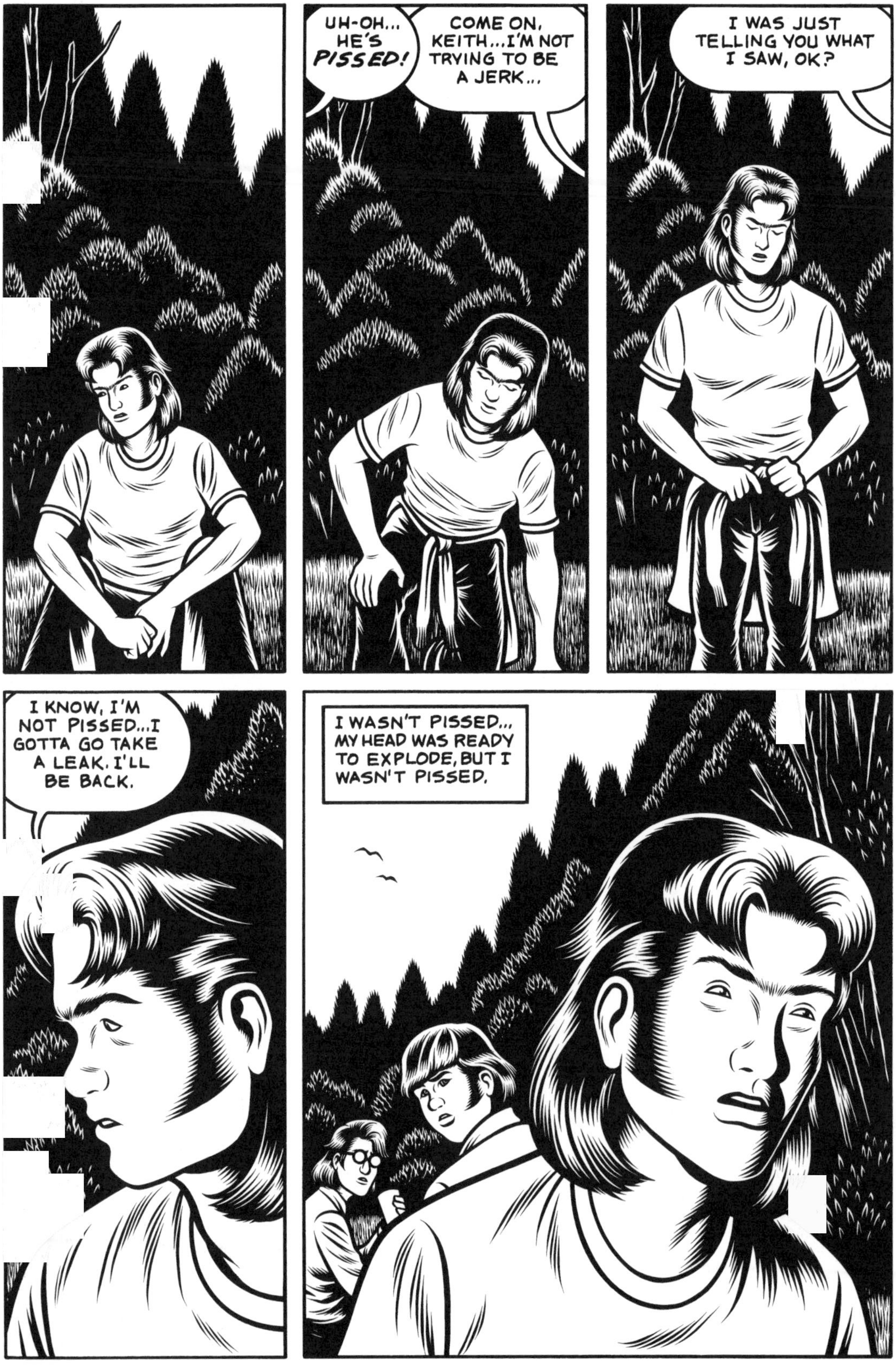

UH-OH... HE'S *PISSED!*
COME ON, KEITH...I'M NOT TRYING TO BE A JERK...
I WAS JUST TELLING YOU WHAT I SAW, OK?
I KNOW, I'M NOT PISSED...I GOTTA GO TAKE A LEAK. I'LL BE BACK.
I WASN'T PISSED... MY HEAD WAS READY TO EXPLODE, BUT I WASN'T PISSED.

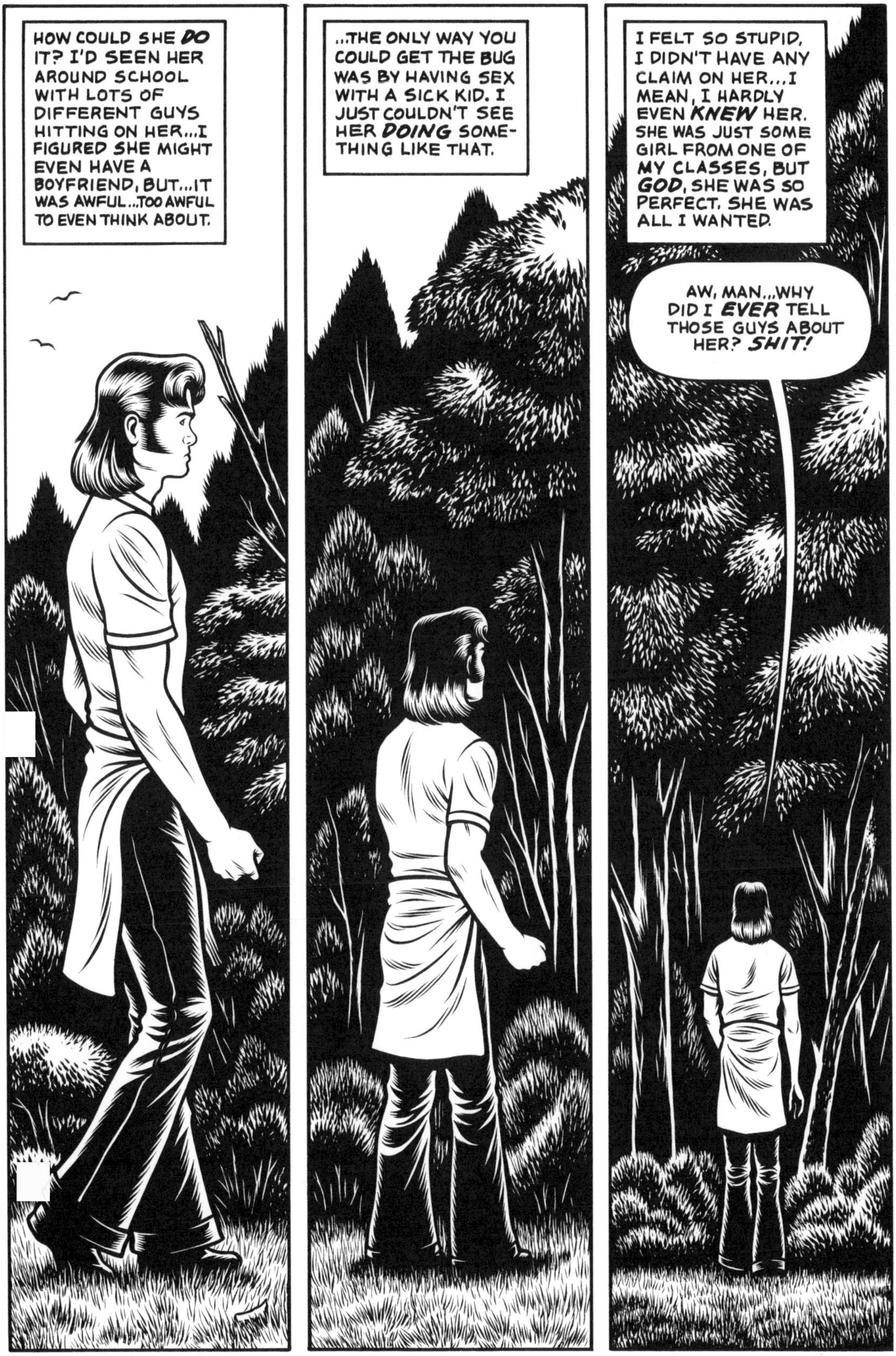
HOW COULD SHE DO IT? I'D SEEN HER AROUND SCHOOL WITH LOTS OF DIFFERENT GUYS HITTING ON HER...I FIGURED SHE MIGHT EVEN HAVE A BOYFRIEND, BUT...IT WAS AWFUL...TOO AWFUL TO EVEN THINK ABOUT.
...THE ONLY WAY YOU COULD GET THE BUG WAS BY HAVING SEX WITH A SICK KID. I JUST COULDN'T SEE HER DOING SOMETHING LIKE THAT.
I FELT SO STUPID, I DIDN'T HAVE ANY CLAIM ON HER...I MEAN, I HARDLY EVEN KNEW HER. SHE WAS JUST SOME GIRL FROM ONE OF MY CLASSES, BUT GOD, SHE WAS SO PERFECT. SHE WAS ALL I WANTED.
AW, MAN...WHY DID I EVER TELL THOSE GUYS ABOUT HER? SHIT!

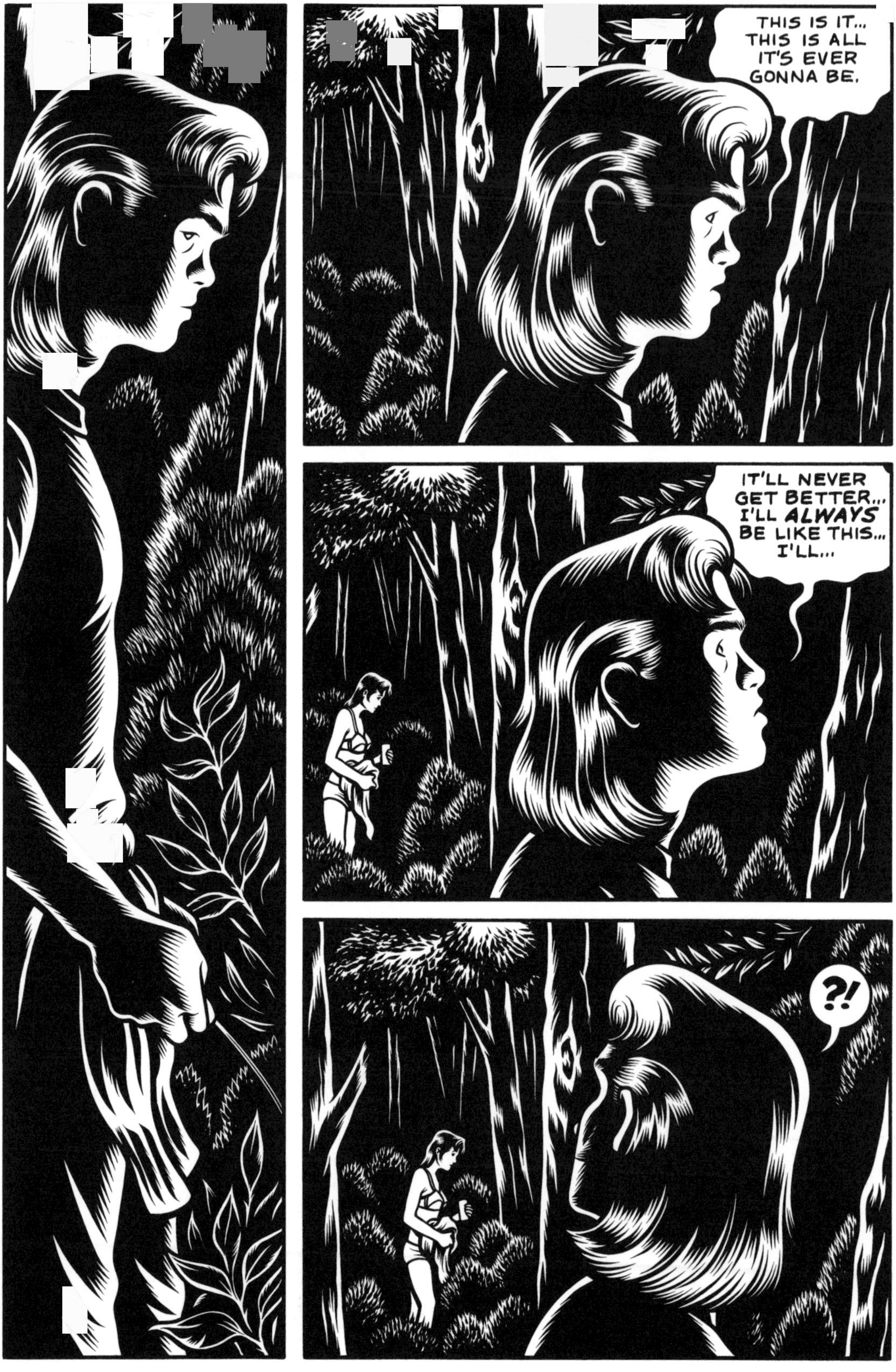
THIS IS IT... THIS IS ALL IT'S EVER GONNA BE.
IT'LL NEVER GET BETTER... I'LL ALWAYS BE LIKE THIS... I'LL...
?!

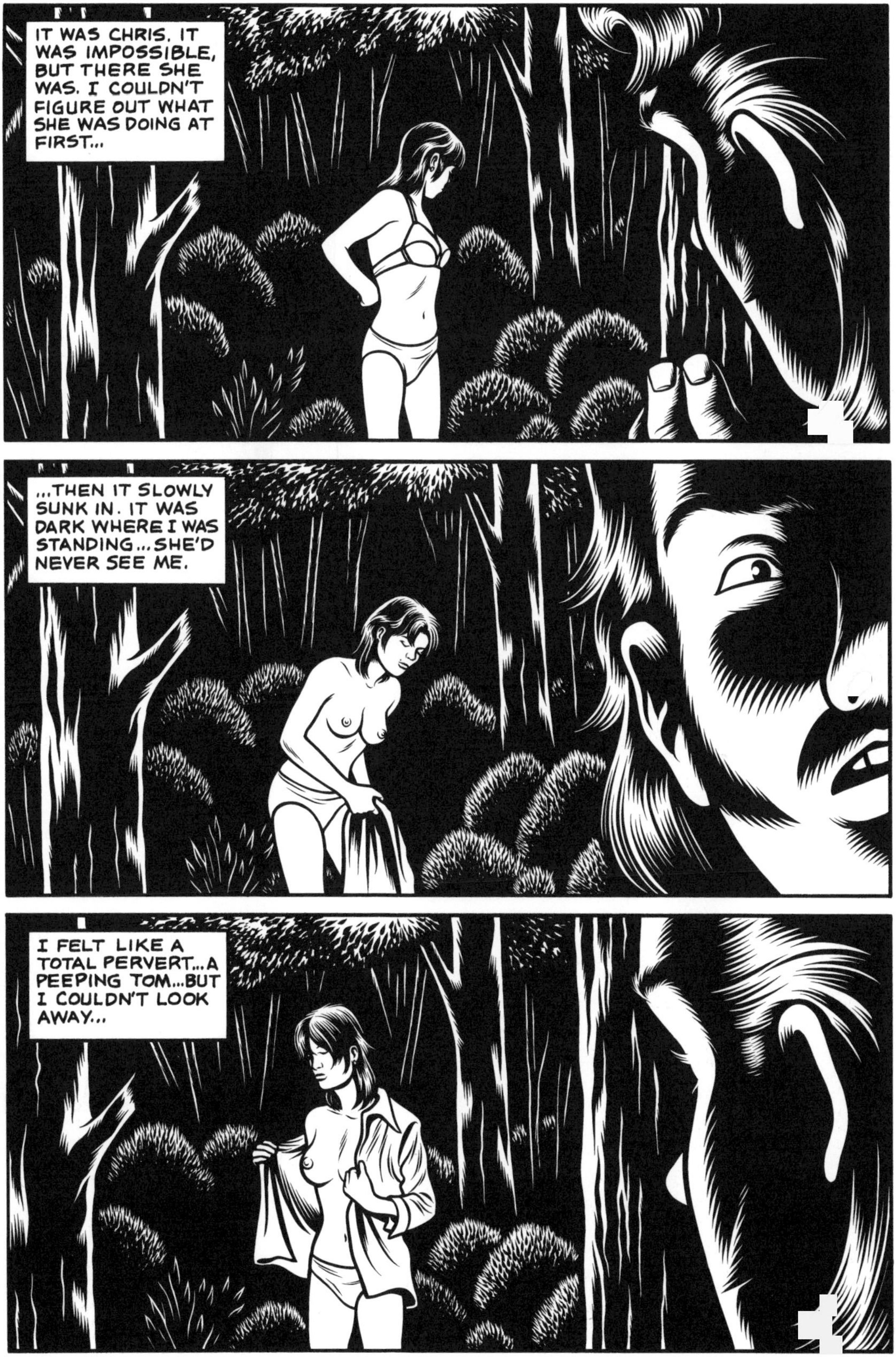
IT WAS CHRIS. IT WAS IMPOSSIBLE, BUT THERE SHE WAS. I COULDN'T FIGURE OUT WHAT SHE WAS DOING AT FIRST...
...THEN IT SLOWLY SUNK IN. IT WAS DARK WHERE I WAS STANDING... SHE'D NEVER SEE ME.
I FELT LIKE A TOTAL PERVERT... A PEEPING TOM... BUT I COULDN'T LOOK AWAY...

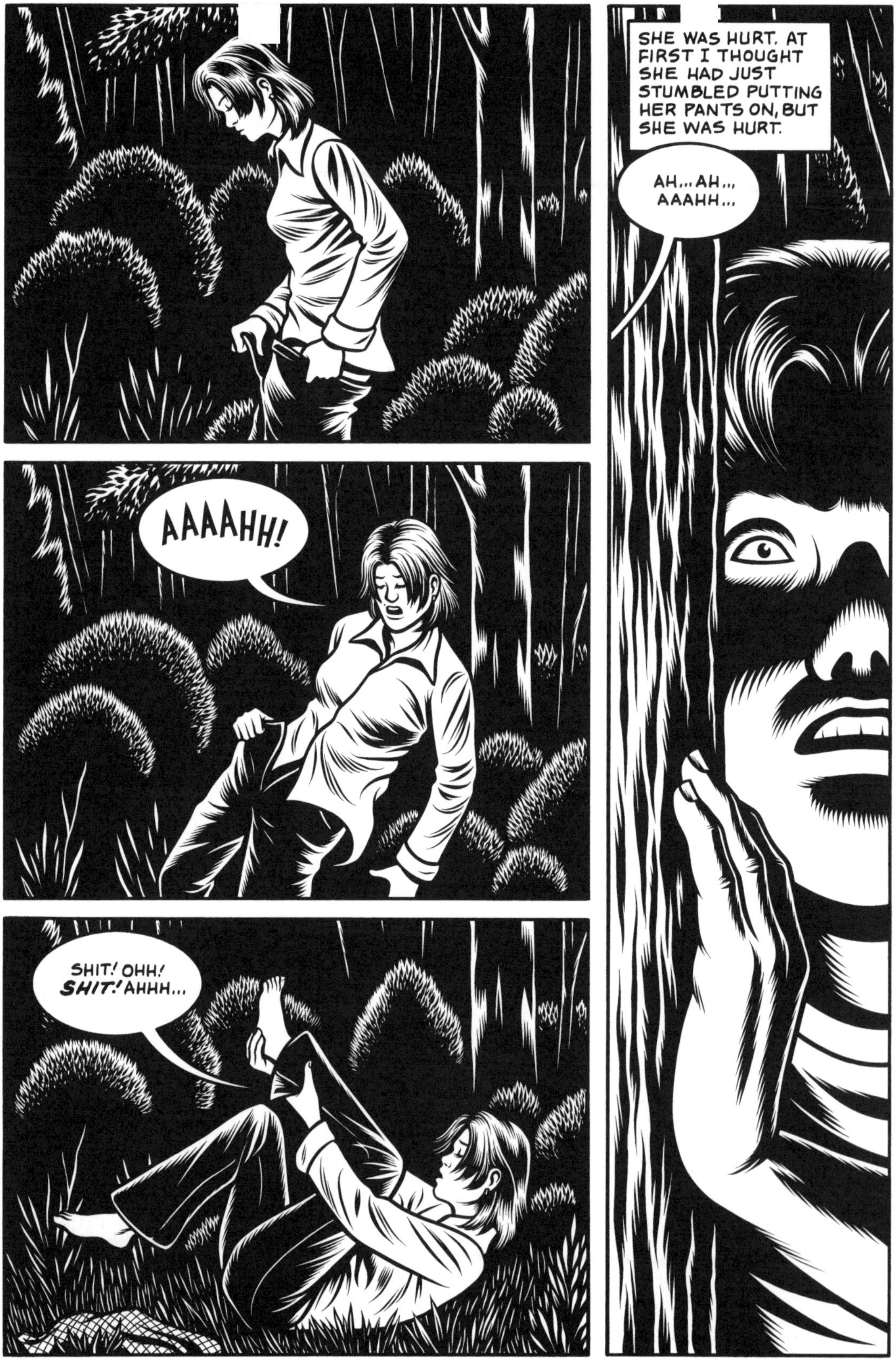
AAAAHH!
SHIT! OHH! SHIT! AHHH...
SHE WAS HURT. AT FIRST I THOUGHT SHE HAD JUST STUMBLED PUTTING HER PANTS ON, BUT SHE WAS HURT.
AH... AH... AAAHH...

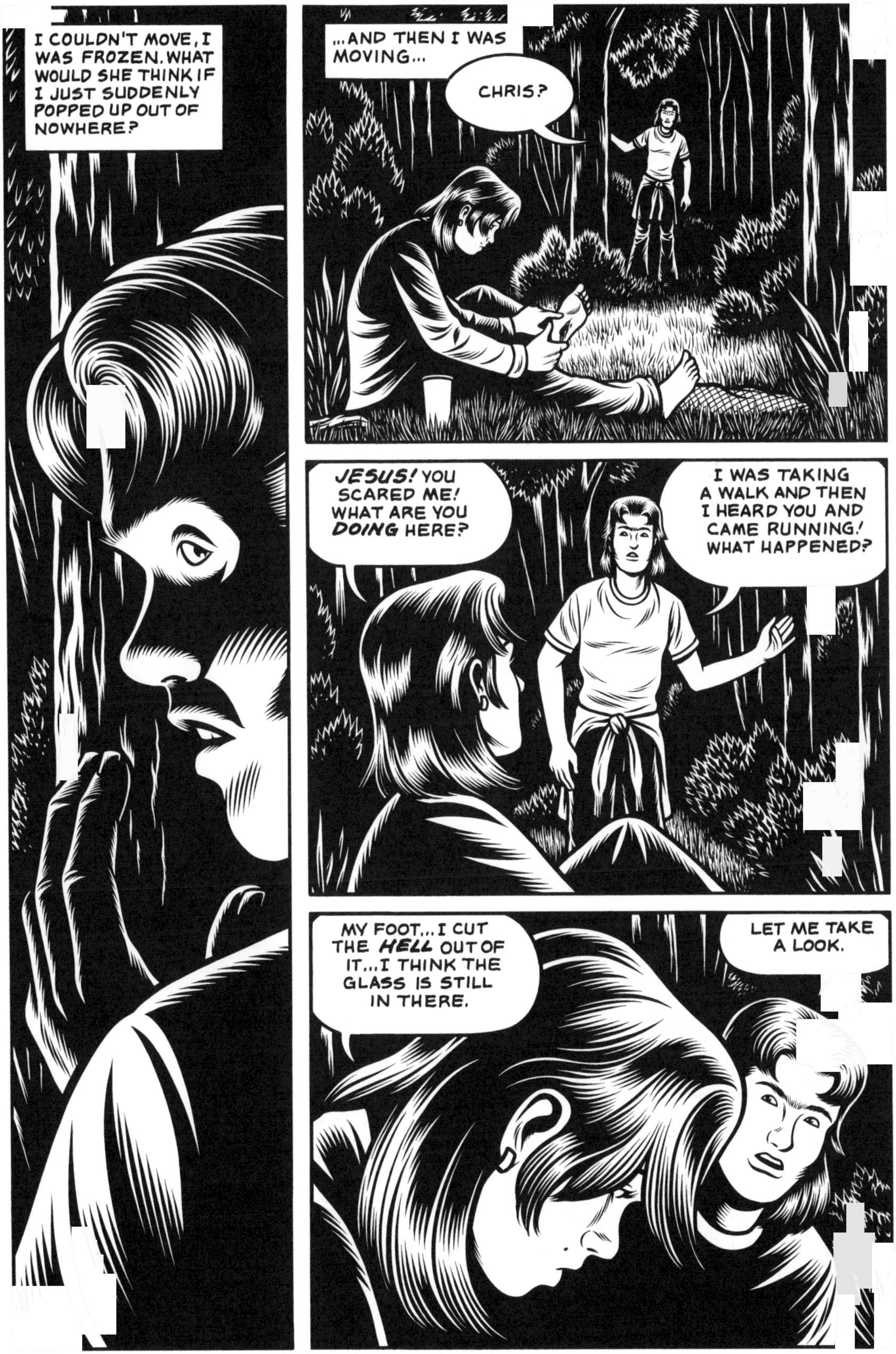

I COULDN'T MOVE, I WAS FROZEN. WHAT WOULD SHE THINK IF I JUST SUDDENLY POPPED UP OUT OF NOWHERE?
...AND THEN I WAS MOVING...
CHRIS?
JESUS! YOU SCARED ME! WHAT ARE YOU DOING HERE?
I WAS TAKING A WALK AND THEN I HEARD YOU AND CAME RUNNING! WHAT HAPPENED?
MY FOOT... I CUT THE HELL OUT OF IT... I THINK THE GLASS IS STILL IN THERE.
LET ME TAKE A LOOK.

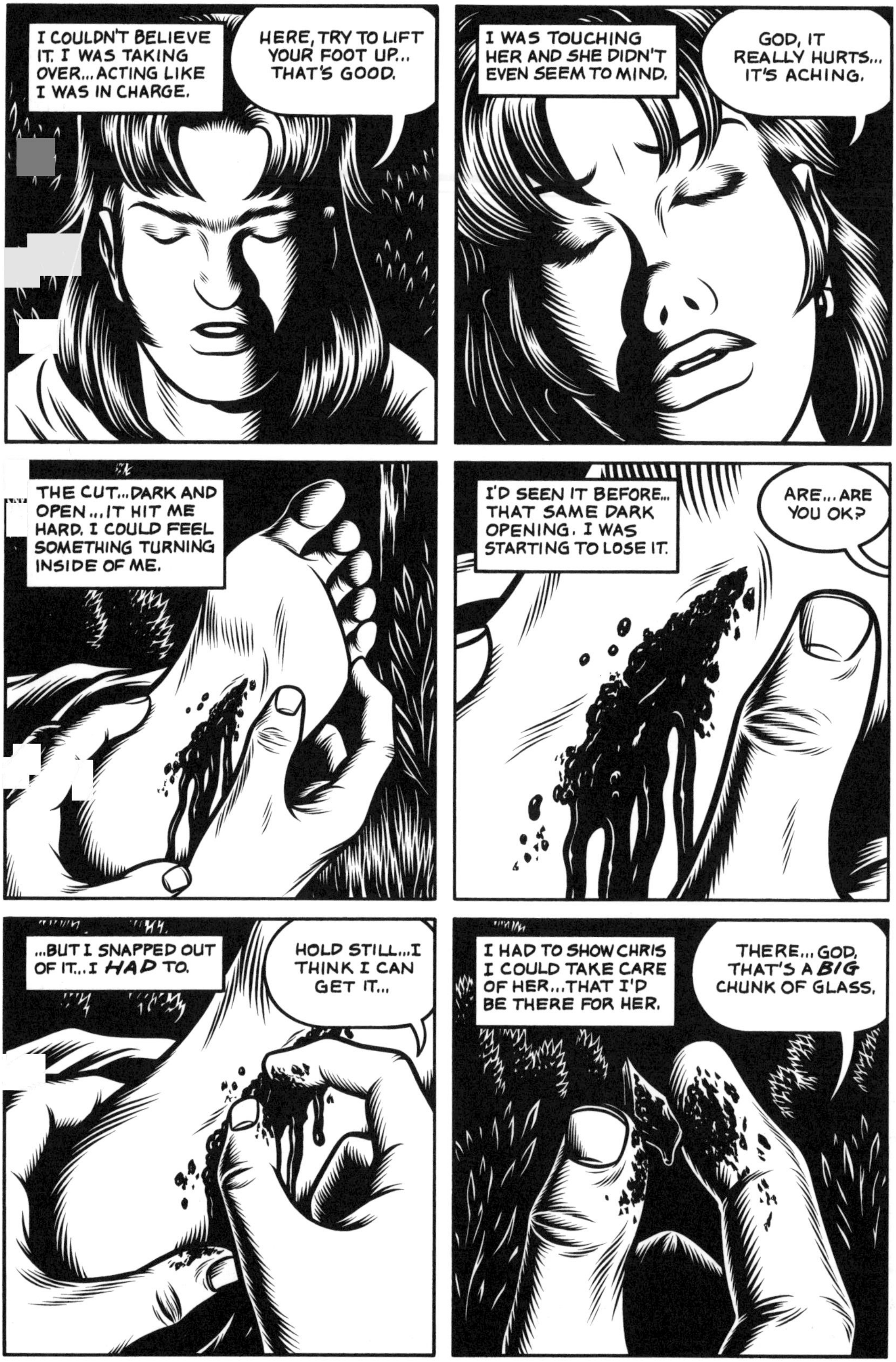
I COULDN'T BELIEVE IT. I WAS TAKING OVER... ACTING LIKE I WAS IN CHARGE.
HERE, TRY TO LIFT YOUR FOOT UP... THAT'S GOOD.
I WAS TOUCHING HER AND SHE DIDN'T EVEN SEEM TO MIND.
GOD, IT REALLY HURTS... IT'S ACHING.
THE CUT... DARK AND OPEN... IT HIT ME HARD. I COULD FEEL SOMETHING TURNING INSIDE OF ME.
I'D SEEN IT BEFORE... THAT SAME DARK OPENING. I WAS STARTING TO LOSE IT.
ARE... ARE YOU OK?
...BUT I SNAPPED OUT OF IT... I HAD TO.
HOLD STILL... I THINK I CAN GET IT...
I HAD TO SHOW CHRIS I COULD TAKE CARE OF HER... THAT I'D BE THERE FOR HER.
THERE... GOD, THAT'S A BIG CHUNK OF GLASS.

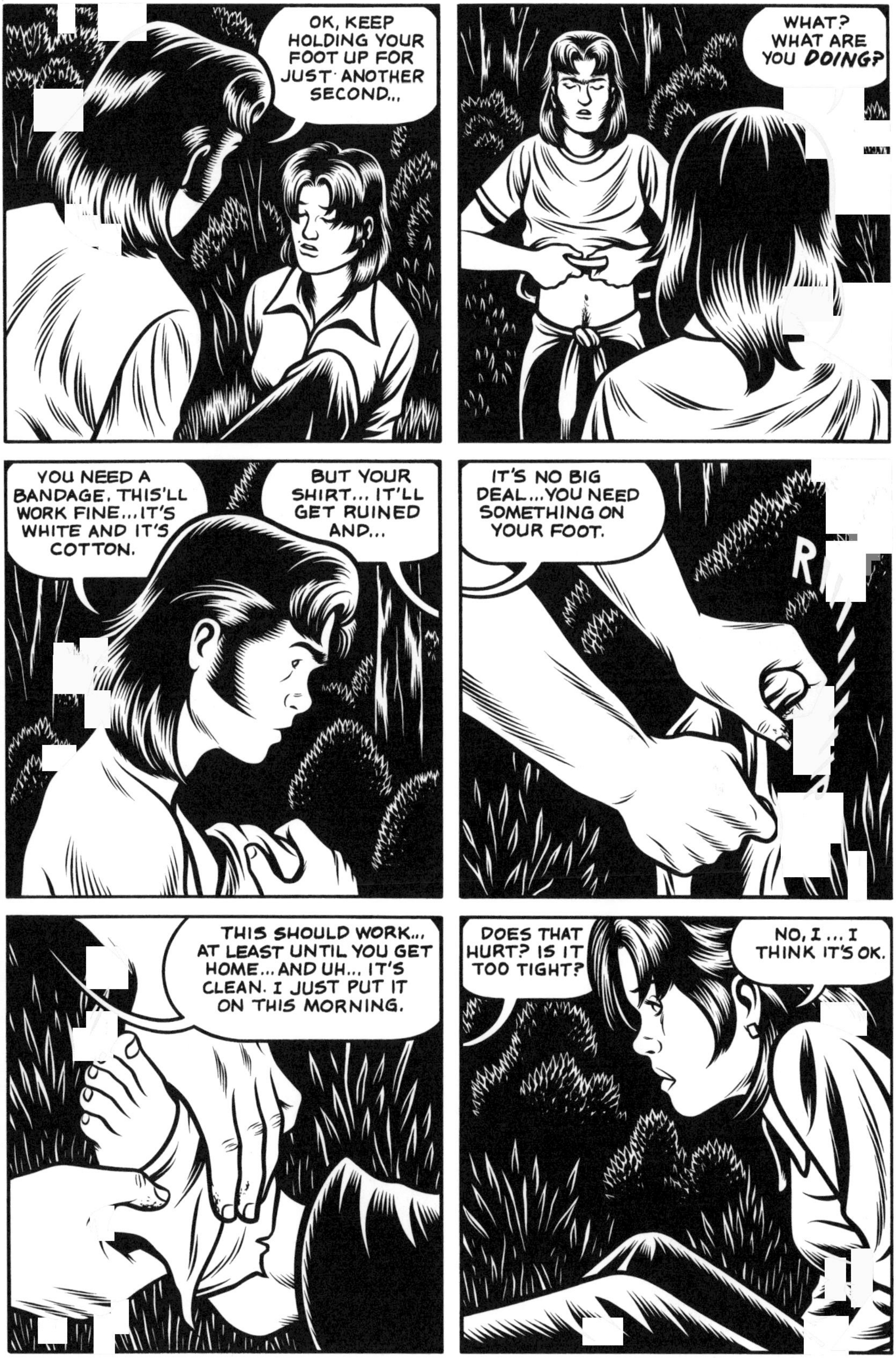
OK, KEEP HOLDING YOUR FOOT UP FOR JUST ANOTHER SECOND...
WHAT? WHAT ARE YOU *DOING?*
YOU NEED A BANDAGE. THIS'LL WORK FINE... IT'S WHITE AND IT'S COTTON.
BUT YOUR SHIRT... IT'LL GET RUINED AND...
IT'S NO BIG DEAL... YOU NEED SOMETHING ON YOUR FOOT.
THIS SHOULD WORK... AT LEAST UNTIL YOU GET HOME... AND UH... IT'S CLEAN. I JUST PUT IT ON THIS MORNING.
DOES THAT HURT? IS IT TOO TIGHT?
NO, I... I THINK IT'S OK.

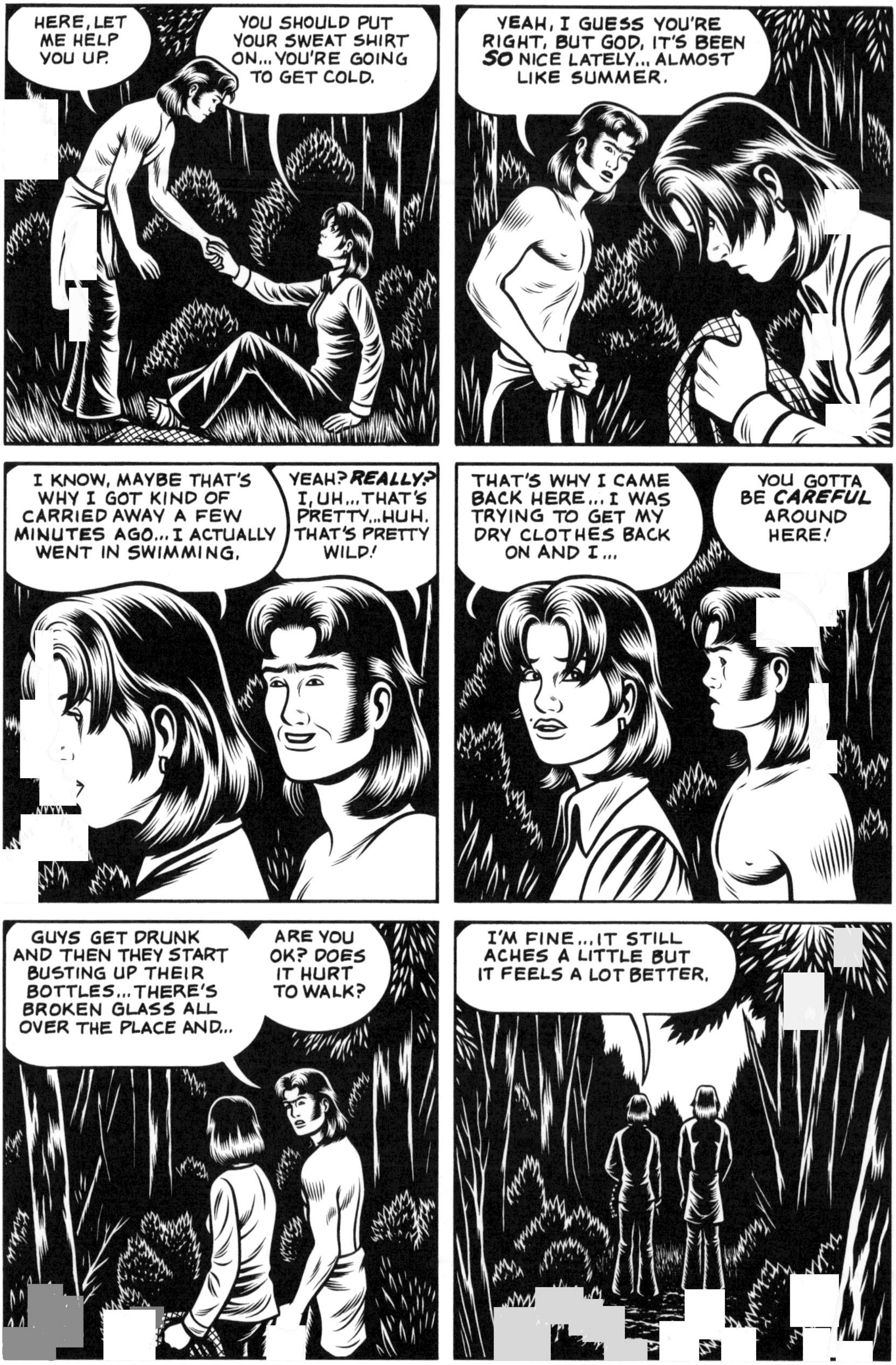

HERE, LET ME HELP YOU UP.
YOU SHOULD PUT YOUR SWEAT SHIRT ON... YOU'RE GOING TO GET COLD.
YEAH, I GUESS YOU'RE RIGHT, BUT GOD, IT'S BEEN *SO* NICE LATELY... ALMOST LIKE SUMMER.
I KNOW, MAYBE THAT'S WHY I GOT KIND OF CARRIED AWAY A FEW MINUTES AGO... I ACTUALLY WENT IN SWIMMING.
YEAH? *REALLY?* I, UH... THAT'S PRETTY... HUH. THAT'S PRETTY WILD!
THAT'S WHY I CAME BACK HERE... I WAS TRYING TO GET MY DRY CLOTHES BACK ON AND I...
YOU GOTTA BE *CAREFUL* AROUND HERE!
GUYS GET DRUNK AND THEN THEY START BUSTING UP THEIR BOTTLES... THERE'S BROKEN GLASS ALL OVER THE PLACE AND...
ARE YOU OK? DOES IT HURT TO WALK?
I'M FINE... IT STILL ACHES A LITTLE BUT IT FEELS A LOT BETTER.

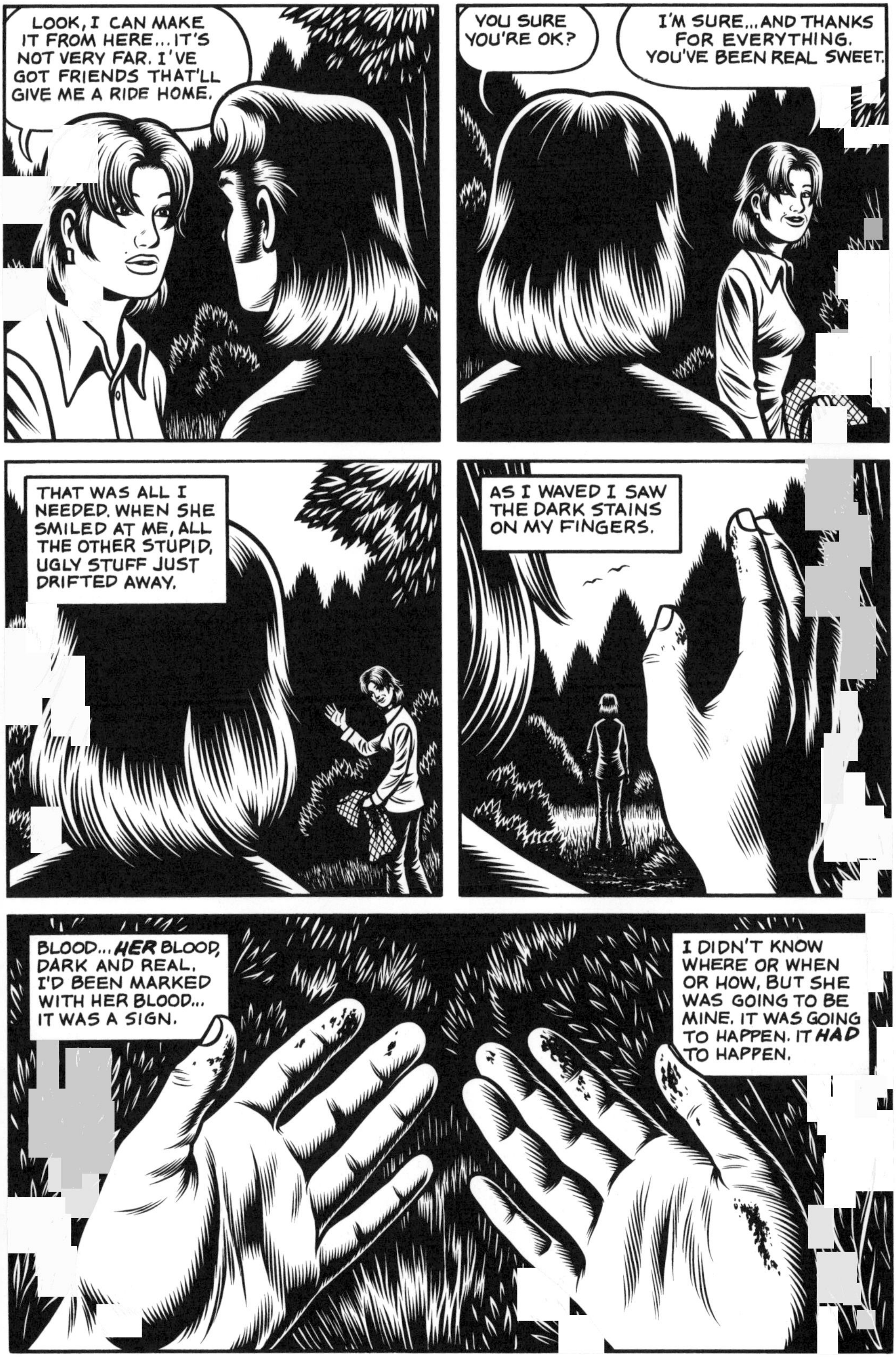
LOOK, I CAN MAKE IT FROM HERE... IT'S NOT VERY FAR. I'VE GOT FRIENDS THAT'LL GIVE ME A RIDE HOME.
YOU SURE YOU'RE OK?
I'M SURE... AND THANKS FOR EVERYTHING. YOU'VE BEEN REAL SWEET.
THAT WAS ALL I NEEDED. WHEN SHE SMILED AT ME, ALL THE OTHER STUPID, UGLY STUFF JUST DRIFTED AWAY.
AS I WAVED I SAW THE DARK STAINS ON MY FINGERS.
BLOOD... HER BLOOD, DARK AND REAL. I'D BEEN MARKED WITH HER BLOOD... IT WAS A SIGN.
I DIDN'T KNOW WHERE OR WHEN OR HOW, BUT SHE WAS GOING TO BE MINE. IT WAS GOING TO HAPPEN. IT HAD TO HAPPEN.

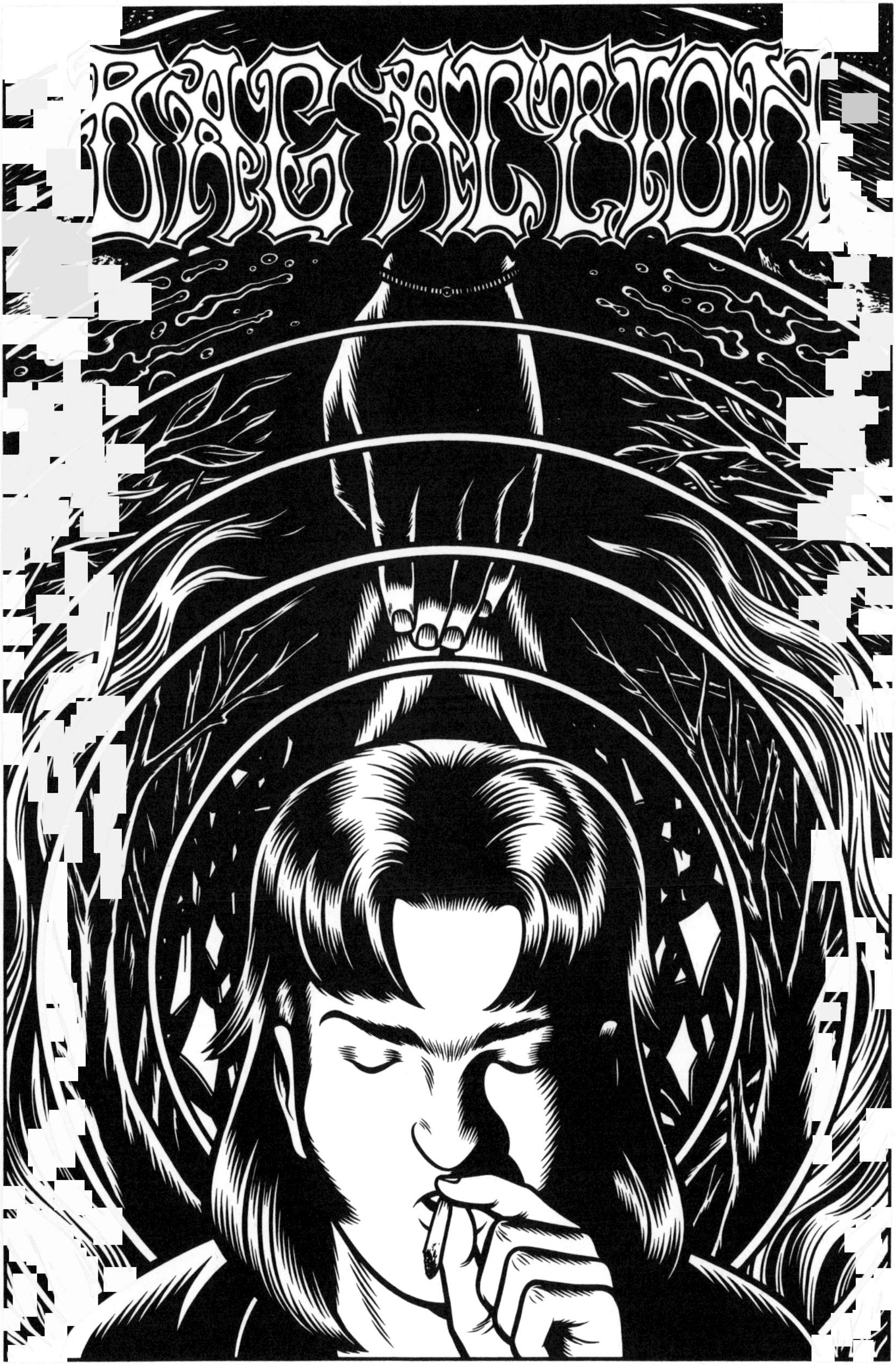

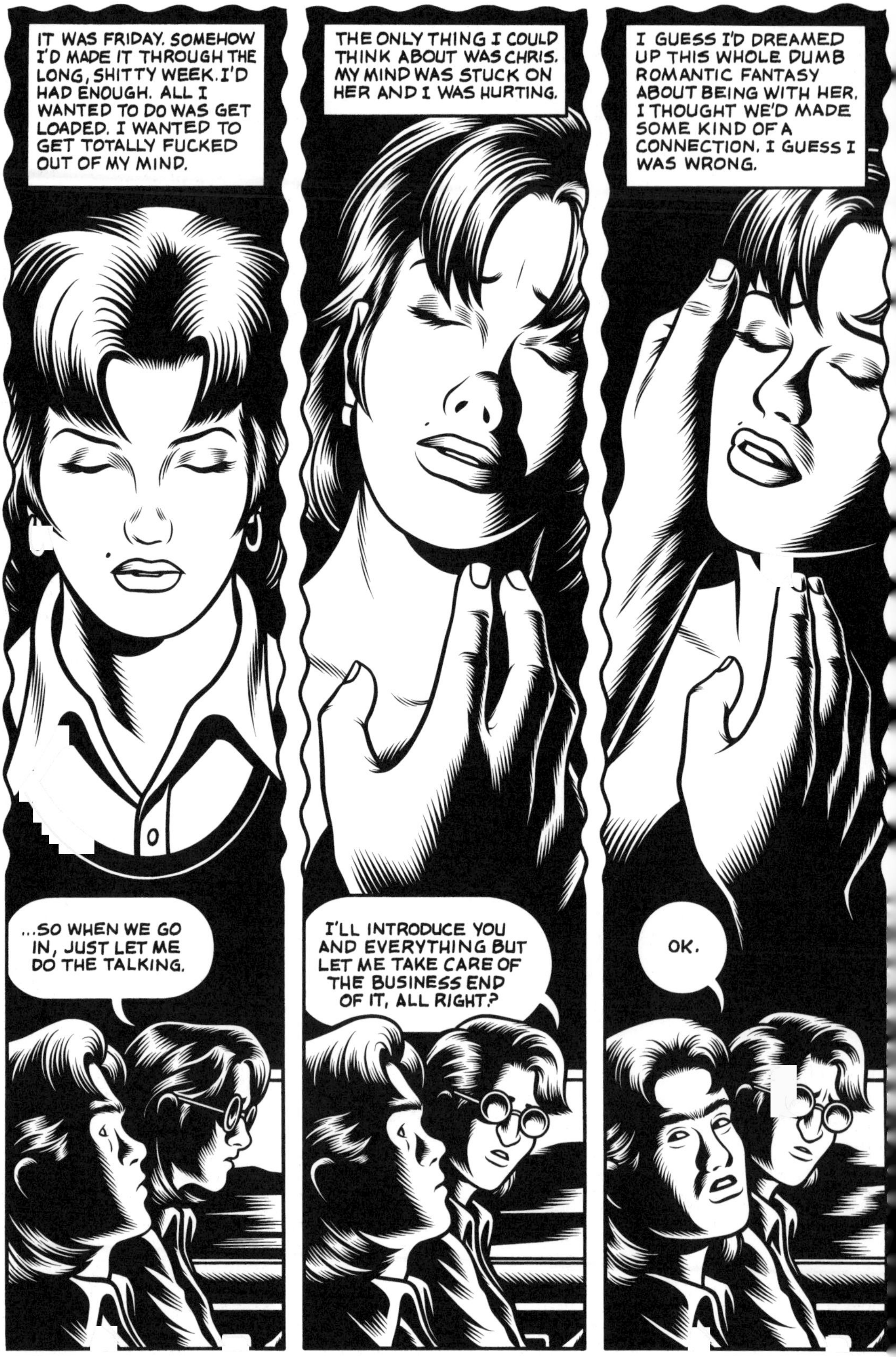
IT WAS FRIDAY. SOMEHOW I'D MADE IT THROUGH THE LONG, SHITTY WEEK. I'D HAD ENOUGH. ALL I WANTED TO DO WAS GET LOADED. I WANTED TO GET TOTALLY FUCKED OUT OF MY MIND.
...SO WHEN WE GO IN, JUST LET ME DO THE TALKING.
THE ONLY THING I COULD THINK ABOUT WAS CHRIS. MY MIND WAS STUCK ON HER AND I WAS HURTING.
I'LL INTRODUCE YOU AND EVERYTHING BUT LET ME TAKE CARE OF THE BUSINESS END OF IT, ALL RIGHT?
I GUESS I'D DREAMED UP THIS WHOLE DUMB ROMANTIC FANTASY ABOUT BEING WITH HER. I THOUGHT WE'D MADE SOME KIND OF A CONNECTION. I GUESS I WAS WRONG.
OK.

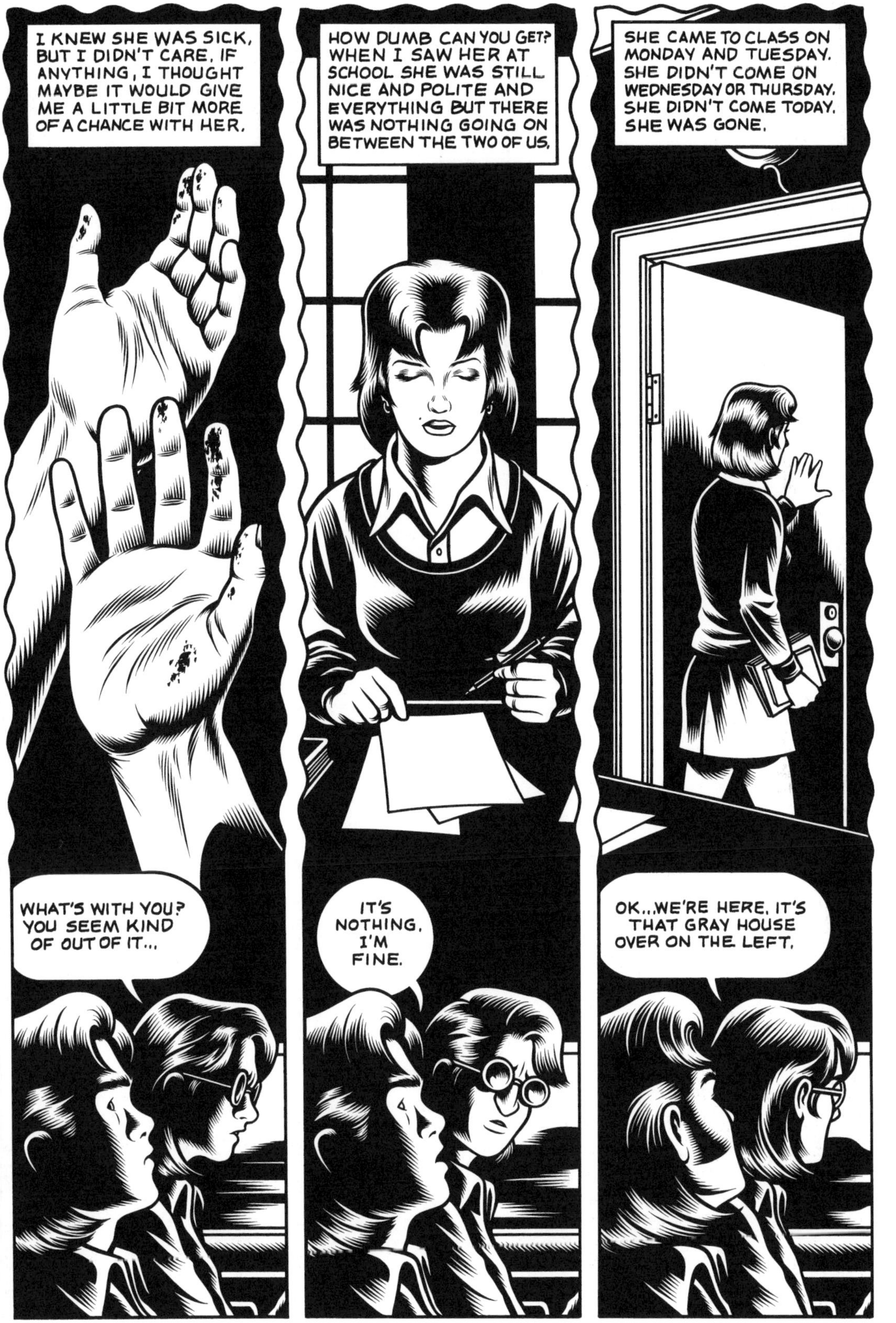
I KNEW SHE WAS SICK, BUT I DIDN'T CARE. IF ANYTHING, I THOUGHT MAYBE IT WOULD GIVE ME A LITTLE BIT MORE OF A CHANCE WITH HER.
HOW DUMB CAN YOU GET? WHEN I SAW HER AT SCHOOL SHE WAS STILL NICE AND POLITE AND EVERYTHING BUT THERE WAS NOTHING GOING ON BETWEEN THE TWO OF US.
SHE CAME TO CLASS ON MONDAY AND TUESDAY. SHE DIDN'T COME ON WEDNESDAY OR THURSDAY. SHE DIDN'T COME TODAY. SHE WAS GONE.
WHAT'S WITH YOU? YOU SEEM KIND OF OUT OF IT...
IT'S NOTHING. I'M FINE.
OK...WE'RE HERE. IT'S THAT GRAY HOUSE OVER ON THE LEFT.

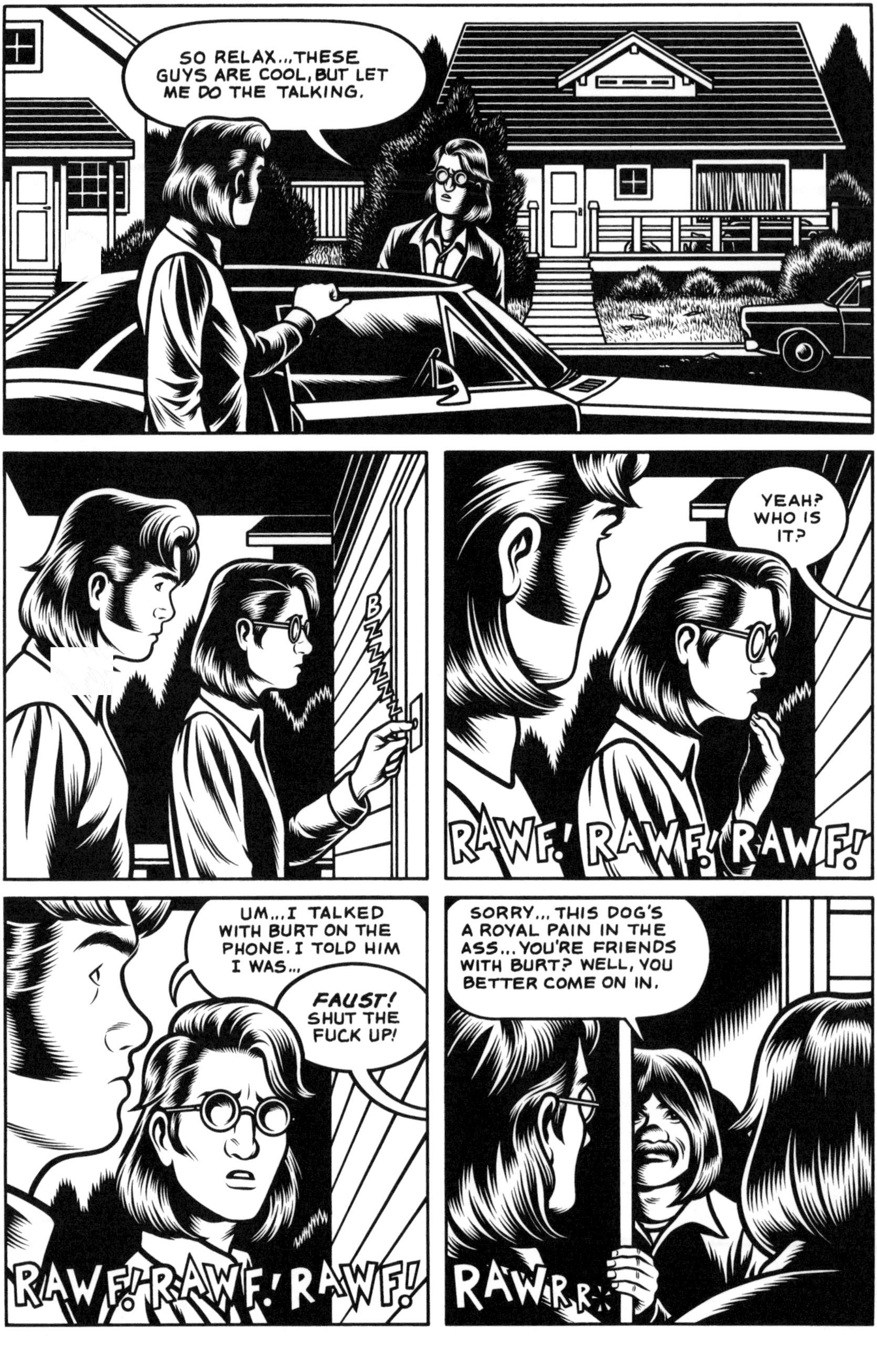
SO RELAX...THESE GUYS ARE COOL, BUT LET ME DO THE TALKING.
BZZZZZZ
YEAH? WHO IS IT?
RAWF! RAWF! RAWF!
UM...I TALKED WITH BURT ON THE PHONE. I TOLD HIM I WAS...
FAUST! SHUT THE FUCK UP!
RAWF! RAWF! RAWF!
SORRY... THIS DOG'S A ROYAL PAIN IN THE ASS... YOU'RE FRIENDS WITH BURT? WELL, YOU BETTER COME ON IN.
RAWRRR

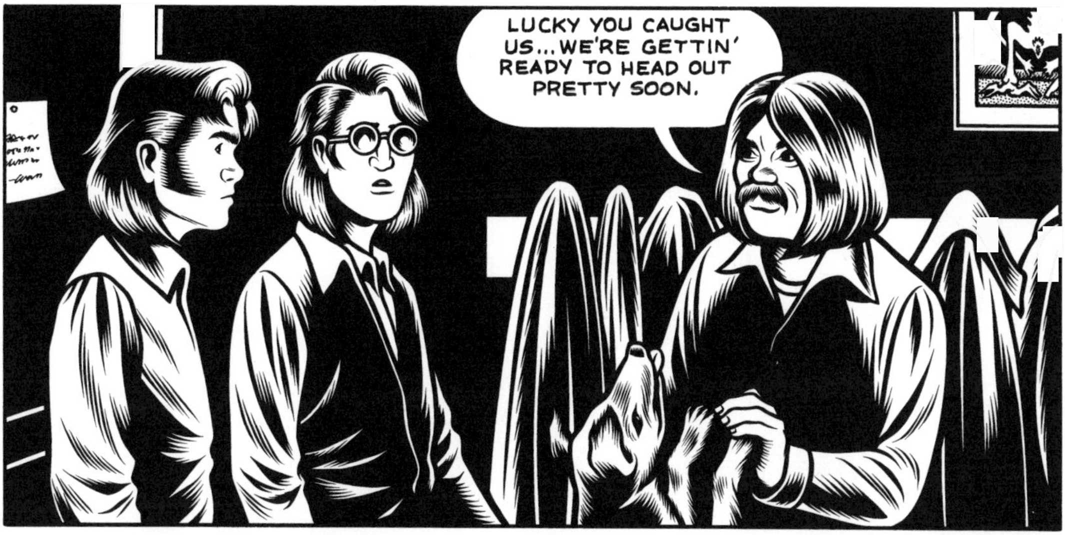
LUCKY YOU CAUGHT US...WE'RE GETTIN' READY TO HEAD OUT PRETTY SOON.

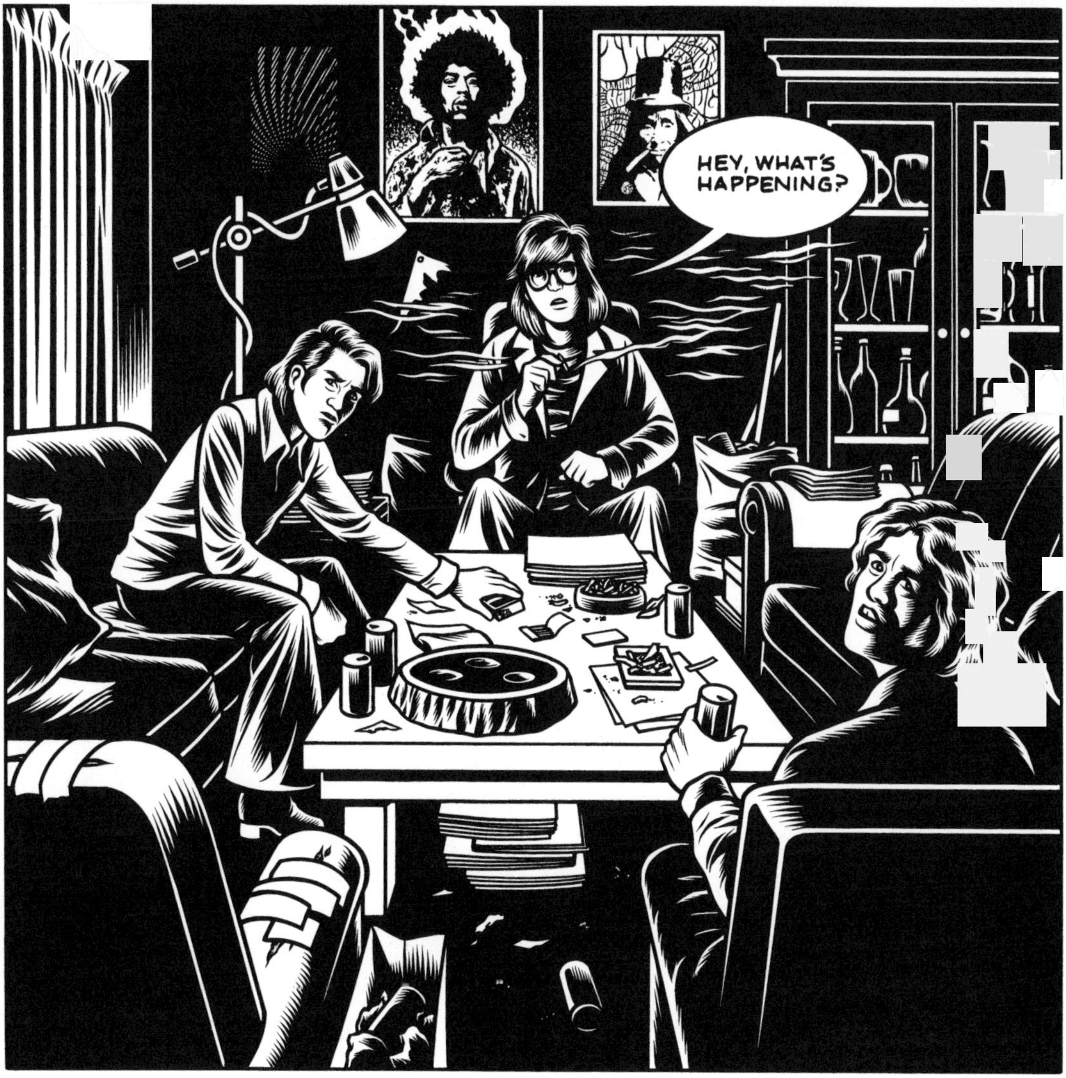
HEY, WHAT'S HAPPENING?

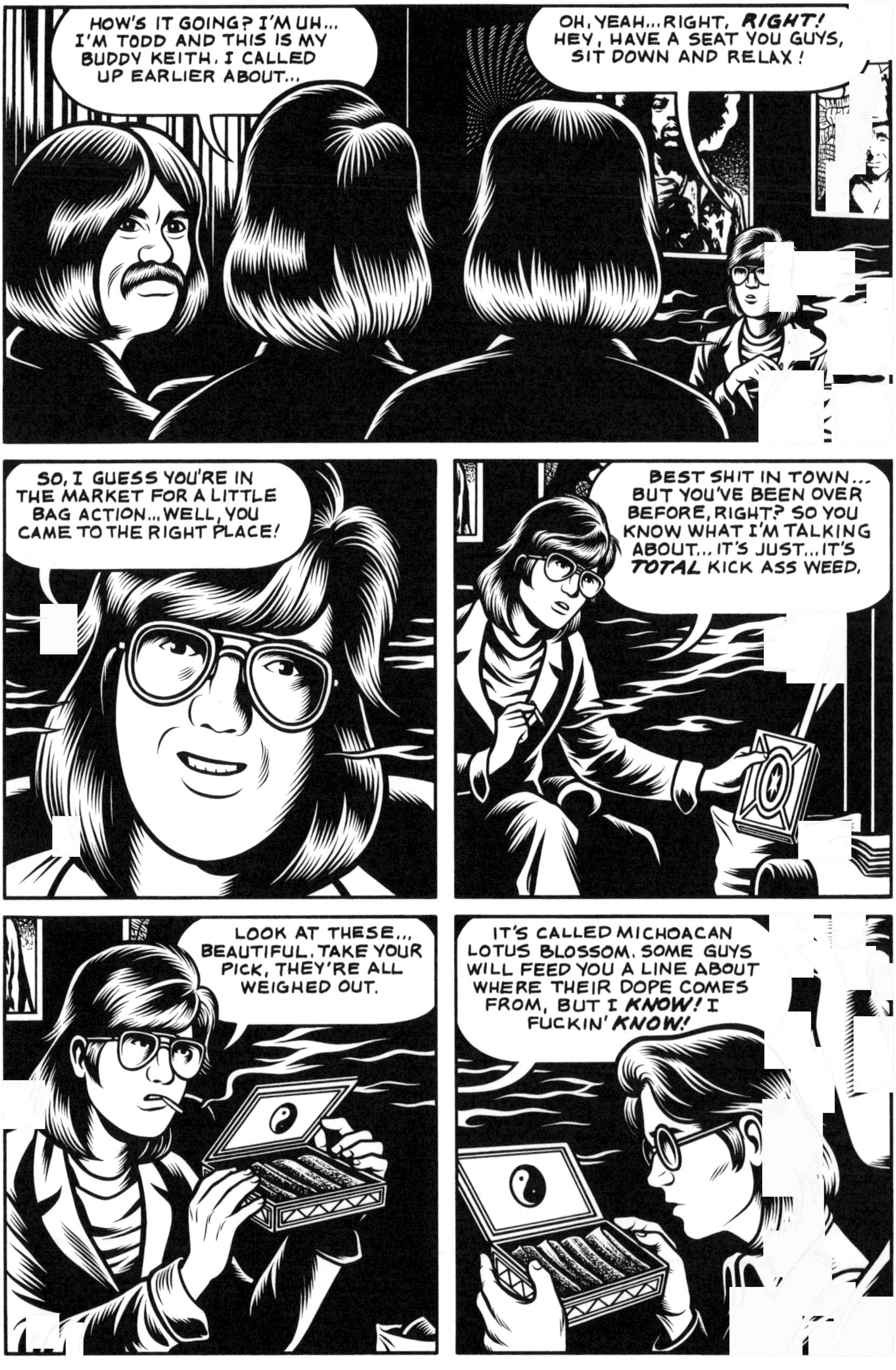
HOW'S IT GOING? I'M UH... I'M TODD AND THIS IS MY BUDDY KEITH. I CALLED UP EARLIER ABOUT...
OH, YEAH... RIGHT, RIGHT! HEY, HAVE A SEAT YOU GUYS, SIT DOWN AND RELAX!
SO, I GUESS YOU'RE IN THE MARKET FOR A LITTLE BAG ACTION... WELL, YOU CAME TO THE RIGHT PLACE!
BEST SHIT IN TOWN... BUT YOU'VE BEEN OVER BEFORE, RIGHT? SO YOU KNOW WHAT I'M TALKING ABOUT... IT'S JUST... IT'S TOTAL KICK ASS WEED.
LOOK AT THESE... BEAUTIFUL. TAKE YOUR PICK, THEY'RE ALL WEIGHED OUT.
IT'S CALLED MICHOACAN LOTUS BLOSSOM. SOME GUYS WILL FEED YOU A LINE ABOUT WHERE THEIR DOPE COMES FROM, BUT I KNOW! I FUCKIN' KNOW!

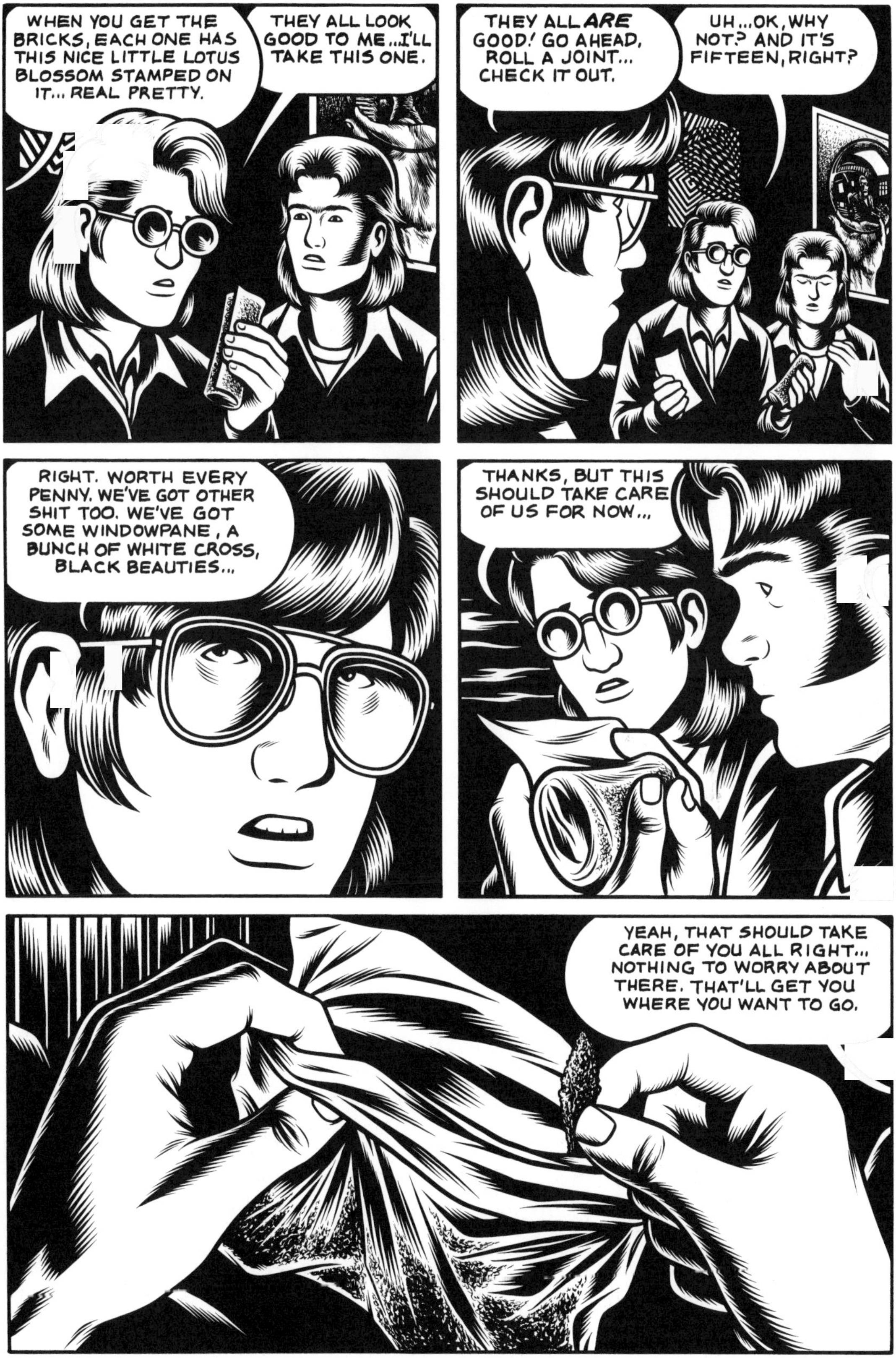

WHEN YOU GET THE BRICKS, EACH ONE HAS THIS NICE LITTLE LOTUS BLOSSOM STAMPED ON IT... REAL PRETTY.
THEY ALL LOOK GOOD TO ME...I'LL TAKE THIS ONE.
THEY ALL *ARE* GOOD! GO AHEAD, ROLL A JOINT... CHECK IT OUT.
UH...OK, WHY NOT? AND IT'S FIFTEEN, RIGHT?
RIGHT. WORTH EVERY PENNY. WE'VE GOT OTHER SHIT TOO. WE'VE GOT SOME WINDOWPANE, A BUNCH OF WHITE CROSS, BLACK BEAUTIES...
THANKS, BUT THIS SHOULD TAKE CARE OF US FOR NOW...
YEAH, THAT SHOULD TAKE CARE OF YOU ALL RIGHT... NOTHING TO WORRY ABOUT THERE. THAT'LL GET YOU WHERE YOU WANT TO GO.

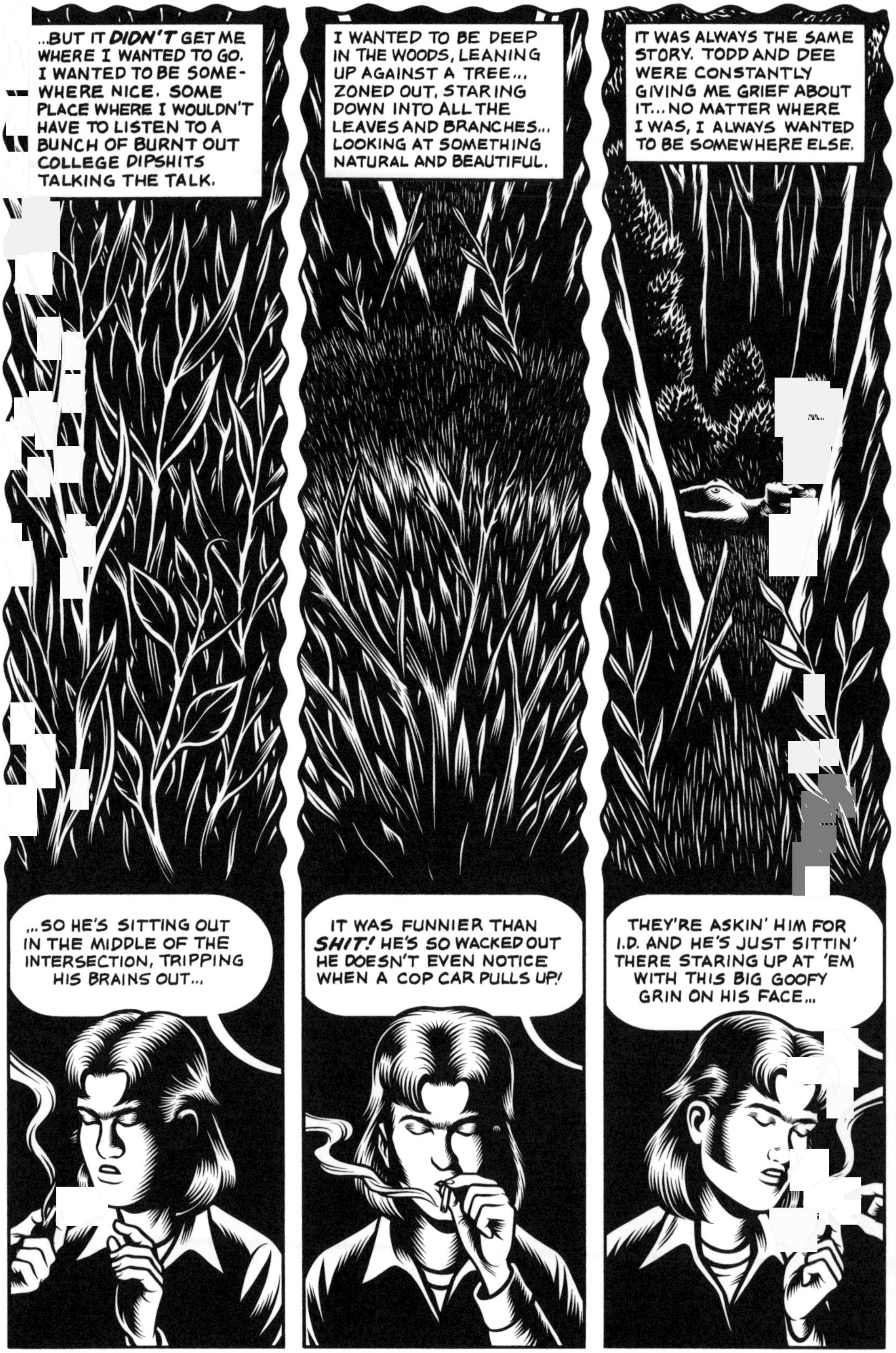
...BUT IT DIDN'T GET ME WHERE I WANTED TO GO. I WANTED TO BE SOME-WHERE NICE. SOME PLACE WHERE I WOULDN'T HAVE TO LISTEN TO A BUNCH OF BURNT OUT COLLEGE DIPSHITS TALKING THE TALK.
I WANTED TO BE DEEP IN THE WOODS, LEANING UP AGAINST A TREE... ZONED OUT, STARING DOWN INTO ALL THE LEAVES AND BRANCHES... LOOKING AT SOMETHING NATURAL AND BEAUTIFUL.
IT WAS ALWAYS THE SAME STORY. TODD AND DEE WERE CONSTANTLY GIVING ME GRIEF ABOUT IT... NO MATTER WHERE I WAS, I ALWAYS WANTED TO BE SOMEWHERE ELSE.
...SO HE'S SITTING OUT IN THE MIDDLE OF THE INTERSECTION, TRIPPING HIS BRAINS OUT...
IT WAS FUNNIER THAN SHIT! HE'S SO WACKED OUT HE DOESN'T EVEN NOTICE WHEN A COP CAR PULLS UP!
THEY'RE ASKIN' HIM FOR I.D. AND HE'S JUST SITTIN' THERE STARING UP AT 'EM WITH THIS BIG GOOFY GRIN ON HIS FACE...

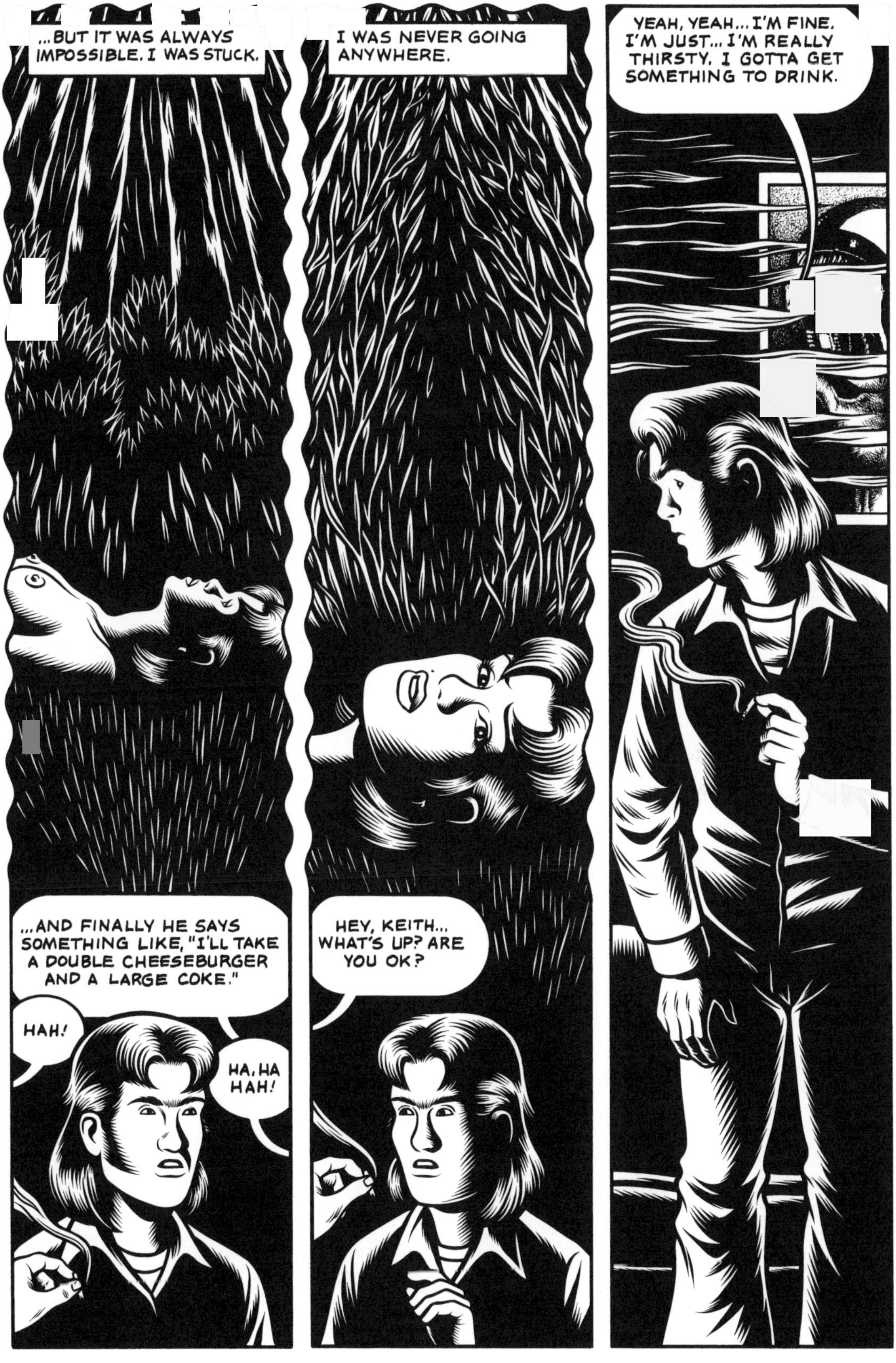
...BUT IT WAS ALWAYS IMPOSSIBLE. I WAS STUCK.
I WAS NEVER GOING ANYWHERE.
YEAH, YEAH... I'M FINE. I'M JUST... I'M REALLY THIRSTY. I GOTTA GET SOMETHING TO DRINK.
...AND FINALLY HE SAYS SOMETHING LIKE, "I'LL TAKE A DOUBLE CHEESEBURGER AND A LARGE COKE."
HAH!
HA, HA HAH!
HEY, KEITH... WHAT'S UP? ARE YOU OK?

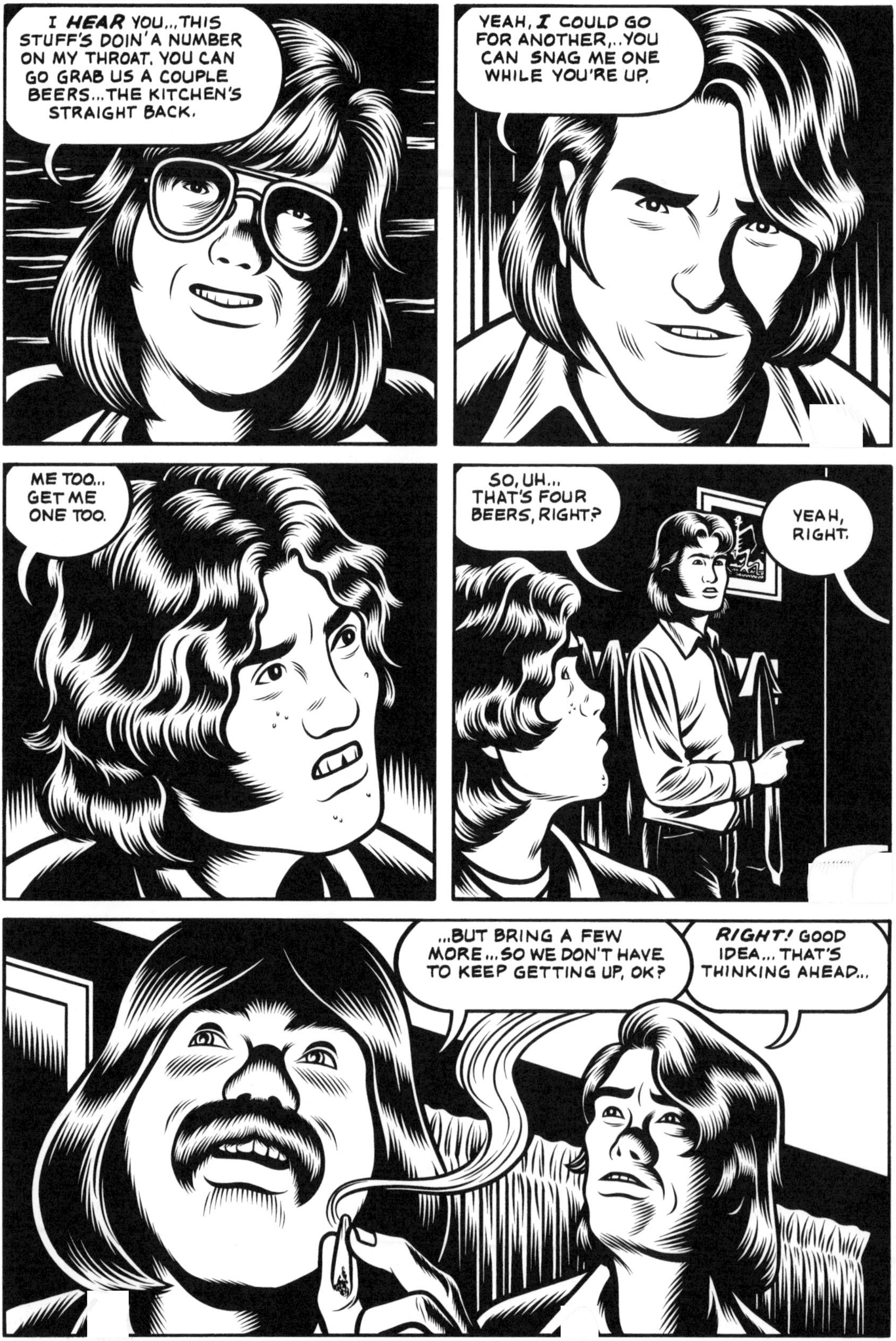
I HEAR YOU... THIS STUFF'S DOIN' A NUMBER ON MY THROAT. YOU CAN GO GRAB US A COUPLE BEERS...THE KITCHEN'S STRAIGHT BACK.
YEAH, I COULD GO FOR ANOTHER... YOU CAN SNAG ME ONE WHILE YOU'RE UP.
ME TOO... GET ME ONE TOO.
SO, UH... THAT'S FOUR BEERS, RIGHT?
YEAH, RIGHT.
...BUT BRING A FEW MORE... SO WE DON'T HAVE TO KEEP GETTING UP, OK?
RIGHT! GOOD IDEA... THAT'S THINKING AHEAD...

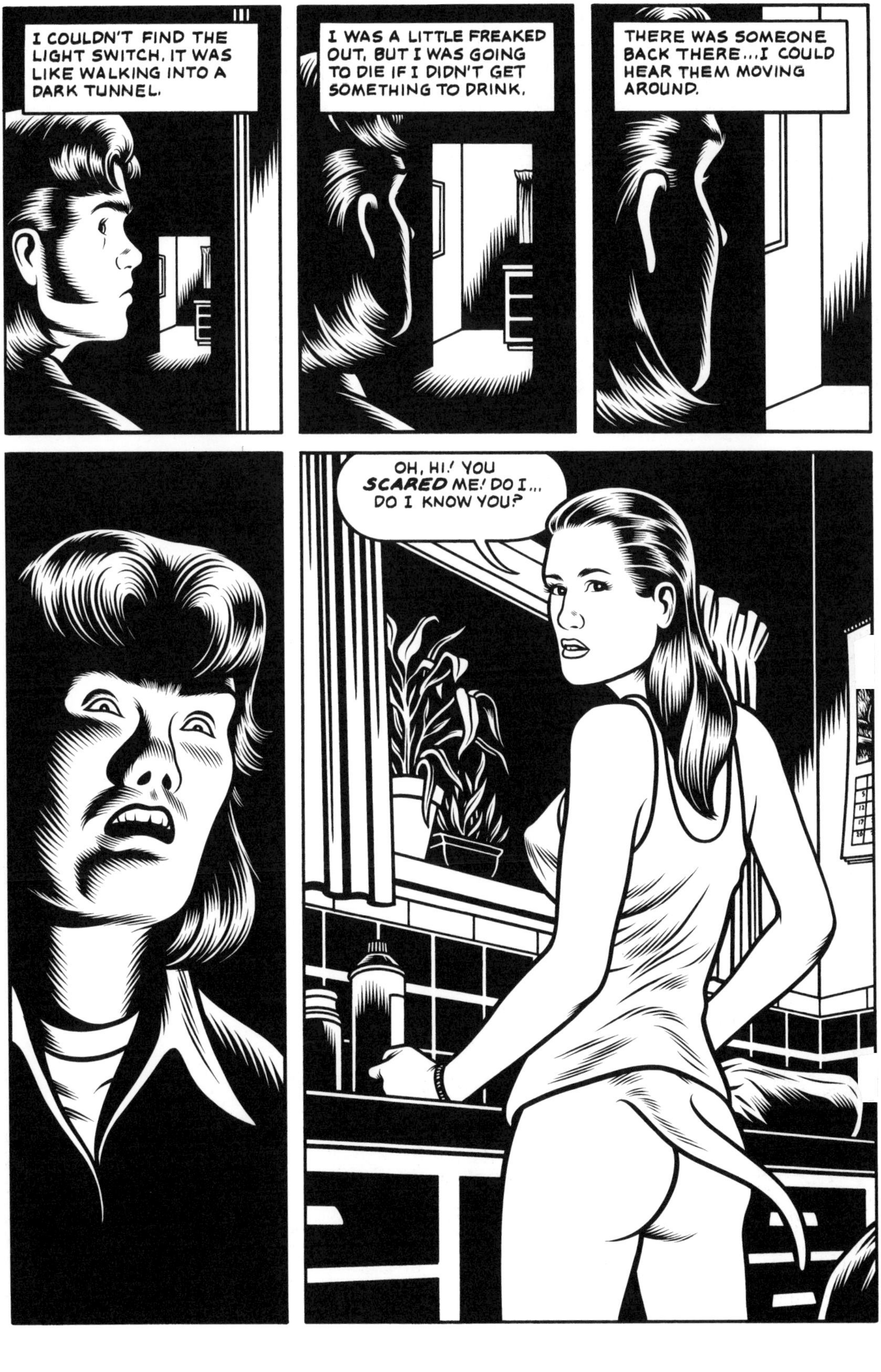
I COULDN'T FIND THE LIGHT SWITCH. IT WAS LIKE WALKING INTO A DARK TUNNEL.
I WAS A LITTLE FREAKED OUT, BUT I WAS GOING TO DIE IF I DIDN'T GET SOMETHING TO DRINK.
THERE WAS SOMEONE BACK THERE... I COULD HEAR THEM MOVING AROUND.
OH, HI! YOU SCARED ME! DO I... DO I KNOW YOU?

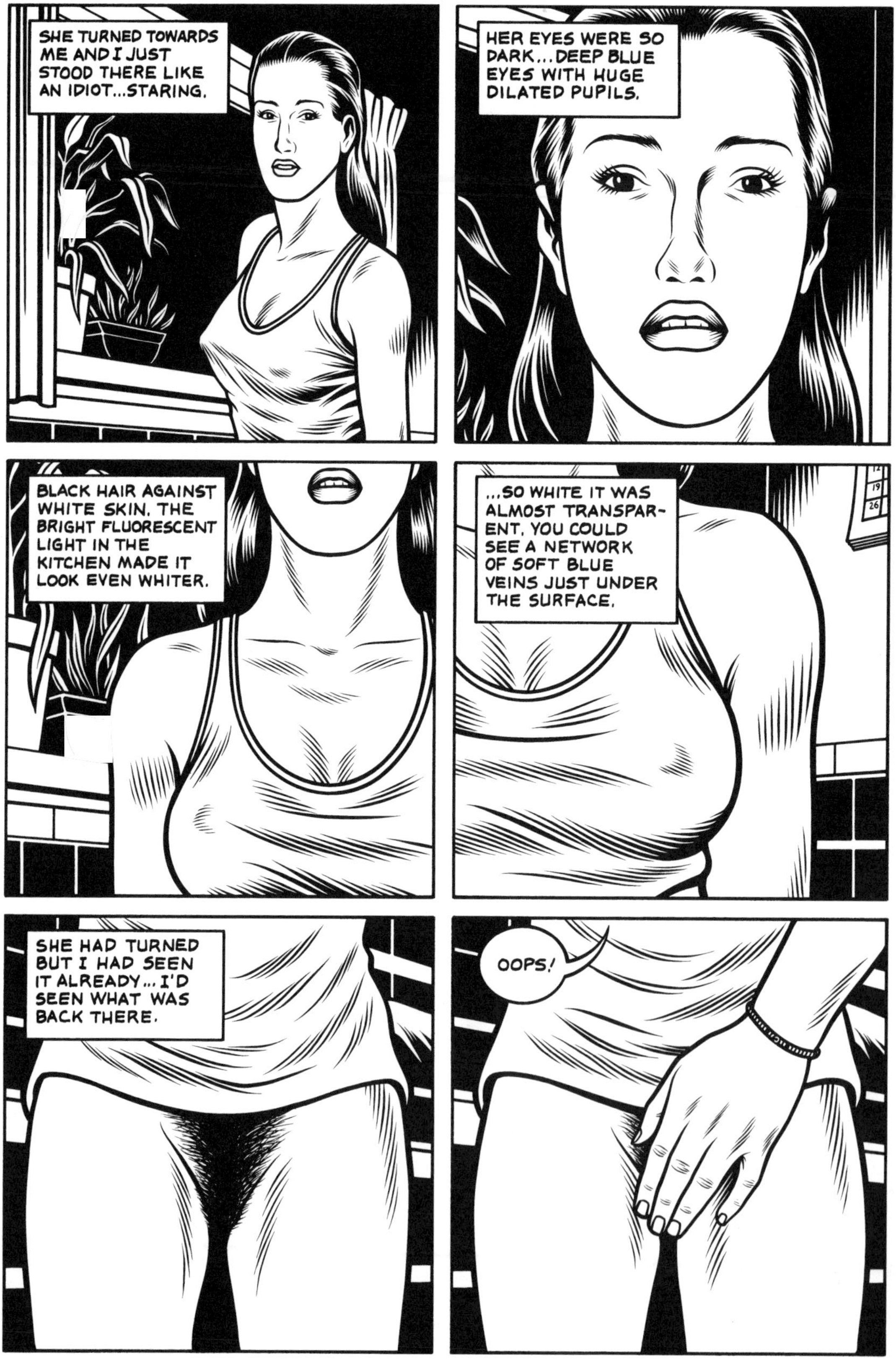
SHE TURNED TOWARDS ME AND I JUST STOOD THERE LIKE AN IDIOT...STARING.
HER EYES WERE SO DARK...DEEP BLUE EYES WITH HUGE DILATED PUPILS.
BLACK HAIR AGAINST WHITE SKIN. THE BRIGHT FLUORESCENT LIGHT IN THE KITCHEN MADE IT LOOK EVEN WHITER.
...SO WHITE IT WAS ALMOST TRANSPAR-ENT. YOU COULD SEE A NETWORK OF SOFT BLUE VEINS JUST UNDER THE SURFACE.
SHE HAD TURNED BUT I HAD SEEN IT ALREADY...I'D SEEN WHAT WAS BACK THERE.
OOPS!

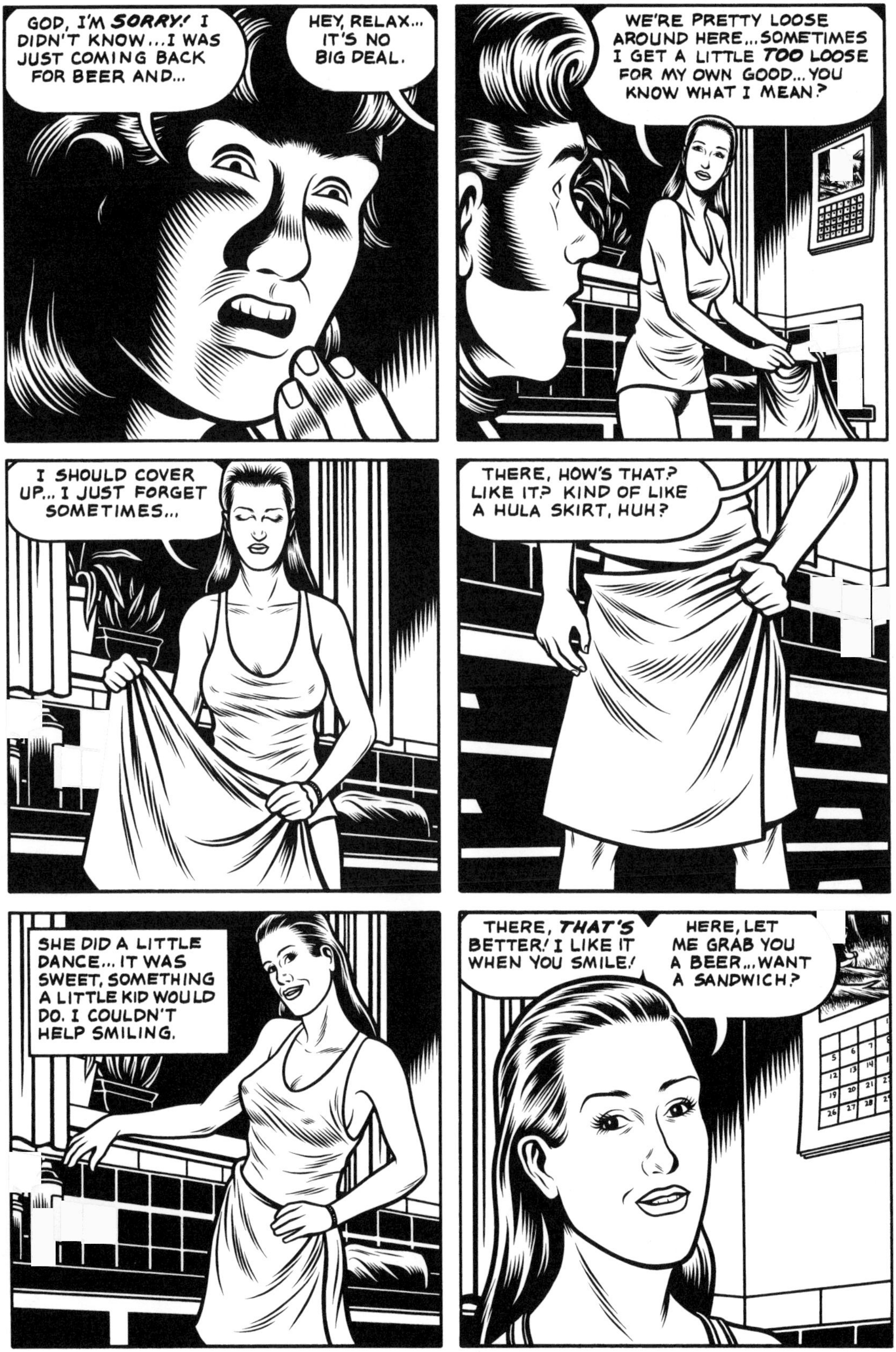

GOD, I'M SORRY! I DIDN'T KNOW...I WAS JUST COMING BACK FOR BEER AND...
HEY, RELAX... IT'S NO BIG DEAL.
WE'RE PRETTY LOOSE AROUND HERE... SOMETIMES I GET A LITTLE TOO LOOSE FOR MY OWN GOOD... YOU KNOW WHAT I MEAN?
I SHOULD COVER UP... I JUST FORGET SOMETIMES...
THERE, HOW'S THAT? LIKE IT? KIND OF LIKE A HULA SKIRT, HUH?
SHE DID A LITTLE DANCE... IT WAS SWEET, SOMETHING A LITTLE KID WOULD DO. I COULDN'T HELP SMILING.
THERE, THAT'S BETTER! I LIKE IT WHEN YOU SMILE!
HERE, LET ME GRAB YOU A BEER... WANT A SANDWICH?

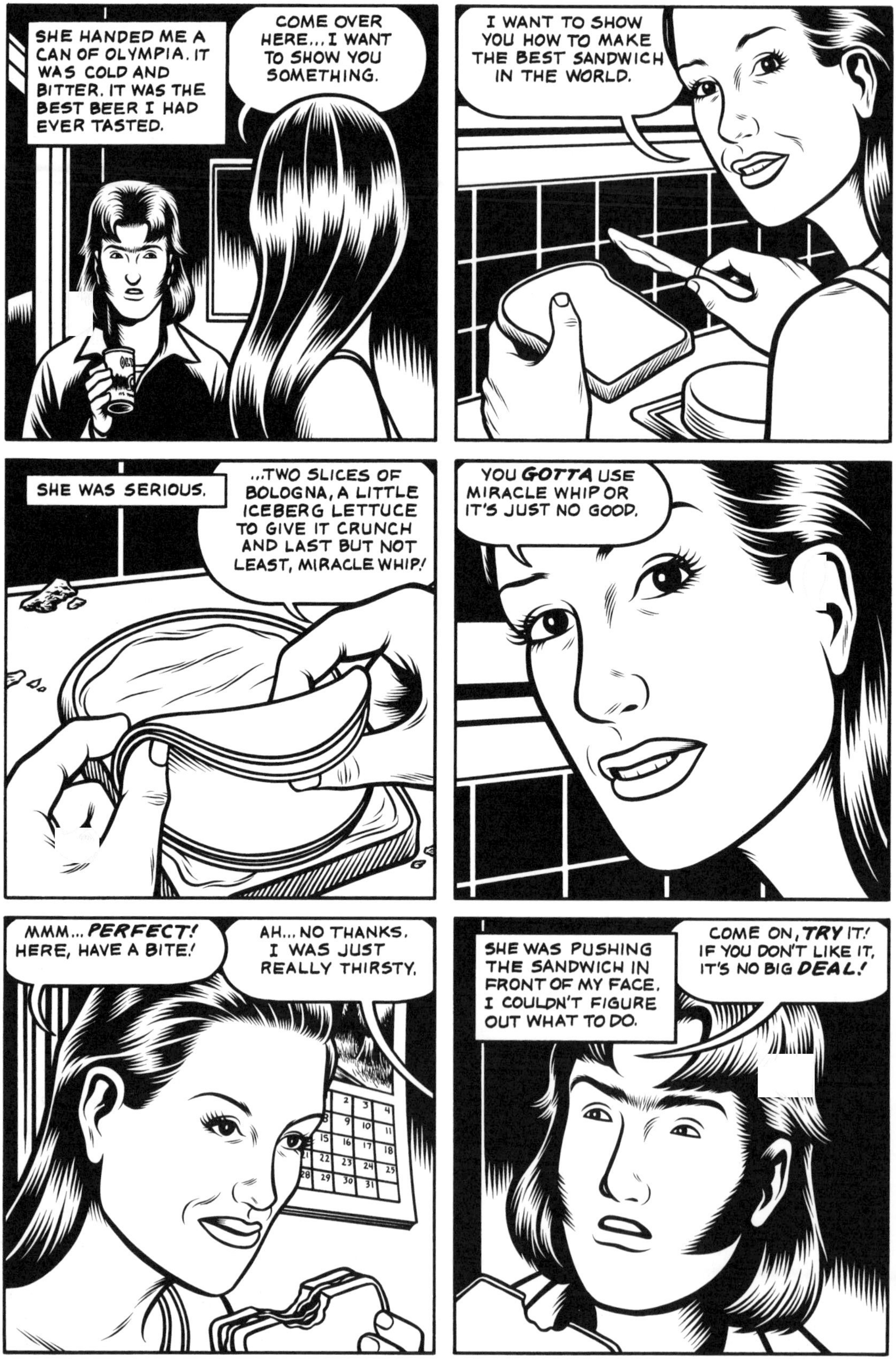

SHE HANDED ME A CAN OF OLYMPIA. IT WAS COLD AND BITTER. IT WAS THE BEST BEER I HAD EVER TASTED.
COME OVER HERE... I WANT TO SHOW YOU SOMETHING.
I WANT TO SHOW YOU HOW TO MAKE THE BEST SANDWICH IN THE WORLD.
SHE WAS SERIOUS.
...TWO SLICES OF BOLOGNA, A LITTLE ICEBERG LETTUCE TO GIVE IT CRUNCH AND LAST BUT NOT LEAST, MIRACLE WHIP!
YOU GOTTA USE MIRACLE WHIP OR IT'S JUST NO GOOD.
MMM... PERFECT! HERE, HAVE A BITE!
AH... NO THANKS. I WAS JUST REALLY THIRSTY.
SHE WAS PUSHING THE SANDWICH IN FRONT OF MY FACE. I COULDN'T FIGURE OUT WHAT TO DO.
COME ON, TRY IT! IF YOU DON'T LIKE IT, IT'S NO BIG DEAL!

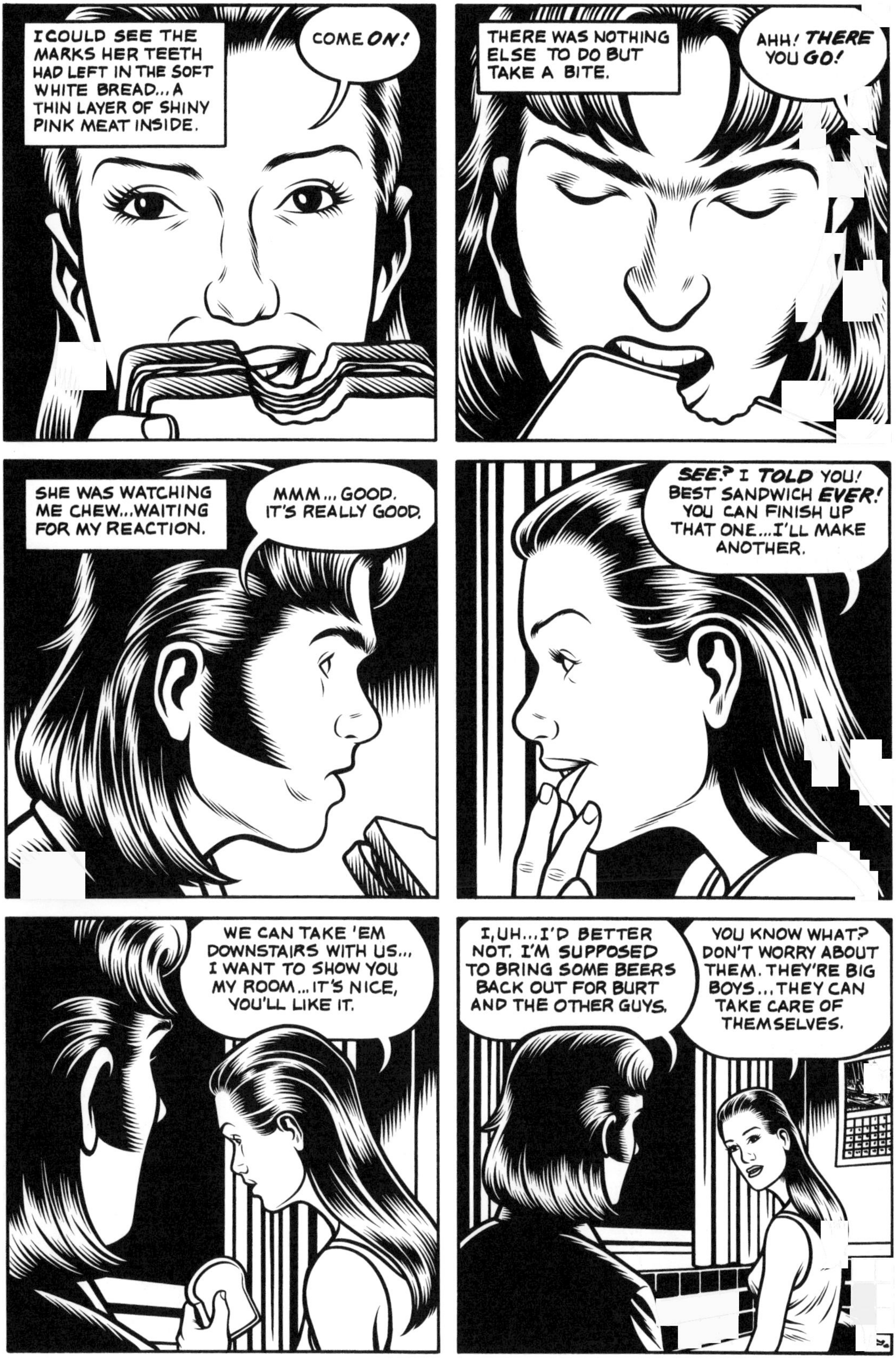
I COULD SEE THE MARKS HER TEETH HAD LEFT IN THE SOFT WHITE BREAD... A THIN LAYER OF SHINY PINK MEAT INSIDE.
COME ON!
THERE WAS NOTHING ELSE TO DO BUT TAKE A BITE.
AHH! THERE YOU GO!
SHE WAS WATCHING ME CHEW... WAITING FOR MY REACTION.
MMM... GOOD. IT'S REALLY GOOD.
SEE? I TOLD YOU! BEST SANDWICH EVER! YOU CAN FINISH UP THAT ONE... I'LL MAKE ANOTHER.
WE CAN TAKE 'EM DOWNSTAIRS WITH US... I WANT TO SHOW YOU MY ROOM... IT'S NICE, YOU'LL LIKE IT.
I, UH... I'D BETTER NOT. I'M SUPPOSED TO BRING SOME BEERS BACK OUT FOR BURT AND THE OTHER GUYS.
YOU KNOW WHAT? DON'T WORRY ABOUT THEM. THEY'RE BIG BOYS... THEY CAN TAKE CARE OF THEMSELVES.

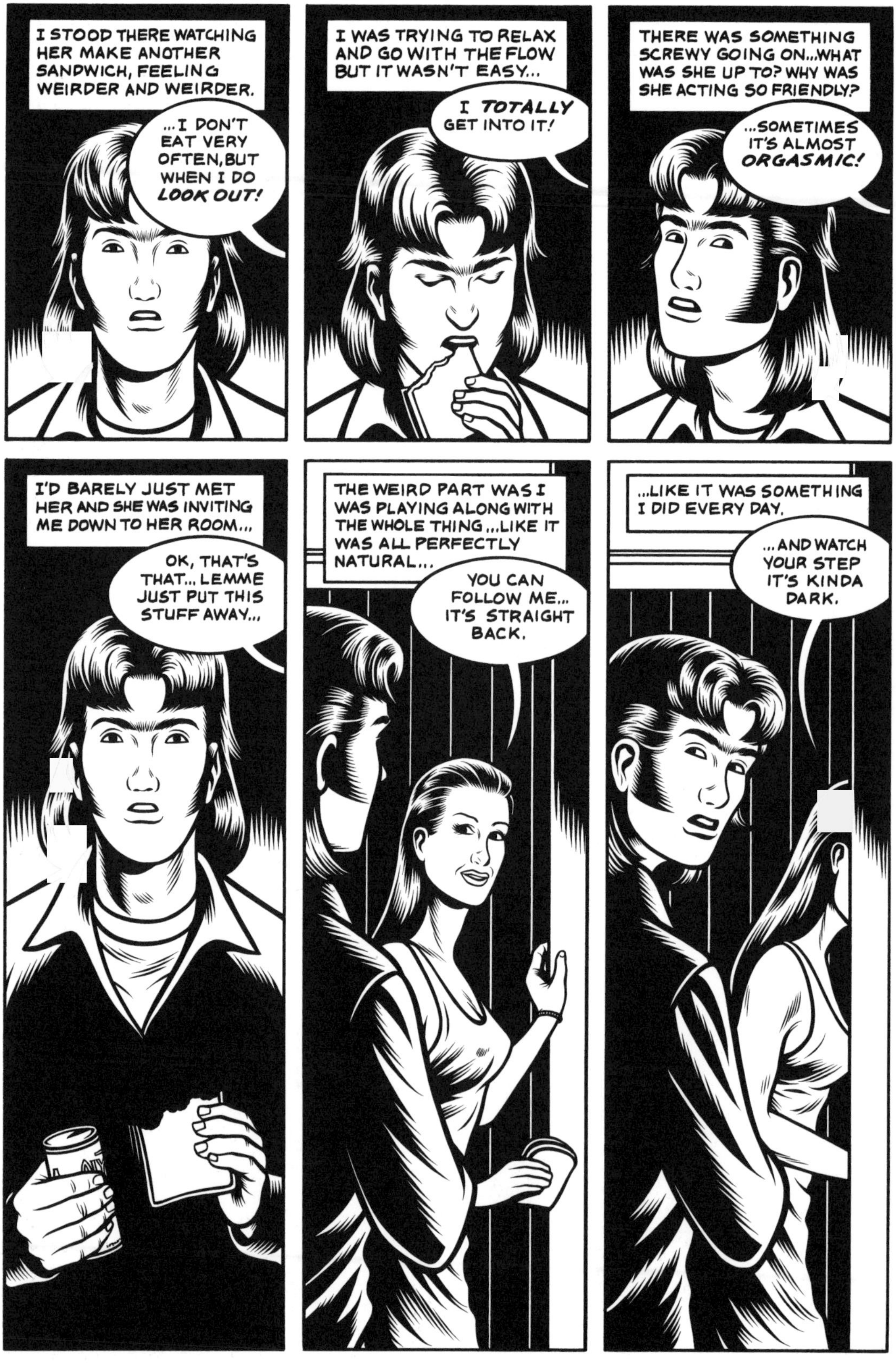
I STOOD THERE WATCHING HER MAKE ANOTHER SANDWICH, FEELING WEIRDER AND WEIRDER.
...I DON'T EAT VERY OFTEN, BUT WHEN I DO LOOK OUT!
I WAS TRYING TO RELAX AND GO WITH THE FLOW BUT IT WASN'T EASY...
I TOTALLY GET INTO IT!
THERE WAS SOMETHING SCREWY GOING ON...WHAT WAS SHE UP TO? WHY WAS SHE ACTING SO FRIENDLY?
...SOMETIMES IT'S ALMOST ORGASMIC!
I'D BARELY JUST MET HER AND SHE WAS INVITING ME DOWN TO HER ROOM...
OK, THAT'S THAT... LEMME JUST PUT THIS STUFF AWAY...
THE WEIRD PART WAS I WAS PLAYING ALONG WITH THE WHOLE THING...LIKE IT WAS ALL PERFECTLY NATURAL...
YOU CAN FOLLOW ME... IT'S STRAIGHT BACK.
...LIKE IT WAS SOMETHING I DID EVERY DAY.
...AND WATCH YOUR STEP IT'S KINDA DARK.

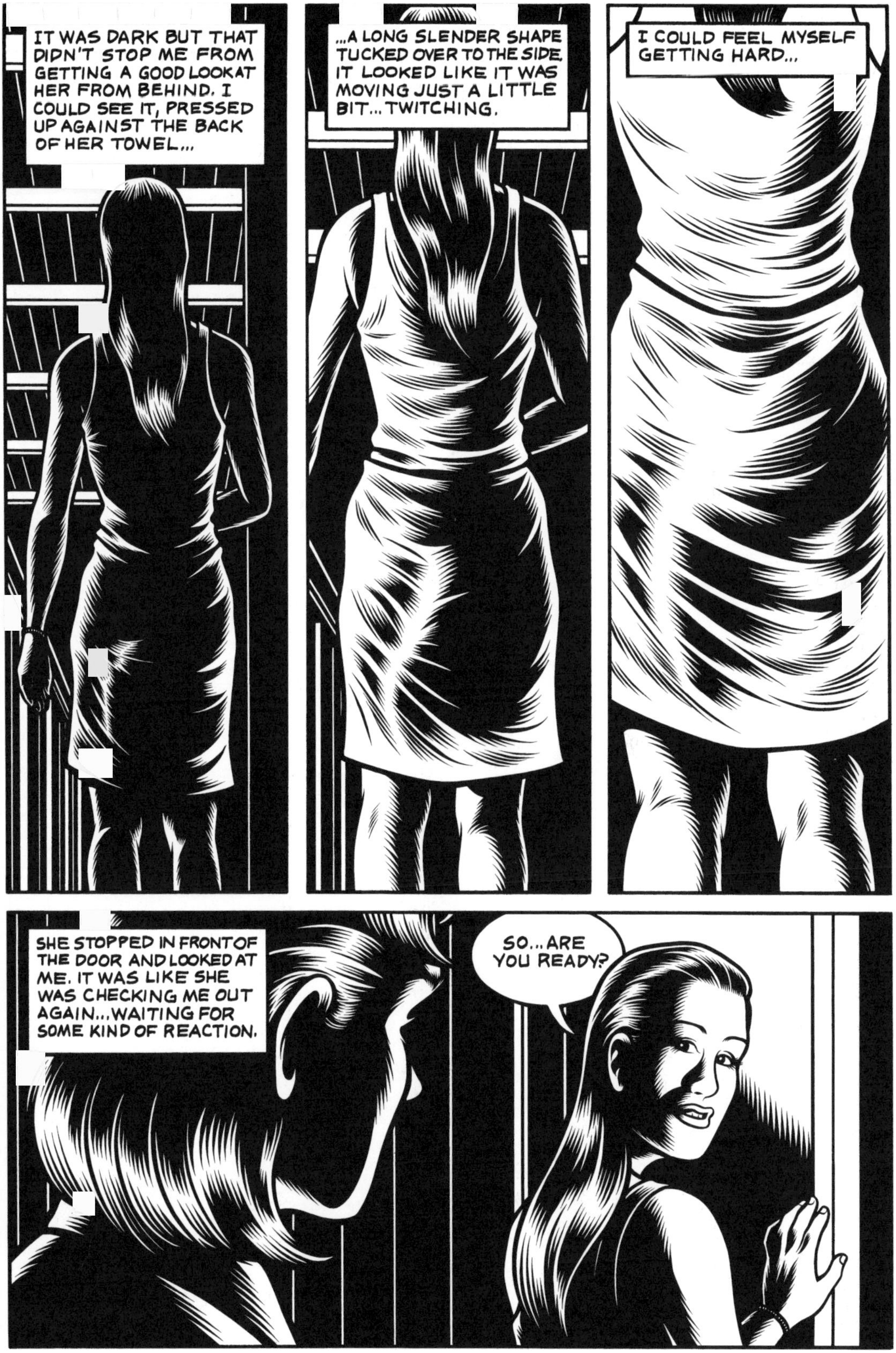
IT WAS DARK BUT THAT DIDN'T STOP ME FROM GETTING A GOOD LOOK AT HER FROM BEHIND. I COULD SEE IT, PRESSED UP AGAINST THE BACK OF HER TOWEL...
...A LONG SLENDER SHAPE TUCKED OVER TO THE SIDE. IT LOOKED LIKE IT WAS MOVING JUST A LITTLE BIT... TWITCHING.
I COULD FEEL MYSELF GETTING HARD...
SHE STOPPED IN FRONT OF THE DOOR AND LOOKED AT ME. IT WAS LIKE SHE WAS CHECKING ME OUT AGAIN... WAITING FOR SOME KIND OF REACTION.
SO... ARE YOU READY?

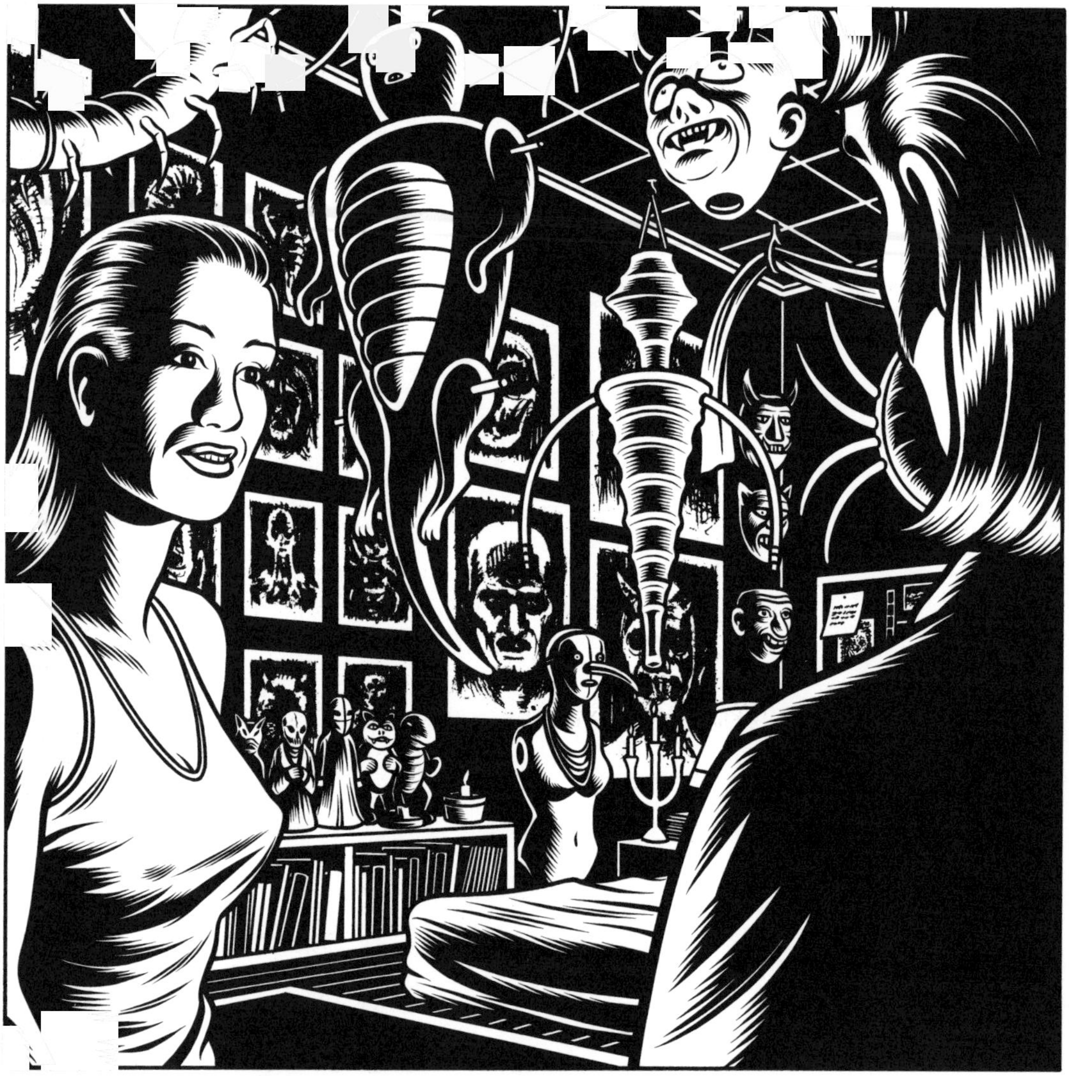

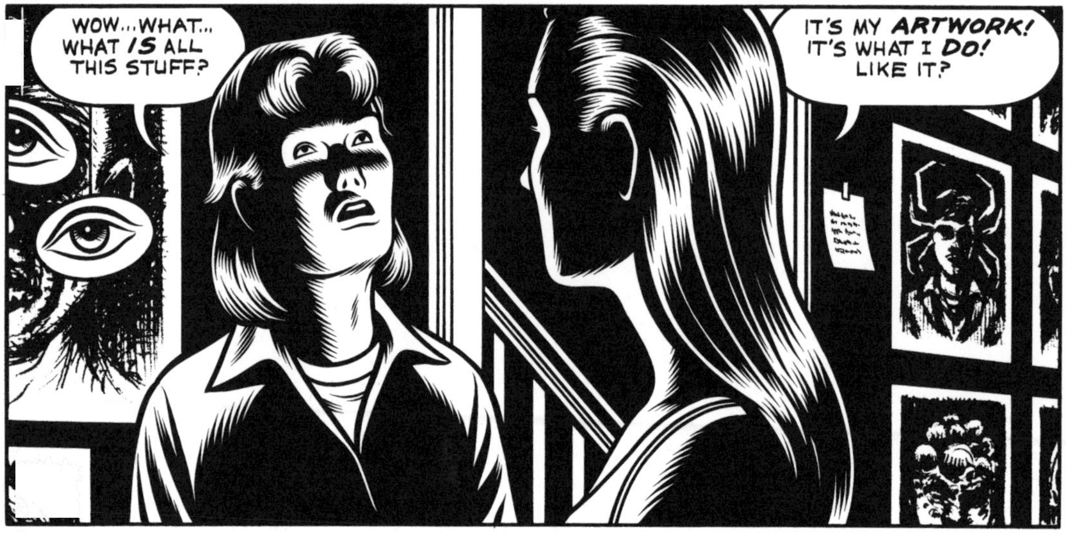

WOW... WHAT...
WHAT *IS* ALL
THIS STUFF?
IT'S MY ***ARTWORK!***
IT'S WHAT I ***DO!***
LIKE IT?

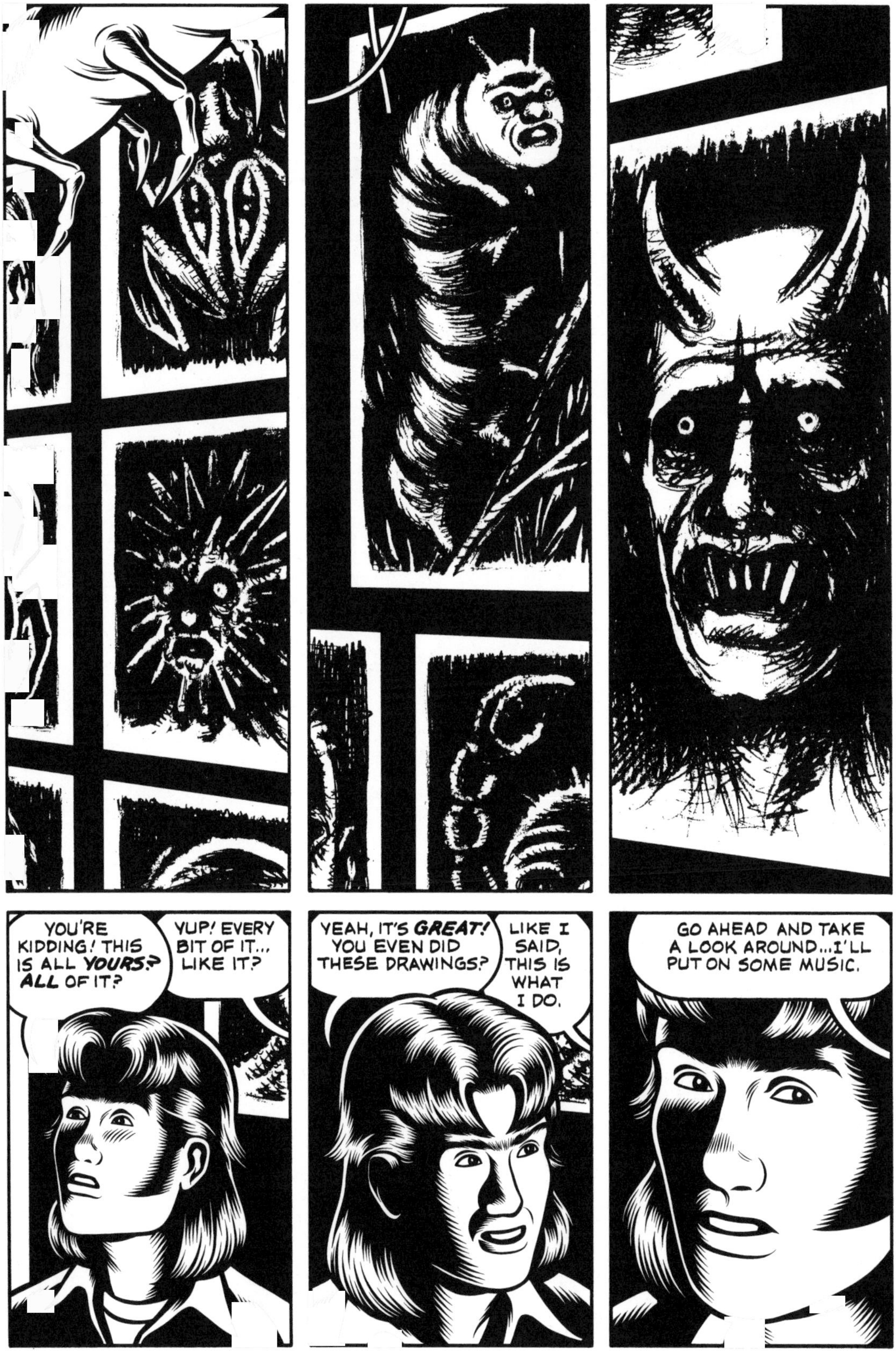
YOU'RE KIDDING! THIS IS ALL *YOURS?* *ALL* OF IT?
YUP! EVERY BIT OF IT... LIKE IT?
YEAH, IT'S *GREAT!* YOU EVEN DID THESE DRAWINGS?
LIKE I SAID, THIS IS WHAT I DO.
GO AHEAD AND TAKE A LOOK AROUND...I'LL PUT ON SOME MUSIC.

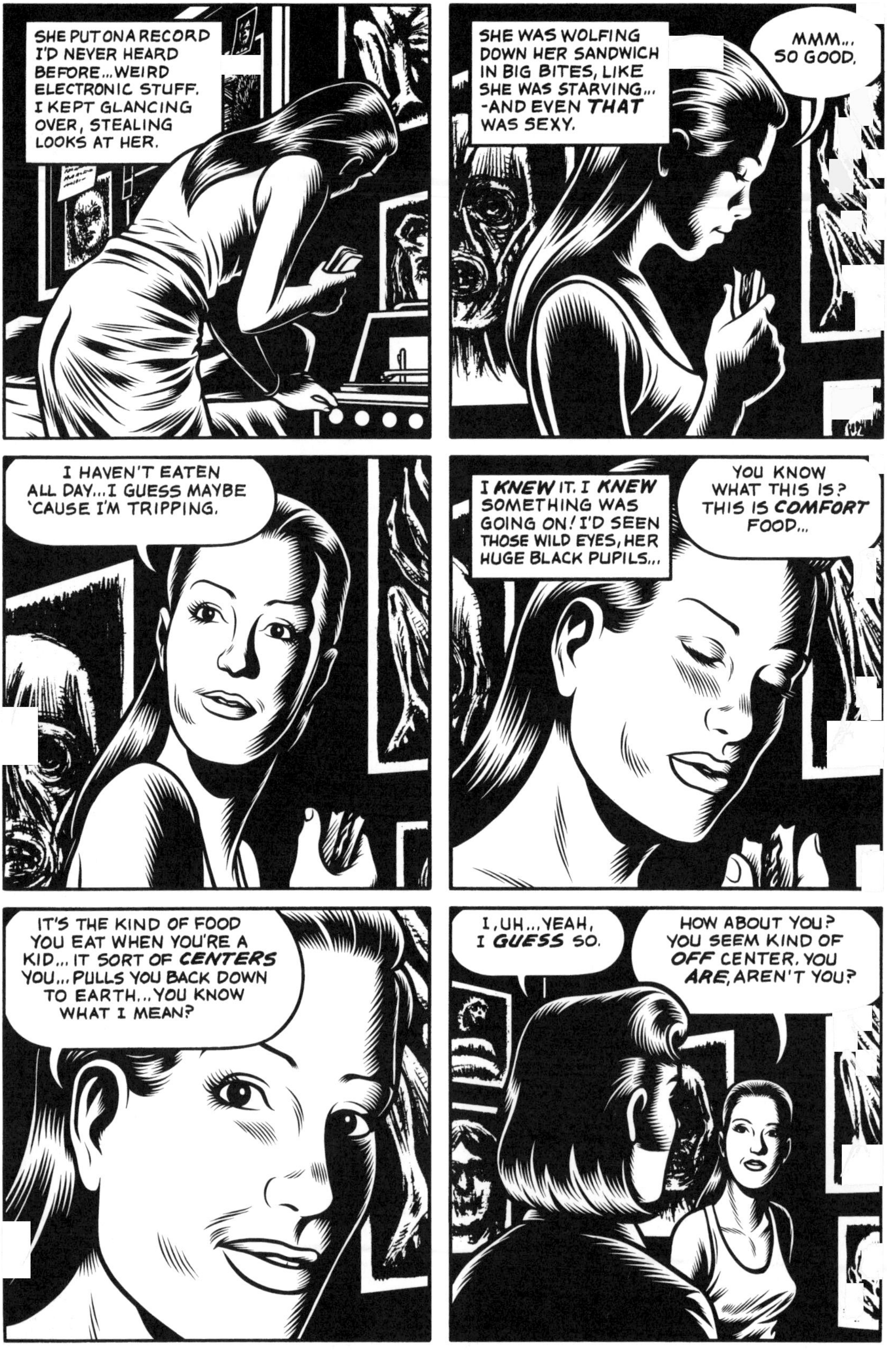
SHE PUT ON A RECORD I'D NEVER HEARD BEFORE... WEIRD ELECTRONIC STUFF. I KEPT GLANCING OVER, STEALING LOOKS AT HER.
SHE WAS WOLFING DOWN HER SANDWICH IN BIG BITES, LIKE SHE WAS STARVING... -AND EVEN THAT WAS SEXY.
MMM... SO GOOD.
I HAVEN'T EATEN ALL DAY... I GUESS MAYBE 'CAUSE I'M TRIPPING.
I KNEW IT. I KNEW SOMETHING WAS GOING ON! I'D SEEN THOSE WILD EYES, HER HUGE BLACK PUPILS...
YOU KNOW WHAT THIS IS? THIS IS COMFORT FOOD...
IT'S THE KIND OF FOOD YOU EAT WHEN YOU'RE A KID... IT SORT OF CENTERS YOU... PULLS YOU BACK DOWN TO EARTH... YOU KNOW WHAT I MEAN?
I, UH... YEAH, I GUESS SO.
HOW ABOUT YOU? YOU SEEM KIND OF OFF CENTER. YOU ARE, AREN'T YOU?

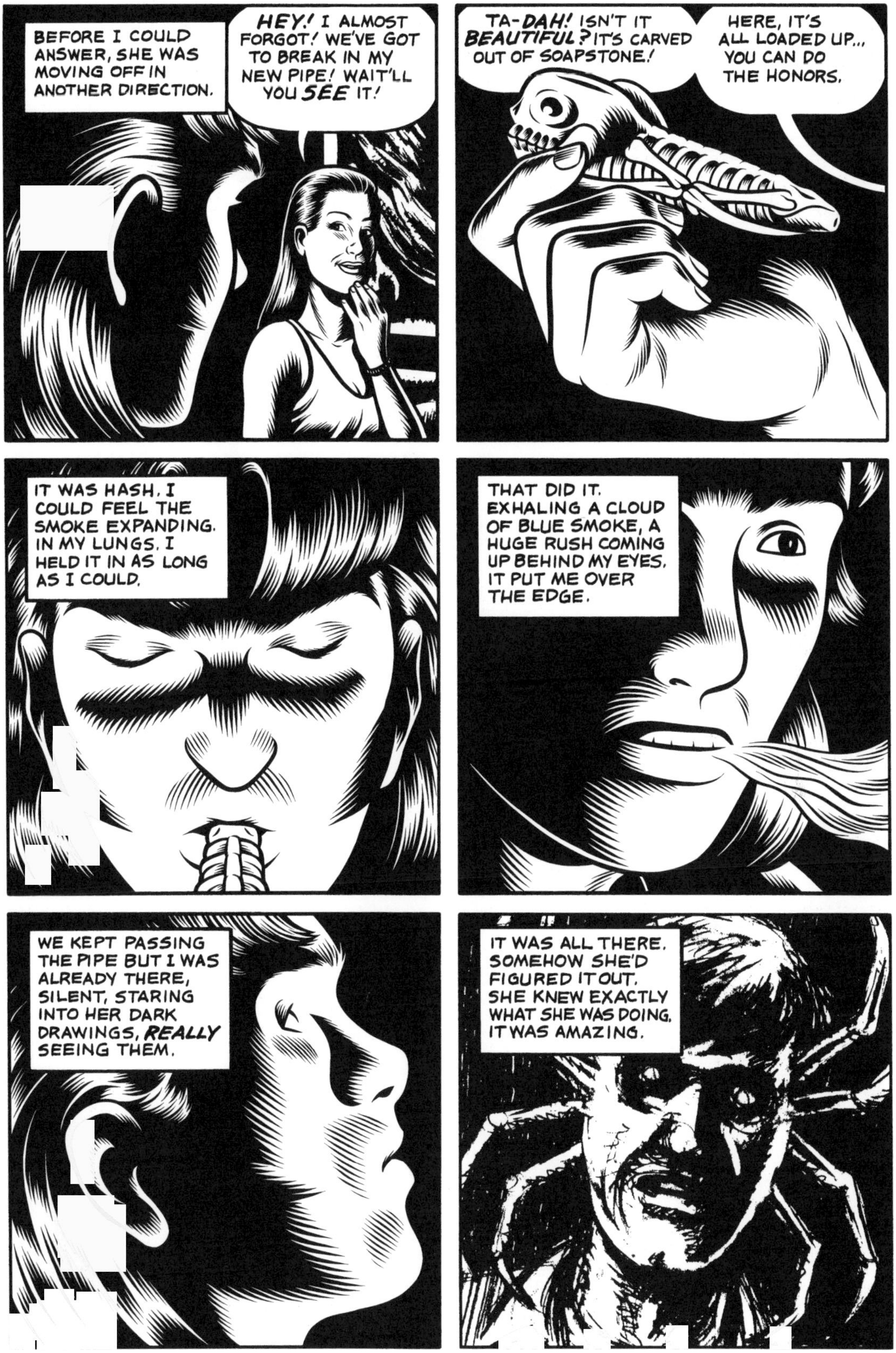
BEFORE I COULD ANSWER, SHE WAS MOVING OFF IN ANOTHER DIRECTION.
HEY! I ALMOST FORGOT! WE'VE GOT TO BREAK IN MY NEW PIPE! WAIT'LL YOU SEE IT!
TA-DAH! ISN'T IT BEAUTIFUL? IT'S CARVED OUT OF SOAPSTONE!
HERE, IT'S ALL LOADED UP... YOU CAN DO THE HONORS.
IT WAS HASH. I COULD FEEL THE SMOKE EXPANDING IN MY LUNGS. I HELD IT IN AS LONG AS I COULD.
THAT DID IT. EXHALING A CLOUD OF BLUE SMOKE, A HUGE RUSH COMING UP BEHIND MY EYES. IT PUT ME OVER THE EDGE.
WE KEPT PASSING THE PIPE BUT I WAS ALREADY THERE, SILENT, STARING INTO HER DARK DRAWINGS, REALLY SEEING THEM.
IT WAS ALL THERE. SOMEHOW SHE'D FIGURED IT OUT. SHE KNEW EXACTLY WHAT SHE WAS DOING. IT WAS AMAZING.

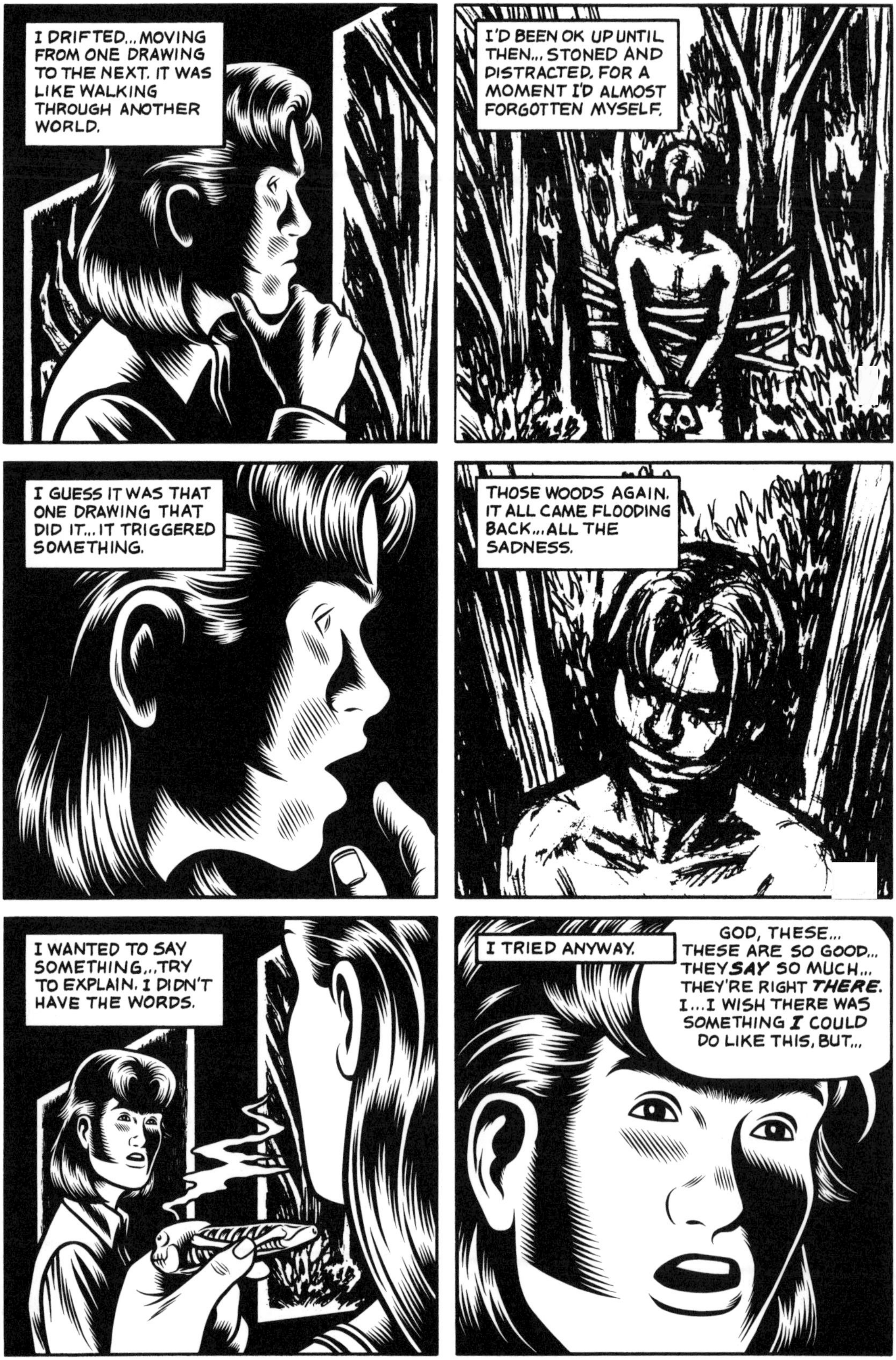

I DRIFTED... MOVING FROM ONE DRAWING TO THE NEXT. IT WAS LIKE WALKING THROUGH ANOTHER WORLD.
I'D BEEN OK UP UNTIL THEN... STONED AND DISTRACTED. FOR A MOMENT I'D ALMOST FORGOTTEN MYSELF.
I GUESS IT WAS THAT ONE DRAWING THAT DID IT... IT TRIGGERED SOMETHING.
THOSE WOODS AGAIN. IT ALL CAME FLOODING BACK... ALL THE SADNESS.
I WANTED TO SAY SOMETHING... TRY TO EXPLAIN. I DIDN'T HAVE THE WORDS.
I TRIED ANYWAY.
GOD, THESE... THESE ARE SO GOOD... THEY *SAY* SO MUCH... THEY'RE RIGHT *THERE*. I... I WISH THERE WAS SOMETHING *I* COULD DO LIKE THIS, BUT...

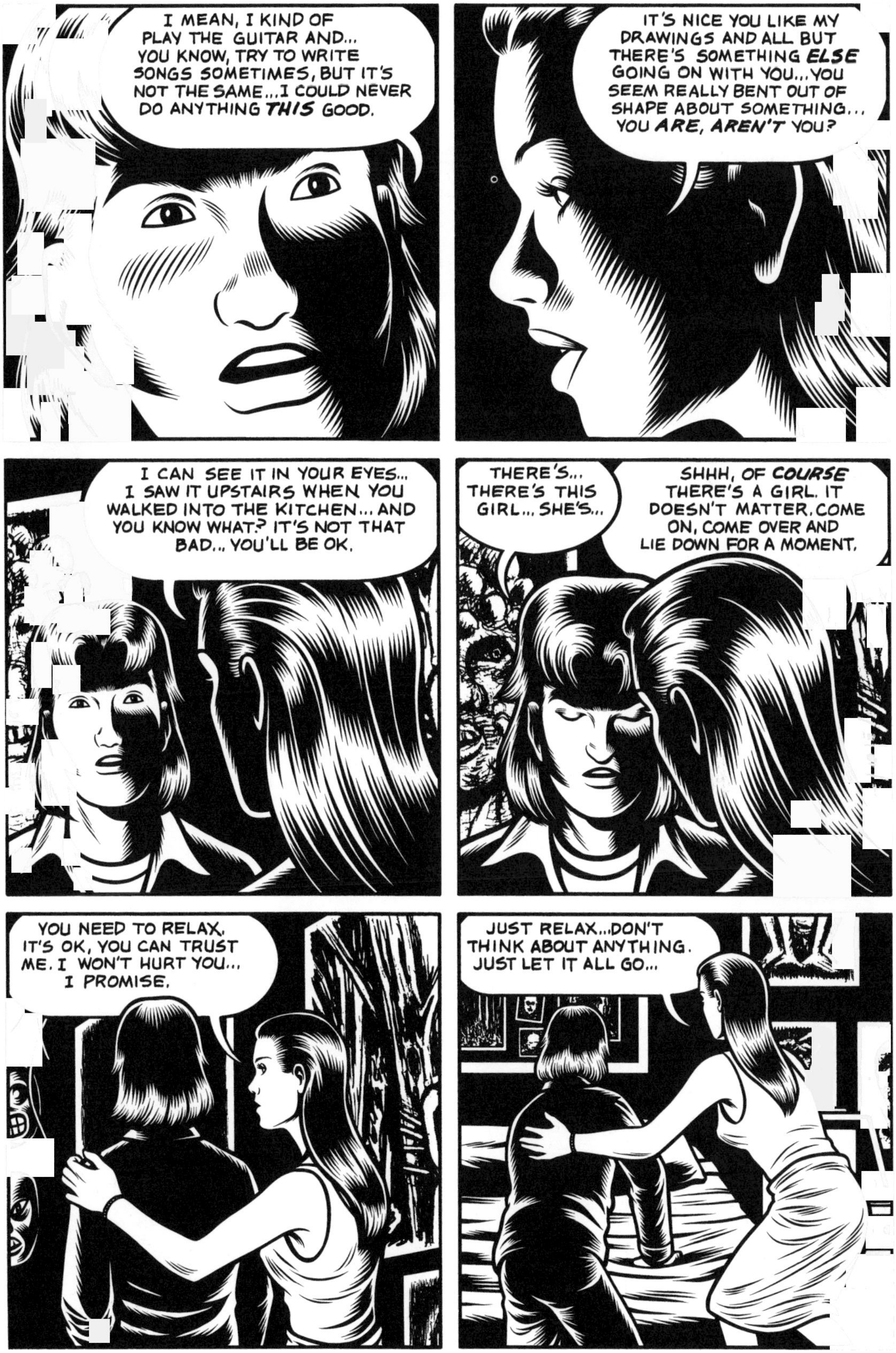
I MEAN, I KIND OF PLAY THE GUITAR AND... YOU KNOW, TRY TO WRITE SONGS SOMETIMES, BUT IT'S NOT THE SAME... I COULD NEVER DO ANYTHING THIS GOOD.
IT'S NICE YOU LIKE MY DRAWINGS AND ALL BUT THERE'S SOMETHING ELSE GOING ON WITH YOU... YOU SEEM REALLY BENT OUT OF SHAPE ABOUT SOMETHING... YOU ARE, AREN'T YOU?
I CAN SEE IT IN YOUR EYES... I SAW IT UPSTAIRS WHEN YOU WALKED INTO THE KITCHEN... AND YOU KNOW WHAT? IT'S NOT THAT BAD... YOU'LL BE OK.
THERE'S... THERE'S THIS GIRL... SHE'S...
SHHH, OF COURSE THERE'S A GIRL. IT DOESN'T MATTER. COME ON, COME OVER AND LIE DOWN FOR A MOMENT.
YOU NEED TO RELAX. IT'S OK, YOU CAN TRUST ME. I WON'T HURT YOU... I PROMISE.
JUST RELAX... DON'T THINK ABOUT ANYTHING. JUST LET IT ALL GO...

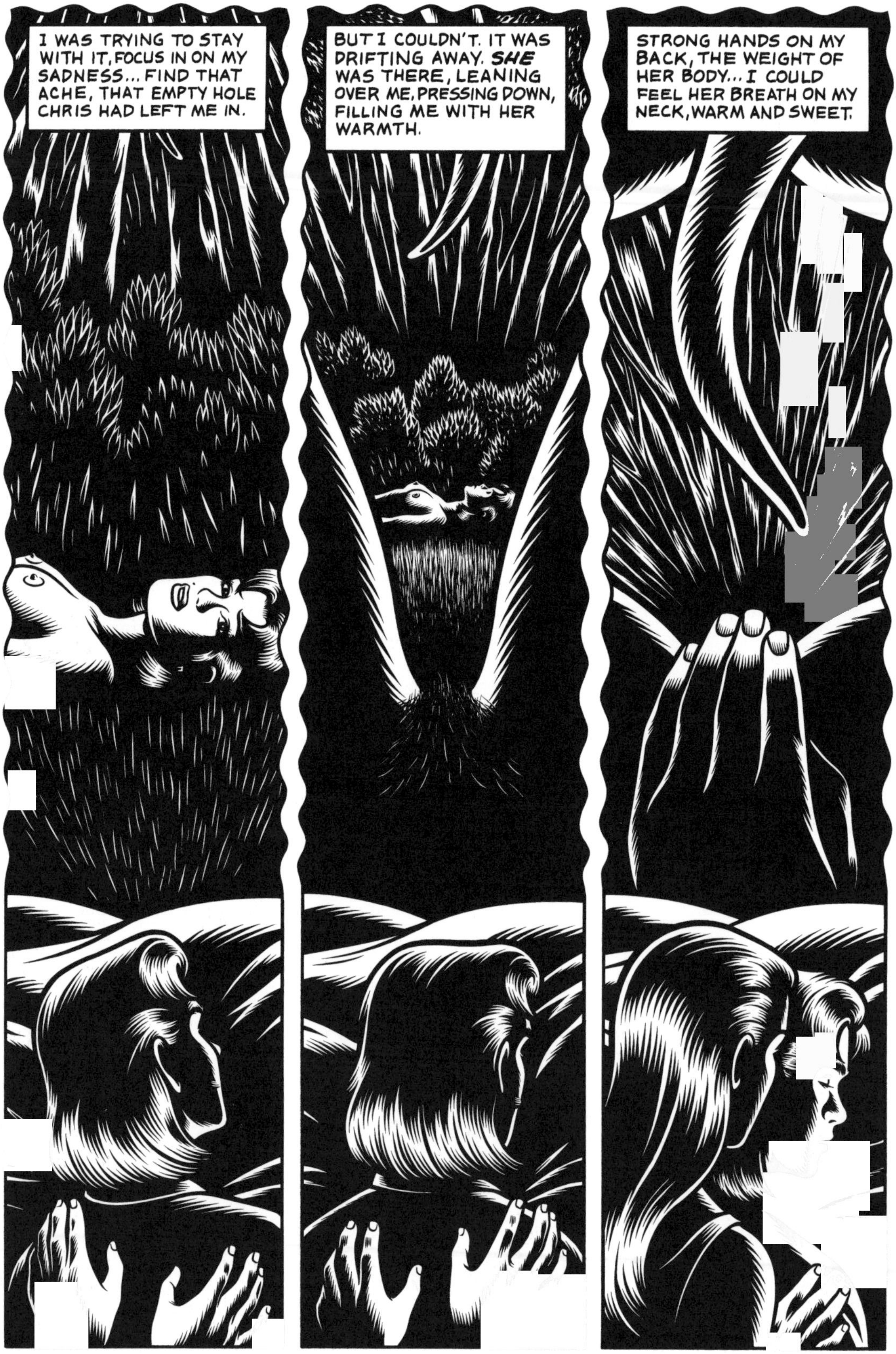
I WAS TRYING TO STAY WITH IT, FOCUS IN ON MY SADNESS... FIND THAT ACHE, THAT EMPTY HOLE CHRIS HAD LEFT ME IN.
BUT I COULDN'T. IT WAS DRIFTING AWAY. SHE WAS THERE, LEANING OVER ME, PRESSING DOWN, FILLING ME WITH HER WARMTH.
STRONG HANDS ON MY BACK, THE WEIGHT OF HER BODY... I COULD FEEL HER BREATH ON MY NECK, WARM AND SWEET.

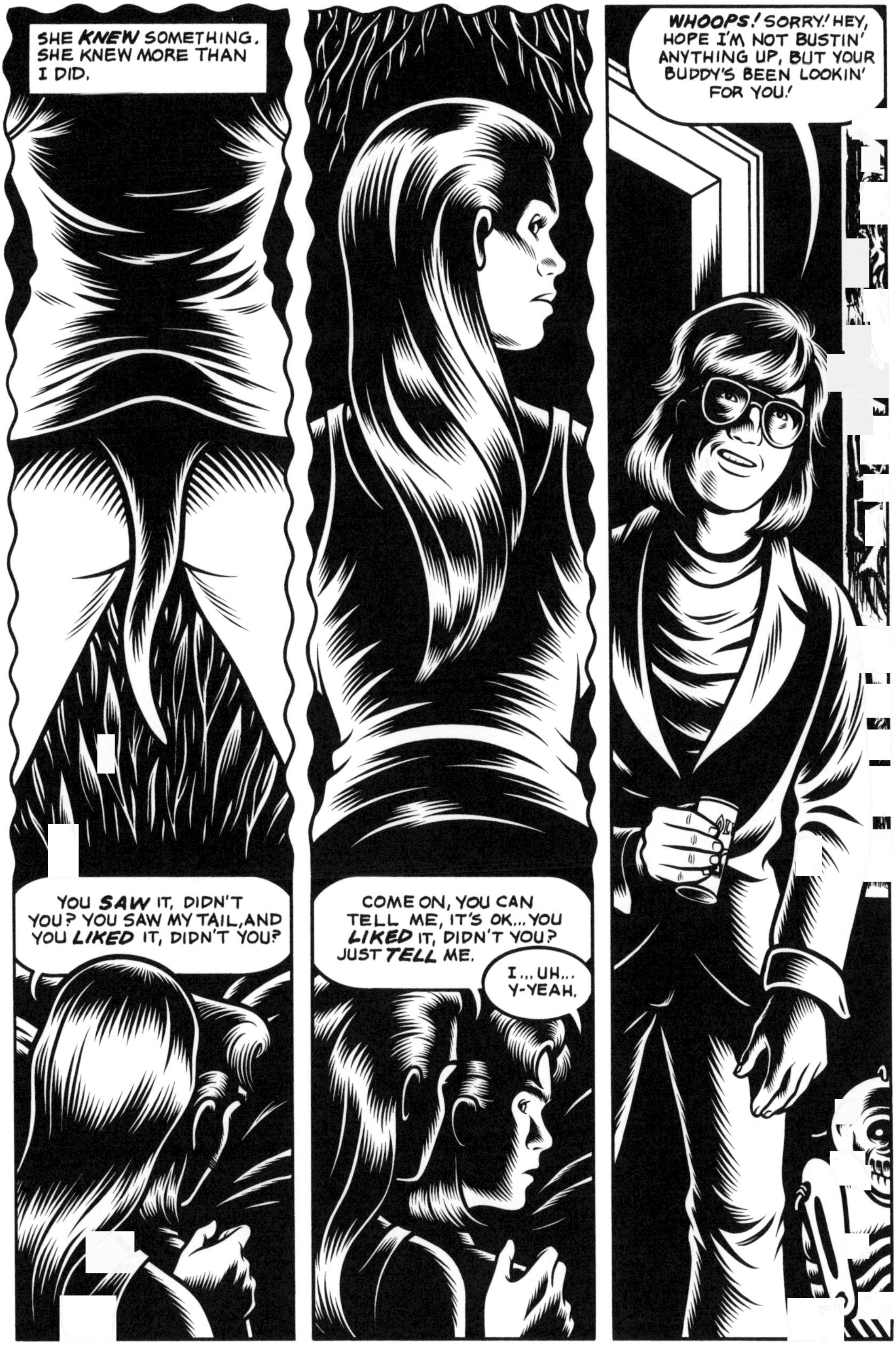
SHE KNEW SOMETHING. SHE KNEW MORE THAN I DID.
YOU SAW IT, DIDN'T YOU? YOU SAW MY TAIL, AND YOU LIKED IT, DIDN'T YOU?
COME ON, YOU CAN TELL ME, IT'S OK... YOU LIKED IT, DIDN'T YOU? JUST TELL ME.
I... UH... Y-YEAH.
WHOOPS! SORRY! HEY, HOPE I'M NOT BUSTIN' ANYTHING UP, BUT YOUR BUDDY'S BEEN LOOKIN' FOR YOU!

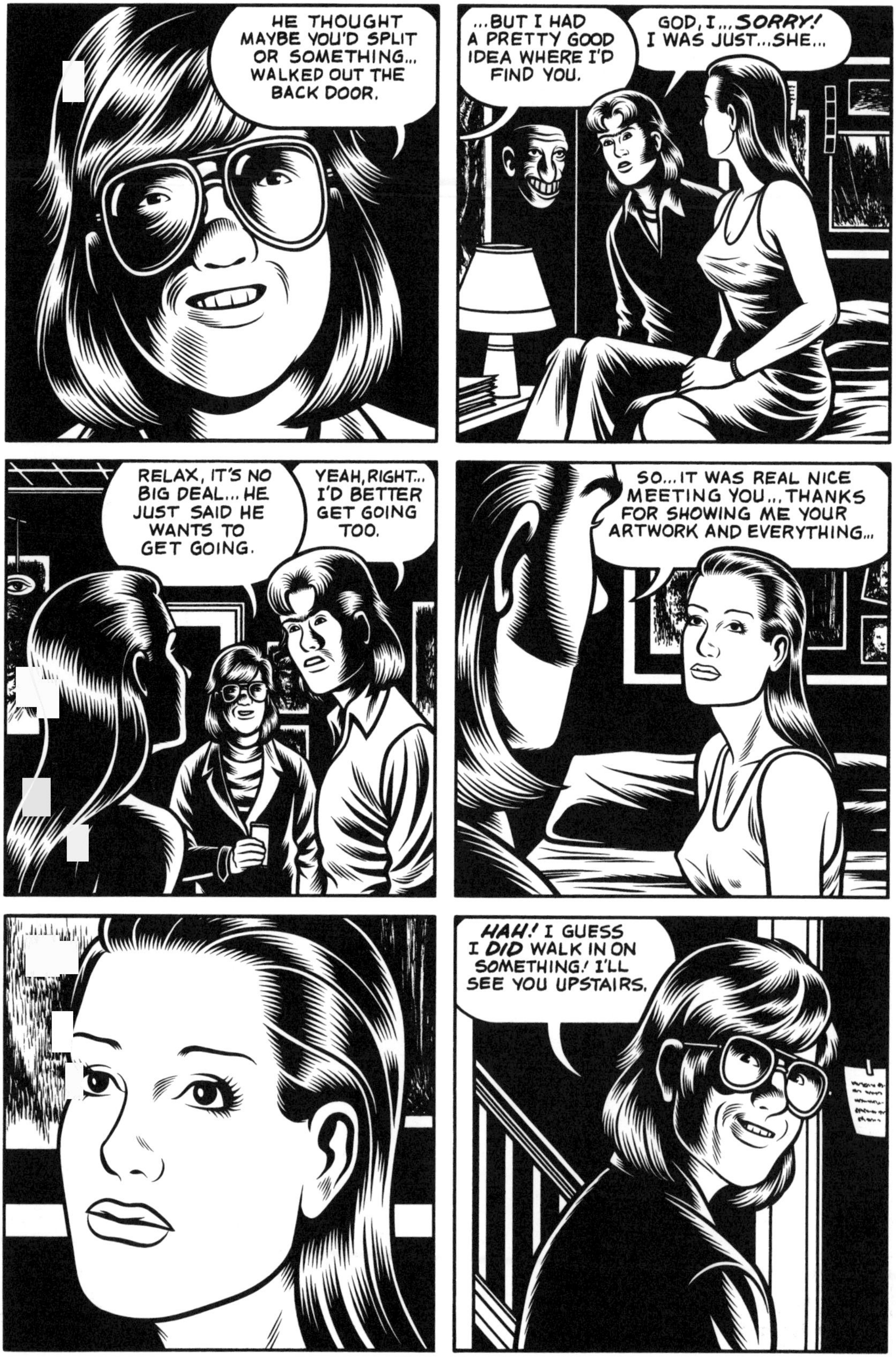
HE THOUGHT MAYBE YOU'D SPLIT OR SOMETHING... WALKED OUT THE BACK DOOR.
...BUT I HAD A PRETTY GOOD IDEA WHERE I'D FIND YOU.
GOD, I... SORRY! I WAS JUST... SHE...
RELAX, IT'S NO BIG DEAL... HE JUST SAID HE WANTS TO GET GOING.
YEAH, RIGHT... I'D BETTER GET GOING TOO.
SO... IT WAS REAL NICE MEETING YOU... THANKS FOR SHOWING ME YOUR ARTWORK AND EVERYTHING...
HAH! I GUESS I DID WALK IN ON SOMETHING! I'LL SEE YOU UPSTAIRS.

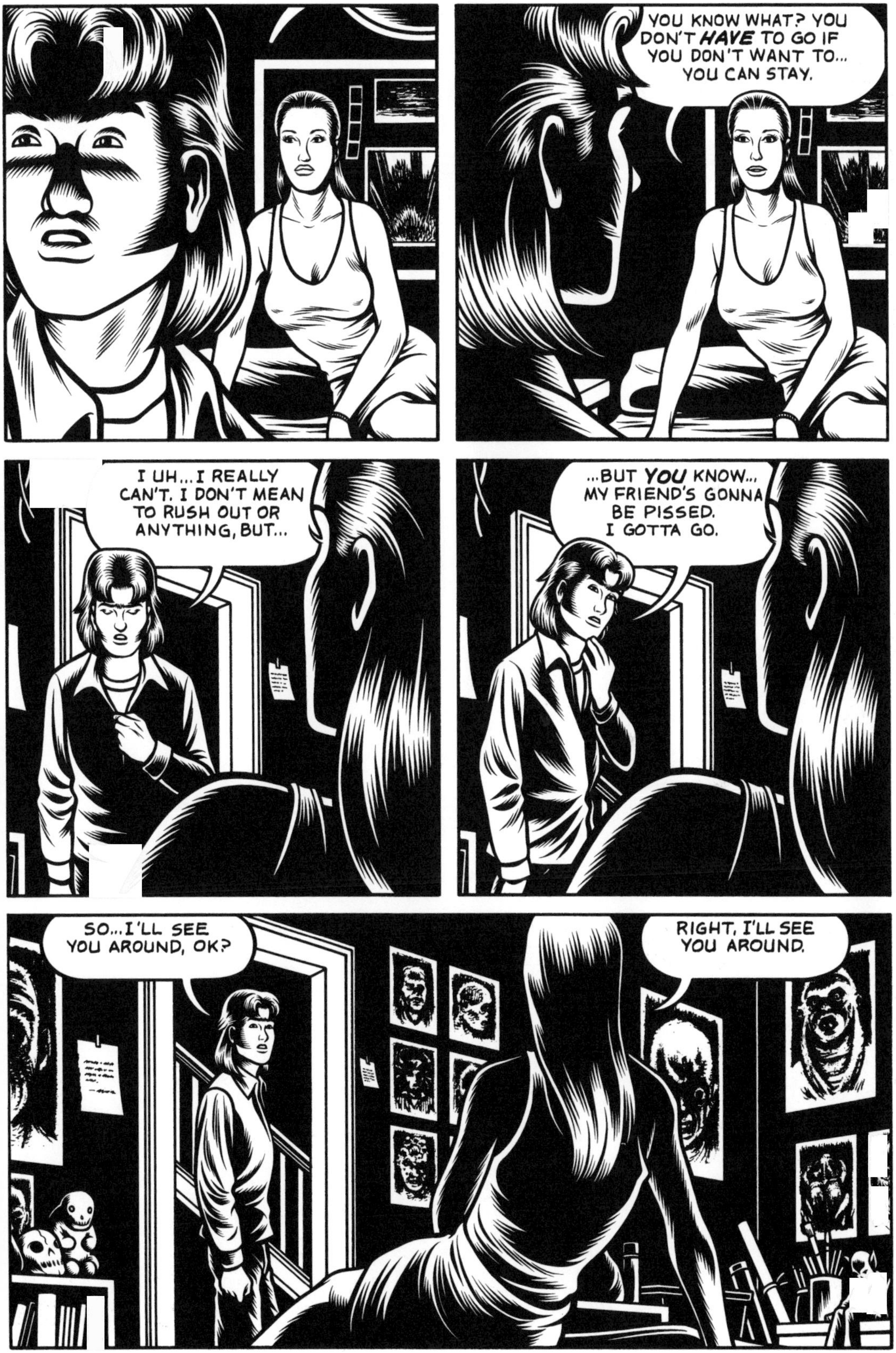
YOU KNOW WHAT? YOU DON'T HAVE TO GO IF YOU DON'T WANT TO... YOU CAN STAY.
I UH... I REALLY CAN'T. I DON'T MEAN TO RUSH OUT OR ANYTHING, BUT...
...BUT YOU KNOW... MY FRIEND'S GONNA BE PISSED. I GOTTA GO.
SO... I'LL SEE YOU AROUND, OK?
RIGHT, I'LL SEE YOU AROUND.

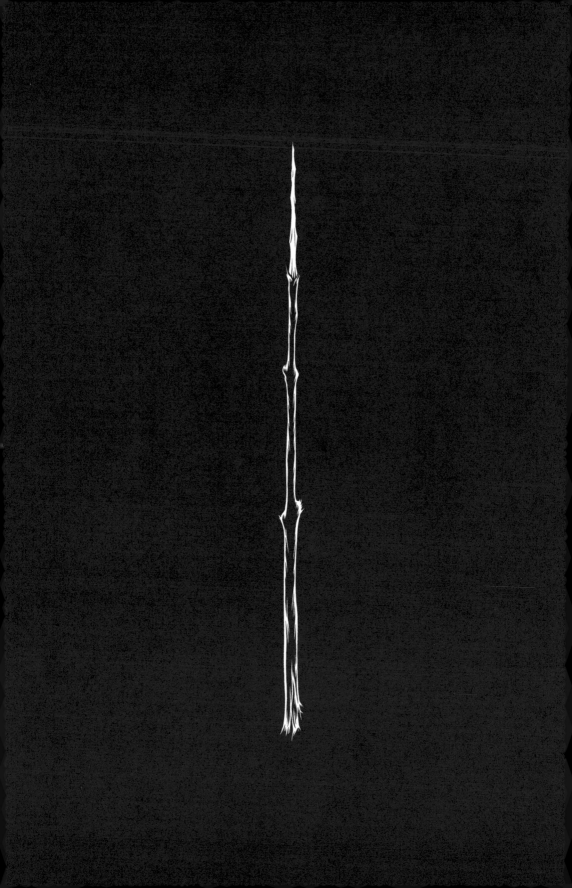

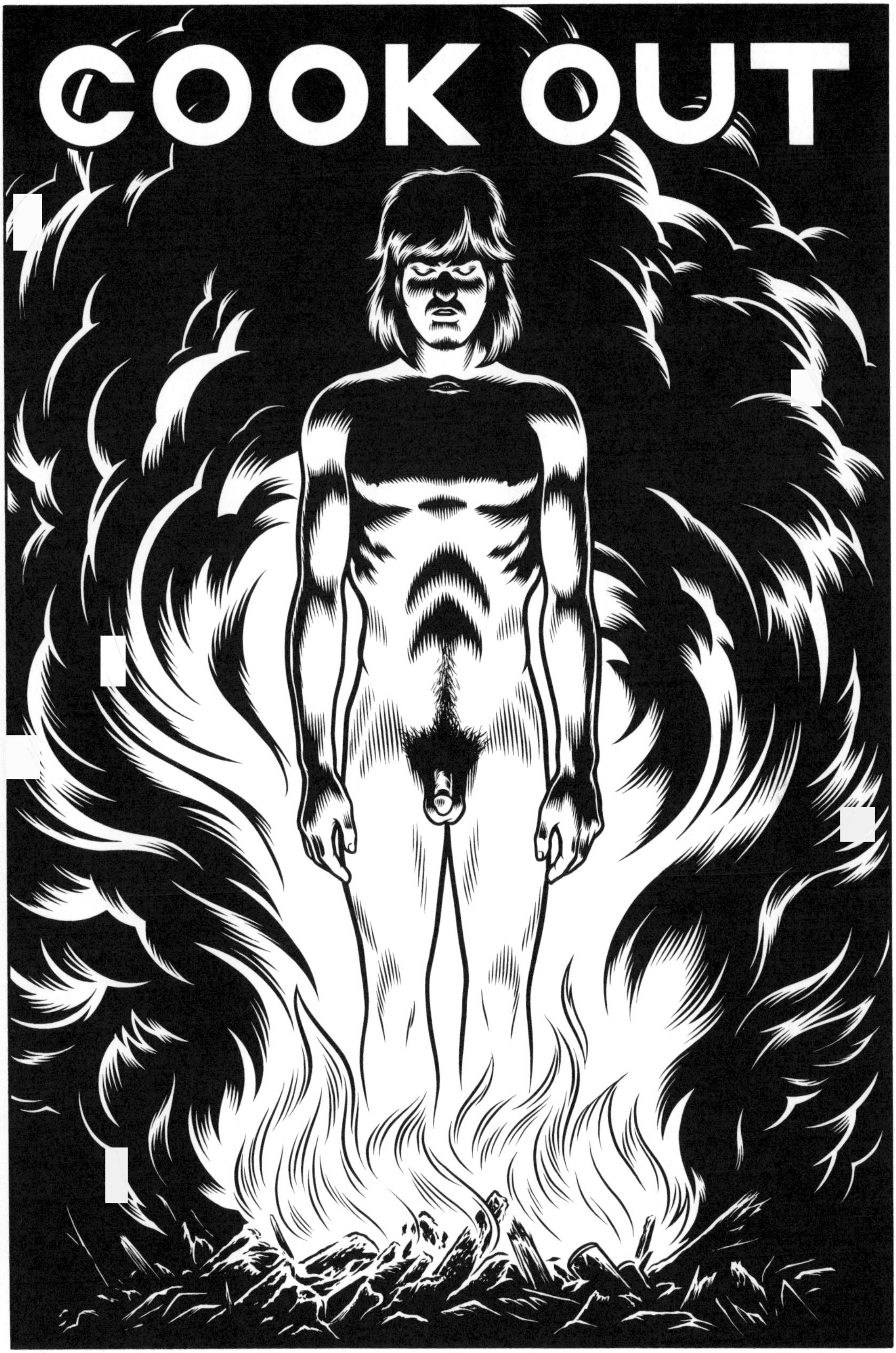
COOK OUT

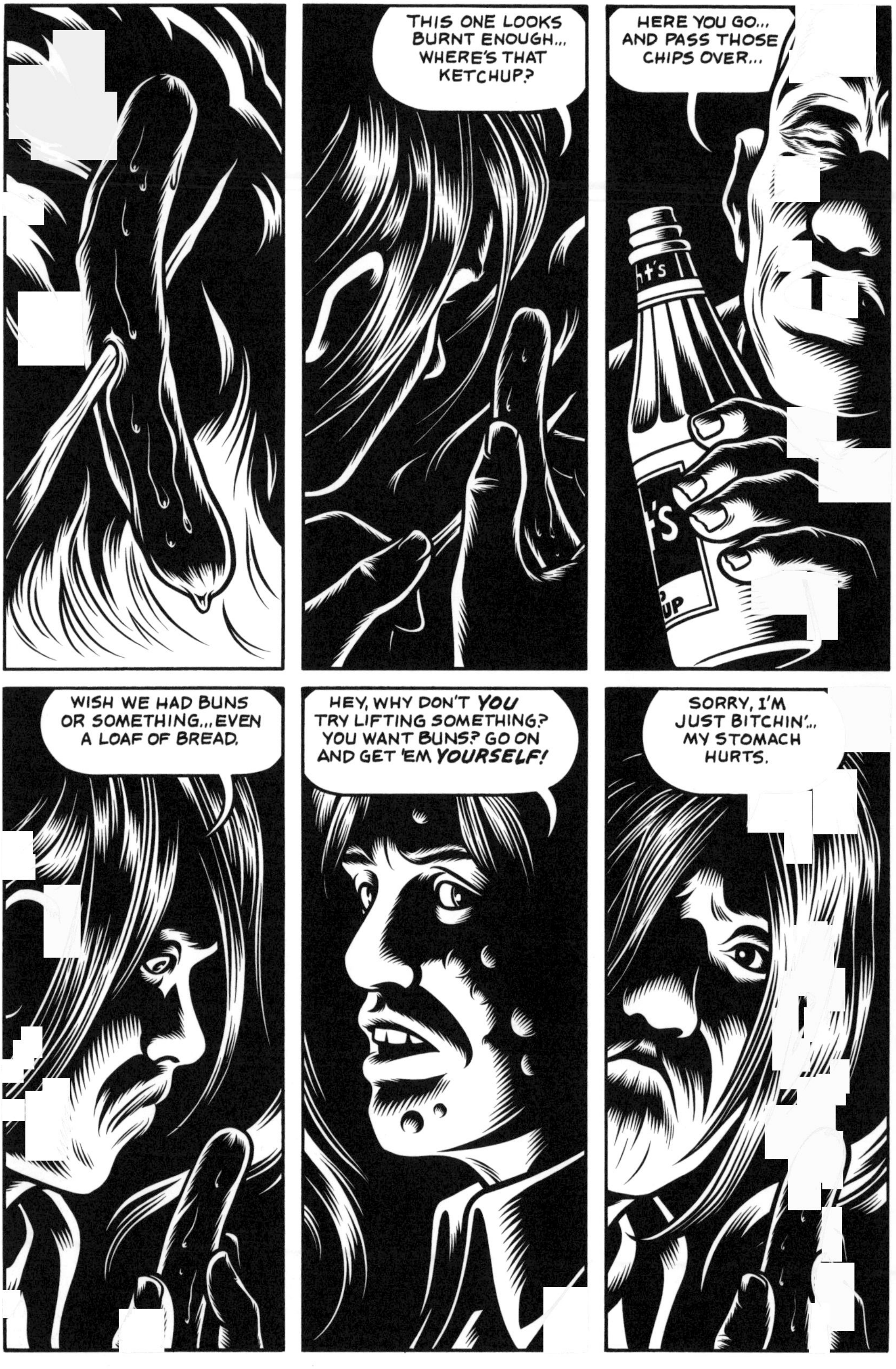
THIS ONE LOOKS BURNT ENOUGH... WHERE'S THAT KETCHUP?
HERE YOU GO... AND PASS THOSE CHIPS OVER...
WISH WE HAD BUNS OR SOMETHING... EVEN A LOAF OF BREAD.
HEY, WHY DON'T *YOU* TRY LIFTING SOMETHING? YOU WANT BUNS? GO ON AND GET 'EM *YOURSELF!*
SORRY, I'M JUST BITCHIN'... MY STOMACH HURTS.

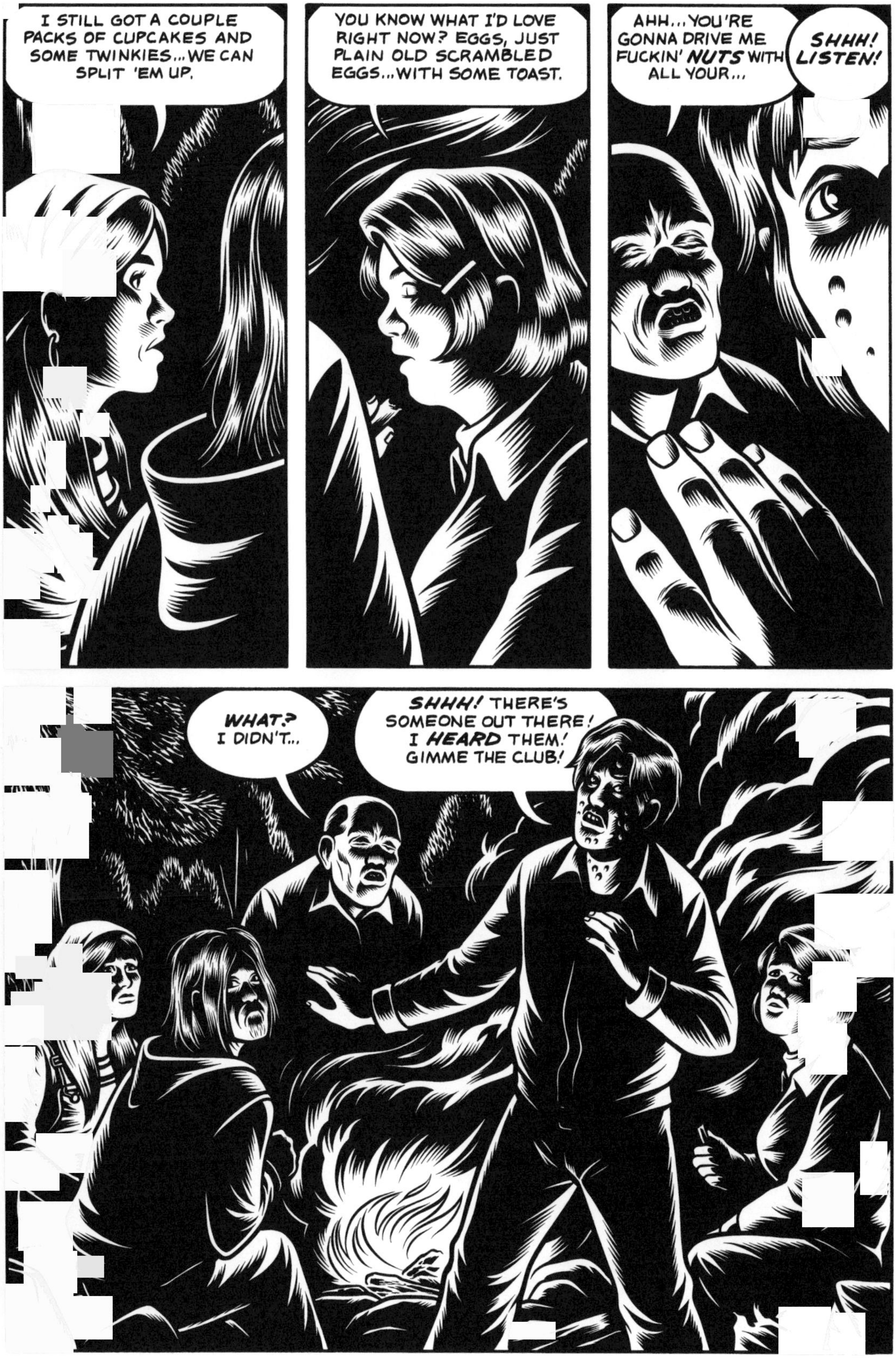
I STILL GOT A COUPLE PACKS OF CUPCAKES AND SOME TWINKIES... WE CAN SPLIT 'EM UP.
YOU KNOW WHAT I'D LOVE RIGHT NOW? EGGS, JUST PLAIN OLD SCRAMBLED EGGS... WITH SOME TOAST.
AHH... YOU'RE GONNA DRIVE ME FUCKIN' NUTS WITH ALL YOUR...
SHHH! LISTEN!
WHAT? I DIDN'T...
SHHH! THERE'S SOMEONE OUT THERE! I HEARD THEM! GIMME THE CLUB!

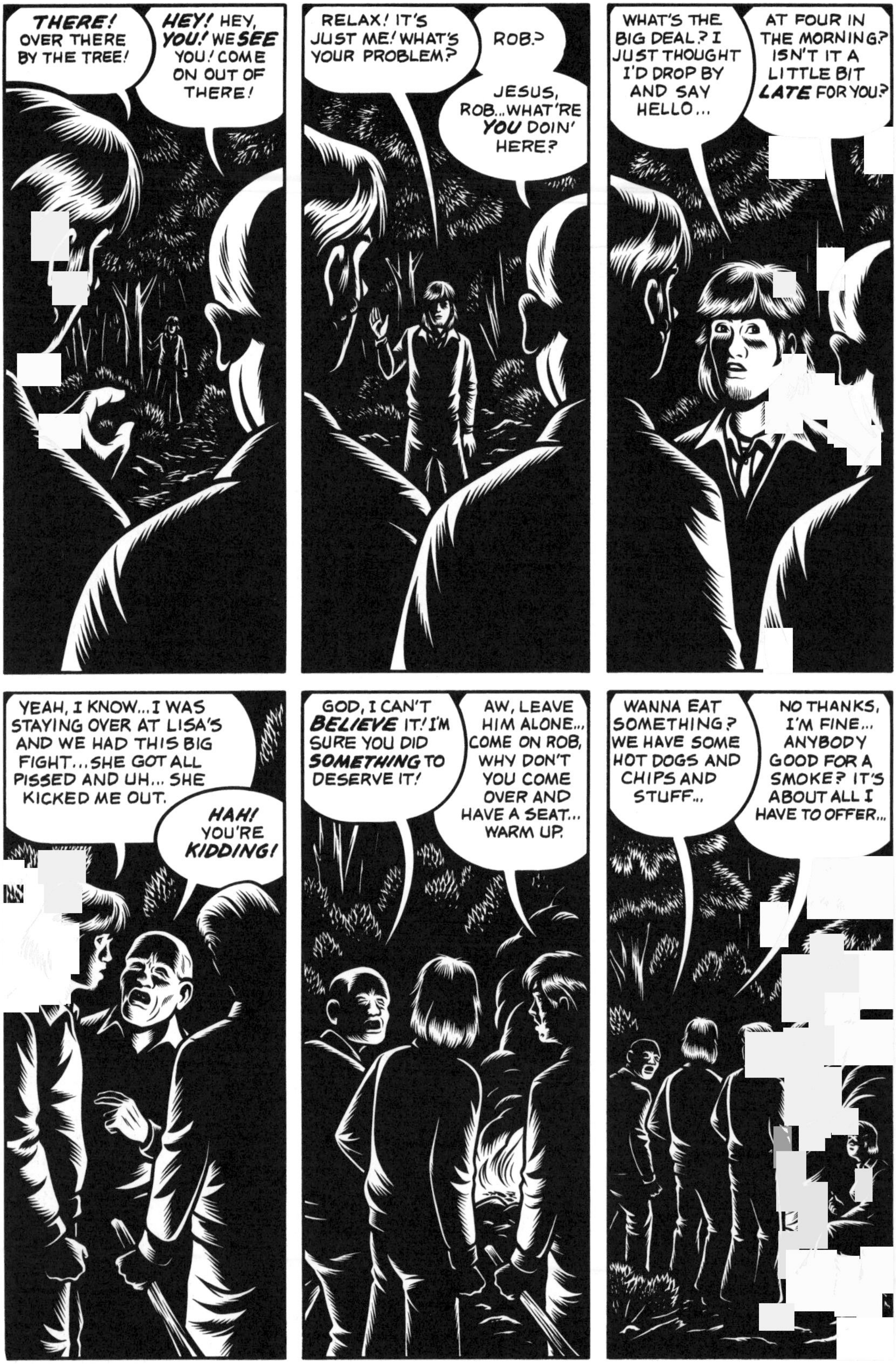

THERE! OVER THERE BY THE TREE!
HEY! HEY, YOU! WE SEE YOU! COME ON OUT OF THERE!
RELAX! IT'S JUST ME! WHAT'S YOUR PROBLEM?
ROB?
JESUS, ROB... WHAT'RE YOU DOIN' HERE?
WHAT'S THE BIG DEAL? I JUST THOUGHT I'D DROP BY AND SAY HELLO...
AT FOUR IN THE MORNING? ISN'T IT A LITTLE BIT LATE FOR YOU?
YEAH, I KNOW... I WAS STAYING OVER AT LISA'S AND WE HAD THIS BIG FIGHT... SHE GOT ALL PISSED AND UH... SHE KICKED ME OUT.
HAH! YOU'RE KIDDING!
GOD, I CAN'T BELIEVE IT! I'M SURE YOU DID SOMETHING TO DESERVE IT!
AW, LEAVE HIM ALONE... COME ON ROB, WHY DON'T YOU COME OVER AND HAVE A SEAT... WARM UP.
WANNA EAT SOMETHING? WE HAVE SOME HOT DOGS AND CHIPS AND STUFF...
NO THANKS, I'M FINE... ANYBODY GOOD FOR A SMOKE? IT'S ABOUT ALL I HAVE TO OFFER...

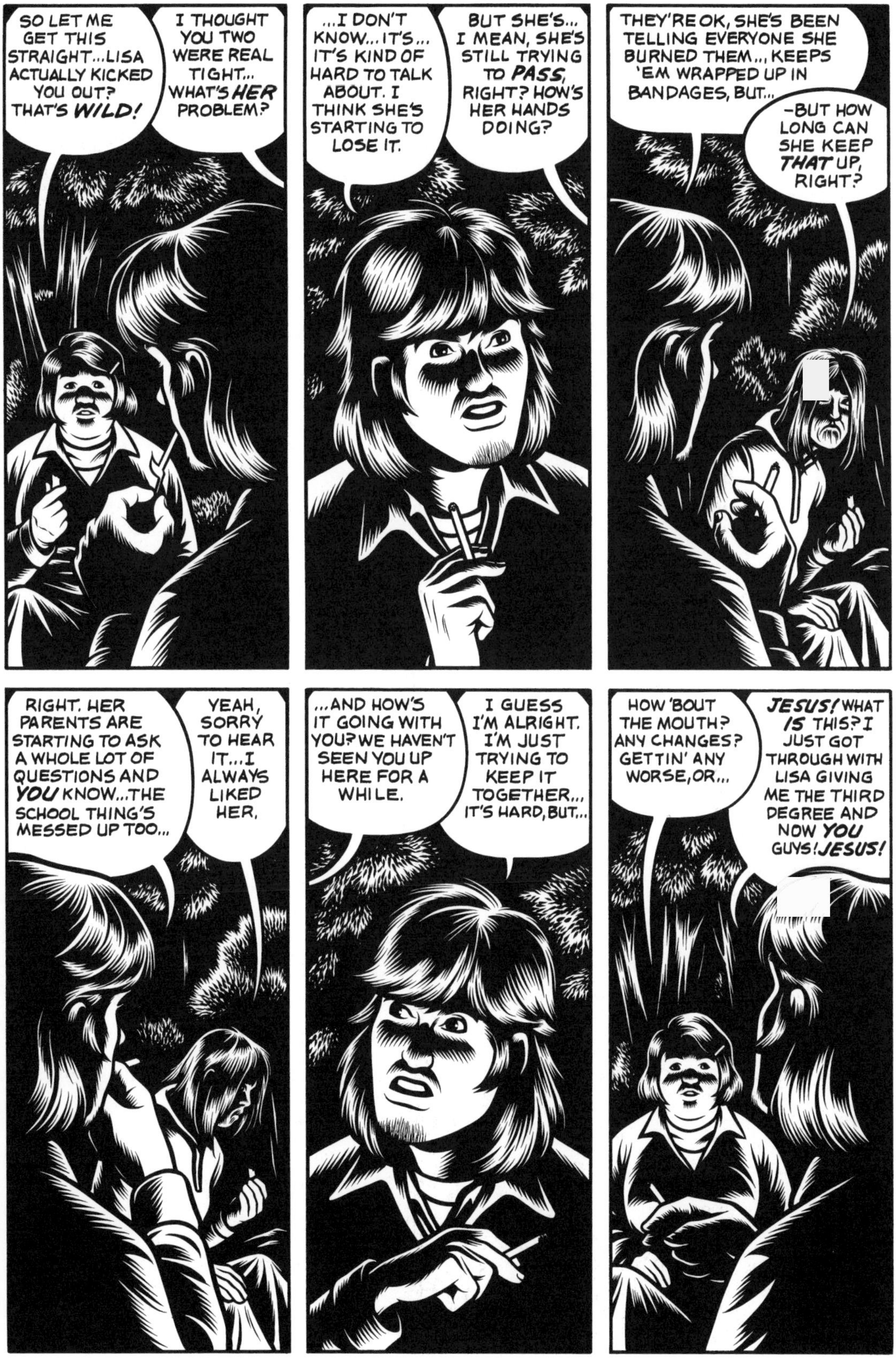

SO LET ME GET THIS STRAIGHT...LISA ACTUALLY KICKED YOU OUT? THAT'S *WILD!*
I THOUGHT YOU TWO WERE REAL TIGHT... WHAT'S *HER* PROBLEM?
...I DON'T KNOW... IT'S... IT'S KIND OF HARD TO TALK ABOUT. I THINK SHE'S STARTING TO LOSE IT.
BUT SHE'S... I MEAN, SHE'S STILL TRYING TO *PASS*, RIGHT? HOW'S HER HANDS DOING?
THEY'RE OK, SHE'S BEEN TELLING EVERYONE SHE BURNED THEM..., KEEPS 'EM WRAPPED UP IN BANDAGES, BUT...
-BUT HOW LONG CAN SHE KEEP *THAT* UP, RIGHT?
RIGHT. HER PARENTS ARE STARTING TO ASK A WHOLE LOT OF QUESTIONS AND *YOU* KNOW...THE SCHOOL THING'S MESSED UP TOO...
YEAH, SORRY TO HEAR IT...I ALWAYS LIKED HER.
...AND HOW'S IT GOING WITH YOU? WE HAVEN'T SEEN YOU UP HERE FOR A WHILE.
I GUESS I'M ALRIGHT. I'M JUST TRYING TO KEEP IT TOGETHER... IT'S HARD, BUT...
HOW 'BOUT THE MOUTH? ANY CHANGES? GETTIN' ANY WORSE, OR...
JESUS! WHAT *IS* THIS? I JUST GOT THROUGH WITH LISA GIVING ME THE THIRD DEGREE AND NOW *YOU* GUYS! *JESUS!*

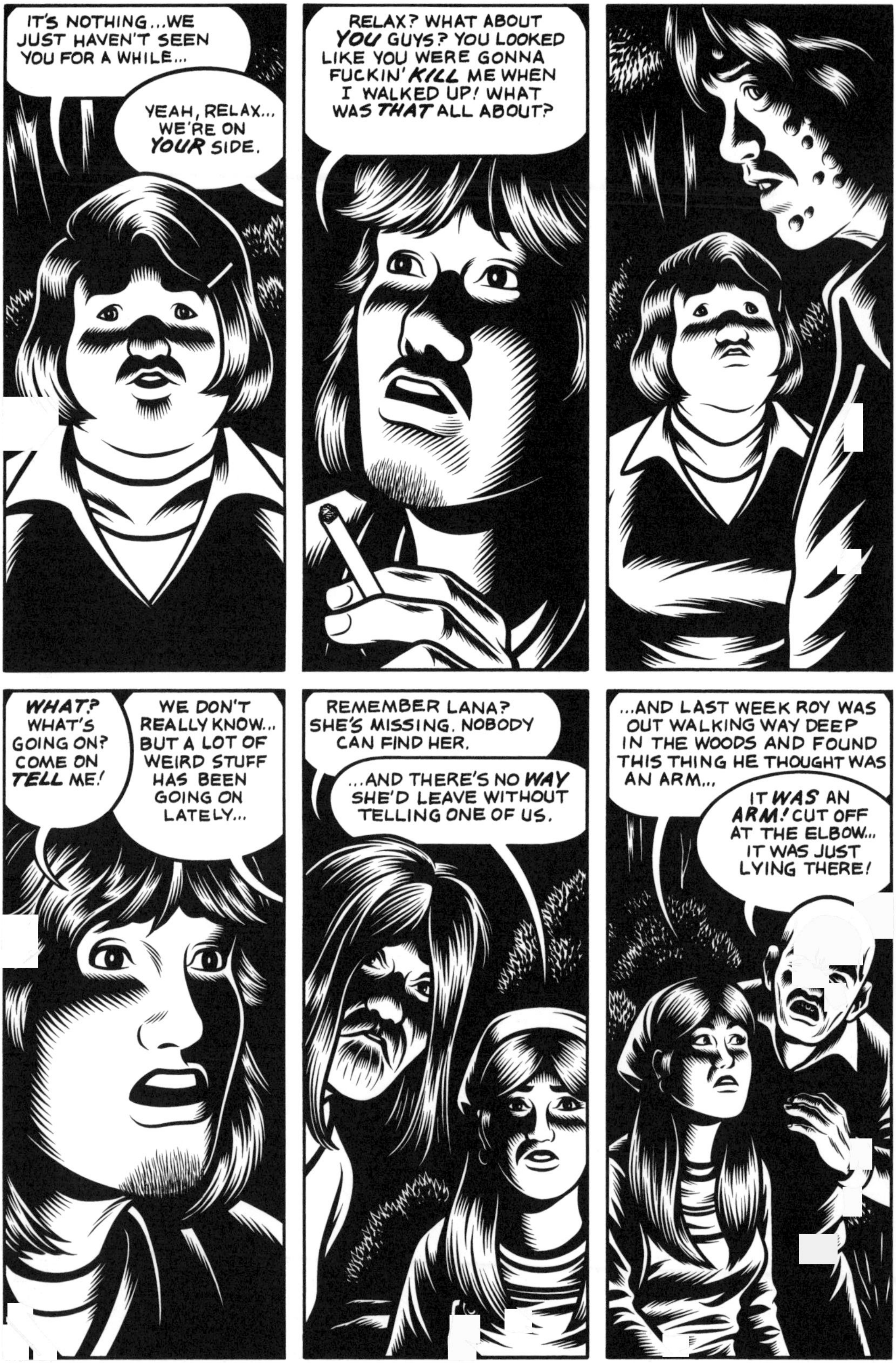
IT'S NOTHING...WE JUST HAVEN'T SEEN YOU FOR A WHILE...
YEAH, RELAX... WE'RE ON YOUR SIDE.
RELAX? WHAT ABOUT YOU GUYS? YOU LOOKED LIKE YOU WERE GONNA FUCKIN' KILL ME WHEN I WALKED UP! WHAT WAS THAT ALL ABOUT?
WHAT? WHAT'S GOING ON? COME ON TELL ME!
WE DON'T REALLY KNOW... BUT A LOT OF WEIRD STUFF HAS BEEN GOING ON LATELY...
REMEMBER LANA? SHE'S MISSING. NOBODY CAN FIND HER.
...AND THERE'S NO WAY SHE'D LEAVE WITHOUT TELLING ONE OF US.
...AND LAST WEEK ROY WAS OUT WALKING WAY DEEP IN THE WOODS AND FOUND THIS THING HE THOUGHT WAS AN ARM...
IT WAS AN ARM! CUT OFF AT THE ELBOW... IT WAS JUST LYING THERE!

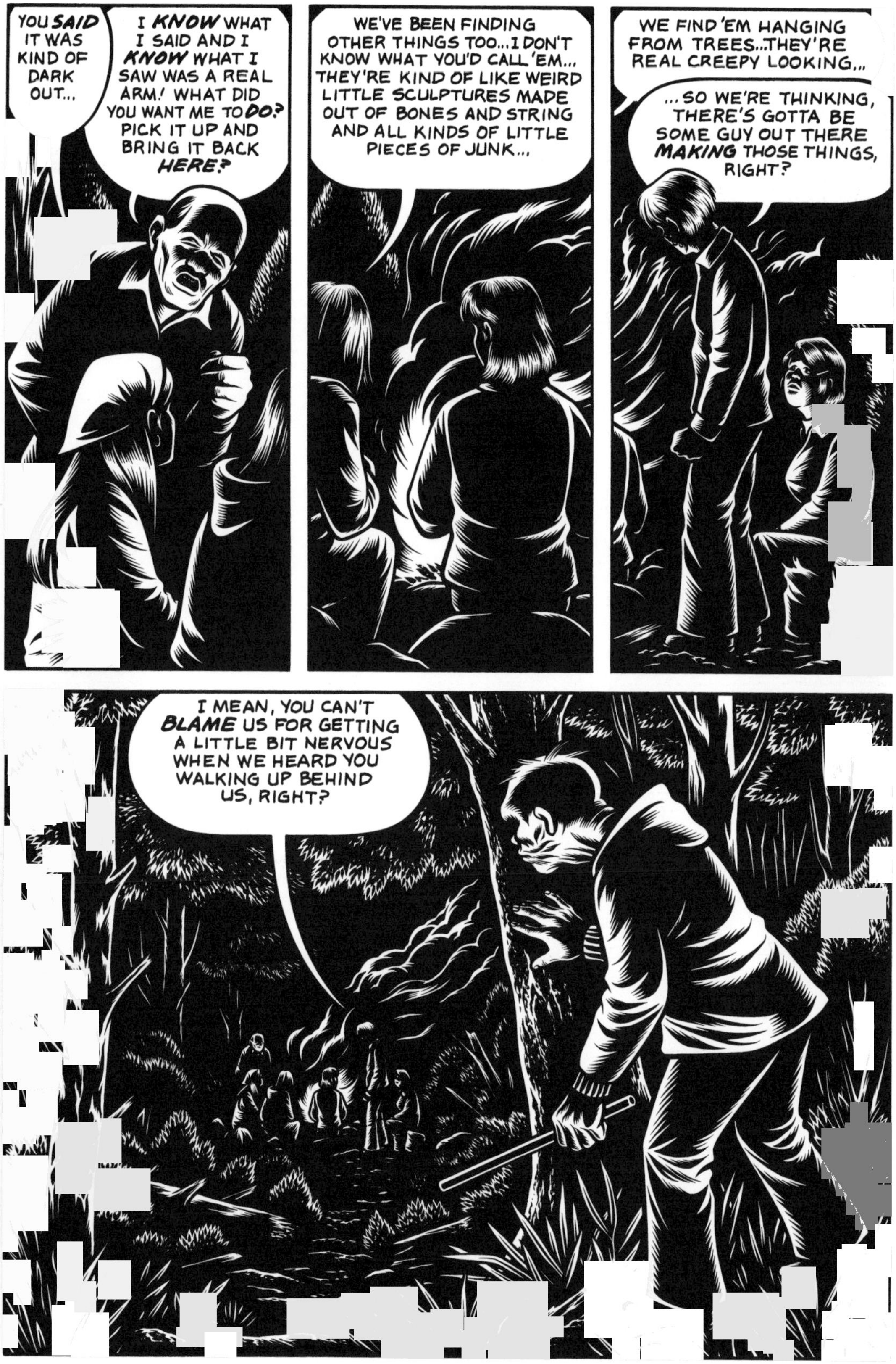
YOU SAID IT WAS KIND OF DARK OUT...
I KNOW WHAT I SAID AND I KNOW WHAT I SAW WAS A REAL ARM! WHAT DID YOU WANT ME TO DO? PICK IT UP AND BRING IT BACK HERE?
WE'VE BEEN FINDING OTHER THINGS TOO...I DON'T KNOW WHAT YOU'D CALL 'EM... THEY'RE KIND OF LIKE WEIRD LITTLE SCULPTURES MADE OUT OF BONES AND STRING AND ALL KINDS OF LITTLE PIECES OF JUNK...
WE FIND 'EM HANGING FROM TREES...THEY'RE REAL CREEPY LOOKING...
...SO WE'RE THINKING, THERE'S GOTTA BE SOME GUY OUT THERE MAKING THOSE THINGS, RIGHT?
I MEAN, YOU CAN'T BLAME US FOR GETTING A LITTLE BIT NERVOUS WHEN WE HEARD YOU WALKING UP BEHIND US, RIGHT?

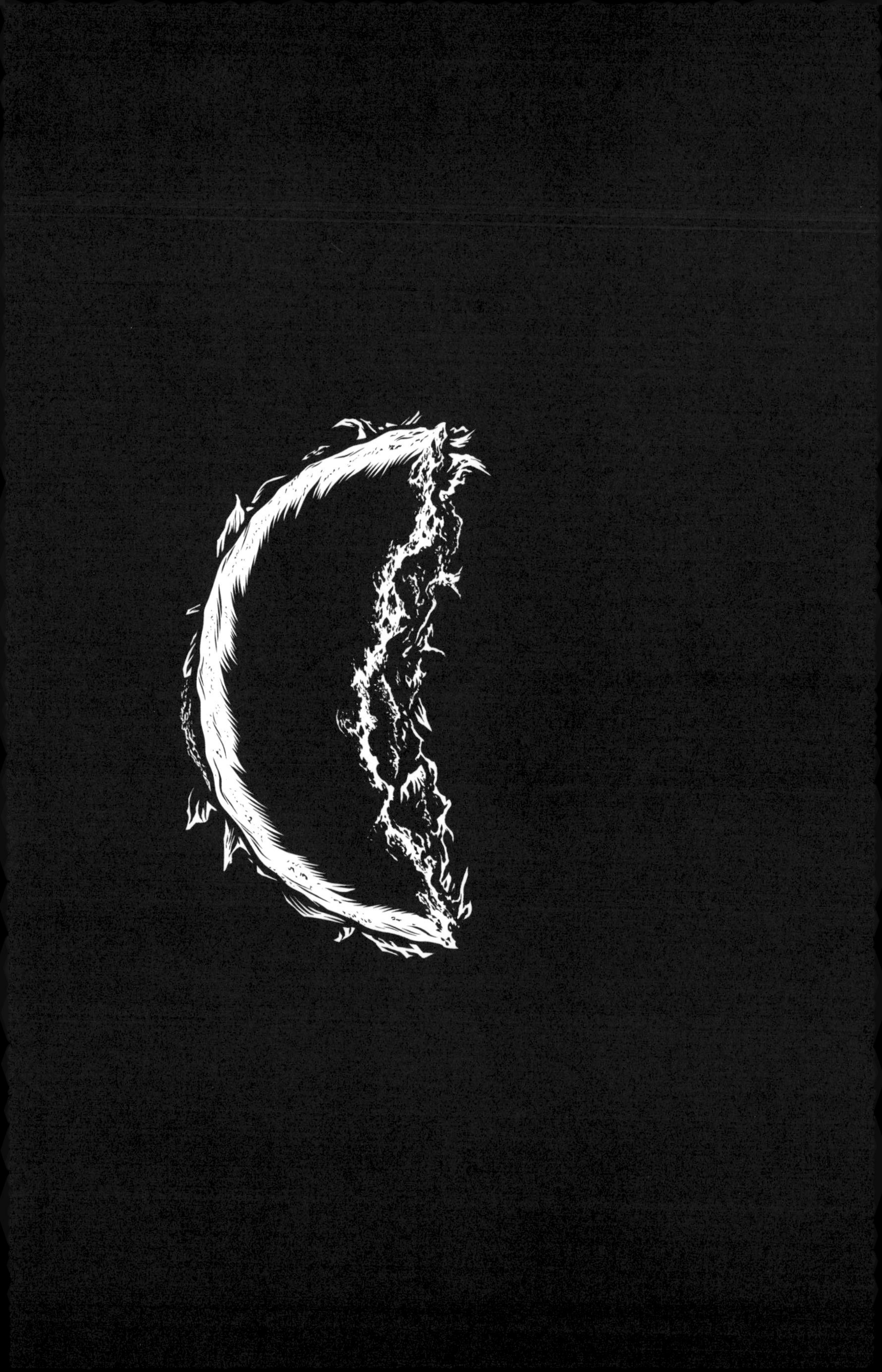

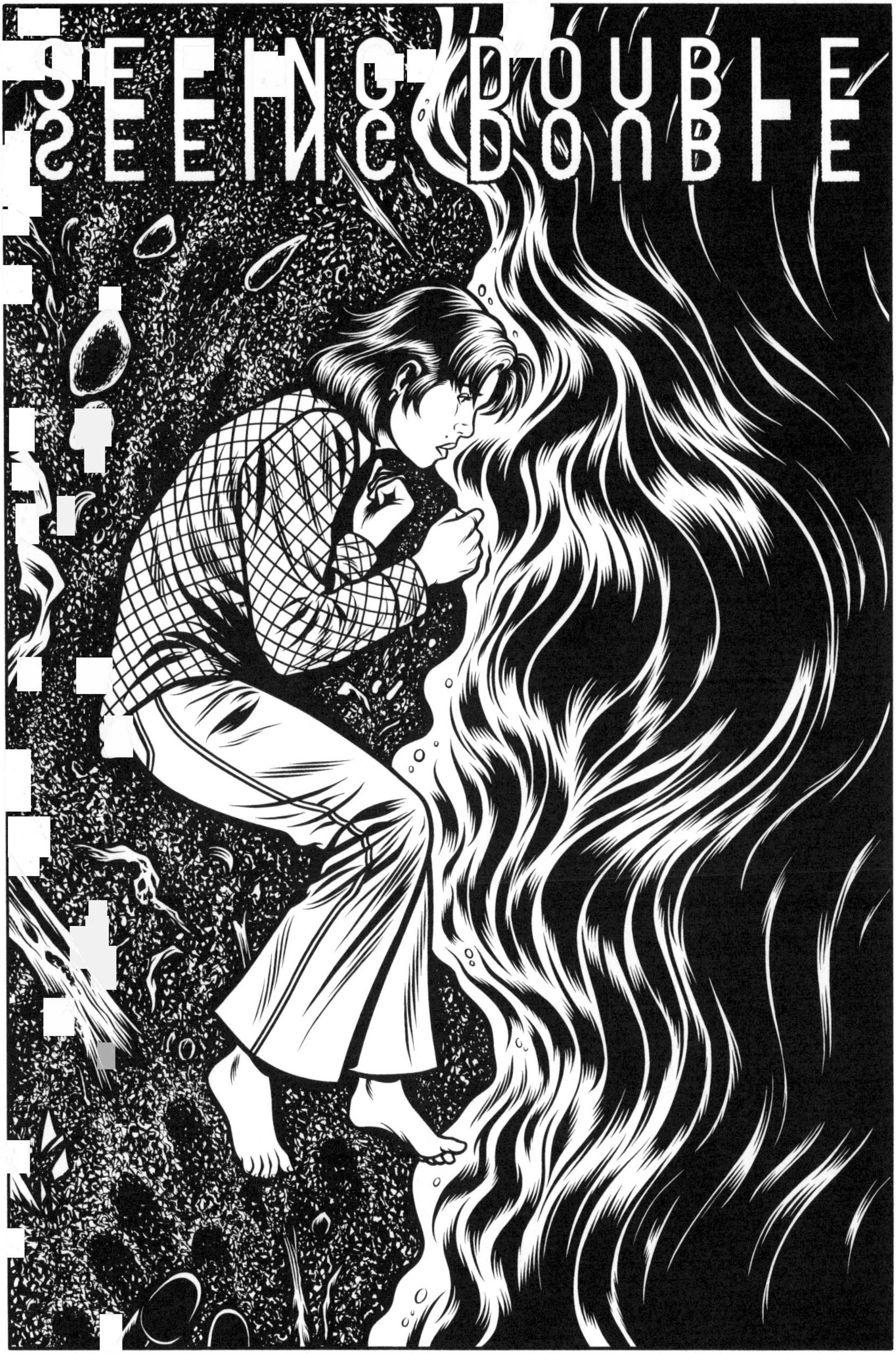
SEEING DOUBLE

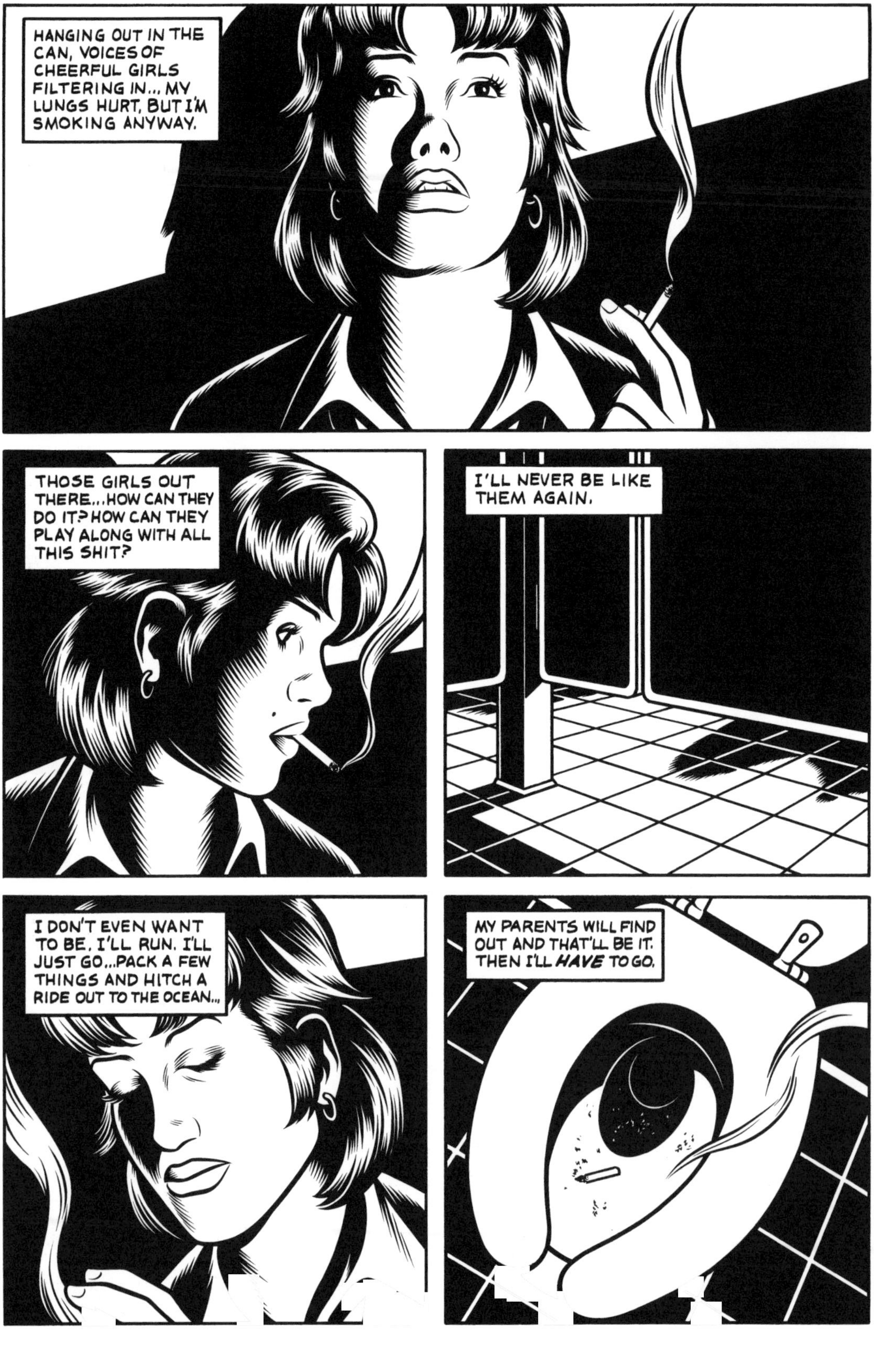
HANGING OUT IN THE CAN, VOICES OF CHEERFUL GIRLS FILTERING IN... MY LUNGS HURT, BUT I'M SMOKING ANYWAY.
THOSE GIRLS OUT THERE... HOW CAN THEY DO IT? HOW CAN THEY PLAY ALONG WITH ALL THIS SHIT?
I'LL NEVER BE LIKE THEM AGAIN.
I DON'T EVEN WANT TO BE. I'LL RUN. I'LL JUST GO... PACK A FEW THINGS AND HITCH A RIDE OUT TO THE OCEAN...
MY PARENTS WILL FIND OUT AND THAT'LL BE IT. THEN I'LL *HAVE* TO GO.

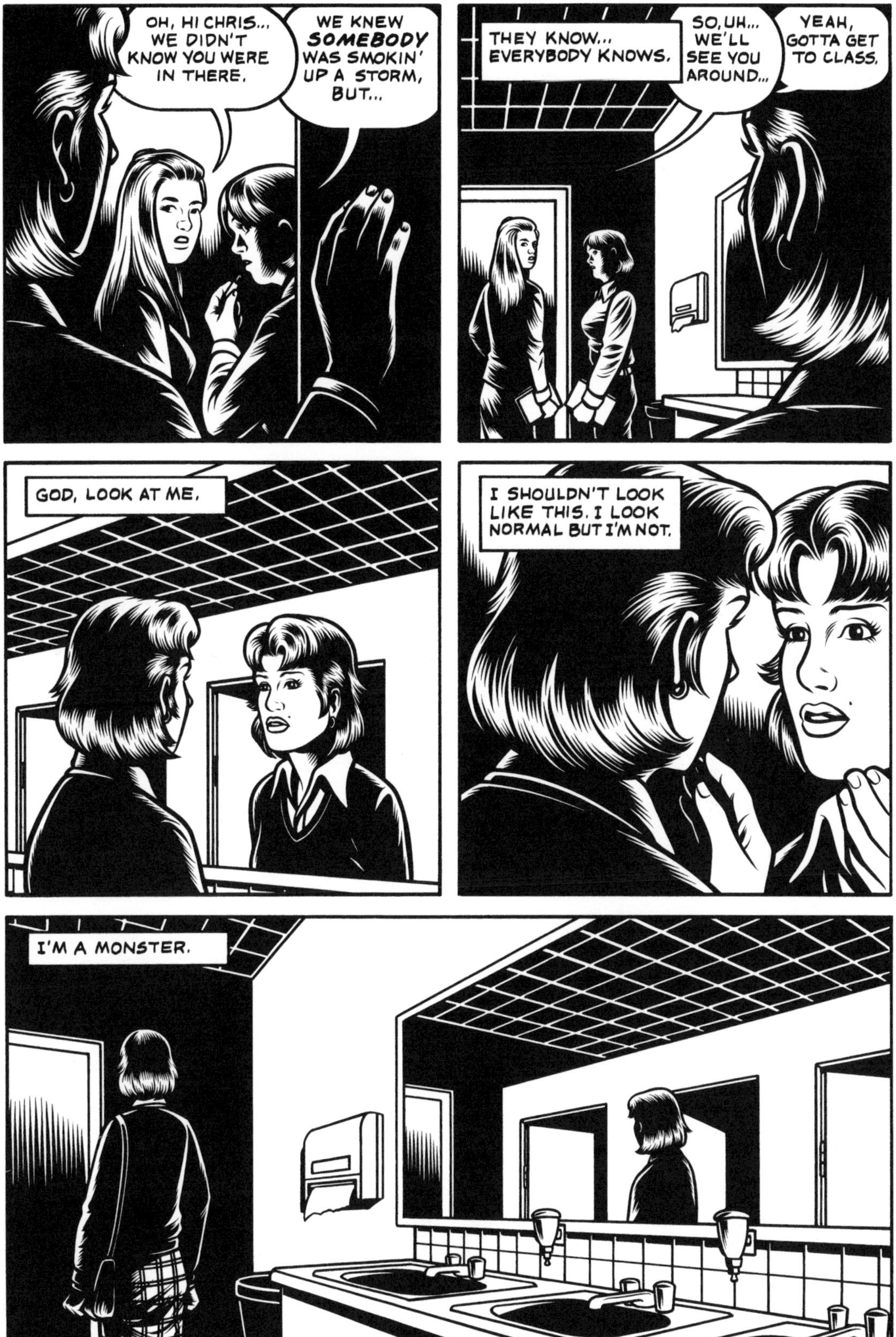
OH, HI CHRIS... WE DIDN'T KNOW YOU WERE IN THERE.
WE KNEW **SOMEBODY** WAS SMOKIN' UP A STORM, BUT...
THEY KNOW... EVERYBODY KNOWS.
SO, UH... WE'LL SEE YOU AROUND...
YEAH, GOTTA GET TO CLASS.
GOD, LOOK AT ME.
I SHOULDN'T LOOK LIKE THIS. I LOOK NORMAL BUT I'M NOT.
I'M A MONSTER.

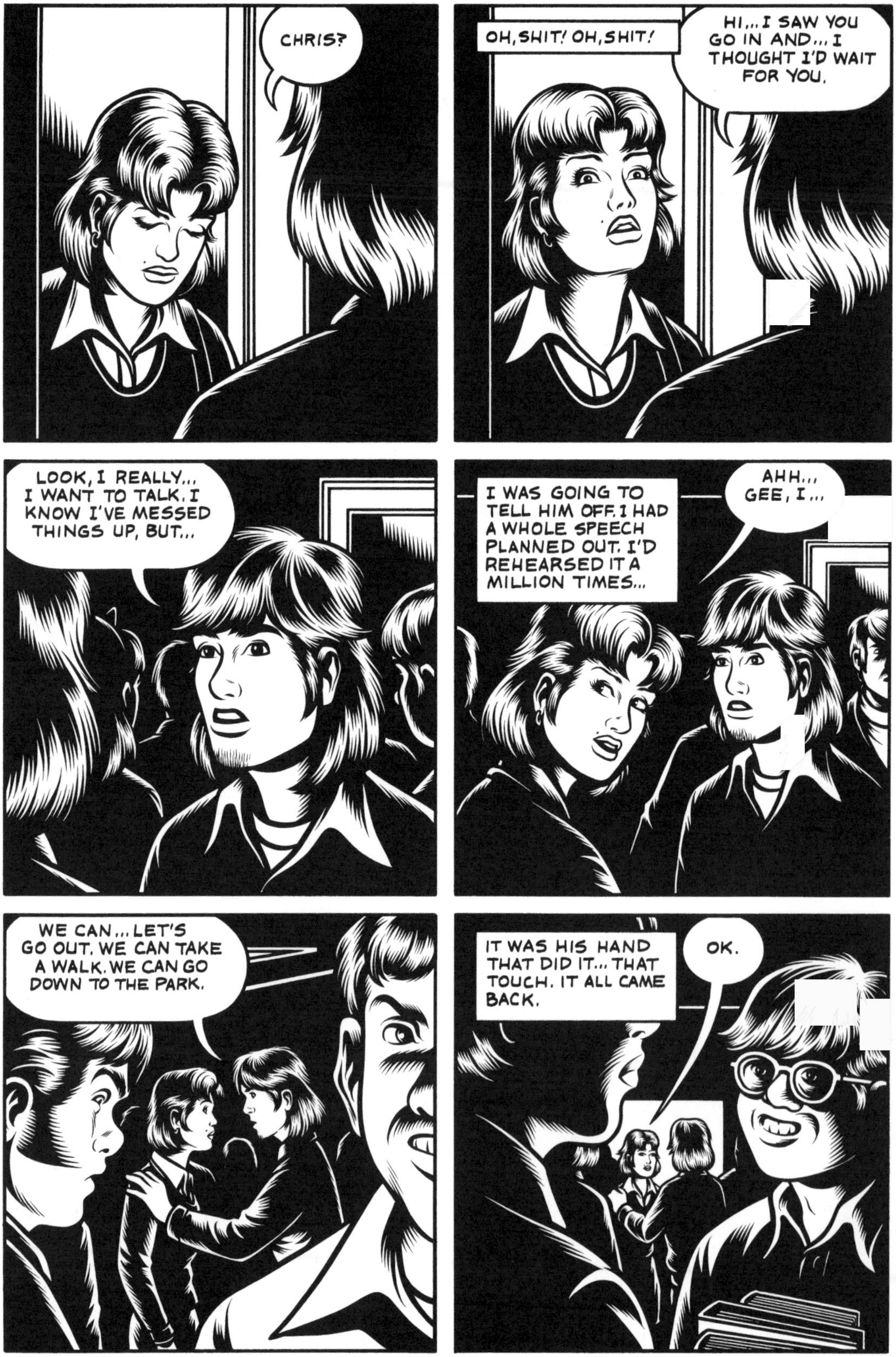
CHRIS?
OH, SHIT! OH, SHIT!
HI... I SAW YOU GO IN AND... I THOUGHT I'D WAIT FOR YOU.
LOOK, I REALLY... I WANT TO TALK. I KNOW I'VE MESSED THINGS UP, BUT...
I WAS GOING TO TELL HIM OFF. I HAD A WHOLE SPEECH PLANNED OUT. I'D REHEARSED IT A MILLION TIMES...
AHH... GEE, I...
WE CAN... LET'S GO OUT. WE CAN TAKE A WALK. WE CAN GO DOWN TO THE PARK.
IT WAS HIS HAND THAT DID IT... THAT TOUCH. IT ALL CAME BACK.
OK.

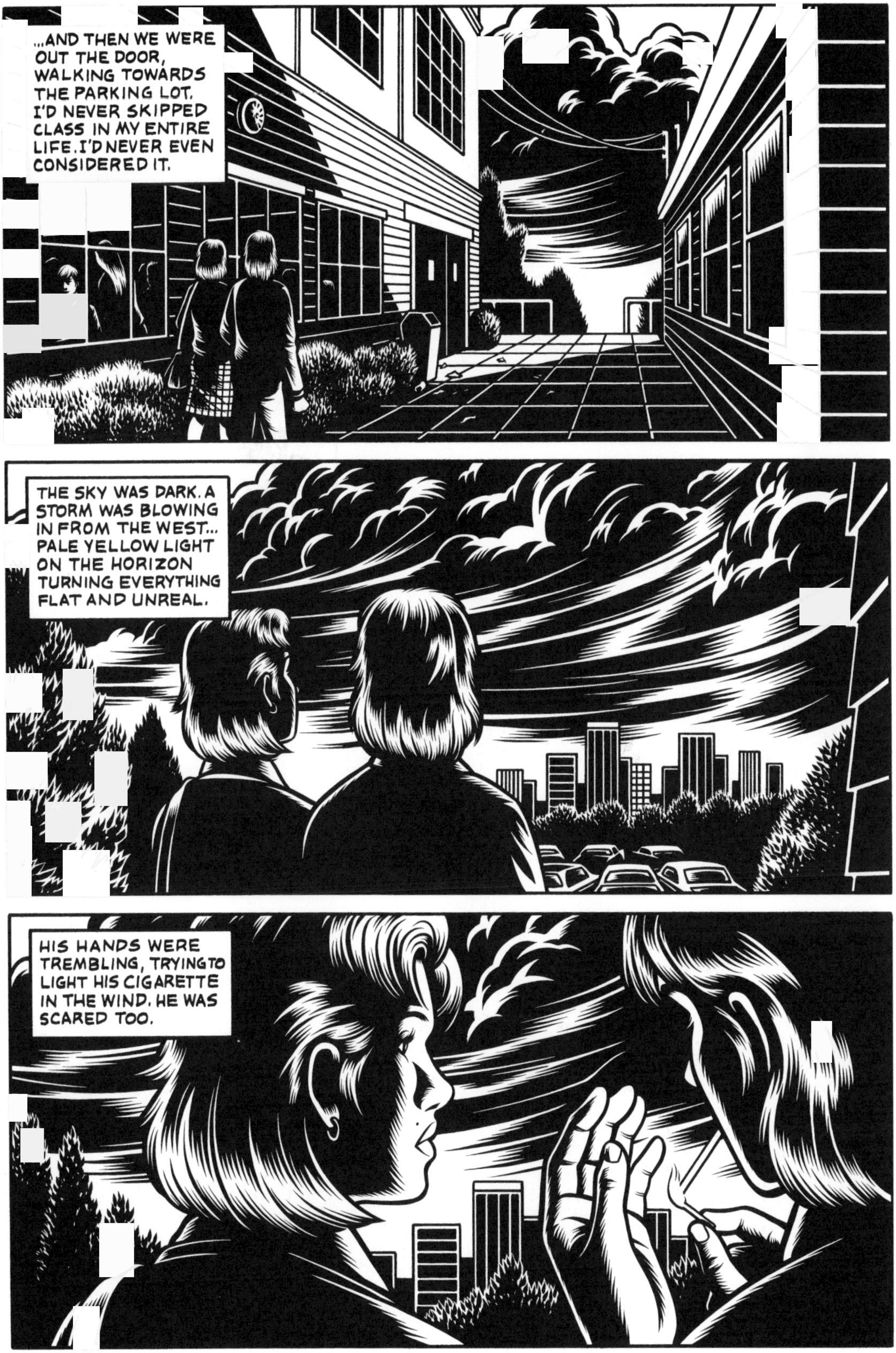
...AND THEN WE WERE OUT THE DOOR, WALKING TOWARDS THE PARKING LOT. I'D NEVER SKIPPED CLASS IN MY ENTIRE LIFE. I'D NEVER EVEN CONSIDERED IT.
THE SKY WAS DARK. A STORM WAS BLOWING IN FROM THE WEST... PALE YELLOW LIGHT ON THE HORIZON TURNING EVERYTHING FLAT AND UNREAL.
HIS HANDS WERE TREMBLING, TRYING TO LIGHT HIS CIGARETTE IN THE WIND. HE WAS SCARED TOO.

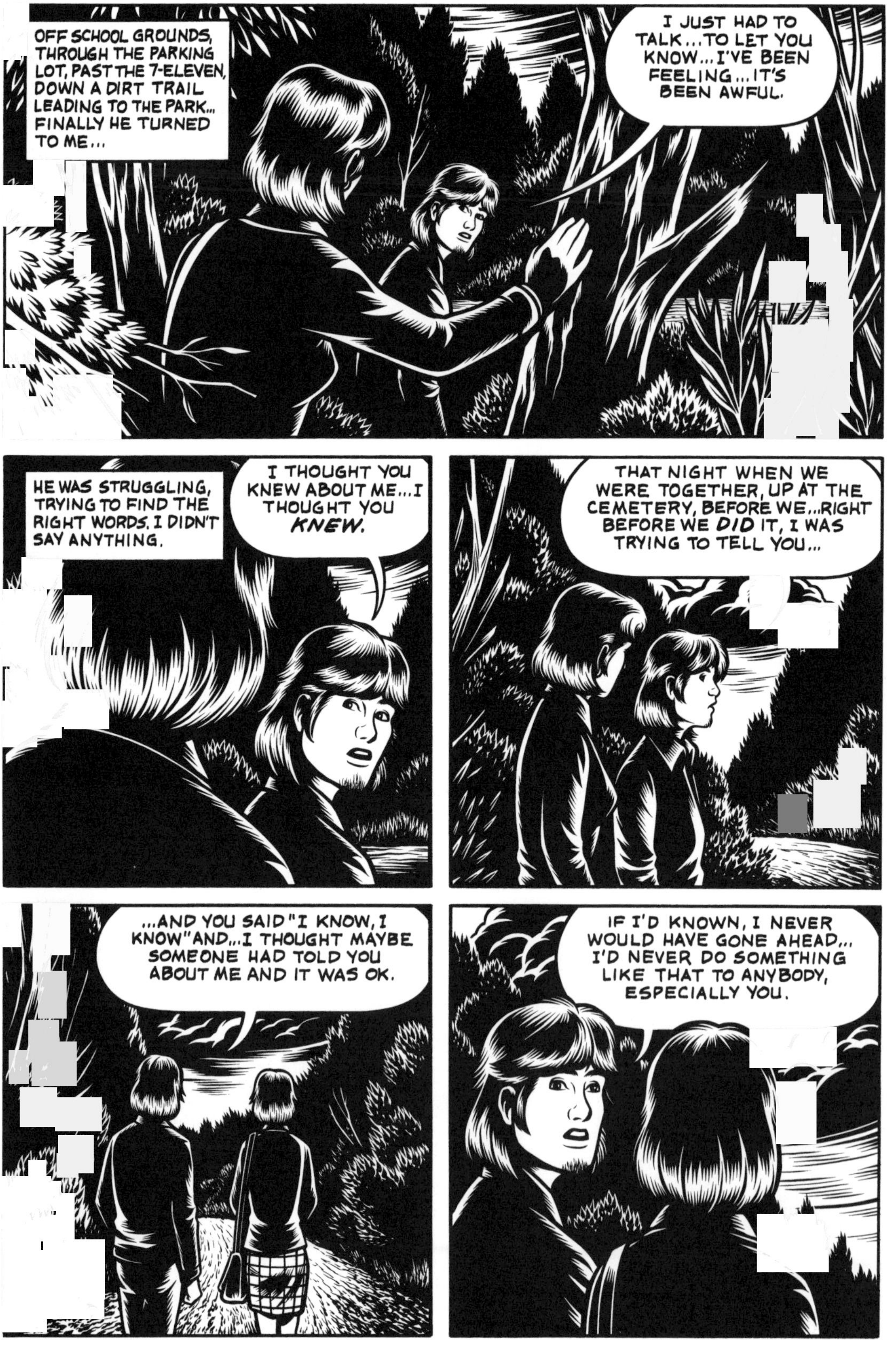
OFF SCHOOL GROUNDS, THROUGH THE PARKING LOT, PAST THE 7-ELEVEN, DOWN A DIRT TRAIL LEADING TO THE PARK... FINALLY HE TURNED TO ME...
I JUST HAD TO TALK... TO LET YOU KNOW... I'VE BEEN FEELING... IT'S BEEN AWFUL.
HE WAS STRUGGLING, TRYING TO FIND THE RIGHT WORDS. I DIDN'T SAY ANYTHING.
I THOUGHT YOU KNEW ABOUT ME... I THOUGHT YOU *KNEW*.
THAT NIGHT WHEN WE WERE TOGETHER, UP AT THE CEMETERY, BEFORE WE... RIGHT BEFORE WE *DID* IT, I WAS TRYING TO TELL YOU...
...AND YOU SAID "I KNOW, I KNOW" AND... I THOUGHT MAYBE SOMEONE HAD TOLD YOU ABOUT ME AND IT WAS OK.
IF I'D KNOWN, I NEVER WOULD HAVE GONE AHEAD... I'D NEVER DO SOMETHING LIKE THAT TO ANYBODY, ESPECIALLY YOU.

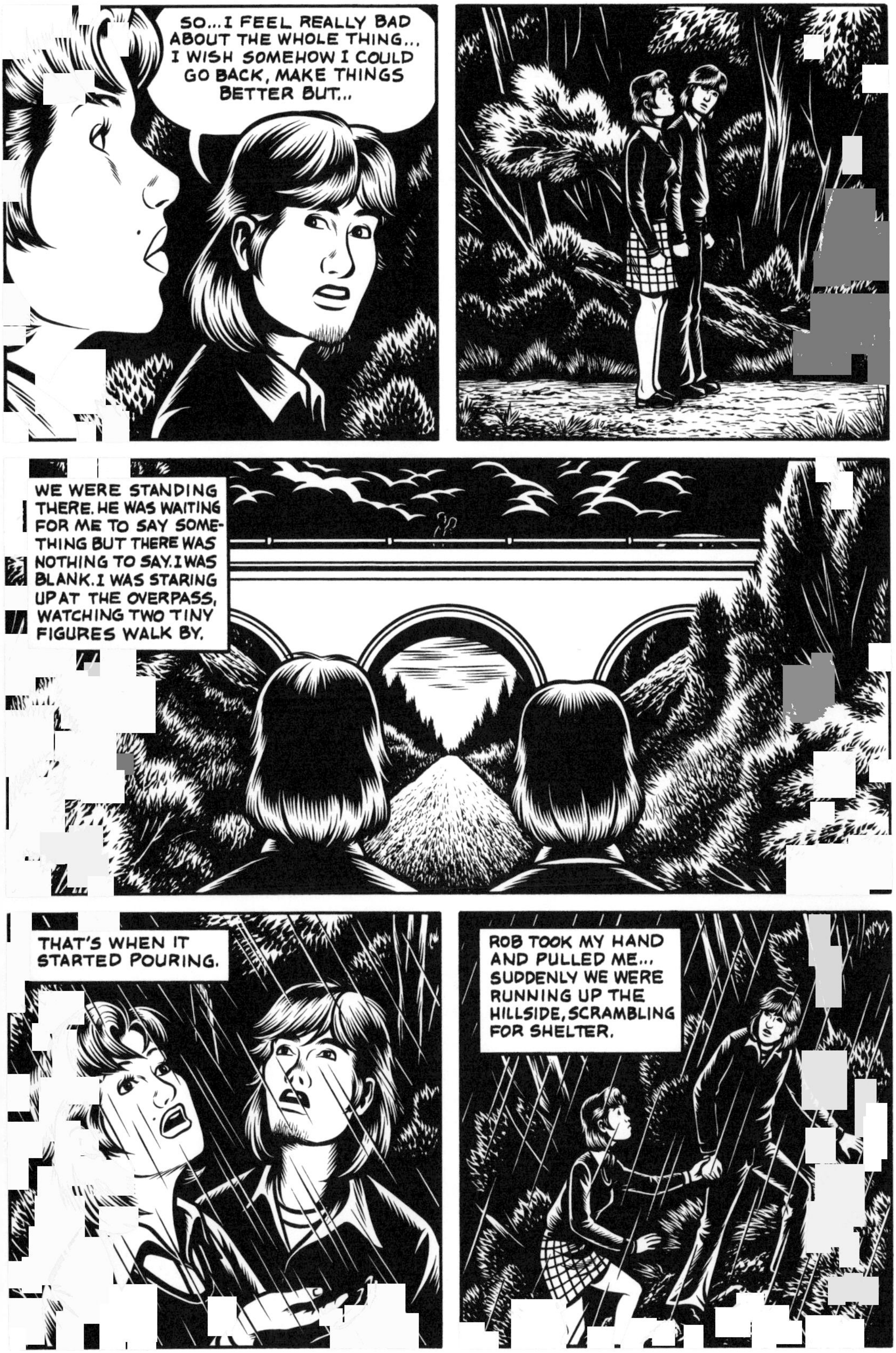

SO...I FEEL REALLY BAD ABOUT THE WHOLE THING... I WISH SOMEHOW I COULD GO BACK, MAKE THINGS BETTER BUT...
WE WERE STANDING THERE. HE WAS WAITING FOR ME TO SAY SOMETHING BUT THERE WAS NOTHING TO SAY. I WAS BLANK. I WAS STARING UP AT THE OVERPASS, WATCHING TWO TINY FIGURES WALK BY.
THAT'S WHEN IT STARTED POURING.
ROB TOOK MY HAND AND PULLED ME... SUDDENLY WE WERE RUNNING UP THE HILLSIDE, SCRAMBLING FOR SHELTER.

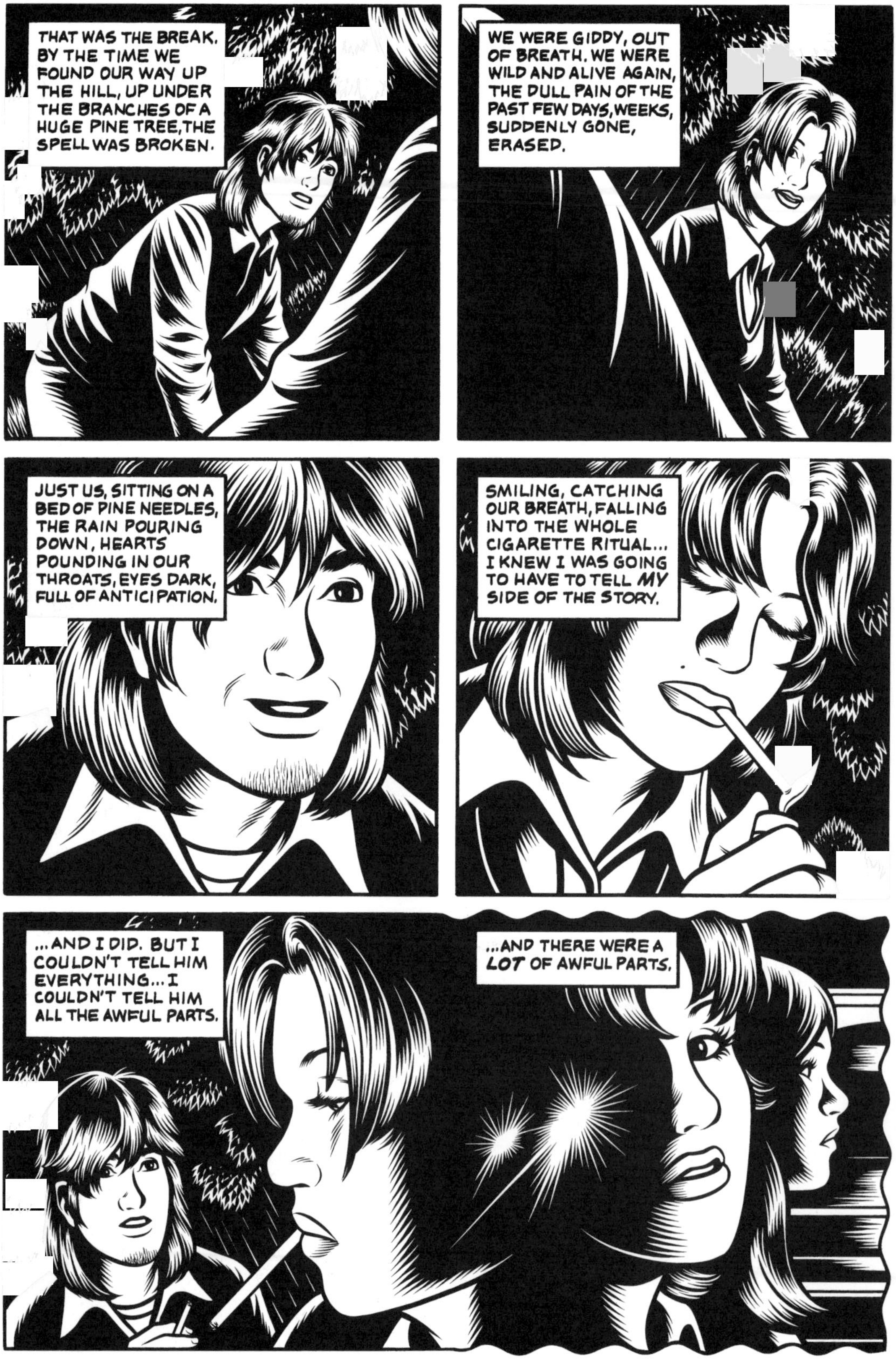
THAT WAS THE BREAK. BY THE TIME WE FOUND OUR WAY UP THE HILL, UP UNDER THE BRANCHES OF A HUGE PINE TREE, THE SPELL WAS BROKEN.
WE WERE GIDDY, OUT OF BREATH. WE WERE WILD AND ALIVE AGAIN, THE DULL PAIN OF THE PAST FEW DAYS, WEEKS, SUDDENLY GONE, ERASED.
JUST US, SITTING ON A BED OF PINE NEEDLES, THE RAIN POURING DOWN, HEARTS POUNDING IN OUR THROATS, EYES DARK, FULL OF ANTICIPATION.
SMILING, CATCHING OUR BREATH, FALLING INTO THE WHOLE CIGARETTE RITUAL... I KNEW I WAS GOING TO HAVE TO TELL *MY* SIDE OF THE STORY.
...AND I DID. BUT I COULDN'T TELL HIM EVERYTHING... I COULDN'T TELL HIM ALL THE AWFUL PARTS.
...AND THERE WERE A *LOT* OF AWFUL PARTS.

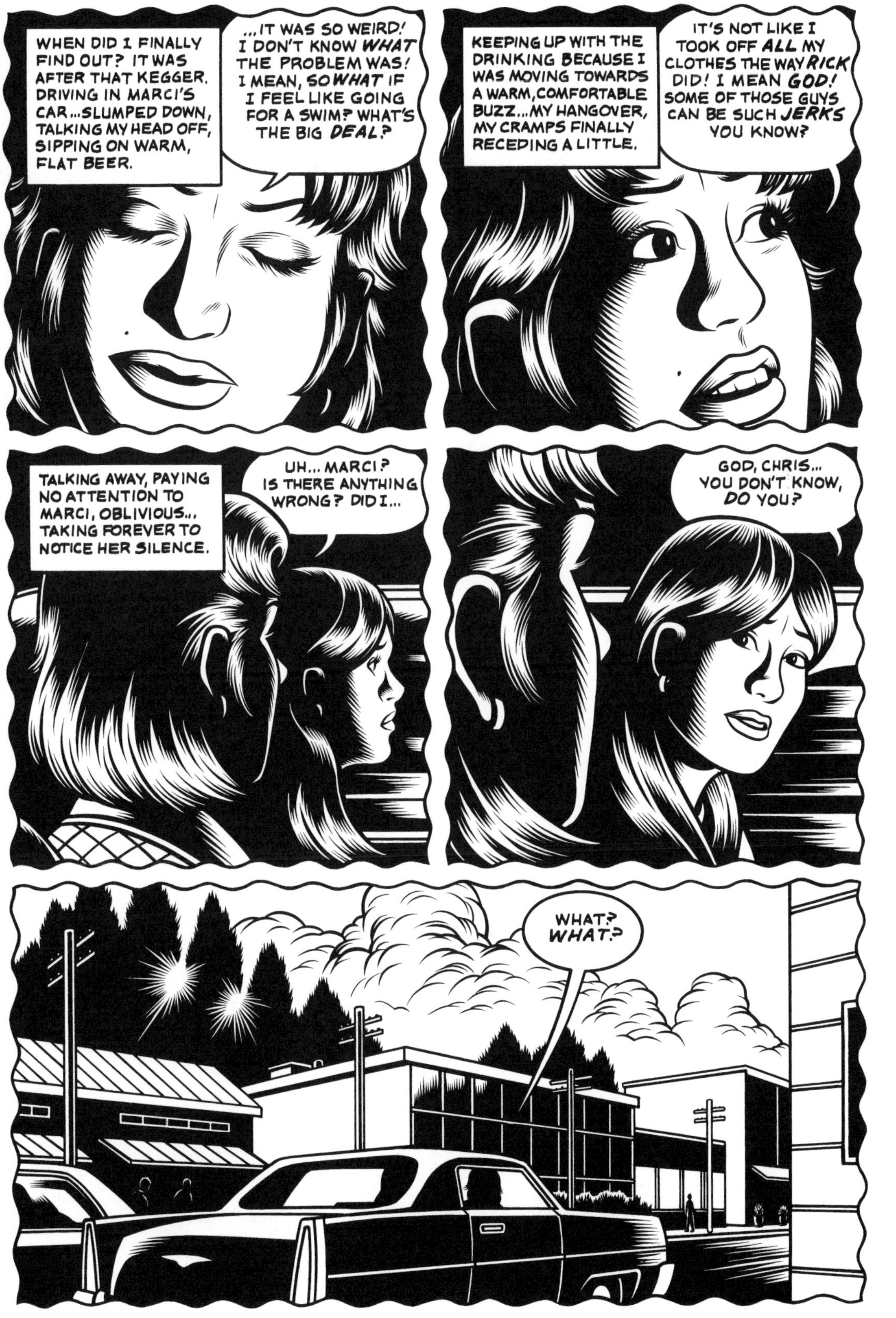
WHEN DID I FINALLY FIND OUT? IT WAS AFTER THAT KEGGER. DRIVING IN MARCI'S CAR...SLUMPED DOWN, TALKING MY HEAD OFF, SIPPING ON WARM, FLAT BEER.
...IT WAS SO WEIRD! I DON'T KNOW WHAT THE PROBLEM WAS! I MEAN, SO WHAT IF I FEEL LIKE GOING FOR A SWIM? WHAT'S THE BIG DEAL?
KEEPING UP WITH THE DRINKING BECAUSE I WAS MOVING TOWARDS A WARM, COMFORTABLE BUZZ...MY HANGOVER, MY CRAMPS FINALLY RECEDING A LITTLE.
IT'S NOT LIKE I TOOK OFF ALL MY CLOTHES THE WAY RICK DID! I MEAN GOD! SOME OF THOSE GUYS CAN BE SUCH JERKS YOU KNOW?
TALKING AWAY, PAYING NO ATTENTION TO MARCI, OBLIVIOUS... TAKING FOREVER TO NOTICE HER SILENCE.
UH... MARCI? IS THERE ANYTHING WRONG? DID I...
GOD, CHRIS... YOU DON'T KNOW, DO YOU?
WHAT? WHAT?

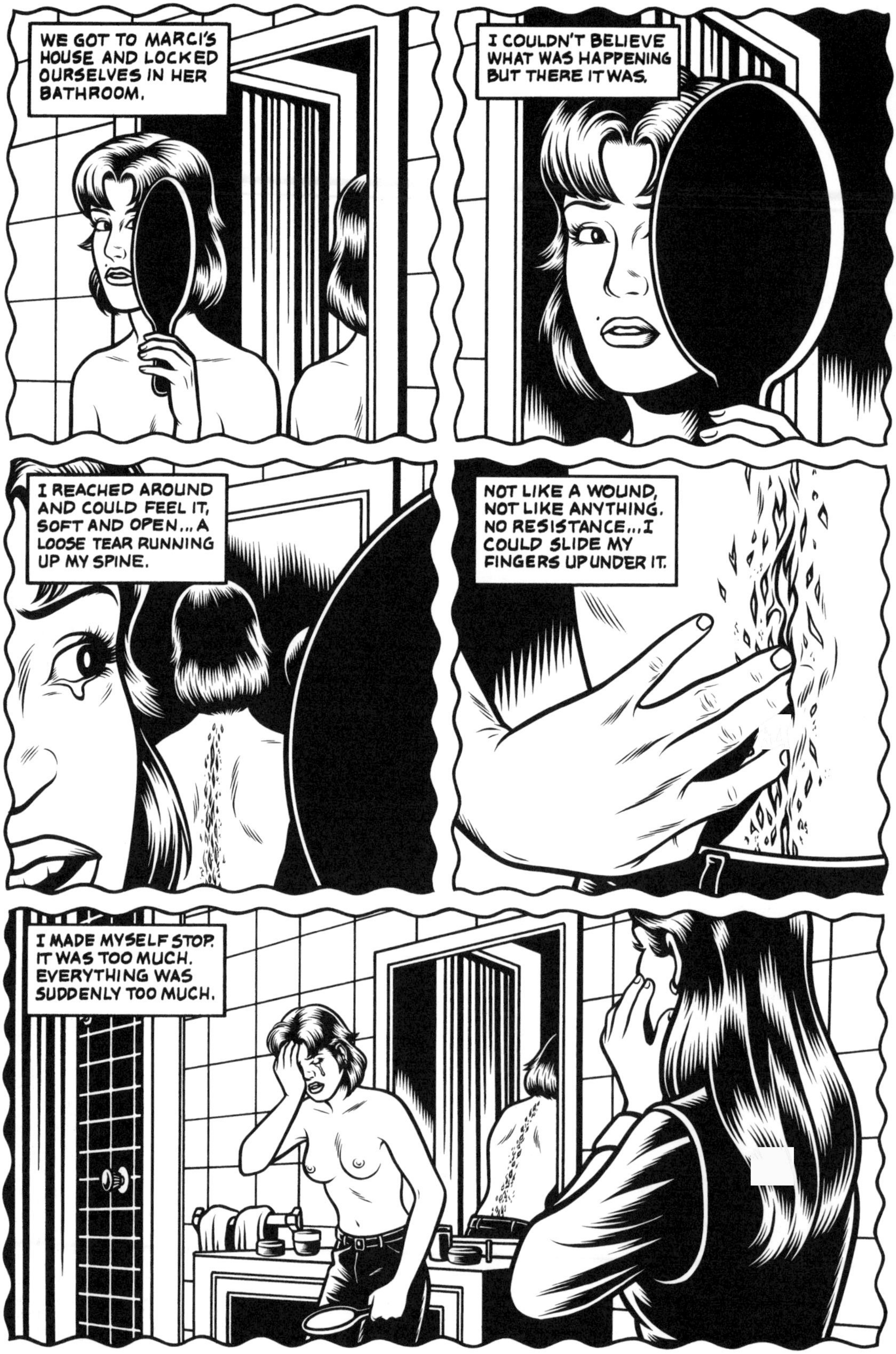
WE GOT TO MARCI'S HOUSE AND LOCKED OURSELVES IN HER BATHROOM.
I COULDN'T BELIEVE WHAT WAS HAPPENING BUT THERE IT WAS.
I REACHED AROUND AND COULD FEEL IT, SOFT AND OPEN... A LOOSE TEAR RUNNING UP MY SPINE.
NOT LIKE A WOUND, NOT LIKE ANYTHING. NO RESISTANCE... I COULD SLIDE MY FINGERS UP UNDER IT.
I MADE MYSELF STOP. IT WAS TOO MUCH. EVERYTHING WAS SUDDENLY TOO MUCH.

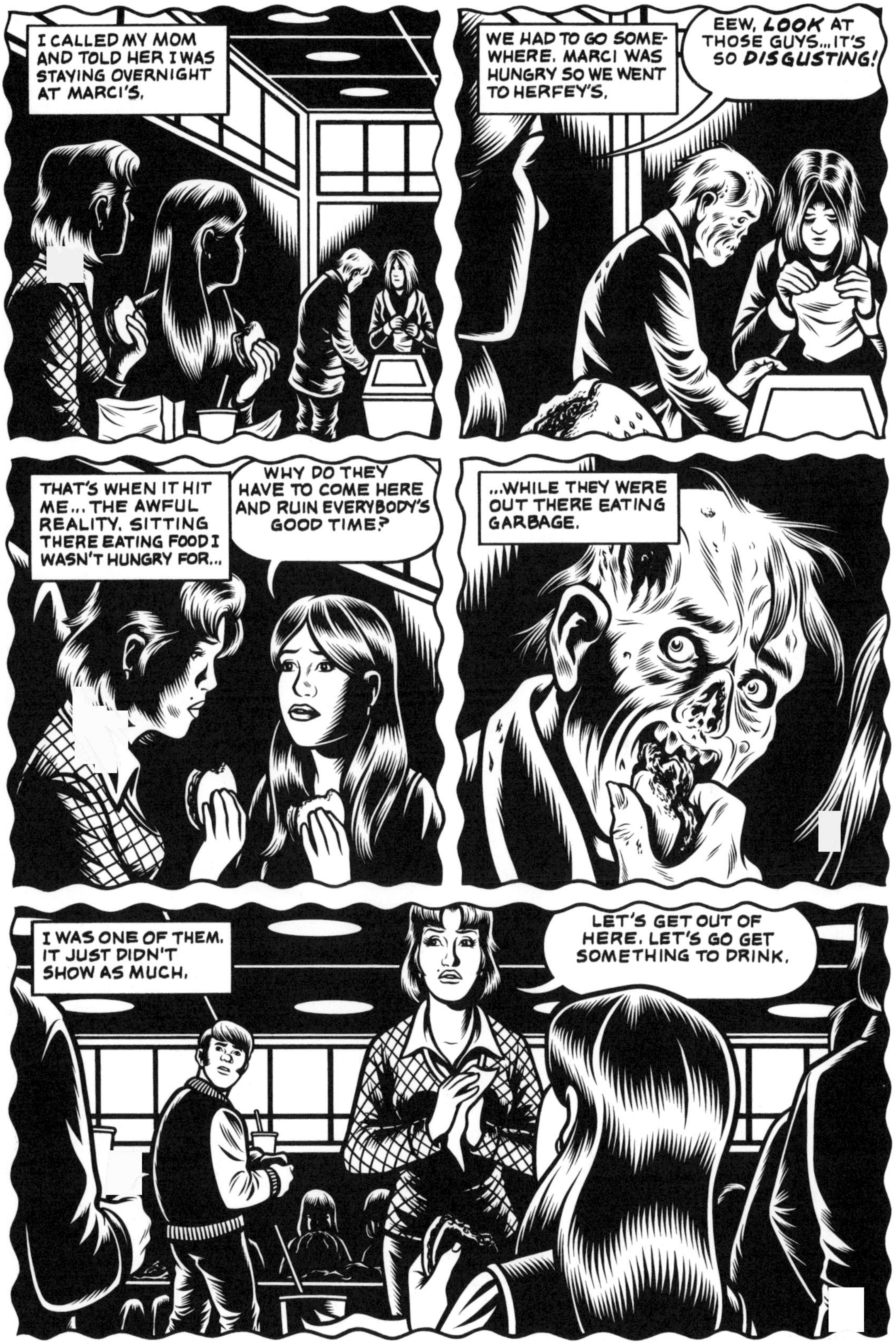
I CALLED MY MOM AND TOLD HER I WAS STAYING OVERNIGHT AT MARCI'S.
WE HAD TO GO SOMEWHERE. MARCI WAS HUNGRY SO WE WENT TO HERFEY'S.
EEW, LOOK AT THOSE GUYS...IT'S SO DISGUSTING!
THAT'S WHEN IT HIT ME... THE AWFUL REALITY. SITTING THERE EATING FOOD I WASN'T HUNGRY FOR...
WHY DO THEY HAVE TO COME HERE AND RUIN EVERYBODY'S GOOD TIME?
...WHILE THEY WERE OUT THERE EATING GARBAGE.
I WAS ONE OF THEM. IT JUST DIDN'T SHOW AS MUCH.
LET'S GET OUT OF HERE. LET'S GO GET SOMETHING TO DRINK.

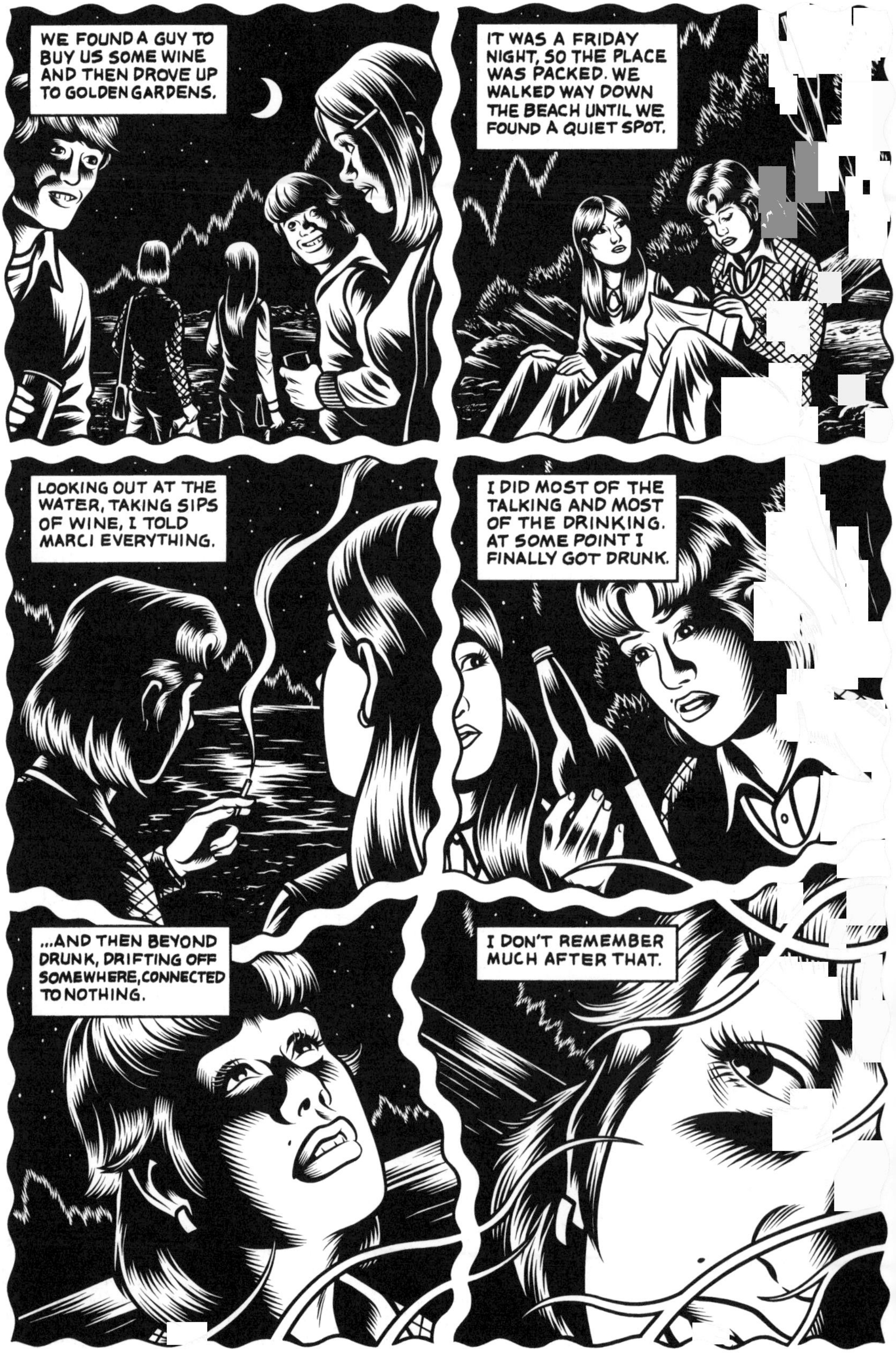
WE FOUND A GUY TO BUY US SOME WINE AND THEN DROVE UP TO GOLDEN GARDENS.
IT WAS A FRIDAY NIGHT, SO THE PLACE WAS PACKED. WE WALKED WAY DOWN THE BEACH UNTIL WE FOUND A QUIET SPOT.
LOOKING OUT AT THE WATER, TAKING SIPS OF WINE, I TOLD MARCI EVERYTHING.
I DID MOST OF THE TALKING AND MOST OF THE DRINKING. AT SOME POINT I FINALLY GOT DRUNK.
...AND THEN BEYOND DRUNK, DRIFTING OFF SOMEWHERE, CONNECTED TO NOTHING.
I DON'T REMEMBER MUCH AFTER THAT.

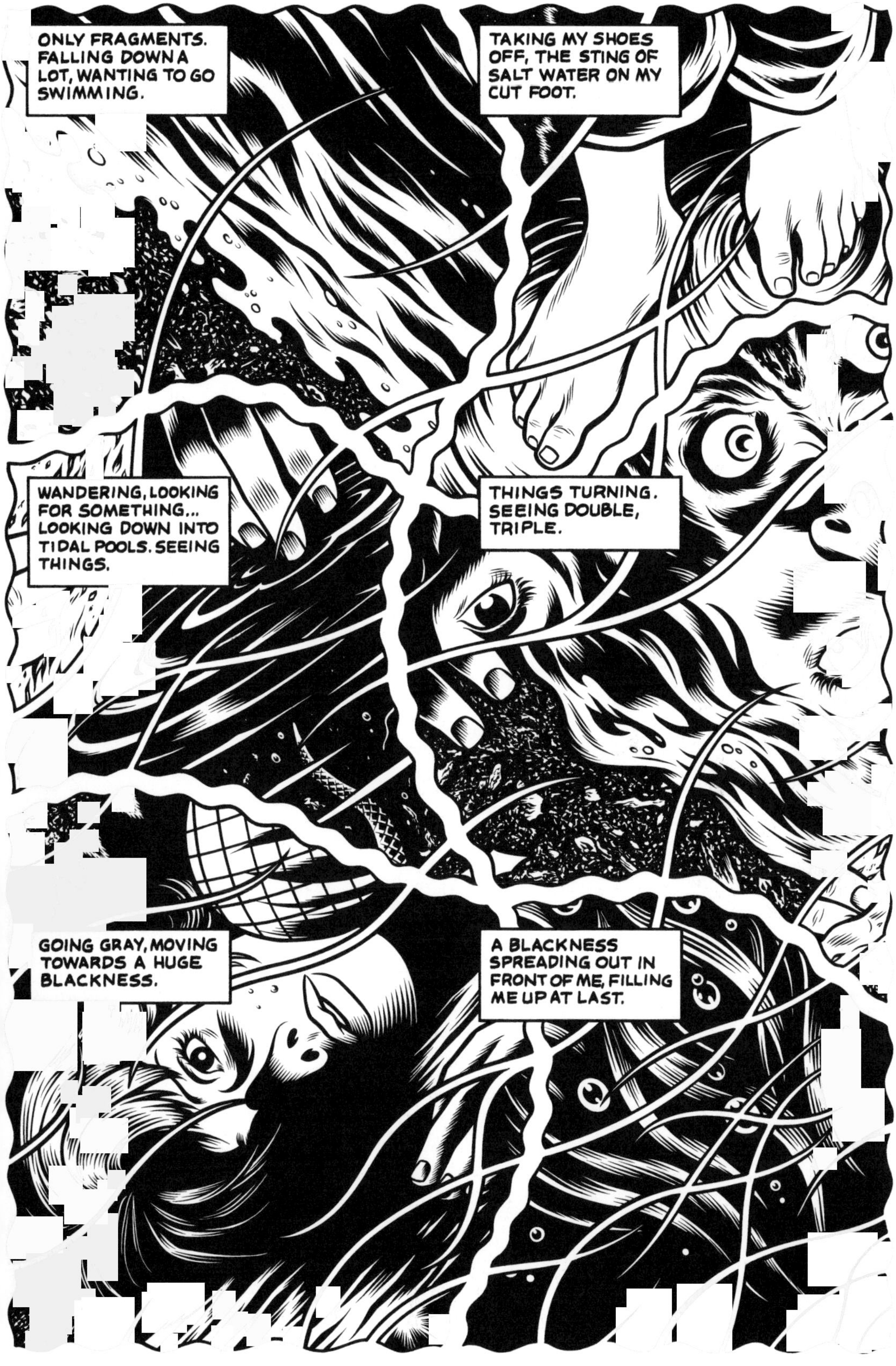
ONLY FRAGMENTS. FALLING DOWN A LOT, WANTING TO GO SWIMMING.
TAKING MY SHOES OFF, THE STING OF SALT WATER ON MY CUT FOOT.
WANDERING, LOOKING FOR SOMETHING... LOOKING DOWN INTO TIDAL POOLS. SEEING THINGS.
THINGS TURNING. SEEING DOUBLE, TRIPLE.
GOING GRAY, MOVING TOWARDS A HUGE BLACKNESS.
A BLACKNESS SPREADING OUT IN FRONT OF ME, FILLING ME UP AT LAST.

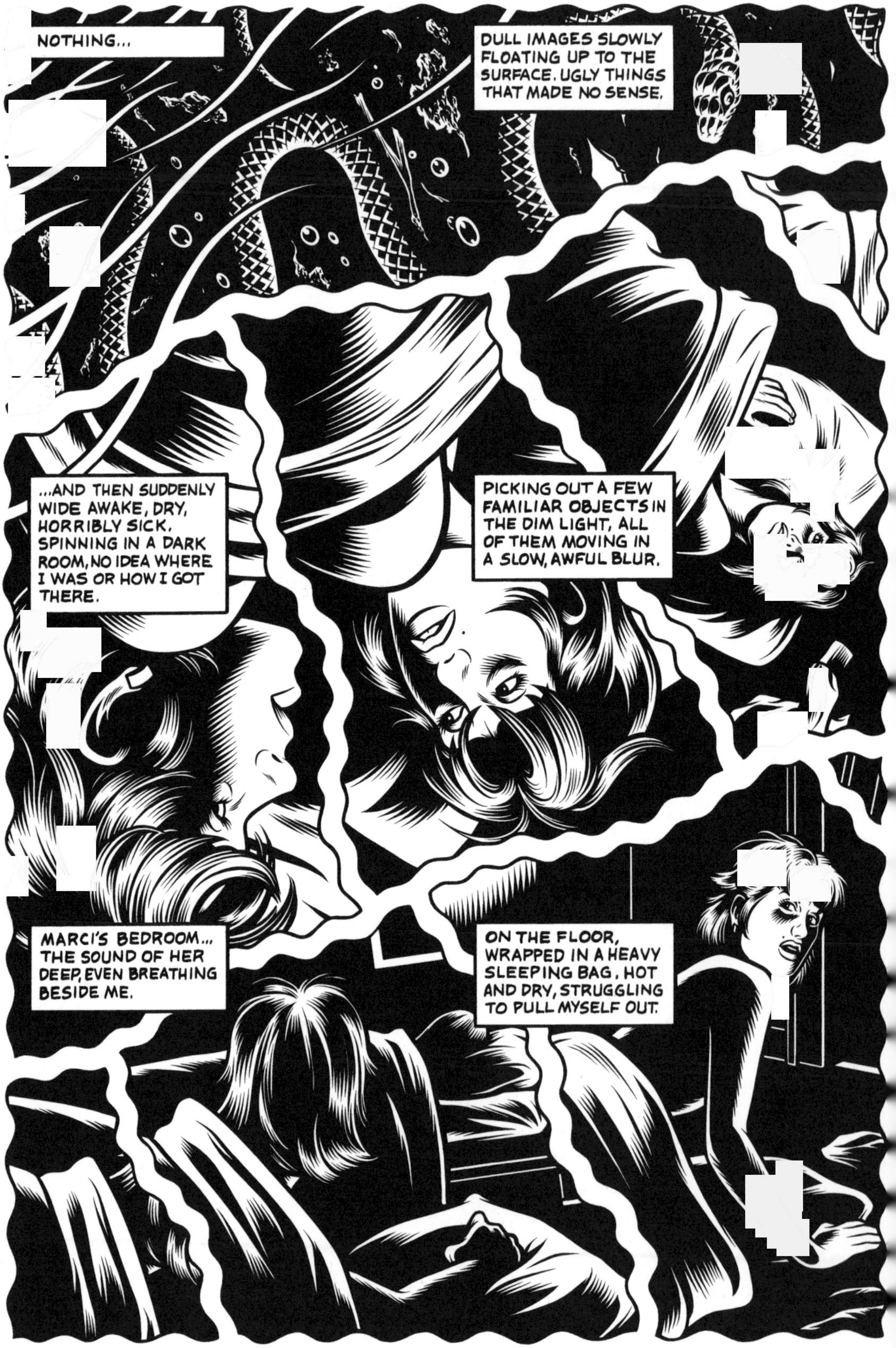
NOTHING...
DULL IMAGES SLOWLY FLOATING UP TO THE SURFACE. UGLY THINGS THAT MADE NO SENSE.
...AND THEN SUDDENLY WIDE AWAKE, DRY, HORRIBLY SICK. SPINNING IN A DARK ROOM, NO IDEA WHERE I WAS OR HOW I GOT THERE.
PICKING OUT A FEW FAMILIAR OBJECTS IN THE DIM LIGHT, ALL OF THEM MOVING IN A SLOW, AWFUL BLUR.
MARCI'S BEDROOM... THE SOUND OF HER DEEP, EVEN BREATHING BESIDE ME.
ON THE FLOOR, WRAPPED IN A HEAVY SLEEPING BAG, HOT AND DRY, STRUGGLING TO PULL MYSELF OUT.

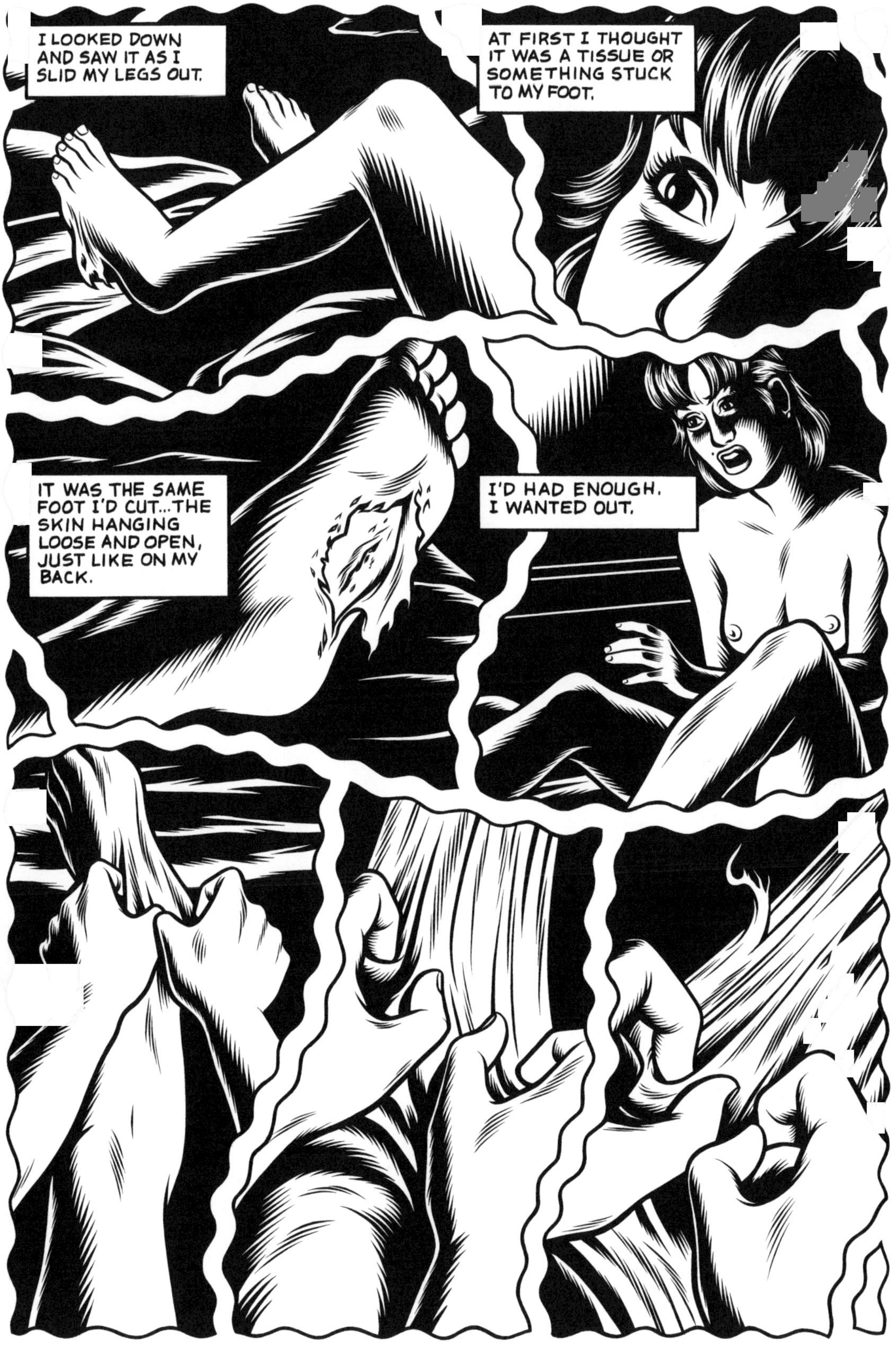
I LOOKED DOWN AND SAW IT AS I SLID MY LEGS OUT.
AT FIRST I THOUGHT IT WAS A TISSUE OR SOMETHING STUCK TO MY FOOT.
IT WAS THE SAME FOOT I'D CUT... THE SKIN HANGING LOOSE AND OPEN, JUST LIKE ON MY BACK.
I'D HAD ENOUGH. I WANTED OUT.

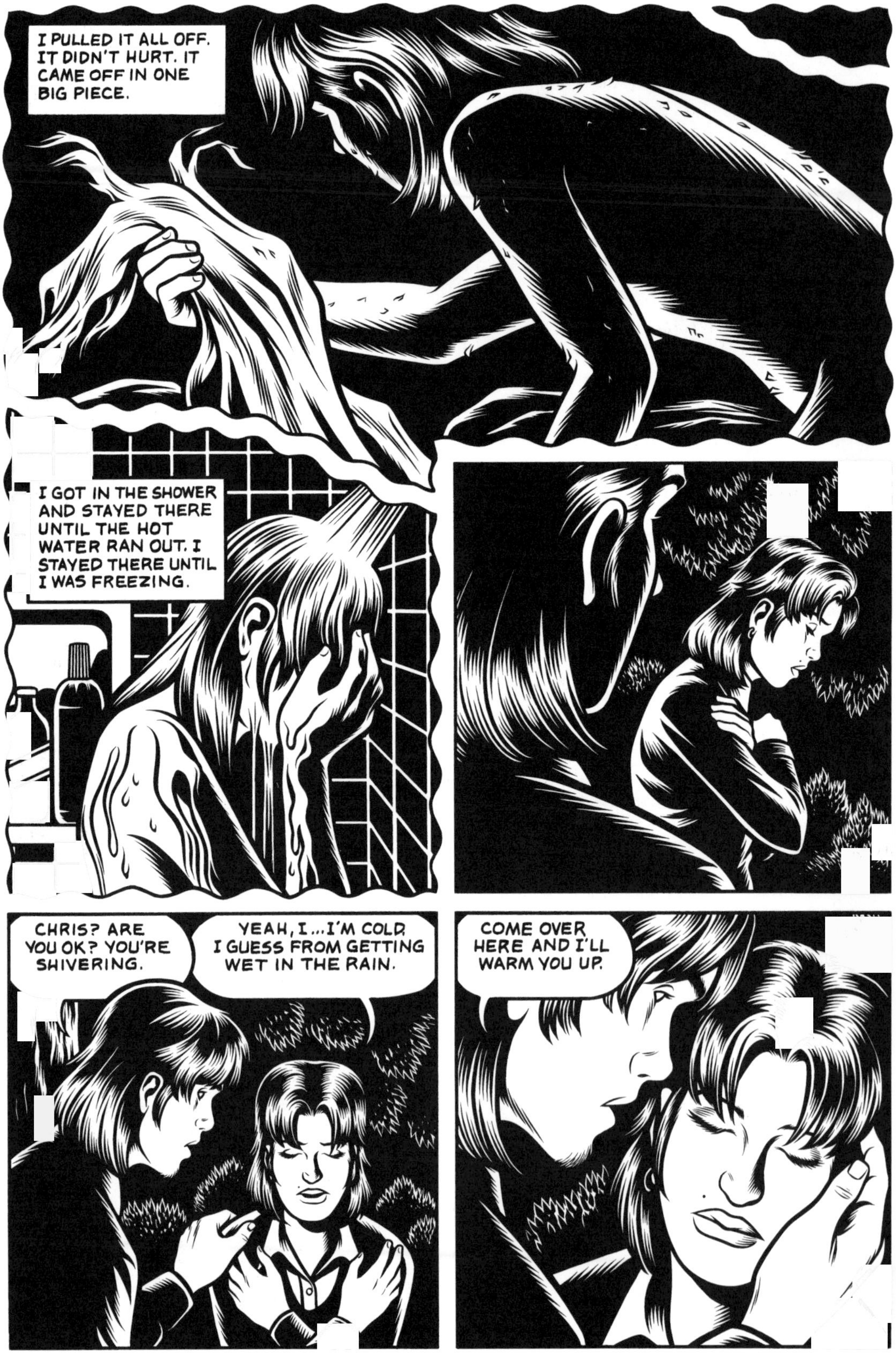
I PULLED IT ALL OFF. IT DIDN'T HURT. IT CAME OFF IN ONE BIG PIECE.
I GOT IN THE SHOWER AND STAYED THERE UNTIL THE HOT WATER RAN OUT. I STAYED THERE UNTIL I WAS FREEZING.
CHRIS? ARE YOU OK? YOU'RE SHIVERING.
YEAH, I...I'M COLD. I GUESS FROM GETTING WET IN THE RAIN.
COME OVER HERE AND I'LL WARM YOU UP.

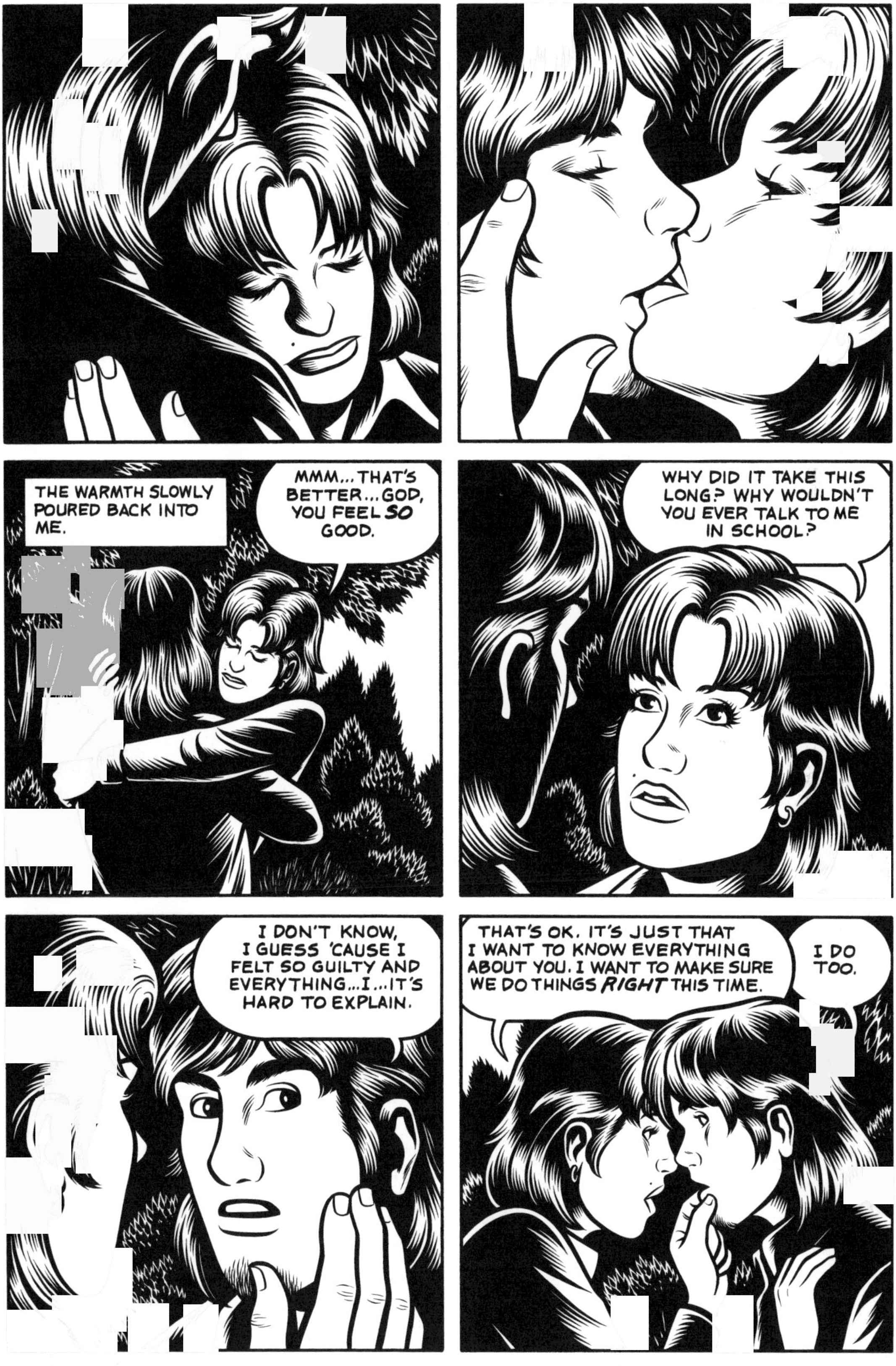
THE WARMTH SLOWLY POURED BACK INTO ME.
MMM... THAT'S BETTER... GOD, YOU FEEL SO GOOD.
WHY DID IT TAKE THIS LONG? WHY WOULDN'T YOU EVER TALK TO ME IN SCHOOL?
I DON'T KNOW, I GUESS 'CAUSE I FELT SO GUILTY AND EVERYTHING... I... IT'S HARD TO EXPLAIN.
THAT'S OK. IT'S JUST THAT I WANT TO KNOW EVERYTHING ABOUT YOU. I WANT TO MAKE SURE WE DO THINGS RIGHT THIS TIME.
I DO TOO.

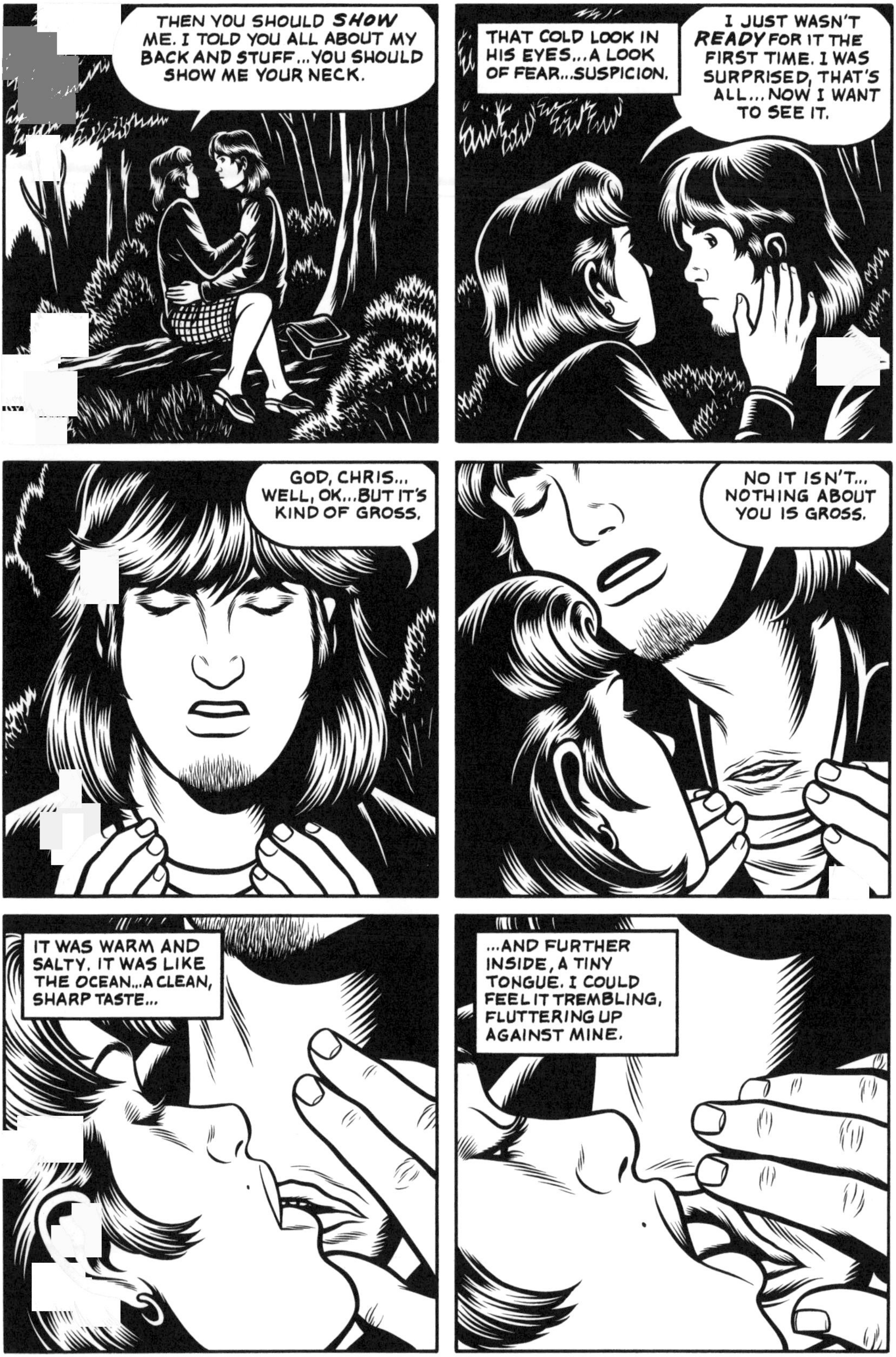
THEN YOU SHOULD SHOW ME. I TOLD YOU ALL ABOUT MY BACK AND STUFF... YOU SHOULD SHOW ME YOUR NECK.
THAT COLD LOOK IN HIS EYES... A LOOK OF FEAR... SUSPICION.
I JUST WASN'T READY FOR IT THE FIRST TIME. I WAS SURPRISED, THAT'S ALL... NOW I WANT TO SEE IT.
GOD, CHRIS... WELL, OK... BUT IT'S KIND OF GROSS.
NO IT ISN'T... NOTHING ABOUT YOU IS GROSS.
IT WAS WARM AND SALTY. IT WAS LIKE THE OCEAN... A CLEAN, SHARP TASTE...
...AND FURTHER INSIDE, A TINY TONGUE. I COULD FEEL IT TREMBLING, FLUTTERING UP AGAINST MINE.

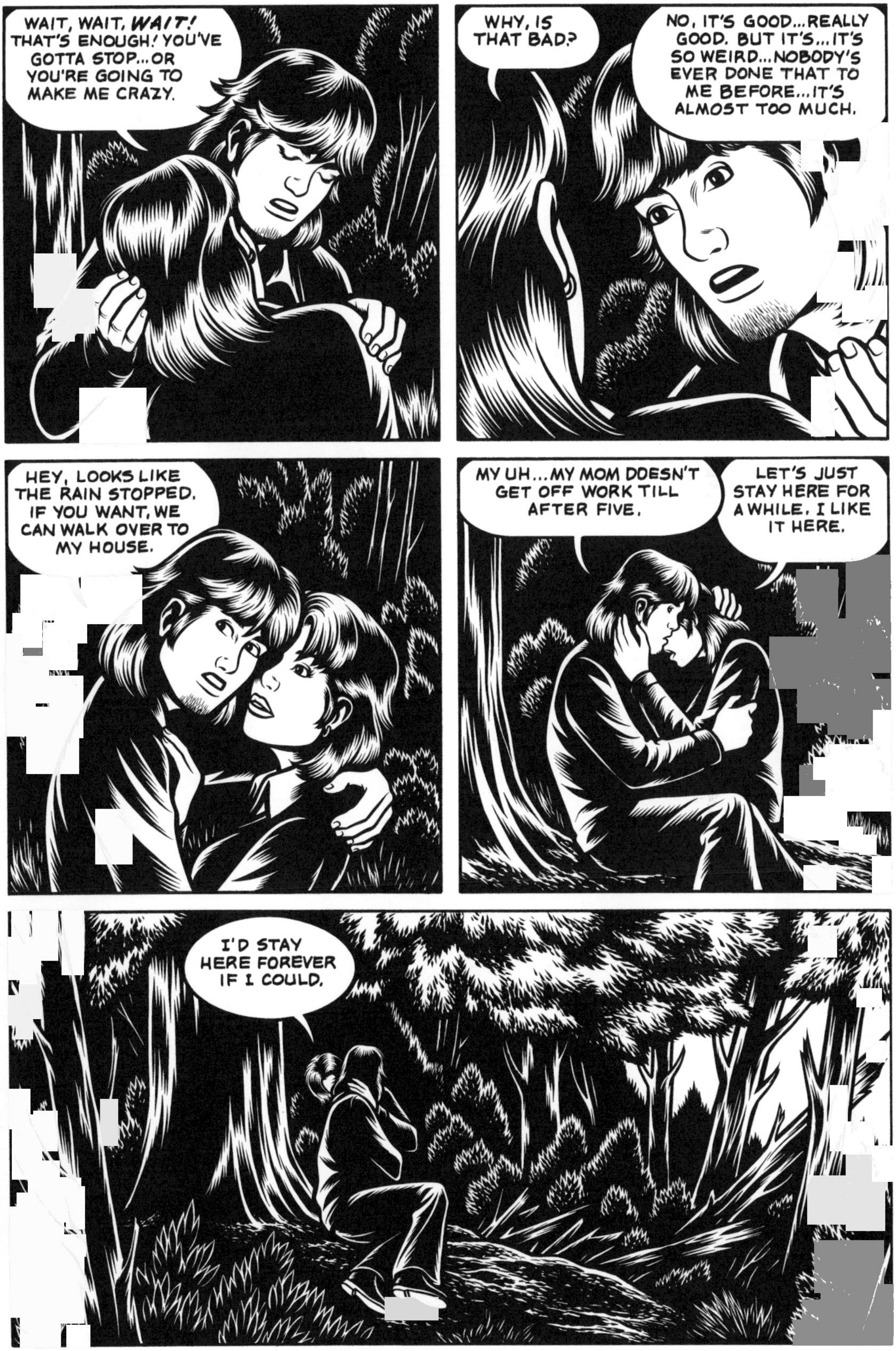
WAIT, WAIT, WAIT! THAT'S ENOUGH! YOU'VE GOTTA STOP...OR YOU'RE GOING TO MAKE ME CRAZY.
WHY, IS THAT BAD?
NO, IT'S GOOD...REALLY GOOD. BUT IT'S...IT'S SO WEIRD...NOBODY'S EVER DONE THAT TO ME BEFORE...IT'S ALMOST TOO MUCH.
HEY, LOOKS LIKE THE RAIN STOPPED. IF YOU WANT, WE CAN WALK OVER TO MY HOUSE.
MY UH...MY MOM DOESN'T GET OFF WORK TILL AFTER FIVE.
LET'S JUST STAY HERE FOR A WHILE. I LIKE IT HERE.
I'D STAY HERE FOREVER IF I COULD.

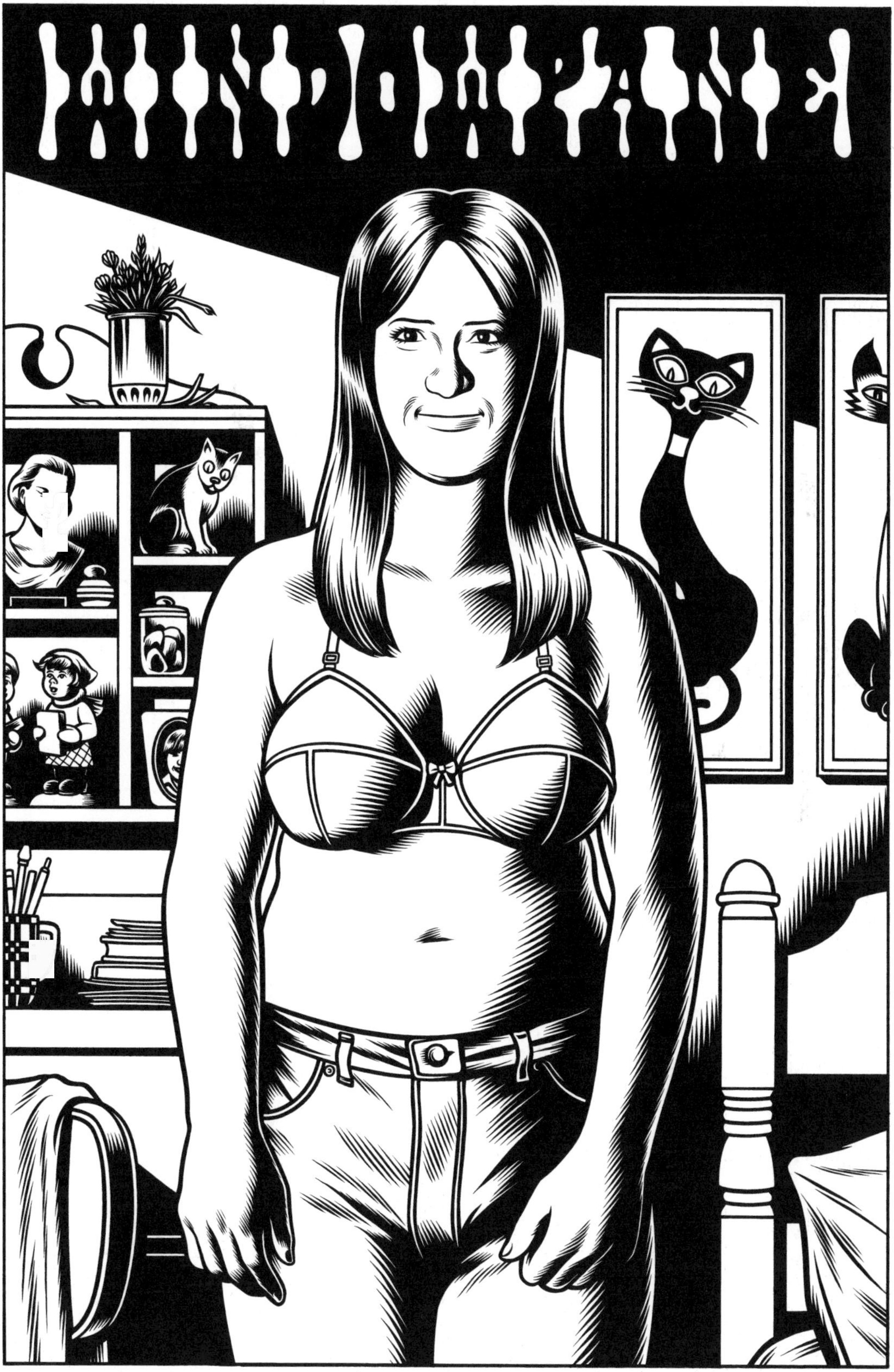

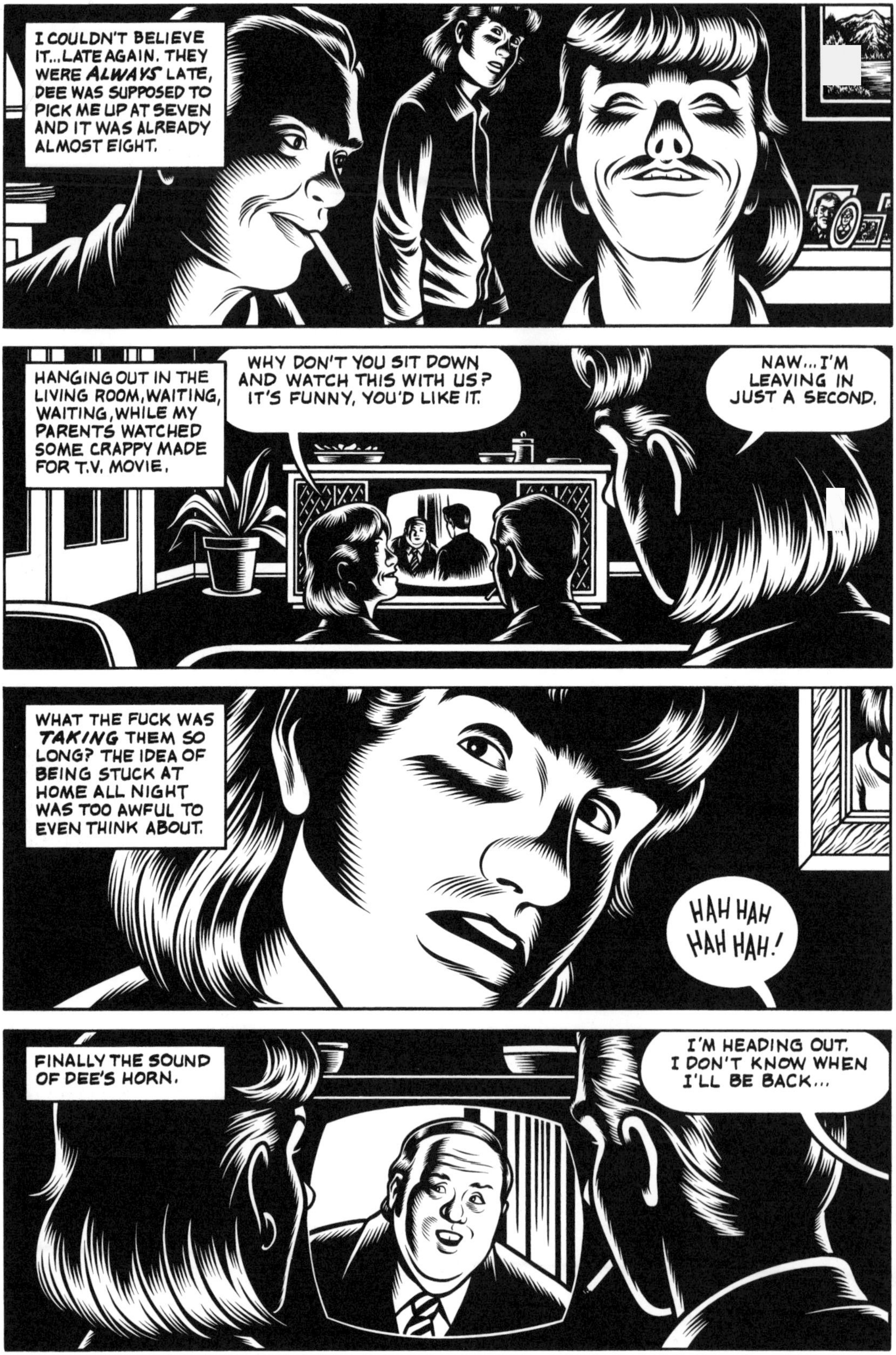

I COULDN'T BELIEVE IT... LATE AGAIN. THEY WERE *ALWAYS* LATE, DEE WAS SUPPOSED TO PICK ME UP AT SEVEN AND IT WAS ALREADY ALMOST EIGHT.
HANGING OUT IN THE LIVING ROOM, WAITING, WAITING, WHILE MY PARENTS WATCHED SOME CRAPPY MADE FOR T.V. MOVIE.
WHY DON'T YOU SIT DOWN AND WATCH THIS WITH US? IT'S FUNNY, YOU'D LIKE IT.
NAW... I'M LEAVING IN JUST A SECOND.
WHAT THE FUCK WAS *TAKING* THEM SO LONG? THE IDEA OF BEING STUCK AT HOME ALL NIGHT WAS TOO AWFUL TO EVEN THINK ABOUT.
HAH HAH HAH HAH!
FINALLY THE SOUND OF DEE'S HORN.
I'M HEADING OUT. I DON'T KNOW WHEN I'LL BE BACK...

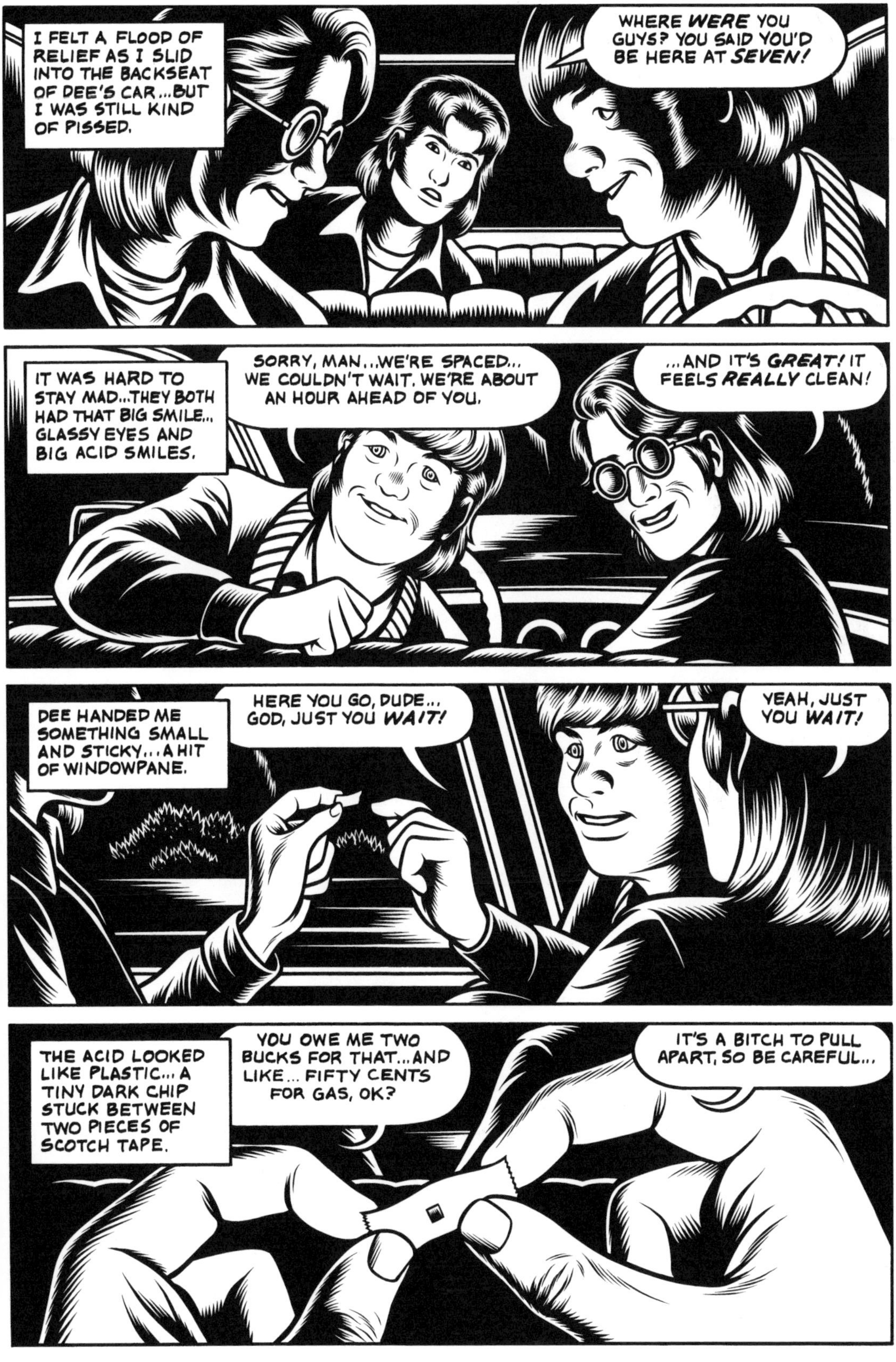
I FELT A FLOOD OF RELIEF AS I SLID INTO THE BACKSEAT OF DEE'S CAR...BUT I WAS STILL KIND OF PISSED.
WHERE *WERE* YOU GUYS? YOU SAID YOU'D BE HERE AT *SEVEN!*
IT WAS HARD TO STAY MAD...THEY BOTH HAD THAT BIG SMILE... GLASSY EYES AND BIG ACID SMILES.
SORRY, MAN...WE'RE SPACED... WE COULDN'T WAIT. WE'RE ABOUT AN HOUR AHEAD OF YOU.
...AND IT'S *GREAT!* IT FEELS *REALLY* CLEAN!
DEE HANDED ME SOMETHING SMALL AND STICKY... A HIT OF WINDOWPANE.
HERE YOU GO, DUDE... GOD, JUST YOU *WAIT!*
YEAH, JUST YOU *WAIT!*
THE ACID LOOKED LIKE PLASTIC... A TINY DARK CHIP STUCK BETWEEN TWO PIECES OF SCOTCH TAPE.
YOU OWE ME TWO BUCKS FOR THAT...AND LIKE... FIFTY CENTS FOR GAS, OK?
IT'S A BITCH TO PULL APART, SO BE CAREFUL...

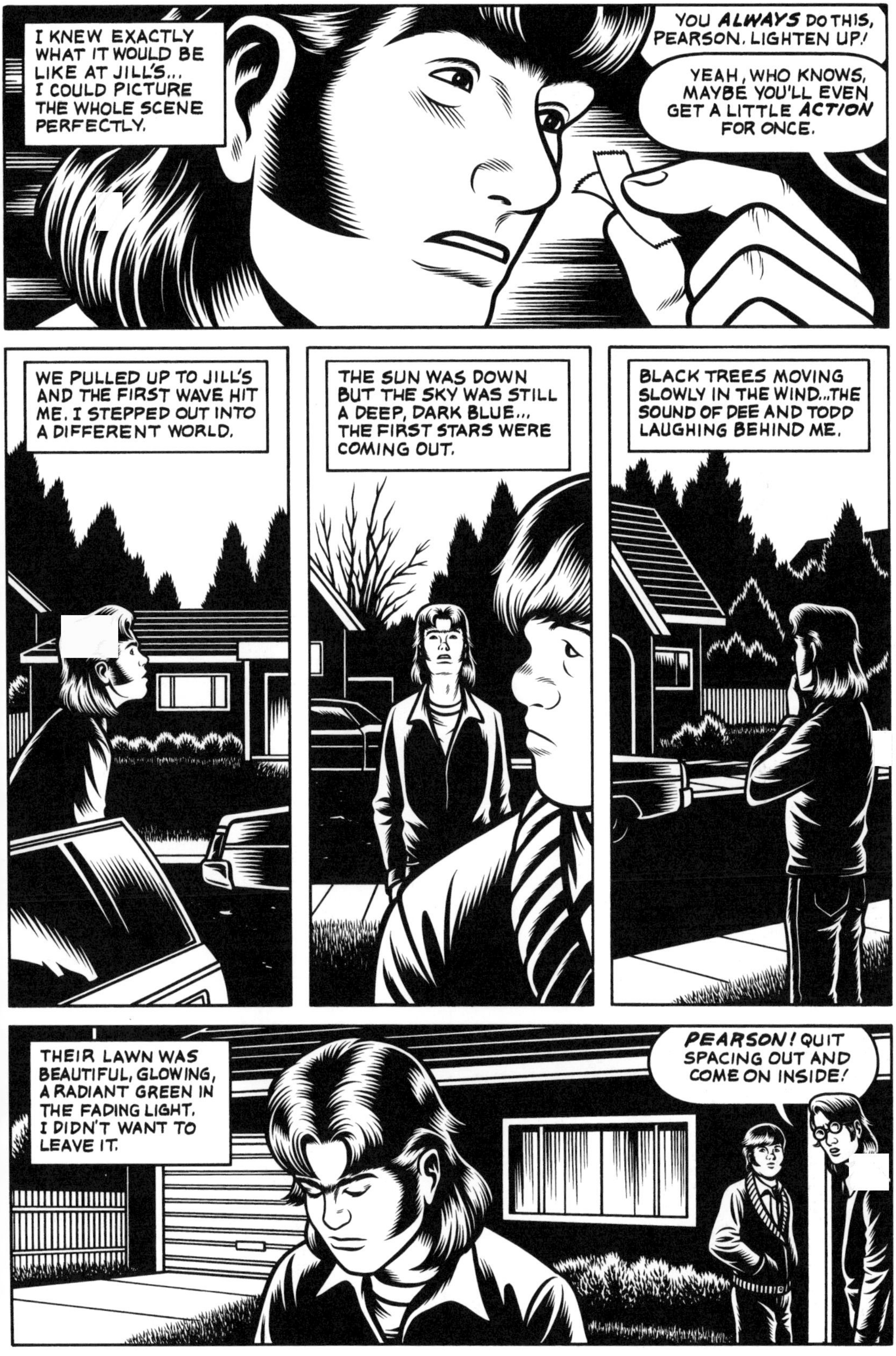
I KNEW EXACTLY WHAT IT WOULD BE LIKE AT JILL'S... I COULD PICTURE THE WHOLE SCENE PERFECTLY.
YOU ALWAYS DO THIS, PEARSON. LIGHTEN UP!
YEAH, WHO KNOWS, MAYBE YOU'LL EVEN GET A LITTLE ACTION FOR ONCE.
WE PULLED UP TO JILL'S AND THE FIRST WAVE HIT ME. I STEPPED OUT INTO A DIFFERENT WORLD.
THE SUN WAS DOWN BUT THE SKY WAS STILL A DEEP, DARK BLUE... THE FIRST STARS WERE COMING OUT.
BLACK TREES MOVING SLOWLY IN THE WIND...THE SOUND OF DEE AND TODD LAUGHING BEHIND ME.
THEIR LAWN WAS BEAUTIFUL, GLOWING, A RADIANT GREEN IN THE FADING LIGHT. I DIDN'T WANT TO LEAVE IT.
PEARSON! QUIT SPACING OUT AND COME ON INSIDE!

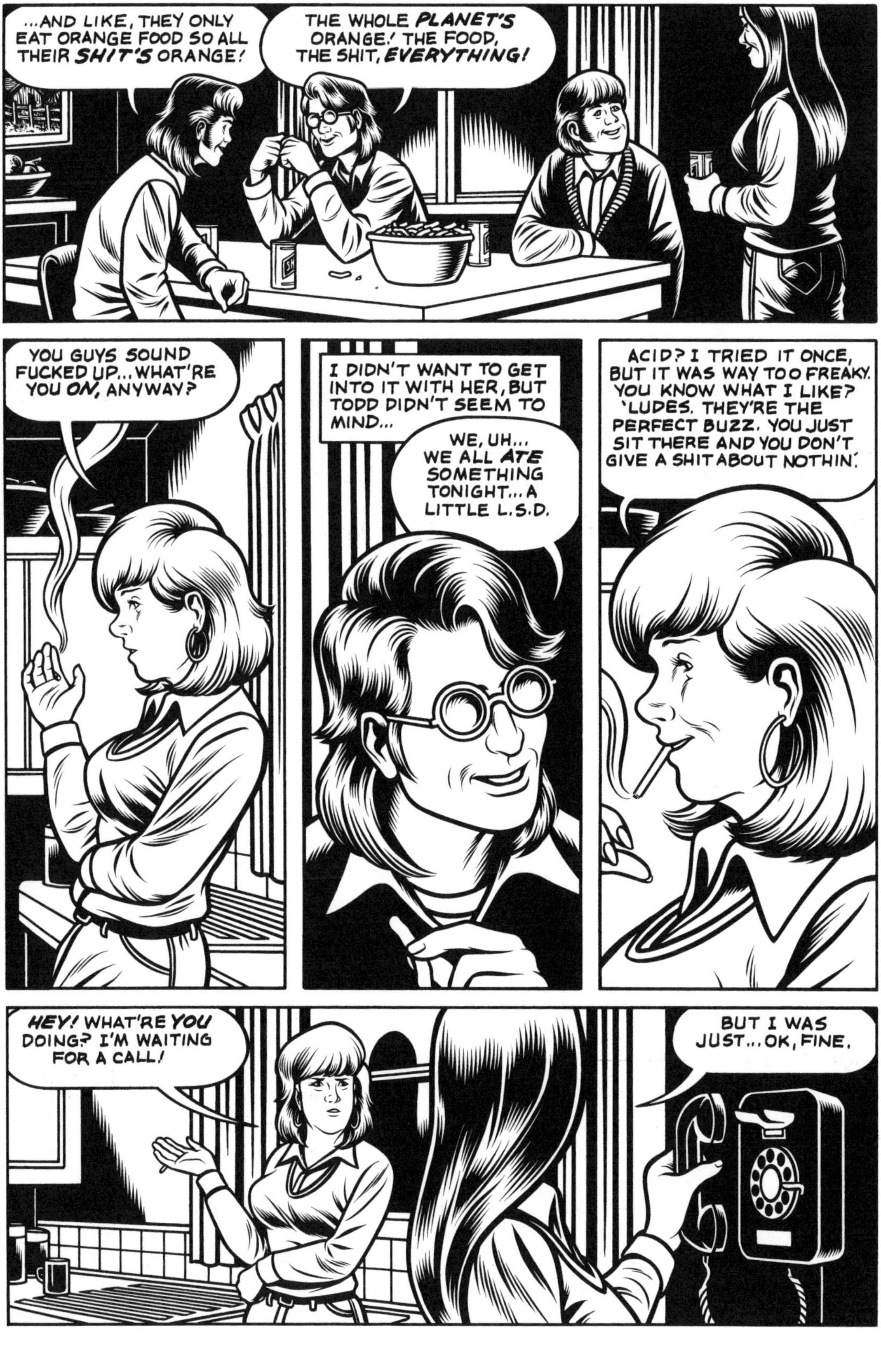
...AND LIKE, THEY ONLY EAT ORANGE FOOD SO ALL THEIR SHIT'S ORANGE!
THE WHOLE PLANET'S ORANGE! THE FOOD, THE SHIT, EVERYTHING!
YOU GUYS SOUND FUCKED UP... WHAT'RE YOU ON, ANYWAY?
I DIDN'T WANT TO GET INTO IT WITH HER, BUT TODD DIDN'T SEEM TO MIND...
WE, UH... WE ALL ATE SOMETHING TONIGHT... A LITTLE L.S.D.
ACID? I TRIED IT ONCE, BUT IT WAS WAY TOO FREAKY. YOU KNOW WHAT I LIKE? 'LUDES. THEY'RE THE PERFECT BUZZ. YOU JUST SIT THERE AND YOU DON'T GIVE A SHIT ABOUT NOTHIN'.
HEY! WHAT'RE YOU DOING? I'M WAITING FOR A CALL!
BUT I WAS JUST... OK, FINE.

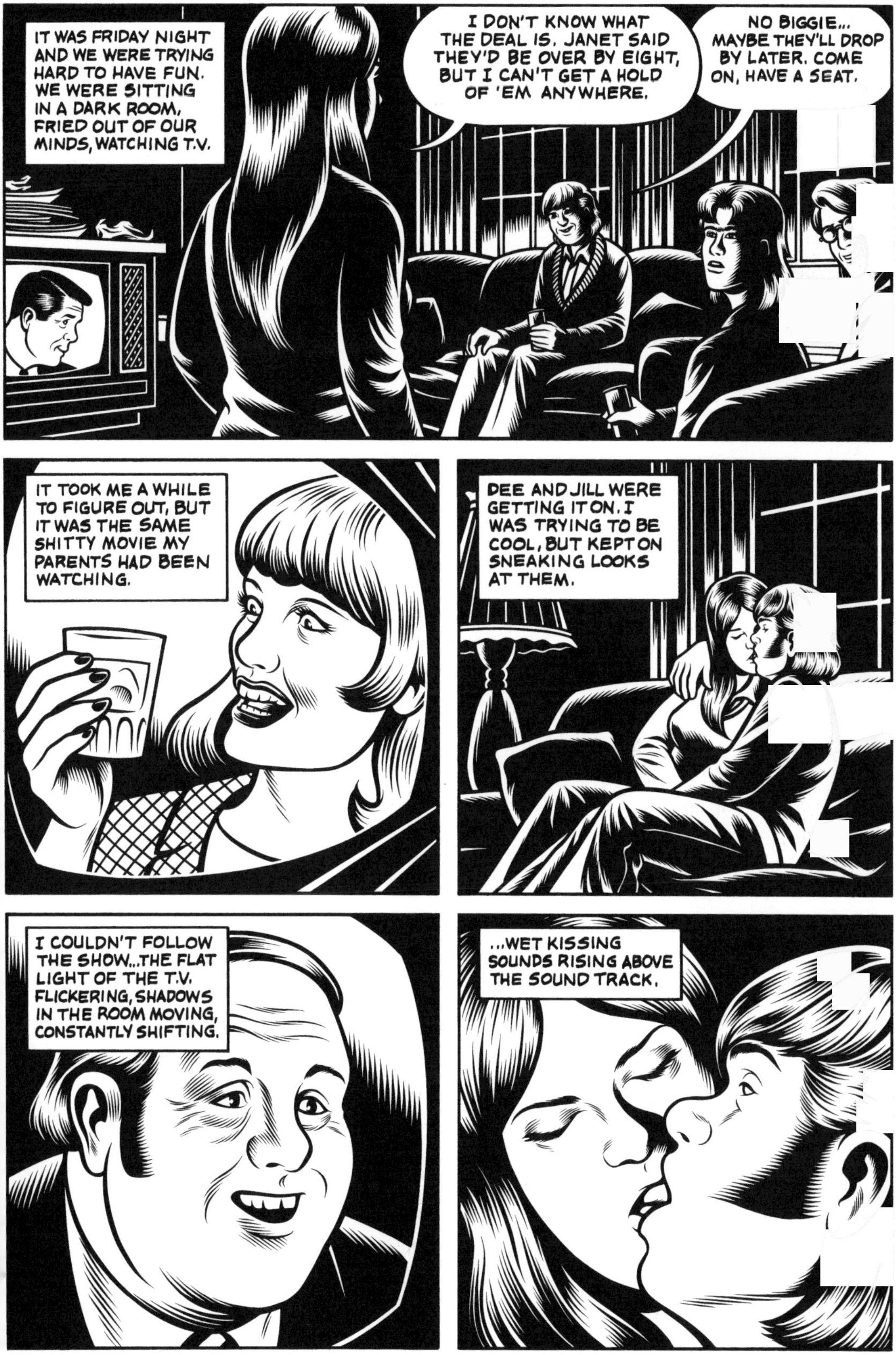
IT WAS FRIDAY NIGHT AND WE WERE TRYING HARD TO HAVE FUN. WE WERE SITTING IN A DARK ROOM, FRIED OUT OF OUR MINDS, WATCHING T.V.
I DON'T KNOW WHAT THE DEAL IS. JANET SAID THEY'D BE OVER BY EIGHT, BUT I CAN'T GET A HOLD OF 'EM ANYWHERE.
NO BIGGIE... MAYBE THEY'LL DROP BY LATER. COME ON, HAVE A SEAT.
IT TOOK ME A WHILE TO FIGURE OUT, BUT IT WAS THE SAME SHITTY MOVIE MY PARENTS HAD BEEN WATCHING.
DEE AND JILL WERE GETTING IT ON. I WAS TRYING TO BE COOL, BUT KEPT ON SNEAKING LOOKS AT THEM.
I COULDN'T FOLLOW THE SHOW...THE FLAT LIGHT OF THE T.V. FLICKERING, SHADOWS IN THE ROOM MOVING, CONSTANTLY SHIFTING.
...WET KISSING SOUNDS RISING ABOVE THE SOUND TRACK.

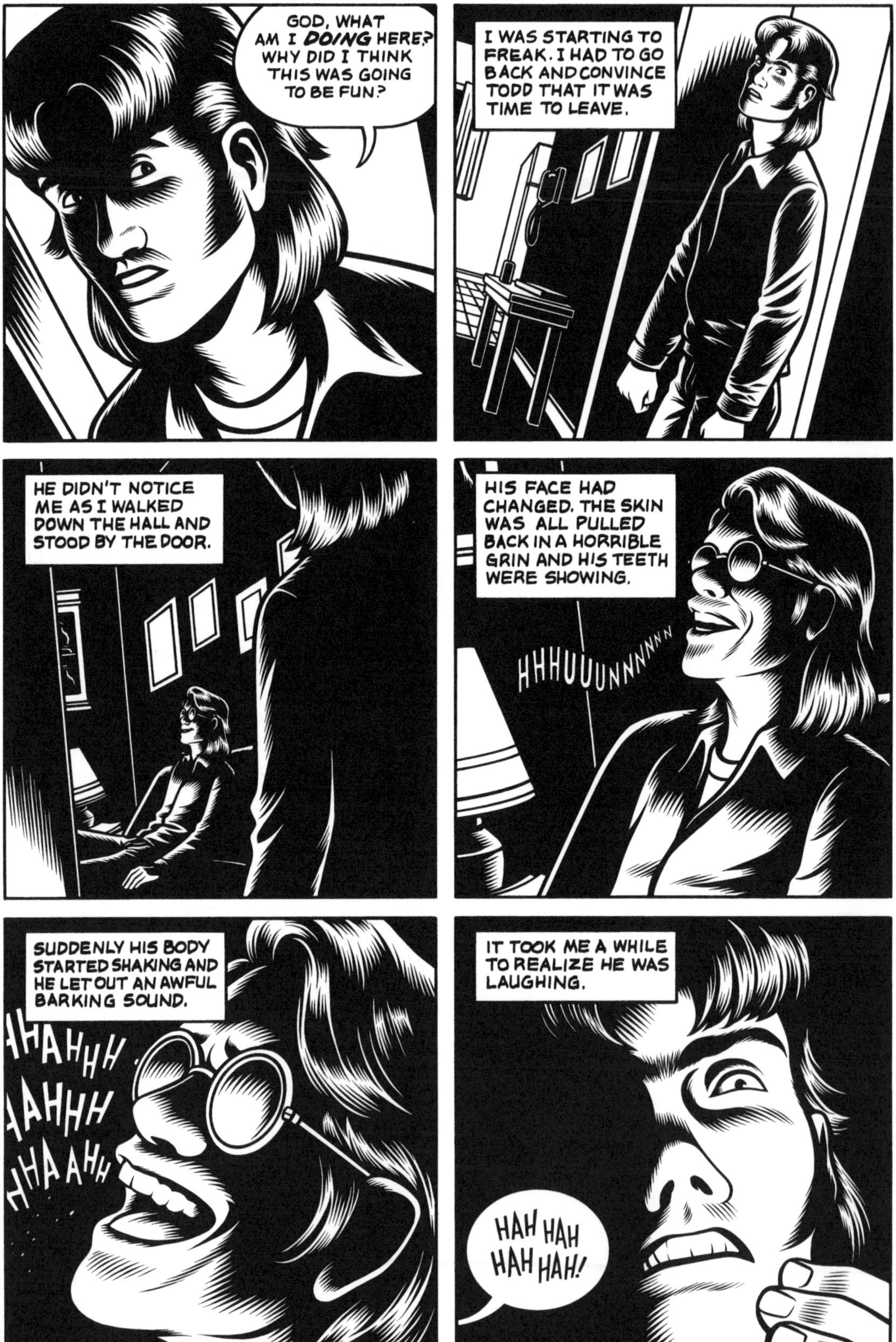
GOD, WHAT AM I *DOING* HERE? WHY DID I THINK THIS WAS GOING TO BE FUN?
I WAS STARTING TO FREAK. I HAD TO GO BACK AND CONVINCE TODD THAT IT WAS TIME TO LEAVE.
HE DIDN'T NOTICE ME AS I WALKED DOWN THE HALL AND STOOD BY THE DOOR.
HIS FACE HAD CHANGED. THE SKIN WAS ALL PULLED BACK IN A HORRIBLE GRIN AND HIS TEETH WERE SHOWING.
HHHUUUNNNNNN
SUDDENLY HIS BODY STARTED SHAKING AND HE LET OUT AN AWFUL BARKING SOUND.
HAHHH
AHHHH
HHA AHH
IT TOOK ME A WHILE TO REALIZE HE WAS LAUGHING.
HAH HAH HAH HAH!

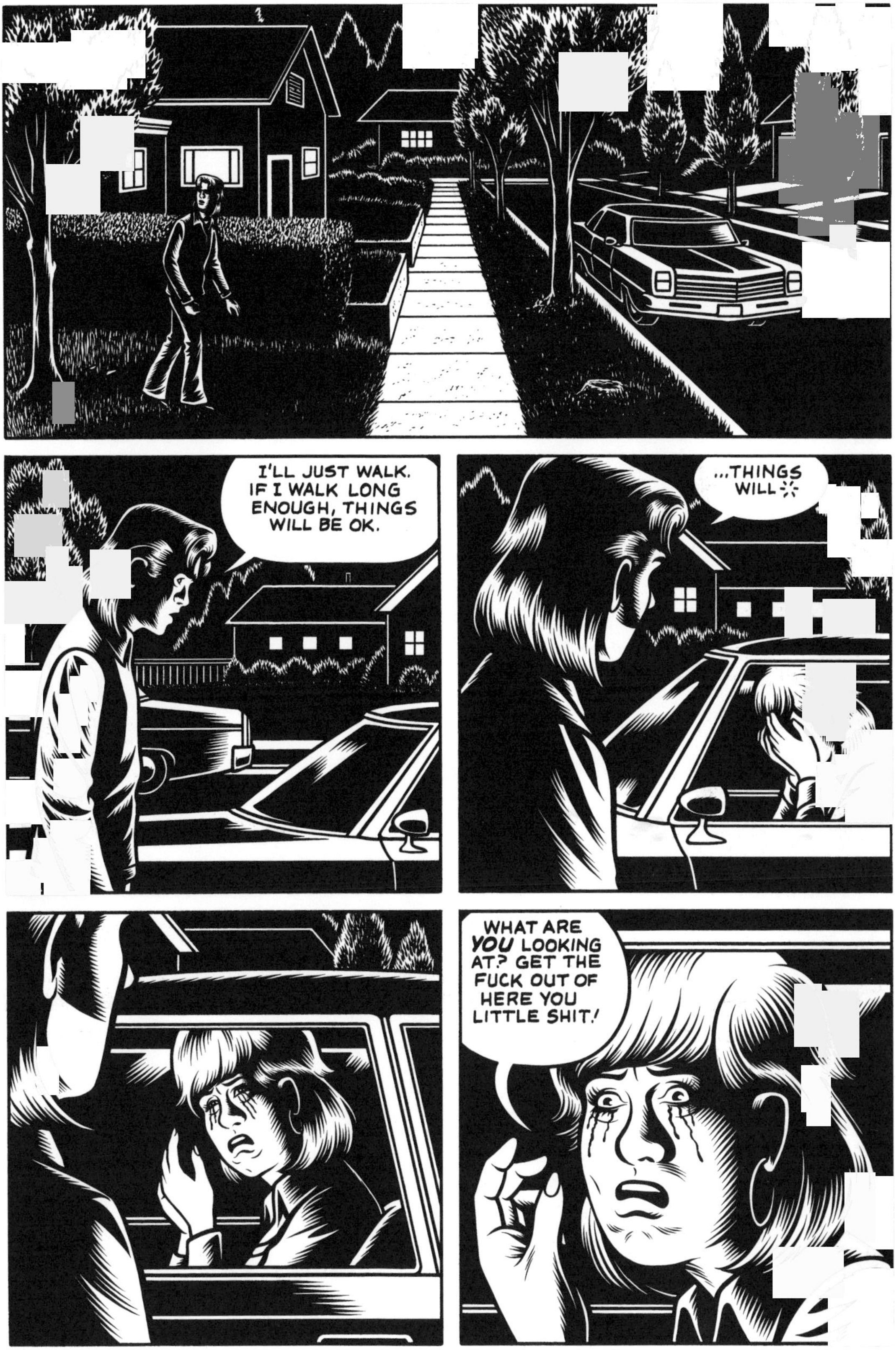
I'LL JUST WALK. IF I WALK LONG ENOUGH, THINGS WILL BE OK.
...THINGS WILL
WHAT ARE YOU LOOKING AT? GET THE FUCK OUT OF HERE YOU LITTLE SHIT!

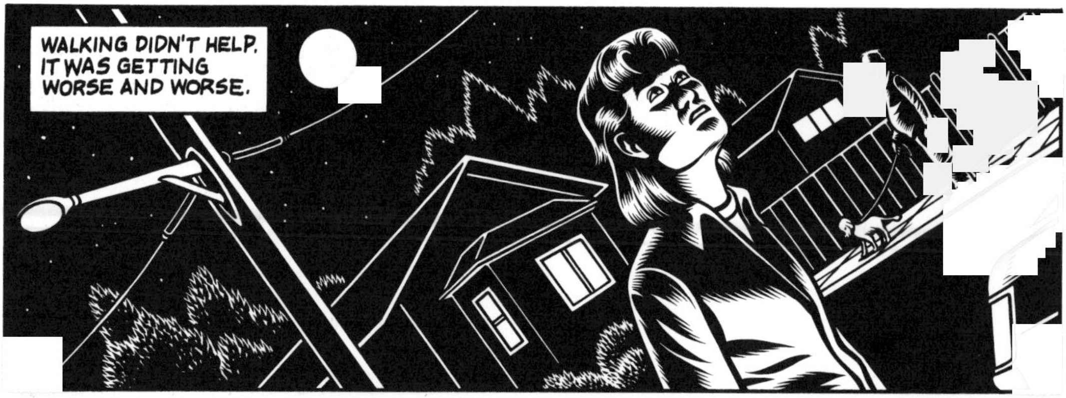
WALKING DIDN'T HELP. IT WAS GETTING WORSE AND WORSE.

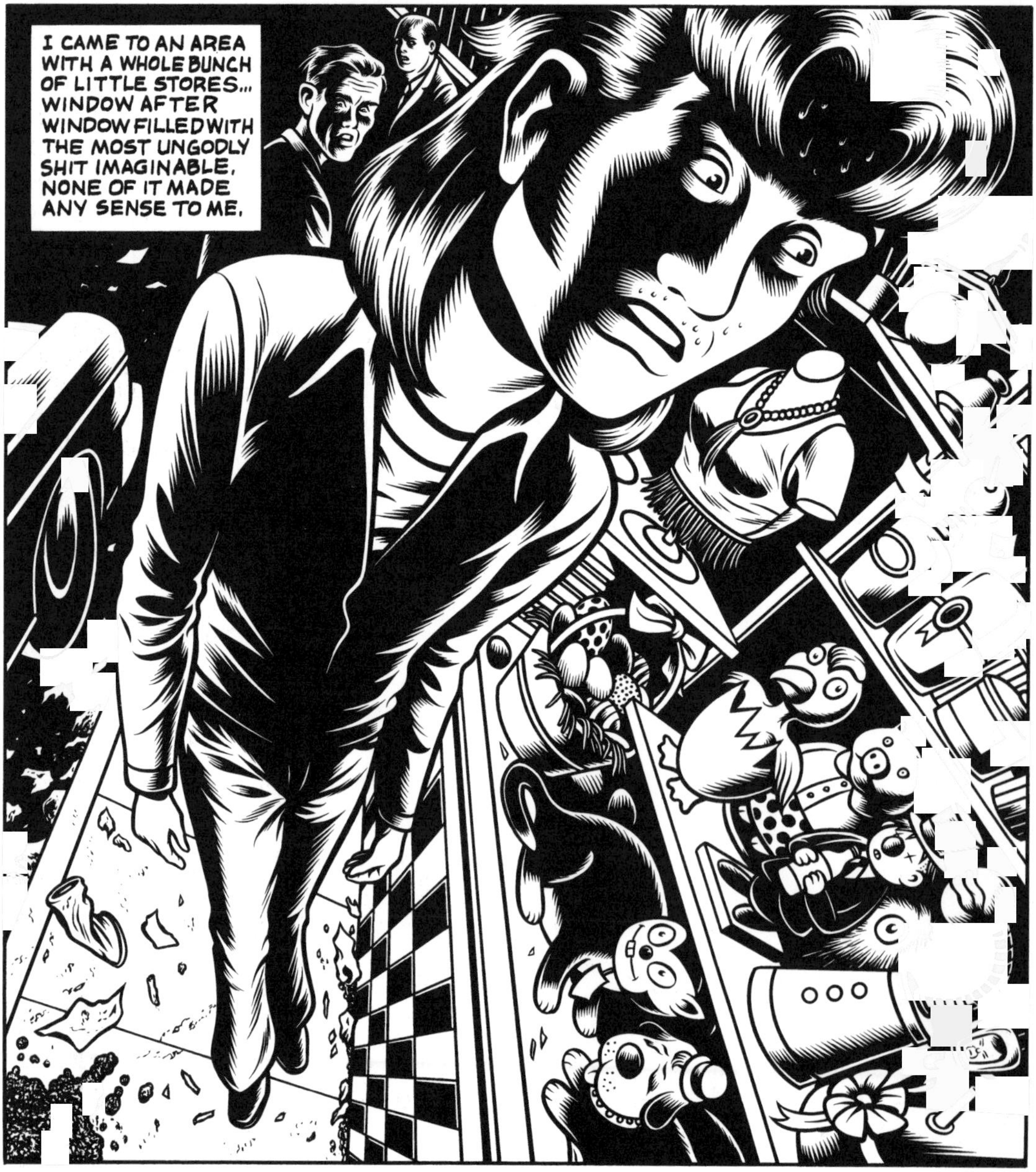
I CAME TO AN AREA WITH A WHOLE BUNCH OF LITTLE STORES... WINDOW AFTER WINDOW FILLED WITH THE MOST UNGODLY SHIT IMAGINABLE. NONE OF IT MADE ANY SENSE TO ME.

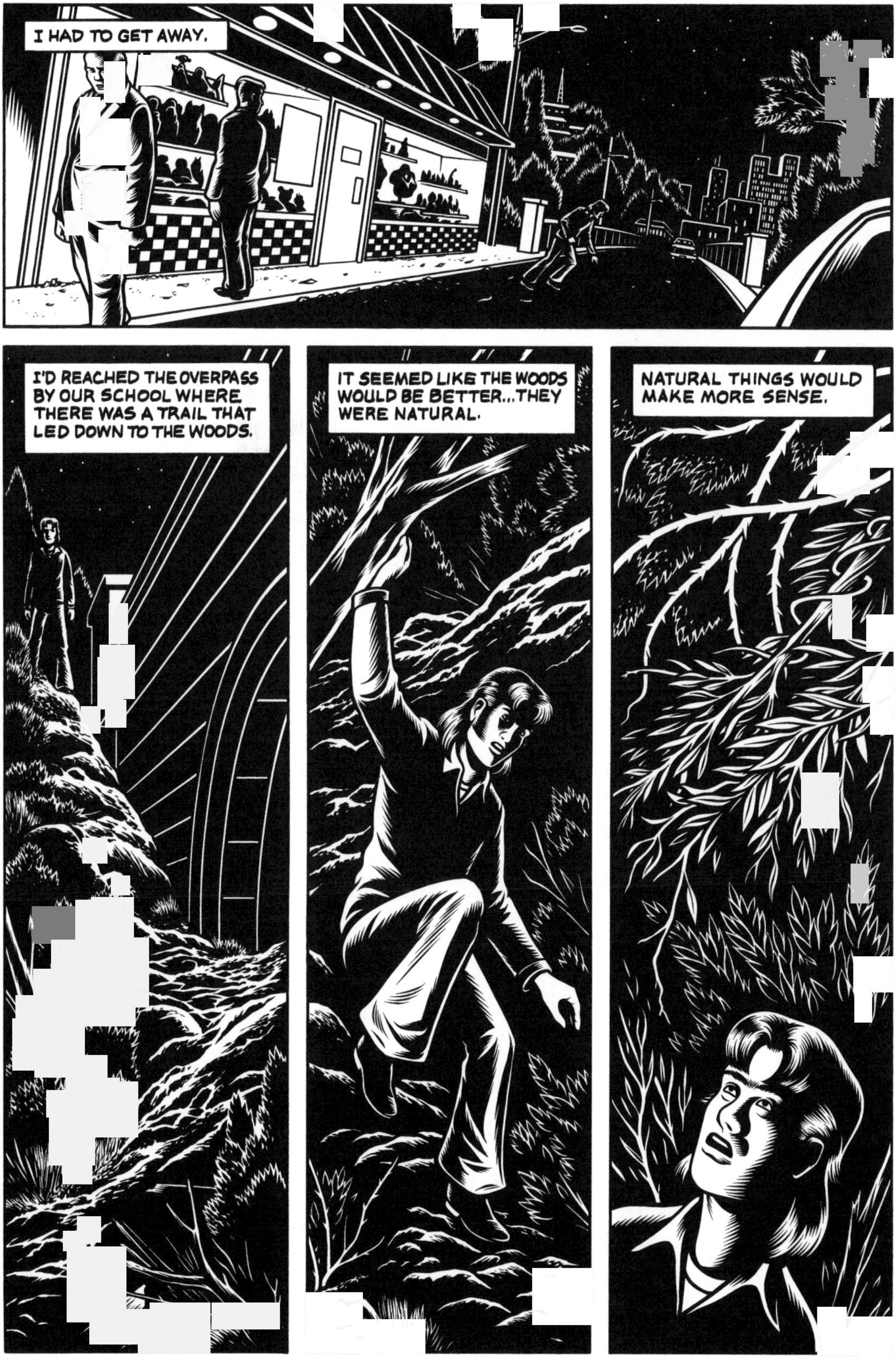
I HAD TO GET AWAY.
I'D REACHED THE OVERPASS BY OUR SCHOOL WHERE THERE WAS A TRAIL THAT LED DOWN TO THE WOODS.
IT SEEMED LIKE THE WOODS WOULD BE BETTER...THEY WERE NATURAL.
NATURAL THINGS WOULD MAKE MORE SENSE.

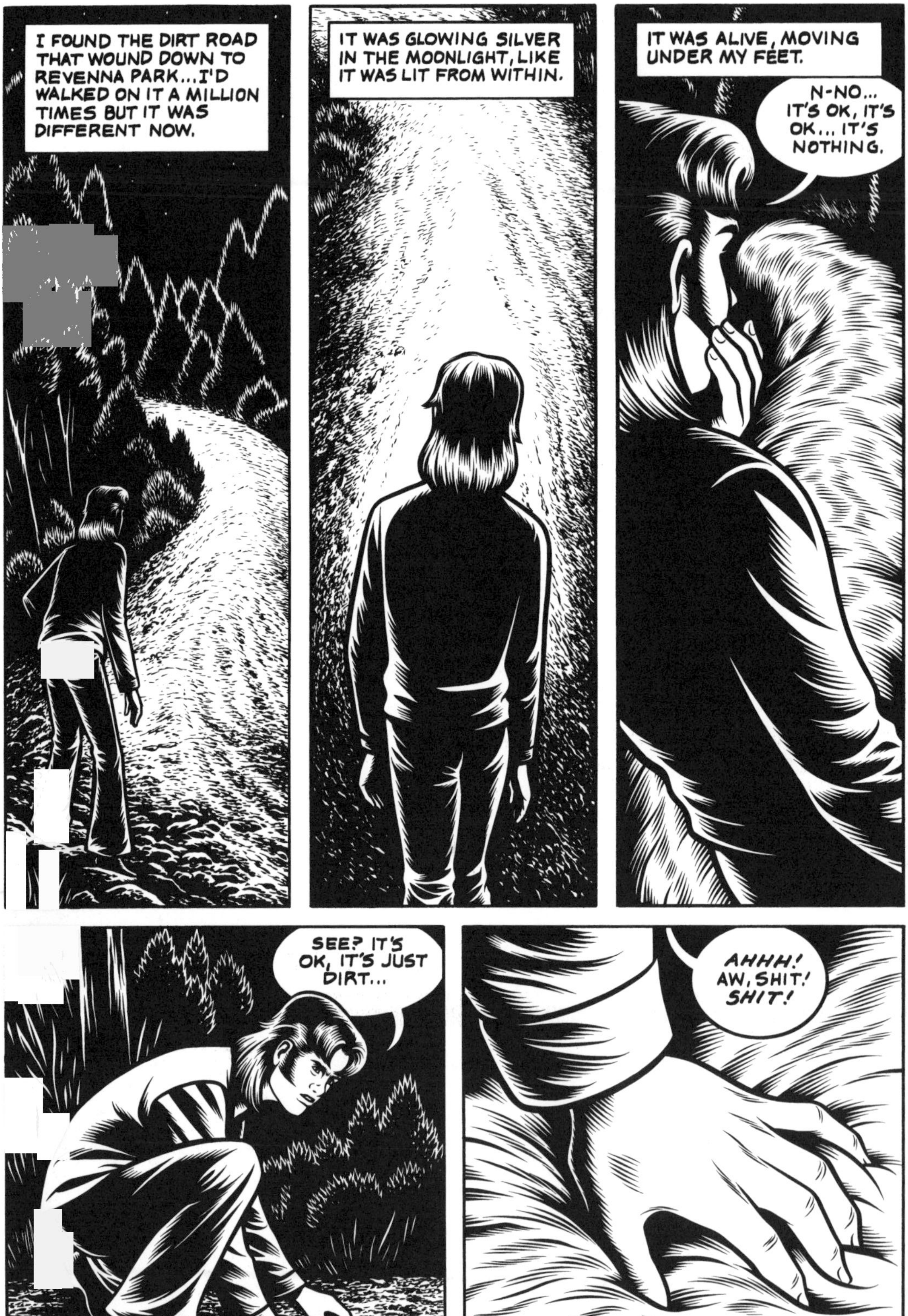
I FOUND THE DIRT ROAD THAT WOUND DOWN TO REVENNA PARK...I'D WALKED ON IT A MILLION TIMES BUT IT WAS DIFFERENT NOW.
IT WAS GLOWING SILVER IN THE MOONLIGHT, LIKE IT WAS LIT FROM WITHIN.
IT WAS ALIVE, MOVING UNDER MY FEET.
N-NO... IT'S OK, IT'S OK... IT'S NOTHING.
SEE? IT'S OK, IT'S JUST DIRT...
AHHH! AW, SHIT! SHIT!

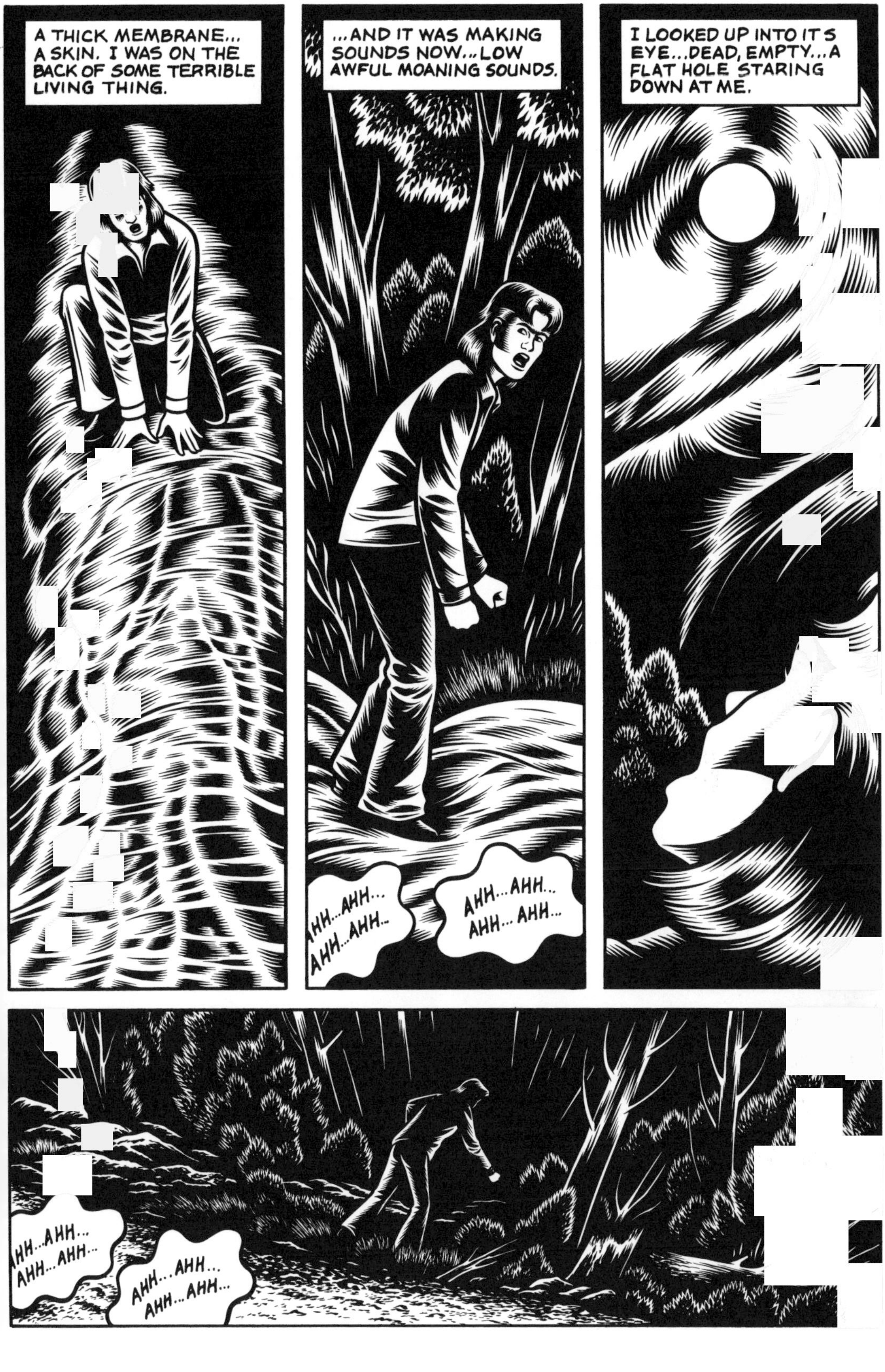
A THICK MEMBRANE... A SKIN. I WAS ON THE BACK OF SOME TERRIBLE LIVING THING.
...AND IT WAS MAKING SOUNDS NOW... LOW AWFUL MOANING SOUNDS.
AHH...AHH... AHH...AHH...
AHH...AHH... AHH... AHH...
I LOOKED UP INTO ITS EYE...DEAD, EMPTY...A FLAT HOLE STARING DOWN AT ME.
AHH...AHH... AHH...AHH...
AHH...AHH... AHH...AHH...

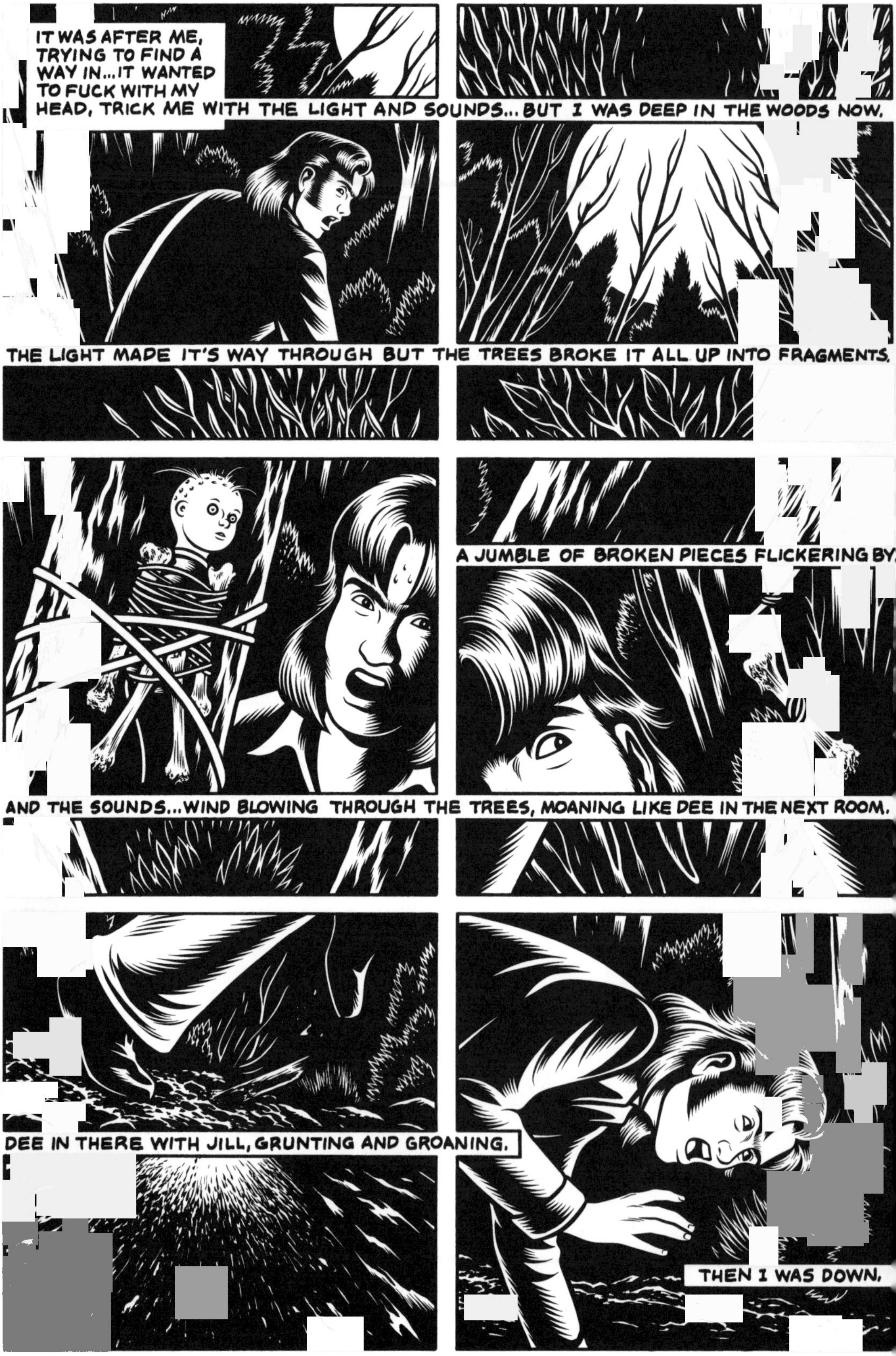
IT WAS AFTER ME, TRYING TO FIND A WAY IN...IT WANTED TO FUCK WITH MY HEAD, TRICK ME WITH THE LIGHT AND SOUNDS... BUT I WAS DEEP IN THE WOODS NOW.
THE LIGHT MADE IT'S WAY THROUGH BUT THE TREES BROKE IT ALL UP INTO FRAGMENTS,
A JUMBLE OF BROKEN PIECES FLICKERING BY.
AND THE SOUNDS...WIND BLOWING THROUGH THE TREES, MOANING LIKE DEE IN THE NEXT ROOM.
DEE IN THERE WITH JILL, GRUNTING AND GROANING.
THEN I WAS DOWN.

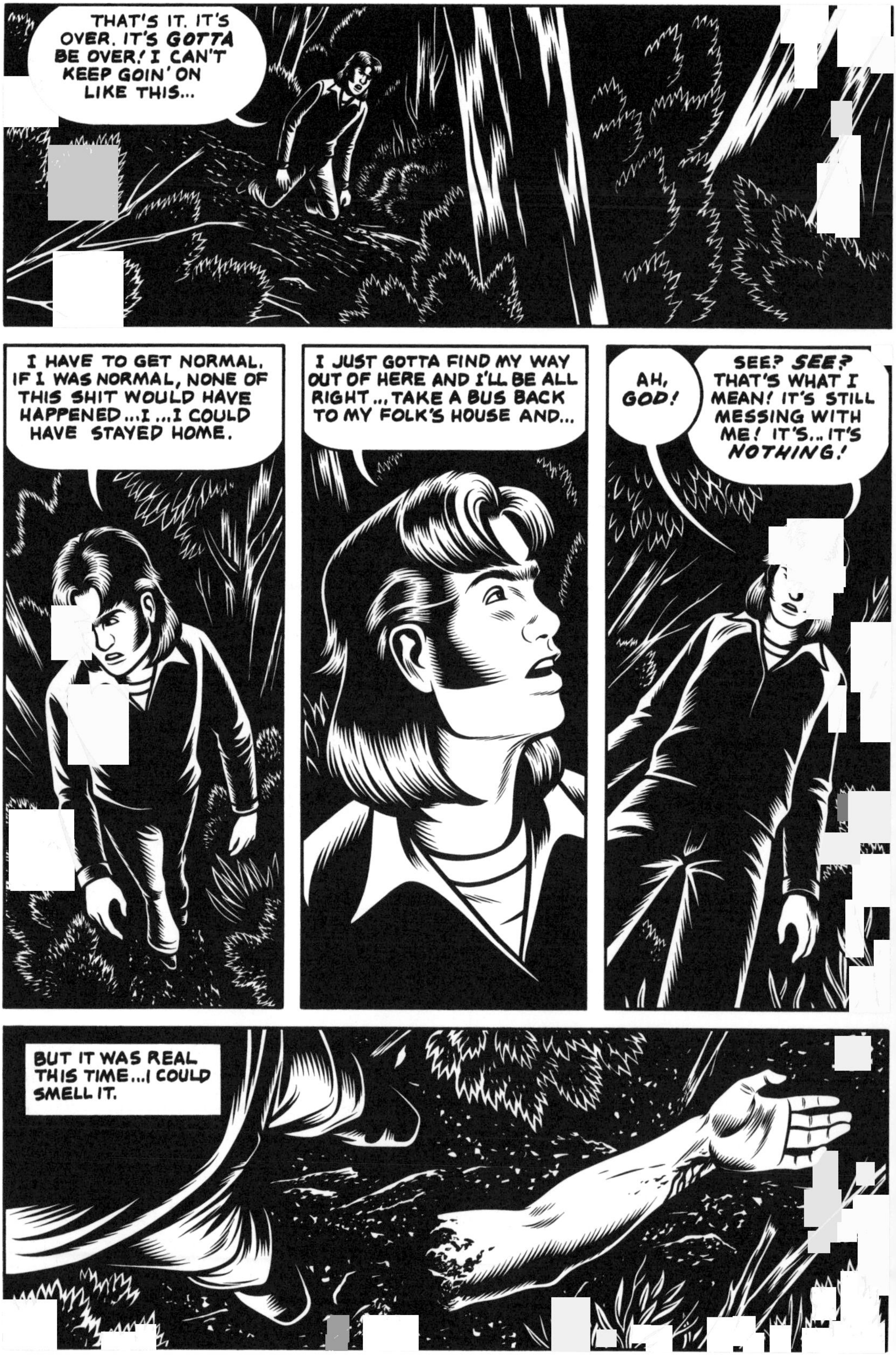
THAT'S IT. IT'S OVER. IT'S GOTTA BE OVER! I CAN'T KEEP GOIN' ON LIKE THIS...
I HAVE TO GET NORMAL. IF I WAS NORMAL, NONE OF THIS SHIT WOULD HAVE HAPPENED...I ...I COULD HAVE STAYED HOME.
I JUST GOTTA FIND MY WAY OUT OF HERE AND I'LL BE ALL RIGHT..., TAKE A BUS BACK TO MY FOLK'S HOUSE AND...
AH, GOD!
SEE? SEE? THAT'S WHAT I MEAN! IT'S STILL MESSING WITH ME! IT'S... IT'S NOTHING!
BUT IT WAS REAL THIS TIME...I COULD SMELL IT.

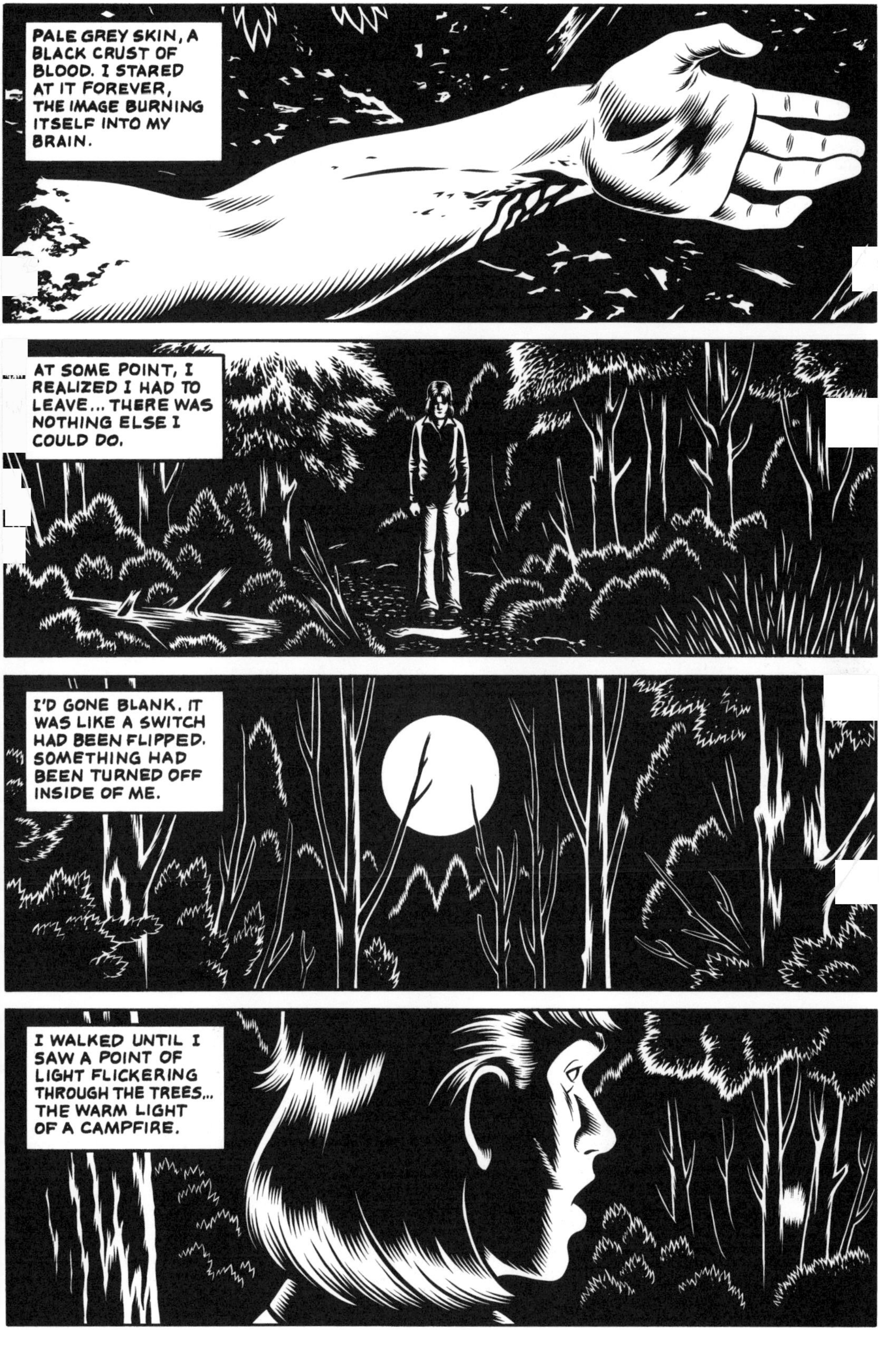
PALE GREY SKIN, A BLACK CRUST OF BLOOD. I STARED AT IT FOREVER, THE IMAGE BURNING ITSELF INTO MY BRAIN.
AT SOME POINT, I REALIZED I HAD TO LEAVE... THERE WAS NOTHING ELSE I COULD DO.
I'D GONE BLANK. IT WAS LIKE A SWITCH HAD BEEN FLIPPED. SOMETHING HAD BEEN TURNED OFF INSIDE OF ME.
I WALKED UNTIL I SAW A POINT OF LIGHT FLICKERING THROUGH THE TREES... THE WARM LIGHT OF A CAMPFIRE.

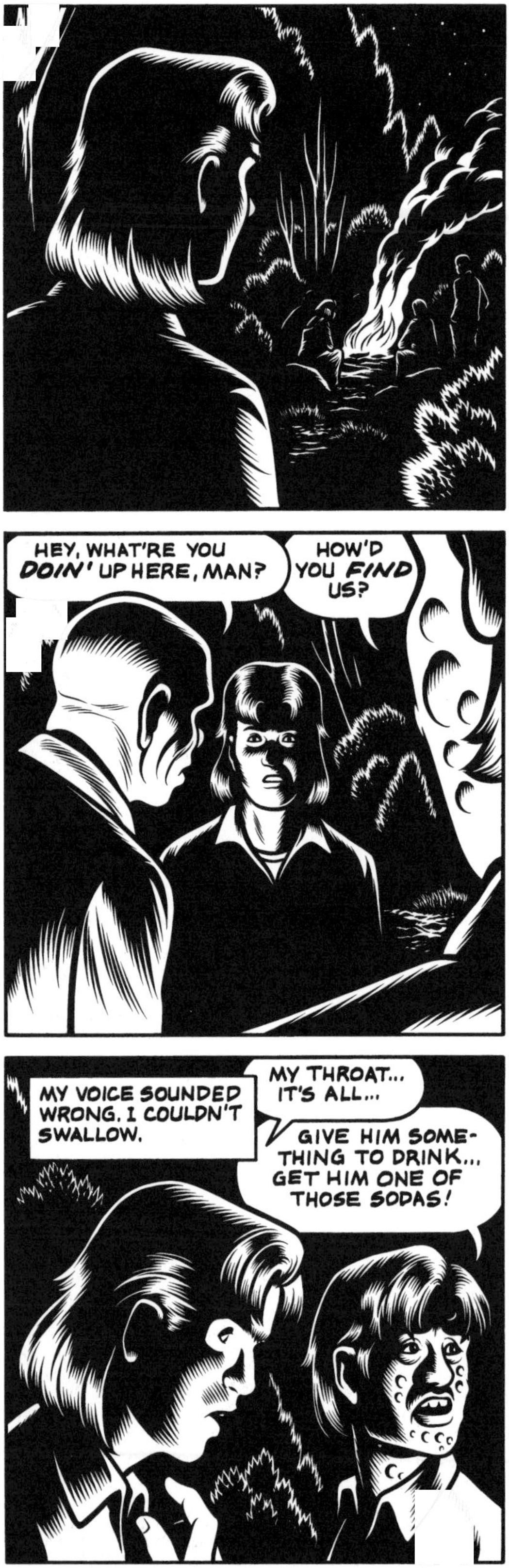
AW, GOD! CHECK IT OUT! IT'S SOME DUDE!
HEY, WHAT'RE YOU DOIN' UP HERE, MAN?
HOW'D YOU FIND US?
I... I SAW... THERE WAS THIS ARM... A DEAD ARM.
DEAD ARM? LOOK AT HIM! THE GUY'S LOADED!
SHUT UP! LET HIM TALK!
MY VOICE SOUNDED WRONG. I COULDN'T SWALLOW.
MY THROAT... IT'S ALL...
GIVE HIM SOMETHING TO DRINK... GET HIM ONE OF THOSE SODAS!
HERE, HAVE A SEAT... YOU CAN DRINK THIS.
AW, MAN... LOOK AT HIS EYES.

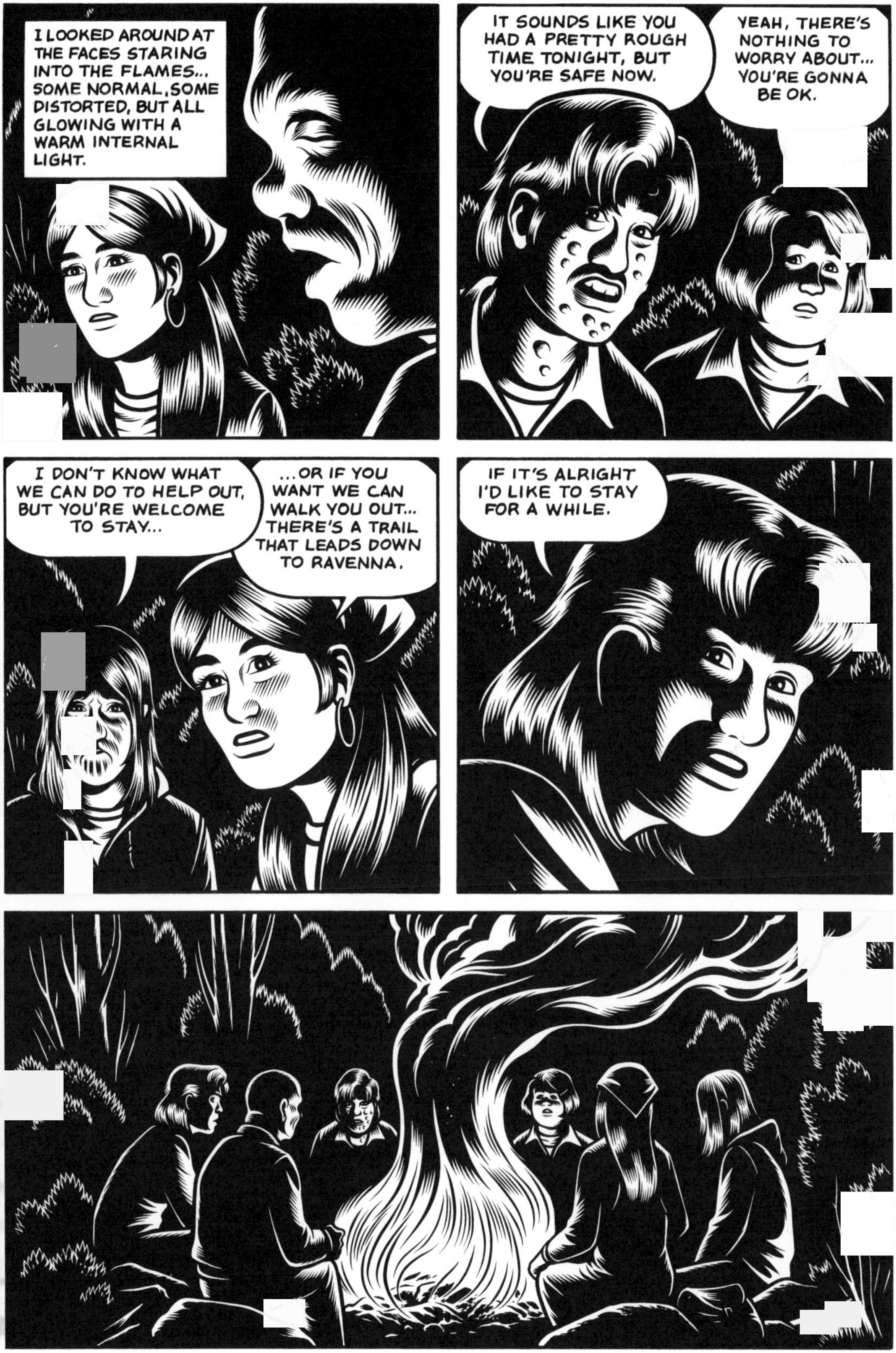
I LOOKED AROUND AT THE FACES STARING INTO THE FLAMES... SOME NORMAL, SOME DISTORTED, BUT ALL GLOWING WITH A WARM INTERNAL LIGHT.
IT SOUNDS LIKE YOU HAD A PRETTY ROUGH TIME TONIGHT, BUT YOU'RE SAFE NOW.
YEAH, THERE'S NOTHING TO WORRY ABOUT... YOU'RE GONNA BE OK.
I DON'T KNOW WHAT WE CAN DO TO HELP OUT, BUT YOU'RE WELCOME TO STAY...
...OR IF YOU WANT WE CAN WALK YOU OUT... THERE'S A TRAIL THAT LEADS DOWN TO RAVENNA.
IF IT'S ALRIGHT I'D LIKE TO STAY FOR A WHILE.

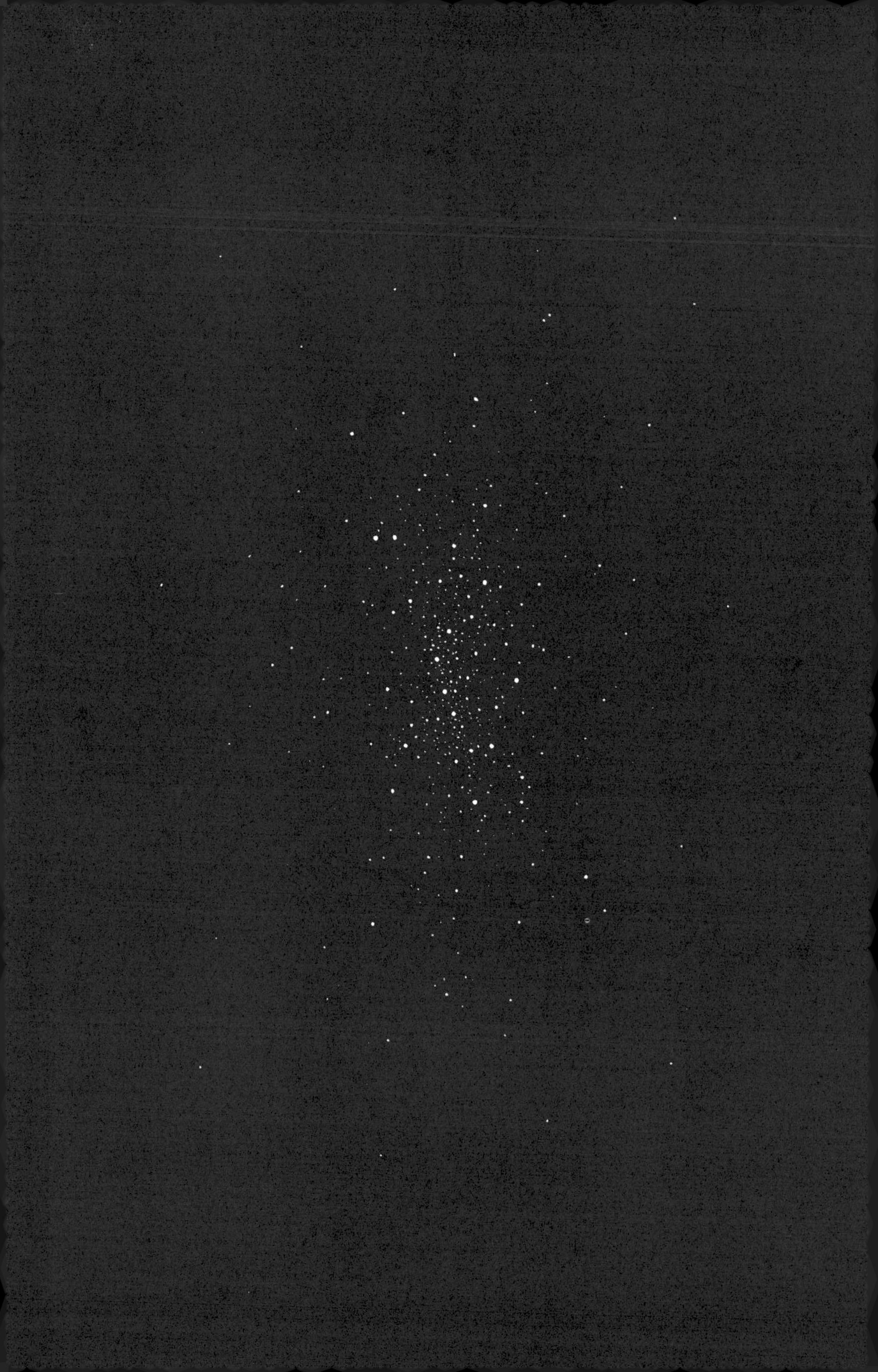

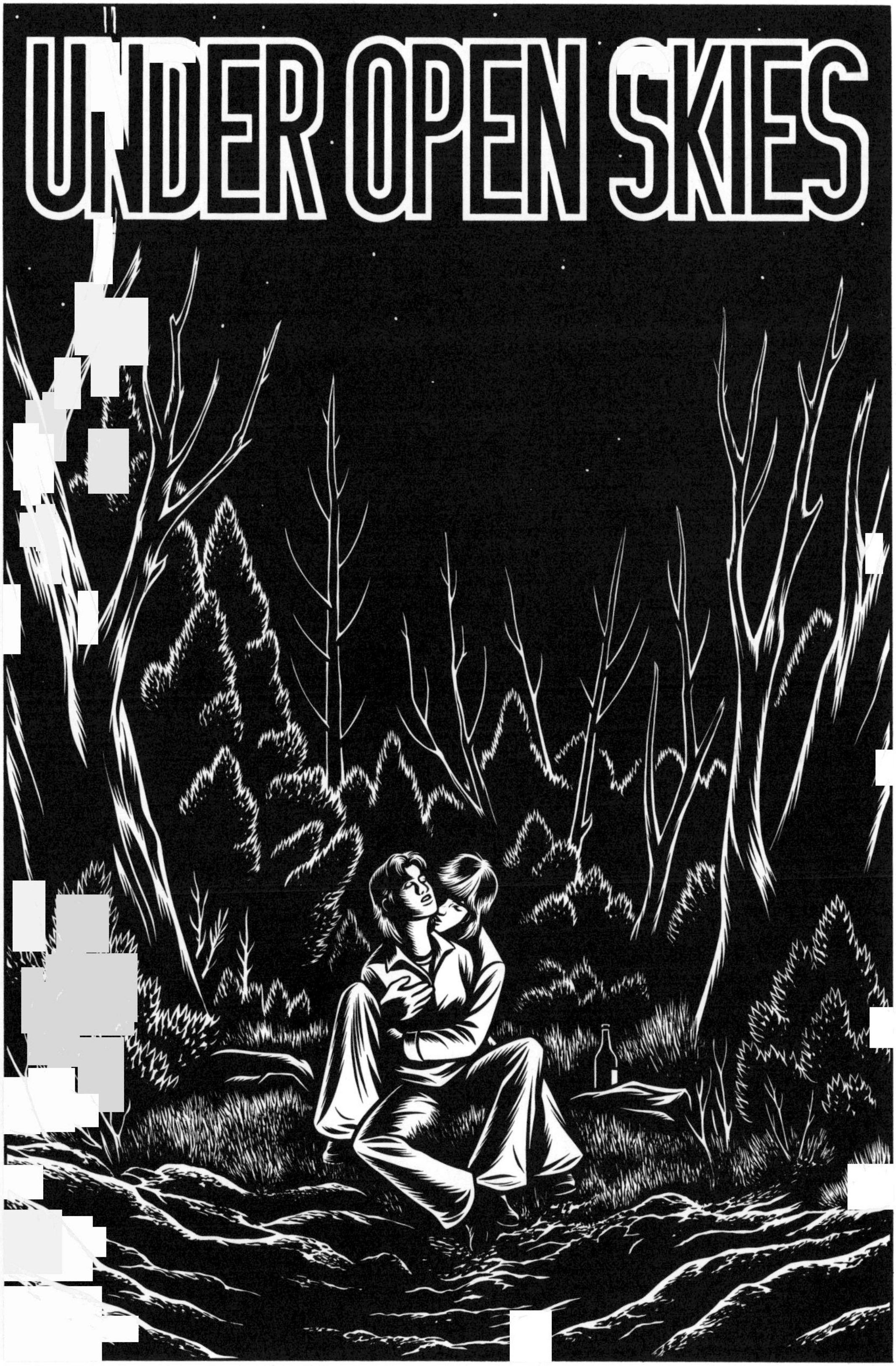
UNDER OPEN SKIES

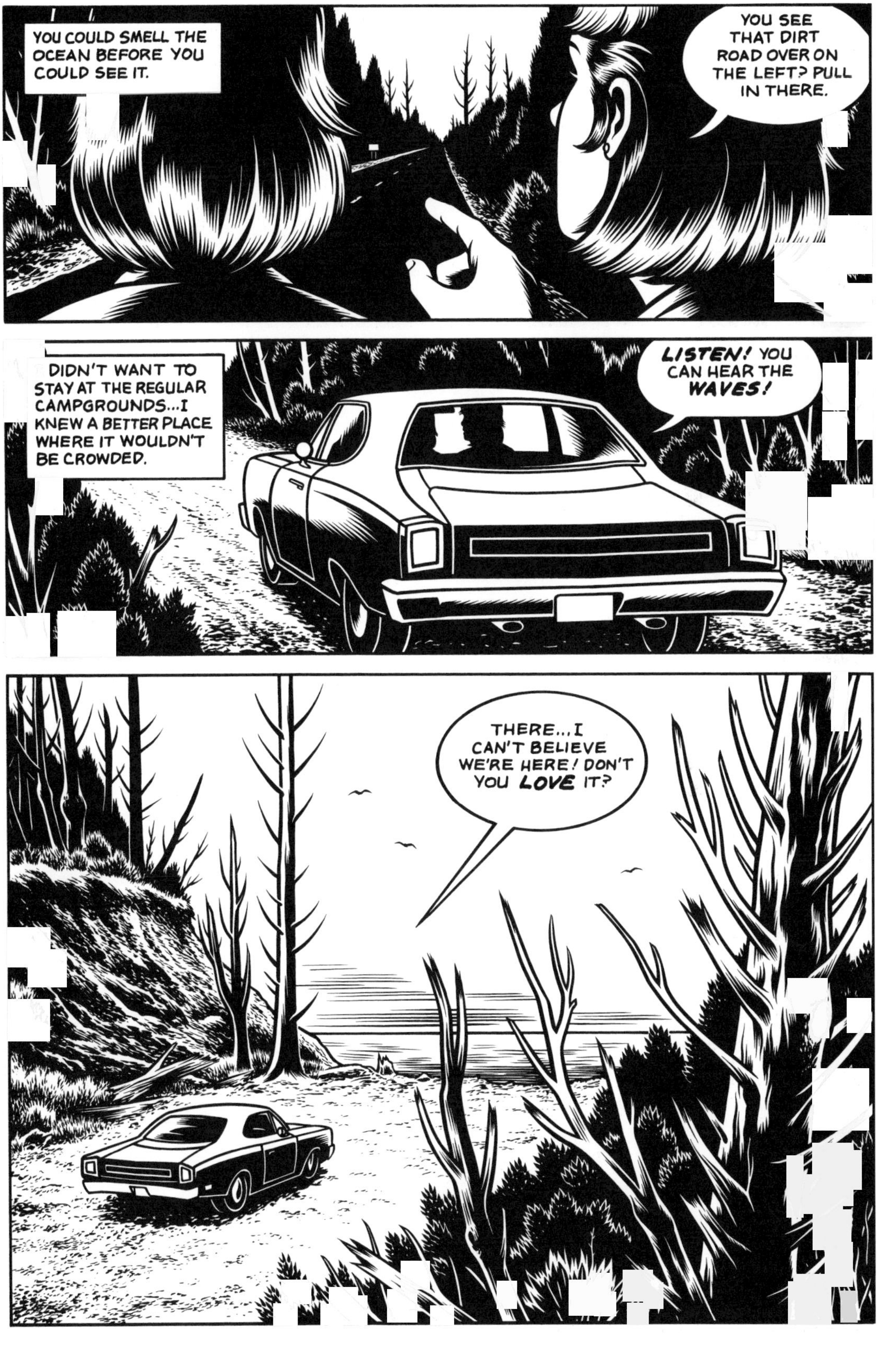
YOU COULD SMELL THE OCEAN BEFORE YOU COULD SEE IT.
YOU SEE THAT DIRT ROAD OVER ON THE LEFT? PULL IN THERE.
I DIDN'T WANT TO STAY AT THE REGULAR CAMPGROUNDS...I KNEW A BETTER PLACE WHERE IT WOULDN'T BE CROWDED.
LISTEN! YOU CAN HEAR THE WAVES!
THERE...I CAN'T BELIEVE WE'RE HERE! DON'T YOU LOVE IT?

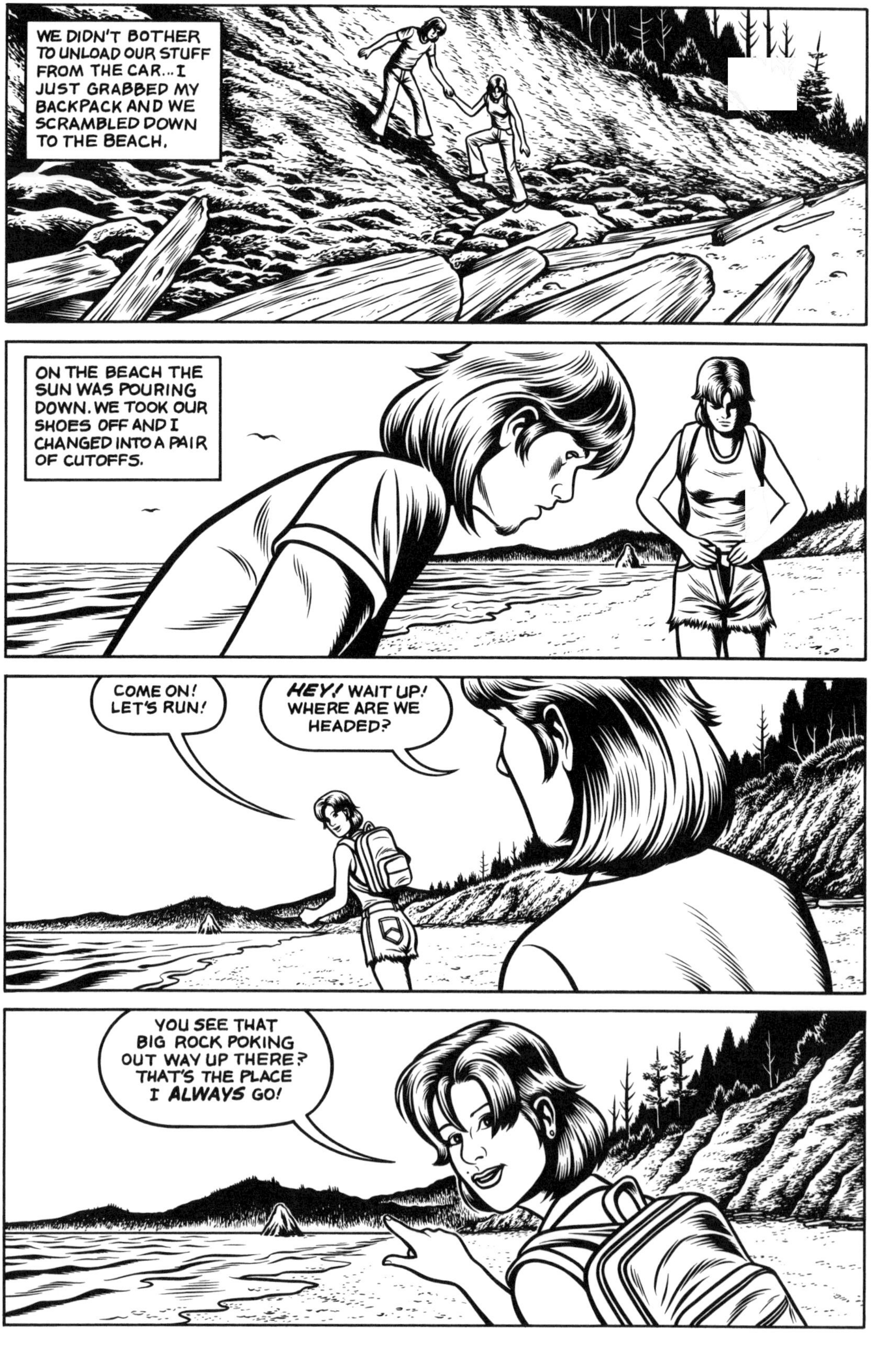
WE DIDN'T BOTHER TO UNLOAD OUR STUFF FROM THE CAR... I JUST GRABBED MY BACKPACK AND WE SCRAMBLED DOWN TO THE BEACH.
ON THE BEACH THE SUN WAS POURING DOWN. WE TOOK OUR SHOES OFF AND I CHANGED INTO A PAIR OF CUTOFFS.
COME ON! LET'S RUN!
HEY! WAIT UP! WHERE ARE WE HEADED?
YOU SEE THAT BIG ROCK POKING OUT WAY UP THERE? THAT'S THE PLACE I ALWAYS GO!

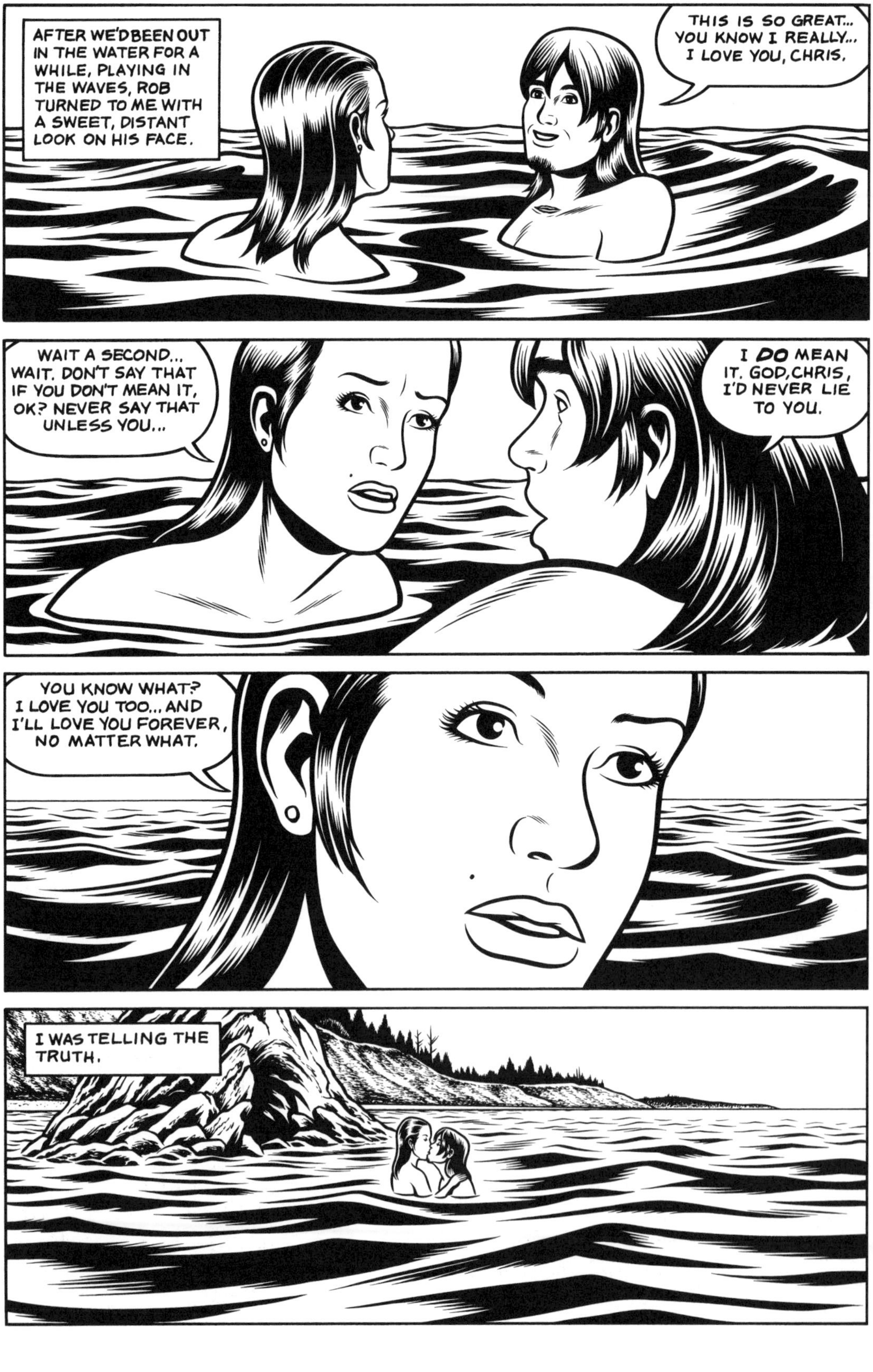
AFTER WE'D BEEN OUT IN THE WATER FOR A WHILE, PLAYING IN THE WAVES, ROB TURNED TO ME WITH A SWEET, DISTANT LOOK ON HIS FACE.
THIS IS SO GREAT... YOU KNOW I REALLY... I LOVE YOU, CHRIS.
WAIT A SECOND... WAIT. DON'T SAY THAT IF YOU DON'T MEAN IT, OK? NEVER SAY THAT UNLESS YOU...
I *DO* MEAN IT. GOD, CHRIS, I'D NEVER LIE TO YOU.
YOU KNOW WHAT? I LOVE YOU TOO... AND I'LL LOVE YOU FOREVER, NO MATTER WHAT.
I WAS TELLING THE TRUTH.

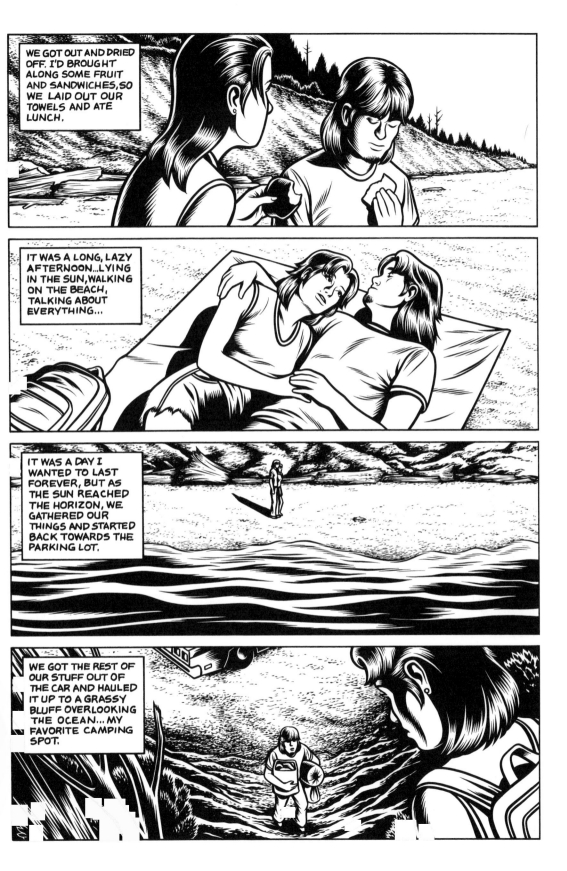

WE GOT OUT AND DRIED OFF. I'D BROUGHT ALONG SOME FRUIT AND SANDWICHES, SO WE LAID OUT OUR TOWELS AND ATE LUNCH.

IT WAS A LONG, LAZY AFTERNOON...LYING IN THE SUN, WALKING ON THE BEACH, TALKING ABOUT EVERYTHING...

IT WAS A DAY I WANTED TO LAST FOREVER, BUT AS THE SUN REACHED THE HORIZON, WE GATHERED OUR THINGS AND STARTED BACK TOWARDS THE PARKING LOT.

WE GOT THE REST OF OUR STUFF OUT OF THE CAR AND HAULED IT UP TO A GRASSY BLUFF OVERLOOKING THE OCEAN... MY FAVORITE CAMPING SPOT.

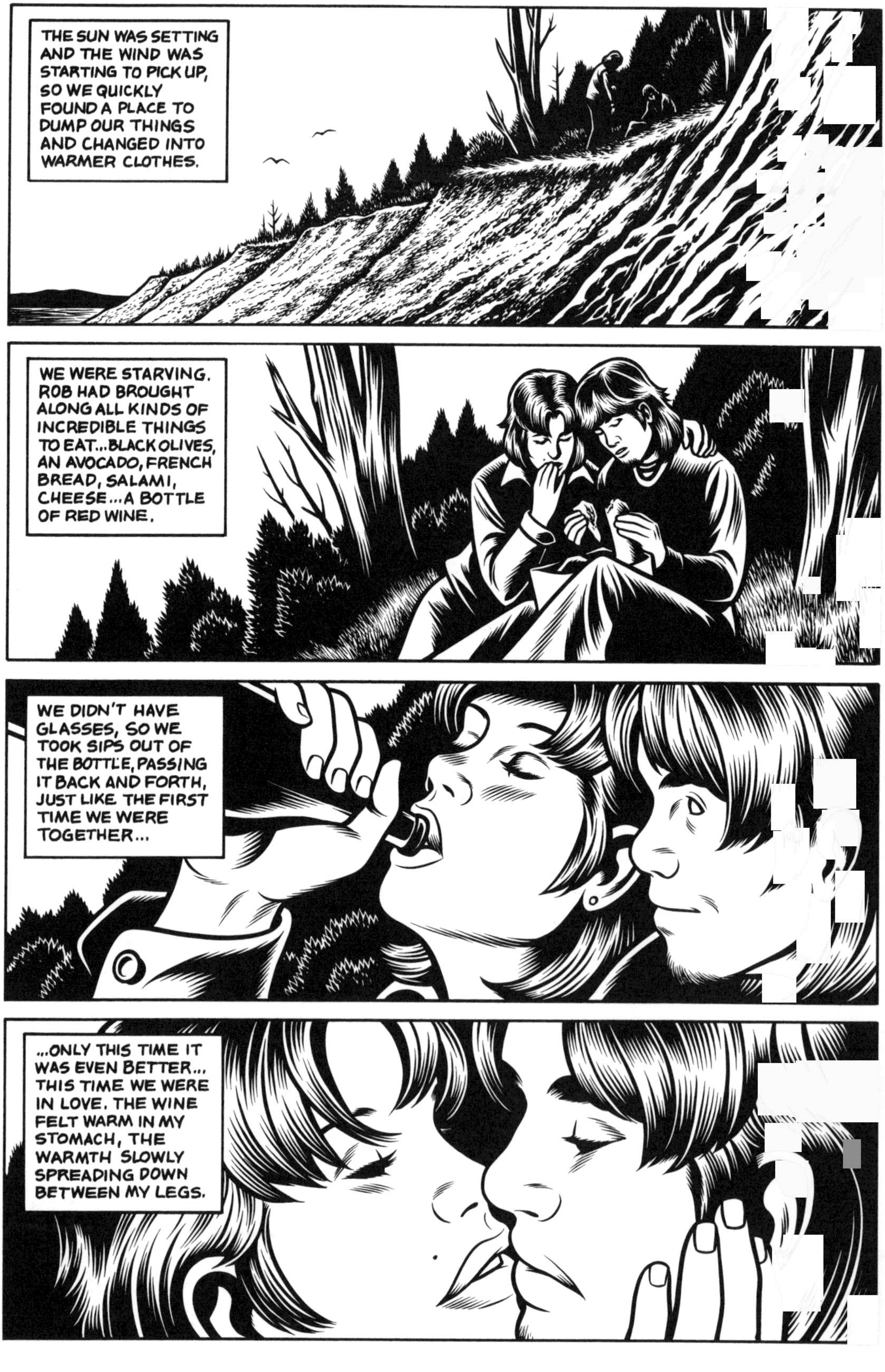
THE SUN WAS SETTING AND THE WIND WAS STARTING TO PICK UP, SO WE QUICKLY FOUND A PLACE TO DUMP OUR THINGS AND CHANGED INTO WARMER CLOTHES.
WE WERE STARVING. ROB HAD BROUGHT ALONG ALL KINDS OF INCREDIBLE THINGS TO EAT...BLACK OLIVES, AN AVOCADO, FRENCH BREAD, SALAMI, CHEESE...A BOTTLE OF RED WINE.
WE DIDN'T HAVE GLASSES, SO WE TOOK SIPS OUT OF THE BOTTLE, PASSING IT BACK AND FORTH, JUST LIKE THE FIRST TIME WE WERE TOGETHER...
...ONLY THIS TIME IT WAS EVEN BETTER... THIS TIME WE WERE IN LOVE. THE WINE FELT WARM IN MY STOMACH, THE WARMTH SLOWLY SPREADING DOWN BETWEEN MY LEGS.

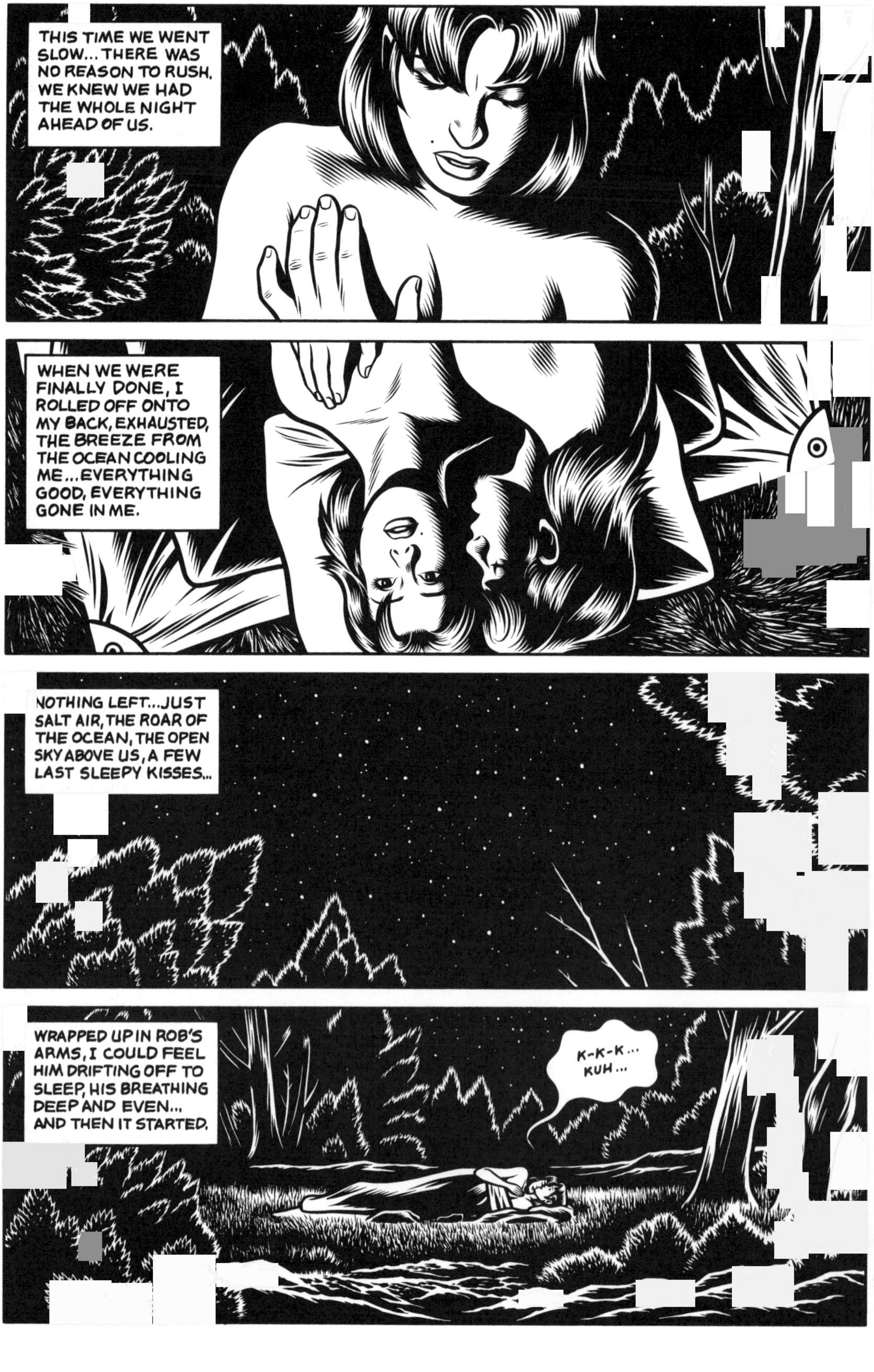
THIS TIME WE WENT SLOW... THERE WAS NO REASON TO RUSH. WE KNEW WE HAD THE WHOLE NIGHT AHEAD OF US.
WHEN WE WERE FINALLY DONE, I ROLLED OFF ONTO MY BACK, EXHAUSTED, THE BREEZE FROM THE OCEAN COOLING ME... EVERYTHING GOOD, EVERYTHING GONE IN ME.
NOTHING LEFT... JUST SALT AIR, THE ROAR OF THE OCEAN, THE OPEN SKY ABOVE US, A FEW LAST SLEEPY KISSES...
WRAPPED UP IN ROB'S ARMS, I COULD FEEL HIM DRIFTING OFF TO SLEEP, HIS BREATHING DEEP AND EVEN... AND THEN IT STARTED.
K-K-K... KUH...

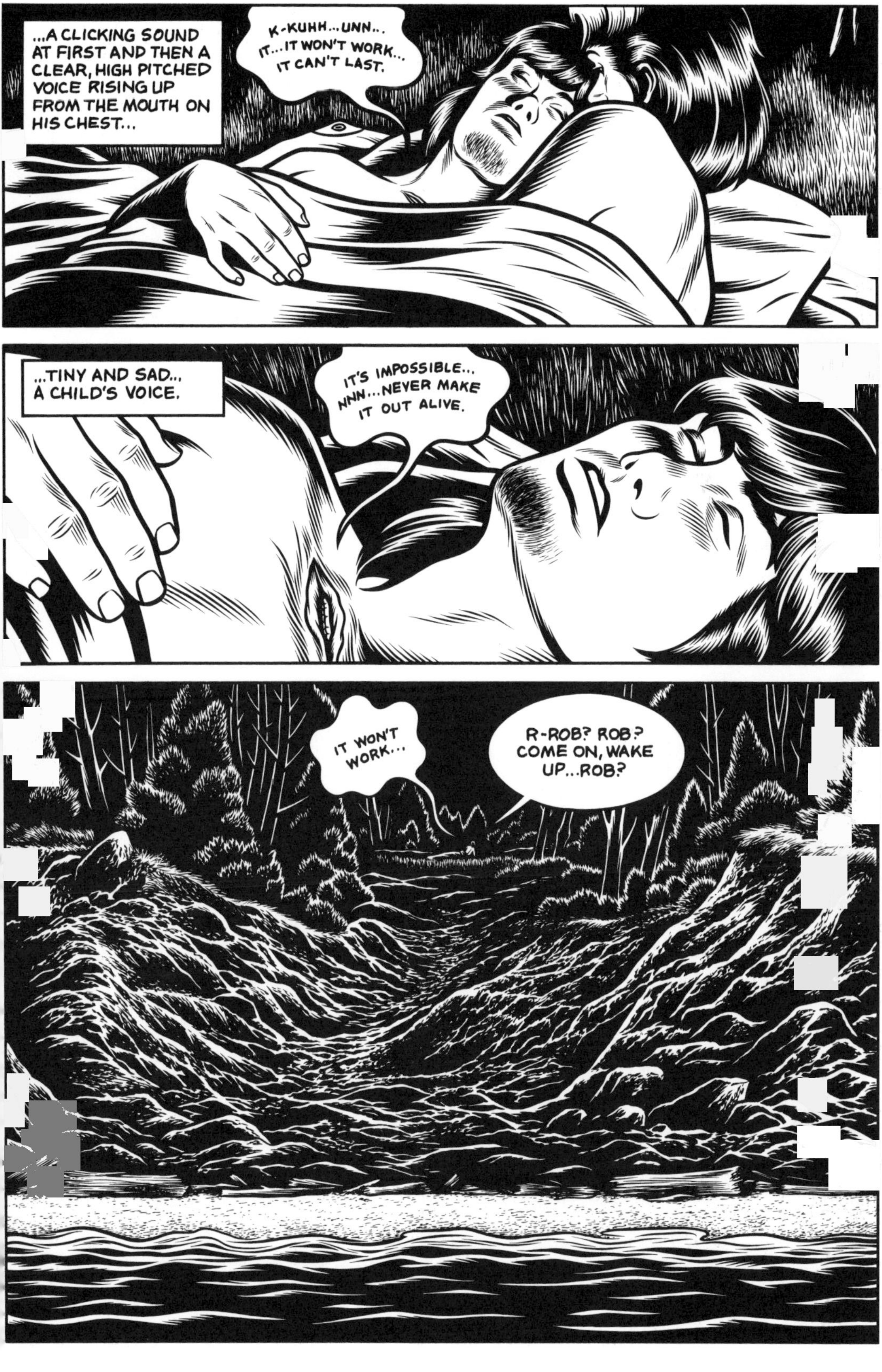
...A CLICKING SOUND AT FIRST AND THEN A CLEAR, HIGH PITCHED VOICE RISING UP FROM THE MOUTH ON HIS CHEST...
K-KUHH...UNN... IT...IT WON'T WORK... IT CAN'T LAST.
...TINY AND SAD... A CHILD'S VOICE.
IT'S IMPOSSIBLE... NNN...NEVER MAKE IT OUT ALIVE.
IT WON'T WORK...
R-ROB? ROB? COME ON, WAKE UP...ROB?

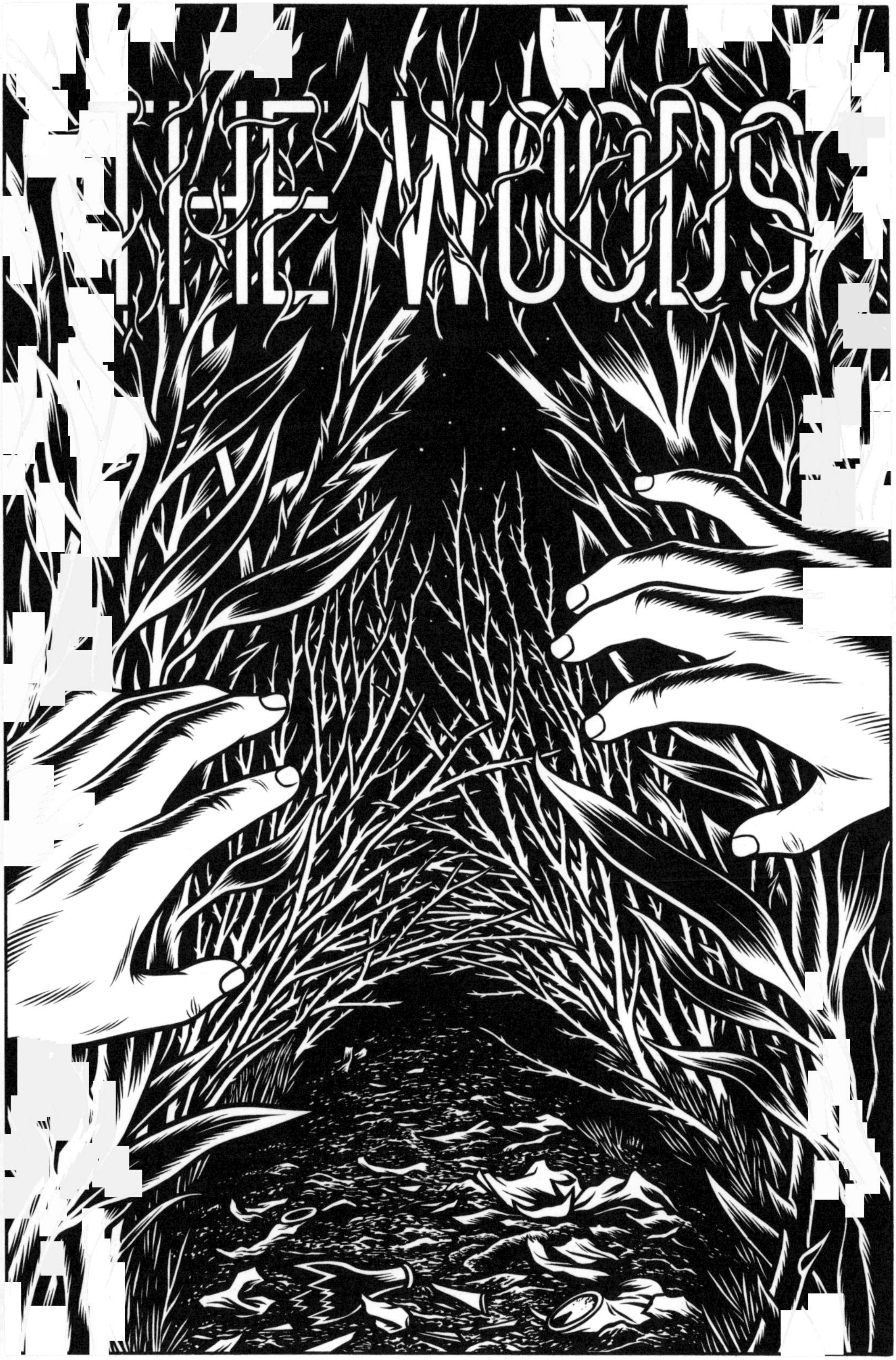
THE WOODS

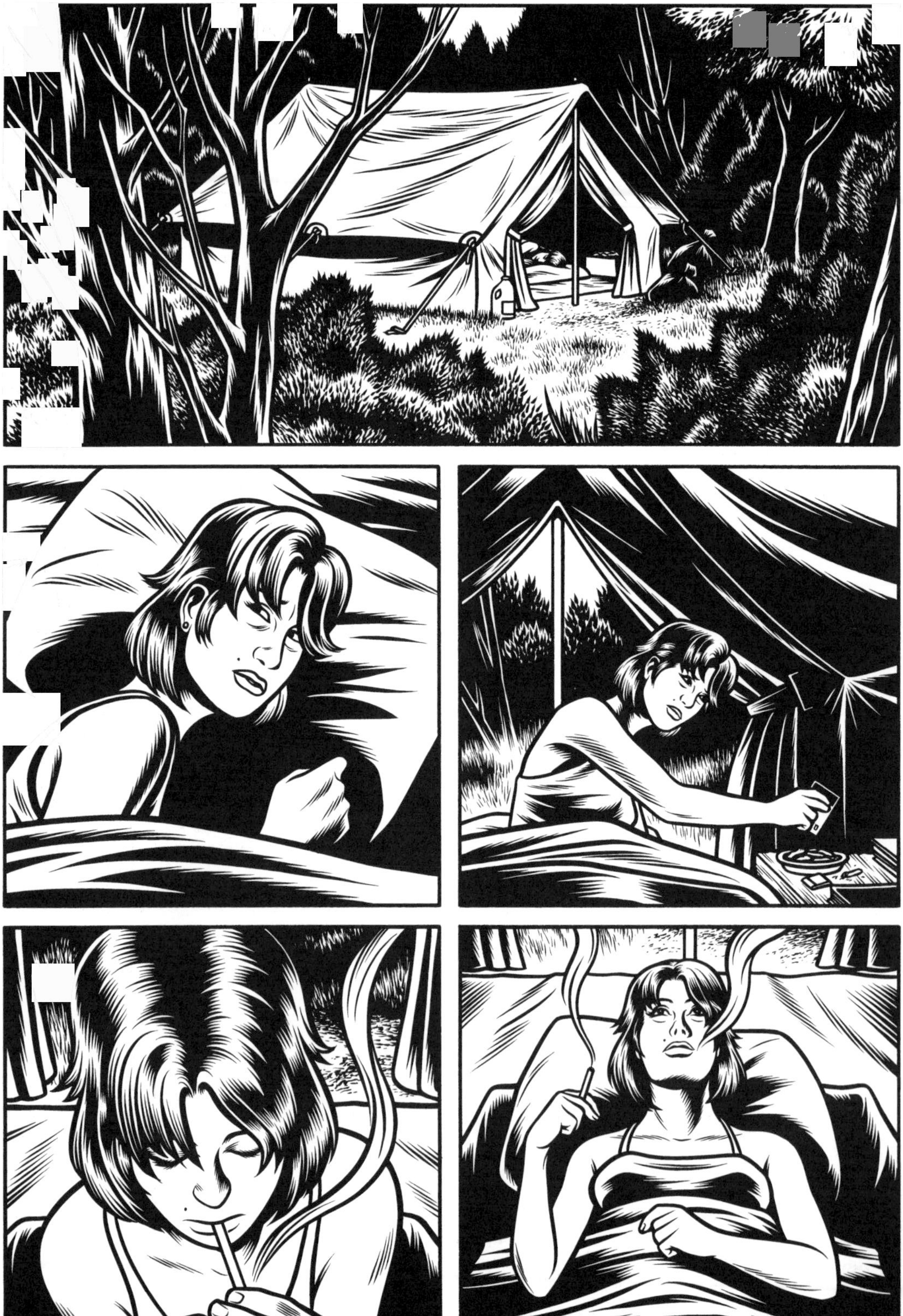

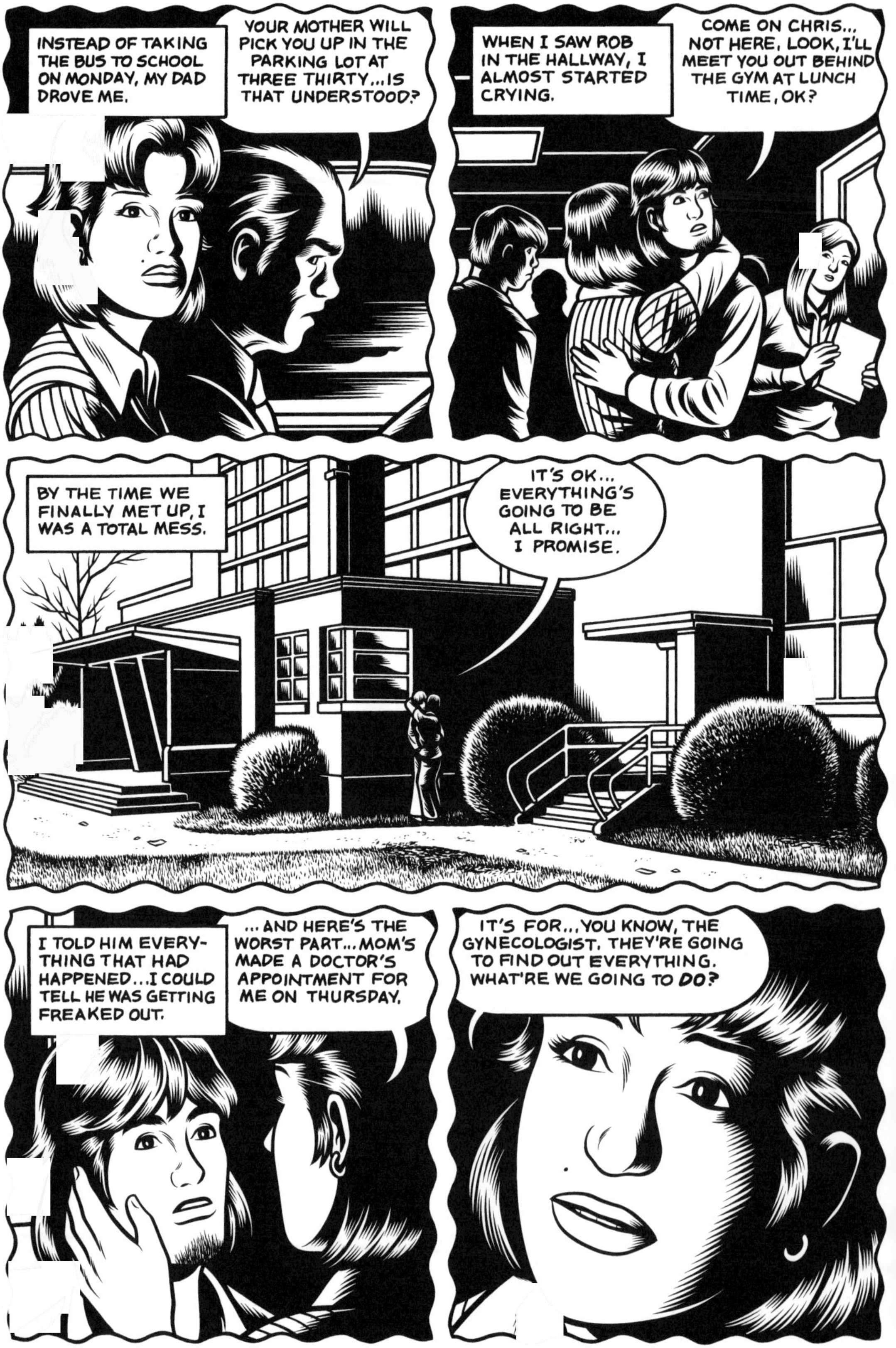
INSTEAD OF TAKING THE BUS TO SCHOOL ON MONDAY, MY DAD DROVE ME.
YOUR MOTHER WILL PICK YOU UP IN THE PARKING LOT AT THREE THIRTY...IS THAT UNDERSTOOD?
WHEN I SAW ROB IN THE HALLWAY, I ALMOST STARTED CRYING.
COME ON CHRIS... NOT HERE, LOOK, I'LL MEET YOU OUT BEHIND THE GYM AT LUNCH TIME, OK?
BY THE TIME WE FINALLY MET UP, I WAS A TOTAL MESS.
IT'S OK... EVERYTHING'S GOING TO BE ALL RIGHT... I PROMISE.
I TOLD HIM EVERYTHING THAT HAD HAPPENED...I COULD TELL HE WAS GETTING FREAKED OUT.
...AND HERE'S THE WORST PART...MOM'S MADE A DOCTOR'S APPOINTMENT FOR ME ON THURSDAY.
IT'S FOR...YOU KNOW, THE GYNECOLOGIST. THEY'RE GOING TO FIND OUT EVERYTHING. WHAT'RE WE GOING TO *DO*?

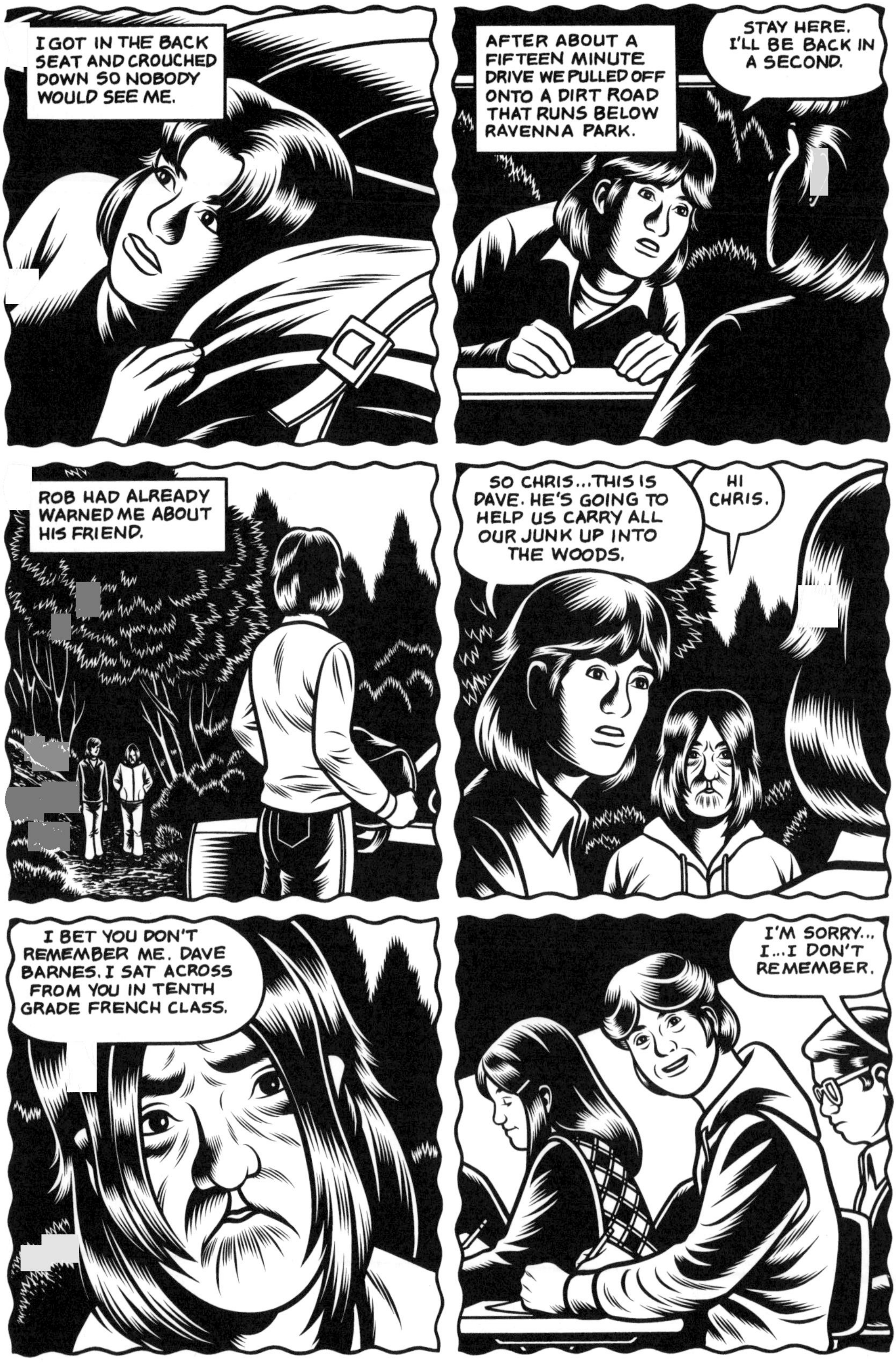
I GOT IN THE BACK SEAT AND CROUCHED DOWN SO NOBODY WOULD SEE ME.
AFTER ABOUT A FIFTEEN MINUTE DRIVE WE PULLED OFF ONTO A DIRT ROAD THAT RUNS BELOW RAVENNA PARK.
STAY HERE. I'LL BE BACK IN A SECOND.
ROB HAD ALREADY WARNED ME ABOUT HIS FRIEND.
SO CHRIS... THIS IS DAVE. HE'S GOING TO HELP US CARRY ALL OUR JUNK UP INTO THE WOODS.
HI CHRIS.
I BET YOU DON'T REMEMBER ME. DAVE BARNES. I SAT ACROSS FROM YOU IN TENTH GRADE FRENCH CLASS.
I'M SORRY... I... I DON'T REMEMBER.

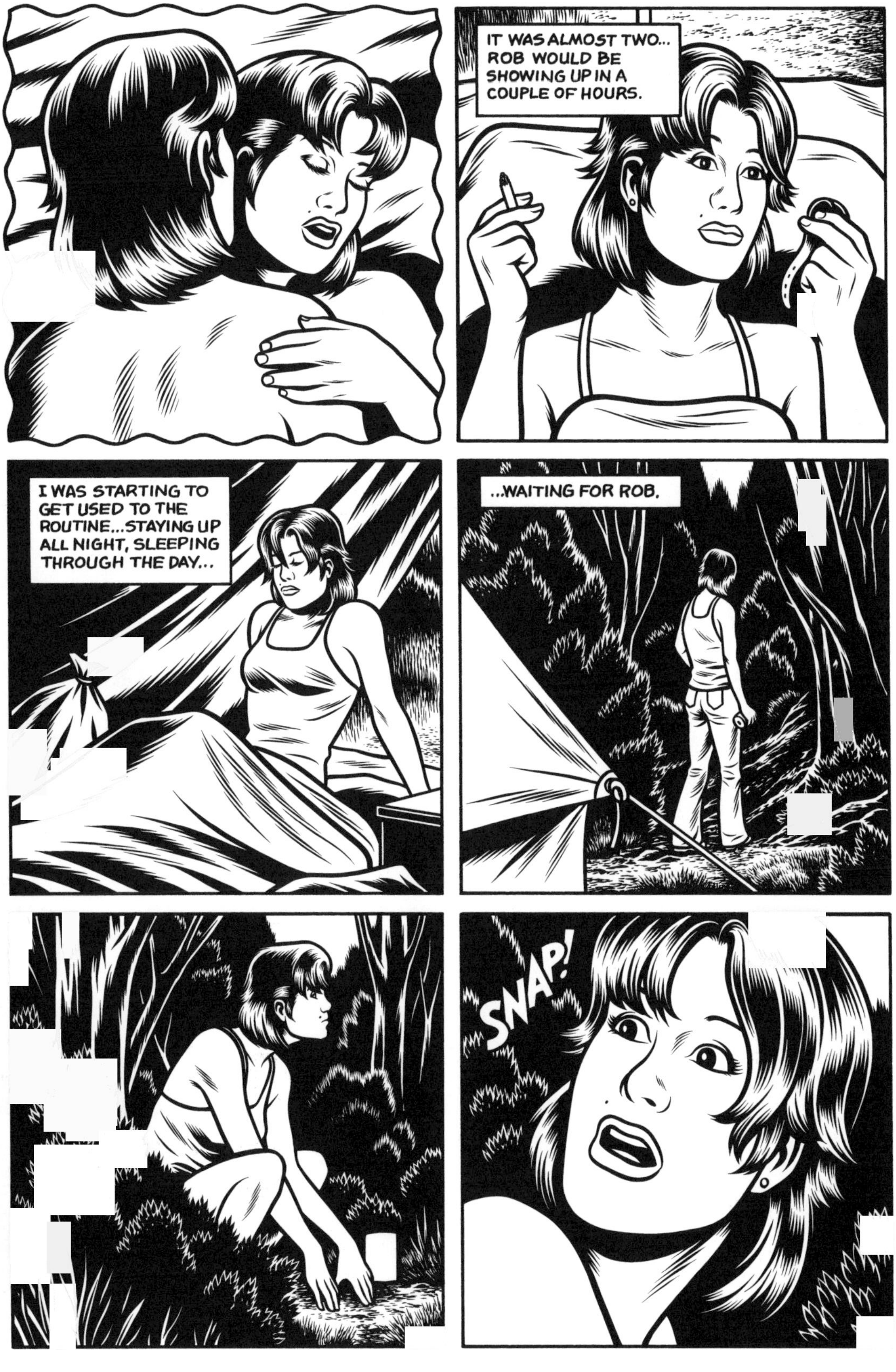
IT WAS ALMOST TWO... ROB WOULD BE SHOWING UP IN A COUPLE OF HOURS.
I WAS STARTING TO GET USED TO THE ROUTINE...STAYING UP ALL NIGHT, SLEEPING THROUGH THE DAY...
...WAITING FOR ROB.
SNAP!

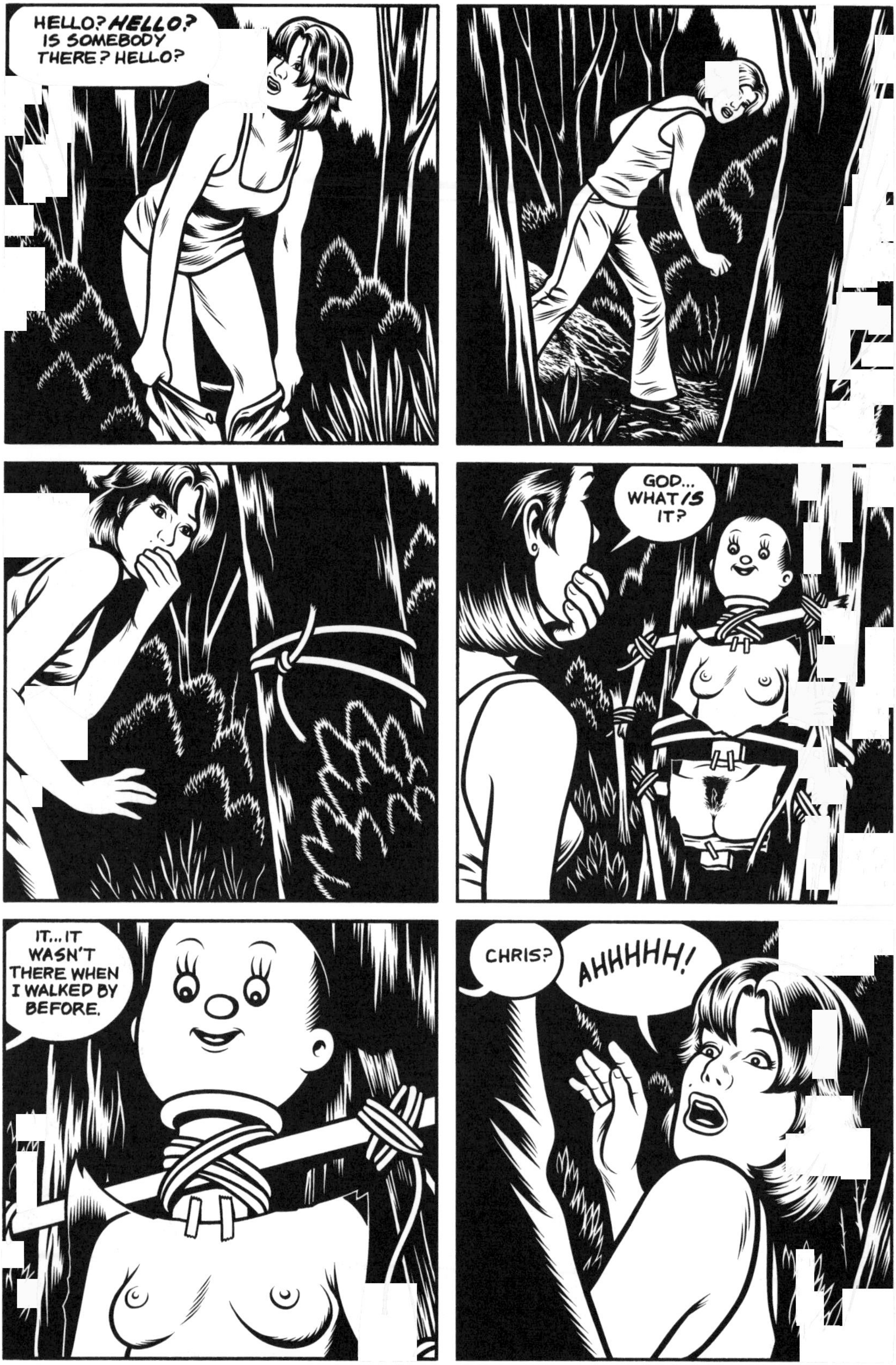
HELLO? HELLO? IS SOMEBODY THERE? HELLO?
GOD... WHAT IS IT?
IT... IT WASN'T THERE WHEN I WALKED BY BEFORE.
CHRIS?
AHHHHH!

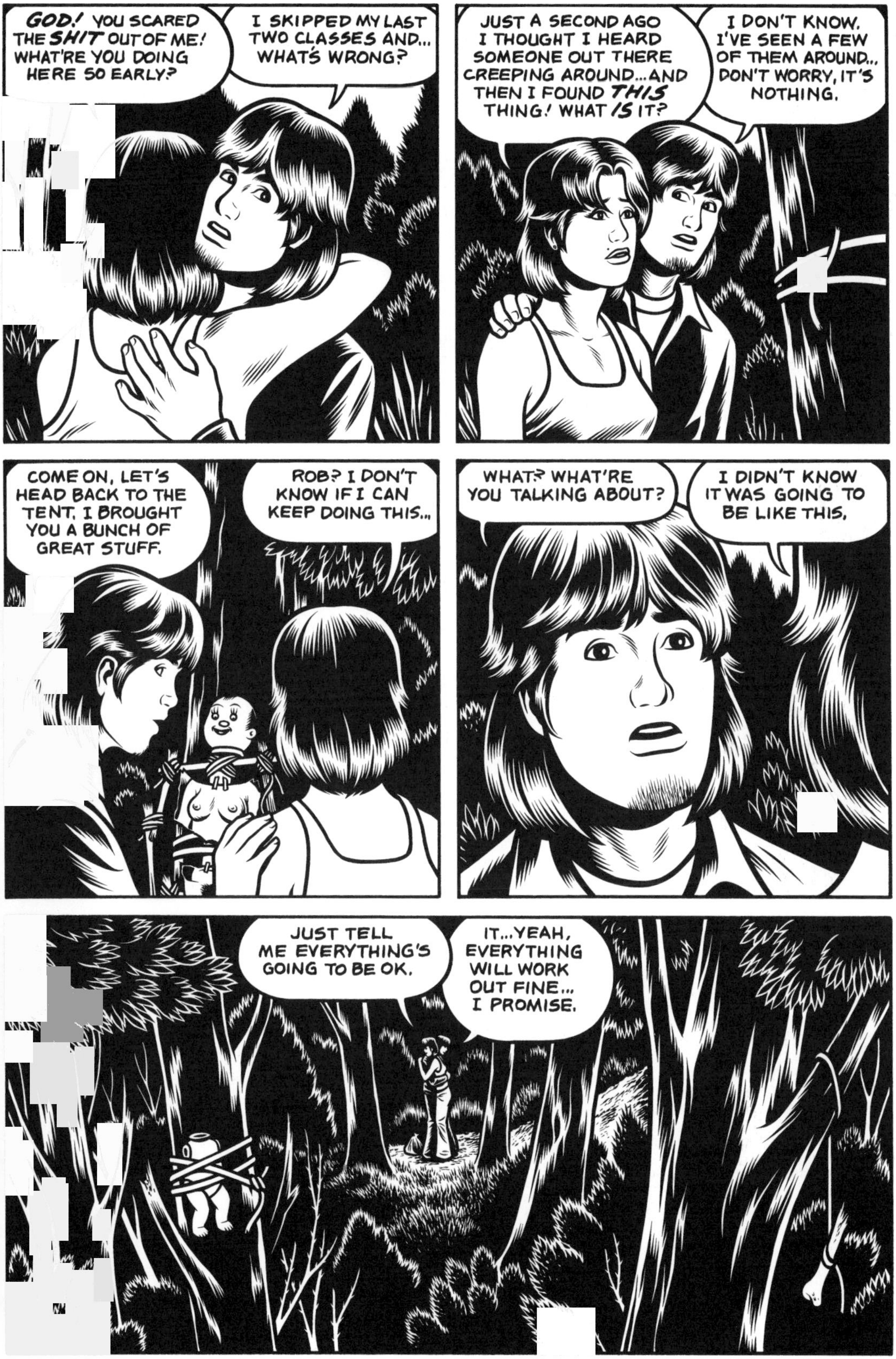
GOD! YOU SCARED THE SHIT OUT OF ME! WHAT'RE YOU DOING HERE SO EARLY?
I SKIPPED MY LAST TWO CLASSES AND... WHAT'S WRONG?
JUST A SECOND AGO I THOUGHT I HEARD SOMEONE OUT THERE CREEPING AROUND...AND THEN I FOUND THIS THING! WHAT IS IT?
I DON'T KNOW. I'VE SEEN A FEW OF THEM AROUND... DON'T WORRY, IT'S NOTHING.
COME ON, LET'S HEAD BACK TO THE TENT. I BROUGHT YOU A BUNCH OF GREAT STUFF.
ROB? I DON'T KNOW IF I CAN KEEP DOING THIS...
WHAT? WHAT'RE YOU TALKING ABOUT?
I DIDN'T KNOW IT WAS GOING TO BE LIKE THIS.
JUST TELL ME EVERYTHING'S GOING TO BE OK.
IT...YEAH, EVERYTHING WILL WORK OUT FINE... I PROMISE.

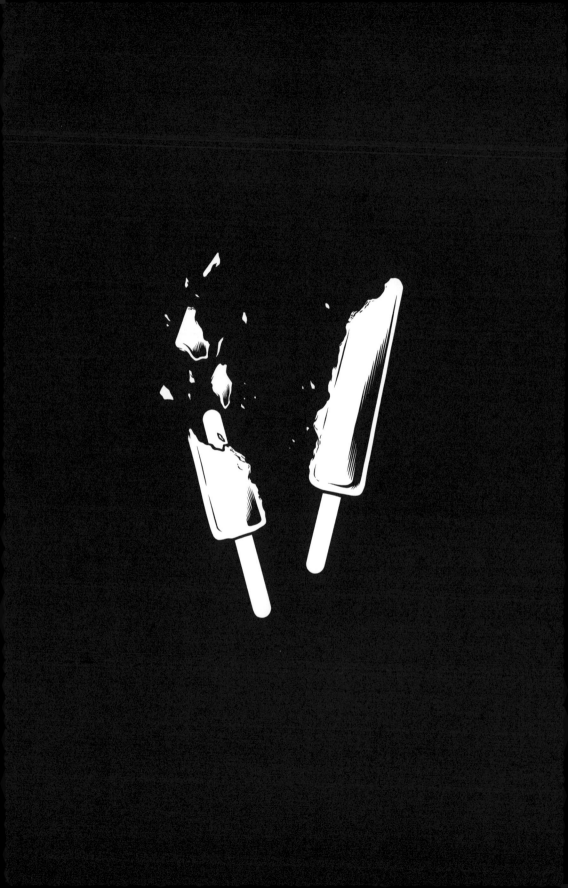

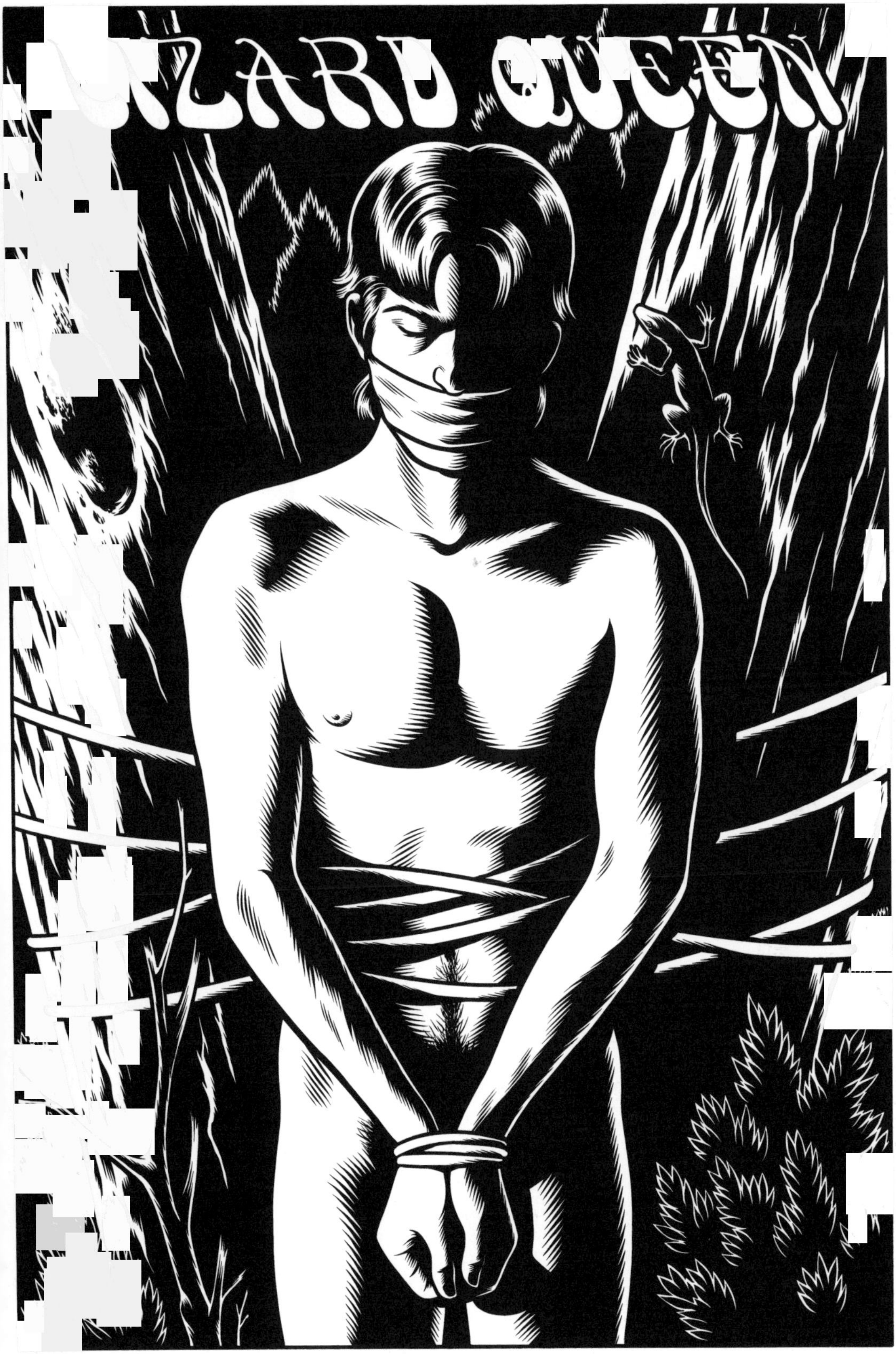
IZARD QUEEN

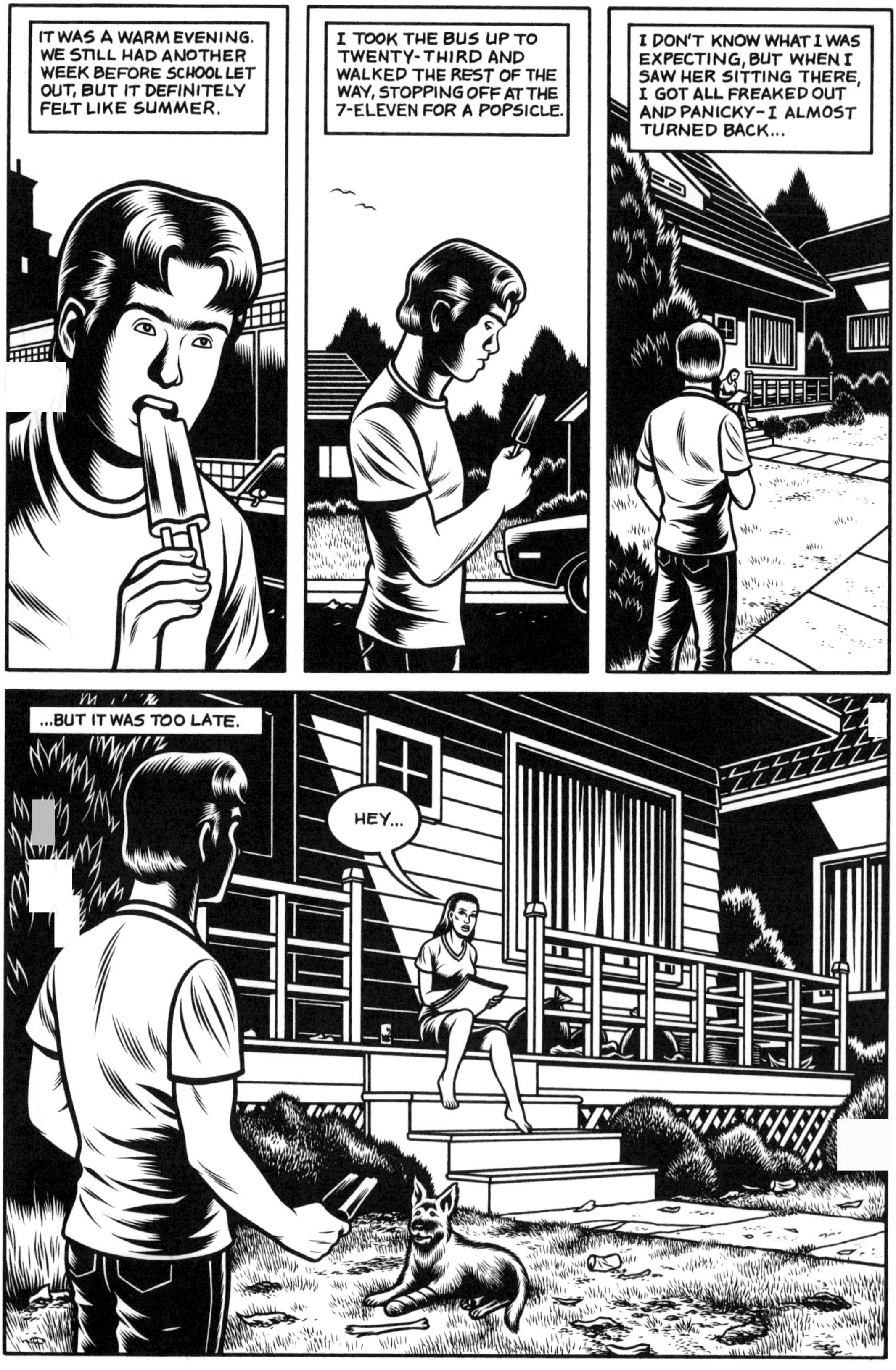
IT WAS A WARM EVENING. WE STILL HAD ANOTHER WEEK BEFORE SCHOOL LET OUT, BUT IT DEFINITELY FELT LIKE SUMMER.
I TOOK THE BUS UP TO TWENTY-THIRD AND WALKED THE REST OF THE WAY, STOPPING OFF AT THE 7-ELEVEN FOR A POPSICLE.
I DON'T KNOW WHAT I WAS EXPECTING, BUT WHEN I SAW HER SITTING THERE, I GOT ALL FREAKED OUT AND PANICKY–I ALMOST TURNED BACK...
...BUT IT WAS TOO LATE.
HEY...

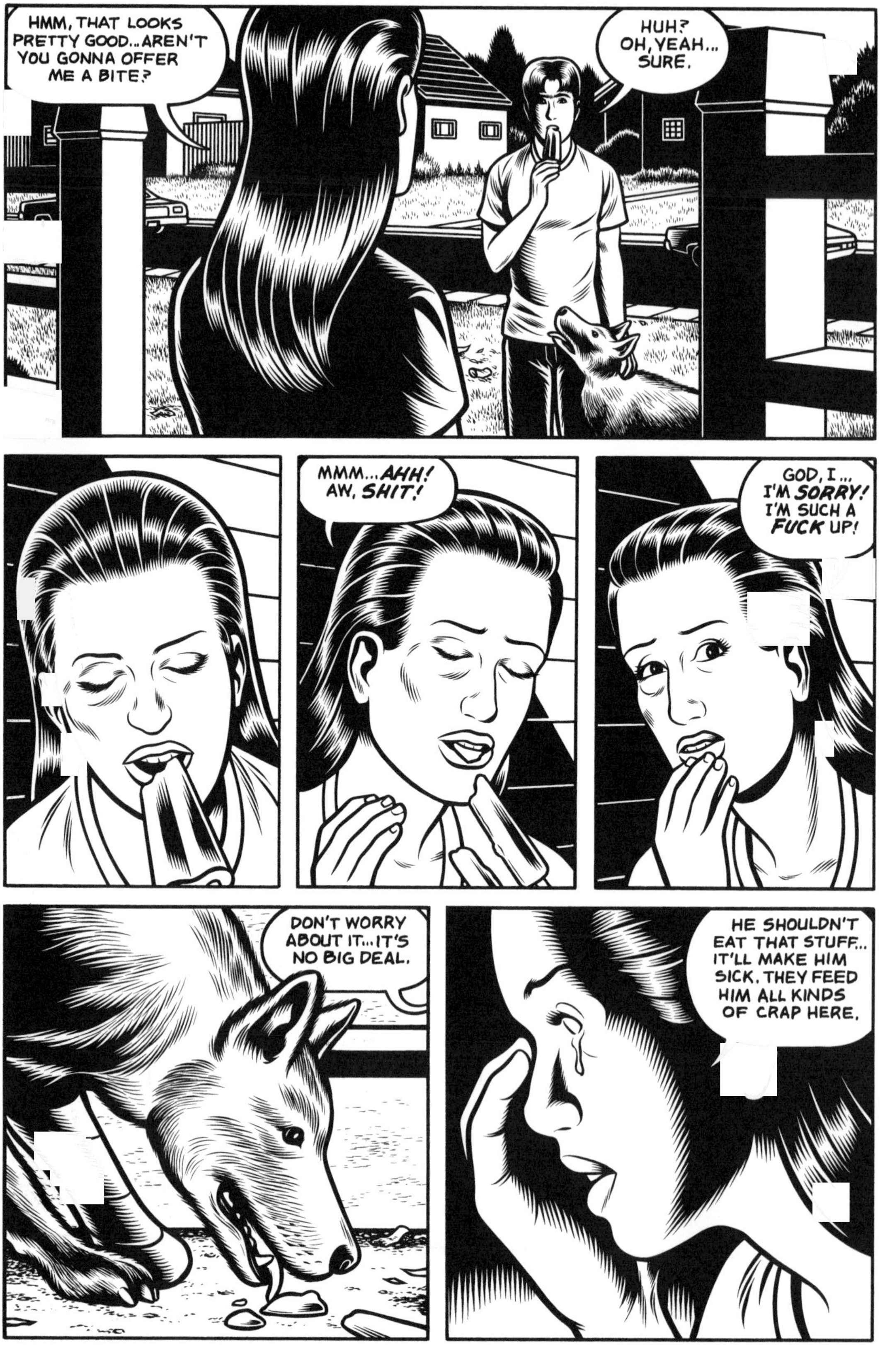
HMM, THAT LOOKS PRETTY GOOD... AREN'T YOU GONNA OFFER ME A BITE?
HUH? OH, YEAH... SURE.
MMM... AHH! AW, SHIT!
GOD, I... I'M SORRY! I'M SUCH A FUCK UP!
DON'T WORRY ABOUT IT... IT'S NO BIG DEAL.
HE SHOULDN'T EAT THAT STUFF... IT'LL MAKE HIM SICK. THEY FEED HIM ALL KINDS OF CRAP HERE.

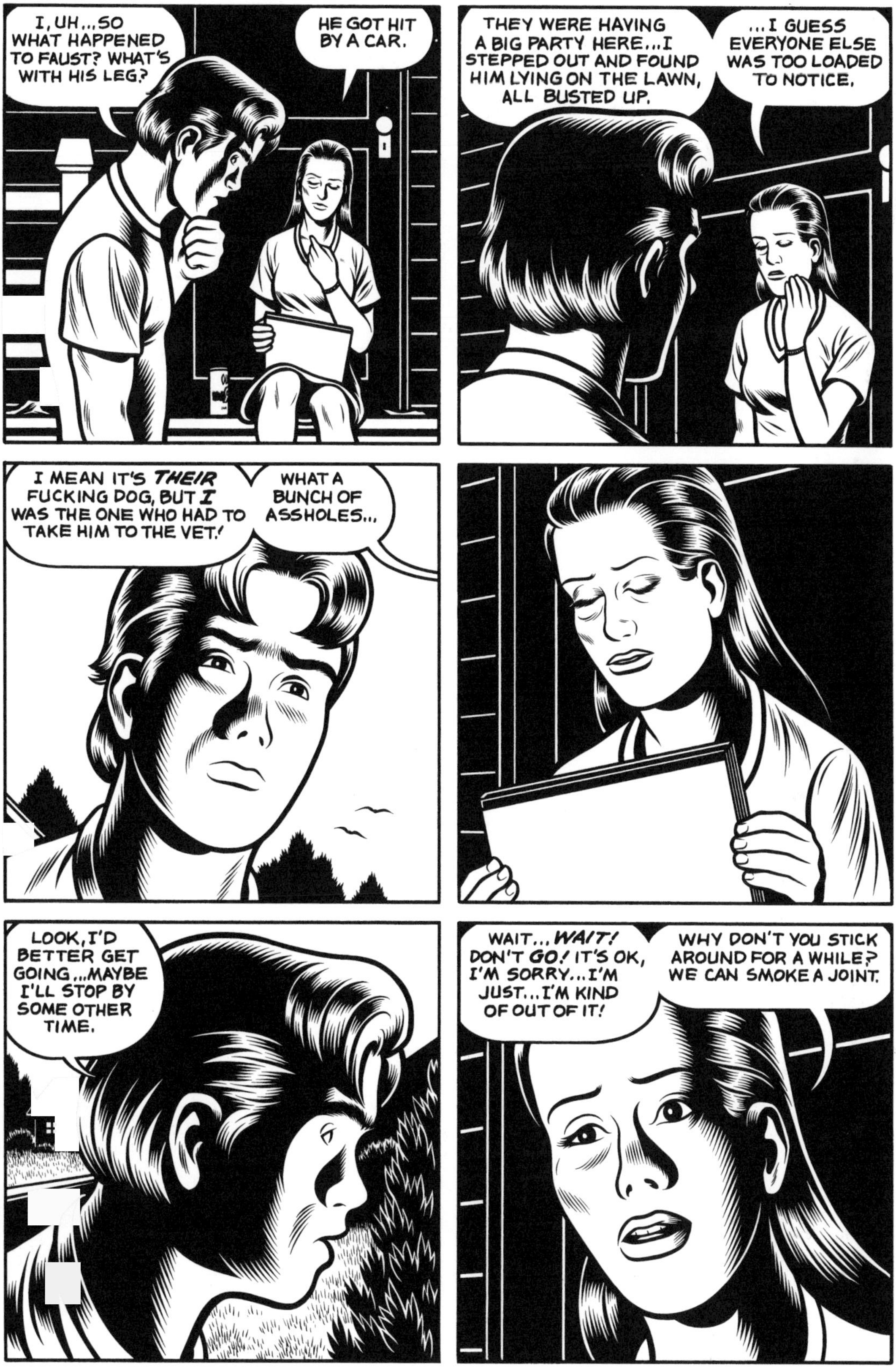
I, UH... SO WHAT HAPPENED TO FAUST? WHAT'S WITH HIS LEG?
HE GOT HIT BY A CAR.
THEY WERE HAVING A BIG PARTY HERE... I STEPPED OUT AND FOUND HIM LYING ON THE LAWN, ALL BUSTED UP.
... I GUESS EVERYONE ELSE WAS TOO LOADED TO NOTICE.
I MEAN IT'S *THEIR* FUCKING DOG, BUT *I* WAS THE ONE WHO HAD TO TAKE HIM TO THE VET!
WHAT A BUNCH OF ASSHOLES...
LOOK, I'D BETTER GET GOING... MAYBE I'LL STOP BY SOME OTHER TIME.
WAIT... *WAIT!* DON'T *GO!* IT'S OK, I'M SORRY... I'M JUST... I'M KIND OF OUT OF IT!
WHY DON'T YOU STICK AROUND FOR A WHILE? WE CAN SMOKE A JOINT.

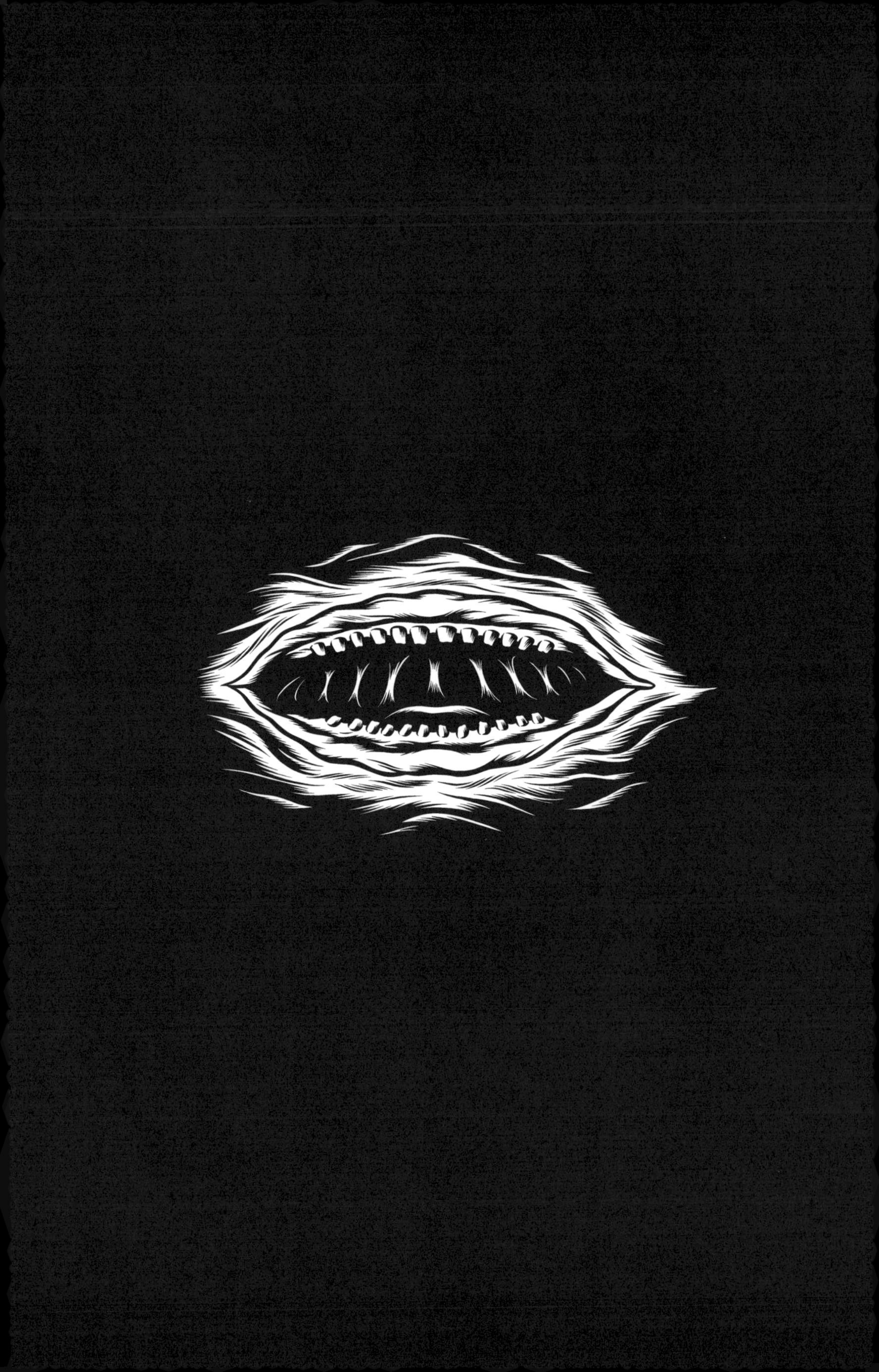

i'm sorry

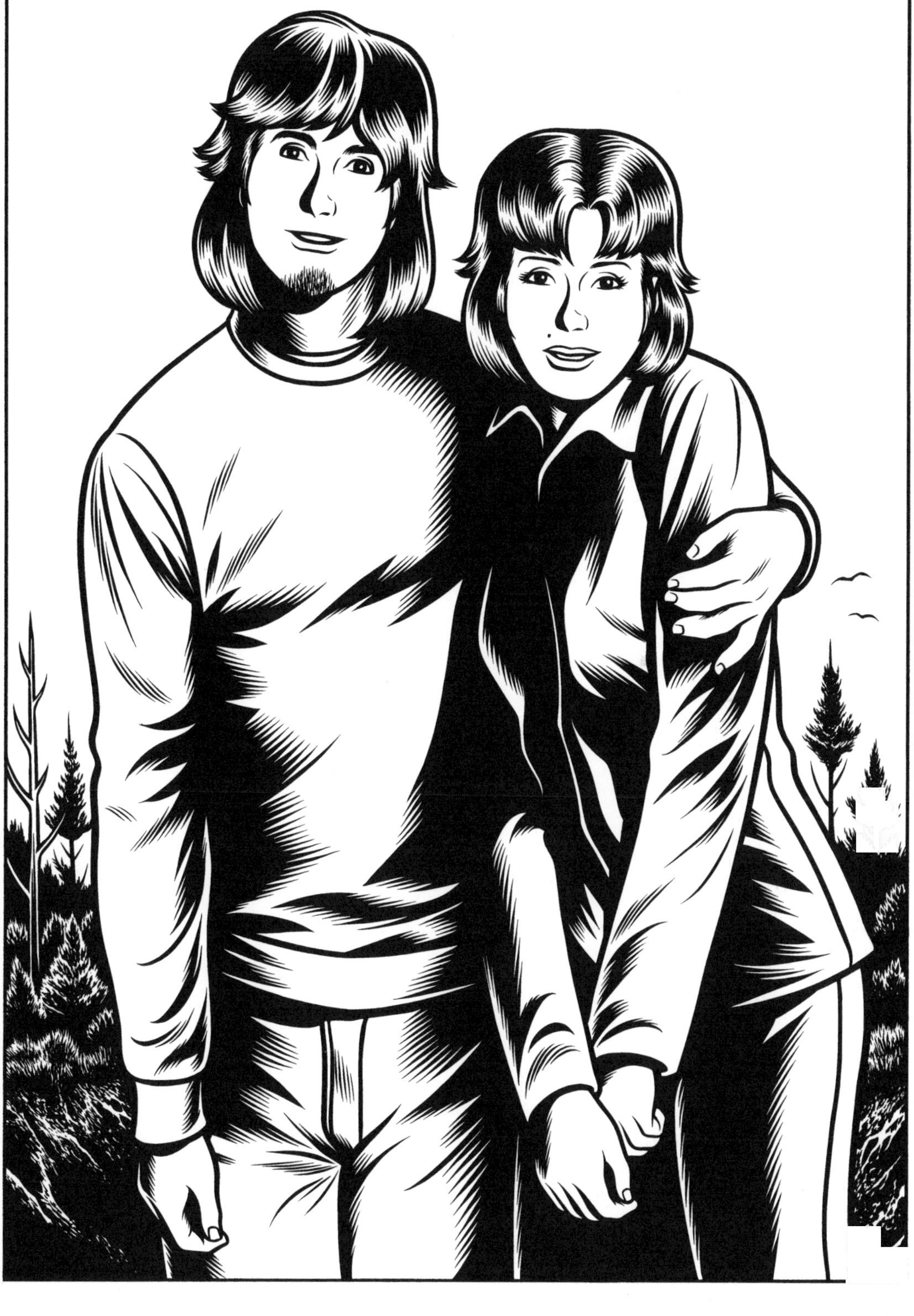

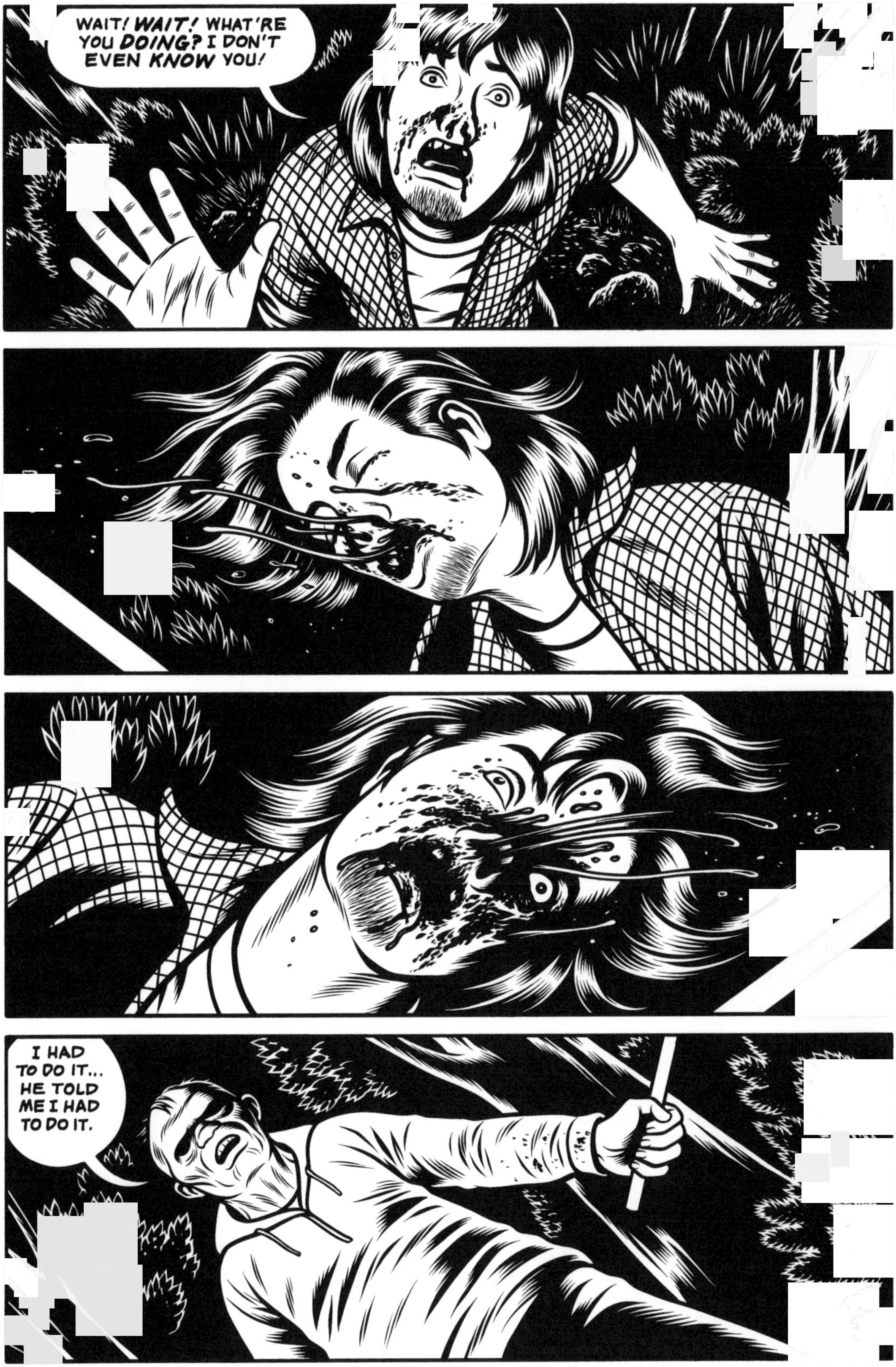
WAIT! WAIT! WHAT'RE YOU DOING? I DON'T EVEN KNOW YOU!
I HAD TO DO IT... HE TOLD ME I HAD TO DO IT.

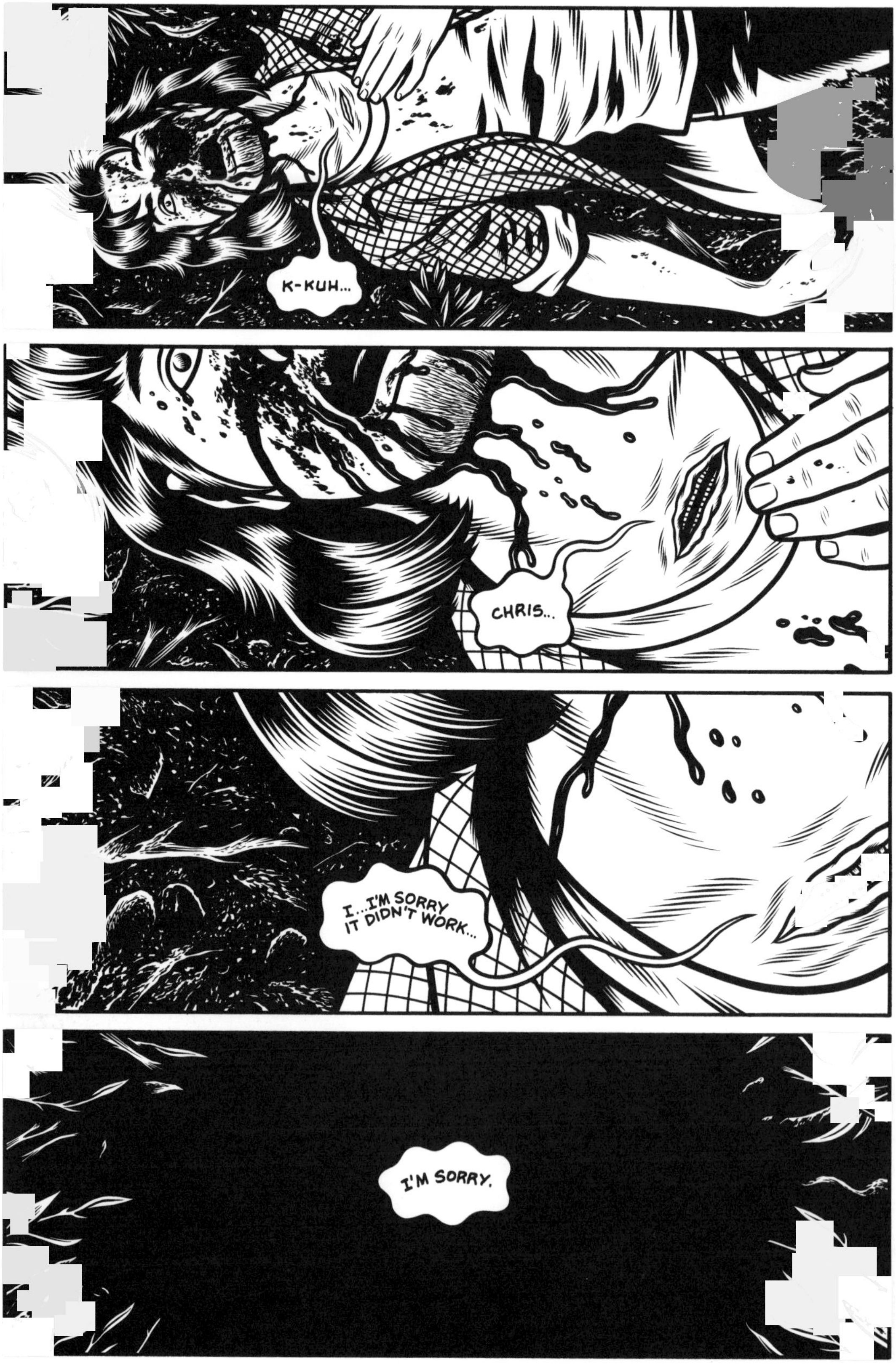
K-KUH...
CHRIS...
I...I'M SORRY
IT DIDN'T WORK...
I'M SORRY.

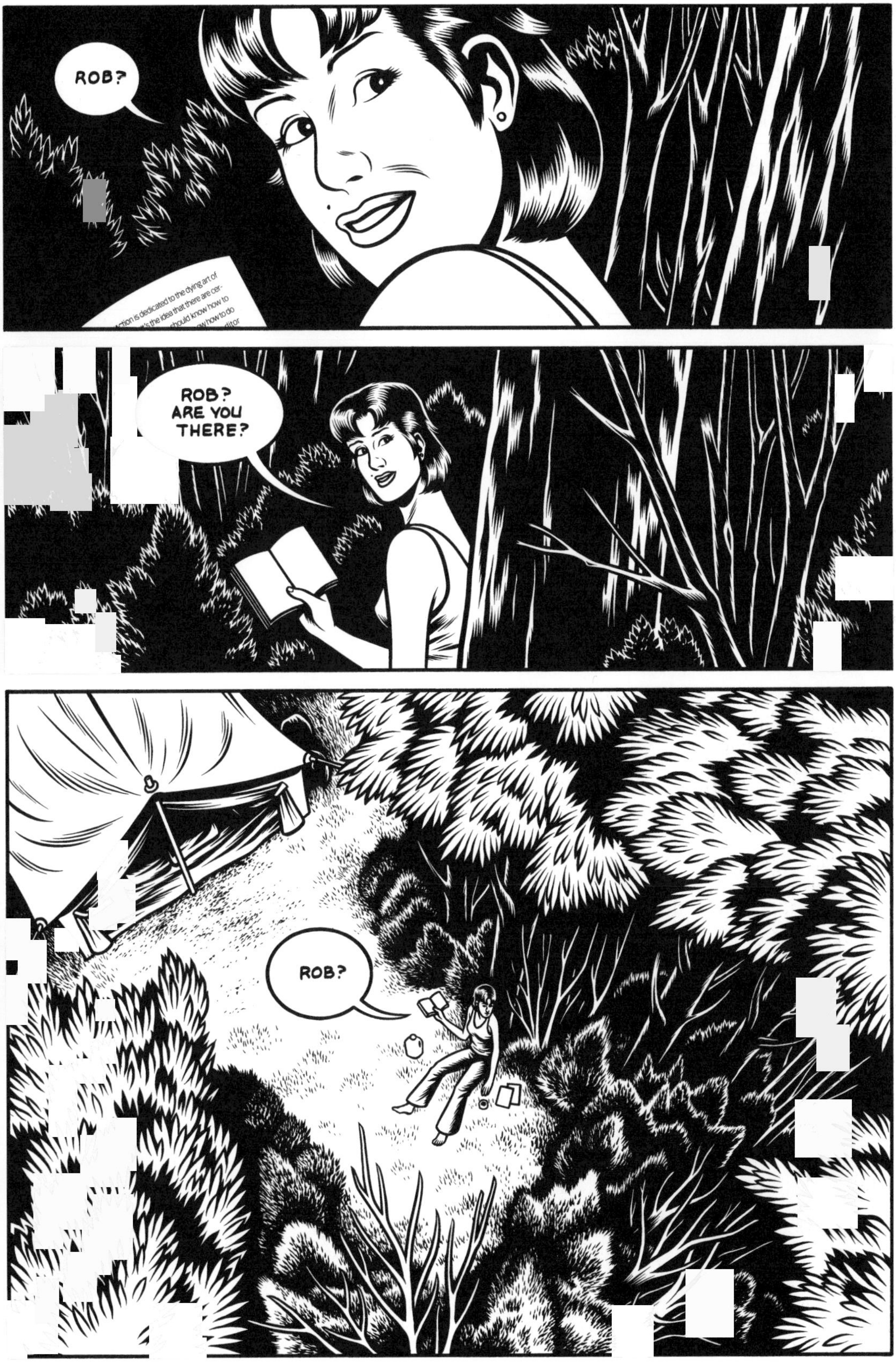
ROB?
is dedicated to the dying art of
the idea that there are cer-
should know how to
how to do
ROB? ARE YOU THERE?
ROB?

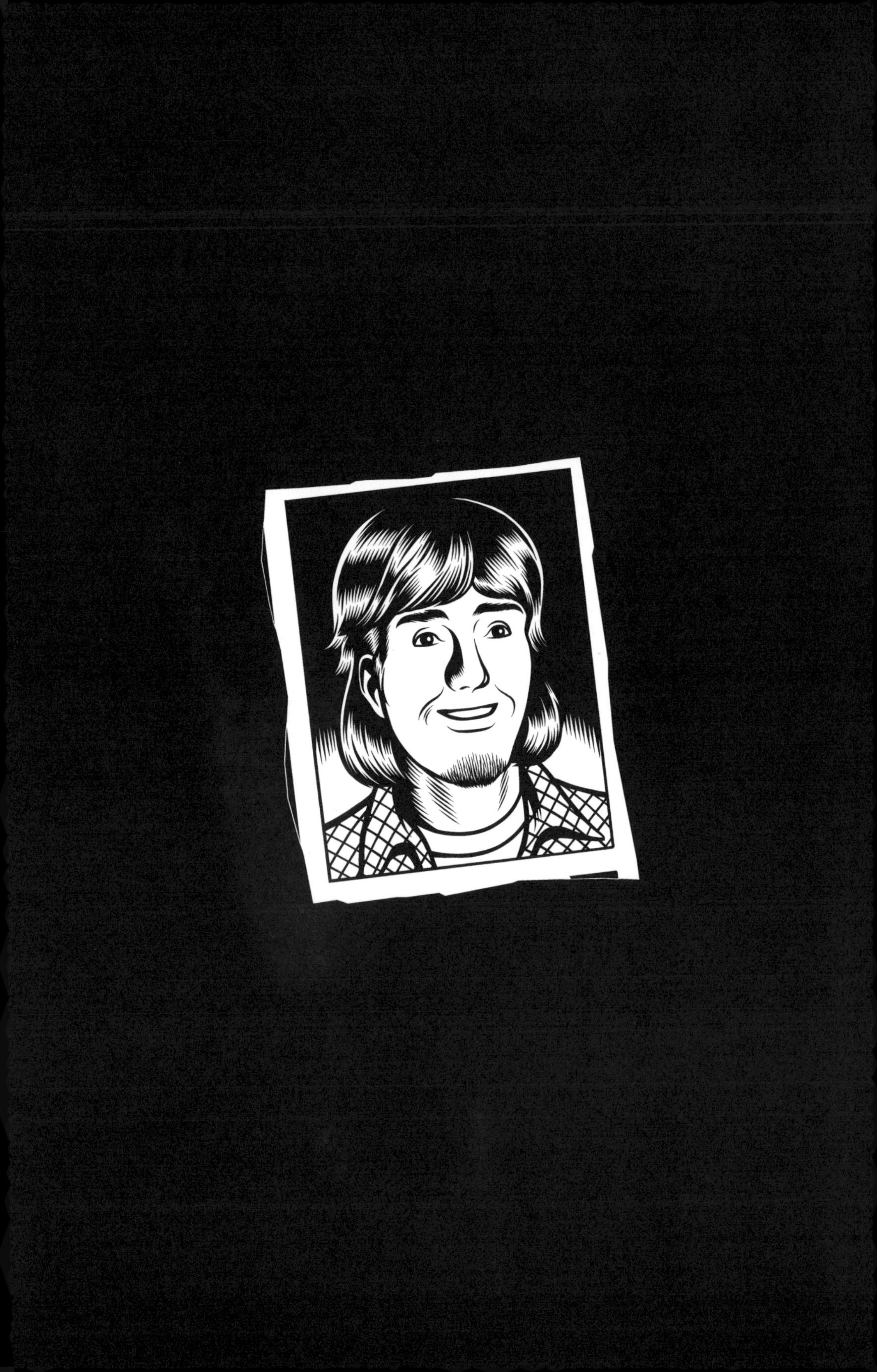

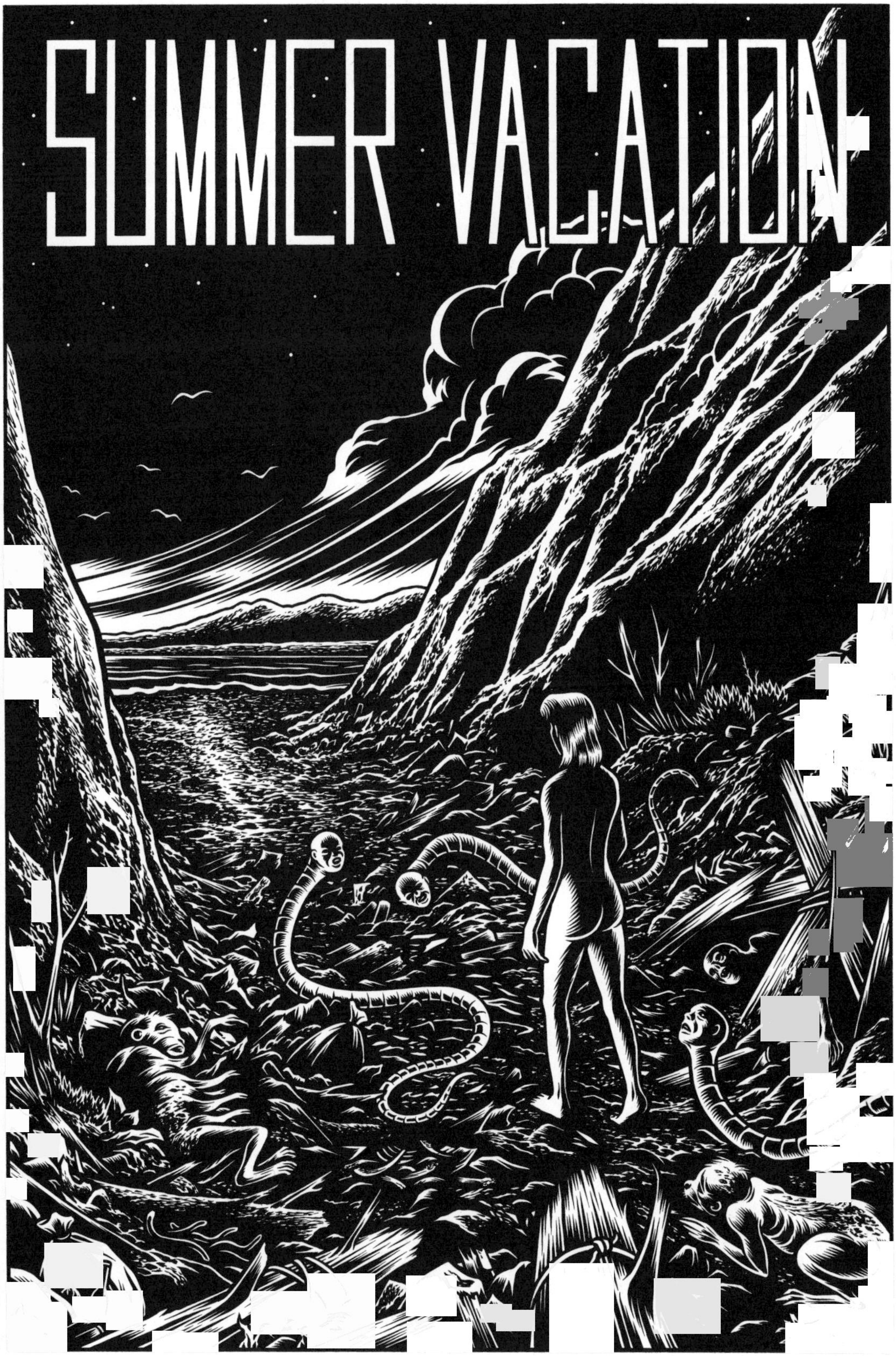
SUMMER VACATION

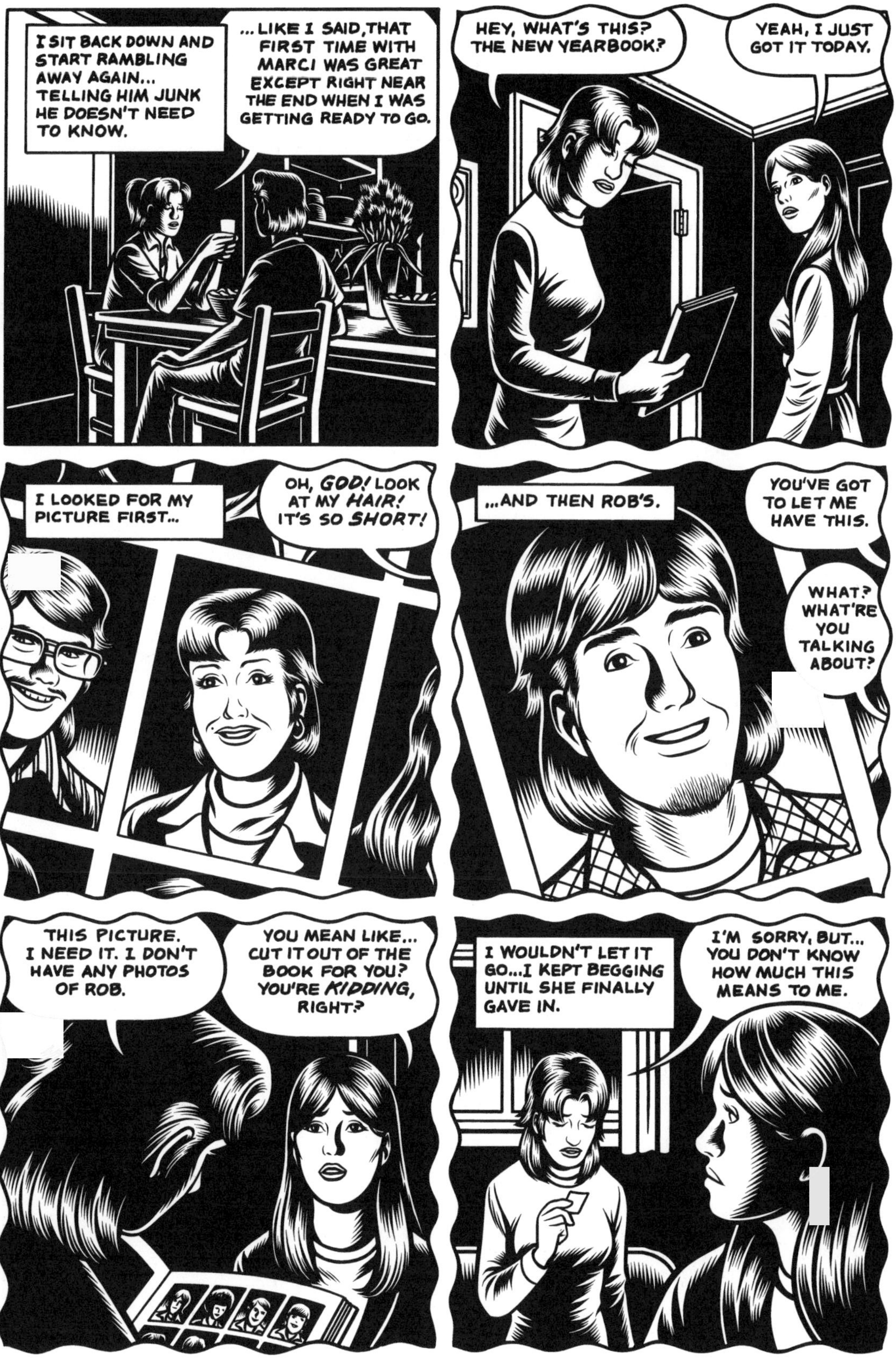
I SIT BACK DOWN AND START RAMBLING AWAY AGAIN... TELLING HIM JUNK HE DOESN'T NEED TO KNOW.
...LIKE I SAID, THAT FIRST TIME WITH MARCI WAS GREAT EXCEPT RIGHT NEAR THE END WHEN I WAS GETTING READY TO GO.
HEY, WHAT'S THIS? THE NEW YEARBOOK?
YEAH, I JUST GOT IT TODAY.
I LOOKED FOR MY PICTURE FIRST...
OH, GOD! LOOK AT MY HAIR! IT'S SO SHORT!
...AND THEN ROB'S.
YOU'VE GOT TO LET ME HAVE THIS.
WHAT? WHAT'RE YOU TALKING ABOUT?
THIS PICTURE. I NEED IT. I DON'T HAVE ANY PHOTOS OF ROB.
YOU MEAN LIKE... CUT IT OUT OF THE BOOK FOR YOU? YOU'RE KIDDING, RIGHT?
I WOULDN'T LET IT GO... I KEPT BEGGING UNTIL SHE FINALLY GAVE IN.
I'M SORRY, BUT... YOU DON'T KNOW HOW MUCH THIS MEANS TO ME.

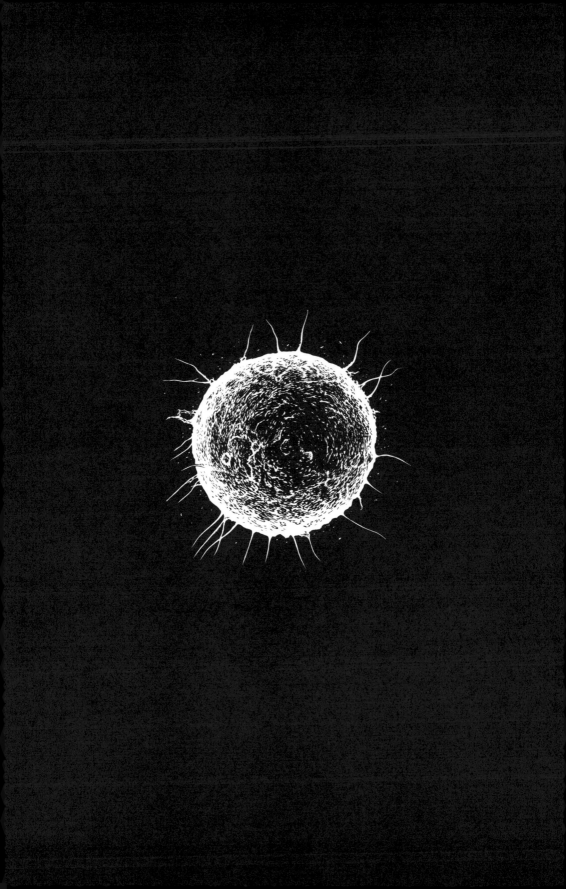

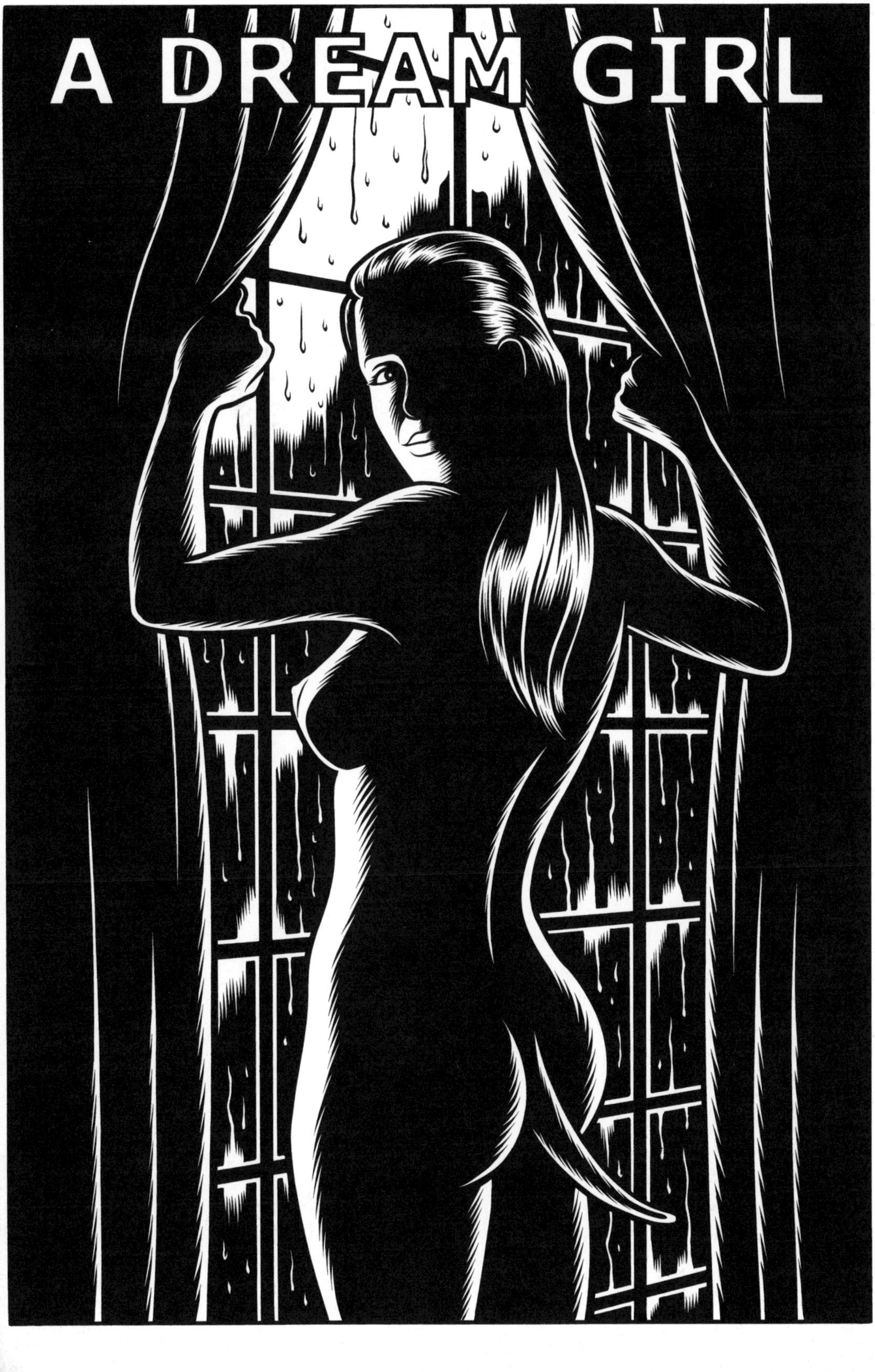
A DREAM GIRL

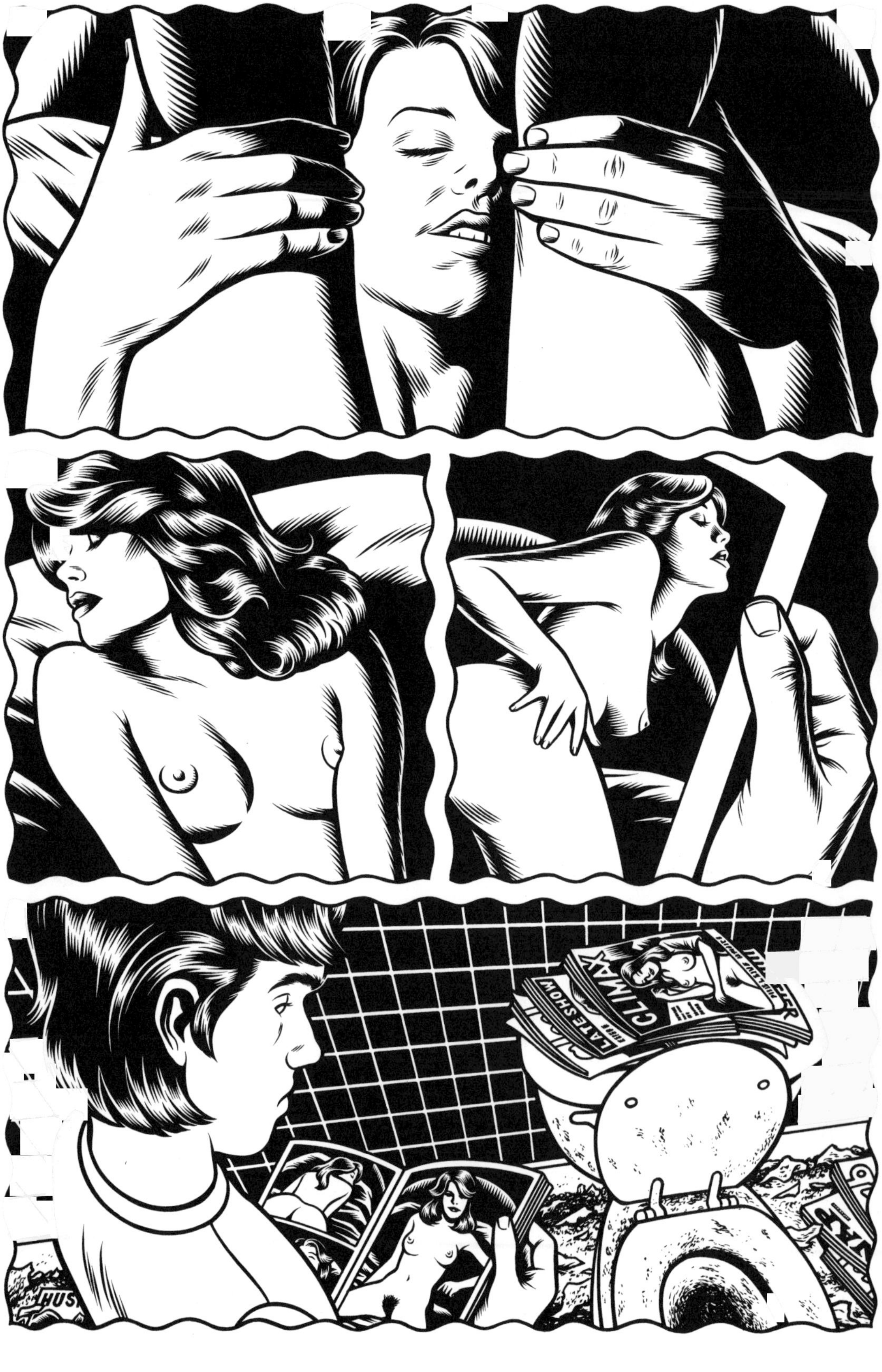
CLIMAX
LATE SHOW

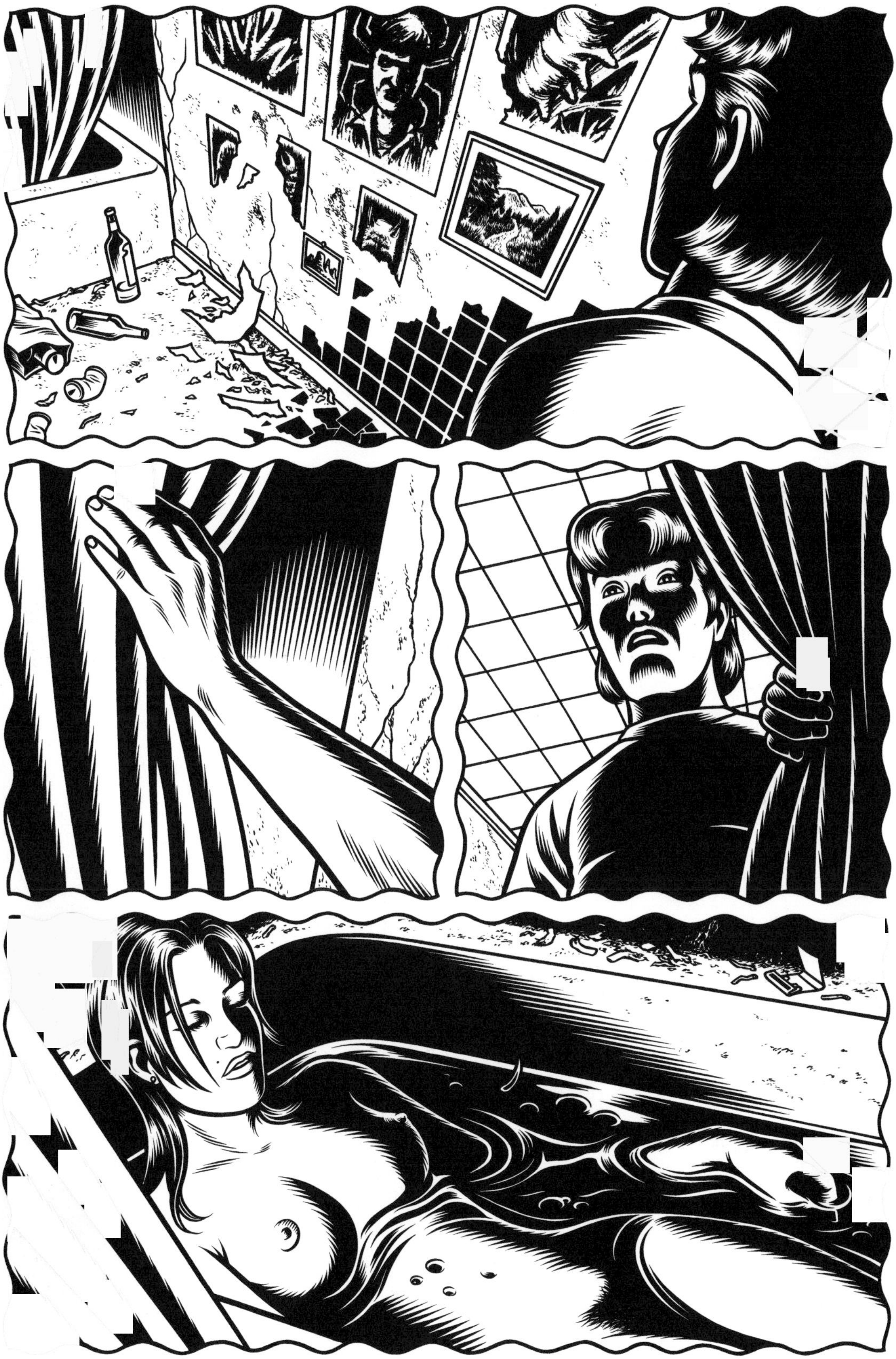

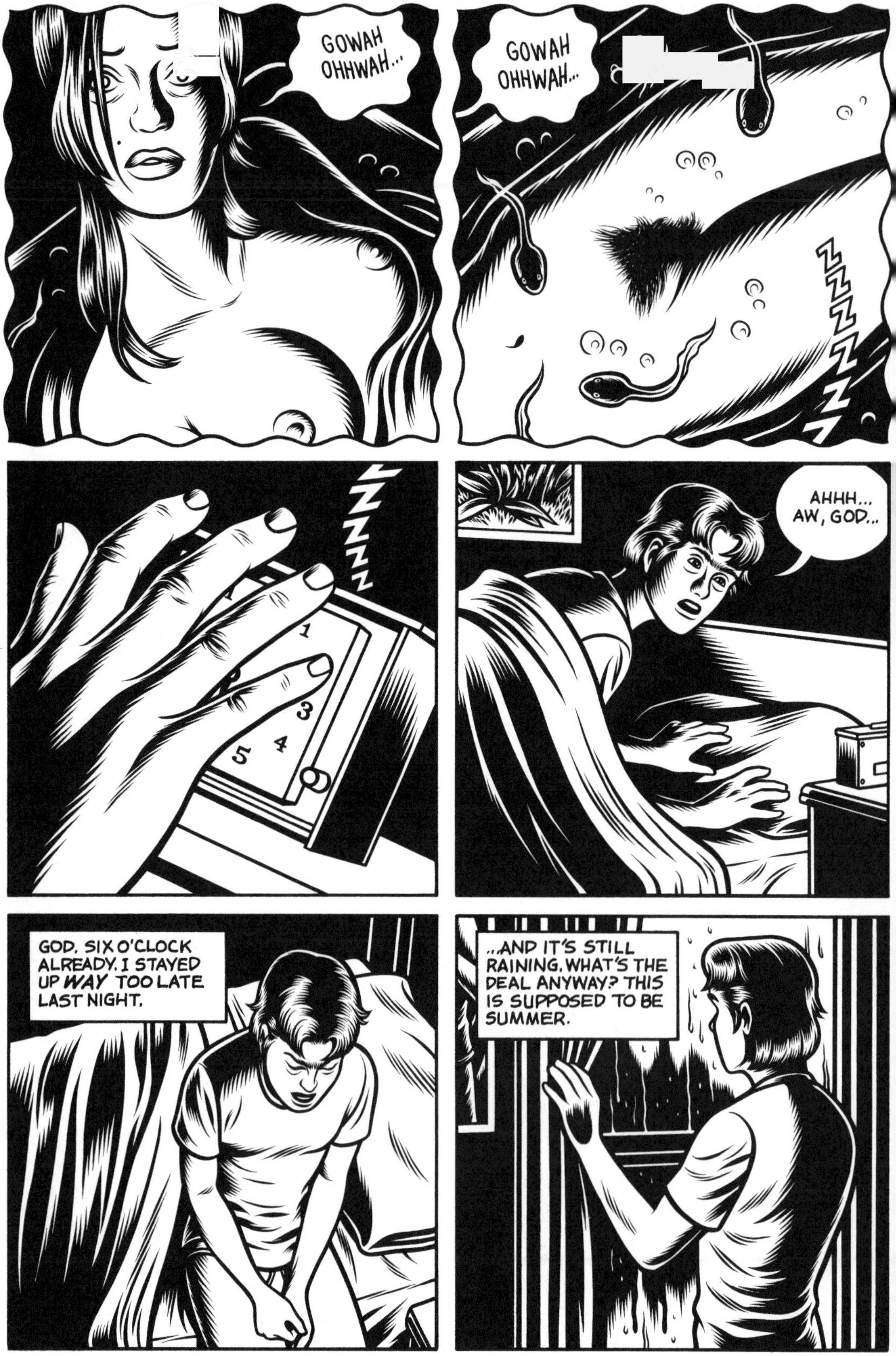

GOWAH OHHWAH...
GOWAH OHHWAH...
ZZZZZZZ
ZZZZZ
AHHH... AW, GOD...
GOD. SIX O'CLOCK ALREADY. I STAYED UP *WAY* TOO LATE LAST NIGHT.
...AND IT'S STILL RAINING. WHAT'S THE DEAL ANYWAY? THIS IS SUPPOSED TO BE SUMMER.

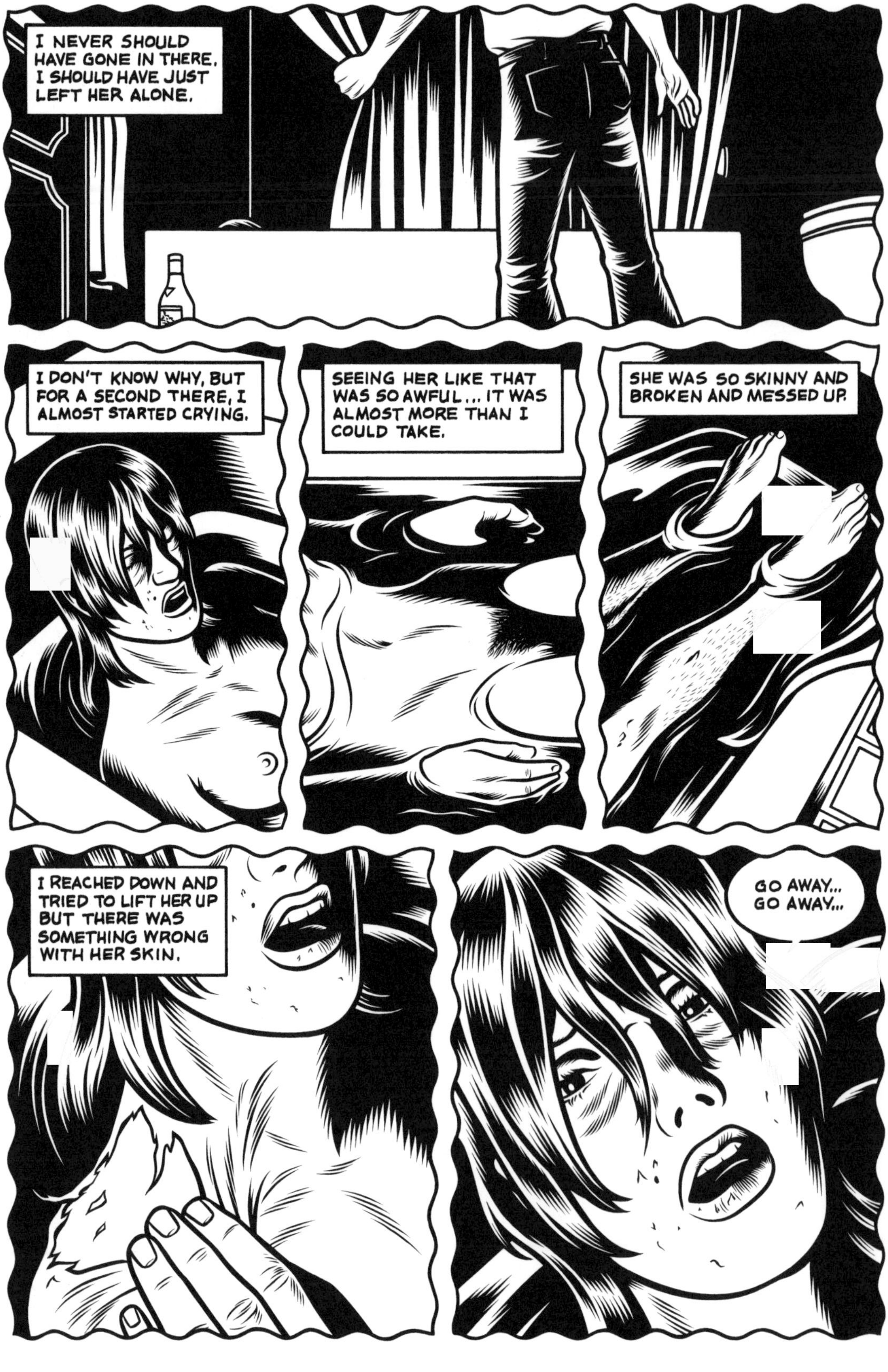
I NEVER SHOULD HAVE GONE IN THERE. I SHOULD HAVE JUST LEFT HER ALONE.
I DON'T KNOW WHY, BUT FOR A SECOND THERE, I ALMOST STARTED CRYING.
SEEING HER LIKE THAT WAS SO AWFUL... IT WAS ALMOST MORE THAN I COULD TAKE.
SHE WAS SO SKINNY AND BROKEN AND MESSED UP.
I REACHED DOWN AND TRIED TO LIFT HER UP BUT THERE WAS SOMETHING WRONG WITH HER SKIN.
GO AWAY... GO AWAY...

THIRD PERIOD. BIOLOGY CLASS...THAT USED TO BE ONE OF THE HIGHLIGHTS OF MY DAY.

SHE WAS SO SWEET AND PERFECT BACK THEN.

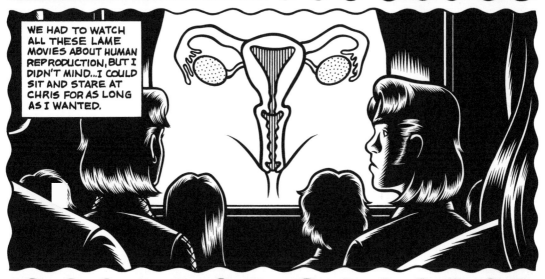

WE HAD TO WATCH ALL THESE LAME MOVIES ABOUT HUMAN REPRODUCTION, BUT I DIDN'T MIND...I COULD SIT AND STARE AT CHRIS FOR AS LONG AS I WANTED.

THOSE MOVIES WERE ALWAYS SO SAFE AND CLEAN...EVERYTHING SIMPLIFIED DOWN TO DIAGRAMS AND ANIMATED CARTOONS...

...MICROSCOPIC PICTURES OF SPERM CELLS SWARMING AROUND A GIANT EGG...

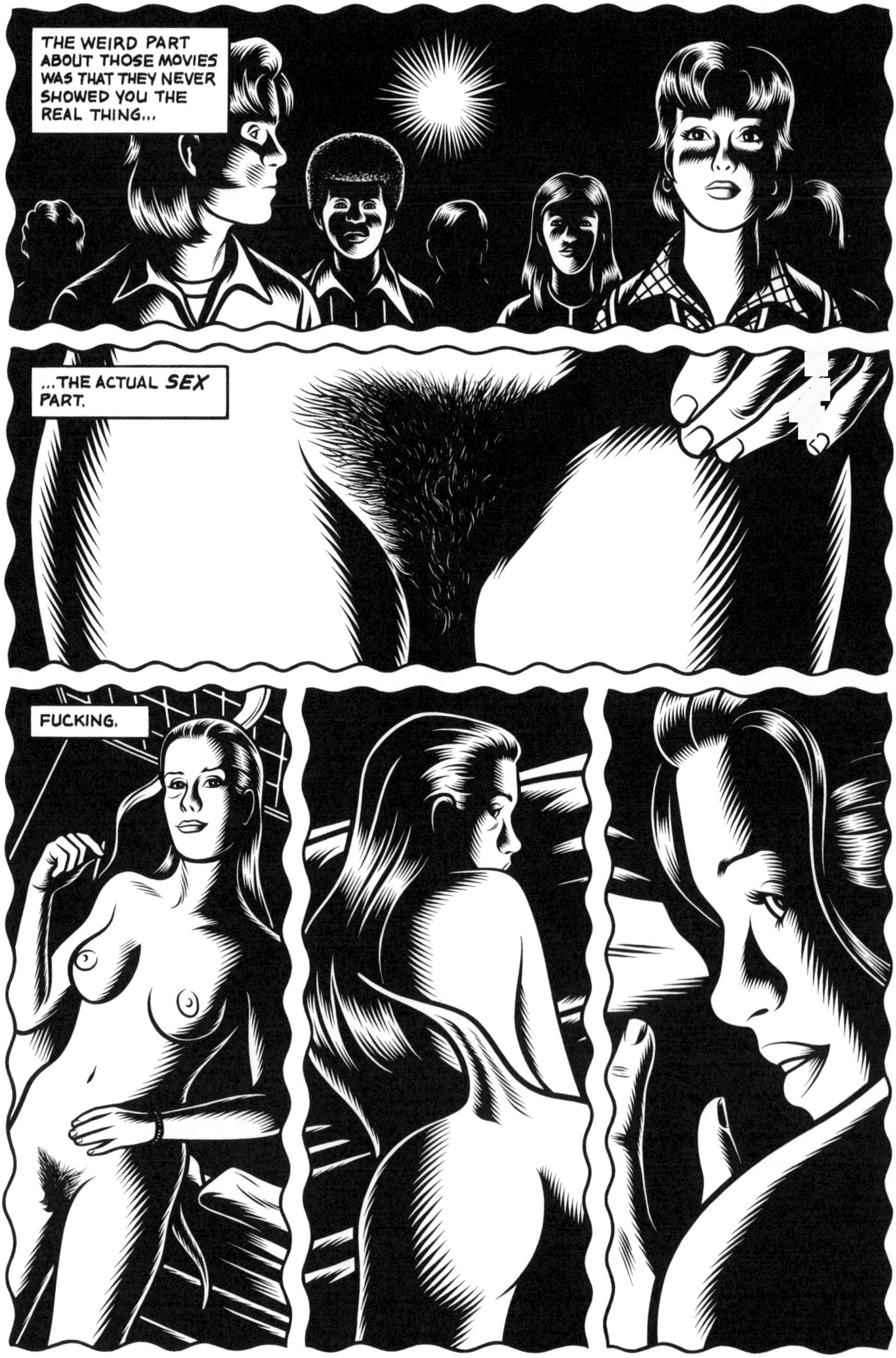
THE WEIRD PART ABOUT THOSE MOVIES WAS THAT THEY NEVER SHOWED YOU THE REAL THING...
...THE ACTUAL *SEX* PART.
FUCKING.

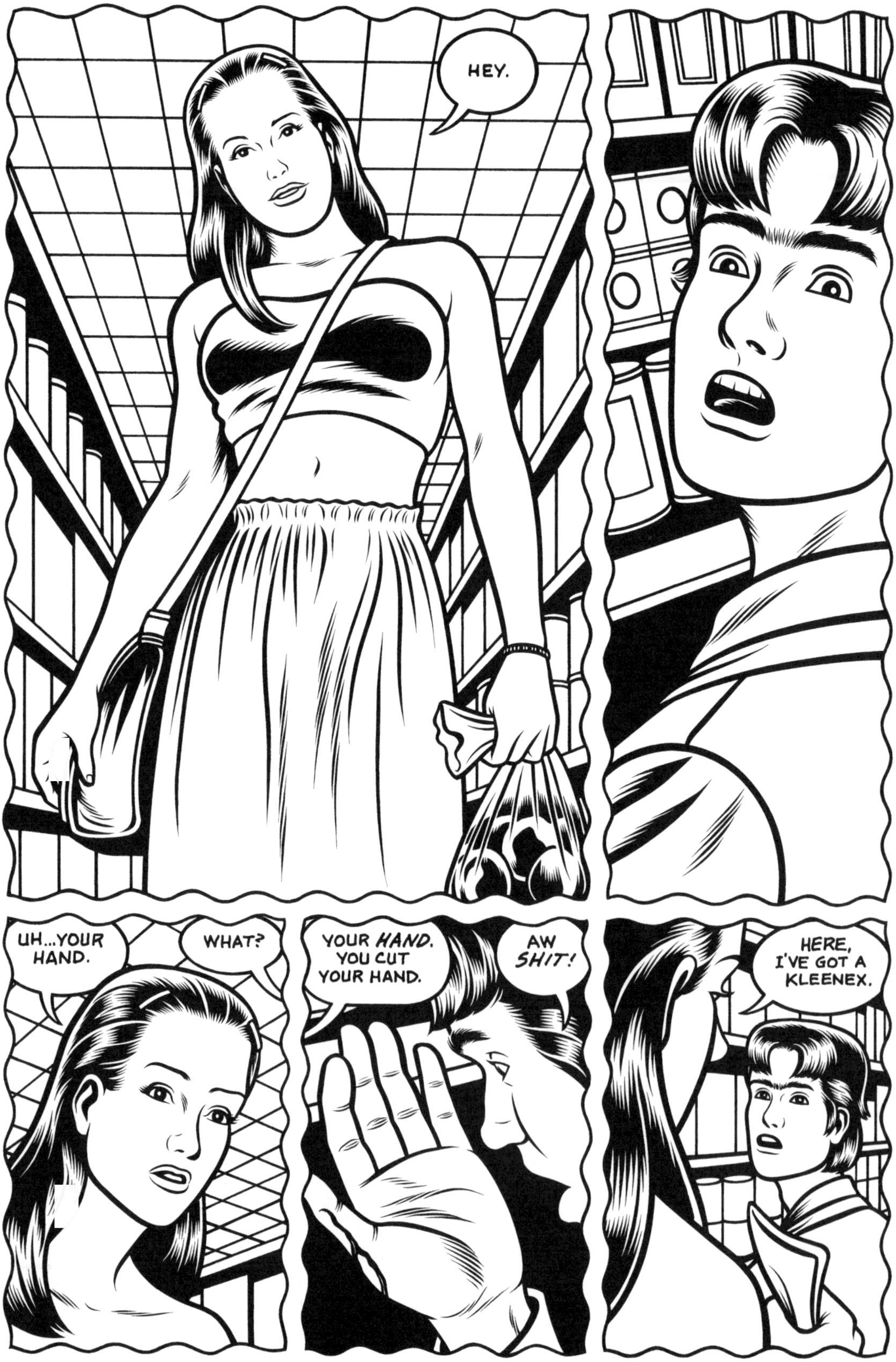
HEY.
UH...YOUR HAND.
WHAT?
YOUR HAND. YOU CUT YOUR HAND.
AW SHIT!
HERE, I'VE GOT A KLEENEX.

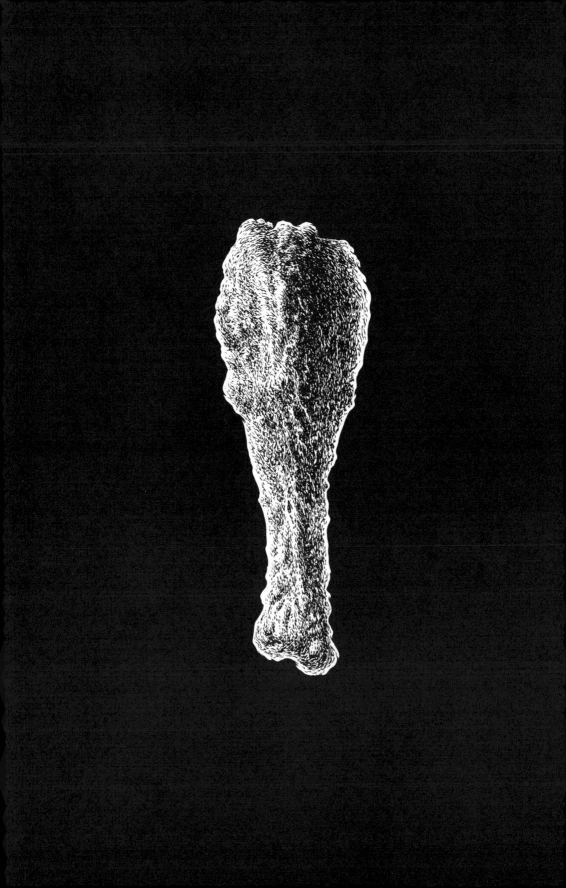

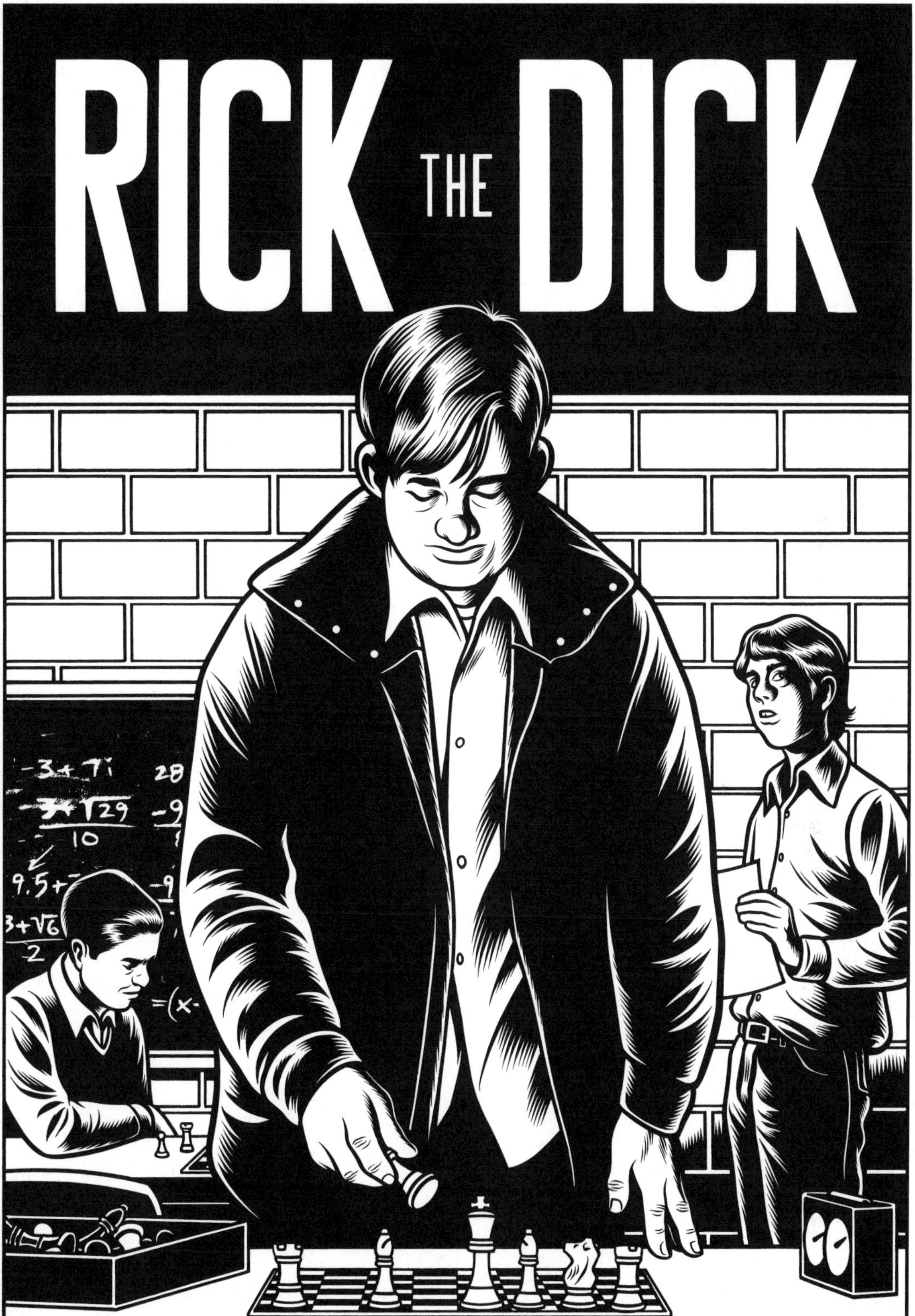
RICK THE DICK

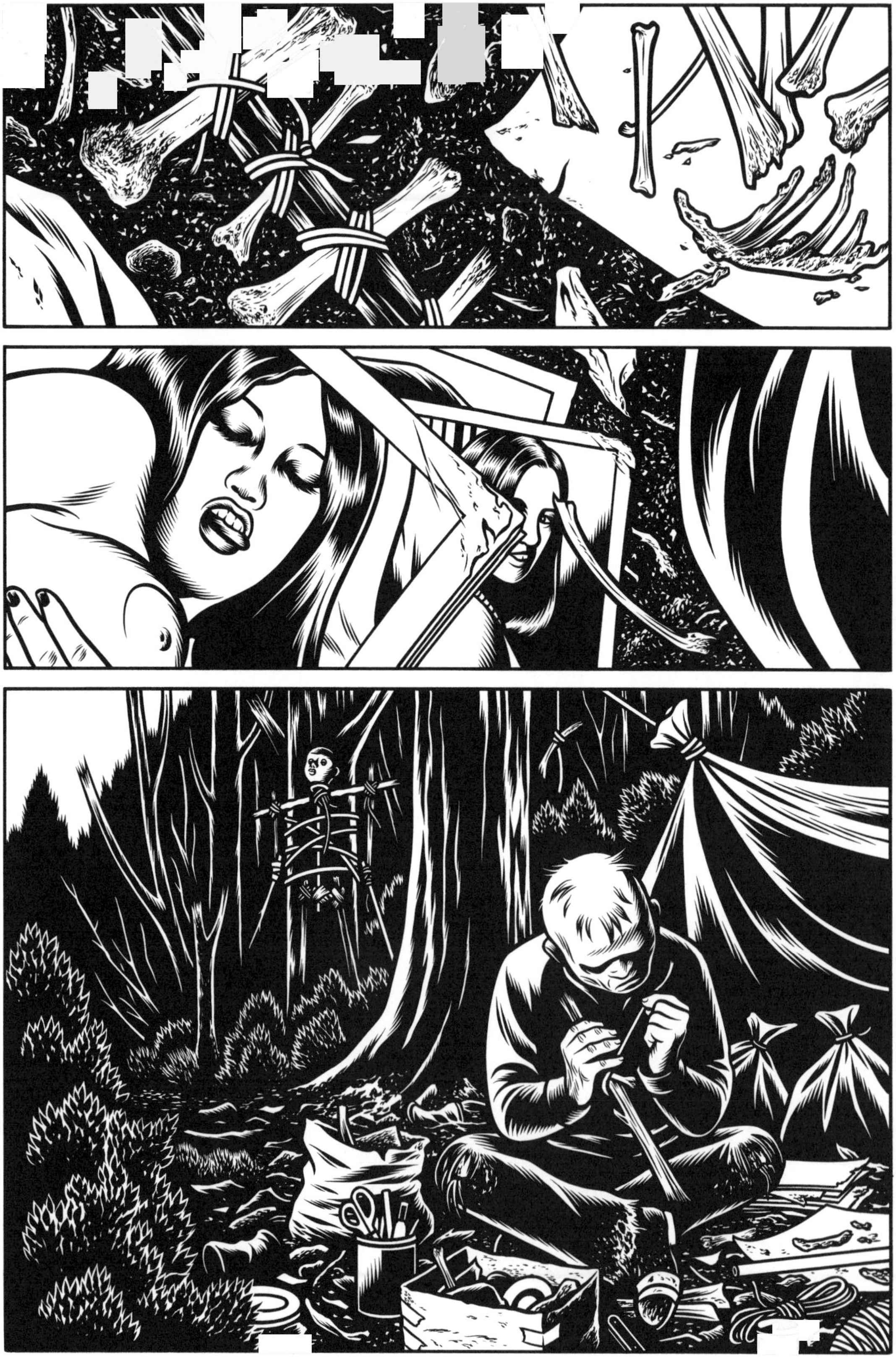

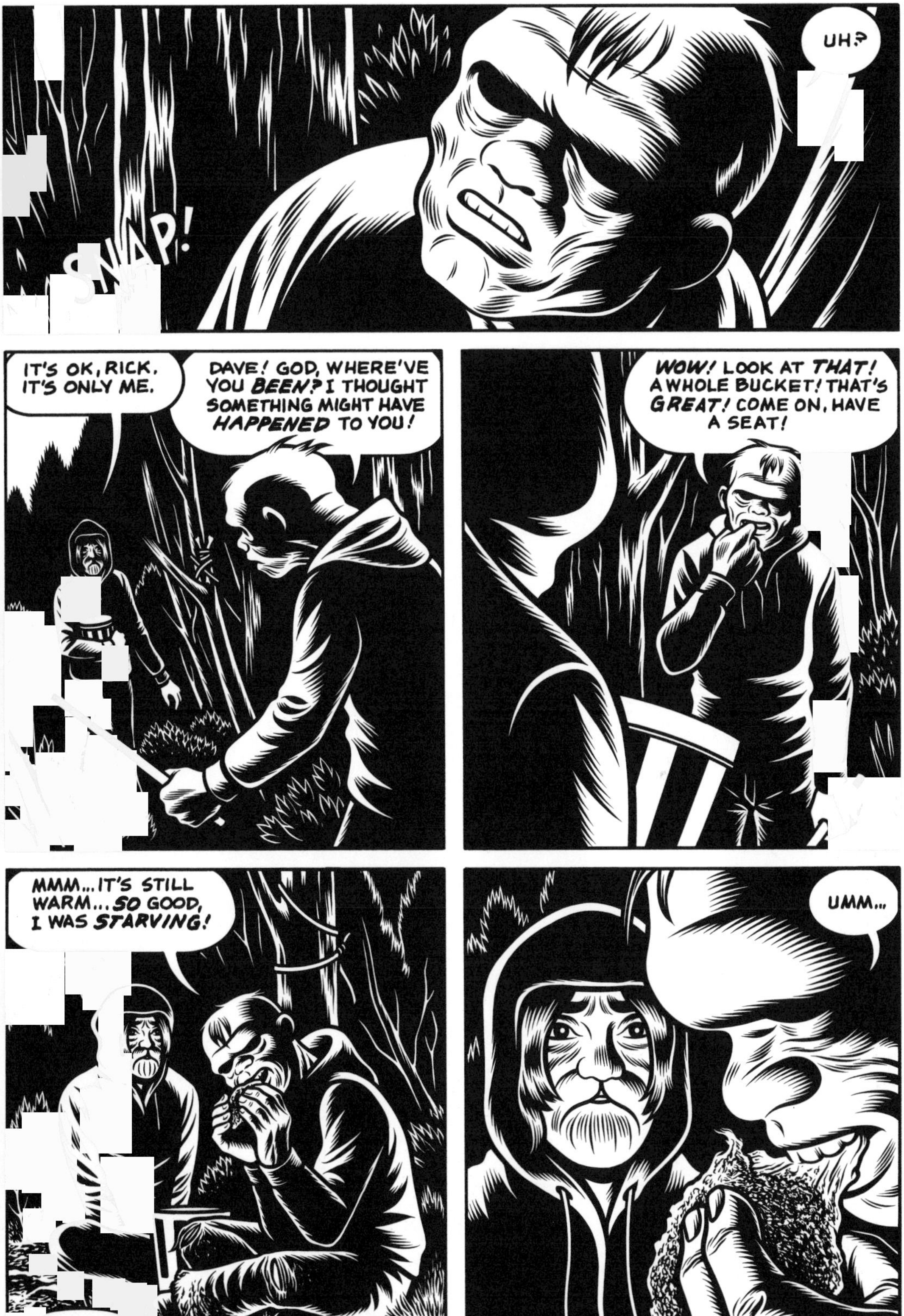
SNAP!
UH?
IT'S OK, RICK, IT'S ONLY ME.
DAVE! GOD, WHERE'VE YOU BEEN? I THOUGHT SOMETHING MIGHT HAVE HAPPENED TO YOU!
WOW! LOOK AT THAT! A WHOLE BUCKET! THAT'S GREAT! COME ON, HAVE A SEAT!
MMM... IT'S STILL WARM... SO GOOD, I WAS STARVING!
UMM...

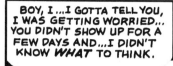

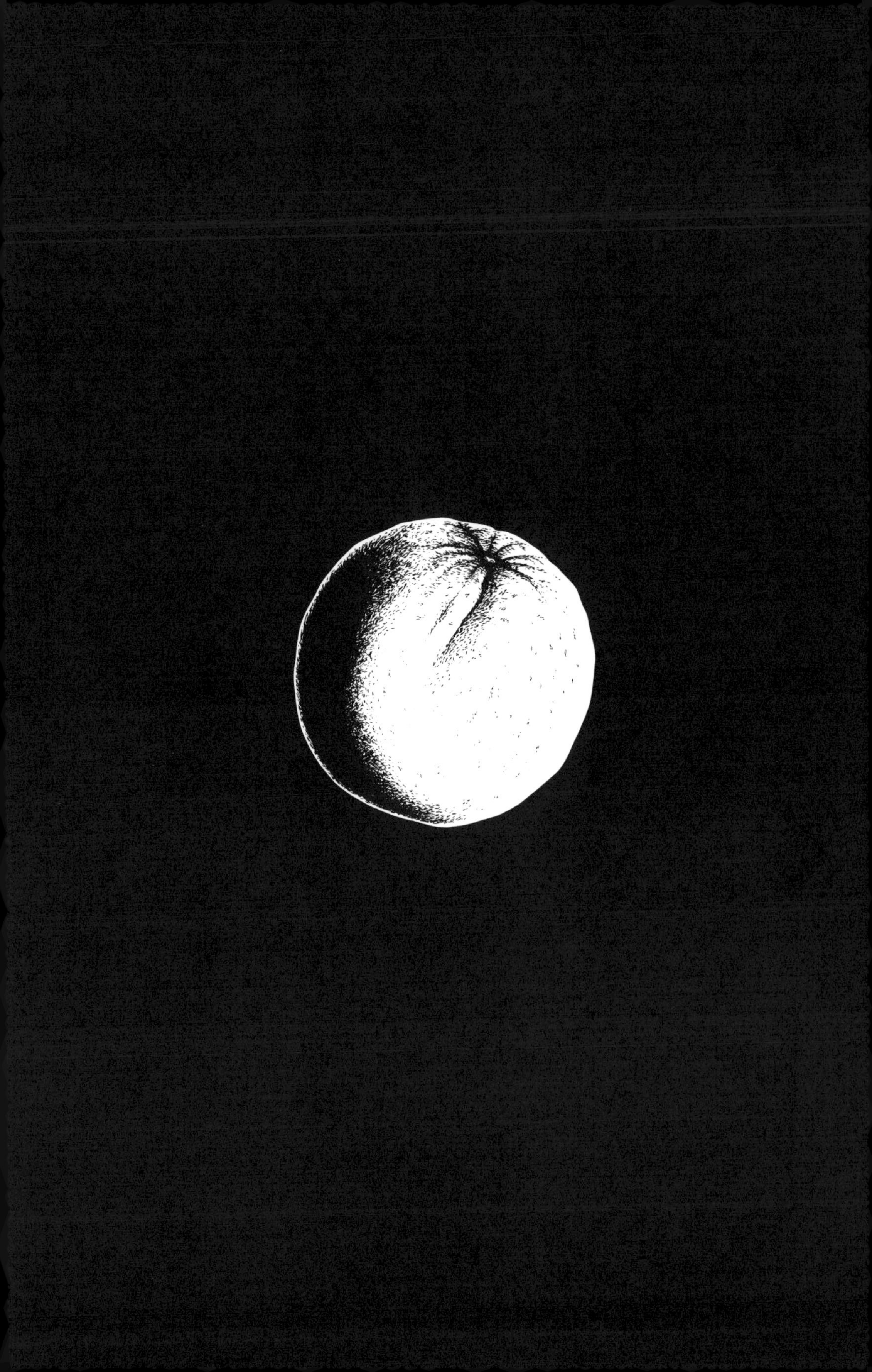

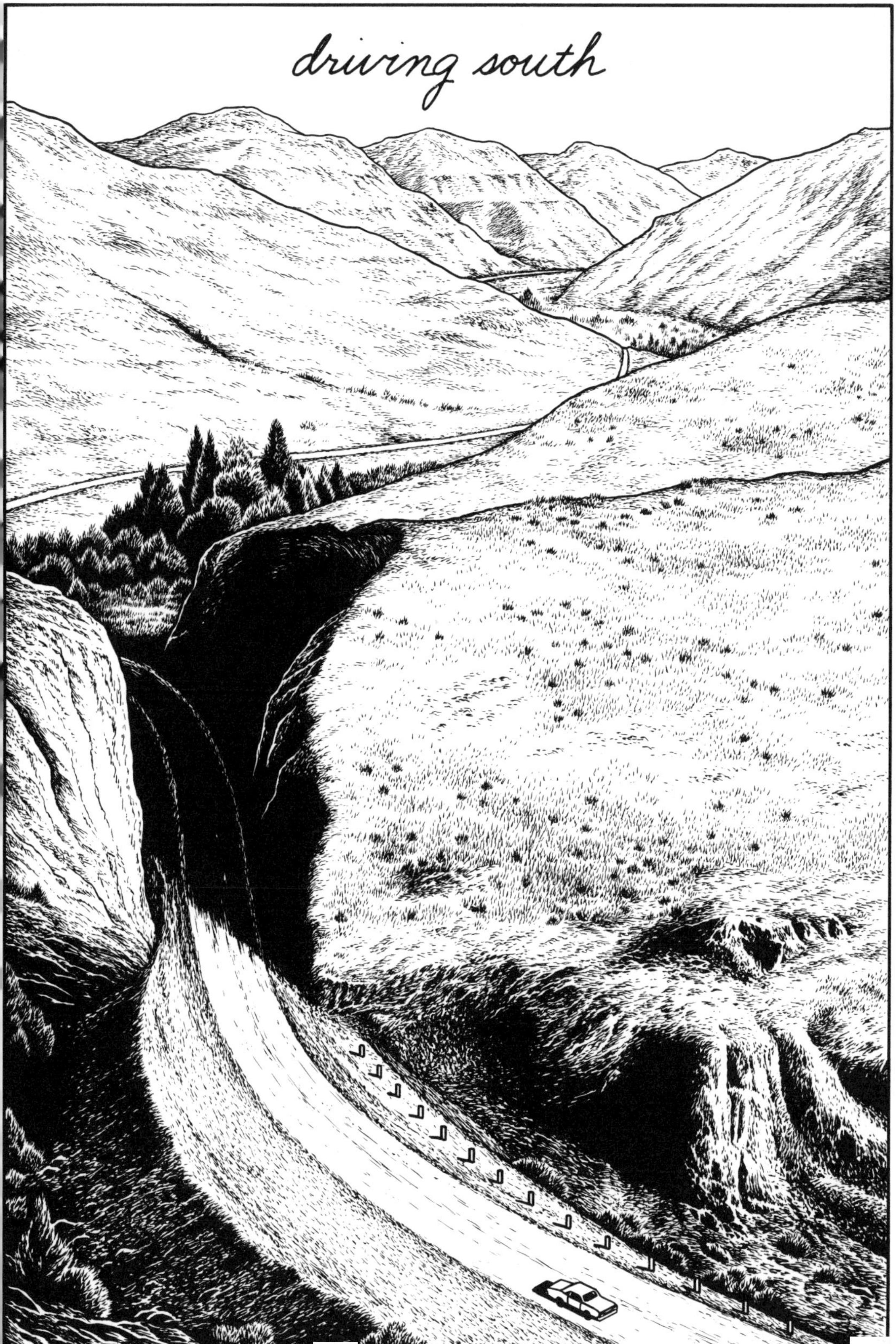
driving south

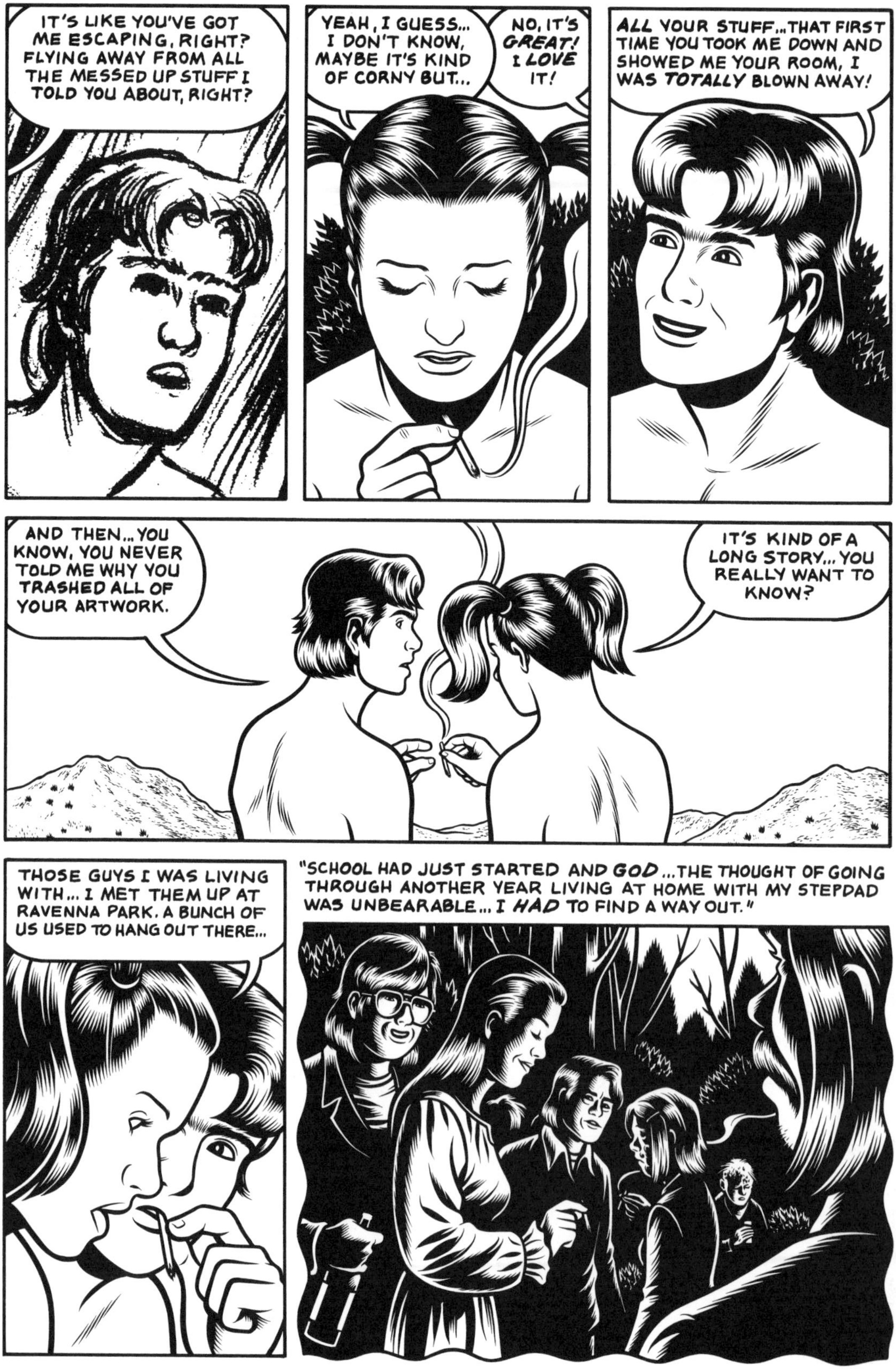
IT'S LIKE YOU'VE GOT ME ESCAPING, RIGHT? FLYING AWAY FROM ALL THE MESSED UP STUFF I TOLD YOU ABOUT, RIGHT?
YEAH, I GUESS... I DON'T KNOW, MAYBE IT'S KIND OF CORNY BUT...
NO, IT'S GREAT! I LOVE IT!
ALL YOUR STUFF... THAT FIRST TIME YOU TOOK ME DOWN AND SHOWED ME YOUR ROOM, I WAS TOTALLY BLOWN AWAY!
AND THEN... YOU KNOW, YOU NEVER TOLD ME WHY YOU TRASHED ALL OF YOUR ARTWORK.
IT'S KIND OF A LONG STORY... YOU REALLY WANT TO KNOW?
THOSE GUYS I WAS LIVING WITH... I MET THEM UP AT RAVENNA PARK. A BUNCH OF US USED TO HANG OUT THERE...
"SCHOOL HAD JUST STARTED AND GOD... THE THOUGHT OF GOING THROUGH ANOTHER YEAR LIVING AT HOME WITH MY STEPDAD WAS UNBEARABLE... I HAD TO FIND A WAY OUT."

"I'D RUN AWAY A COUPLE OF TIMES... EVEN TRIED CAMPING OUT IN THE WOODS WITH SOME FRIENDS BUT I COULDN'T TAKE IT..."

"...TOO SCARY."

"ANYWAY, THESE OLDER GUYS WOULD SHOW UP WITH THEIR DOPE AND THEIR BIG BOTTLES OF WINE AND WE'D PARTY WITH THEM."

"THEY WERE KIND OF NERDY... GUYS WHO'D NEVER HAD GIRLFRIENDS... BUT THEY SEEMED OKAY."

HEY, IF YOU'RE SERIOUS, YOU COULD MOVE IN WITH US...

...THERE'S AN EXTRA ROOM IN THE BASEMENT. IT'S YOURS IF YOU WANT IT.

"SO I MOVED IN. IT WASN'T BAD... ALL I DID WAS GET STONED AND WORK ON MY ART ALL DAY."

"I KEPT THINKING THERE WAS GOING TO BE A PAYBACK, SOME KIND OF SEX THING, BUT AS LONG AS I WAS NICE TO THEM AND CLEANED A FEW THINGS UP, EVERYTHING WAS COOL."

HEY, LIZ! HOW ABOUT GRABBIN' ME ANOTHER OLY!

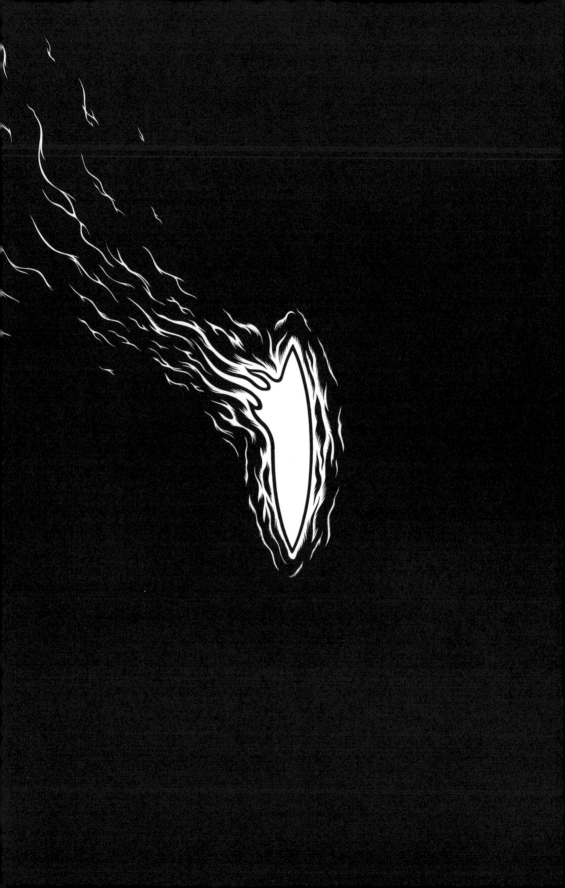

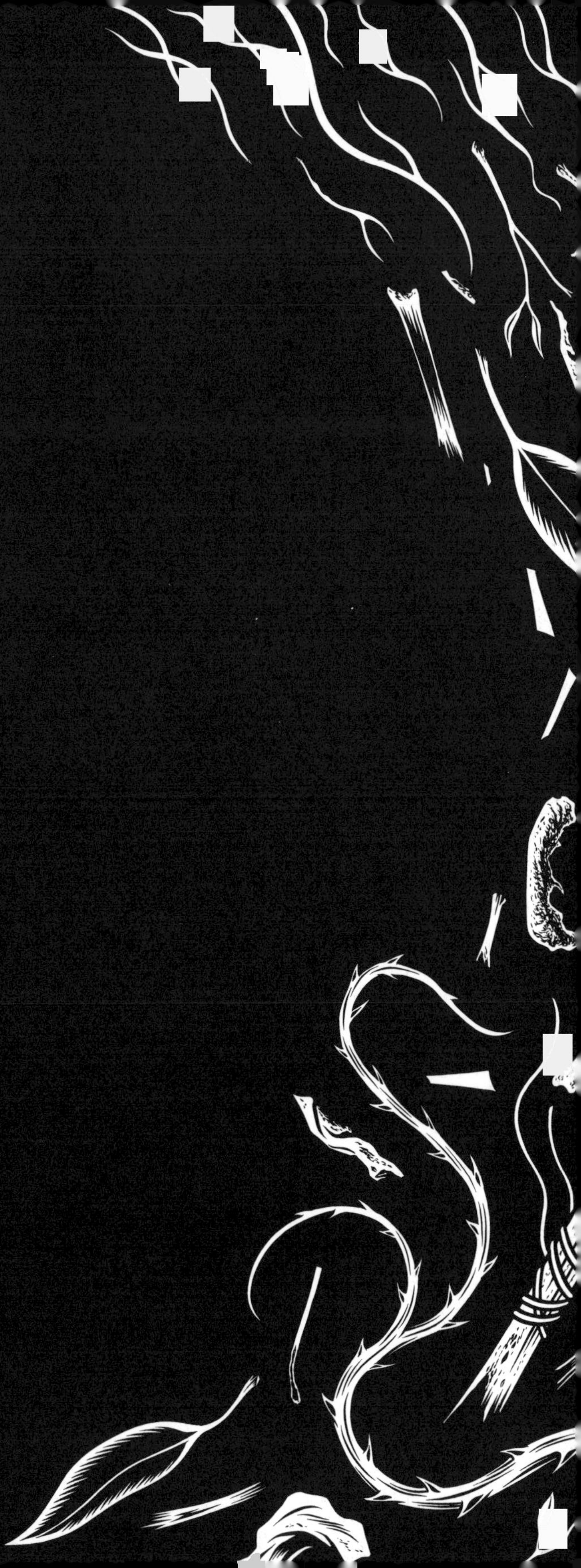

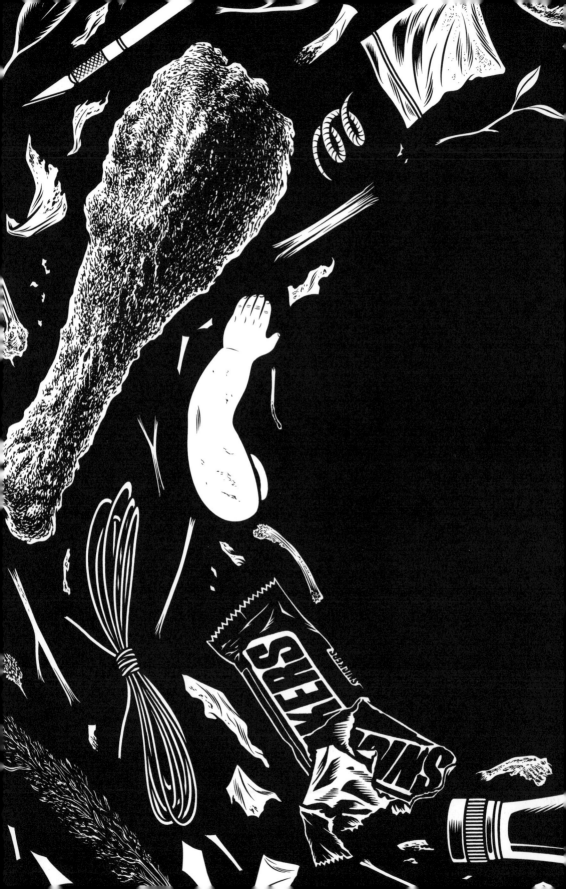

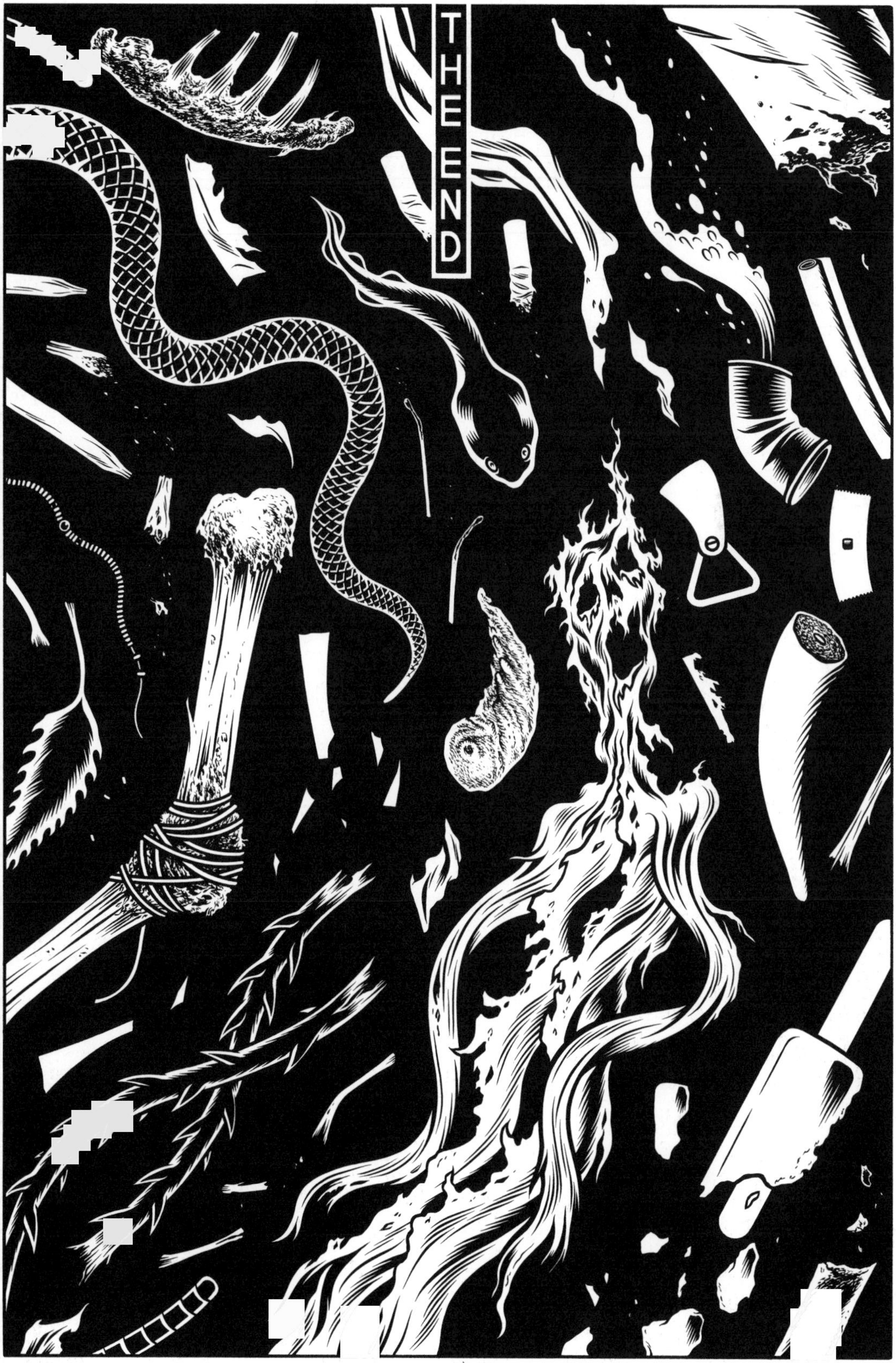
THE END

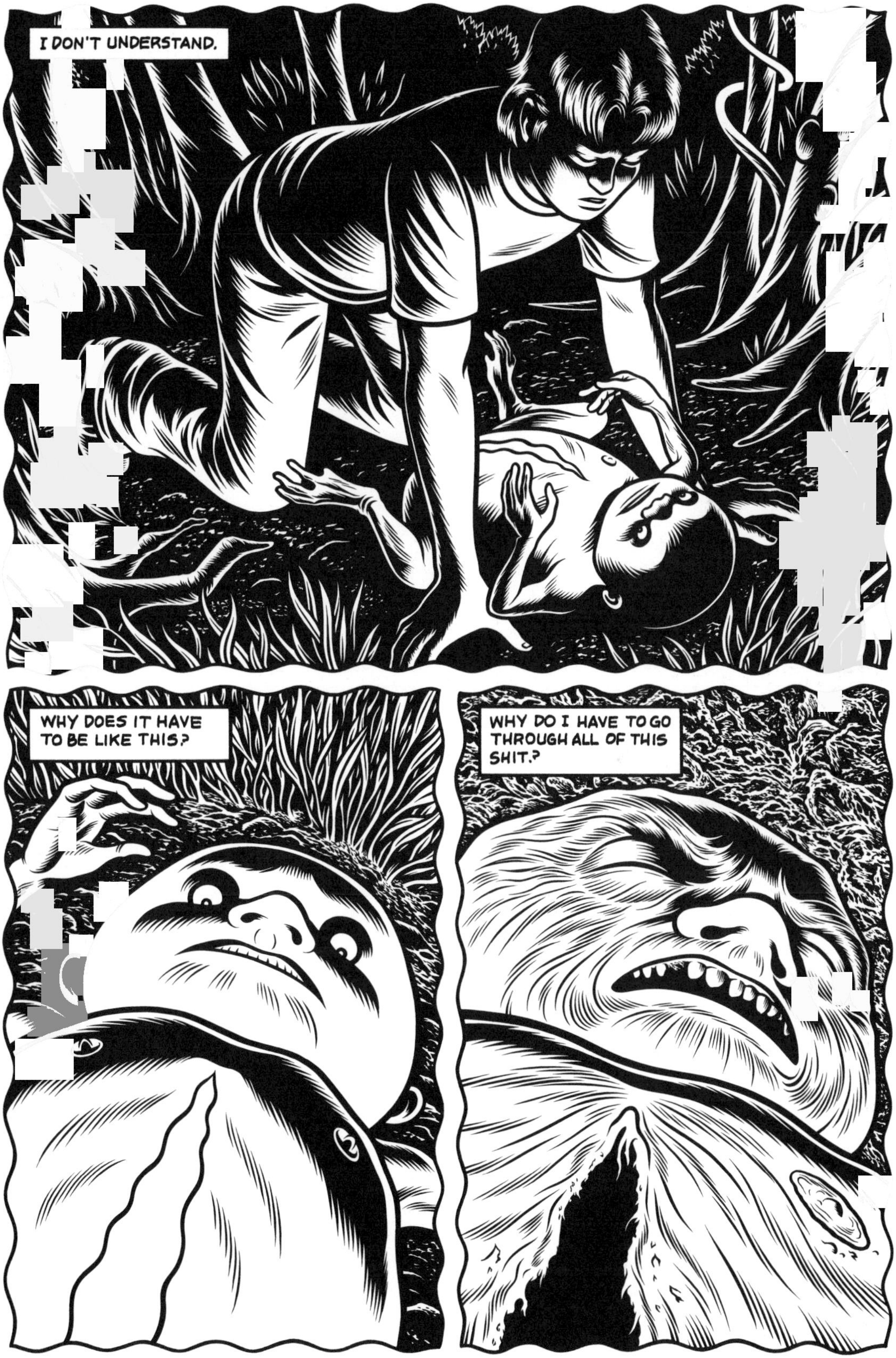
I DON'T UNDERSTAND.
WHY DOES IT HAVE TO BE LIKE THIS?
WHY DO I HAVE TO GO THROUGH ALL OF THIS SHIT.?

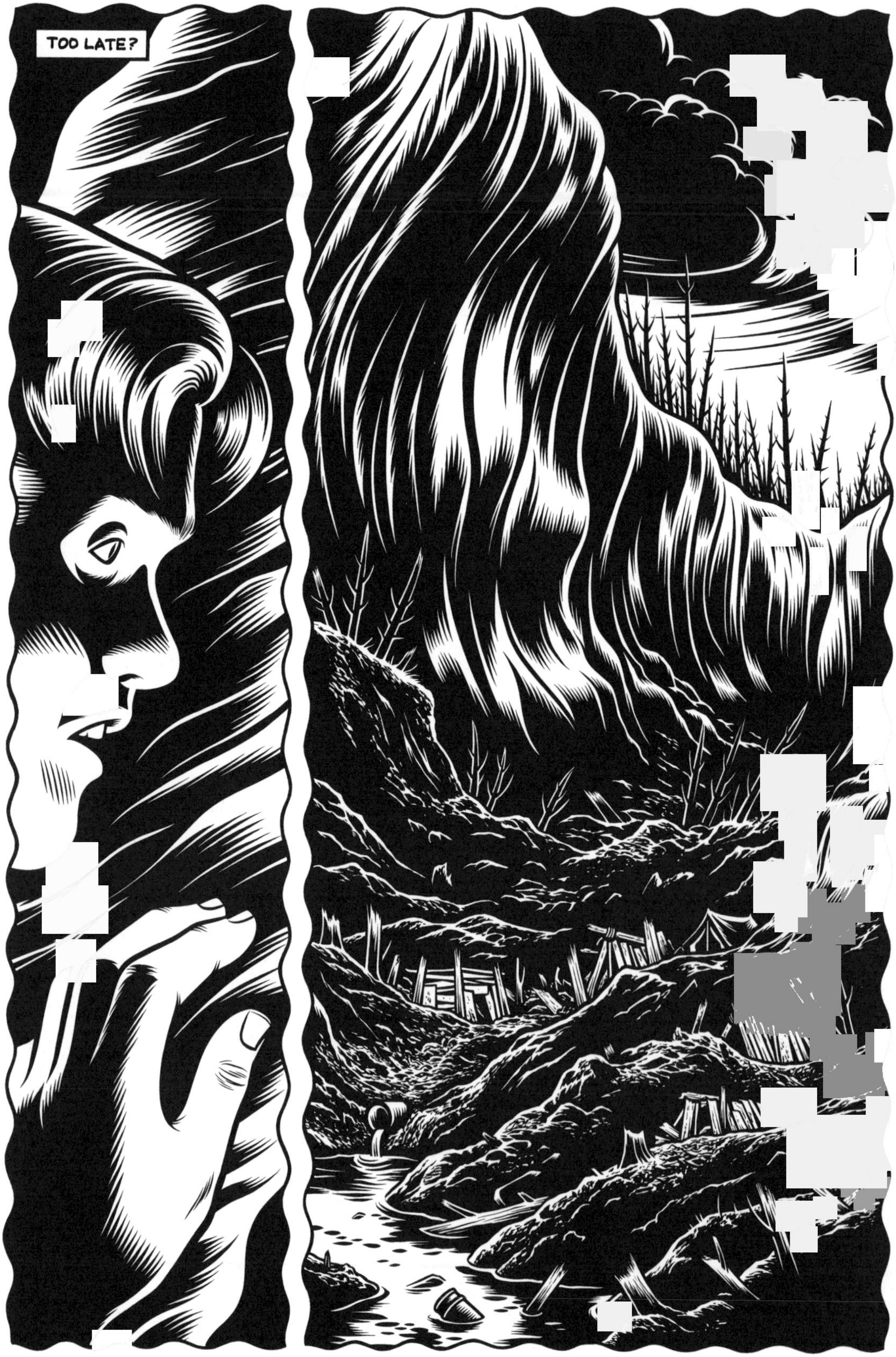
TOO LATE?

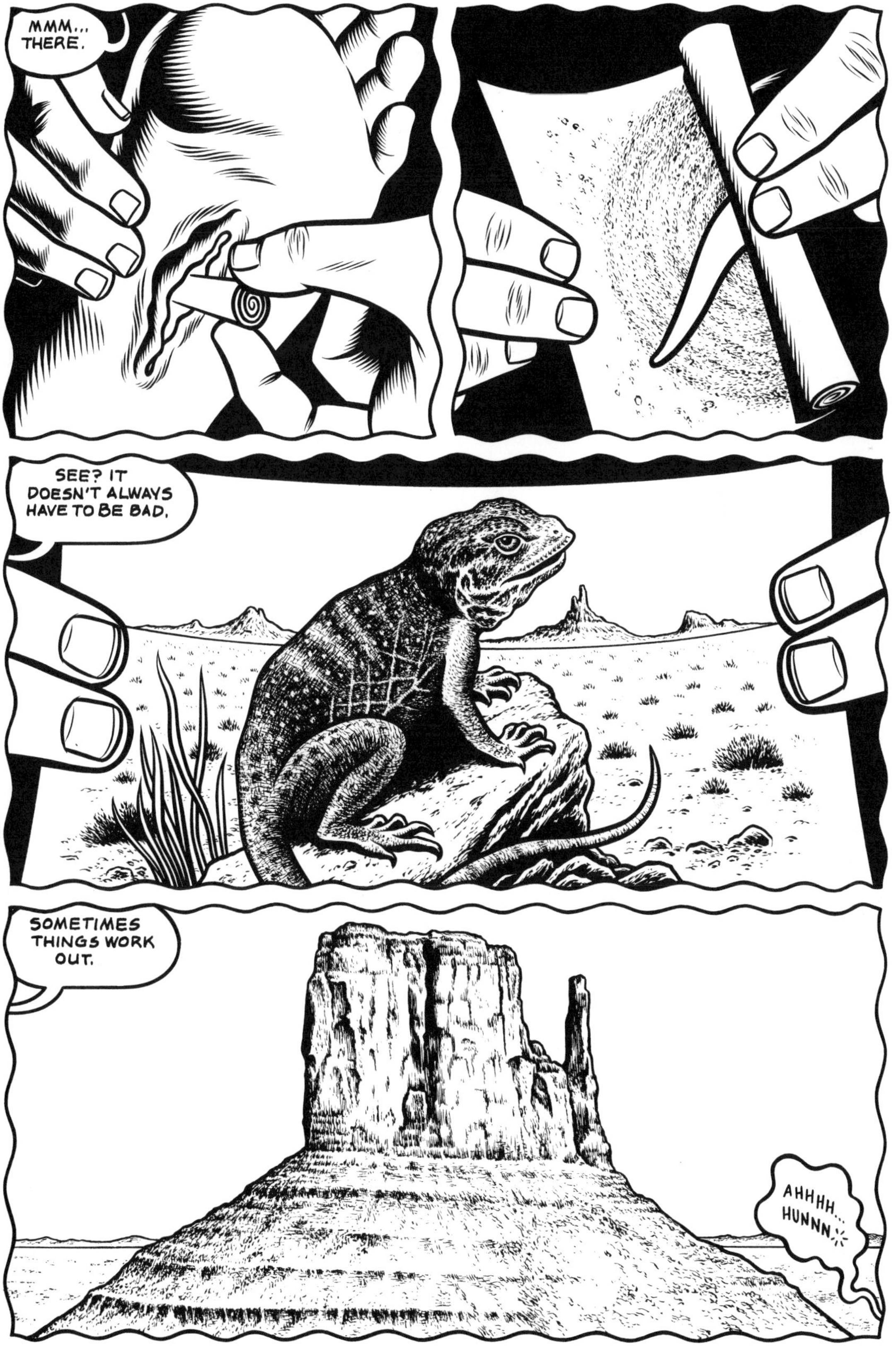
MMM... THERE.
SEE? IT DOESN'T ALWAYS HAVE TO BE BAD.
SOMETIMES THINGS WORK OUT.
AHHHH... HUNNN.

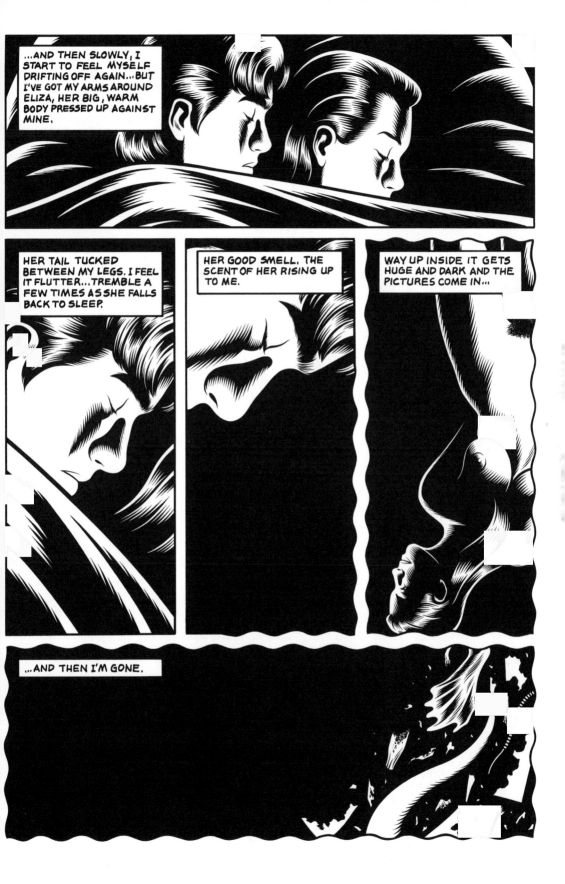

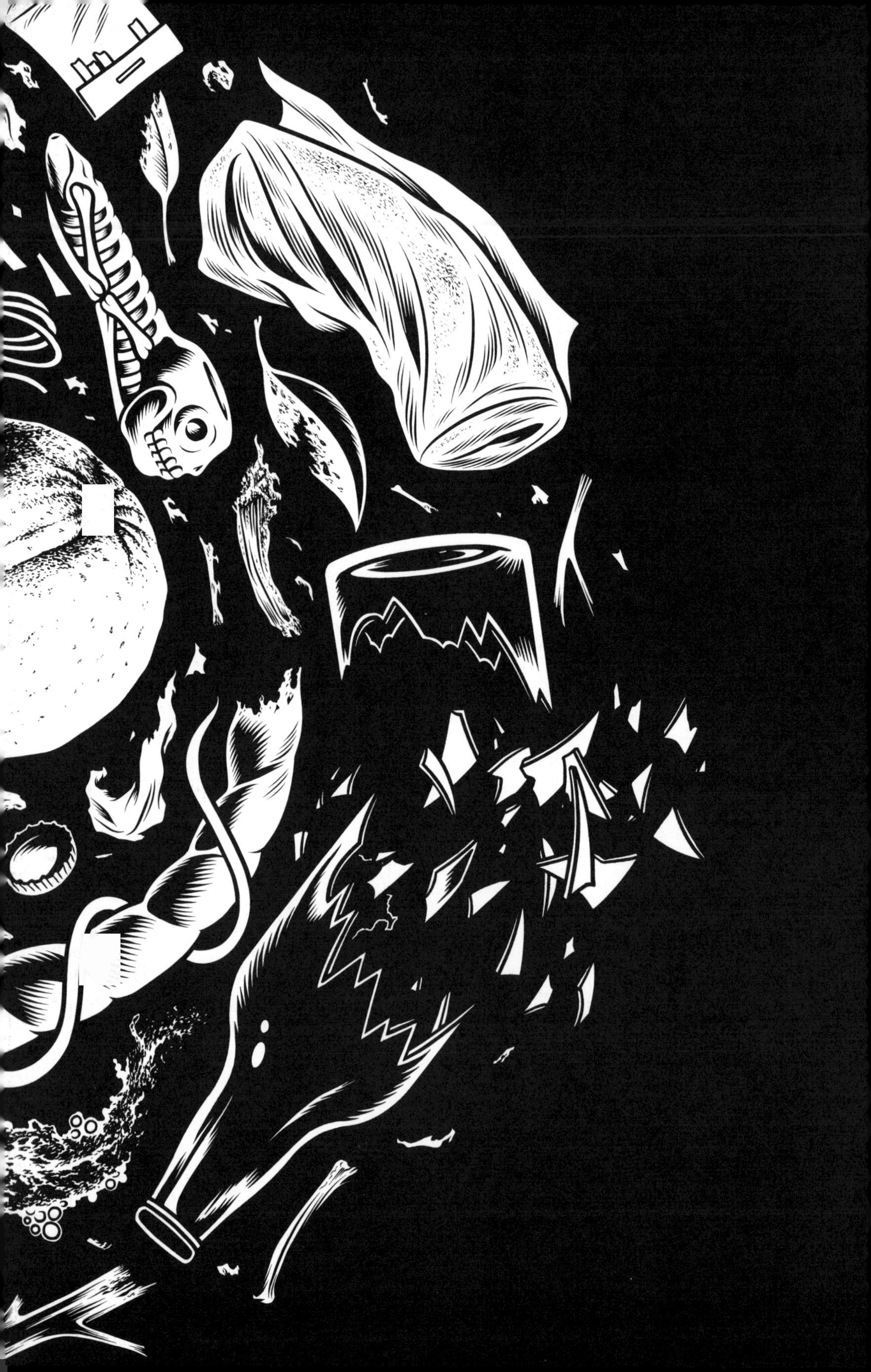

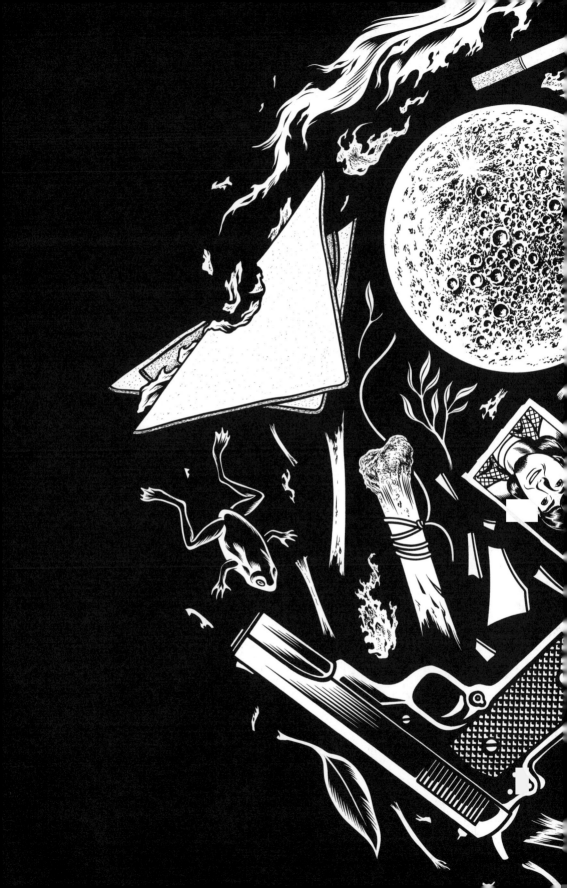

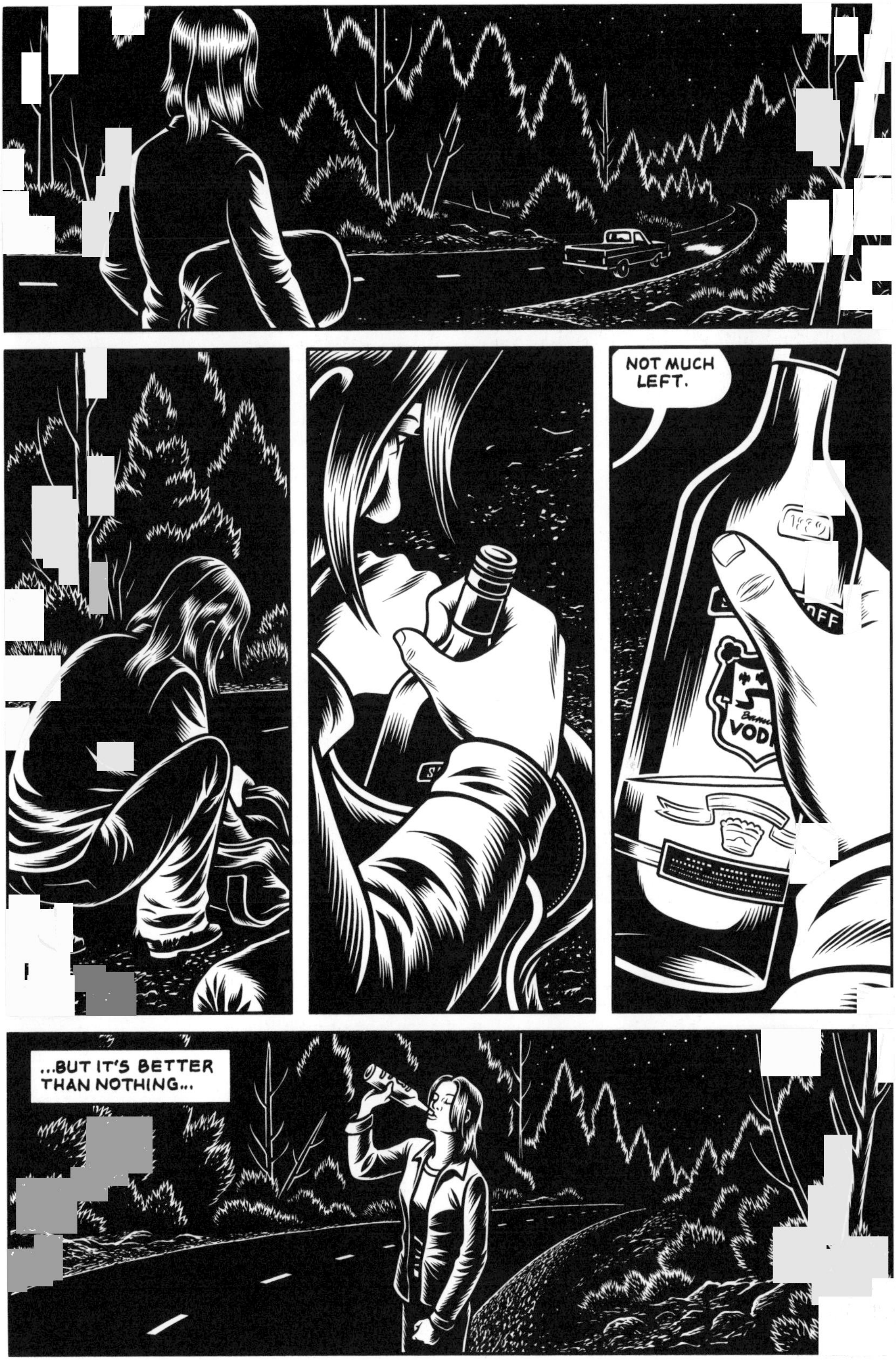
NOT MUCH LEFT.
...BUT IT'S BETTER THAN NOTHING...

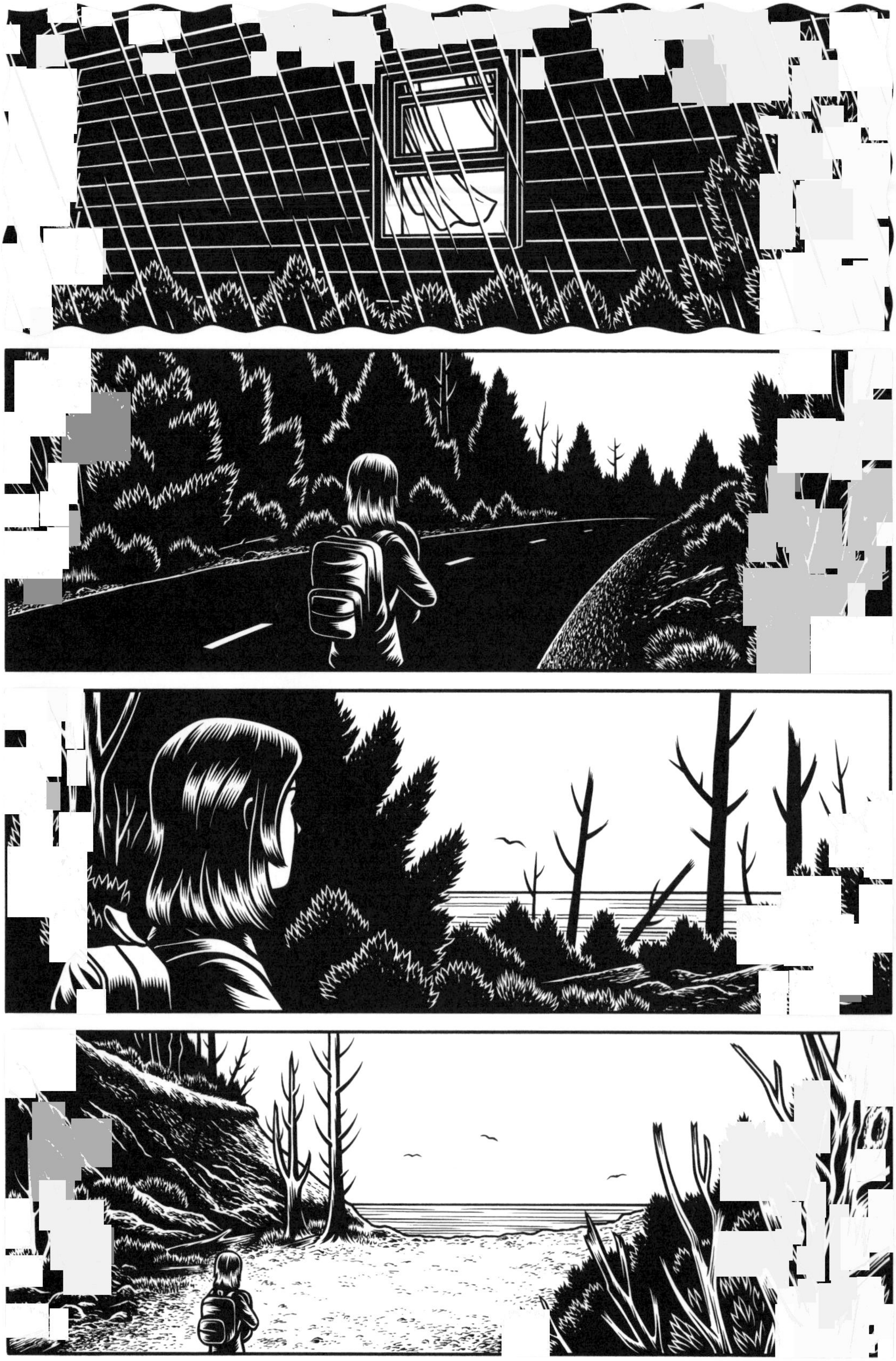

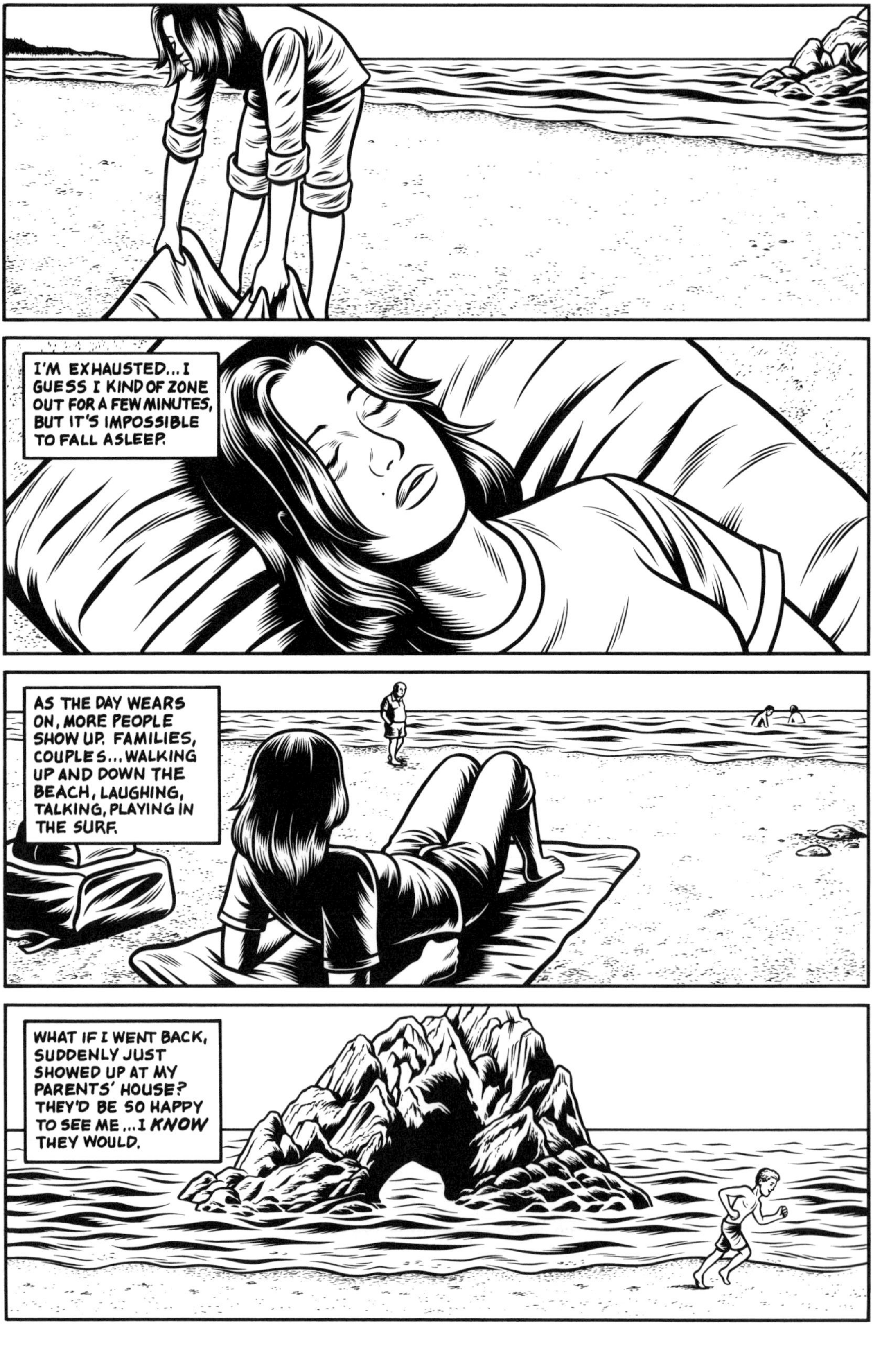
I'M EXHAUSTED... I GUESS I KIND OF ZONE OUT FOR A FEW MINUTES, BUT IT'S IMPOSSIBLE TO FALL ASLEEP.
AS THE DAY WEARS ON, MORE PEOPLE SHOW UP. FAMILIES, COUPLES... WALKING UP AND DOWN THE BEACH, LAUGHING, TALKING, PLAYING IN THE SURF.
WHAT IF I WENT BACK, SUDDENLY JUST SHOWED UP AT MY PARENTS' HOUSE? THEY'D BE SO HAPPY TO SEE ME... I *KNOW* THEY WOULD.

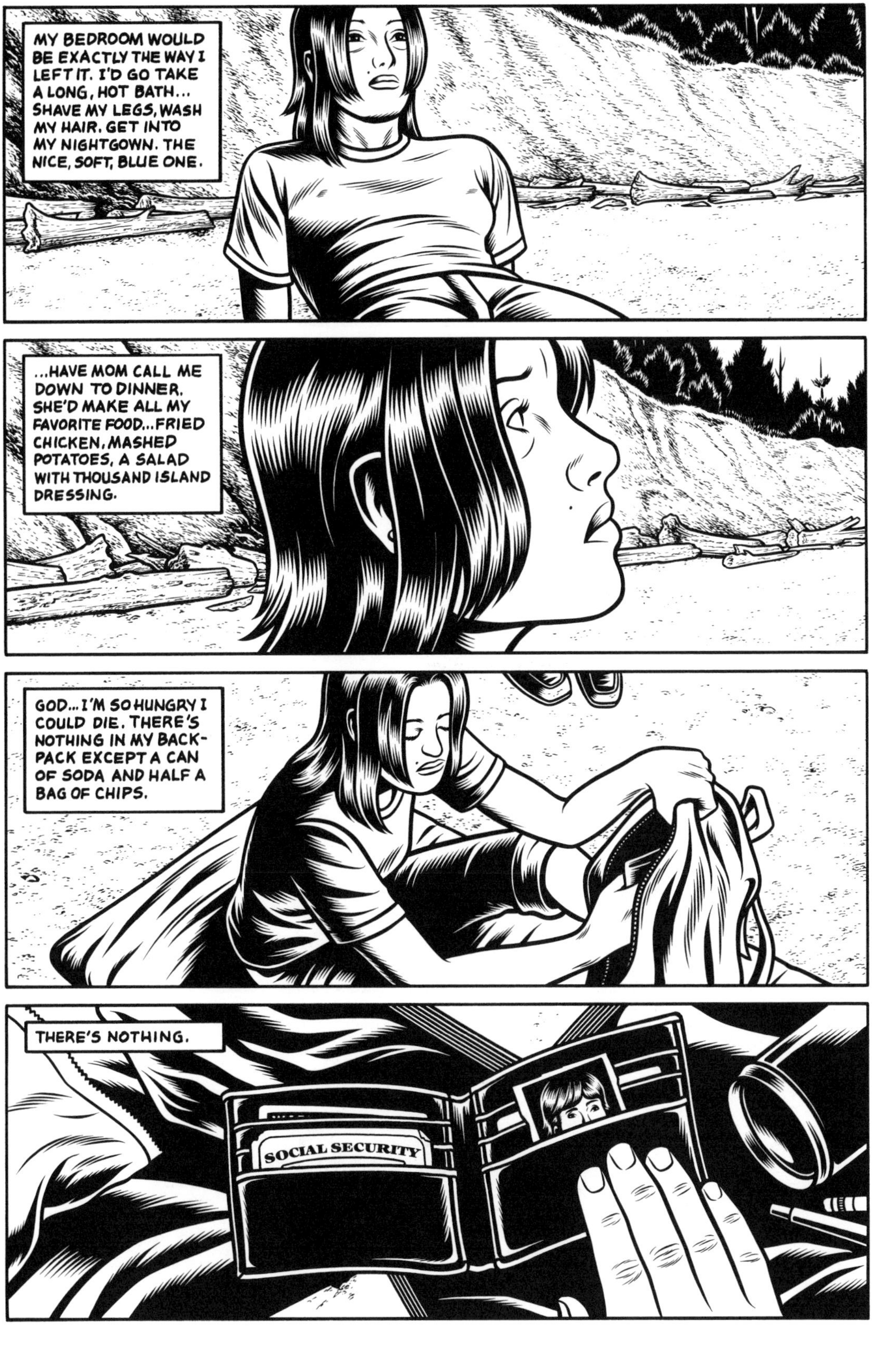
MY BEDROOM WOULD BE EXACTLY THE WAY I LEFT IT. I'D GO TAKE A LONG, HOT BATH... SHAVE MY LEGS, WASH MY HAIR. GET INTO MY NIGHTGOWN. THE NICE, SOFT, BLUE ONE.
...HAVE MOM CALL ME DOWN TO DINNER. SHE'D MAKE ALL MY FAVORITE FOOD...FRIED CHICKEN, MASHED POTATOES, A SALAD WITH THOUSAND ISLAND DRESSING.
GOD... I'M SO HUNGRY I COULD DIE. THERE'S NOTHING IN MY BACK-PACK EXCEPT A CAN OF SODA AND HALF A BAG OF CHIPS.
THERE'S NOTHING.
SOCIAL SECURITY

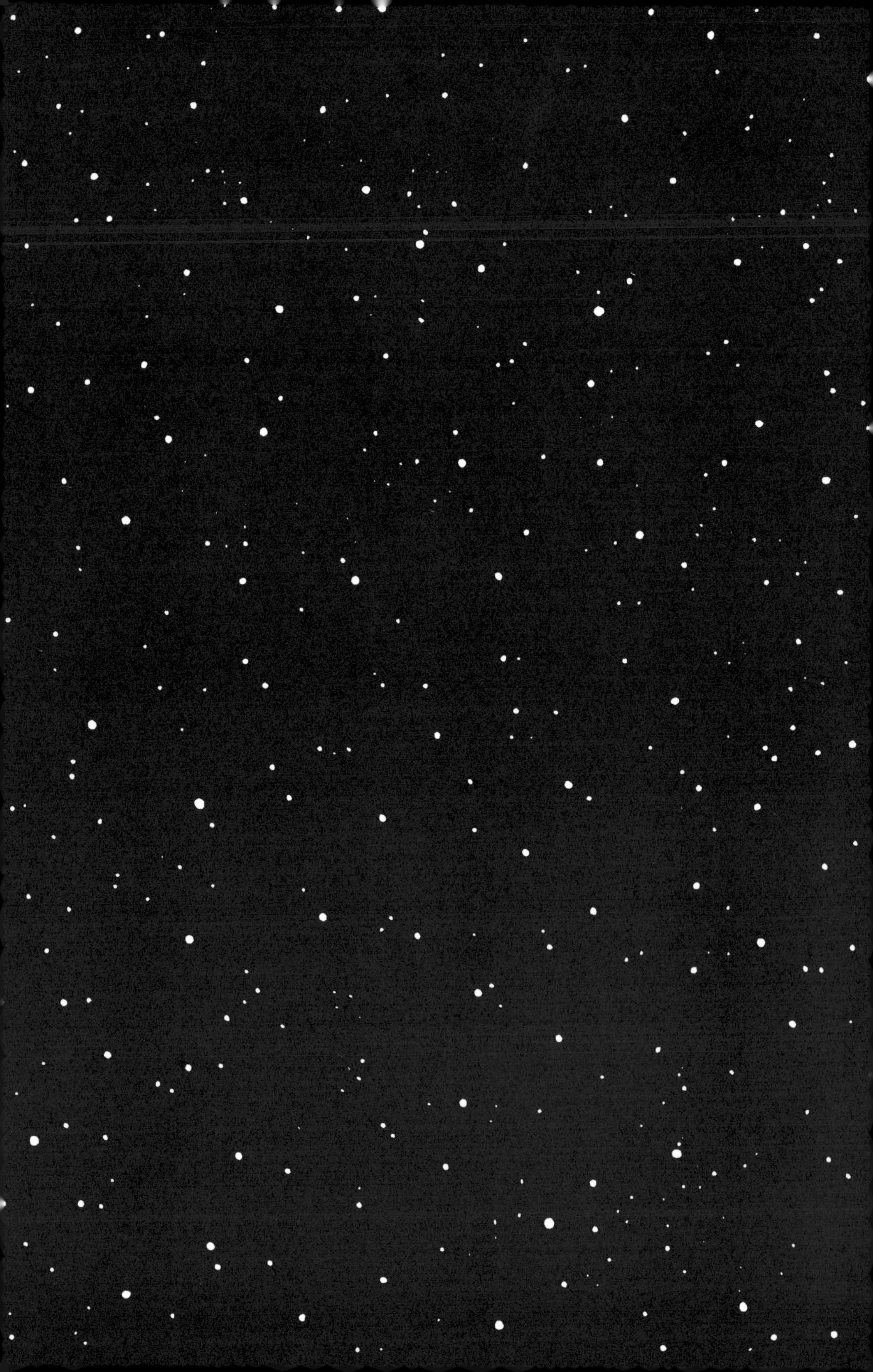

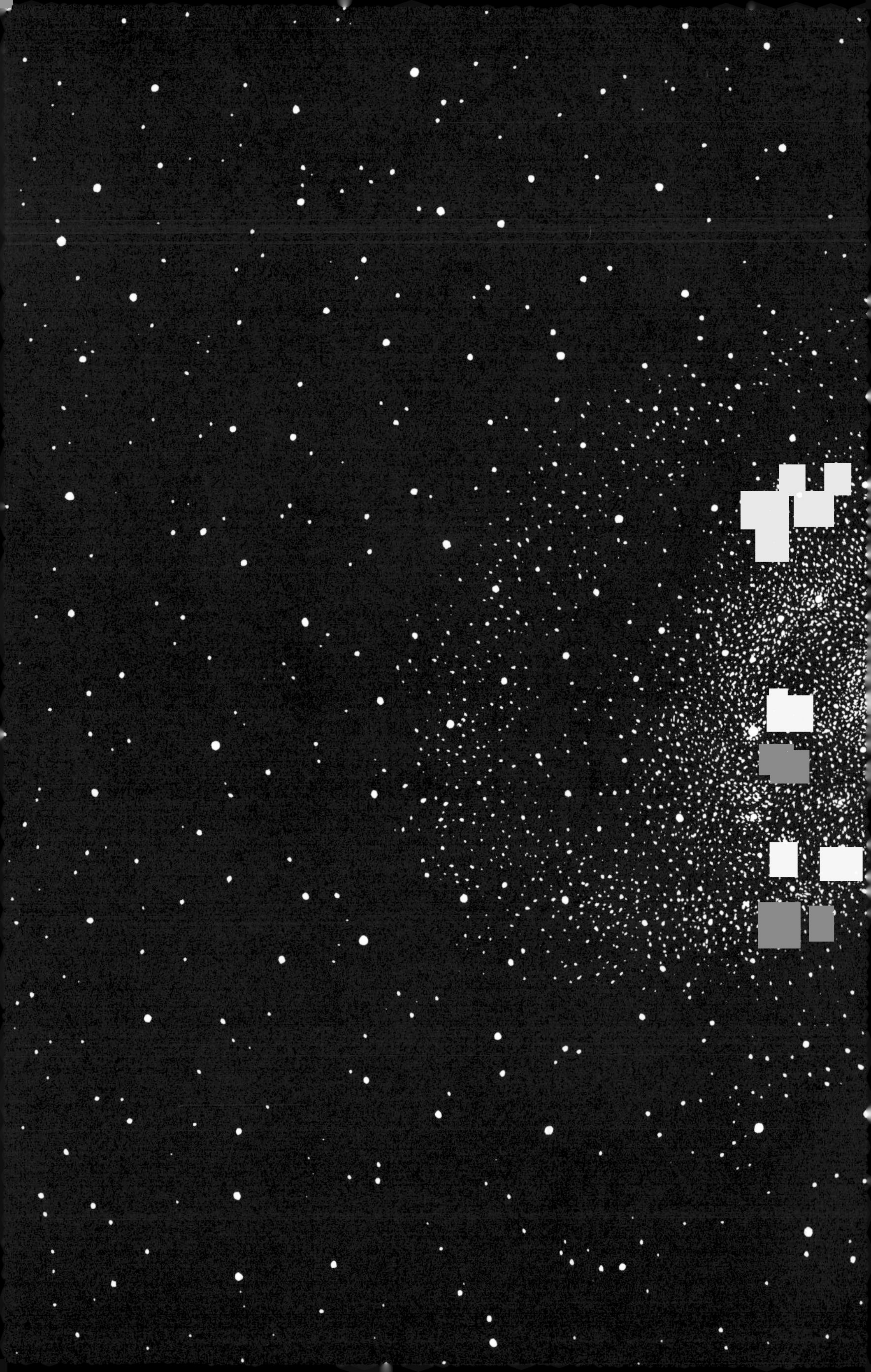

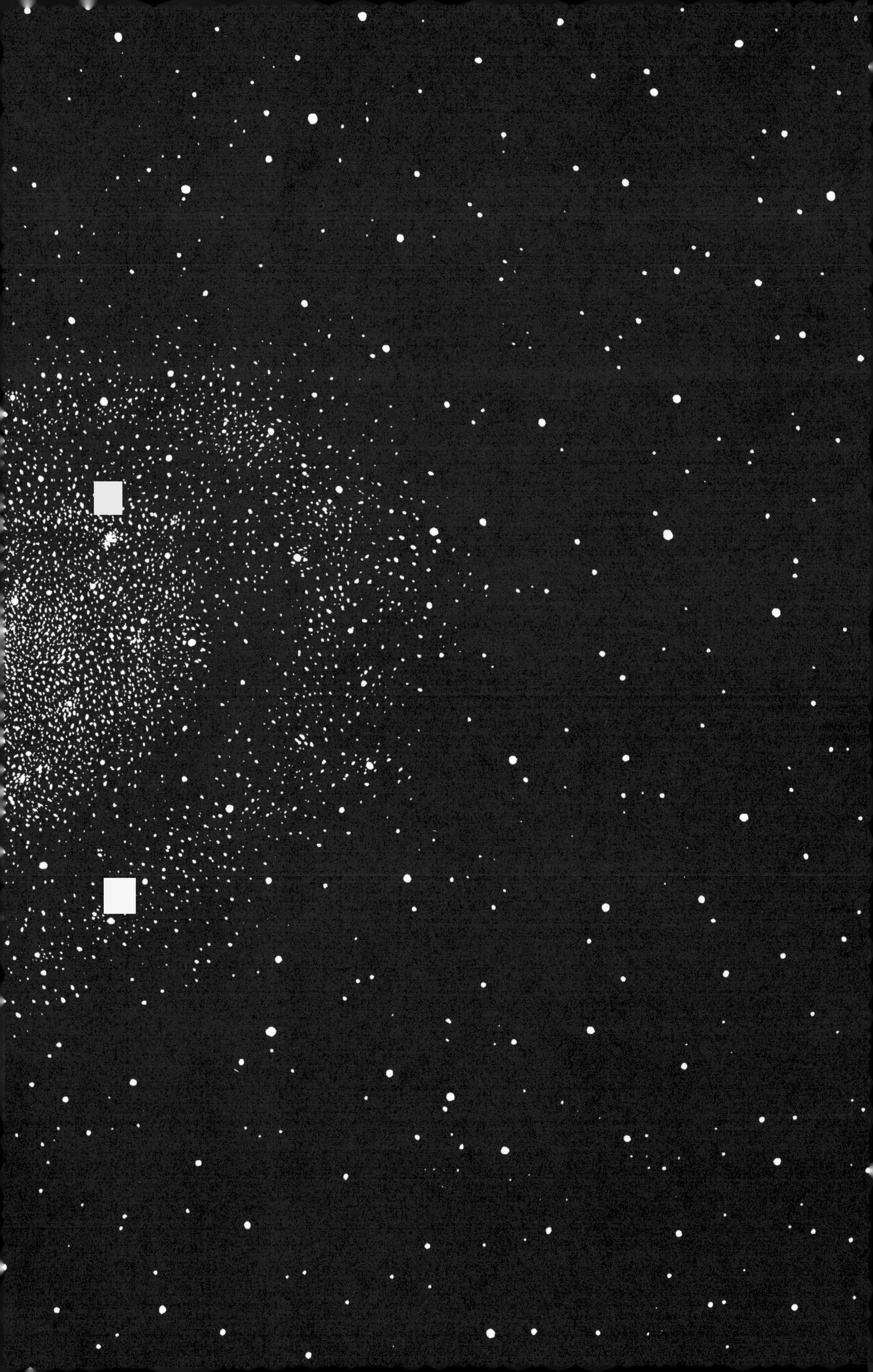

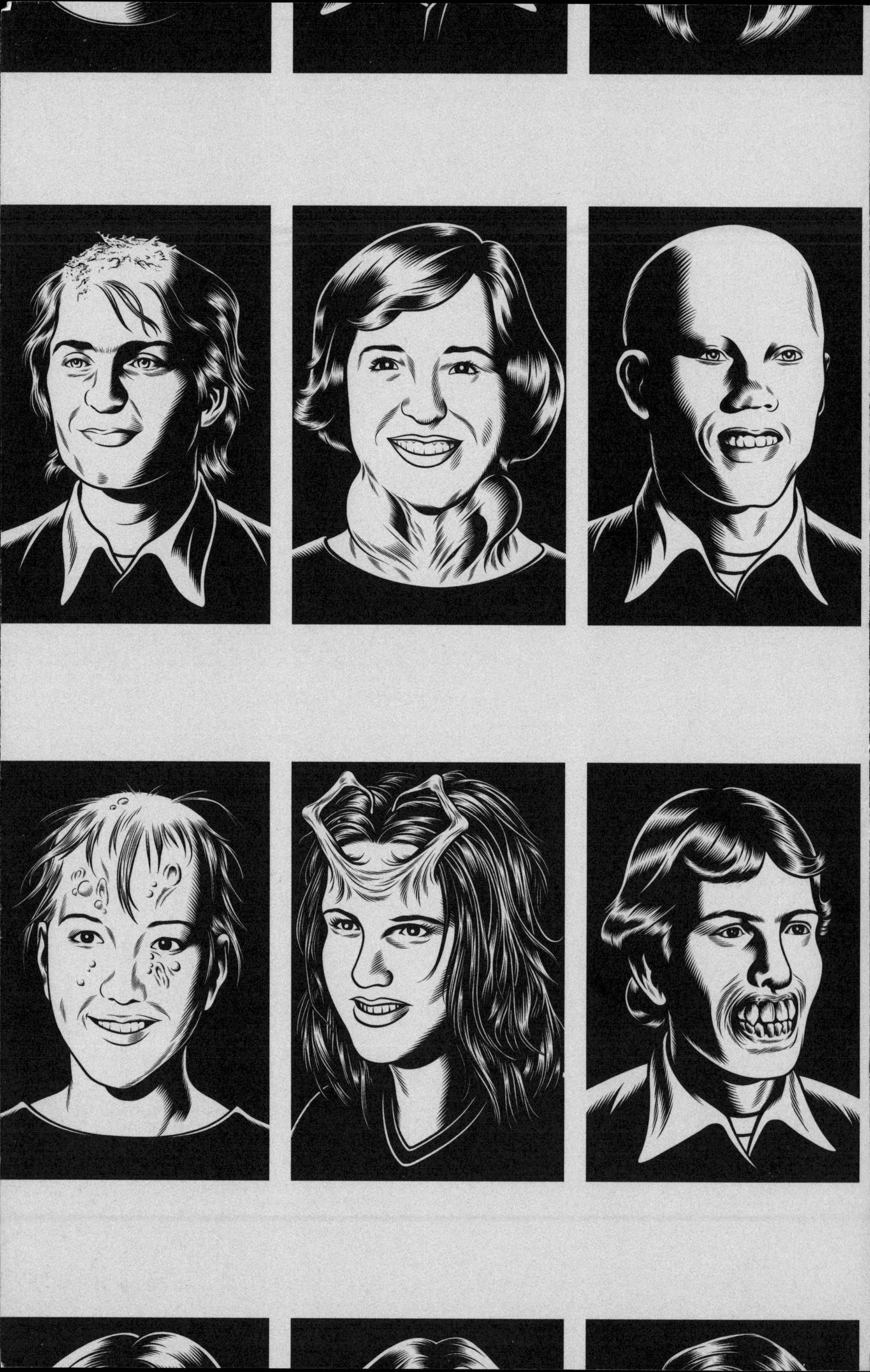